READER'S DIGEST

CONDENSED BOOKS

FIRST EDITION

THE READER'S DIGEST ASSOCIATION LIMITED
25 Berkeley Square, London W1X 6AB

**THE READER'S DIGEST ASSOCIATION
SOUTH AFRICA (PTY) LTD**
Nedbank Centre, Strand Street, Cape Town

Printed in Great Britain by Petty & Sons Ltd, Leeds

Original cover design by Jeffery Matthews F.S.I.A.D.

For information as to ownership
of copyright in the material in this book see last page

ISBN 0 340 26689 9

Reader's Digest
CONDENSED BOOKS

DAUNTLESS
Alan Evans

INTRUDER
Louis Charbonneau

GOING WILD
David Taylor

DINAH,
BLOW YOUR HORN
Jack Bickham

COLLECTOR'S LIBRARY
EDITION

In this Volume:

DAUNTLESS

by Alan Evans (p.9)

When David Smith, commanding the light cruiser *Dauntless* and seaplane carrier *Blackbird*, is ordered to harass the Turkish-held coast of Palestine, the task seems routine. But then Smith's orders are changed dramatically: a German brigade is racing south, and he must stop it at all costs. With the unexpected help of the Australian cavalry, a band of British mutineers and a fiery young nurse, Smith's force swings into battle in this thrillingly action-packed story of the Great War.

INTRUDER

by Louis Charbonneau (p.171)

Imagine a twisted criminal in control of a powerful computer—manipulating the central data system for an entire city. Imagine this power used to work a deadly, private revenge. Could such a terrible nightmare come true?

The catastrophic accidents that strike the people of Hollister seem unrelated at first. But terror mounts as it becomes increasingly clear that someone is tampering with computer programmes on which the city's vital services depend. Unless the mysterious intruder can be stopped, Hollister will be brought to its knees . . . . This story is chillingly relevant to today.

Going Wild

by David Taylor (p.313)

Dr. David Taylor has one of the world's most unusual professions—he's a zoo vet, travelling thousands of miles every year to treat his exotic patients. Whether it's fish or fowl, zebra or whale, Taylor is ready to cope with any emergency. Life wasn't always so exciting: as an ambitious young vet, Taylor found himself tending poodles and budgerigars. *Going Wild* tells how he broke into the challenging world of zoo medicine, and describes the fascinating adventures of his new career.

Dinah, Blow Your Horn

by Jack Bickham (p.387)

In a small American town in the early 1900s, a railroad strike threatens the security of the whole community. Amid argument and turmoil, thirteen-year-old Bobby Keller witnesses the growing anger and resentment of the workers towards the railroad company and its police. And it looks like cowardice to him when his own father tries to avoid taking a stand with the rest.

To save his family's self-respect, Bobby risks everything in one daring exploit. He also learns the painful lessons of trust, love and growing up.

DAUNTLESS

A CONDENSATION OF THE BOOK BY

Alan Evans

ILLUSTRATIONS BY COLIN ANDREW
DRAWINGS BY GINO D'ACHILLE
PUBLISHED BY HODDER & STOUGHTON

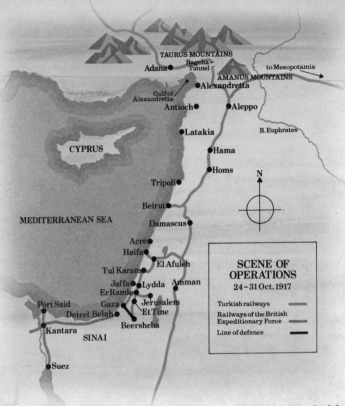

In 1917 General Allenby's army, poised on the threshold
of Palestine, is ready to launch an attack
against the Turks. Then comes the grim news that five
thousand crack German troops, the Afrika Legion, are
speeding south to reinforce their ally.
Time is desperately short, and Commander David Smith, RN,
harrying the enemy coast with his small flotilla, is
given urgent orders: Find and stop the Afrika Legion!
All Smith's daring and ingenuity are called upon to meet
this challenge, as on land and sea his little force
fights to the death against a strong and cunning enemy.

1 Make or Break

Commander David Cochrane Smith pencilled the date at the top of the notepad: 24.10.17. It triggered the thought—General Allenby's army would attack the Gaza-Beersheba line in a week, on the 31st. This would be a battle vital to the entire future of the war. Thoughtfully, he laid the notepad down and stared out across the water.

He stood right in the stern of HM Seaplane Carrier *Blackbird*. Until the war she had been a fast cross-channel packet. Now she had accommodation for four Short seaplanes in the big barn of a hangar the dockyard had built on her after end. His own ship, the light cruiser *Dauntless*, sailed a quarter-mile to starboard. Both ships were on a course almost due south, with the morning sun blazing out low over the sea from the coast of Palestine and lifting above the eastern horizon.

Smith's figure in white drill trousers and jacket was slight, seemingly frail, but that was deceptive. He was thin-faced, not handsome, pale blue eyes watchful under the peak of his cap. He was probably as happy that morning as he would ever be. He had a command and was grateful to Rear Admiral Braddock, who had got him *Dauntless* and had given him *Blackbird* as consort. Smith and his seaplane carrier were to act in support of Allenby's army, while Braddock concentrated on organizing convoys to combat the menace of U-boats in the Mediterranean.

Smith suspected the old admiral had fought to get this command

9

for him, and he was right. Smith was unpredictable. Admittedly he had won two decisive actions recently, one in the Pacific and one in the North Sea, but in the first he had outraged a neutral government, and in the second had defied his immediate superior. There were many who said he was a hothead and a rebel, but Braddock had won his fight all the same. The admiral was a friend. Smith was unmarried, had few friends, and was bleakly aware of it.

Now Smith stood aboard *Blackbird* and told himself that this command was make or break for him. He was far from a conventional naval officer. Brought up in a village shop in Norfolk by adopted parents—a retired chief petty officer, Reuben Smith, and his wife, Hannah—his career had been chequered, highlighted by success, but marred by scandal. If he made a success of his part in Allenby's campaign then his critics would be silenced and he would go forward on the floodtide of victory. And there *would* be a victory. There had to be. The allies needed it in this third year of the war and Allenby had been sent out to get it.

The carrier had reduced speed to ten knots and one of the Shorts was wheeled out of the hangar, its big, boxlike floats resting on a trolley. It stood fifteen feet high, a biplane with its wings folded back, but now that it was clear of the hangar the riggers swung out the wings and rammed the locking pins into the sockets on their leading edges. The Short changed from a nesting bird to one ready to fly. Smith saw Lieutenant Chris Pearce checking that those pins were secure, as he always checked since the day he had seen one hanging loose as he had been about to take off.

Pearce was a pilot as well as the captain of *Blackbird*, a tall, good-looking young man who had worn an engaging grin when Smith first met him, three weeks before. But now he looked drawn and edgy, tired. Smith was startled. He had not seen Pearce for days: he worked him and his four flying crews hard, but still the man should not look so worn. Pearce had come to him with reports of near-brilliance. But it was a highly-strung brilliance and, in Smith's short experience of him, he had proved increasingly nervy and erratic.

Now Pearce turned, lifted a hand signalling that he was ready and Smith joined him, took a leather flying helmet and climbed up into the Short. That was all the flying gear they needed in these last days of the Mediterranean summer. He put notepad and map on the seat of the observer's cockpit. Pearce stood in the pilot's cockpit in front of him, reaching up for the hook on the derrick purchase dangling on the end of its wire. The armourer passed up four 16-pound anti-personnel bombs. "All we've got left, I'm afraid, sir," he said. Smith set the bombs down  on the floor of the cockpit, the Lewis gun nudging his back. He nodded his readiness as Pearce looked round questioningly.

Pearce faced forward, lifted a hand, the winch hammered and the derrick lifted the Short and swung it out over the side to hang above the sea. Events moved rapidly now. *Blackbird* could launch a seaplane in forty-five seconds. The Short dropped down to the sea off *Blackbird*'s port quarter and seamen standing on her wide rubbing strake used long poles to boom off the fragile seaplane from the steel side. For a second it dangled less than a foot above the wave crests slipping beneath the floats as *Blackbird* pulled slowly away, then Pearce yanked the toggle release that slipped the hook and the Short smacked down on the sea.

Shorts were big, ungainly birds but reliable. They flew and flew. They were forty feet long and the wings spread sixty-three feet. Under the mid-section there were two big floats with a smaller float at each wing tip and another on the tail. The Short sat back on the tail float now it was on the sea. Pearce turned the tap on the compressed air cylinder in his cockpit, and the Maori engine kicked and fired. He ran it up, taxi-ing, then shoved forward the control column until the tail float lifted off, and hauled back as the Short reached flying speed. They rose into the air, and eased around in a gently-banking turn until they were headed east, towards the distant coast of Palestine. Ten minutes later they crossed the coastline at fifteen hundred feet.

Allenby's orders had been short and to the point: capture Palestine. The land that lay under Smith now would be the battleground. To his left and far to the north, was Syria, ahead the hills of Judaea lifted in a blue wall, and on the right, in the distant south, was the desert of Sinai. The Turks had ruled Palestine for centuries. When the war started they advanced through Sinai and threatened the Suez Canal. But they were beaten back, and in the last year the British army under Murray had fought its way up through the Sinai desert. Now, however, the Turks had with them five thousand soldiers of the German Asia Corps to supply a technical stiffening.

The Short turned south, following the thread of the railway and pointing its nose towards the Gaza–Beersheba front line sixty miles away. German engineers had strung fortifications across the thirty miles between Beersheba, the fortress at the southern end of the hills of Judaea, and Gaza, up on the coast. They boasted the line was impregnable. And, now that Allenby had taken over from Murray, he had no choice except to attack it. His army crouched ready on one side of the line, Palestine lay on the other, and he had his orders: take Palestine.

Rear Admiral Braddock's orders to Smith were simple: harass the enemy.

"Harass the enemy." For the last two weeks *Dauntless* and *Blackbird* had raced up and down this coast from Gaza to the Gulf of Alexandretta, three hundred miles to the north. *Dauntless* shelled installations, drove the coastal traffic of dhows and small craft into the shallows, then set them afire or blew them up. *Blackbird*'s Shorts reconnoitred, and bombed the railway whenever they could. The railway that ran down from Alexandretta to the Gaza–Beersheba line was the sole artery sustaining the enemy there. Although damage to the track could be made good in a day, any delay meant a break in supplies to the enemy army.

This was not Smith's first flight in those two weeks, because he needed to see for himself—he could not always send others. So here he was with Pearce, looking for trouble and ready to make it; hence the four bombs, all that remained after the Shorts' repeated attacks. Trouble was not hard to find. A week ago one of the Shorts was hit by gunfire and forced down into the shallows off the coast.

Smith had sent an armed party in the motorboat to lift the pilot and observer out of the surf. They had been very lucky.

The Short droned on at a steady sixty knots and the old Arab town of Lydda slid under the port wing. The Turks had a garrison a mile or so north of it, but Smith saw no troops on the move. The railway ran on southwards. Smith stood up and leaned to one side to peer ahead. There was no train in sight. The spur line coming from Jaffa on the coast swung southwards to join the main line at Lydda station, a half-mile south of the town itself. Ahead, a further mile south of the station was a German anti-aircraft battery.

Pearce had not forgotten this. The Short banked away well clear of the guns, turning westwards towards the coast and picking up the line of the railway from Jaffa. Smith smacked the pilot's shoulder and pointed at a trailing plume of grey-black smoke some seven or eight miles ahead. Pearce pushed up the goggles to rub irritably at his eyes, then pulled the goggles down again. He peered in the direction Smith indicated and his scowl was wiped away by a grin. He eased the nose of the Short down in a shallow dive. It was the train that had run once a day from Lydda to Jaffa and back again until *Dauntless* and *Blackbird* set out on their rampage. Now, after an interval, it was trying again. The Short dropped out of the sky towards it. Smith groped down by his feet as they overhauled the train, eight trucks, all of them loaded, then the tender stacked with logs, and the engine, its tall chimney belching out smoke. The Short was down to two hundred feet or so, sweeping forward over the train, and Smith could see the dark faces of the men on the footplate of the engine turned up to him.

He was standing again, holding the bomb over the side of the cockpit, yanking out the pin and seeing the fan of the tail start to revolve. He let it go as they raced towards the locomotive. He saw a soldier on the footplate with a rifle at his shoulder.

The Short was past in a blink and tearing away ahead of the train as the bomb burst, in front of the engine but wide of the track. Smith groped for another as the Short's port wing dipped in as tight a turn as the unwieldy craft could produce, and the nose pointed once more at the train. The Short wasn't overtaking the train now but closing it and Smith had to allow for their increased combined speeds. He worried at the pin, got it free and let the bomb go. He saw the bomb fall ahead of the train and wide again, and swore. He'd botched it. Next time. . . . He reached down, lifted the third bomb.

Pearce turned the Short and they overhauled the train again. It was steaming more slowly as it climbed a long slope. Sand dunes on the right of the track and orange groves on the left, the train sliding up at Smith, beneath him, the engine coming up—now!

The bomb burst in the dunes, hurling up sand, yards from the track though level with the engine. One to go.

The Short was banking right-handed above the crest of the hill. Smith caught a quick, wheeling glimpse of Jaffa a mile or more past the crest of the hill. A minaret stood above the walls of the old town perched on the edge of the sea. Then the smaller township, just half a dozen neatly laid-out streets, deserted now, that lay a half-mile north of Jaffa. What was it?—Tel Aviv. And then the two ships, far out at sea, patrolling. And all the time he scanned the sky, head turning. He checked, stiffened, then tapped Pearce's shoulder.

The Short levelled out and Pearce twisted around in his seat. He peered in the direction Smith indicated and found what Smith was pointing out. It was like a small black insect, high in the sky and coming up from the south where the German Asia Corps had an airfield. But Pearce put up his thumb, then made a downward thrusting gesture. So he thought there was time to finish the attack.

Smith hesitated, then nodded. He was a novice observer while Pearce was a highly-experienced pilot—and he didn't want to let the train off the hook. The Short's nose tilted down steeply as Pearce set it diving along the track, only a dozen feet above it.

The train was stopped. Smith saw the men leap from the footplate and scurry towards the orange groves, but his attention was all for the locomotive itself. For the last time he yanked out the pin and let go the bomb. The engine flashed beneath him and in that instant the bomb burst. Looking past the tail of the Short he saw dust rising. The Short turned, climbing slowly now, and as the dust blew away he saw the bomb had fallen short of the train but on the track. There was a hole now and twisted rails.

That was enough. This was yet another day when the train would not arrive at Jaffa, when a repair gang would have to replace the track, when he had, in the spirit of his orders, harassed the enemy . . . .

Pearce lifted the Short, then sent it plunging. Smith turned around and gripped the Lewis, cocked it and peered up through the ring sight at the German plane diving down after them.

Far out of range, but for how long? They were over the sea now, levelling out close above the waves and heading for *Dauntless* and *Blackbird*. Smith squinted up at the Fokker monoplane, watching as the black aircraft swung slowly from one side of the Short's rudder to the other, steadily closing. He wondered uneasily if they had hung on too long. If it came to a fight the seaplane would have no chance, being slower and less manoeuvrable than the Fokker.

It was just in range of the Lewis now but Smith was not an expert shot and so he waited, took his eyes off it for a moment as he felt the Short bank to starboard. He saw they were near to *Blackbird* and Pearce was turning into the wind to set the seaplane down. The carrier was stopped, and *Dauntless* was starting to patrol around her.

Smith swung back to peer over the Short's tail, could not see the Fokker, searched frantically but for only a split-second because the enemy was boring in from his right hand. He pivoted in the cockpit, swinging the Lewis around, got the Fokker in its sights, lost it, brought the sights on again—and fired as the German fired. He saw no signs of a hit on the Fokker but splinters were snapping off their own tail and fuselage, and something cannoned off the Lewis sending the shock jarring up his arm. The Short was descending slowly, and the Fokker snarled over them and away, then banked to come back at the Short again. They were skimming the surface of the sea, the heels of the floats rubbing into the short waves. The floats dug in, the feathers of spray dropped away and the Short was down, taxi-ing towards *Blackbird*.

The Fokker was flying through a sky pocked with bursting shells from *Dauntless*, but the firing ceased as the Fokker closed on the Short. Smith had the gun steady in his hands and the Fokker filled the big ring sight. The Short, too, was a sitting duck. He swallowed at the thought and fired.

He thought this time the burst had scored, was sure he saw pieces flying from the Fokker that swerved and showed its side before it straightened again. The German pilot could fire only one brief burst and then flashed over Smith's head again, turning and climbing, the shells from *Dauntless* bursting around him. He plunged down towards the sea, then fled for the shore, tucked right down on the surface of the sea.

Pearce edged the Short alongside *Blackbird* with the engine ticking over. Smith secured the Lewis with shaking hands and wiped the sweat from them on the front of his white shirt. *Dauntless* had launched her gig and it was pulling towards the Short. He could see Leading Seaman Buckley, who had served with him in the Pacific and the Channel, at the helm, the look on his face half-anxious, half-irritated at Smith getting involved with a German fighter plane. Smith grinned. Buckley had a certain licence because of long acquaintance, dangers and hardships shared.

The Short was close under *Blackbird*'s lee now. The derrick was swung out and dangled the purchase block and its hook. A heaving line was secured to that hook and a seaman on *Blackbird*'s deck held the rest of the line, ready to throw it. Smith watched the seaman attentively. Any man who missed the line when it was thrown could expect hard words—the line then had to be recovered and thrown again while the carrier lay stopped, which was wasteful of time and effort, and often dangerous.

The seaman threw the line, snaking it out across the ruffled sea. It fell on the fabric aft of the cockpit. Smith dived after it, sprawled precariously along the fuselage, grabbed at it and caught it. He worked back into the cockpit, then clambered past Pearce to haul in the line and thus bring down the hook of the derrick purchase. He hooked onto the ring on the upper wing and lifted a hand. As the derrick took the strain the Short's engine died.

Smith looked at Pearce and told him, "We cut it too fine, Chris."

"Well, we got back, sir," Pearce was breathless and he fumbled with the strap of his helmet, not looking at Smith.

"With a hell of a lot of holes and by the skin of our teeth." He paused, then asked softly, "Is anything wrong, Chris?"

"No, sir. Nothing."

Pearce was lying. "This isn't the time nor the place," Smith murmured, "but if you'd like to have a talk—"

"No, sir! There's nothing." Pearce was quick in his denial. "Everything's fine."

16

But Smith said ruthlessly, "You look dog-tired and you're on edge. Maybe you're driving yourself too hard. When you're not on the bridge or flying, you're down in the hangar." He paused, then: "I don't want you flying again for a while."

Pearce looked at him now, startled, and protested, "Sir! I'm *all right!* It was just that blighter looked a lot farther—" His voice was rising but it cut short as he saw the gig alongside the seaplane, the men in her looking up at him curiously.

Smith said quietly, "You see what I mean." He stood up and swung a leg over the side of the cockpit. "That's an order. No flying." He went down into the gig.

The bow man shoved off, and Smith sat in the sternsheets of the gig, looking back as the Short was swung inboard, then lowered onto the waiting trolley. Now they could fold the wings and shove it into the hangar that filled the after half of *Blackbird* to within fifty feet of her stern. The hangar made her a queer-looking ship, a bit like a floating boot, but she could make twenty knots and Pearce swore that once you got some way on her she handled like a destroyer. He admitted also that in a strong wind and at slow speed the slab-sided hangar acted like a sail and made things tricky.

Smith turned and faced forward as the gig closed *Dauntless*. She was a light cruiser, commissioned only two years before. Of four thousand tons, she was four hundred and fifty feet long and no more than forty in the beam, slender, graceful and fast; she had steamed twenty-nine knots in her trials and could still do so. She mounted three 6-inch guns, one forward of the bridge and two aft.

Smith was delighted with her, gained fresh pleasure from each sight of her. He knew she had her faults, that to give her speed she was lightly armoured, and that when steaming at speed it was hell's own job to work the forward 6-inch because of the seas breaking over her bow. He forgave her those, as a man might accept the faults of a beautiful woman he loved. Yet *Dauntless*'s faults, particularly her lack of armour, could possibly be the death of him and the three hundred and fifty men aboard her.

Buckley ran the gig neatly alongside *Dauntless* and Smith started to climb the ladder. On deck a party under the command of Lieutenant Griffith waited to hoist in the gig. A dark, soft-spoken Welshman, Griffith had made a brave reputation in the Dardanelles as a forward observer ashore. Now he asked, "Any luck, sir?"

Smith answered, "Caught the train on its daily run to Jaffa."

"Again? They must be fed-up. Give 'em a fright, sir?"

"Not as bad as that Fokker gave me." He grinned at the laughter and climbed up to the bridge.

The two ships headed southwards with *Dauntless* leading, following the coastline, searching for targets. The land south of Jaffa was sand dunes, some a hundred feet high, stretching inland like a low mountain range. Two hours later they were passing Gaza, the coastal end of the Gaza–Beersheba line, and the coast was greener.

Two British monitors were anchored five miles out, low in the water like crocodiles, lobbing 6-inch shells into Gaza as part of the build-up to Allenby's attack. The land artillery with Allenby's army was also pounding Gaza. His army stretched all the way back to the manmade harbour at Deir el Belah, ten miles to the south, and beyond. A pall of red dust hung permanently over the land, churned up by the hooves of eighty thousand horses, camels and donkeys. This army had built its own railway from Kantara, on the Suez Canal, as it fought its way across Sinai; Deir el Belah was its forward railhead. It was a tough army with confidence in itself. Not cockiness; it respected the Germans and Turks for the fighters they were, but it had fought them from Egypt into Palestine and beaten them all the way. It was ready to beat them again.

The same mood of confidence ran through Smith's command. There were only six days now to Allenby's attack. Smith was not looking forward to it with eager anticipation because the first result of battles was a casualty list. But this time the final result *had* to be different, not a tragic failure like the Dardanelles nor an unending, murderous struggle like that in France and Flanders. This time they would achieve a victory, drive the Germans and Turks out of Palestine, and *Dauntless* and *Blackbird* would play an important part in it.

And yet . . . three years of war had left Smith wary of over-optimism. Although he knew the attack would be on the 31st, the rest of his command only knew it must be soon. Yet Kressenstein, the German commander, must also know that. He would have made his own plans. . . . Now, as the two ships headed southwards for Port Said, Smith was uneasy.

ADELINE BRETT, twenty-one years old, small, pretty and blonde, climbed out of the thick oven-heat in the Number Two forward hold of the steam tramp *Morning Star*. The marine sentry, rifle with bayonet fixed, turned the key in the padlock and swung open the doors in the barbed wire surrounding the hold. Adeline passed through and stood outside on the deck for a moment, blinking in the strong sunlight. The white cotton shirt and drill trousers were plastered to her body with sweat. They were men's naval issue, laboriously tailored, but still too big for her. Now she eased them from her skin, and held up her face to the wind of passage; *Morning Star* was making all of her best speed of twelve knots, smoke billowing from her single funnel, sparks and coal dust and soot raining down aft. The old ship was alone, and running for her life.

The girl hitched at the canvas medical haversack slung from her shoulder. She remembered their first dawn at sea, when the thump of an explosion had brought her running from her bunk to the rail of the *Morning Star*. There she watched as the old destroyer, their escort, back broken by the torpedo, sank in minutes. *Morning Star* had not stopped to help survivors or invite another torpedo. She had run, was still running. And somehow, miraculously, she had lost the German submarine.

. Adeline Brett smiled at the young marine sentry and passed under the bridge towards her cabin in the superstructure. In the cabin she opened the haversack, checked its contents and made good its deficiencies of bandages, dressings and pills from a chest she dragged out from under the bunk. Adeline Brett was a nurse.

At the beginning of her career she had cycled down from the big house in Hampshire to the little cottage hospital, just a young girl of good family helping out. In that long-ago summer she was the schoolgirl daughter of a rich man, meeting and mixing with the wealthy and famous, one of her uncles a press baron and another in Parliament. But when the war came she went to France, where an army surgeon, a veteran of the Boer War, took a liking to her and schooled her. From France she went as a member of a small volunteer team to Gallipoli and then, with what was left of it, to Salonika. There the war and disease took its toll and within a month the team had disintegrated and she was left alone. Then she found this strange unhappy ship.

Now she worked quickly, neatly, packed the haversack so it was ready again, and hung it on a hook. She turned the taps to run water into the basin, stripped off the shirt—washed, worrying about the men of the battalion imprisoned below. She was the sole woman aboard this ship and caring for four hundred infantrymen locked away behind barbed wire. She dried her face and looked at herself in the small mirror, her reflection shivering with the vibration of the old ship's engines. Her lips tightened, and she turned away from the mirror. By nightfall, she thought, they should all be safe in the harbour at Port Said.

2 *The Battalion*

Smith was in his cramped little hutch of a sea cabin at the back of the bridge, a seven-foot steel cube holding a bed, a small desk and a chair. His report lay before him unfinished as he brooded over Chris Pearce, wondered what ailed him. Should he ask for *Blackbird*'s captain to be relieved, request a medical report? But either of these could prove damaging to Pearce's career and up to now it had been outstanding. Besides, Pearce's performance was still adequate and you could hardly relieve a man of his command because he was no longer outstanding. But Smith should be able to rely on him totally, and he could not. Something was wrong, eating away at him, but the way he had reacted to Smith's questioning showed that, whatever it was, he was determined to keep it to himself.

Smith sighed with frustration, then picked up his pen. They were bound for Port Said and with luck there would be shore leave— that might work a change in Pearce. Meanwhile the report for Admiral Braddock had to be finished before they got in.

Port Said was barely two hours away when the messenger came running from the wireless office aft. Smith took the signal, and went through to the charthouse next door.

"There's a steamer in trouble," he said. "Engine's broken down on her way to Port Said. We've been ordered to assist. Course?"

He handed the signal to Henderson, the navigator, who plotted the position of the ship on the chart muttering, "*Morning Star.*

What's she doing out there on her own?'' He pointed at the signal. "And RDF indicates U-boat in that area!"

Smith thought that the Radio Direction Finding report had probably been made the previous night when the U-boat had surfaced to charge batteries and could rig her wireless aerial. She must have gone from that area now or she would not have passed by a target like *Morning Star*. But she might well return. He said dryly, "Could complicate things a bit." As he went out onto the bridge he, too, wondered why a solitary ship lay out there without escort.

Dauntless altered course and *Blackbird* followed, both ships increasing speed to twenty knots. Even so it would be dusk when they came up with *Morning Star*. When they were still fifty miles away Smith ordered *Blackbird* to launch a seaplane. The Short lifted into the air to go scouting ahead, sent to find *Morning Star* and patrol around her, watching for the U-boat.

Close on two hours later they sighted the Short, flying in a wide circle around the steamer. *Morning Star* was a tramp of three to four thousand tons. As the sun sank, *Blackbird* stopped to recover the Short. *Dauntless* went on, slipping towards the tramp at ten knots. There was a sea running now, her bow nodding as she rode it.

Ackroyd, the first lieutenant, was on the bridge. Square-shouldered and square-faced, a dour Yorkshireman, impatient of fools and paperwork, he already had enormous respect for Smith, who in the last weeks had proved himself a seaman. But the rumours of unconventional behaviour, insubordination and scandal, made him wary. Now he said, "Signal from *Blackbird*, sir. The Short reports smoke, probably a convoy, to northward."

Smith nodded, eyes on the ship ahead.

Ackroyd muttered, "What's that row?" Faintly across the sea came the sound of yelling. He lifted his glasses then said incredulously, "That's wire strung around her hatches and bridge!" Then a light flashed from the bridge of the *Morning Star*.

The signal yeoman read: "SOS.... Prisoners escaping."

Ackroyd said, "What the hell? *Prisoners?*"

As *Dauntless* came astern of *Morning Star*, Smith saw through his glasses what looked like barbed wire laced around her foredeck and bridge, and a crowd milling just forward of the bridge, heaving

21

and swaying. He let the glasses fall on their strap: "Send the sea-boat! Armed!" And as he dashed back to his cabin: "I'll go!"

In the cabin he discarded the glasses, snatched the Webley pistol on its belt and buckled it around him, slid down the ladder and ran aft. *Dauntless* was pitching in the swell, the cutter already in the sea and her crew gone down into her. He glanced across at *Morning Star* and saw flickering spurts of flame, heard the rattle of rifle fire. He grabbed for the dangling line and dropped hand over hand. He caught a fleeting glimpse of *Blackbird* making ready to pass a tow to the disabled tramp steamer.. He wondered, suppose the U-boat turned up now? He swore as he dropped into the boat and fell across a thwart. Buckley, holding the line, a rifle slung from one shoulder, apologized: "Sorry, sir."

Smith answered, "Not your fault." Pushing past him, Smith snapped at the midshipman, "Get on with it! Shove off! Oars!" He sat down with a thump. The cutter thrust away from *Dauntless*'s side and headed for the *Morning Star*. He saw the midshipman was Bright, the lumpish one whose clothes were too small for him so the buttons of his jacket strained. Bright? A misnomer? He was the one always falling over things, always bewildered. The cutter soared and plummeted as she closed the *Morning Star*. Smith said, "Smart work, Mr. Bright. You were very quick." He had been.

"Th-thank you, sir." The evening was cool but Smith saw the boy was sweating. Nervousness? Smith murmured, "You're doing well. Lay us alongside." A little encouragement would not go amiss.

The side of the *Morning Star* was hanging over them now as she rolled. Heads showed over her bulwarks and a Jacob's ladder spilled down and was grabbed by one of the cutter's crew. Smith pushed between the men to get at the ladder, hung on to it and started to climb. The ladder swung as *Morning Star* rolled, and he was jerked out over the sea then thrown in against the rusty, riveted plates. He climbed steadily, aware that there had been shooting aboard this ship only minutes before and that his Webley was still in its holster. Then he saw the faces above him, one topping a seaman's blue jersey and bareheaded, the other wearing the round cap of a marine. He swung a leg over the rail as the marine held out a steadying arm. The marine carried a rifle with bayonet fixed in his other hand.

Smith stood just under the bridge and took a quick glance round. All the covers were on the hold except the two nearest to him and there was barbed wire strung in a fence across the deck. Marines were posted by it, a guard on the wired-in hold, rifles with fixed bayonets held at the ready. Two more marines sat on the deck, one of them wiping at a bloody nose and the other nursing his right wrist. Smith's glance returned to rest on the captain of marines who stood before him, saluting. Smith returned the salute and the marine said breathlessly, "Brand, sir."

"Smith. Commanding *Dauntless*. I heard firing a minute ago. What's going on?"

Captain Brand was a muscular young man, broken-nosed. His was a face that might easily break into a wide grin but now he looked a tough nut. "The prisoners tried to break out," he said.

Smith asked, "Germans? Turks? Where are they from?"

"Salonika, sir." Brand dabbed at a cut on his forehead and said hesitantly. "They're not *exactly* prisoners, sir, though my orders were to treat them as such." He saw Smith's exasperation and finished quickly. "They're British soldiers, sir."

British! And not *exactly* prisoners . . . . "So they tried to break out?" Smith prompted.

Brand wiped again at the blood that streamed from his cut. "We're quartered right aft. I heard the shouting and ran forward with a few of my men and found the prisoners trying to break past the sentries, I ordered my men to fire over their heads."

Smith said, "And that drove them below." He was staring at the wire strung around the hold, a gap of six feet or so torn in it.

Brand said flatly, "It did not. More of them kept coming up out of the hold and they were shoving us back. But then the major came running up. He got them below again."

"Major?" Smith asked, "What major?"

"Taggart, sir. He's the only officer with them and he's in the hold with them now." Brand paused, then added, "God knows what would have happened if all of them had got out. They'd gone mad!"

"All?" Smith asked, "How many men are you holding?"

"Close on four hundred, sir."

Smith said, "I want to see."

Buckley and a half-dozen men from the cutter were behind him now, rifles held across their chests, peering suspiciously about. They followed him as he picked his way through the trodden tangle of wire strewn on the deck. At one side of the gap was a door in the wire, closed and padlocked. There a ladder poked its top rungs out of the hold and Smith moved to it, hearing Brand coming behind him.

Smith peered down into the hold below. He said, "Four hundred men in this hold?"

Brand said, "Yes, sir. And in the other one forward. The dockyard at Malta worked through the night to fit bunks, and hooks for slinging hammocks. There wasn't a troopship available and we had to sail the next morning to embark the battalion at Salonika."

Smith said. "It's a poor substitute for a trooper."

Brand said honestly, "It's bloody awful, sir."

"What did she last carry?"

"I don't know. But she's been a cattleboat before now."

And still was. Smith stared down into the hold. The only light was from small blue bulbs, scattered sparsely around the sides of the hold.

He called, "Major Taggart!" His voice echoed in the hold, came back to him a hoarse whisper. He saw faces turned up towards him, faces so close together they were like a mosaic.

A voice answered from below: "Yes?"

"I am Commander Smith. His Majesty's cruiser *Dauntless*. I'm coming below." Smith swung onto the ladder and started down into the gloom. The smell of packed humanity rose up around him. The ladder ended in a small clear space of deck, where a score of men were drawn up shoulder to shoulder. An officer stood bareheaded in front of them, his tunic hung open, thrown on hurriedly. He was only a shade taller than Smith but broader, deep-chested, black-haired and black-browed. He stood to attention. "John Taggart, Major, Composite Battalion."

Smith held out his hand, but stared past him at the men crouched on the bunks that were built in tiers, four above each other. More men squatted on the 'tween-decks and another ladder led down into a hold still further below. Smith saw blue lights down there also, glistening on faces slicked with sweat like oil.

He himself ran with sweat already. The inside of the hold was airless and humid. He asked the major, "Captain Brand only knows your men tried to break out. Can you add to that?"

Taggart was angry, curt. "Two or three of them were standing on the ladder getting a lungful of clean air. Then the girl screamed for help and—"

Smith broke in: "Girl? What girl?"

"This one!" The voice came from behind and above him and he spun on his heels to see her coming down the ladder, to step onto the deck beside him. She was small, her curly blonde hair cut short, dressed in a pair of men's white drill trousers and a white shirt that made her seem even smaller than she really was.

Taggart said, "This is Miss Adeline Brett. She's the nurse attached to us. In fact, apart from a dozen orderlies, she's the only medical help we have."

She glanced up at Smith, and asked coldly, "You command the cruiser? And so you command here?" And when Smith nodded: "Then you must do something for these men."

It was more an order than a request and Smith was not used to taking orders from a slip of a girl. He said shortly, "I understand this—disturbance began when you screamed for help."

The girl's brow lifted fractionally. "Did it? I did scream and I'm sorry. I'd been here to see to a man who had fallen from the ladder and I was walking aft to my cabin when a sailor grabbed me. I pulled away, and because it was a shock, I screamed. But that was stupid. I lost my head for a moment." She was passing it off coolly, but at the time she must have been terrified.

Smith saw the shirt was torn at the neck and showed a white shoulder. Taggart asked quietly, "Who was it?"

Adeline Brett shook her blonde head. "I don't know. It was dark under the superstructure. He ran away aft."

Taggart growled, "One of the crew?"

"Obviously." The girl did not seem interested. "I came to see if these men need attention. With your permission, John?"

Taggart nodded and she moved to the front rank of the men behind him, pulled cotton wool and a bottle from the haversack slung from her shoulder and said briskly, "Hands, please."

The first man held out his hands. Smith saw they were torn and bloody. He said. "They tore down the wire with their *hands?*"

Taggart glanced sidewise at him and said dryly, "They've been faced by wire before."

Smith looked at them and at the men beyond them, faces stacked in rows as the tiers of bunks climbed the sides of the hold. Soldiers. They wore thick khaki serge uniforms, trousers bound around with puttees. They had discarded their tunics but they still wore heavy collarless, khaki wool shirts. And they were eerily quiet.

He asked Taggart, in a voice so low only the other could hear, "Who are these men? Why are they here?"

Taggart glanced at Smith, seemingly surprised by the question, and asked cynically, "You mean, you care why?"

Smith said softly, savagely, "I saw Jutland and other actions before and since, a sight more than four hundred men killed and a lot of them were men I knew and liked. We're sacrificing the cream of a generation and it sickens me. Now answer my question!"

The cynicism was wiped from Taggart's face. He looked straight at Smith then said slowly, "When you've served with men for a long time—but I don't need to tell you. I'd do anything for them but in fact I can do little. Of course you care. My apologies."

"Not necessary." Smith thought Taggart was a good soldier and a good man, an instinctive judgment. But Taggart hesitated now, as if uncertain where to begin.

"We were ordered to attack—" He stopped and shook his head and after a moment started again. "It goes back to before Salonika. In Flanders some of the regiments that were badly cut up were combined into composite battalions. *This* was a composite battalion, formed from survivors of a dozen regiments. From Flanders they sent it—us—to Gallipoli and at the end of that they took us across to Salonika." He paused, then amended, "I took them across to Salonika. Our old colonel had been killed in Gallipoli. We went to Gallipoli with a strength of eight hundred and thirty-four and we left for Salonika with six hundred and two."

The girl, Adeline Brett, was swabbing at the torn hands of one of the men. He stood patiently, meekly, as she lectured him: "You should have more sense! All of you! Going mad like that! I can look after myself." Smith believed it. Even so, she looked very small and very young.

Some of the men looked as young. One seemed little more than a boy but there was a bitterness about his young face. Smith noticed him because he sat a little apart from the others, despite the crowding in the hold.

Taggart said, "In Salonika we soon got a new colonel. We didn't see much of him but even then it was too much. I ran the battalion. I'd come to it in 'fifteen when they formed it—it really was my battalion. Then we were ordered to attack to straighten a salient in the line on the Vardar river in Salonika. We were assaulting prepared positions and under crossfire from machine guns. It was hopeless. The attack failed. We went in with nearly six hundred effectives and we came out with four hundred. They pulled us out of the line and in the back area the colonel called a conference of all officers at a farmhouse. He rode up from the rear and told them to wait there while he spoke to the men. They were bivouacked a half-mile away and he rode down and called them out on parade. He sat on his horse in front of them, so drunk that he had to use both hands to hold on. He cursed and shouted at them and told them the attack had failed because they'd not pressed it home. He called them cowards, and they stood there, what was left of them, dog-tired, some of them asleep on their feet."

Taggart stopped, his gaze distant now. He said, "We don't leave men in the field, nor weapons if we can save them. We'd brought back thirty or forty rifles and pistols and the men had been told to bring them to the parade to hand them in. Someone used one of those weapons to shoot him."

Smith had been watching the young man who sat alone, but now

27

his gaze snapped back to Taggart, shocked. "You mean—dead?"

Taggart said sardonically, "Three shots in the chest at close range. They knocked him back off the horse and he was dead before he hit the ground. That's why they are all here."

Smith asked, "All? But surely only one man—"

"—fired the shot." Taggart nodded. "Right. But nobody would admit he saw it. The weapon belonged to a dead man. That's why the whole battalion was put aboard the *Morning Star* and sent to Cyprus. But the people there didn't want four hundred men who had been involved in mutiny and that is why they are bound now for Port Said. The army doesn't know what to do with them."

Smith said, "If the officers were at a farmhouse half a mile away, how do you know what happened?"

Taggart's face was expressionless. "I was there, the only officer present. I had a horse and I'd followed the colonel. That's why I'm here now: I didn't see who shot the colonel, either. I'm as much a prisoner as my men."

It was very quiet when Taggart finished speaking. Smith could hear their breathing, feel their eyes on him. Now he knew the reason for Taggart's wariness, their watchfulness; they kept a secret to themselves and from the world.

"Commander Smith!" The hail came from the marine officer, Brand, leaning over the hatch. "The ship's master is here, sir, Captain Jeavons."

Smith answered, "I'm coming!"

"So am I," Taggart said grimly. "I want to talk to him."

Adeline Brett's voice came softly but clearly. "Do you find it uncomfortable down here, Commander?"

She turned towards him and Smith thought she might be quite a pretty girl if she was not in that mannish get-up. He said, "I've known better places."

"The first couple of days are the worst." She too was watching him now. She went on, "You are in command. Something must be done for these men."

She was pushing Smith and he did not like it. He replied shortly, "As you say, I command. And I will decide what needs to be done." He turned to the ladder but her parting glance told him she was not impressed.

He climbed out of the hold followed by Taggart and picked his way through the barbed wire. A party of marines wearing leather gloves were starting to unroll a new coil of wire, to repair the gap. Smith growled, "Belay that." They halted in the work and glanced at Captain Brand. He looked puzzled, but nodded.

Buckley waited anxiously beyond the wire with the half-dozen seamen from *Dauntless*'s cutter, hefting their rifles and peering curiously at the wire. The ship's master stood near the bridge. He might have been fifty, no more, but he looked an elderly man, his broad shoulders sagging. He held out his hand, "Jeavons, sir. Master. *Bloody* business! Thank God you turned up, sir. We left Salonika with an old destroyer for escort but a U-boat sank her the first night out. They said there was no escort available and we had to crack on at full speed. We were doin' that already." He mopped at his sweating face with a handkerchief. "Then the engines broke down. What with reports of a U-boat in the area, and us lying stopped with that murdering gang below forward and the cargo we've got aft . . . if a torpedo hit that lot—" He ran out of breath.

Smith was sorry for him, one more man worn down by three years of war. But there was a U-boat out somewhere in the darkness. He asked only two questions.

"What is this cargo aft?"

"What's left of what we brought out from England. They unloaded the forward holds to fit them for the prisoners but the two after holds are crammed with ammunition for Port Said, high explosive."

"And what's wrong with your engines?"

Jeavons shrugged. "Just steamed too far too fast. The chief said he could get them going by tomorrow but who knows what might happen before then? Suppose a torpedo—"

"I see your point." Smith cut him off. "We're taking you in tow and will escort you to Port Said."

Jeavons asked, "Will you leave a good-sized party aboard, sir? More marines?"

"No, I will not. There's no question of Major Taggart's men trying to take over this ship."

Jeavons burst out, "You weren't on the bridge when they crashed through that wire! You didn't see their faces."

Taggart said, hard-voiced, "I'll answer for them. From now on I'll sleep in the hold."

Smith turned on Captain Brand. "I want those men out on deck for the rest of the night. Rearrange your wire if you like, and post every man you've got as sentries but those men come on deck and stay there."

Brand said hesitantly, "I was given written orders, sir, and they were explicit—"

"No doubt. And you had to carry them out." But Smith added, "Now I am the senior officer present and in the light of the conditions I'm giving you fresh orders."

"Thank you, sir." Brand sounded grateful and relieved. "I don't like this job."

Jeavons grumbled, "You're taking a lot on yourself, Commander."

Smith said pointedly, "Your ship, for one thing. Now I'm going back to mine." He strode to the rail.

Taggart appeared beside Smith and said simply, "Thank you."

Smith shrugged. "The least I could do. They've had a bad time." Smith held out his hand. "Goodnight, Major Taggart."

Taggart hesitated, still guarded, but gripped the hand.

Then the flash lit the northern horizon. Their heads whipped around to stare. Someone on deck said hoarsely, "God Almighty!" The flash died away and the sound of the explosion came rumbling across the sea.

Smith said softly, "There's a convoy out there." He dropped down the ladder to the cutter. Now they knew where the U-boat was at work.

Midshipman Bright swung the head of the cutter towards *Dauntless*, where she lay less than a cable's length away. Once aboard *Dauntless*, Smith went to the bridge. The cruiser was already under way and when he looked across at *Blackbird* he saw she would soon be ready to take the tramp in tow.

Ackroyd said, "Bit of a mystery ship, sir?"

She was. Smith wondered about the four hundred men aboard *Morning Star*, all that was left of a battalion of nearly nine hundred, and about Taggart. He must know the danger of his involvement in the plot. And plot it was—an unknown number of men were lying to shield a murderer and Major Taggart was a party to it. He would be lucky to be cashiered and dismissed, was more likely to end up behind bars, and that was a tragedy because he was a good man.

Smith only said, "Tell you about it later. We'll be rid of her at Port Said." And he would be glad of that.

Lieutenant Cherrett, the signals officer, came hurrying up with a signal he had decoded. It was from Braddock: "Make all speed Port Said. Report estimated time of arrival."

Smith dictated his answer to Cherrett, then prowled out to the wing of the bridge. Why the sudden urgency when Braddock knew Smith was headed for Port Said anyway? What had changed in a few brief hours? Smith was uneasy now and he shifted restlessly about the bridge as the night closed around the ships, hurrying as best they could.

3 A Killing Machine

The three ships anchored in the outer harbour of Port Said before the dawn, a light from the shore stuttering instructions and signals as they stole in over the still water. The signal yeoman read them. "Admiral's coming off now, sir . . . accompanied by General Finlayson. . . ."

As the yeoman read on, signal after signal, Lieutenant Ackroyd said, "That looks like the admiral's picket boat now, sir."

It did. A pinnace was pushing out from Braddock's armed yacht, *Phoebe*, anchored in the basin. Smith ordered, "Rig the accommodation ladder. I'll see them in my cabin aft."

The signals were still flickering out: times to be ready for ammunition and supply lighters, water tenders, the oiler for *Dauntless* and the coaling lighters for *Blackbird* and *Morning Star*.

Ackroyd said grimly, "They're in a hurry."

Smith nodded. The men aboard *Dauntless* and *Blackbird* had hoped for leave ashore, but those hopes were obviously to be dashed.

He dropped down the ladders from the bridge to fo'c'sle and then to the upper deck and strode aft, past the engine-room ratings coming up with spanners, hammers and other gear to receive the oiler. The accommodation ladder was rigged just in time for the admiral's pinnace, swinging around the stern of *Dauntless* and slipping in alongside.

Braddock was first up the ladder, nearly seventy but climbing steadily. He was broad, solid, black-bearded, almost always stern and now grim. Smith saw that look and knew there was trouble.

General Finlayson followed Braddock. Smith had met him once at his headquarters in Deir el Belah where he commanded the army on the coast. He was a Scot, stocky, with a face burned by the sun, tough and competent, a fitting commander for an army that had fought hard and won.

Behind Finlayson came one more officer, a lieutenant colonel of a line regiment, a man of Smith's height, wiry, lean and brown.

Smith led them to his main cabin and saw them seated. This after cabin tapered towards the stern but widened to better than twenty feet. It was really a suite: a sleeping cabin and bathroom opened from it. There was a dining table, sideboard, desk, cupboards, several armchairs. Smith never saw it while at sea. It was stuffy, even though whirring ventilators circulated the air.

Braddock said, "Saw your wireless reports. You've been busy."

"Yes, sir," answered Smith.

Braddock only nodded approvingly but that was enough. He set high standards. Now he glanced across at Finlayson.

The general took his cue. "You know that Allenby has a tough nut to crack, that he faces an army of greater size, defending entrenched and fortified positions. You may know also that we and the Turks have committed every man we can to the Gaza–Beersheba front; there can be no question of reinforcement by either side."

He glanced questioningly at Smith, who nodded. He knew the scales were finely balanced. Finlayson went on, "We've received a report from London. It came out of Germany but it's rated as authentic. The Germans have trained a force of brigade strength, some five thousand men that will function as a unit, with its own guns and a very high proportion of machine guns. They are all highly-trained, crack troops and because of that and their high fire-power you can treble their numbers when you assess them as a fighting force. The Germans call them the Afrika Legion."

Finlayson paused, then continued. "The Afrika Legion is on its way, headed for the Gaza-Beersheba line."

Smith looked at Braddock. Finlayson had explained the situation but the admiral would give Smith his orders. Braddock said simply, "Find it. The Afrika Legion is coming to Palestine by rail. You must find it. We must know when it arrives in this theatre of the war."

Smith was on the point of saying, "We'll try." But he did not. No marks would be awarded for effort, the Afrika Legion was a killing machine. It could turn the potential victory into a stalemate, the campaign into a long, bloody war of attrition like France and Flanders. He said, "Yes, sir."

Braddock asked. "No questions?"

"No, sir."

Braddock grunted, stirred uneasily in the chair, then went on. "Colonel Edwards, here, will also be looking for the Legion. He can pass among the Arabs, done it before. You'll put him ashore south of Jaffa tomorrow night."

Smith glanced at Edwards. The lieutenant colonel was sprawled in his armchair. He had a hooked nose that gave added strength to his handsome face. There was a rakish air about him of self-confidence and Smith disliked him on sight. "I'll find the Legion if it's there," Edwards said arrogantly. "Just have to grease a few palms, maybe cut a throat or two, but I'll find it."

Finlayson snapped, "I want information, not senseless killing!"

Edwards smiled. "All part of the game, sir."

"It's not a *game!*"

"I'm sorry, sir," said Edwards, but he did not sound contrite. "It's a war. But it's a war behind the lines, too, so if the odd throat gets cut you can't be surprised."

Finlayson eyed him with open distaste but then a knock came at the door and it opened to show Lieutenant Ackroyd, cap under arm, looking at Smith. "Sorry to interrupt, sir, but there's a boat alongside from *Morning Star*. Her master and a young lady have come aboard. She says her name is Miss Adeline Brett and that the general will know of her. She insists on speaking to him, sir."

That damned girl! Smith thought. He glanced at Finlayson.

The general said evenly, "I've heard of the young lady. I can spare her a few minutes."

Smith nodded at Ackroyd who turned and beckoned. They entered the cabin, the girl leading the way. Jeavons came behind her, snatching off his cap and peering about him uneasily.

Finlayson stood. "Miss Brett, I am General Finlayson."

He indicated his chair. Adeline Brett sat in it stiffly, hands on its arms, and said as stiffly, "I believe you hold the responsibility for the ordering of the *Morning Star*."

Finlayson nodded. "That is correct," he said dryly. He nodded towards Smith and the others. "This is Commander Smith's ship and his cabin, but if you wish to speak privately I'm sure he will—"

"That isn't necessary." The girl shook her blonde head. "I'm glad Commander Smith is present because he will be able to verify what I have to say about the conditions aboard *Morning Star*. May I go on?" And when Finlayson nodded she told him about the heat, the crowding, the barbed wire and the bad food. She paused to glance at Smith for confirmation. When he nodded impassively she finished, "Those men are held prisoner although no charge has been brought against a single one of them. They were turned away from Cyprus. Now, while we're talking, those men are locked below in the holds. You might have noticed a certain stuffiness in this cabin. You should try five minutes in that hold!" She was leaning forward in the chair now, voice lifted in anger.

Finlayson leaned back against the table, his face showing only patience. He asked, "And what do you want of me?"

"That you give the order to bring them ashore."

Finlayson shook his head, answered quietly, "No. I am aware of the facts of the case, such as are known, as I'm sure you are. Those men were embarked on *Morning Star* under orders and I am bound by those orders. The ship is to sail again, to Deir el Belah, and the battalion stays aboard her."

Adeline Brett took a breath. "Very well. Then these are some other facts of which you may *not* be aware. My father—"

Finlayson pushed away from the table. He did not raise his voice but there was anger in it now as he broke in, "I know about your father and your uncle, *and* their friends, *and* their influence in Parliament and the press, but that weighs nothing with me. I will not be blackmailed. I have always tried to do my duty without fear or favour."

There was a moment of silence. Only the ventilators hummed as the soldier glared at the white-faced girl.

Then Finlayson said flatly, "Good evening to you, Miss Brett." And that was final, dismissive.

She stood up and went to the door and Smith moved quietly to open it. As she passed him he said softly, "Wait." He turned and found Edwards at his back.

The colonel lounged past him to the door, his eyes on the girl. "I'll just get a breath of air," he drawled as he went out.

Smith turned reluctantly back to the cabin. Jeavons was saying nervously, "None of that was my idea, sir . . . but I do want those men and the cargo put ashore. See, sir, I know my agents will have another waiting for me at Tangier in no more than a week."

Finlayson said, "You have my sympathy, Captain. But your agents are contracted to deliver that cargo, and that includes the battalion, at a place to be stipulated. There was no time clause. That contract means that the *Morning Star* is under orders as much as any ship of war, virtually hired by the Admiralty. You leave for Deir el Belah today, escorted by Smith here on his way to Jaffa. If your engines aren't repaired in time he'll tow you."

Braddock nodded.

Jeavons looked from one to the other, then said heavily, "Very well. But you'll give me your word that you'll take off these men as soon as possible?"

Finalyson said, "You have my word." Jeavons put on his cap and left. Finlayson shifted in his seat and muttered, "That damned Edwards—drink and women! Whenever he's in Cairo it's one damned woman after another." His gaze fell on Smith and he was momentarily embarrassed and looked away. Then he cleared his throat and turned to Smith again.

"You endorsed Miss Brett's comments regarding the conditions aboard *Morning Star*. Maybe you think I'm being unnecessarily severe. Remember this: one of those men killed his commanding officer and some, if not all, know who fired the shots. Yet every one has denied knowledge under oath. Some or all are therefore involved in mutiny under arms." Finlayson jabbed a stubby finger at Smith. "Remember this, too: there was mutiny in the French army this summer. Now I don't believe Allenby's army will mutiny, not any part of it. But suppose we put Taggart's battalion ashore here, even under guard? Questions will be asked: Why are they held? How many are innocent and why are they held? I don't want those questions asked, because doubt could be fatal. I have to choose between the army and the battalion and I've chosen. Clear?"

"Yes, sir." Smith paused. "But this battalion, sir—can I ask for something?"

Finlayson said, exasperated, "Good God! What now?"

Smith said, "Sir, when I went aboard *Morning Star* I countermanded some of the orders given to Captain Brand."

"You did, eh?" Finlayson scowled at Braddock, who in turn scowled at Smith.

Smith pressed on doggedly, "It seemed to me the conditions aboard that ship were unfit for animals, let alone men." Finlayson's lips tightened but Smith persisted. "I had to board *Morning Star* because the men had broken out despite the wire and the marines. What really held them back and what holds them now is their discipline and the presence of the one officer with them, Major Taggart. There's no reason they should be kept in the hold, nor that the food should be so bad. Sir, if orders could be given before *Morning Star* sailed, then—"

Finlayson waved him into silence and said dryly, "I heard you don't waste time. I'll have my aide see to it."

"Thank you, sir. Er—would you care for a drink?"

Finlayson said, "Thanks, I think you owe me one."

As he and Braddock were savouring neat scotch, Smith remembered Edwards and the girl and excused himself.

Out on the deck there was commotion among the oiling parties as the oiler came alongside. Jeavons waited disconsolately at the head of the accommodation ladder, but Smith had to search for Adeline Brett, finally spotting her in the dark shadow of the superstructure and almost hidden by Edwards. He was leaning over her but as Smith stepped up Edwards eased away. His teeth showed in a smile as he said to the girl, "Another time."

"Possibly," she answered, "but very unlikely."

Edwards countered easily. "All things are possible."

Then Midshipman Bright appeared at the run. He halted before Edwards. "I'm to show you your cabin, sir. Your bag's gone below."

36

Edwards said acidly, "There was a bottle or two in that bag. I trust your heavy-handed sailor didn't break them. But lead on, little admiral." He followed Bright forward.

Adeline Brett faced Smith boldly. "I suppose you think that was a dirty trick, the way I tried to bully Finlayson?"

Smith answered, "It wasn't bullying. It was attempted blackmail and it was a dirty trick."

"I'm not sorry. I did it for the battalion."

"The end justifying the means?"

"Any means." She waited but when Smith did not answer she pressed him, "Well?"

He said, "The other day I had to order a seaplane to search for a train. They found the train but the seaplane was shot down. We got her crew back unharmed, but suppose they had been killed? What should I write to their next-of-kin? So sorry, but the end . . . ?"

She peered up at him. "You had to send them, of course, even knowing there was a risk."

"Yes."

"Then surely that was a case of the end—"

Smith said harshly, "I just mistrust the—catch phrase. In war one man's means can be another man's bloody end."

Adeline Brett was silent for a moment. "I agree with you." Then she smiled lop-sidedly. "I also agree with me, but then I'm a woman."

Smith stared down at her and thought he would not disagree with that.

Her eyes fell and she said quietly, "You asked me to wait."

He had forgotten, but he cleared his throat and said, "The general has been thinking it over. The battalion will be allowed on deck and he'll arrange for fresh food to be sent aboard." Then as she stared at him he said hurriedly, "Here comes your boat . . . you'd better get away. Jeavons looks to be ready."

Now, behind them, Braddock stood at the door of the cabin. Smith took the girl's arm and handed her over to the master of the *Morning Star*, saw them both start down the ladder. Her voice came up to him, quiet but clear, "Thank you."

Braddock appeared at Smith's elbow. "Where's Edwards?"

"Gone to his cabin, sir."

Braddock growled. "The bloody man's a show-off. All that talk of cutting throats is said for effect but it's also true. He's a killer. Finlayson detests him because he's a long way from your conventional army officer."

Smith thought that Finlayson probably did not like *him* either, because he too came with a reputation of being unorthodox. Did Finlayson lump the pair of them together, he and Edwards?

But Braddock was rumbling on. "He's a brigand. Before the war he was some sort of trader here. And he certainly didn't learn to use that knife in the British army."

Smith asked, "Knife?"

"You'll see. I've seen him in his Arab get-up." Finlayson was waiting now at the head of the accommodation ladder: Braddock went on quickly, "Two bits of news for you: you'll be getting some help from an old French battleship coming from Malta: *Maroc*. She's slow but she mounts four 12-inch guns and she'll be under your orders. The other thing is that we've heard the three German ships in the Sea of Marmara have been exercising but they're back in port now." That was *Goeben, Breslau* and the big cruiser *Walküre*, which had run through the Dardanelles to seek sanctuary with Turkey early in the war. Imprisoned now in the Sea of Marmara by a force of British capital ships, they flew Turkish colours, were ostensibly Turkish ships, but their commanders and crews were German. "All three of them locked in there. Thank God. Still, it must be hard. . . . They have some fine seamen."

"Yes, sir. Particularly in the U-boats."

Braddock cocked an eye at him. "You know that's heresy? That they're supposed to be treacherous and cowardly?"

Smith grinned at him, knowing his man now. "Yes, sir."

Braddock turned towards the ladder, but paused to say seriously, "You've got to find this Afrika Legion. We've got to stop it somehow. It could scupper the whole campaign."

"I know."

Braddock nodded, and went down the ladder after Finlayson.

DAYLIGHT CAME, and the men of *Dauntless* and *Blackbird* toiled on. The oiler cast off and was replaced by the ammunition lighter. At Smith's orders Ackroyd had sent a large party over to *Blackbird* to help with the back-breaking, filthy job of coaling ship. "Thank God we burn oil," Ackroyd said from the heart. Like most of them, he'd had his share of coaling ships.

Smith had been busy with the chart, making plans, and now sent for Pearce and his gang from *Blackbird*. His gang were the four flying crews, an exclusive little club who messed together aboard *Blackbird* and went ashore together. As they climbed the accommodation ladder another lighter was towed alongside *Blackbird*, carrying a Short seaplane, wings folded back along the fuselage. That would be the replacement for the one they had lost just over a week ago.

Ackroyd said with distaste, "What is *that*? And who painted it that *bloody* funny colour?"

Smith thought "bloody" was right; the fabric of the wings and fuselage was mottled red to pale pink.

Pearce explained wearily, "She's a rebuild job. I went ashore to sign for her when it was still dark. They told me she'd been badly shot up. Still needs work done on her engine but I said we'd do it; couldn't wait. I suppose some colouring got into the stuff the riggers slopped on her. The chaps I took with me spotted some initials painted just below the cockpit. DLLR. So they've christened her Delilah."

Ackroyd led Pearce and the fliers into the main cabin. The four pilots, Cole, Beckett, Kirby and Rogers, were all flight lieutenants of the Royal Naval Air Service. And the observers, three of them lieutenants but volunteers from the army: Hamilton of the Artillery, Wilson of the Norfolks, and Burns from the Rajputs. Last was a small midshipman called Maitland.

Smith paused for a minute and watched as the Short was hoisted aboard *Blackbird*. If the plane had had to be rebuilt he wondered grimly what had happened to the pilot with the initials DLLR. He turned and entered the cabin as Pearce was saying, voice high and impatient, "I know you don't believe me but there's a day not far off when there will be aircraft with accurate bombsights. Aircraft big enough, fast enough to sink capital ships! I'm telling you—"

As Smith entered the cabin, he broke off, scowling, running fingers through his hair. The gang looked embarrassed at what they thought were Pearce's wild flights of fantasy, but Smith watched him and wondered. He grinned at the pilot. "But for the moment, Chris? If you attacked a capital ship in a Short?"

The gang chuckled and Flight Lieutenant Cole said, "Pray, for one thing."

Pearce shrugged. "You'd have to sit a Short on the funnel and you'd be shot to bits trying it. Unless—" He stopped.

Smith prompted, "Unless—?"

But Pearce would not be drawn. "You'd have to be lucky."

Smith let it go. "Sit down, gentlemen, please."

He told them about the Afrika Legion, and the task set *Dauntless*. "But particularly you. If the Afrika Legion comes then we— you—must find it." He looked at them, ordinary young men of assorted sizes, but all with serious, selfconscious expressions now. "Well, don't look so worried. You're only going to fly. I'm not asking you to do any real work like the rest of us aboard these ships."

That sent them back to their ship in a more cheerful mood but Smith knew the task he was setting them and its dangers.

He went to the bridge and the navigator, Henderson, said, "That was bad luck." And when Smith looked at him questioningly: "They were hoisting that Short aboard *Blackbird*. It swung and knocked one of the hands from the lighter into the harbour. Poor chap drowned."

Smith shook his head. He had watched the Short hoisted in and had not seen the accident. The man had slipped unnoticed out of life. He hoped Pearce was collecting the evidence. Inevitably there would be a court of inquiry.

Morning Star had signalled that her engines were ready to take her to sea and *Blackbird* had completed coaling ship. So a bare few hours after entering Port Said, Smith led his little squadron to sea again, grimly aware that Allenby's victory was now in serious jeopardy. They had to find the Afrika Legion.

He walked out to the starboard wing of the bridge as *Dauntless* turned onto the northerly course that would take her to Deir el Belah and beyond to Edwards's landing south of Jaffa. Astern of her, and ahead of *Blackbird*, steamed *Morning Star* with her cargo of ammunition and the silent, waiting men of Taggart's battalion. He wondered which might prove the more explosive.

40

4 The Search

In the blazing heat of that afternoon, 25th October, *Morning Star* plodded into the anchorage at Deir el Belah. Smith watched from the bridge of *Dauntless* as the tramp passed inside the anti-submarine nets while *Dauntless* and *Blackbird* steamed on, bound for Edwards's landing place near Jaffa but altering course a few points to port as if bound for Cyprus. That was for the benefit of the Turk observers watching from Gaza.

There were many ashore at Deir el Belah who watched *Dauntless*'s clean lines as she slipped by. One was Sapper Charlie Golightly of the Royal Engineers. He was the driver of an engine that puffed up and down between Kantara on the Suez Canal and the railhead at Deir el Belah each day, hauling the train that brought supplies and reinforcements up from Kantara and took down wounded. The train stood in a siding now, close by the sand dunes that lined the shore, while a score of yards away Charlie reclined in a deckchair under a clump of palms. In the shade he was sweating only slightly. Short, moon-faced, bald and fifty, only the heat and his work prevented his plumpness from running to obesity. He sucked at a cigar, and a glass of cold beer stood in easy reach by his chair.

Albert had brought him the beer, chilled in the box of ice Charlie had taken aboard at Kantara. Albert had also cooked a meal and was now washing the dishes. Albert was an Egyptian boy of fifteen with a wide smile who was Charlie's fireman when he drove the train, and his servant when he was at ease. Charlie had named the boy Albert. "Never mind what your ma called you. Now you're with me you'll have a Christian 'andle. You do as I tell you an' we'll get on all right." Now, through a gap in the dunes, they watched *Dauntless* pass.

Albert sat back on his heels, wiped wet hands on a rag and smiled up at Charlie. "Fine ship."

"Fine ship?" Golightly sucked on the cigar. "Ah! Ships and women. Either one'll get you into deep water. Steer clear of them both, except when you has to—if you see what I mean. Any feller needs a bit o' home comfort now and then, after the day's work."

41

That made him thoughtful. The day's work? It was time he gave some thought to it. He clasped his hands under his round little belly and pondered logistics. Militarily speaking, Sapper Golightly's only concern with logistics was driving his train, but his present interest was not military. Charlie was in his thirty-second year of service, and in all that time he had neither sought nor been offered promotion. But for many years now he had been making provision for his old age. From a succession of stores and depots, and while transporting supplies between them, he had taken a toll. He would have his pension, of course, and the rents from half-a-dozen houses he had bought in Bermondsey over the years. But what he yearned for was a pub.

So—logistics? His gaze rested on his tent, stacked full of souvenirs of the war, from Turkish helmets to water-bottles, bayonets and pistols. From there his gaze drifted to the engine whose tender had a false bottom that could be loaded from underneath. In Port Said there were plenty of buyers for souvenirs and from Port Said he brought back scotch, purchased remarkably cheaply because it was stolen, to trade for more souvenirs. He was making a profit but he knew that soon the army would move forward, the trip from the front would lengthen and thus his turnover would reduce. Maybe he should concentrate on the smaller souvenirs that fetched a higher price, like the pistols . . . .

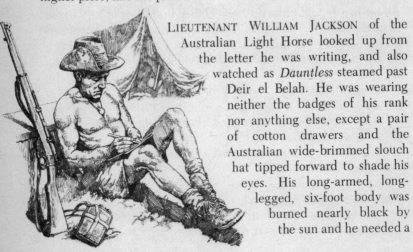

LIEUTENANT WILLIAM JACKSON of the Australian Light Horse looked up from the letter he was writing, and also watched as *Dauntless* steamed past Deir el Belah. He was wearing neither the badges of his rank nor anything else, except a pair of cotton drawers and the Australian wide-brimmed slouch hat tipped forward to shade his eyes. His long-armed, long-legged, six-foot body was burned nearly black by the sun and he needed a shave. He glanced at his watch, remembering that his troop was detailed for a working party, and bawled, "Troop Sergeant Latimer! Get 'em out on parade!"

From the tents around him came cursing, obscenities. No one appeared but a voice bellowed, outraged, "What the flamin' hell are you at, Jacka? We've done enough this week!"

Jackson took no notice; it was always the same. He stared at the palms and the glint of sunlight on the little lake they surrounded. Water. The horses, called Walers because they came from New South Wales, had gone mad when they finally fought their way out of the desert of Sinai and found grass. The army had been told that in this coming battle they would have to go for twenty-four hours or more without water. Well, they were used to that after Sinai. Getting used to it had not been funny.

He returned to the letter, writing quickly. Before the war he had worked on his father's sheep station and had grown up on horseback; Australians were natural horsemen. He finished the letter: "Your loving son, Bill".

Men were emerging from the tents now. Some were in riding-breeches, others in shorts. All were in sleeveless flannel singlets. Jackson owned a tattered tunic and was lucky because many officers did not, owing to the unending patrols and skirmishes. Some of the men were clean-shaven but most were as black-jowled as he was. But every man had his rifle, bayonet and bandolier of ammunition, all his equipment clean and serviceable. And there was nothing wrong with the Walers, the troopers saw to that.

Jackson dragged on his breeches and reached thoughtfully for his boots. The troop had just lost a couple of horses in a tussle with a patrol of Turkish cavalry. No remounts had come up but there was an English yeomanry regiment a mile down the road. When it got dark maybe he could take some of the boys down there. . . .

A CLEAR NIGHT and the sky filled with stars. Smith came onto the bridge of *Dauntless* as she thrust steadily through a smooth sea. *Blackbird* kept station a cable's length astern. The two ships had steamed out of sight of the land and only turned towards the enemy coast south of Jaffa when the sun set. Henderson emerged from the chartroom and said, "Twenty minutes, sir."

Smith nodded, then asked, "Has Colonel Edwards been told?"

Ackroyd said sourly, "I sent young Bright to wake him ten minutes ago. He told Bright to go to hell."

Edwards had refused the hospitality of the wardroom, preferring to sit with his boots up on the bunk in his cabin, steadily making his way through a bottle of whisky that stood at his elbow. By noon the bottle had been empty and he slept.

Now Ackroyd muttered, "He's a rum chap. But whatever he's got on his conscience, it doesn't trouble him. He sleeps like a baby."

Smith wished he had Edwards's facility. He had tried to sleep in his little sea cabin but had lain instead with his eyes open thinking about the Afrika Legion, and the trains packed with those tough, elite soldiers hurrying towards Palestine.

He asked, "Is Jameson ready?" Lieutenant Jameson was a boxer, a tough middleweight, quick and cool. More importantly he was a good officer, a fine seaman and was to command an armed party in the cutter to set Edwards ashore.

"Yes, sir."

"I'm going along. You know what to do. Patrol till we return but if something goes wrong and we don't come off again then you report to the admiral and carry on with the search for the Legion as ordered. No rescue attempts."

"Aye, aye, sir." Ackroyd did not like this but saw the sense of it. If an armed party was taken, then the coast would be alerted and any rescue attempt would be suicidal.

Smith said, "I'm going for a word with Edwards." He left the bridge, made his way to Edwards's cabin. The curtain was drawn across the door and Smith called, "Colonel Edwards?"

"Who is it?"

"Commander Smith."

"I'm changing. Come in."

Smith entered and drew the curtain behind him. Edwards stood scowling by the desk, shirtless, tunic in hand. Smith had seen many a drunk and, whisky or no, Edwards was stone-cold sober. He asked, "Getting close?"

"Less than twenty minutes. We'll put you ashore where you indicated. If there's anything else we can do—?"

Edwards shook his head. "I've got all I want. But you can put my

44

case ashore next time you're in Port Said. There'll be my kit in it."
He dipped his hand into the suitcase and held up a full bottle of
whisky. "And this. So tell your chaps to go easy, will you?"

He caught Smith's deliberately neutral stare and laughed. "You
fight your war, Commander, and I'll fight mine. I'm a temporary
gentleman, not Finlayson's style at all. Before the war I got a
banker's draft from home once a quarter so long as I stayed out
here. There'd been some trouble with a girl or two. The draft was
just enough to exist on, so I started dealing in anything that would
turn a few quid. After the war it'll be different—the Arabs will be
grateful to anybody who helps them kick out the Turks. I'll be
somebody around here. And the women?" He pointed a finger.
"Look, when I get out of that desert I need a woman. I risk my neck
every minute I'm out there so I think I'm entitled to all I can get.
Money. Influence. And women." He paused, then: "So?"

But Smith only said, "You've got about ten minutes." He pushed
through the curtain and climbed to the upper deck.

HE WAITED BY THE RAIL with Jameson and the cutter's crew, all
armed with pistols. *Dauntless* was turning her starboard side to the
distant coast to make a lee for the cutter. The way was coming off
her; she was stopping. The shore was in darkness but to the northeast there were lights marking the old Arab port of Jaffa.

Someone among the crew of the cutter sucked in a startled
breath, then muttered, "Blimey! Thought it was a ghost!" Edwards
came to them silently out of the gloom, wrapped in white robes
from head to foot. He halted by Smith, who now saw the knife in
its sheath, thrust through his belt. Edwards saw the glance and
drew the knife, hefted it casually. It was long and curved, wicked
looking. Edwards's eyes glittered below the headdress as he said,
"The only friend I trust."

Smith said shortly, "Put it away and don't fool about."

Edwards chuckled, but he obeyed.

Dauntless stopped and the cutter was lowered. The crew climbed
down a net thrown over the side and into the boat. Edwards followed them easily and Smith went last. He settled in the sternsheets and the cutter got under way. So did *Dauntless*, her grey
steel hull sliding past, with *Blackbird* astern of her.

The crew rowed steadily, knowing they had a two-mile pull to the shore. As they closed it, Smith asked, "This is the place?"

Edwards nodded, "Good enough. Anywhere along here."

Smith knew the coast was not defended here, only lightly patrolled by the Turks, because there was nothing inland but sand dunes for five or ten miles. But he searched the shore with his glasses to detect any signs of movement as they steered for a gap in the rockbound coast. The cutter slipped through a neck of swirling water between the rocks. The beach ahead was deserted. Smith could see Edwards was leaning forward, ready to go. Smith asked, "Suppose you meet someone in the dunes?"

Edwards did not look at him, watched the shore over the bending and straightening backs of the cutter's crew, but he said casually, "His throat or mine. And I'll bet it's his."

The cutter grounded, Buckley leaped over the side and held the bow as Edwards jumped ashore and walked quickly up the beach without pausing or looking back. He reached the dunes and his pale figure was lost to sight. Smith ordered, "Shove off."

They turned and headed back out to sea. Smith thought Braddock was right: Edwards was a brigand, a cut-throat. He was also a brave man. Did it matter that this was only to further his own ambition for money, influence, women . . . ?

Smith shifted uneasily, admitting to himself his own ambition to succeed in his career—and hadn't he risked that career more than once for a woman? But he and Edwards were not two of a kind, he was sure of that.

BEFORE DAWN the ships were back on patrol off Haifa, and *Blackbird* began launching the Shorts in the first grey light, the start of a long day for the gang. They flew reconnaissance patrols throughout the daylight hours, striking inland to Lydda, swinging north up to the Turkish camp at El Afuleh, then westward down to Haifa and still following the railway, searching. When a returning seaplane was sighted, another flew off to take up the hunt before the first came down on the sea.

After the sun had set, the ships hurried northward, and the next dawn found them off the Gulf of Alexandretta. The gulf was twenty miles wide and ran inland for thirty. Smith watched its northern Turkish shore lift slowly out of the sea as *Dauntless* steamed northward across the gulf's mouth. They were three hundred miles north of Deir el Belah and Cyprus lay seventy miles southwest.

Henderson, the navigator, said, "The chart shows minefields across the mouth of the gulf with only one probable cleared channel along the northern shore, about a mile out. And the Turks have coastal batteries on that shore."

Smith nodded: he had seen the channel on the chart and the guns in the Turkish batteries commanded it.

The line of the railway ran north from Lebanon, inland of the Amanus mountains, and then swung around the head of the gulf. Once through the new Bagcha tunnel the railway turned westward along the northern shore of the gulf and so to the town of Adana. That was the northern limit of Smith's search because north of Adana the railway ran inland, beyond the range of the Shorts.

There was no sign of the Afrika Legion at Adana so the two ships steamed south again and the Shorts continued their searches. Traffic on the railway was normal. In the late morning *Blackbird* signalled that the replacement Short that had been christened Delilah was ready for a test flight. Pearce had not flown for two days now. Smith looked across, saw Flight Lieutenant Beckett in its cockpit and Lieutenant Hamilton climbing into the observer's seat.

Ackroyd said, "He's going along for the ride. Or maybe Beckett wants ballast aboard."

Smith smiled. "Hamilton will provide plenty of that." The lieutenant of artillery bulked large as he sat down in the cockpit.

Blackbird's speed was falling away, the Short was hooked on, lifted by the derrick. At that moment Hamilton inexplicably stood erect, just as the derrick swung. He wavered, arms flailing, then toppled over the side and fell to the deck beneath the dangling Short.

Beckett shouted an order from the cockpit and the evolution continued. It was the right thing to do—others would cope with Hamilton. As the Short was lowered into the sea, men aboard *Blackbird* rushed towards the inert figure on the deck. Smith snapped, "Pass the word for the surgeon!"

The Short engine burst into life and Delilah, the mottled pink and red of her like a flame running across the sea, took off. Merryweather, the surgeon, a burly young man who played rugby for his country, charged up the ladder and onto *Dauntless*'s bridge. Smith told him of Hamilton's fall. "Will you need to go aboard?"

Merryweather asked, "Can I have a word with Maginnis?"

Smith nodded and told the signalman: "Make to *Blackbird:* 'Am coming alongside. Surgeon to speak to SBA.' "

As *Dauntless* closed to within a score of yards, Maginnis came onto the wing of *Blackbird*'s bridge. He was the sick-berth attendant aboard *Blackbird*; she carried no doctor. He was Glaswegian and an unlikely nurse. Broad and squat, long-armed and with huge hands, he looked more like a gorilla.

Merryweather spoke through the trumpet to Maginnis on *Blackbird*. "What's his condition?"

Magginis's deep growl came over the sea. "Ach! He banged his heid but the skull's a'richt. He's got a bump like an egg, that's a'. Concussion, mebbe. Ah'm keeping him in his bunk wi' some tea an' aspirin."

So Hamilton was all right. Smith was relieved but then he bellowed through cupped hands, "What the hell did he think he was doing, standing up as she was hoisted out."

Maginnis shrugged his shoulders. "He disnae ken, sir. Canna remember daein' it. Didnae believe it when we telt him. He's only a soljer, ye ken."

Dauntless took station ahead of *Blackbird* again and Beckett flew Delilah round the ships for an hour as they steamed southward. When he finally set the Short down and was back aboard *Blackbird*, Pearce signalled: "Aircraft excellent. Needs only minor adjustments before operational. Estimated available four hours."

Smith grunted, "Acknowledge." Then: "No!" That was not enough. "Make: 'Well done. We need your painted lady.' " No harm in patting Pearce's back and thereby those of the mechanics and riggers who had laboured to get Delilah into the air.

The reports came in from the other Shorts, signalled to Smith in *Dauntless*, where he read them and pored over the map. He was certain the Afrika Legion had not yet arrived. He was also certain as to his next move. When the Legion did come they would be held up at the bottleneck north of Adana. The broad-gauge track from Constantinople ceased at the Taurus mountains. The Turks and Germans were building tunnels to link it with the broad-gauge track on the other side, but they were not yet ready. Meanwhile the Legion would be slowed to a snail's pace on the metre-gauge line and the road connection. There he would find them.

So in the early evening he told Ackroyd, "We'll fly one more patrol down to Lydda and Jaffa and if that draws a blank we'll head north towards Adana at twenty knots."

Cole was the pilot and Wilson of the Norfolks went as his observer. The Short was Delilah. They took off with something over two hours of daylight remaining. Their mission was to fly twenty miles down the coast to Haifa and from there follow the railway up to Lydda. From there they would return and seek out the ships.

Smith was on *Dauntless*'s bridge at the estimated time of the Short's return. Right on time a lookout reported, "Aircraft bearing Red three-oh!" At that distance it was unidentifiable, but as ships and aircraft closed the gap it was seen to be Delilah.

Smith told the Signal Yeoman, "Make to *Blackbird*: 'Prepare to recover seaplane. Captain coming aboard.' " He wanted to hear Wilson's report in person, even though he was so certain they would have drawn a blank that his course north was already laid off.

So as *Blackbird* swung out of her station astern and stopped to make a lee for the Short, so *Dauntless* slowed, stopped also, lowered the gig, and Smith went down into it. Its crew pulled across to *Blackbird*, and Smith watched Delilah turning into the wind to come down on the sea.

There was something wrong.

As the gig came up astern of *Blackbird*, the Short was down and taxi-ing, engine snarling. Wilson should have been ready to grab at

49

the heaving line on the derrick purchase but the observer sat slumped in the cockpit, head lolling. The boom of the derrick was swung inboard again, and a seaman snatched the line; whipped it around him under his arm, grabbed at the hook and was swung out above the Short. The steam winch chuntered and the seaman went down on the end of the wire, balanced on the cockpit coaming by the pilot, then hooked on. The seaplane's engine died, the winch hammered and Delilah was hoisted inboard.

The gig ran in alongside *Blackbird* and Smith climbed aboard.

Now that he was only yards away from the Short he could see the
rents torn in the fuselage around the observer's cockpit. The pilot
was on deck, Pearce holding him by the arm. Chris looked no better
for his rest from flying, was still nervy, tired. He turned, saw Smith
and led the pilot over to him. Cole had pulled off the leather helmet
and goggles. His hair was sweat-matted to his head.

Smith asked shortly, "What happened?"

Cole swallowed. "We didn't see the Afrika Legion. Flew in up
the line, circled around Lydda, headed for Jaffa and home, only

saw the one train all the time. Then a Fokker dived on us. You know how it is, sir. They've got more speed and manoeuvrability. This chap must have been new though, thank God: he never got his sights on us. Wilson gave him a few bursts from the Lewis and that kept him off. In the end he just fired one burst at long range and flew away. Just that one burst, but it cut Wilson to pieces below the waist. They'll have a job cleaning that cockpit—"

Smith cut in harshly, "What about the train you saw?"

"The train?" Cole shoved fingers through his hair. "That was just north of Lydda. We dropped the bombs, missed, but one burst ahead and made them stop and get out of the train. The second time we buzzed down low, right over them and I saw them clearly. They were Turks, no doubt of it. Then that bloody Fokker." He shook his head.

Pearce asked, "What about Delilah?"

Cole brightened a little. "Marvellous. Still hard work, like all these Shorts, but she's the pick of our bunch." They began to talk the technicalities of flying and Smith recognized it as a manoeuvre on Pearce's part to take Cole's mind off Wilson.

Smith looked over to the Short. Surgeon Merryweather had arrived from *Dauntless* and was now up on one side of the observer's cockpit, Maginnis on the other. After a moment Merryweather climbed down to the deck, shoulders hunched. He turned and caught Smith's eye, shook his head wearily.

So Wilson was dead. Maginnis and the others were extricating his body from the cockpit, working gently, voices hushed. Wilson had been a volunteer, seconded from the Norfolks as an observer. He was the son of a farming family, a likeable young man, shy but with an eagerness to fly. He had wanted to become a pilot.

Smith's gaze swung back to Mike Cole, standing weary and dejected before him. "It wasn't your fault," he said quietly. And to Pearce who was scowling angrily at Delilah, "I think Mike has earned a drink, Chris."

"Aye, aye, sir." Pearce recovered himself, took Cole by the arm and led him away. "Come on, Mike."

Smith watched them walk forward and out of his sight. The hands now folded back the wings of Delilah and began pushing the seaplane on its trolley into the gloom of the hangar. Right by the entrance stood a drum of fuel they had used for the Shorts, and Smith frowned. But he heard voices, glanced over the side and saw the whaler that had brought Merryweather, and the gig still waiting for himself. It was time he got back to his ship.

He faced forward. Suddenly Delilah twisted on the trolley, and a wing nudged the drum of fuel, sending it toppling, crashing onto the deck. At that same instant a flame flickered at the tail of the Short and there came a yell of "Fire!"

Smith ran at the drum that rolled slowly back and forth with the motion of the ship, a pool of petrol spreading beneath it. Two of the fitters came running and Smith gasped, "Over the side!" The gig and the whaler mercifully lay the other side of *Blackbird*. They shoved at the drum and Smith's feet slipped in the petrol on the deck. He sprawled and rolled out of the way of the other two. Suddenly flames whipped past him along the petrol trail and licked at the drum as the fitters were heaving it over.

The explosion was muffled but the yellow flame lifted high above the side. Then it was gone. He felt a hand on his arm, saw Pearce helping him to his feet. "The fire——?"

"Out, sir."

The two fitters slumped to one side. Smith went to them with Pearce. The flame had burned both men. As Pearce retched, Merryweather appeared with Maginnis at his heels. The surgeon took one look and sucked in his breath.

Smith dragged Pearce aside and demanded, "What are the orders regarding ready-use fuel?"

Pearce blinked, "Orders, sir? I——I don't think——"

"How long had that drum stood about, half-full and open?"

"I——don't know, sir. I didn't notice."

Smith rubbed at his face, tried to damp down his anger. "You didn't notice? What the *hell's* wrong with you, Chris?"

Pearce had been shaken but now the shutter came down, his face went blank. "There's nothing wrong, sir."

Smith said savagely, "For God's sake, Chris! Two men are lying there between life and death because of *stupidity!*"

Merryweather looked up. "I'll have to get them to *Dauntless*."

Smith nodded and told Pearce, "Signal *Dauntless* to come alongside and take off two serious cases of burning."

Pearce left, running. Merryweather and Maginnis were kneeling over the fitters. Smith walked into the hangar: he found little sign that there had been a fire, just a smoke-blackened streak on the deck. And Delilah? Surely the fire had started in Delilah? He saw a rigger stooped under the fuselage and went to crouch beside him. He asked, "This is where it started?"

The rigger glanced at him. "Yes, sir. I saw it start, just a little flame. I had it out in seconds but by then it had caught on the petrol on the deck. Can't make it out. Looks as if a bullet passed through here—" He poked a finger in the hole in the wooden spar, the fabric burned from it. He said doubtfully, "Might have been a tracer, but for the wood to smoulder all that time—" He shook his head. "I just can't credit it."

They straightened together and Smith said, "The Short—what caused it to swing?"

"Damned if I know *that*, either, sir. She was coming in just like normal, the trolley wheels didn't jam. She just—swung."

There would be a court of inquiry, of course. First the drowned man, and now this. Smith walked out of the hangar and onto the deck.

He watched as Merryweather and Maginnis carefully wrapped the two burned men in clean, white sheets, then Merryweather turned to his bag, took out a hypodermic and injected both men. He saw Smith and said, "They're both unconscious and in shock. Those jabs will stave off the pain when it comes, for a while."

Smith asked, "What's your opinion?"

The surgeon rubbed at his face and sighed, "Not much chance aboard *Dauntless*, but if we can get them to Deir el Belah there's a big forward hospital where the burns men are top class."

As the night closed around them, *Dauntless* came alongside, and the two ships were briefly secured while the burned men, lashed to stretchers, were swung over by a derrick to a waiting party that hurried them below to the sick bay.

Smith climbed to the bridge. He was certain Adana was the place to look for the Afrika Legion. His task was to find the Legion and if he delayed now, went south to Deir el Belah and so missed them, then he would be called to account.

The ships eased apart and Henderson asked, "Course, sir?"

Smith hesitated, then said, "I want a course for Deir el Belah. And revolutions for twenty knots. Pass that to *Blackbird*."

Dauntless slid away from *Blackbird*, starting to work up to twenty knots. Every second on this course took him farther from Adana, but he could not let those men die. Smith watched the carrier taking station astern, a shadow of a ship in the night. Doubt was racking him now.

5 A Quiet Little Run up the Coast

Dauntless and *Blackbird* raced through the night to make the passage back to Deir el Belah in just four hours. Smith conned *Dauntless* as she closed the darkened anchorage, a rectangle of sea enclosed by anti-submarine nets. A drifter patrolled at the opening in the nets, and when her challenge had been answered *Dauntless* slipped past her and through the gap.

Deir el Belah was no port but an Arab village and an oasis. In the anchorage, ships discharged their cargoes into lighters to be carried ashore by men of the Egyptian Labour Corps. There was a ship discharging in the anchorage now, both ship and lighter alive with the figures of men labouring under big lamps.

Dauntless steamed gently on past two M-class monitors, each with its single 6-inch gun, like a pointing finger, and there lay *Phoebe*, Braddock's armed yacht. *Morning Star* lay at the far end of the anchorage, almost lost in the darkness beyond the lights of the discharging ship. Smith could see a guard boat, a motor launch, puttering around her. Then Taggart's battalion was still aboard her—and Adeline Brett? There was a blur of white moving on the deck of *Morning Star* that might be—

He ordered, "Stop both!"

Dauntless came to anchor. The land prickled with a thousand lights, the fires of the army, but one particular light stuttered at *Dauntless* a succession of signals: an oiler waited for her, a coaling lighter for *Blackbird*, and Braddock wanted to see Smith on shore, at army headquarters.

Smith told Ackroyd, "We sail in two hours. Pass that to *Blackbird*." He had to go back to the search. He dropped down the ladders and hurried aft to his main cabin where he shaved and dressed in fresh white drill. When he returned to the deck the first of the burned men was being lowered on a stretcher into a big, white launch with a red cross that had come alongside.

Merryweather was there and turned a worried face to Smith. "I'd like to go to the hospital with them, sir."

Smith nodded. "You've got two hours." He added gently, "Cheer up, Doc. No man could have done more than you."

Smith went down into the motorboat that lay astern of the launch. The boat headed for the shore and the temporary jetty. Smith walked rapidly along its echoing planks and up through the gap in the dunes. He passed a train on a siding, its engine softly hissing, and took the dusty palm-fringed road towards army headquarters.

CHARLIE GOLIGHTLY, in the shadow of the engine, glanced absently at the white-uniformed figure striding up the road, then turned back to business and Albert. "You say this feller was goin' round asking questions about scotch?"

Albert nodded vigorously. "Corporal say a big man. Captain Jeffreys. Corporal say this man from Pip Emma."

"Provost Marshal," muttered Charlie. He did not like the sound of it. "We'll give things a rest for a bit."

Albert nodded knowingly, "Big fighting soon."

Charlie said shortly, "Fighting's the army's business." He was only concerned with his own. "It's this Jeffreys feller I don't fancy." He hesitated, not wanting to take a loss on a transaction. He decided, "There's one more lot o' scotch at Port Said. We'll fetch that, then pack it in."

LIEUTENANT BILL JACKSON, standing tall in the darkness, watched Smith pass and thought he must be the captain of the cruiser. He remembered the talk of her hell-raising commander; there was a driving energy in the way this man had hastened up the road.

A big trooper slouched up to the fire nearest Jackson, scowled at it morosely and spat into it. Jackson rasped, "You're supposed to keep it going, Jasper, not put it out!"

Without turning the trooper grumbled, "Aw, give it a rest, Jacka.

We're all sick o' this job." He threw wood on the fire and walked away, hands in the pockets of his patched breeches. Jackson grinned sympathetically. These men of his were a handful when out of the line as now. There were men from sheep stations but also from many other jobs and backgrounds, such as teachers and lawyers. Their only uniformity was their toughness and soldiering skill, and in that they were the best.

And they would be in the attack. Jackson's grin faded. Maybe they were too good he thought, because when the attack came they would be right at the front.

FINLAYSON'S HEADQUARTERS lay north of the village of Deir el Belah in a tent the size of a large bungalow. It stood in a crowded, tented town. Smith had to wait for a convoy of camels to pass before he could cross to the HQ. They rocked by under mountainous loads roped to the big saddles, their high crosstrees sticking up front and rear, 350 pounds to a load that included two galvanized iron tanks of fresh water. In the day the roads and tracks built by the army carried little traffic but now they were crowded with column after column of camels, mules, horses and lorries all moving eastward while night hid them from the Turks.

An aide led him through an anteroom in the tent where a dozen clerks hammered at typewriters by the light of paraffin lamps. Beyond was a room with a wide table spread with maps. Finlayson and Braddock straightened from stooping over the maps and as Smith crossed to the table Braddock said, "How are those two burned men?"

"They have a chance, sir."

"Bad luck, that."

"Yes, sir." Two men he knew and liked might die. But Braddock knew how Smith felt. There was nothing more to say.

Finlayson said, "We've studied your wireless reports and so have my intelligence staff. Anything to add?"

Smith hesitated, marshalling his thoughts, then said, "From Adana down to Gaza is roughly three hundred miles as the crow flies but the railway is about five hundred miles long because of the way it winds about. There are stretches the Shorts can't reach but they have twice flown over the accessible areas and seen nothing. Five thousand men and their equipment means a dozen trains at least and they would be seen. They won't be hanging about in the dead ground we can't reach, because Kressenstein will ram them down to the Gaza-Beersheba line as fast as he can. The summer is ending and he knows General Allenby's attack must come soon." He paused then finished positively. "At this moment therefore I don't believe the Afrika Legion has cleared Turkey."

Finlayson was nodding and smiling. "I told you my staff studied your reports. They reached the same conclusion but they went a stage further. Since the Turks and Germans are desperately short of rolling stock on that railway, if they want to maintain their rate of supply to the front line they can't turn over a dozen trains to the Legion. They'll have to bring it down piecemeal and that means it will be too late."

Smith said uneasily, "With respect, sir, maybe the Germans have thought of a way around that one."

Finlayson's fingers drummed testily on the map. "We bring you good news, then you try to put a damper on it."

"Only giving my opinion, sir."

Finlayson grunted, glanced at Braddock. "I'd like the search to go on. When they do arrive, we want to know."

Braddock nodded and Smith said, "I propose to sail north immediately and patrol off the Gulf of Alexandretta. I believe the break in the line at the Taurus mountains will slow them up and that's where we'll find them." They discussed it for a few minutes and then Braddock agreed. Smith asked, "Any word from Edwards, sir?"

Finlayson shook his iron-grey head. "Nothing. I'm not surprised because clearly the Legion isn't there to be found." Under the lamplight he looked older, tired, but he seemed less tense than when Smith had entered. He said, "The date for the attack is confirmed, final. The build-up is exactly on time and Allenby will have the advantage of surprise. About two weeks ago a certain staff officer got lost in the desert in no-man's-land. A Turkish patrol saw him and shot at him so he ran for it, but he dropped his briefcase. The Turks found it covered in blood and stuffed with maps from a staff meeting—maps that showed a plan for an attack on Gaza." Finlayson chuckled softly. "It worked. The Turks have reinforced

Gaza. And Allenby will attack at Beersheba." His smile faded. "We need a victory. God willing, this time we shall have it."

Smith asked, "What about *Morning Star*, sir?"

Finlayson said bitterly "I could have done without her and that battalion! A team of investigating officers came up from Cairo and spent a day aboard her. They found out nothing. After the attack I'll have the men brought ashore and interrogated again. A man has been murdered and the murderer must be found and tried. Justice must be done."

He sighed, then said dryly, "Meanwhile, I've had your suggestions acted on. Go and see for yourself if you don't believe me."

THE MOTORBOAT headed for *Morning Star*, passing close under *Blackbird*'s stern, and Smith smelled the lingering stench of the fire, borne on the breeze from the black cavern of the hangar. *Blackbird* was coaling and Smith saw men from *Dauntless* working aboard her.

The launch patrolling around *Morning Star* turned to intercept the motorboat. The Lewis gun mounted forward in the launch was manned and as she came alongside the lieutenant commanding her called across the gap, "What boat is that?"

Smith stepped to the side where he could be seen and answered, "*Dauntless*. Commander Smith. What are your orders?"

The lieutenant called, "To keep everyone away except those on my list."

"What list is that?"

"The admiral gave it to me but it came from General Finlayson. Your name is on it, sir."

The launch swung away. Smith was surprised that his name was on the list of those authorized to board. Finlayson must have assumed that he would return to ask about the men aboard *Morning Star*.

The boat was swinging around under the stern of *Morning Star*. The pink-faced midshipman at her helm looked down his nose at the grime on the ladder the tramp had rigged. Smith climbed it nevertheless, found one of Captain Brand's marines on guard at the head of it and asked him, "Major Taggart?"

The marine peered, recognized him. "The major's forrard, sir."

Smith walked past the superstructure and found that the entire deck forward of the bridge was now a large cage of barbed wire. There was a door in the wire where a marine sentry stood guard and Smith could see another sentry on the fo'c'sle. The deck inside the cage was covered with the bodies of sleeping men. In the dim light Smith saw Taggart rise and pick his way through the others to the wire. The sentry let him through.

Taggart said, "They've shipped extra stoves, army cooks and fresh food, so we're eating much better. We've got drill uniforms in place of the serge and we're allowed on deck. I'm very grateful."

Smith muttered something, embarrassed. Over Taggart's shoulder he saw that one other man was awake, sitting with his head propped against the bulwark, staring unseeing across the deck. Smith thought he recognized him. Hadn't he been the only man in the hold not to watch Smith that first night? To change the subject he nodded towards the man, and asked Taggart, "Who's that?"

Taggart answered casually, "Garrett. He's a bit young. I use him as a runner so as to keep my eye on him." He went on quickly, taking Smith's arm, "Come on, we'll go where we can talk."

They passed the superstructure and crossed the deck away from the marine sentry at the head of the ladder. A rectangular, tarpaulin-covered shape was lashed to the deck. Smith glanced at it curiously and Taggart explained, "Adeline's wagon for carrying her supplies or wounded. There's a harness but most of the time we haven't had a horse or mule so we've man-hauled it. That's easy enough, it's light and well-sprung." They halted, leaned on the bulwark and looked out over the anchorage to where *Dauntless* lay, *Blackbird* astern of her. For a time they were silent then Taggart said, "Good-looking ship."

Smith said simply, "She's beautiful." Then he turned and asked casually, "Any trouble?"

Taggart shook his head. "The feller that tried to grab Adeline, Captain Jeavons put him ashore. We've had no more trouble."

Smith looked past him. "They are a remarkably disciplined body of men." That didn't say a part of what he meant. "I mean—" He searched for words.

Taggart glanced sideways at him. "I think I know what you

mean. They hold together, fight together. Loyal to king and country and all that, but above all they are loyal to themselves because they're infantrymen and they've soldiered together a long time. So damn this talk of mutiny."

Smith remembered the faces in the hold: he had seen strain but in none of them either viciousness or fear. What Taggart had just told him confirmed the impression he had gained, that in a unit under Taggart the men of his battalion would be a force to reckon with. But that would not happen because, no matter whether the murderer among them was found or not, the battalion would never fight again as a unit. Sooner or later it would be split up.

Taggart's gaze slid past Smith. He went on hurriedly, "Sorry if Adeline gave you the rough edge of her tongue the other night. She feels for the men—she's a grand girl when you get to know her."

Smith said dryly, "I'll give her the benefit of the doubt."

"You can do it now."

Smith turned and saw Adeline Brett coming towards them, a dressing gown wrapped around her slim figure, her hair tousled. She stopped before them, pushed at the blonde curls with one hand and said. "A boat came alongside and woke me. I couldn't get off to sleep again." She looked at Smith. "Was that you?"

He nodded. "Sorry."

She shrugged that aside. "I doze a lot in the day now because I haven't much to do."

Taggart caught the girl's eye on him and he asked Smith abruptly, "You're off soon?"

Smith looked across to *Blackbird* and saw the coaling lighter being towed away. "Very soon."

"I'll see you again, maybe." Taggart walked forward and left Smith and the girl alone.

She said, "I want to thank you."

"It's been said already." Smith was gazing after Taggart. "He's in trouble up to his neck. He knows who did it and when the truth finally comes out they'll know he lied to shield the man and they won't be easy on him. He's an officer and can give no excuse." His eyes came down to the girl. "Do *you* know?"

"I wasn't there when the colonel was shot."

"That's not what I asked. Do you know who did it?"

She answered angrily, "The colonel was a drunken fool! John Taggart had seen the position they were to attack. He told the general it was hopeless but his battalion would still take it! The colonel was safely behind the line when the attack went in and he didn't even see the wounded come back, but *I* saw them!" She shuddered.

Smith waited, then pressed her again. Because Finlayson was right and this secret was a poison. Taggart would suffer for it, and many others. "Do *you* know who did it?"

Adeline hesitated, then: "I—have a suspicion but it's no more than that. I wouldn't tell anyone." That was final.

He said, "I have to go." She walked with him to the head of the ladder, guarded by a marine sentry. He paused awkwardly. "As Taggart said, 'See you again'."

She smiled but with lips tight-pressed and he wondered if she was laughing at him. But she asked, "What's your name?"

"David."

She set her hands on his shoulders, put up her face and kissed him. "Thank you, David." She walked away. The marine sentry stared blankly out into the night as Smith glared at him, then turned and descended the ladder. The marine grinned.

The motorboat crept alongside *Dauntless* and Smith quickly forgot the battalion, Taggart and Adeline Brett. He saw the launch from the shore hooked onto the foot of the ladder. It had brought Merryweather back to the ship, but Braddock was also aboard it. As the boats rubbed together Braddock leaned over the side of the launch and growled, "They've just brought in an Arab with a message from Edwards. Another throat-cutter by the looks of him, but the word from Edwards is that there's a supply dump by the railway at Lydda guarded by a company of Germans. Know anything about it?"

Smith shook his head. "There's an anti-aircraft battery just south of Lydda," he explained, "so we give it a wide berth."

Braddock grunted. "Don't know if it means much." Then, "You still think this Afrika Legion might arrive in time to ruin things?"

"Yes, sir."

Braddock muttered, "I hope to God you're wrong."

The launch headed away and Smith climbed aboard *Dauntless*.

He had his orders, both ships had completed with fuel and the search for the Afrika Legion would go on. Either this detour to Deir el Belah would have done no harm and they would find the Legion at Adana—or a court martial would break him.

Before sunrise, when the first light was a pink edging to the hills of Judaea, *Dauntless* led *Blackbird* out of the anchorage as quietly as they had come and headed for Alexandretta.

TELEGRAPHIST LOFTY WILLIAMS curled his long frame to lean his head in at the door of *Dauntless*'s galley, blinking after the glare of the afternoon sun. "Wotcher, Cookie. Any chance of a wet?"

Leading Cook Matthews, sweating rivers in the heat of the galley, jerked his head at the big kettle of tea that stewed on the stove. "Help yourself." He watched as Lofty produced the two pint mugs from behind his back and poured tea the colour of gravy into the mugs, added sugar and a spoonful of condensed milk. Matthews asked, "What's goin' on, then?"

Lofty eyed the tea. "Looks a drop o' good." He sipped and swore as he burned his tongue. "What's goin' on? Nothing much, mate. Not like them first two weeks when the ol' man was shooting everything that showed itself ashore."

Matthews nodded. "We've got a fire-eater there. I've heard one or two tales about him. Quiet feller, but—"

"Ah! Still waters, mate." Then Lofty added thoughtfully, "He's been quieter than ever this trip. I was talking to that Buckley, you know, the big killick as came with him. He says the skipper's too quiet."

"So?"

Lofty shrugged. "So nothing. Except that the balloon'll be going up ashore pretty soon and maybe Smith knows when that will be. We'll be busy then. But now? Nothing. Just a quiet little run up the coast."

He walked aft, adjusting to the motion of *Dauntless* so that he did not spill a drop from the mugs even when climbing down the ladders to the lower deck.

At the wireless office he edged in through the thick pall of tobacco smoke from the pipe of Leading Telegraphist Bailey, who sat slouched in one chair with his feet propped up on another and the headphones pushed comfortably down so the earpieces rested against his jaw.

Bailey took the pipe from his mouth, glanced up at the clock and said, "Blimey, you're early. Are we sinking?"

"Just thought I'd get a wet before I started." Lofty was to take over the watch at four. It was now five minutes to. He offered a mug and asked, "Anything goin' on?"

Bailey shook his head and sipped at the tea. "Routine."

"Just what I was telling Cookie. A quiet little run—"

He stopped as Bailey's feet slammed down from their resting place on the chair and he shoved the mug aside, reached out to the Morse key and rattled off an acknowledgement. Someone was calling *Dauntless*. He picked up a sharpened pencil and began to print neatly on the signal pad. The signal was in code.

Lofty nipped out of the office and halted at the first cabin he came to. The curtain that served as a door was drawn back and Lieutenant Cherrett, the signals officer, lay on his bunk, a magazine open on his chest, snoring gently. Lofty reached in, shook Cherrett's foot and as he opened sleepy eyes, said, "Beg pardon, sir. Signal coming in. Coded."

Cherrett grumbled, "Probably some highly-secret request for the number of teetotallers on board." But he went quickly to the wireless office, sat down with the signal and started decoding.

Minutes later he was racing for the bridge. To Ackroyd, who had the watch, he panted, "Captain?"

Ackroyd jerked his head towards the sea cabin. "In there. What's the rush?"

Cherrett threw at him: "*Walküre*'s out!"

6 *Dawn Rendezvous*

Why?

Smith was snatching some much-needed but uneasy sleep when Cherrett brought the signal. After the initial moment of shock, that question came first to his mind. Why had *Walküre* broken out?

The signal advanced no theories. *Walküre* had evaded her watchers and passed through the Dardanelles under cover of darkness the previous night. Her destination and present position were unknown. *Dauntless* and *Blackbird* were to proceed to a rendezvous just west of Cyprus, where they would be joined by the old French battleship *Maroc* and her two escorts at first light. They would then search, sweeping westward, with Smith in command—as Braddock had told him three days before.

He went into the chartroom with Henderson and laid off the new course. Twelve hours of steaming would see them there at dawn to meet *Maroc*. Their dash to the Gulf of Alexandretta would have to wait. Dangerous as the Afrika Legion was, a German warship at large in the Mediterranean constituted an even greater threat.

He returned to the bridge with Henderson, who said, "*Walküre*'s a funny sort of ship. With twelve 8.2-inch guns, and fifteen thousand tons, she's too big for a cruiser. Yet she's too small for a battle cruiser or a battleship."

Ackroyd shrugged square shoulders and said with heavy humour, "A pocket-sized battleship."

That brought grins to the faces on the bridge and Henderson said, "Some pocket."

Ackroyd mused, "Wonder if she's after the convoys?"

It was a possibility. Smith said, "Maybe." But guessing was a waste of time. They had to *know*.

It was night once more and the two ships were racing through a rising sea when Cherrett came running again with a signal. *Walküre* had been sighted west of Crete headed due west. Now it made sense of a sort and Ackroyd said tentatively, "The Adriatic?"

Smith nodded. It was possible for *Walküre* to fight her way into the Adriatic and join the Austrian fleet at Pola, where it had lain since the start of the war doing almost nothing. That might be the idea to an adventurous ship's captain who might persuade the Austrians to engage in active operations with himself. The Allies had trouble enough in the Mediterranean trying to counter the U-boat threat. If the Adriatic boiled up it would stretch still further the naval reserves that were already strained to breaking point.

But the next signal came as an anti-climax. Their orders were unchanged: Smith's little squadron, once assembled at the rendezvous, would sweep westward—but now only to form part of a screen of ships in case *Walküre* tried to return to the Aegean. Smith went to his bunk and tried to sleep but only dozed restlessly, and he was up and on the bridge again before the dawn.

Ackroyd had the watch and greeted Smith. " 'Morning, sir. Only one signal an hour or so back from *Maroc*, confirming she'll be at the rendezvous on time but she's had to send back one of her escorts with engine trouble. She's carrying on with the other one. That's SC 101, American submarine-chaser.''

Smith nodded and took the mug of scalding hot, bitter coffee that Buckley brought him. The American submarine-chasers were new to the Mediterranean. They were little more than big motor launches, a hundred feet long with a single 3-inch gun forward, a Y-gun aft for lobbing depth charges over the side and a speed of only some seventeen knots. He asked, "What about us?"

Henderson came out of the charthouse, holding a mug of cocoa. "We'll be on station in another fifteen minutes, sir."

"Good. That's right on time." *Maroc* had done well, too. She was slow and elderly and the powers that be had set her a tall order when they sent her to keep this rendezvous on time.

The Afrika Legion. . . . He should have been close to the Gulf of Alexandretta by now and instead he was two hundred miles off and getting farther away with every second. But maybe Finlayson's intelligence officers were right, that the Legion would be too late now, anyway. He shifted restlessly as *Dauntless* crashed on through seas now big and oily. Astern of *Dauntless* came *Blackbird*. She was a good seaboat and was plugging on well. But Smith was uneasy, because he still felt he could not trust her young captain, Chris Pearce.

He finished the coffee and balanced the mug on the shelf below the screen. By the time the sun was up his little squadron would be together and sweeping westward in a long line.

ACKROYD ASKED, "Any sign of *Maroc*?"

Dauntless and *Blackbird* were about on station now, and reduced to fifteen knots. The sun was close under the rim of the sea astern and visibility was lengthening with every second, even though mist and lowering clouds seemed to fur the edges of everything.

The port lookout called, "There she is, sir! *Maroc*! Thirty on the bow!"

Smith set his glasses to his eyes and saw her coming out of the mist about three miles away, the outline blurred, but her size could not be hidden. The twin funnels, the tripod mast—

Ackroyd said, "Make the challenge, Yeoman."

"*No!*" Smith shouted it. "*Hard astarboard! All guns load!*"

Pandemonium broke loose as Smith jabbed his fingers on a button and klaxons blared through *Dauntless*. The ship emerging out of the mist was as big as *Maroc* but there the resemblance ended. *Maroc* had three funnels and no tripod mast. This was *Walküre*.

Dauntless was coming around, heeling in the turn. Smith saw the crew of her forward gun skidding on the tilting foredeck as they strove to load and bring it into action. Now *Walküre*'s long guns fired. Smith remembered the carrier astern, whirled round and saw her still holding her course. Was Pearce slavishly waiting an order to turn? He rapped at the signal yeoman. "Make to *Blackbird*: 'Turn sixteen points. Take evasive action. Enemy bears three miles west.'"

And no more than three. That salvo of hers would soon fall—

The salvo plunged into the sea a cable's length from *Dauntless*'s starboard quarter. The bugles were blaring and the deck was alive with racing men. Ackroyd went to take command of damage control. The signal yeoman reported, "*Blackbird* acknowledges, sir." He added, "An' she's turning!"

It was high time. "Wireless to C in C Eastern Med and all HM ships: 'Am in action *Walküre*. My position—' get that from the pilot—'enemy course and speed due east fifteen knots.'"

Second Officer Jameson said, "Guns requests—"

Smith snapped, "Yes, dammit! All guns commence!"

Seconds later the two after 6-inch guns fired together and the vibration sent the mugs under the screen rolling across the bridge. Smith had ordered, "Full ahead both! Starboard ten!" and *Dauntless* was now tearing away to the south. He was out on the starboard wing of the bridge, seeing *Walküre*'s guns fire. Her outline was blurring again through the gauzy draperies of the mist as the distance between the two ships widened. Smith looked for the fall of that salvo, casting a hasty glance around at *Blackbird*. She made a fine target for *Walküre*'s shells with that haystack of a hangar, and the bombs below her deck. Pearce should have turned sooner. If *Walküre* hit her—

The shock threw him into Henderson, sent the pair of them slamming into the screen, and the sea fell across their shoulders and almost drove them to their knees. The salvo had burst to port close alongside, hurled sea water aboard in tons and heeled *Dauntless* over but she was running on an even keel again now.

Smith snapped at Jameson, "Damage reports?"

"Nothing yet, sir."

The after 6-inch guns fired again and Smith fumbled for the glasses, searched for *Walküre*. He saw her stern on, insubstantial as the mist itself on that blurred horizon. *Walküre*'s guns also were firing now from her after turrets. She and *Dauntless* were on widely diverging courses. Soon *Dauntless* would be out of range of those big guns in the enemy cruiser but then she would be out of sight also. He could not let that happen. He had stumbled on *Walküre*— now he must not lose her.

A salvo howled overhead and burst off the port bow, well clear of *Dauntless*, but straddling *Blackbird*. Deafened, he heard only distantly Jameson's bellow, "They've dropped one on *Blackbird*!" Smoke was pouring from the carrier's deck forward of the bridge on the starboard side and trailing from a hole just above the waterline. The shell had penetrated the deck and smashed on out of *Blackbird*'s side.

Smith ordered, "Port ten!"

"Port ten, sir! . . . Ten of port wheel on, sir!"

The cruiser's knife-edge stem swept around through a semicircle until Smith said, "Meet her. . . . Steer two-oh degrees."

He stared out over the bow at *Walküre* dead ahead. He heard somebody cheer on the deck below. Did they think he was steaming to attack the huge cruiser? That would be madness—*Dauntless* stood no chance at all in a stand-up fight against that heavily-gunned, heavily-armoured ship. But if they were to keep *Walküre* in sight in this visibility he would perforce have to stay within range of her guns. And now, additionally, he had to draw her fire to give *Blackbird* a chance.

68

He told the signal yeoman, "Wireless to C in C and HM ships: 'Maintaining contact with enemy. Enemy's course east, speed twenty knots.'" He watched *Walküre* through the glasses, the lenses shaking his image as the forward 6-inch gun saw her again, and fired. "Starboard ten," he ordered, to take *Dauntless* out of the path of the next salvo. "Meet her . . . steer that."

Henderson said, "I think that round of ours fell short, sir."

Smith grunted assent. *Walküre* was still in reach of the 6-inch, just, but the range-taker would be having trouble reading ranges in the mist. *Walküre* was pouring out smoke now. She was definitely making a run for it. Her latest salvo fell abeam of *Dauntless*, hurling up huge spouts of water about three cable-lengths away.

Jameson said, "Damn! Lost her!"

Smith peered into the mist. He swept the glasses along the horizon but saw nothing, not even *Walküre*'s smoke. He swore softly but made himself ask casually, "What's our speed?"

Henderson answered, "Twenty-two knots, sir."

"Good enough." Still carefully casual. *Walküre*'s best speed was about twenty-five knots but she would not work up to that for some time, so she would not get away from *Dauntless*. Provided she did not change course.

He managed to maintain his cool tone when he said, "There she is." The mist had thinned or *Walküre* had pushed out of it. But there she was, now broadside on and her guns firing.

The forward 6-inch slammed again. The gun crew was having a bad time with *Dauntless* steaming at this speed and in this sea, the bow wave coming inboard to break over them in sheets of spray.

Jameson said, "Range is closing, sir!"

Walküre's salvo burst to starboard, a good cable's-length astern of *Dauntless*. Then *Walküre* disappeared.

This time Jameson swore. "What the hell does her skipper do for an encore? Pull rabbits out of a hat?"

Smith managed to laugh though it was far from funny. The sea and that hazy horizon were unchanged but *Walküre* had gone as if she had sunk beneath the waves. Where was she bound for, anyway? When *Dauntless* had come on her, *Walküre* was headed eastward towards Cyprus. What for? To bombard the shore and whatever shipping she might find? Or had she intended a change of course that would send her tearing down towards Port Said and the convoys?

Smith shifted restlessly. Where *was* she? Only mist and the empty sea lay ahead of *Dauntless*. The sun was up now, a watery sun but sparkling lights from the sea, still very low so Smith had to squint against it. How long since they saw her? If she had doubled back on her track and headed westward she could be hull-down over the horizon and lost to him when the mist lifted.

There was an uneasy silence on the bridge, all of them aware of the danger of losing *Walküre*. He said quietly, "Starboard ten. Meet her. Steer that."

"Course eight-five degrees, sir!"

Now *Dauntless* was heading eastward, which had been *Walküre*'s course when last sighted. Smith glanced out over the starboard quarter and could just make out *Blackbird*. He hoped she was far enough from *Walküre* to be safe. Smith stepped out to the port wing of the bridge and leaned on the screen beside the lookout. The sun was sucking up the mist so now they had glimpses through gaps in it of a clear-edged, empty horizon.

The lookout bawled in Smith's ear, "*Port quarter! My God!*"

Smith whipped around, saw *Walküre* burst out of the mist almost astern of *Dauntless* and steaming straight for her. He shouted, "Starboard ten!" As *Dauntless* heeled to that order he thought how she had nearly caught them, had turned back to port in a wide circle that would have brought her broadside on to *Dauntless* but for that last change of course.

Then the bridge gratings bucked under his feet, flame towered from a hit aft and the blast threw the port lookout into Smith, sent both of them staggering. Smith pushed away and saw smoke boiling up right aft. *Walküre*'s captain *had* caught them.

The ship's heeling turn meant Smith could no longer see *Walküre* from where he stood. He plunged back across the bridge to the starboard wing, felt the deck shiver and heard the slam of a 6-inch gun firing from aft. He waited for the other to fire but it did not. He could not see the damage in the stern for the smoke there but he could see *Walküre* only too well; she was turning to starboard to fire broadsides and at a range of barely three miles.

He ordered "Port ten," to send *Dauntless* swerving away once more. The 6-inch aft fired again and at the same instance the salvo from *Walküre* howled in. *Dauntless* thrust through a curtain of spray, seemed to shake herself free, and was in the open sea again.

A report came up from Ackroyd that the aftermost 6-inch gun was dismounted; the one still in action was the gun mounted on the superstructure above Smith's main cabin.

In the mad minutes that followed as *Dauntless* swerved and ran for her life, the surviving 6-inch gun aft slammed away and the salvoes from *Walküre* came howling in. Twice they fell terrifyingly close alongside so the men below deck heard them like hammer-blows on the thin steel shell of the cruiser. She survived, but Smith knew that one of those salvoes must land on her soon. The mist that had hidden *Walküre* would no longer save *Dauntless*. The sun was wiping it away from the surface of the sea like steam wiped from a mirror. Visibility for gunnery was excellent now and *Walküre* bulked huge under her black trail of funnel smoke.

"Ship bearing Green nine-oh!" yelled the starboard lookout.

Smith lifted his glasses and saw a ship hull-up on the horizon. It was the French battleship *Maroc*, and closer, something like a mile ahead of her, was a much smaller vessel. That would be the American sub-chaser, SC 101, the battleship's solitary escort. Doubtless she had gone scouting ahead when they heard the gunfire, her captain making the most of the small advantage in speed that his little craft had over *Maroc*.

Smith said, "Yeoman! Make to *Maroc*: 'Enemy bears northwest four miles.' "

The searchlight above the bridge blinked out the signal but before it was done Smith saw it was superfluous. Jameson said, "*Walküre*'s firing on *Maroc*, sir!"

Maroc was already turning, presenting her side to the enemy. A column of waterspouts rose short of her and as she steamed clear, flame winked from fore and aft turrets. Smith swung the glasses, searching for *Walküre*, found her and saw she was turning. He ordered, "Port ten!"

Walküre had turned away eastward again. She had held *Dauntless* almost in her grip but now that she faced *Maroc* with her four 12-inch guns she dared not fight on, the odds were loaded against her. Smith wondered how her captain must feel, first of all to have

71

got this far unseen, only for *Dauntless* to blunder onto him, to turn under cover of the mist and almost catch the cruiser at point-blank range, and then. . . . "Meet her. Steer oh-six-oh. Revolutions for fifteen knots."

Now *Dauntless* was following *Walküre*. *Walküre*'s after-turrets still fired at *Maroc*, and the French battleship had turned in pursuit, was returning the fire as the range opened between them. It was a long-range duel between the big ships, and both ships achieved some near-misses.

The sub-chaser had fallen back to patrol abeam of *Maroc* and one salvo from *Walküre* fell around the cockleshell craft. Smith held his breath until he saw her pushing out of the smoke and spray. He said, "Make to the chaser: '*Walküre* flying Turkish colours. Understand USA not at war with Turkey.'"

An answer came from the chaser inside a minute: "Submit your last signal should be addressed to *Walküre*."

Smith laughed with the rest of them on the bridge. Whoever commanded the chaser had a cool head and a sense of humour. He asked, "Who is her captain?"

Henderson had already checked the list. "Lieutenant Petersen. That's with an 'e', s-e-n, sir." Smith nodded and Henderson added, "Suppose he's Norwegian by origin."

If he imagined a tall blond Viking, he was wrong.

HARRY PETERSEN was dark and blue-chinned, short and broad. He stood in his cramped wheelhouse now and scowled at the smoke that marked *Walküre*, hull-down over the horizon. She was no longer firing and *Maroc*'s guns had fallen silent.

Young Ensign Cleeve on the deck below turned and laughed. "Well, it sure was exciting while it lasted. Goodbye *Walküre*."

Petersen took the stubby pipe from his mouth, tamped down the tobacco with a horny forefinger and clamped his teeth around the stem again. "We might see her again."

It was a procession now, *Dauntless* shadowing *Walküre* while *Maroc* and the chaser tried vainly to keep up. *Blackbird* was there, too, but hardly faster than the French battleship now. Petersen knew only one ship could keep up with *Walküre* and that was *Dauntless*.

ACKROYD, filthy with soot and grime, reported to Smith in person. "Fire's out, sir. The shell didn't penetrate; exploded on impact but the gun and its crew are a total loss."

He did not go into details and Smith could imagine the scene of carnage around the gun after a direct hit from one of those shells. But it might have been worse. Suppose that shell had torn through the armoured deck and exploded below, leaving *Dauntless* a crippled hulk? Suppose an entire salvo—

He tried to black out the pictures from his mind. The loss of the gun crew was bad enough; he had known the men personally, as he knew every man aboard *Dauntless* and *Blackbird*. In the ringing silence after the guns' firing he experienced the familiar reaction. The excitement, the concentration that gripped him when in action, these were past now and the coldness crept in on him.

Jameson said, "*Blackbird* reports she's making water but her pumps are coping and she's making repairs, can steam fifteen knots."

Smith nodded. *Blackbird* was three or four miles astern. Again he was uneasy about Pearce. Why had the man been so slow to react?

Smith swung up into his chair behind the bridge screen. "Resume normal working." This would be a long shadowing operation, he was certain. He could see *Walküre*, just a speck under her smoke, safely out of range. *Dauntless*, with her advantage of speed, could comfortably shadow *Walküre* like this indefinitely, but her captain had already shown he would not accept that. They had to watch out.

All through the morning the tailing went on, eastward at around twenty knots. To the south lay Cyprus and to the north Turkey, but both were hidden below the rim of the sea. There were only *Dauntless* and *Walküre* now, tearing through the big seas: the others had slipped astern, out of sight. Soon the weather moderated, the wind easing, the sea falling away to a long swell and *Blackbird* wirelessed that she had worked up to twenty knots.

The pursuit went on. The sun was overhead now, glittering on the sea so it hurt the eyes. The German ship was tiny with distance and blurred by smoke and heat shimmer that made it tremble in the lenses of the glasses.

Later Henderson emerged from the chartroom to say, "She might turn any time now, sir."

He meant that *Walküre* had steamed past Cyprus and now could turn south towards Port Said and the convoy routes. The night would cloak *Walküre* long before she reached those destinations and Smith dared not lose her like that. But he had anticipated this moment and only nodded acknowledgment of Henderson's words. "She won't turn," he said. "She's headed for Alexandretta."

There was silence on the bridge, then Ackroyd asked, "What would she want there?"

Smith shook his head. He didn't know what she was up to. There was nothing at Alexandretta for *Walküre*. But, "She was headed eastward when we ran into her," he said. "If she was bound for Port Said or the convoy routes, why should she go north-about around Cyprus?"

Walküre held on to the eastward and when the coast of Turkey was sighted it was certain she was bound for Alexandretta. Ackroyd and Henderson looked at Smith, still sitting easily in the chair, and exchanged glances of puzzled respect behind his back. She finally altered course but only to edge in towards the northern shore. Smith ordered, "Revolutions for ten knots."

Walküre was on a course to take her through the gap in the Turkish minefields that closed the twenty-mile mouth of the gulf, running under the protecting muzzles of the batteries there. Smith got down from the chair, stretched and leaned his arms on the screen to set the glasses to his eyes again. He watched the big cruiser haul away, shrink and finally disappear into the gulf. It was twenty-five miles from the mouth to the small port of Alexandretta.

He lowered the glasses. "Starboard five." While *Dauntless* started on a steady patrol across the entrance to the channel, signals went out telling the Allied navies that *Walküre* was trapped in the Gulf of Alexandretta and *Dauntless* held the door.

"Well, she's safe now," Ackroyd said, scowling into the gulf.

Smith answered grimly, "We'll see about that."

An hour later *Blackbird* heaved up over the horizon under a pall of smoke as her stokers laboured to keep her engines pounding. A huge hole had been torn in her hull just above the waterline. Smith watched her come on. She might make twenty knots, but only in fine weather and that was not good enough for the consort to a fast light cruiser like *Dauntless*. That hole had to be mended soon, and he must have another talk with Pearce. . . .

Putting Pearce from his mind he ordered, "Make to *Blackbird*: 'Prepare to launch two seaplanes.'"

Smith wanted to see *Walküre*, where she lay, whether she was anchored or still shifting about the gulf. Something would have to be done about her; she could not be left as a threat, another German warship constantly to be guarded.

"*Blackbird* acknowledges, sir." Ackroyd said.

Only twenty-four hours before they had been on a mission that would have brought them here anyway. The Afrika Legion.

"Tell Pearce that one of the Shorts is to reconnoitre the railway from Adana to the Bagcha tunnel. I'll fly in the other up the gulf as observer."

He walked out to the wing of the bridge. One seaplane had already been pushed out of the hangar.

Ackroyd appeared at his shoulder. "Wireless from *Maroc*, sir." He handed a flimsy to Smith: *Maroc* estimated her arrival at the gulf at 1900 hours. "That'll turn the key in the lock," he added cheerfully.

That it would. *Walküre's* captain would not be mad enough to steam out into the fire from *Maroc's* 12-inch guns. Ackroyd said, "Surely *Walküre* must have known she'd be bottled up here. Or did she hope to get this far without being spotted?"

Smith pointed out, "She nearly did." If *Dauntless* had been an hour later at the rendezvous, *Walküre* would already have passed and been on her way safely eastward to Alexandretta.

The gig headed for *Blackbird*. She was stopped now, one seaplane in the water, tethered by lines and boomed off from the ship's side by the long poles. He could see four 65-pound bombs slung horizontally under the fuselage, and Flight Lieutenant Rogers in the pilot's cockpit. Rogers was known to his brother fliers as "Captain Webb", after the famous Channel swimmer, because he had only too often crashed in the sea and had to swim for it. Beyond him, aboard *Blackbird*, a second seaplane had been hoisted from its trolley, pilot and observer already aboard. Delilah. He recognized Hamilton back from the sick bay, sitting in the observer's cockpit.

Cole was the pilot. Of course. Delilah was his darling and he and Hamilton were a team.

"Oars!" The gig slipped up to Rogers's Short and bow grabbed for and caught a strut, hauled the gig in alongside a boxy float. Smith stepped over the side of the gig with a steadying hand clutching the float strut. Rogers passed down a flying helmet from the pilot's cockpit. Smith snatched it, slung his cap into the boat, yelled, "Lose that and I'll stop your grog for the rest o' the war!" He saw the crew laughing as he hauled himself up into the cockpit and the gig sheered away.

He had to lift the map and sketchpad from the seat before he plumped down into the cockpit. Rogers opened the top on the compressed air cylinder and the engine fired, rose to a thunder as they ran across the sea. The vibration eased to a thrumming, the spray was gone and they were airborne and climbing, tilting on one wing as they headed for the Gulf of Alexandretta.

All three sides of the gulf that opened out before them were backed by mountains, to east and south the shore was thickly wooded and to the north clothed in brush. They were halfway up the gulf now and right ahead was the little town of Payas with its old castle. Smith's chart aboard *Dauntless* had shown thirty fathoms all along the gulf except for close inshore, so *Walküre* had plenty of room to manoeuvre and anchor. . . .

There she was! He leaned forward and thumped Rogers's shoulder and pointed. *Walküre* lay near the head of the gulf at anchor, smoke only wisping from her two funnels, and close by her lay the big German freighter *Friedrichsburg*, which had been trapped here from the early days of the war. Rogers turned the Short towards *Walküre*. He was not wasting any time. Circling about would only lose them what little element of surprise they had.

The nose of the Short dipped as Rogers put her into a shallow dive. Smith rose in his seat to see the better, braced against the wind that tore at him, searching *Walküre* for signs of damage. He thought she might have been hit forward but he could not be sure till they were closer. The Short's dive steepened and her speed mounted. Smith could make out the details of *Walküre* now, the big-gun turrets, one forward, one aft and two either side of the centre line—and she *had* been hit forward!—the 5.9s and 3.4s, these last with barrels at high elevation pointing up at him.

Smith gulped, eyes still scurrying over the ship, seeking more signs of damage, finding none but seeing instead the flames winking from the guns along her deck. He clung to the cockpit coaming as Rogers threw the Short heavily about the sky in an attempt to put off the gunners. Shells were bursting around them. The Lewis jammed into Smith's back, painfully reminding him that it was there. He turned and cocked it, aimed it down over the side of the cockpit, squeezed the trigger as the Short pulled out of the dive. *Walküre* still lay far beneath them but in the face of that gunfire they would never get closer.

He felt the jerk as Rogers let go the bombs, 65-pounders, too big to be carried in the cockpit. Smith swore as he saw them fall, one to starboard and two to port of *Walküre*. Three misses. *Walküre* was anchored and still they could not hit her. Pearce had said, "Sit the Short on the funnel"—but the gunfire made that impossible. But only three bombs? Where was the fourth?

Walküre was sliding swiftly away astern of them now, her guns still hammering away. Smith leaned out, peered down and saw the fourth bomb hanging below the fuselage, looked up and saw Rogers working at the toggle release. The engine was hiccoughing and Smith saw oil flying on the wind. Right ahead of them was the big freighter; Rogers was easing the Short around to pass close above her stern. Smith felt the lurch as the bomb dropped away. It burst, right on the water line of the *Friedrichsburg* and under her stern. He saw a chunk of steel plate spinning skyward and turned to slap Rogers's back. *That* was a hit.

Rogers glanced over his shoulder, gave a quick, excited grin, then returned to his flying. Smith dropped down in his seat. They had not hit *Walküre* but he was not disappointed; they *had* hit the freighter—a pointed reminder that she was still in the war. He had seen *Walküre* at anchor and knew now that she would not be coming out for a while. And in a few hours *Maroc* would be up. . . .

He stopped making plans. The engine of the Short was still hiccoughing and now Smith became aware that there were great holes torn in the fuselage and they were only four or five hundred feet above the waters of the gulf.

He looked back and saw *Walküre* and the freighter, the latter marked by a tendril of smoke, but both of them tiny now. The Short was still close on twenty miles from the open sea, *Dauntless* and *Blackbird*. Their maximum speed was eighty knots but they weren't making anywhere near it. He looked over the side of the cockpit, down at the white wave crests beneath him, the Short's shadow sliding over them, cast sharp by the sun. They were making fifty, possibly sixty knots, so they had to stay in the air for twenty minutes.

The Turks had launches patrolling the gulf; none of them in sight at the moment but if the Short came down here it would mean a prison camp for Rogers and himself. Twenty minutes. . . .

DAUNTLESS AND *BLACKBIRD* were in sight now to the north. *Maroc* and the chaser had still not arrived. In minutes Smith could see they were steaming south from the north headland at the mouth of the gulf, patrolling.

Now the Short's engine died. In the silence, with only the wind's sighing through the wires strung between the two wings, Smith heard Rogers say, "Hell!" as he eased the nose of the Short down so that it glided towards the sea. Smith squinted at the ships. *Blackbird* steamed astern of *Dauntless* but the gap between them was widening. Had the cruiser increased her speed or—? No, *Blackbird* was stopping and now Smith could see the reason: a seaplane coming down out of the north. That was Cole and his pal Hamilton in *Delilah*. But what were they doing here? They were supposed to be flying a reconnaissance all the way to the Bagcha tunnel, a round trip of about three hours.

Rogers shouted, "Hang on!"

They were slipping just above the surface of the sea now, Rogers turning the Short into the wind, straightening her, keeping her nose down. The floats touched so gently as to raise only a feather of spray, then they were slowing, stopping. They were down but not yet home and dry. The seaplane bobbed and swung on the choppy sea as the wind pushed at it, Rogers was using the rudder in an attempt to keep the Short into the wind but not succeeding. Smith stood up to see over his head: *Dauntless* was cracking on speed towards them now with her stern tucked down and a big white bow-wave. Slender and graceful, despite the stains and scars of battle. In a few minutes she would be up with them.

The Short lurched under him and he lost his balance and sat down with a bump. The floats, riddled with bullet holes, had filled with water and sunk so that the fuselage collapsed on the sea. The tail of the Short went under. Rogers shoved up out of his seat to sit on the fuselage, blaspheming steadily and pulling off his shoes. "She's going to sink in a minute, sir."

He was right. The weight of the engine and the water-filled floats dragged down the Short's wings and fuselage inside a few minutes. In that time *Dauntless* came up, stopped and lowered a boat. It picked up Smith and Rogers as they paddled around with their shoes hung around their necks but the Short had gone.

As they sat in the boat Smith said ironically, "I suppose this swimming home is standard procedure for you."

"Captain Webb" Rogers took it philosophically, "Oh well, sir. It could have been a lot worse."

Smith agreed. "If we hadn't got this far we'd be prisoners."

"Not only that, sir. Those lumps of shell that went through her might easily have gone through us."

Smith swallowed sickly. He remembered Cole talking about Wilson who was killed while flying as his observer over Lydda, ". . . cut him to pieces below the waist."

The boat was alongside *Dauntless* and he climbed the ladder and thrust his shoes into the first pair of hands he saw. "Give them to Buckley and tell him I want another pair and some clothes."

Rogers followed him up to the bridge where Ackroyd waited, face serious. Someone handed out towels. Smith peeled off his shirt, asked Ackroyd, "Why did Cole return early?"

"They were hit, sir." He paused, then went on, "Hamilton's dead, Cole is hurt pretty badly. They've sent him over to us for the surgeon to handle." Smith was still for a second then went on rubbing at his face with the towel. First Wilson, now Hamilton. The big lieutenant of artillery had seemed indestructible. He and Cole had been closer than brothers. Now Hamilton was dead and Cole was hurt.

"There's some good news, sir." Smith towelled his chest, saw Ackroyd smiling now. "Signals, sir."

Smith leafed through the signals and saw the reason for that smile. The British armoured cruiser *Attack* would arrive in thirty-six hours. Another French battleship, *Océan*, would arrive soon after. A transport was to be sent from the Adriatic carrying four Italian torpedo boats with electric motors for silent night attack, ideal for slipping into the gulf over the minefields and slamming torpedoes into *Walküre*. Smith looked up and grinned. Ackroyd said, "One way or the other we've got her."

Smith agreed. Buckley came with clothes draped over one arm and said, "They've sent Hamilton's map and notebook over with Cole, sir. And it seems Cole wants to talk to you."

At that moment a seaman brought a canvas-wrapped packet to the bridge. "Come over with the pilot, sir. For you."

Smith nodded at Buckley. "Open it."

He grabbed his clothes from Buckley and started dressing as Buckley unwrapped the packet. It held a map clipped to a board and a notepad spotted with blood.

This was Hamilton's map, Hamilton's notepad. The notes were in Hamilton's bold, scrawled hand. Of the anti-aircraft battery on the northern shore of the gulf, the bouncy crossing, "Up and down like a see-saw". Then: "Beautiful, the sunlight on the mountains and the ravines so deep and dark." And then: "Adana station: Germans at Adana! More than a company! Five hundred! Flat cars with guns. Caught them napping! Not a shot fired and I could count the buttons on their shirts! Good old Delilah!"

That was the last entry. Smith slowly folded the map and put the notepad inside it. He looked up to see Rogers and Ackroyd staring at him. "They found the Afrika Legion," he said.

Ackroyd burst out, "That's bloody marvellous!" Then as he saw Smith's set face, "Isn't it?"

Smith did not answer him but said to Rogers, now dressed in shirt and trousers lent by Jameson, "Let's go and see Cole."

He lay in a cot in the sick bay, his face as white as the sheet tucked up around him. Merryweather came to meet them at the door. "He wants to talk to you." He sighed bitterly. "There's nothing I can do for him. I can't understand how he's still alive."

Smith heard the catch of Rogers's breath. Merryweather stood aside and Smith moved forward to kneel by the cot. Cole's head turned, eyes looking for him. Smith said softly, "Hello, old son."

Cole whispered, "Hamilton? How is he?"

"He'll be all right," Smith lied.

"Good." Cole smiled. "I was worried about him."

He was silent, then Smith prompted, because he had to ask, he had to know. "What happened?"

Cole whispered, "Got over Adana. Hell of a trip—up and down like you were in a bloody great lift. But Delilah took it like a bird. She's a beauty! And Adana. Train there. Lot of Germans. Hundreds! . . . Afrika Legion. Must be. Guns. Got right down low, buzzed them. Not a shot fired at us. Then—anti-aircraft, I suppose. Found I was still flying or Delilah was flying herself. Couldn't see Hamilton or hear him. Don't remember much about the rest. Saw *Blackbird*. Kept dozing off but got down. Delilah got us down. Is she all right?" He peered anxiously at Rogers.

"A few holes, that's all," he answered.

"Great." Cole was silent, eyes closed.

Smith waited, watching the pilot. He felt a touch on his arm, turned his head and saw the surgeon point at the door where Midshipman Bright waited. Smith glanced back at Cole but the surgeon was bent over him, one hand moving in a gesture of dismissal. Smith and Rogers rose and left the sick bay.

Bright said, "Sorry to interrupt, sir, but the first lieutenant said to fetch you. There's a local boat alongside and that Arab chap has come aboard, the one we put ashore south of Jaffa."

"Where is he?"

"In the cabin he had before, sir. He asked if his kit was still aboard and then if he could use the cabin. An' he said he wanted to talk to you so the first lieutenant said you would see him all in good time, sir, when you were ready."

Smith's lips twitched as he pictured Ackroyd telling Edwards that and enjoying it. He said, "Very good," and turned to Rogers. "What's the state of aircraft? How many available? Two?"

"Yes, sir." Rogers was unhappy, his mind on Cole. "Captain Pearce said Delilah wouldn't be ready to fly for a few hours but the other two are on standby."

The gig took Rogers back to *Blackbird* and Smith strode aft to Edwards's cabin. The soldier sat on the bunk in his white robes, his tunic across his knees. He looked thinner, his cheeks sunken, dust ingrained into his skin. He had pulled off the headdress and his hair was matted. Whisky stood on the desk and he held a glass in one hand while he rummaged in the pocket of his tunic with the other. He pulled out his cigarette case and a photograph came out of the pocket with it and fell to the deck at Smith's feet.

Smith stooped and picked up the photograph, rose slowly. It showed the head and shoulders of a young woman, a half-smile on her full lips. He asked neutrally, "Friend of yours?"

Edwards tucked a cigarette in his mouth, took the photograph, glanced at it and grinned. "Livvy? Not exactly a friend, old boy. More a sort of tenant. When I met her in Cairo she was living in some scruffy married quarter. I've got a flat I only use when I can get to Cairo and that's not often, so I let her have it. Her husband doesn't get to Cairo much either, so it works out very well." He gulped at the whisky and sighed appreciation. "Livvy's a nice little piece, though now she's hinting at a divorce and giving me those 'what-about-it' looks. To hell with that." He tossed the photograph carelessly onto the desk and showed his teeth in a grin. "I want you to send a signal to Finlayson. I've found the Afrika Legion."

"So have we." Smith held out Hamilton's map and pad, saw the grin wiped from Edwards's face. "We've located a half-battalion or so at Adana but we don't know whether that's an advance guard, rear-party or what. We'll send your signal, of course. It's just as well we're here to send it." That was said casually, but he knew the message had got home. But for *Dauntless* and her wireless it would have taken Edwards a week or more to reach Finlayson with his information. But then Smith said honestly, "Congratulations. It was a tremendous piece of work. You're an extraordinary man."

Edwards nodded complacently, accepting the compliment. "I'll make damn sure I get the credit for it, too, because it'll count for something when the war's over. It's like money in the bank." He sucked whisky and muttered, "I was lucky to get out at all. I was coming down from Adana when I saw these ships and I found an old pal to bring me out in his boat." He squinted up at Smith. "You don't seem overjoyed by *your* success."

Smith said flatly, "I'm not. For one thing, it cost the lives of two good men." There was another reason, a spectre that had haunted him since he began the search for the Afrika Legion, but he asked, "What did you find?"

Edwards filled his glass. "I first got word of them at Lydda where they have a supply dump. From Lydda I worked round the gulf to Adana, by train all the way, riding and hiding how I could, greasing palms. I saw some of the Legion pass through Adana— that was the rearguard your chaps saw. I also found a railway clerk at Adana I'd used before. The Germans had warned him they'd shoot him if he talked. I told him I'd give him away if he *didn't* talk and that coupled with a big bribe opened his mouth."

He drank more whisky, glanced at the photograph on the desk and drawled, "Ye-es, Livvy old girl, I'm for Cairo after this. I need a rest, a bed and you-know-what." He looked up at Smith, "That other girl, Adeline, was it? Where is she now?"

Smith said, expressionless, "Get on with it."

Edwards laughed. "Sorry. Not stepping on your toes am I?" But when Smith didn't answer he shrugged and went on. "The Legion's in a hurry and travelling light, so they've been able to cut down on the trains. Everything is being cleared from the railway to let them through." Smith listened, apprehension growing.

Edwards said, "They'll pick up some supplies at Lydda and should all be at Beersheba by early on the thirty-first. That's in two days' time. They're to relieve the Turks at Beersheba so that they can be sent to reinforce Gaza."

Smith stared at him. So the Turks and Germans still believed the main attack would fall on Gaza as General Allenby had meant them to. Beersheba was the real key to Allenby's plan of campaign. The attack on Gaza would be a feint while the real attack would be at Beersheba, to take it and roll up the "impregnable" Gaza–Beersheba line from that flank. The plan called for surprise and Allenby would clearly have achieved that. But it also demanded that Beersheba be taken before the end of the first day, before it could be reinforced, and before the attackers had to withdraw for more water. And that first day was 31st October, the day when the Legion would arrive. Smith said thickly, "I'll send a signal."

Edwards stared at him and said, "It's worse than I thought?" He knew Allenby's attack would take place soon and that the Legion might endanger its success. But he had not been told the details.

Smith said, "I'll explain later."

As he walked to the wireless office he thought it could not be worse. Early on the thirty-first, the Afrika Legion would be at Beersheba: five thousand picked men, highly trained, heavily armed with machine guns and field artillery.

And one of the spectres that had haunted Smith since he began his search now stood at his shoulder. Right from the start he had asked himself the question he dared not voice: When they found the Afrika Legion—what could they do about it?

He still had no answer.

7 "They'll Bury Me There–And I Won't Be The Only One!"

Smith went aboard *Blackbird* and saw Pearce in his cabin.

"Why didn't you turn when *Dauntless* did, when *Walküre* opened fire? Were you waiting for an order from me?"

Pearce stared down at his desk. "No, sir."

"I'd hope not. I expect you to show some initiative in a situation like that. So?"

Pearce looked up and said honestly, "I just couldn't seem to think for a moment."

Smith asked, "Have you any excuse?" But there could be no excuse. "Any reason?" He let his gaze drift to the photograph on the desk, suddenly aware that Edwards had the same photograph— of Olivia Pearce, Chris's wife.

Pearce's eyes followed his to the photograph, glanced quickly at Smith, then away. "No reason, sir."

Smith said, watching him, "Colonel Edwards came off in a boat an hour ago."

Pearce was astonished but that was his only reaction. "The one who acts as an Arab? How on earth did he wangle that?"

"Some old pal he met." Smith decided that Pearce did not know about Edwards but was clearly worried about his wife. "You can't go on like this, Chris. I'll give you leave as soon as I can. Meanwhile I want to see an improvement. If I can help in any way, just ask."

The offer was there. Pearce could unburden himself if he cared to, but he only said, "Thank you, sir."

Smith had to leave it at that. He told Pearce about the Afrika Legion. "Braddock has ordered us back to army HQ in Deir el Belah as soon as *Maroc* comes up to take over here. I intend to leave Ackroyd in command and fly back, taking Edwards with me."

Pearce brightened, was on familiar ground. "It's a hell of a long flight, sir, and all of it over the sea!" He shrugged. "But the Shorts have got the endurance and this northerly wind will help."

THE TWO SHORTS charged heavily across the sea, lifted off, and headed southward. Smith sat behind Kirby in one, while Beckett flew the other with Edwards as passenger. *Maroc* and the chaser should arrive soon, and then *Dauntless* and *Blackbird* could start back for Deir el Belah.

It was a long flight and his thoughts were not pleasant company. He had almost missed the Afrika Legion because he had run to Deir el Belah with the two men burned in the fire aboard *Blackbird* instead of sailing north to Alexandretta. He had let sentiment affect his judgment and if the Legion had slipped south unseen, it would have been his fault. His concern over those two men might have set at risk the lives of thousands committed to the attack on the Gaza-Beersheba line. He had come to Palestine believing this to be a time of crisis in his career, make or break, and he might have been broken, had survived only by luck.

Night fell early in the flight and they flew on in darkness. But the wind did not fail them, and neither did the Shorts. They droned on down the coast past Gaza, marked by the gun-flashes pricking the night, and came to Deir el Belah. A line of buoyed lights had been laid across the anchorage for them and the Shorts turned into wind, and one after the other slid down to settle on the sea. A decked-over lighter took the seaplanes aboard and set Smith and Edwards, who was still in his Arab robes, ashore.

They walked up through the gap in the dunes. In the darkness a locomotive slowly clunk-clunked among the sidings, halted with a hiss of steam and a squealing of brakes. Smith saw the sapper on the footplate as he passed, the man's round face shining with sweat. They trudged rapidly up the road, both of them stiff and weary.

The wind set the palm fronds waving and clashing above their heads and brought to their ears the thunder of the guns before Gaza. In the night muzzle-flashes flickered against the dark sky.

An aide met them at Finlayson's headquarters and ushered them hurriedly through the anteroom into the tent where Smith had seen Finlayson and Braddock before. They stood over the map now as if they had never moved. A tall lieutenant of the Australian Light Horse stood by the table, and Jeavons, master of the *Morning Star,* waited a little apart. He looked straight and spruce now, and had a smile for Smith. Major John Taggart was there also. He nodded, still wary in the presence of the others.

A haggard Finlayson performed the introductions. The lean, hard Australian was Lieutenant Jackson. Finlayson quickly got down to business, outlined for all of them the Afrika Legion's background, then: "The Legion is on its way to reinforce Beersheba and will pick up supplies and ammunition at Lydda on the night before the thirty-first. The Flying Corps are going to try a bombing raid but the guns of Lydda will keep them high and it will be difficult to hit the dump or cut the railway line." He rubbed at tired eyes and looked at the officers grouped round the map. "The Legion must be stopped and the one place it might be done is at Lydda. A force must strike inland to destroy the dump and demolish the track."

In the silence Smith heard the beating of moths against the lamp. He said, already disliking the idea, "A landing?"

"A raid," Finlayson corrected him. "We haven't the ships, the men, or the time for a conventional landing." He looked at Edwards. "Could you guide a small force through the dunes and on to Lydda, a night landing and a night march?"

Edwards hesitated, then: "I could. But it's heavy going for troops in the sand, and it's ten miles from the nearest point."

Finlayson brushed that aside impatiently. "We know that. I'm talking of mounted men, a single troop of horse. We know from your own reports that there are guardhouses along the road from Jaffa to Er Ramle which lies across your route to Lydda. There is also a Turkish regiment in reserve camped on that road. Therefore, a troop of horse could not pass through. Correct?"

Edwards nodded, licking his lips.

Finlayson went on: "Our plan is this. There is a Turkish garrison camped just south of Jaffa and another regiment five miles north—about a mile north of the Auja river." His finger moved deliberately across the map, marking them. "There's a ford at the mouth of the river with only one machine-gun post. Major Taggart's battalion will land there from *Morning Star* in three motorized lighters in daylight after a preliminary bombardment by *Dauntless* on the evening of the thirtieth—that's tomorrow. They will establish a bridgehead, acting in all respects as if preparing the way for a full-scale landing on the next day."

He looked up. "The Turks have feared a landing north of Gaza and have guarded against it. While this will be a lot farther north, they will certainly react with all the force available. That will pull in the regiment from north of the Auja, the garrison at Jaffa, and the regiment on the Jaffa–Er Ramle road. The way will then be clear for Mr. Jackson's troops to land south of Jaffa. They must reach the railway and the dump before first light and at least demolish the track—and if possible destroy the dump."

He paused, gazed round at them and asked quietly, "Questions? Colonel Edwards?"

Smith glanced sideways at Edwards and saw sweat on his face, though the night was chill. Edwards said, "There's a chance. The dump—" He hesitated, then said, "It's guarded by a company of Germans and they're not rear-echelon troops. They'll fight. . . ." His voice trailed away.

Finlayson said bitingly, "I asked for questions, not a recital of obstacles to be surmounted. This raid must be attempted." His eyes shifted round the room. "Mr. Jackson?"

The tall Australian shrugged. "We'll give it a go."

Finlayson said grimly, "You'll have to. Major Taggart?"

Taggart asked, "Has anyone got a better idea?" He waited but no one spoke. He said, "I know what you want, sir."

Finlayson rubbed at his forehead with the tips of his fingers. "Thank you, gentlemen. I can think of no alternatives. The chances of success are small but we must make the attempt." He looked straight at Taggart. "Will your men obey orders?"

Taggart answered coldly, "Yes, sir."

Finlayson said, "Arms will be sent out to the *Morning Star* tomorrow but ammunition will be carried aboard the lighters. The battalion will not transfer to the lighters till the moment of landing and will land at your orders or those of Commander Smith—" now he stared at Smith "—who will use whatever force is necessary to impose discipline and enforce the landing."

Taggart said angrily, "That won't be necessary."

"I trust not. But the landing must be made."

There was a silence for a moment as the threat hung in the air. Now Smith knew the reason for the change in Finlayson. He had weighed the possible gain to Allenby's army against the lives of Jackson, Taggart and their men, and had the guts to give the order.

Now he asked, "Captain Jeavons? You're happy with this—ah—*unusual* extension of your contract?"

The master of the *Morning Star* asked in his turn, "I'll take my orders from Commander Smith?"

Finlayson nodded. "He will command the operation."

"That's good enough for me. I've heard a lot about him." Then Jeavons said bluntly, "Those lads of Major Taggart's, they're all right when you get to know them. I can't hardly credit that they're hiding a murderer—"

"That will do!" Finlayson cut him short and looked sharply at Jackson who showed no surprise. "Keep that to yourself."

Jackson drawled, "It's a bit late, sir. I've heard rumours."

"Stop them."

"Yes, sir."

Finlayson forced a smile. "Captain Jeavons, I think everyone knows you have a cargo waiting for you at Tangier. In forty-eight hours you will be on your way. You have my word on it. That ammunition in the after holds will be unloaded as soon as it's light."

"Thank you, sir."

Jeavons took his leave and the rest of them got down to detailed planning. But it was an uneasy cooperation. Smith was immediately aware of the hostility of mistrust that separated the three soldiers, Jackson, Taggart and Edwards. Taggart was guarded and Jackson spoke hardly at all, but his dislike of Edwards showed clearly. Edwards's description of the defences that would face Jackson and Taggart was detailed; he was an expert, had observed everything. But he spoke mechanically, his mind was clearly elsewhere. Smith wondered what he was scheming.

They worked under the yellow light of the lanterns while the aides came and went. Each time the flap of the tent opened it let in a swirl of red dust, and all the while came the muffled tramping of the convoys of horses, camels and trucks that headed eastward through the night, towards Beersheba.

When the conference broke up an aide said he had tents for Edwards and Smith. Edwards took up the offer and curtly ordered the aide to find him a bottle of whisky. His arrogance and mocking grin were gone. Now he stalked away, silent, withdrawn.

Smith went aboard *Morning Star* with Taggart to be met by Adeline Brett, her dressing gown wrapped around her.

"David! That *was* you in the seaplane?" He nodded and thought she seemed pleased to see him, but then she turned to Taggart. "What did Finlayson say? Is he moving the men ashore?"

Taggart said wryly, "In a manner of speaking." He glanced around at the marine sentry at the head of the ladder.

Adeline caught that glance and said, "Come into my cabin."

She curled into an easy chair and the two men sat on the lower bunk. Smith leaned back against the bulkhead, his cap hooked on one knee. Taggart started to tell Adeline Brett of the task set the battalion. Smith closed his eyes as he listened and the words ran together to form a murmur of sound that lulled him.

Adeline Brett's whisper came, "It'll be nothing short of murder putting those men ashore."

Taggart said, "There's no help for it. There's too much at stake and this has to be tried by somebody."

Smith struggled to open his eyes and saw her turn to him, pleading, "David? Isn't there some other way?"

He had to answer, "No." His eyes closed again and his cap slipped to the deck. Taggart's voice murmured on. . . .

Adeline Brett lowered her face into her hands as she listened to Taggart trying to reassure her and failing because he could not lie. She feared for the pair of them. She feared for all those who would be thrown ashore. Taggart ran out of words, was silent. She raised her face to look at him and the young commander sprawled limply, half-sitting, half-lying across the bunk.

Taggart followed the direction of her glance and said softly, "I gather he's only snatched what sleep he could in the last few days."

The girl said, "Then let him sleep here." And when Taggart hesitated, "You're not worried about my reputation, John? I've been the only woman with the battalion for months. No one will talk and I wouldn't care if they did."

So he lifted Smith's legs onto the bunk, and the girl spread the blanket over him. Taggart went out to sleep on the deck among his men and she climbed to the upper bunk but could not sleep, and lay thinking of the man in the bunk below.

"DAVID?" He woke muzzily, hearing her softly calling his name, just able to see in the faint moonlight from the open scuttle that she knelt by his bunk. He realized he was propped up on one arm, the other thrust out defensively and she held that outstretched hand.

He asked, "What's the matter?" his voice slurred. He wondered where he was, then remembered. He should not be here with this girl.

"You cried out." Her face was close; the blonde curls were tousled but he thought she was beautiful.

He said, "I must have been dreaming." He couldn't remember what about but he knew he had been afraid. She rose to sit on the bunk at his side. He could hear her breathing, the catch in it. He reached out and for a moment she held back but then he drew her to him, felt the warmth of her body through the thin stuff of her nightdress. He forgot the morrow.

Later he thought that for her sake, for appearances, he should rise and dress and go out to sleep on the deck. But she lay close to him, his arms about her, and he slept.

MAROC cruised off the Gulf of Alexandretta with the US Submarine-Chaser No. 101 as the sun climbed above the Amanus mountains and struck sparks from the waters of the gulf. Maroc was old and slow but she commanded the narrow channel with her 12-inch guns. Walküre was a ship in a bottle and Maroc the fat cork jammed in its neck. The American, Harry Petersen, sat in a deckchair by the wheelhouse of the chaser, his pipe between his teeth and one big hand wrapped around a mug of coffee. He watched a reconnaissance plane flying back from the head of the gulf.

Young Ensign Cleeve came on deck, peered sharply up at the aircraft then saw Petersen relaxed and asked, "British, sir?"

Petersen nodded. "Dawn reconnaissance from Cyprus. Went in 'bout a half-hour ago."

The biplane closed the ships, circled lazily and a signal lamp blinked from the observer's cockpit. The chaser's signalman read: "*Walküre* . . . at . . . anchor . . . no . . . steam . . . *Friedrichsburg* . . . staging aft . . . making repairs."

Cleeve said glumly, "It doesn't look as though she's coming out." He glanced across at *Maroc*, at the long barrels of her guns and added, "Don't know as I blame them."

Petersen chewed on his pipe and thought the captain of *Walküre* must know that the blockading force would grow stronger and he must eventually be attacked. *Walküre* was no longer in the Dardanelles with the batteries and gunboats to protect her. Here she was vulnerable. But she had not broken out of the Dardanelles just for an airing. What the *hell* was she doing here?

SMITH WOKE with the sunlight streaming through the scuttle. For a moment he was lost then remembered where he was, threw back the blanket and stood up. Adeline Brett's dressing gown lay on the upper bunk but the bunk was made up. He dressed and splashed water on his face from the basin in the corner and stepped out of the cabin. The marine sentry at the head of the ladder glanced quickly at Smith then faced front, face inscrutable under the round, flat cap. Smith returned his salute and growled, "Good morning!"

Aft, *Morning Star*'s deck swarmed with men of the Egyptian Labour Force unloading the ammunition from the after holds. He walked forward and halted under the bridge at Adeline Brett's shoulder. She turned and they smiled at each other but there was a shyness between them now and she quickly turned to watch Taggart. He sat on the bulwark, legs dangling, talking to the men of the battalion who squatted around him on the deck.

Taggart was saying: ". . . So that's what we're going to do, and why. As soon as the chaps working aft have finished, we'll be drawing arms." He paused. The men sat very still and watched him grim-faced. "Any questions?"

In the silence Smith noticed a number of faces he recognized.

The youngster, Garrett, with that cold, bitter stare. . . . A carroty-haired corporal at the front said flatly, "No questions, sir, but to me it looks a right bastard."

There was a long growl of agreement. Taggart nodded. "It is." He waited, looked around. "No more? Then carry on."

Smith stared at the faces, the eyes on Taggart, and knew that these men would follow him. They would go ashore sweating with fear and praying the soldier's prayer: "Not in the face or the guts, O Lord!" But they would follow the major.

As Taggart walked past Smith and Adeline Brett he said hoarsely, "Couldn't blame them if they shot *me!*"

Smith took his leave of Adeline Brett awkwardly, but gently. After a hurried breakfast he went ashore in a gunboat loaded with ammunition from the holds. He halted on a lighter beached close by the jetty: it was all one big hold, a hundred feet long and twenty wide, with an engine aft. A score of carpenters were setting up stalls to take the horses and hold them safe during the sea passage. Smith saw Jackson among them and went down to him, eyeing the work and testing its strength. He said, "It looks all right."

Jackson pushed back the slouch hat and rubbed sweat from his brow with the back of his hand. "It's the only thing about this caper that does," he said bitterly. "I wouldn't trust Edwards an inch but I've got to and he's been on the bottle all night. I've got a good bunch o' blokes and I don't fancy risking any one of 'em. But there's a few thousand men waiting in front of Beersheba tonight so if it's possible to blow that dump and track then we will. I just wish there was another way."

Smith answered from the heart. "So do I."

He spent the rest of the morning at the camp at Deir el Belah, hastening the work of unloading the *Morning Star*, the shipping of arms for the battalion and the conversion of Jackson's lighter. The sweat turned the red dust that hung on the air into a paste on his face. Only at the end did he find a few minutes to go to the hospital. He did not see the injured fitters but their doctor told him, "They're over the worst. The burns are severe but we can mend them. Fortunately their faces weren't touched. In a month or so we'll ship them home. That cheered them no end. You did well to bring them in so soon. We got them only just in time."

That was some comfort.

It was noon when *Dauntless* led *Blackbird* in through the gap in the anti-submarine nets. All eyes in the anchorage turned to watch the two ships enter harbour. The 6-inch gun right aft in *Dauntless* was a twisted wreck, the deck torn and buckled around it. *Blackbird*'s side wore a crude patch like some huge poultice and the funnels of both ships leaked smoke from scores of holes punched by splinters. They were a battered pair but Smith was proud of them.

A launch took him out to his ship and the pipes shrilled as he climbed aboard. He told Ackroyd, "We sail as soon as possible." *Dauntless* disembarked her wounded over one side while the ammunition was taken aboard on the other. Sacks of mail for the ship's company came aboard also. There was a brief hiatus when the bugles sounded the "Still" and the dead, Cole among them, were lowered into the lighter, the ship's company standing at attention. Then the bugles blared again and the work went on.

Some time later Smith went aboard *Blackbird*, and made his way to Pearce's cabin. The door stood ajar. Smith tapped, pushed his head around it, and saw Chris Pearce seated behind his desk. A cleaning rod lay before him and he was loading a Webley pistol which he dropped into a drawer as Smith entered.

Smith told him about the planned operation. "I want *Blackbird* repaired and seaworthy by tomorrow." He paused, watching Pearce and asked, "You think you can do it?" Chris Pearce was more gaunt and hollow-eyed than ever, but the nervous edginess had gone. There was a cold hardness about him that reminded Smith of Garrett, the young soldier in Taggart's battalion.

Pearce answered, "Yes, sir." He was silent a moment, then: "I kept something back the other day when you asked if I was worried about anything. I was. I hadn't heard from Livvy—that's my wife, sir. For a long time I had—suspicions. Then about three weeks ago, the day we sailed, I got a letter from a so-called friend in Cairo . . . and they weren't just suspicions any longer. Since then I've been waiting for some leave to go to see her. But there's a letter from her today that saves me the trouble. She wants a divorce. There's this soldier—" He stopped there.

Smith said quietly, "I'm sorry, Chris. I'd like to be able to give you leave, but—"

Pearce was shaking his head. "I told you, her letter makes it clear that would be a waste of time."

After weeks of torment the blow had fallen. He was too calm by far and Smith didn't like it. He said baldly, "She told you who this soldier is."

Pearce didn't even blink. "She identified him very clearly. He's Edwards, that imitation Arab."

"What's the pistol for?"

"Just cleaning it, sir." He met Smith's gaze frankly, too frankly, a man with his mind made up.

Smith said deliberately, "I'll need you and I'll need him. You'll give me your word that you won't try something stupid or I put you ashore under guard. Do I have it?"

Pearce said quietly, "I won't do anything stupid, sir. Livvy was everything to me, but I'm not going to hang for Edwards."

"You're not answering my question!"

"Accidents happen, sir, and it is wartime."

"Don't be a fool, Chris!" Smith stared at Pearce, realizing he meant what he said and would act on it. Pearce met Smith's eyes calmly, he was not insane. He could send Pearce ashore and report to Braddock—but the operation had to come first.

Pearce said, "I know you need us both. So long as you do—you have my word, sir."

Smith reasoned with him, raged at him—and accomplished nothing. His only consolation was that Pearce could do nothing for a time—at least, not until this operation was over: then it would be up to Smith to act quickly. He returned to his ship and plunged into his work, but with one more worry to plague him. The operation itself was bad enough, without Pearce coldly plotting murder.

SAPPER CHARLIE GOLIGHTLY lay in the grove of palms hard by the siding watching the officer from the provost marshal's staff. Jeffreys, Charlie knew it had to be Captain Jeffreys, stood a score of yards away, by Charlie's engine. The captain, flanked by two burly military policemen, was tall and hook-nosed with cold eyes. He hefted a bottle of the whisky Charlie had smuggled up from Port Said and was asking Albert where Sapper Golightly could be found. Albert pointed up the road towards the main camp but

Jeffreys did not believe him, Charlie could see it on his hard face. A third MP crawled out from under the engine's tender.

Charlie knew he could not stay in the palms. He could not stay in the army either or in Palestine, because Jeffreys would hunt him down and Charlie was too old to go to prison. He shuddered at the thought and the fat moneybelt under his shirt dug into him. His business here was finished, the sooner he moved on the better. So he eased back until he was hidden by the trunks of the palms and he could climb on to shaky legs and hurry through the grove. He stopped at its edge and peered out at the *Morning Star*. He knew she was due to sail for Tangier this very day.

Charlie started down through the gap in the dunes, wanting desperately to look back but knowing that was the last thing he must do. If Jeffreys saw a man with his head turned as he hurried away. . . . He reached the beach and shoved through the throng unloading the boats, his eyes flickering till he saw one boat almost empty and pushed towards it. He clambered aboard as they ran it out. Nobody took any notice.

When the boat ran alongside the *Morning Star* he climbed the dangling ladder with his heart in his mouth.

" 'Ere! What are you up to?"

The challenge shook Charlie. But then he turned and saw the owner of the voice: Sapper Barney Cockcroft. He was another old soldier with a crime sheet as long as his arm, but it would have been as long as his leg as well if Charlie hadn't helped him now and then with guile and a little perjury. So Charlie looked him in the eye and said, "You never seen me, Barney, no more'n anybody else did. Like I done for you afore now."

Barney returned his stare, then closed one eye and turned his back. Seconds later Charlie was wheezing down steep and narrow iron ladders. In five minutes he was in a dark little room with one grimy scuttle that gave him a view of the anchorage. Drums of red lead and white spirit stacked around him showed this was the paint store. From what he had seen of this old bucket nobody did much painting so he was safe here for the time being. And later? He would cross that bridge when he came to it. He sat down slowly on a drum of paint, patted the money belt and thought about Tangier.

IT WAS ALMOST TIME. *Blackbird*, *Morning Star* and the four lighters had all signalled that they were ready to proceed. Smith waited on the torn quarterdeck of *Dauntless* with Taggart, Jackson and Edwards, who were all to sail aboard *Dauntless* so that they could discuss final details. They were silently watching the launch coming off from the shore bearing Finlayson and Braddock. Ackroyd stood behind Smith.

Edwards broke the silence. "The old bastard isn't going to change his mind and call it off." The whisky smell hung around him.

Taggart answered shortly, "He can't."

Edwards laughed with some of the old arrogance but there was bitterness in it. "I started this war with the intention of being a rich man at the end of it. I've made some useful friends among the Arabs. I told them I'd pledged my life to the defeat of the Turks so they could set up their Arab state. I pledged my life but I didn't mean to give it, just *lend* it until Johnny Turk was finished. Now I'm going to be kept to my word." He looked at Smith. "Bloody luck. Maybe your albatross has something to do with it."

Smith stared at him, not understanding. "My—what?"

"That Delilah, the bad-luck seaplane." And as Smith still stared: "I heard some of your men talking about it."

Ackroyd broke in. "I haven't heard the talk myself, sir, but I understand it's been going around."

"What has?"

"Well, Delilah was a rebuild job, had already been shot to bits once. She drowned a man at Port Said as soon as we got her. Then Hamilton fell out of her. Wilson was killed. Two fitters were caught in the fire that started in her. Then Hamilton again and Cole. Maybe she's bad luck."

Smith could not believe it. These were skilled technicians, not ancient mariners with tarry pigtails. He said irascibly, "I'll see the first man you catch spreading that tale."

There was an uneasy silence. Jackson eyed Edwards and asked laconically, "Reckon you'll be sober when we go ashore?"

Edwards leered at him. "Stone cold, old boy." The leer slipped away and he muttered, "Stone cold. I mean it. They'll bury me there and I won't be the only one—"

96

Jackson said contemptuously, "Shut up! You make me sick."

Taggart eyed him coldly, "You'd better keep your mouth shut as well, Mr. Jackson."

Jackson looked at Taggart and Edwards. "A right caper this is goin' to be. Out of all the millions in the British army I draw you two. One slobbering drunk and another with a mob that shot their CO."

Edwards fumbled at the knife in his belt.

Smith pushed in among them, shoved Taggart back and with the heel of his hand cut Edwards's hand from the knife. He snapped, "That's enough from all of you."

"That was rank insubordination!" Taggart was pale with fury.

Jackson said calmly, "What are you going to do? Bust me and send me home?"

Smith shook his head. "No. This operation goes ahead. You all have your orders. I have mine and I'll carry them out."

He turned his back on them, sick at heart. The launch hooked on to the foot of the ladder and Finlayson and Braddock climbed to the deck. Their visit would of necessity be brief; the ammunition lighter was casting off and it was time to sail. Finlayson must have sensed the tension in the group, Smith thought, as he shook their hands, spoke with each of them in turn. Probably he put that tension down to the impending operation. Perhaps he was right.

Smith followed the admiral to the ladder. Braddock said to him, "Two things: complete wireless silence, of course, from the moment you sail. And you command this operation but you will *not* go ashore! That is an order. Understood?"

It was said clearly: Ackroyd and all of them heard it. Smith could only answer, "Aye, aye, sir."

The salutes were exchanged, the pipes shrilled, the marine guard presented arms and Braddock and Finlayson went down into the launch. Minutes later *Dauntless* was under way and leading the little squadron of *Morning Star* and the four lighters towed by the tramp out through the opening in the nets. There was a scattering of cheers from the deck of *Blackbird*, taken up by the soldiers thronging the dunes to watch the ships depart. The crew of *Dauntless* were cheering and so were Jackson's troopers in the lighter. The men of the battalion, spread around the decks of the tramp now that she was stripped of her barbed wire, cheered as loud as any.

Ackroyd grinned. "Quite a send-off!"

Smith did not smile. He said quietly, "It won't work."

Ackroyd glanced across at him, had hardly heard the words. He temporized, preferring to hope. "It's a gamble but—"

"It's not just a hundred or a thousand-to-one against. It won't work." Smith swung to face him. Responsibility had passed from Finlayson to him because he had to land those men who cheered now, and its weight showed in his face.

His voice was savage. "Taggart's diversionary attack may clear the way for Jackson, but at the same time it will destroy any element of surprise. The guard on the dump will be alerted and they won't stand meekly by while Jackson blows up the railway and if he tries to attack the dump he'll be taking on odds of three to one. He knows it. So do Taggart and Edwards. They know also that we can put their men ashore but we'll never get one of them off again because the Turks will bring up guns to make it impossible."

He paused, then finished flatly, "There is only one sure way of stopping the Afrika Legion and that is to strike the railway and the dump with overwhelming force and total surprise."

He turned away to face forward, staring blindly out over the bow at the sunlit sea. There must be a way to rescue some of them from the slaughter. *Must* be.

THE SHIPS steamed southward as if headed for Port Said until Deir el Belah had slipped below the horizon. Then they turned and headed northward out of sight of the land.

Smith shifted about the bridge, huddled into himself. He knew it would be impossible to take off any of the landing force but still he sought a way. He visualized the two landing places. First the Auja river, with enemy batteries pouring a murderous cross-fire down on the beaches. Then saw again the rockbound coastline where they had landed Edwards, the distant lights of Jaffa and one light like a descending star that was the train from Lydda. . . .

He halted in his restless pacing across the bridge, his thoughts racing, then stepped to the engine-room voicepipe and spoke to the engineer, "Chief, I want you to find a volunteer for me. . . ."

When he had finished he turned back to the bridge to find Henderson, who had the watch, eyeing him curiously. Smith listened absently as the yeoman read a signal from *Morning Star*, his mind busy with details now, all the pieces of his plan dovetailing into place. Then a phrase caught his attention and jerked his head round. He waited till the yeoman had finished and Henderson ordered, "Acknowledge," then said, "Read that again."

Henderson grinned and read: "Stowaway. Sapper Golightly. C. Engine-driver, Royal Engineers. States ordered to Tangier to find availability railway sleepers and lines but orders mislaid. Request instructions." Henderson was laughing now. "Cheeky blighter, whoever he is."

Smith grinned, excitement restoring his humour. "Make to *Morning Star*: 'Heave to. Sending boat for stowaway.'"

CHARLIE GOLIGHTLY clambered aboard to be met by the master-at-arms who took him forward and up to the bridge at the double, barking at him, "Where's your cap?"

"Lorst it." Charlie stumbled on the ladder.

The master-at-arms caught him by his belt and rammed him up the ladder. "You'll lose a sight more than that if you say one wrong word up 'ere. Our bloke eats wrong 'uns. Get *hup!*" He thrust Charlie into Smith's sea cabin, bellowed, "Sapper Golightly, sir!" and closed the door behind Charlie, who for one gut-sinking moment thought he was in a cell. Then his gaze focused on the officer seated at the desk. This slight, wiry, thin-faced man smiled and Charlie was briefly relieved.

Smith saw a round, open face devoid of all viciousness or guile, the natural camouflage of a regular soldier with thirty years of undetected crime behind him. Smith said, "I've heard your story and that you're an engine-driver."

Charlie said quickly, "Yessir! Drove 'em all over for the army for the last twenty year. All kinds. So on account of my experience an' that, they asked me to go to Tangier to see what . . ." his voice faded. The thin face before him had stopped smiling and Charlie remembered the warning of the master-at-arms.

99

Smith said, "I think I can promise you no more than a reprimand. But first you've got to tell me the truth."

Charlie swallowed and told him the most favourable version of the truth he could contrive, then waited and sweated.

Smith grinned to himself, his suspicions confirmed. "No doubt the provost marshal takes a serious view of your crime. But I'm going to ask you to do something for me, and if you agree, I'm certain you'll get away with a ticking-off. If you don't agree then I must send you back to Deir el Belah at the first opportunity to be dealt with. Understood?"

Charlie jumped in eagerly, "I'm your man, sir!"

"Wait till you hear what you have to do," Smith answered dryly, then told him.

Some minutes later the master-at-arms took a thoughtful Charlie Golightly below to the messdeck. Then Smith told Henderson, "Pass the word for Major Taggart, Colonel Edwards and Lieutenant Jackson. And the first lieutenant."

They found him in the charthouse with the large-scale map of Palestine spread before him. When they were all present he said abruptly, "I'm changing the plan." He told them what he intended to do, and saw his excitement take alight in their faces.

Oddly enough it was Edwards, his drunken depression forgotten, who spoke for all of them. "It's still a hell of a gamble but this way at least there's a fighting chance."

Smith looked at each of them. "We sink or swim together in this. No more backbiting." And when they nodded stiffly he told Taggart, "Tell Mr. Jackson about the battalion. What really happened."

Taggart grumbled obstinately, "He thinks he knows."

Smith's patience was cracking. "I don't give a damn what he thinks! Tell him the truth as you told me!"

Taggart swallowed his pride and recounted the story of the colonel's shooting. When they had heard him out Jackson rubbed at his jaw and said wryly. "They still sound a funny mob to me, but at least they had their reasons."

Taggart snapped, "That's right! And I'll tell you this: they've been caged too long and they're ready to fight *anybody*."

So now there was a guarded truce between Taggart and Jackson, which was better than nothing. Smith looked at Edwards, who said confidently, "You can rely on me to carry out my orders." All his arrogance had returned and Smith wondered at the change in him.

Ackroyd said doubtfully, "Will the general agree to this, sir?"

"I'm not asking him." Ackroyd scowled worriedly at the enormity of this. Smith said, "Wireless silence, remember?"

Taggart chuckled softly. "Not so much turning the blind eye, more: 'none so dumb as he who will not speak.'"

Smith said grimly, "You and your battalion know something of that." He glanced at his watch. "There's a lot to do."

They set to, working against the clock and Smith knew every second brought them nearer to committal. He concentrated on his planning for now, on his own account, he had taken into his hands the lives of the five hundred men to be landed, and the thousands who waited before Beersheba.

8 The Raid

There was a chill dampness to the night and the sky was overcast. Smith sat at the helm of the cutter with Edwards on one side of him and Lieutenant Jameson on the other. Edwards still wore his robes and carried the villainous knife. Three of Captain Brand's marines from *Morning Star* were crowded into the stern-sheets but Brand crouched in the bow along with Buckley.

Ackroyd had pointed out, "With respect, sir, the admiral's order was that you were not to go ashore."

Smith had answered solemnly, "In that operation. This is a different plan." It was Smith's plan and he was going ashore.

A black frieze of dunes loomed against the dark with the thick silver line of the surf underlining it. That line was broken some three hundred yards to Smith's left where lay the mouth of the Auja river. The cutter ran into the surf, bucked and pitched, then crashed in on the beach. That crash landing half-threw Buckley over the bow, Brand with him. Smith made them out, standing in water to their knees and hauling on the bow of the boat.

Smith called, "Oars!" Whispering was pointless in this thundering surf. He shoved Edwards forward after the marines and clambered over the thwarts as the rest of the cutter's crew plunged into the sea to wade in. Edwards jumped into the surf and slipped like a shadow across the beach. Brand and his three marines followed, Brand with pistol in hand, the marines with rifles at the trail. Smith brought up the rear with Buckley panting at his shoulder.

Then boots began to slip in the soft sand; they were into the dunes. Edwards turned to his left and headed towards the mouth of the river. Smith was up with the marines now, his breath coming fast. He saw Edwards reach one hand down to the sand, lift up the loop of telephone wire and then the flash of the knife. Now the machine-gun post was cut off from Jaffa, four miles to the south and from the Turkish regiment just a mile away inland.

Edwards was crouching, edging further into the dunes. Then he swung left towards the sea again and a glimpse of the river close to his right. The Turkish machine-gun post must be. . . .

Edwards halted, went down on one knee and flapped a hand, signalling, "Down". Smith knelt beside him, Brand and his marines up close, faces blank with tension. Edwards pointed at the rise of the dune ahead of them, his meaning clear: just over the crest. Brand gestured and the marines spread out, hefting their rifles. Smith had told them: "No shooting, use the butt if you must."

Edwards crawled forward, knife in hand, and the line of them followed a yard behind. He inched up to the crest of the dune, edged his head above it, was still, then without turning beckoned with the knife. They all eased up to the crest. Smith saw the surf, the beach, and then the Turks in their machine-gun nest below him. There were three of them in a semicircular earthwork built of timbers and sand. Two lay wrapped in blankets or greatcoats, and one stood by the machine gun that pointed out to sea, his head resting on his folded arms. After scores of nights spent peering at a black and empty sea the man dozed.

Smith briefly stared out to sea. He could not make out the lighters but they should be there lying off, waiting. He scrambled over the crest and at his movement they were all up and over, plunging down into the nest. There was no work for the rifle-butts, nor for Edwards's knife. The two huddled Turks were buried under

Brand and his marines. Buckley fell on the one who stood by the machine gun and slammed him down onto his back with a big hand across his mouth. Smith pointed his pistol an inch from the horrified eyes and Edwards hissed something. The Turk lay still. •

Smith tried to keep his voice steady. "Good. They're all yours, Mr. Brand." He left Brand to secure the prisoners and threw at Buckley, "Bring up Mr. Jameson and the cutter's crew."

As Buckley ran off along the beach Smith dragged a torch from his pocket, pointed it out to sea, and flashed the dot-dash of the "A". Brand came up beside him, breathing heavily and said with satisfaction, "All secure, sir."

"Very good." Smith said. "They'll send out a party to check along the wire when they don't get an answer from this post during the night. So when the rest of your marines come ashore, send a good NCO and some men to lay an ambush for them."

"I know the man to send," answered Brand.

Smith hurried on, "Colonel Edwards will show you the ford. Take two men and set up a defensive screen."

Edwards leaned on the earthwork, but now he stirred impatiently, "Where are the boats?"

Smith snapped, "I told them to lie off. No point in their being seen before *we* got ashore. Now get *on!*"

Edwards's head jerked round at the rasp in Smith's voice, then he scrambled out of the earthwork with Brand and two marines doubling after him. The third marine dropped to one knee just below the crest of the dunes, keeping watch.

Smith stared into the darkness. Was there a square shape? Suddenly there they were, ugly and unwieldy floating boxes butting in towards the river's mouth. One, two—four of them!

Buckley ran out of the darkness to his left with Jameson and the cutter's crew. Smith said, "Come on!" He swung out of the machine-gun nest and trotted towards the river's mouth. Then he ran inland along the bank for some fifty yards and halted where a track led down through the dunes to the water's edge. Edwards waited there, peering out to sea.

Smith hurried up the river bank that rose gently to about twenty feet, made out the figure of Brand kneeling below the crest and dropped down beside him. Brand glanced at him and said softly,

"All quiet, sir. I've one man *there*, the other *there*." He pointed to left and right.

Smith could not see them; there was no sound, nor movement. He realized Jameson now crouched at his shoulder, and said, "Take your orders from Captain Brand."

Jameson nodded; he already knew that he and his men were to form part of the defensive screen in case a Turkish patrol came that way. Smith ran down the bank again to stand beside Edwards who held a masked torch, its glow pointing seaward. They waited by the ford as the lighters ran into the mouth of the river. Smith could hear the putter of the first lighter's engine. A shift of the wind brought the smell of horses to Smith's seaman's nostrils. He wondered how Jackson and his troops had coped with their mounts on the long run from Deir el Belah.

He flashed the "A" again and the engine of the lighter stopped. She slid on gently and grounded on the ford. There was a trampling and clattering aboard her. Smith saw a horse's head lifted briefly above the bulwark and a voice came clearly, "*Hold still, yer flamin' cow—!*"

The ramp was coming down and Smith waded out towards it. He reached the lighter as the ramp hit the water and drenched him in spray. He saw a man, tall, slouch-hatted, striding down the ramp into the water, heaving on the reins of the horse that followed him gingerly. Smith recognized Jackson and waved with the pistol, "Head for Edwards! On the bank! See him?" Edwards in his robes was a pale blur.

Jackson answered laconically, "I see him." He waded towards the shore. The horse bucked as it plunged into the water but as it became surer of its footing it followed him more easily. A trooper towing his horse was following Jackson over the ramp and the others came after him. The second lighter slid in close alongside the first and grounded with a *thump!* Its ramp crashed down and Taggart, carrying a rifle across his chest, ran over it to jump into the water and head for the bank. Smith pushed on, seeing the third lighter and beyond it the fourth, creeping in. And there against the far bank lay *Dauntless*'s motorboat.

Smith splashed out to the other bank and was met by Lieutenant Griffiths, the gunnery observer, who reported with satisfaction, "Our marines are deployed at the top o' the bank, sir. Sergeant Harriman's up there. The whole country seems quiet but the Vickers is set up with a good field o' fire."

Smith nodded and began to retrace his passage across the ford, pushing his way among the men of Taggart's battalion who streamed towards the shore in a stumbling, breathless, silent, mob.

All four lighters were aground now and the bank swarmed with men, their boots scuffing, trampling in the sand. Everything was working out. Compared to this, Finlayson's planned landing near Jaffa would have been a shambles. He ran past them to where the Australians stood holding their horses' heads. Edwards was standing by Jackson, and he held the reins of two horses.

Smith asked, "Ready?"

"Yes." Then Jackson added, "—sir."

Smith took a breath. Now for it. He said to Edwards, "Hold the thing still." Smith had ridden horses but knew he was no horseman. He found a stirrup and clawed himself up into the saddle, gathering the reins.

Edwards mounted with the ease of practice and Buckley said, "Sir?" Smith stared down at Buckley, remembering him too late. He himself was astride the only spare horse.

But Jackson said, "Jasper Beaver! You put this sailor up behind you! Mount!"

The troopers mounted as one and the voice of Jasper Beaver complained, "Aw, God! Come on, Buckley, chum. The ol' neddy ain't going to like this but he'll stick it." Smith saw Buckley hauled up behind the big trooper, then they all went up the bank together with Smith clinging on for dear life.

The track was faint, following the line of the river as it curved to run south and then turned eastward again. There the track joined another that ran due south.

Jackson said, "Phil!" A man wheeled out of the ranks to wait at the junction to guide the foot-soldiers coming on behind. The rest of the troop turned onto the main track and rode on south.

Edwards led the horsemen at a fast canter, a muffled thrumming of hooves in the sand, a squeak of leather and jingling of harness. They passed a hump of ground and briefly the track descended before lifting again. Now Smith could see the ground falling away on either hand, to his left to a plain, to his right down to the sea. *Dauntless* was out there, somewhere.

There was a village ahead, a dark scattering of houses on both sides of the track. They dashed through it. Stealth was impossible.

Smith's legs and rump were sore. The track was climbing again now and crossed the Jaffa–Tulkarum road. They rode on up a long, gentle rise, lifted over the crest, and trotted down on the other side for two hundred yards. There they halted. They had ridden some three miles.

Smith slid off the horse and shoved the reins at the nearest trooper. He hobbled stiffly forward, rubbing his thighs, to stand by Edwards. Buckley was coming up, walking as gingerly as himself.

He looked around. The railway track was empty. It ran away down to his right, twin lines of dull silver in the night, towards the distant black hump of Jaffa: Here on this rise the line coming up from Jaffa swung in a curve, then ran away downhill to his left, towards Lydda. It would take them to the dump there, fast. And, if they were lucky, bring them back again.

The Australians had dismounted, one man from each section of four holding the horses, the others gathering behind Jackson, who ordered, "Flankers out." Troopers broke away from the group and trotted off, two up the line and two down it, and were lost in the darkness. The horse-holders led their Walers across the railway track and into the orange groves that grew close and thick.

Smith called, "Follow me!" He ran down the track towards Lydda for a hundred yards, Jackson and his troops at his heels swearing as they stumbled in the darkness. Smith halted and panted, "*That* one!" Two troopers crossed the track, axes glinting in their hands and a moment later the blades *chunked* into an orange tree. The furious chopping sounded loud in the stillness.

Smith ran back to where Buckley waited and stared down towards Jaffa. From *Dauntless* he had seen the pinprick glow of the train go past into the town—but what if it did not return? Somewhere a jackal howled. From far to the south came the mutter of the guns before Gaza and their flashes lit the sky. But now there was a moving light, a tiny red glow that crept up the hill from Jaffa towards him. Thank God.

A crash away to his left drew him back to Jackson and his men who were hauling the felled tree across the rails. Smith gasped, "The train's coming! Where's that trooper—" Then he saw the man on hands and knees close to where the tree lay, pushing the contents of his haversack into a heap, scraping a match. Three of the troopers lay down beside the little fire, their rifles under them.

Smith glanced around. The others had retreated out of the firelight. Smith backed away from it, pulled the Webley from its holster and sank down. His gaze went back to the little fire that lit the tree and the sprawled figures of the seemingly sleeping men. Then his head jerked around. The pulsing glow was in sight. The train moved slowly after the long haul up from Jaffa, smoke from its chimney lifting against the sky as it trundled towards him. It was close enough for him to see the driver outlined against the glow of the firebox.

The train ground to a halt only feet from the felled tree. The outraged driver jumped down, advanced into the firelight where one of the prone figures stirred sleepily. The driver stopped short, peering and Smith shoved himself up, shouted, "Now!" He ran at the footplate, grabbed at the handle and pulled himself aboard. There was a fireman, and a soldier swinging a rifle and backing away across the footplate in the face of the Webley. Smith snarled at him, "Keep still!" The man still fumbled at his rifle. Then Edwards appeared from the other side of the engine, materializing like a ghost in his white robes. He shoved the gaping fireman aside, laid the blade of the knife across the soldier's throat and tore the rifle from his slackened fingers. Jackson came crowding in after Edwards, grabbed first the fireman, then the soldier and bundled them off the footplate to the little knot of troopers waiting by the track.

Smith jumped down and started back past the tender. As the darkness closed in, Buckley came trotting up from the rear of the train.

"Right y'are, sir! Eight trucks and not a soul aboard. Only these two at the front are loaded."

Smith halted and took stock. They had the train without raising an alarm; that was one more step along the way.

Jackson appeared on the top of the wood-stacked tender and leaped across to the first truck. Troopers climbed up to join him and started hurling sacks and crates over the side into the orange grove. Smith called up, "They've got to be out of sight!"

A voice answered impatiently, "Aw, we know that."

Smith grinned and called up to Jackson. "Quick as you can! I'm going to look for Taggart!"

Jackson lifted a hand in acknowledgment. Smith ran up the slope to the crest, peered back along the trail they had followed from the Auja river. It was too soon for Taggart but—something moved out there in the darkness. There was a rhythmic whispering that might have been wind in trees but there was no wind. A thick snake coiled up the hill towards him, and as it came on out of the night it grew legs. The whispering was the scuff of boots in sand and the laboured breathing of Taggart's battalion.

Smith ran down to meet them and fell in by Taggart who marched at their head, stepping out at a rapid pace. The Australian troopers left behind as markers now rode out on the flank, and Smith told them to report the battalion's arrival to Jackson. He asked Taggart, "What about the men?"

"They're all right," Taggart jerked out between panting.

"Any stragglers?"

"We don't—have—stragglers."

Smith could not believe it. It had been a killing march: Taggart must have doubled them for some of the way. And the men who carried rifles were the lucky ones; others humped machine guns.

He halted on the crest to watch them go by. All the faces were like Taggart's, drawn and sweat-streaked, mouths gaping as they panted, eyes wide and fixed on the back of the man in front. He saw why there had been no stragglers. Here and there pairs of men supported another shambling along, head down, between them. But nobody interrupted that quick pace set by Taggart.

And at the side of the column moved the sergeants and warrant officers, hurrying up the length of their respective companies. "Keep closed up! Keep the step an' keep closed up! Not far now!" Smith watched the last company come up to the crest and called, "Well done!" Some eyes slid his way, blinked with recognition. That was all. And at the tail of the column came the battalion's medical orderlies towing their little cart with its stretchers and cases, Merryweather the surgeon at their head and—

Smith burst out incredulously, "What are you doing here?"

Adeline Brett did not check her pace any more than the soldiers had but she wiped at a tendril of hair that clung to her sweating brow and answered, "I should think it was obvious."

Smith strode along beside her and glared across at Merryweather, "Are you out of your mind?"

Merryweather said defensively, "I didn't find her till I was aboard the lighter, sir. Somehow she was ashore before me."

They were over the crest and marching rapidly down on the train. The battalion was already lining out along it, a confused mass of figures in the dark.

Adeline Brett said quickly, "You have duties to attend to, Commander. It was not my intention to distract you from them. We'll go along as best we can, help when we can. If you'd only stop thinking of me as a woman, I'd present no problem."

Smith grabbed her arm, pulled her out of the column. Stop thinking of her as a woman? That was very difficult. He said, "I don't want you involved in—I don't want—"

She said softly, "I know what to expect, David. I've seen dead and wounded before, too often."

He knew that. He looked beyond her to the men who were clambering into trucks now, looked ahead to the morrow's dawning, when these men would need her. He said, "I'm very glad you've come. Take care, that's all."

It was her turn to stare, bewildered at the sudden change.

Then he saw a short, plump figure easing its fat legs out of the tail of the little cart. Adeline Brett followed his gaze and explained, "We had to put him in there. He couldn't keep up."

Smith said, "I don't care how he got here as long as he does the job." He called to the groaning figure, "Come on!" Then he turned and ran and Charlie Golightly waddled after him.

He found Taggart marshalling his men into the trucks. Smith said, "Three companies, no more. The rest stay here with Jackson. Come up to the cab and ride with me, or—"

"I'll ride with the men."

Smith nodded. He had thought that would be Taggart's decision. It would have been his. He ran to the head of the train and in the glow that seeped out round the edges of the firebox

109

door he saw Charlie Golightly on the footplate of the engine. Smith clambered aboard. Buckley hovered in the background near Edwards who leaned on the far side of the cab.

Golightly said gloomily, "Right bloody lot this is. They run it by praying by the look of it."

Smith frowned, "Can you drive it?"

"Well, sir, it's not what I've been used to. An engineer like me, I'm used to a proper way o' doing things and—"

Smith broke in, "*Can you make the thing go?*"

Charlie Golightly tried to step back from that icy glare but found Buckley behind him. Aboard *Dauntless* Smith had said, "You don't have to come. I'm not giving you an order. If you come I'll do all I can for you. Or you can go in the cells now and take your chance back at Deir de Belah."

Prison had seemed chillingly close to Charlie just then, but now it seemed solid and safe by comparison. He stood on the footplate and wondered if he could come out of this alive. Charlie said, "I c'n drive it all right. It's just been a bit neglected, like."

Briefly Taggart appeared by the cab. "Ready."

Smith answered, "Right." He turned on Charlie Golightly. "Full ahead." Charlie wound off the brake, and eased over the regulator handle. The engine wheezed, jerked with a rattling of couplings, then eased forward. They were moving.

Smith shoved past Charlie to lean out over the side of the cab and look back. He saw Jackson and his troopers lined out along the track. Somewhere in the orange groves were a hundred or more of Taggart's battalion, but the rest, three hundred of them, were packed into the trucks behind him. He could see them standing, heads and shoulders above the sides of the trucks, lurching as the train moved forward. And Adeline Brett was somewhere among them.

He swung back into the cab. "Can't we go faster than this?"

Golightly sniffed and rubbed at his nose with a fat hand. "I should say so. But I don't want her to run away down this hill 'cause this officer 'ere—" he jerked his head at Edwards, "—he tells me there's a bend at the bottom. After that I'll let her out for what she's worth and Gawd 'elp us all."

The train rocked as it swung round the curve, then straightened

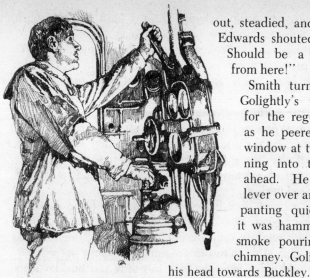

out, steadied, and chuffed on. Edwards shouted, "That's it! Should be a straight run from here!"

Smith turned and saw Golightly's hand grope for the regulating lever as he peered out of his window at the track running into the darkness ahead. He eased the lever over and the train's panting quickened until it was hammering along, smoke pouring from the chimney. Golightly turned his head towards Buckley.

"Chuck some wood on!" he yelled.

Buckley staggered across the footplate, clawed down an armful of logs from the tender, kicked open the firebox door and fed the logs into the furnace. The red glow lit them all, Buckley sweating as he threw in the logs, Edwards hawk-faced and eyes glittering, Charlie's round face professionally watchful.

The little old engine was giving all she had, and probably running faster than she had in twenty years. Not even Jackson's horsemen could have stayed with her now. Smith enjoyed a brief moment of exhilaration, then was jerked back to reality as Edwards pointed, and shouted, "Beit Dejan!"

Smith peered past him and saw a cluster of houses away to the right of the track. He asked, "How far now?"

"Halfway. Another ten minutes at this rate, if that!"

Ten minutes or less in which to skim over the plan again to see if he had forgotten anything. But plan as he might, an operation like this was dependent on luck, necessity its sole justification. Smith was gambling with the lives of three hundred men only because he had to. The lives of thousands hung on the outcome. Not for the first time that night he was afraid.

Suppose they were too late, that the Afrika Legion had already passed through, the supply dump stripped bare and the whole reckless adventure nothing but a waste of lives?

He tried to shake off the haunting possibility but failed. The Legion was pressing on as fast as it could. Only by sea could it have moved faster with all its equipment and supplies—the thought raised in him again the suspicion that he had overlooked something . . . something obvious.

"Slow down! We're getting close!" That was Edwards.

Smith heard Golightly say, "Keep clear o' that brake 'andle, Mr. Buckley, if you please. I might want it any time now."

The speed of the train fell away. Suddenly Edwards said, "Here it is! Stop her!"

The stone parapet of a bridge came up out of the darkness, flicked past, was gone. Now the brake was winding on, beginning to bite. Charlie Golightly knew his job: with just the barest of jerks the train came smoothly to rest in a sighing of steam.

Smith dropped down from the cab, Edwards and Buckley leaping after him. He dared not waste a second. The smoke and sparks from the engine's chimney would have marked them—the train was expected at Lydda station, not here. Soon the sentries at the dump and the station would start to wonder.

A half-mile away across the dark countryside to the left and north were the scattered lights of Lydda. But Edwards was pointing at another light, off to the southeast. "The dump," he said. "A quarter-mile away, no more, and fairly open country."

Just ahead the track curved to run south. In half a mile it joined the main line at Lydda station and the two lines, the main and the spur from Jaffa, made a V as they ran down to the junction. The wood and the dump it hid lay in that V.

Smith turned to find Taggart at his shoulder. Beyond him the men poured in a cataract of shadows over the sides of the trucks. Figures came running out of the night, stumbling in the darkness. They halted in a semicircle behind Taggart, his warrant officers and sergeants.

Taggart turned on them. "Ack company deploy and move up on the right of the dump *now*. Charlie company deploy and move up on the left *now*. I'll lead Beer company in the centre and we'll give you five minutes start, then head straight for the light." His finger pointed at the solitary light marking the dump. "No firing till we're fired on, then rapid and *get in!* Flare men in the rear of Beer company with Sergeant Carmichael and the demolition party." He paused, went on: "Ten rounds rapid, then we'll do the work with the bayonet." He paused again, then finished. "This is to show *them.*" His head jerked at those far behind him, Finlayson, the whole military machine that had locked him and his men away in the hold of the *Morning Star.* "Carry on!"

The group dissolved, the men trotting back to their companies and Taggart glanced at Smith. "Those are all the orders they need. They know what they're doing."

Buckley murmured to Smith, "That Arab feller, sir."

Smith turned and saw Edwards in his robes drifting, spectral, in the engine's shadow. "Colonel Edwards! You come with me."

Edwards said flatly, "Not on your life. My orders were to guide the attacking force to the dump and I've done that. I agree your plan gives a fighting chance of taking the dump, but getting out again is another matter. When your attack goes in you'll raise the countryside and that regiment north of the Auja will come down like the hammers of hell. I'm an Intelligence officer. I'm too valuable to risk in that kind of scrap." He finished cynically, "Don't worry about me. I'll make my own way home."

Smith thought that Edwards must have seen his chance when he had disclosed his plan back aboard *Dauntless.* Smith said softly, "I told you that we sank or swam together in this and that means right to the end. Besides, we may need you on the way back." He glanced at Taggart. "I want him guarded."

Taggart hesitated, then turned and saw Garrett, his runner, at his heels. "Put this officer in the front truck," he ordered, "along with the Vickers and its crew. You can all keep an eye on him."

Edwards exploded, "Don't be ridiculous! Surely you can see—"

Smith finished, "If he tries to escape, shoot him."

Edwards glared but Garrett's rifle was trained on his chest and Garrett said, "Into the truck—sir." There was unmistakable menace in the words; Garrett would shoot.

Edwards muttered under his breath but recognized that menace and climbed into the truck, followed by Garrett.

Smith looked up at Golightly where he stood on the footplate.

113

"So far you've done all I asked. Now stay there and be ready to go. There are twenty men with you."

Golightly stared uneasily into the darkness. He cleared his throat. "I won't leave her, sir."

For a moment the night was quiet, the men of B company still . . . and in that silence the thought came to Smith: was it coincidence that *Walküre* broke out as the Afrika Legion headed for Beersheba? If not, what was her purpose? What could she do—?

The silence and the train of thought were broken as the long line of B company moved forward and he followed them, Buckley at his side. Taggart was a moving blur ahead of his men. The last of a random battalion, he had made them into a unified fighting machine, with a heart and inner loyalty of its own.

Great clumps of cactus made gaps in the long line, but the men washed around each clump and formed up again. A blacker edge of darkness rose against the sky as they advanced. That was the wood, hiding the dump. Edwards had said the Germans had strung barbed wire between the trees and hung it with empty tins. The battalion would have to get through it.

The wood was close now. Off to the right a German voice called, uncertain, then after a moment's paused called again, a definite challenge. The line was trotting now and Smith went with them. Flame spat briefly away to the right and was answered by a volley. Taggart bellowed, "Get in! Get in!"

The line was ragged now because the men were running and the faster ones got ahead of the others. Above the pounding of the booted feet Smith heard shouting from inside the belt of trees. The line halted, the men kneeling before him. The wire was a web between the trees and the tins jangled together as the kneeling men thrust rifles through the wire and fired furiously in "ten rounds rapid". Others with gloved hands and cutters were snatching at the wire, cutting, the strands parting with a dull thwang and trailing. The men around him were bawling madly, "In! In! In!" The bayonets were coming out, grenades exploded. Away to the left a machine gun hammered.

Taggart was right forward against the wire. He turned back as he shouted: "Sergeant Carmichael! Flares!" Then he lurched forward, staggered then recovered. Smith lost sight of him as the men came up off their knees and poured through the gap cut in the wire in a yelling, cursing flood. Smith went with them, swung right when the flood split on a square bulk that was ranked piles of crates and sacks under the sagging roofs of camouflage nets. A single shot was fired, then a flare burst overhead, brilliant blue-white and smoking. Smith saw the men of the German guard, half-dressed as they had run from their tents, saw them only for the blink of an eye, then Taggart's men were on them.

He moved in a narrow lane that ran through the dump, stumbling over the bodies of men, with other panting, running men on either side of him. There was firing all around the dump, a continuous rattle of musketry, and now and again the thump of a grenade and the smell of it caught at the throat. Inside the confines of the wood, in the narrow lanes, was bedlam. The Germans were fighting well, as always. They had been surprised in the night, not knowing who their attackers were nor whence they came, but still they fought. Smith, feeling remote, an onlooker, retained a memory of charging, clashing figures, of men fighting hand to hand, even wrestling on the earth. Of a man charging huge out of the darkness, bayonet uplifted like a sword and Buckley stepping in to beat him down with the butt of the rifle. Of Taggart turning to face Smith, lifting his rifle and firing, it seemed, directly at him but in fact at a German coming up behind him.

Running on under the ghostly light of the flares. A private crouched with bayonet pointed at Smith, who croaked, *"Dauntless!"* The bayonet swung away and ahead were trees with barbed wire dangling. This was the far perimeter of the dump. He realized it was over. The firing had ceased. Taggart showed at Smith's side and said huskily, "Well, we've done it."

They had taken the dump and were astride the railway line to Gaza and Beersheba.

9 Dawn Patrols

The newly determined Pearce had demanded and got from Admiral Braddock two hundred Egyptian labourers to shift the coal and stores in *Blackbird* from starboard to port, listing the ship so that the shell hole in the hull was clear of the water. Blacksmiths and army engineers worked with *Blackbird*'s crew to fit a more seaworthy patch on her side. They took aboard fuel for the Shorts and bombs that Pearce begged from the Royal Flying Corps. He kept them all at it because Smith had said, "I'll need you."

An hour before dawn *Blackbird* sailed north at full speed. She only slowed to launch the three remaining Shorts. At first light their wings were spread and they were hoisted out. Kirby was the first pilot away with Burns as his observer. Then Rogers and Maitland in *Delilah* and last was Beckett with one of the riggers called Phillips, chosen from a dozen volunteers. Heavy with bombs they laboured across the sea and lifted slowly, heading north. Pearce had told them: "Reconnoitre the railway and the dump at Lydda. Then look for *Dauntless* off the mouth of the Auja river."

LIEUTENANT HARRY PETERSEN was asleep in the little wheelhouse of the patrolling submarine-chaser. He woke when the hand gently shook his shoulder, and he squinted up into the young face of Ensign Cleeve, who said softly, "Starting to get light, sir."

Petersen pushed up out of his old deckchair, and stepped up beside the quartermaster at the wheel. He saw their course was northwest by north, looked up and narrowed his eyes to penetrate the darkness. There was just a hint of grey in that darkness now. Cleeve said, "*Maroc* three cables on the starboard bow, sir."

Petersen grunted, made out the shadowy bulk of the old French battleship as she plodded across the mouth of the gulf ahead of them, saw her against the lighter sky of the eastern horizon. Somewhere beyond that horizon the sun was lifting behind the Amanus mountains and soon its rays would be sweeping over the gulf and out across the sea. It would be lighter already far up where *Walküre* and the freighter lay.

Cleeve asked, "Do you think we'll see some action today, sir?"

Petersen thought about it. The French battleship, *Océan*, coming up from Malta, might be here by noon, and the cruiser *Attack* would certainly arrive before the day was out but they would be just another bolt on the door. They were all waiting for the torpedo boats that were able to slip into the gulf and over the

116

minefields with their electric motors. *Walküre* would defend herself but even if she were successful she'd know her time was limited. So she might come out then and make a fight of it.

He said slowly, "Not today. And when she does come out we'll only be looking on." He explained with weary patience to the disappointed Cleeve, "Because this bucket hasn't even got a torpedo. She's anti-submarine, remember? Besides, *Walküre* is technically a Turkish warship and the US isn't at war with Turkey." Then he asked, "Anything from *Maroc*?"

"No, sir."

Petersen growled. "I don't like getting all my information secondhand." The chaser's wireless was only a tactical set for manoeuvring, its range barely five miles. The light was growing now and Petersen could make out details of *Maroc*'s rigging. The sea was calm and quiet, there was no wind and hardly a ripple on the surface of the black water except for those from *Maroc*'s bow and the white water at her stern. . . .

"*Torpedo running across the bow to starboard!*" The port lookout yelled, pointing out into the dark.

Petersen lunged forward, eyes frantically searching the sea as he shouted, "Action stations!" and hit the button of the hooter that blared through the ship. Then he saw the line of foam drawn across the sea and running towards *Maroc*. He bawled at the crew of the 3-inch gun on the foredeck. "Fire!" He pointed out to port. "At any damn thing!"

They'd have a job to hit a U-boat even if they saw it, but that wasn't the point. The gun would draw the eyes of *Maroc*'s lookouts so they might see the torpedo's track. But Petersen had a sick feeling that, even if they did, it would be too late now for *Maroc* to do anything. He snapped, "Hard over left rudder! Full ahead!" As the chaser's head came around he swung out of the wheelhouse by one hand from the doorframe as he searched ahead, along the torpedo's track for its point of origin.

He ordered, "Meet her! Steer that!" He could see no periscope, just a point on the sea where the line of bubbles had begun. Somewhere there lay the submarine. He saw young Cleeve dashing aft to the Y-gun, so called because it was shaped like a Y, its arms able to throw a depth charge out on either side of the chaser.

As they were coming to the beginning of the torpedo track he turned to bawl at Cleeve, "Fire!" A depth charge shot up and out over the side to plummet into the sea as another slid over the stern. The crew of the Y-gun were reloading as Petersen told the quartermaster, "Hard right, rudder!"

A flash came to starboard of them, from *Maroc*, a leaping, soaring flame that lit the sea and seared the eye. Blast snatched the cap from Petersen's head and punched him in the chest. Then the sound of the explosion came, not so much a sound as a blow to the ears. Petersen could see *Maroc* burning in half-a-dozen places along her hull—but there were two hulls now. Her middle had been blasted out as the magazines blew up and now her bow and stern stuck up separately and ever more steeply from the sea as they burned and sank. The stern went down with a rush even as Petersen watched, horrified.

He ran his hand through his hair and ordered hoarsely, "Midships!" Water still boiled where the two depth charges had exploded but there was no debris, nothing. He turned to see Cleeve at the Y-gun on the fantail, his mouth gaping as he stared at *Maroc*. Petersen yelled at him. "*Fire!* Mr. Cleeve! *Fire!*"

The Y-gun lobbed depth charges wide over the stern of the chaser. They exploded, hurling water at the sky, but there was no trace of oil, of the U-boat. He swung back to stare again at *Maroc* and this time the blast from her plucked him loose from his hold on the doorframe and sent him sprawling across the deck. The four men crewing the forward gun joined him in a heap. The flash had been even brighter than before, their ears rang. The bow, all that was left of *Maroc*, had disintegrated and disappeared in that one monstrous, flaming explosion. The sea was empty and dark again now and the chaser the only ship on it.

But not alone. Somewhere below the surface lay the submarine that had sunk *Maroc* without leaving a solitary survivor—no man could have survived those terrible explosions. Petersen had dropped four depth charges without result. He was on a cold trail now, with the U-boat creeping farther away with every second.

Only one hope remained. He ordered, "Hard left rudder! Steer due west." The chaser's head came around until she was headed out to sea. So they ran away from the gulf and the light until, when they were a mile west of the sunken *Maroc,* he ordered their speed reduced to five knots, and they turned again to steer due east. All of the boat was hushed as the lookouts stood with the glasses to their eyes and the chaser crept back towards the gulf with her engines barely ticking over.

Very quietly Petersen said, "Keep a good lookout all around." He knew this was a long shot. The light was growing fast. For the moment, though, the chaser crept over a still-dark sea: she showed no blaze of white at bow or stern. She was not a big boat, and set low in the water, surely hidden by the darkness.

He sensed someone beside him and turned to see Cleeve standing by the wheelhouse steps. Cleeve asked softly, "D'ye think the bastard's still there, sir?"

Petersen said, "Maybe. He knows he hit the bull's-eye because he felt those explosions but he doesn't know whether he's sunk her or not. He hasn't heard a depth charge for more than ten minutes so maybe he'll think we've gone to look for survivors. So it might be worth coming up for a quick look. There might be another sinking in it for them if we've stopped to pick up men."

Cleeve said, "I see." He licked his lips and started, "Sir—"

Petersen continued, "Of course, he might have worked all this out, then gone a stage further and just be waiting for us somewhere."

Young Cleeve swallowed. "Yes, sir."

"Which is why I ordered a lookout kept all round. I—" Petersen stilled suddenly, the glasses set to his eyes, "Port five . . . steady. She's dead ahead an' a half-mile away!"

He heard Cleeve scampering aft to his post at the Y-gun as he watched the slender periscope standing out of the sea with the smallest feather of white water at its base as the submarine moved slowly ahead. He asked casually, "Got it?"

The voice of the layer on the 3-inch gun came back across the quiet deck, "Right." He waited for the order to fire but Petersen did not give it. The chaser slipped on slowly and the gunlayer was certain the U-boat, its periscope clear and steady in his sights, must see them.

But Petersen knew differently. The periscope stood against the growing light while the chaser was still out in the darkness with

119

the night behind her. So he waited as Ensign Cleeve chewed at his lip and the gunlayer, swearing under his breath, carefully kept the sight laid on that white feather of water where the periscope cut the sea.

Then Petersen snapped, "Fire!" And: "Full ahead!"

The layer and the engineer were both ready. The gun slammed and the shell fell just short of the periscope, or hit it. When the water that had been kicked up fell, the sea was empty but the gun was loaded again, fired. Now the chaser was almost on top of the U-boat. Cleeve shrieked at his crew and once more the Y-gun hurled depth charges over the side, and as they exploded Petersen set the chaser turning, lining her up to run in again.

That was when the U-boat came wallowing to the surface off the starboard beam, her bow down, stern high and listing over. The 3-inch fired before Petersen's order, slamming a shell into the black hull. Petersen threw at the quartermaster, "Hard right rudder!" He wanted to circle around the U-boat in easy range of the chaser's 3-inch gun and machine guns. He told the men who manned them, "Lay on the conning tower and fire as soon as anybody shows." Forward of her conning tower the U-boat carried a bigger gun than the 3-inch and she must not be allowed to use it.

The 3-inch was punching holes in the steel skin of the submarine and she listed farther so he could see into the conning tower as it lay over towards him. A man crouched in the hatch with the cover held open above his head. The machine guns chattered and the hatch cover slammed down. Then the 3-inch shifted its aim to the conning tower and shells burst on and around the hatch, penetrating the side of the tower.

The submarine was still listing, and the hatch was underwater now. The conning tower disappeared as she capsized and lay there briefly, bottom up. The 3-inch fired into her again and again until she slid below the surface for the last time with the oil running from her like blood from a wound, a death wound. Only then did the gun cease firing. Its crew stood around grinning a little uncertainly. They had not sunk a U-boat before, not many people had. Petersen was not smiling, not looking particularly pleased that his command had sunk a U-boat. Men had died. That they were Germans no longer seemed to matter. He ordered, "Secure that gun. Steer east-northeast. We'll look for survivors from *Maroc*."

They were as certain as he that it was a fruitless quest but it was undertaken in case of a miracle. So there was no celebration aboard the US Submarine-Chaser No. 101, which had just sunk her first submarine and so gloriously justified her existence. She ran down to the patch of flotsam that marked the grave of *Maroc* and the crew lined her sides, searching among the litter for signs of human life. They found none, though they patiently quartered the area. Finally Petersen abandoned the search; there was no point in going on. He looked up from the surface of the sea as the lookout at his elbow pointed and said huskily, "Cap'n! On the bow!"

Petersen squinted out over the chaser's bow as she crept towards the Gulf of Alexandretta. He was staring into the first rays of the sun showing over the Amanus mountains, sending shafts of light sparking blindingly up from the sea. He heard Cleeve say, "Sir, I can't see anything out there. We've—"

Petersen cut him off. "You were hoping to see some action. It looks like you'll get your bellyful."

It was Cleeve's turn to strain his eyes into the rising sun. Then he breathed, "Oh, my God!" Still distant but menacing, sharp and black in silhouette, *Walküre* came thrusting out of the gulf.

10 The Afrika Legion

The dump was theirs but this was still only a beginning.

Taggart was bellowing, "Sarn't Major! Ack and Beer companies man the perimeter! Marine guards at the corners! Even numbers face *out* and odd numbers face *in!* Charlie company sweep through from north to south—and I want outposts! Commanders of Number One sections to me!"

They came at a run and Taggart gave his orders. Then, as the sections scattered to take up their outpost positions, Taggart turned on Smith and explained, "Odd numbers to face in to pick up any birds flushed by the beaters of Charlie comp'ny. There might be one or two hiding under the netting." His tone was calm but his eyes glared. He turned to Smith. "We were lucky. Hardly lost a man. Incredible, and all down to surprise. By God, we owe you something. Finlayson owes you. . . ." He rubbed at his face and walked away.

Smith found his pistol was empty. When had he fired it? He could not remember. He reloaded with fumbling fingers as he strode behind Taggart to the northern perimeter of the dump. Charlie company were falling in there.

Men of A company were bellied down under the trees on the northern perimeter. Taggart halted there, Smith beside him, and they stared out to the north and the east. To their right the railway track ran down from the north and it was deserted, but for a dozen kneeling figures about two hundred yards away. Smith could make them out in the growing light.

Taggart said, "That's Carmichael's demolition gang. They know what they're doing."

Smith nodded. Sergeant Carmichael was a quick bow-legged Scot. He had been a shot-firer in a pit in Scotland before the war and he'd done a lot of demolition work with the Engineers. He and his gang carried ten big packs, loaded with charges, coils of slow and fast fuses and a handful of detonators.

Just the other side of Lydda, to the northeast of them, was a Turkish garrison and it would be wide-awake now after the firing at the dump. Smith looked over his shoulder, over the prowling figures of Charlie company sweeping through the dump, to where the darkness hid the railway station. It was only a quarter-mile away, and there would be troops there too, if only a guarding platoon. Then three miles farther south lay Er Ramle where there was the German anti-aircraft battery and the Turks had cavalry.

Taggart read Smith's mind: "We haven't got long." He shrugged inside his stained and ripped tunic. "It's turned cold."

The day was coming. There was a thin line of orange light along the Hills of Judaea where they lifted out of the plain in the east. Smith's eyes focused on the lights, yellow in the approaching dawn, that marked Lydda. "Where are the outposts?"

Taggart pointed towards the town. "Straight out a couple of hundred yards there's a corporal and two men. Others out on either side and in the rear."

Smith moved towards a gap in the wire, "I'll walk out that way." Taggart was the soldier and this was his business. Smith knew he was wasting Taggart's time standing there.

Taggart said, only half-jokingly, "Don't get lost."

Smith answered, "I won't." He picked his way through the flattened wire and started to walk towards the lights. He found Buckley was dogging him as always and grinned to himself. The day was coming on them quickly now, and visibility lengthened with his every stride. He could see the railway lines stretching straight and dull-silver, running away to the north.

"Who goes there?" The challenge came sharp from a cluster of cactus below a slight rise in the ground.

Smith answered, "*Dauntless!*"

"Advance an' be recognized!"

Smith walked on and a khaki figure rose up from among the cactus. The soldier said, "Hullo, sir." He jerked his head, indicating the rise. "Corporal's up top."

"Thank you." Smith passed through the cactus and climbed the slope to where the corporal lay, peering over the crest. A private lay a couple of yards away. Both had rifles tucked into their shoulders. The corporal took in Smith with a quick glance then faced forward again, but not before Smith caught a glimpse of a face covered in sweat and dust with a fringe of carroty hair poking out from under the pushed-back cap. Smith remembered him. At Taggart's briefing aboard *Morning Star* he had said: "It looks a right bastard."

It still did. They weren't out of things yet by a long chalk. Smith waited silently with the two soldiers as daylight grew. Carmichael's gang still worked close by, spaced along the railway track at thirty yard intervals. Carmichael's voice came to him, though Smith could not make out the words. A minute later the Scotsman trotted back towards the dump, his team behind him.

The corporal, peering over the crest, said huskily, "They're just coming out, sir. On the road this side o' the town. See 'em?"

Yes. Tiny, antlike figures were moving out of Lydda, a marching column, and was that a horse at their head? But then his attention was distracted and he cocked his head, listening.

Smith said, "Can you hear a train?"

Now they all heard it, like distant, panting breath. The corporal muttered, "Strewth!" Then, "Anything been said about water, sir?"

Smith saw the tunics of the two soldiers were black with sweat. They could easily have sneaked a drink but they had not. Discipline. He said, "Take a mouthful, no more." He unslung his own bottle and let the water wash round his mouth before he swallowed. It was water from *Dauntless* and he wondered briefly if he'd ever see her again.

Rifle fire spattered briefly, distantly behind him, to the south of the dump. That would be a curious patrol from the station. A Vickers rattled and the rifle fire ceased. He told Buckley, "Go and relieve our rear sentry. And send him up here."

The man came up and dropped down beside the corporal. In the silence they heard the train more loudly, closer. . . .

"Here she comes." That was the corporal.

Smith's mouth was already dry again. The train had passed the body of marching men and would arrive in less than a minute. He ordered, "At the train. Six hundred yards. Ten rounds rapid."

The three rifles cracked and stuttered as smoke wisped from the barrels. Smith saw the train slowing and said, "Five hundred!" There was a pause in the firing as the soldiers thumbed at the backsights. The train stopped and there were men jumping down from the wagons. In this leaden light they were not so much men as moving dots but you could see the colour of their uniforms.

The corporal said, "My God! They're Jerries!" And carried on firing. Smith stared at the men who were running towards him now. Here and there a section halted as one to kneel and fire, then rise and run on. They had been hurriedly thrown into action but were moving like a well-oiled machine. These were the men Smith had sought, the Afrika Legion.

Men fell on the plain between the clumps of cactus, but the line came on and there was another behind it. A file ran up the railway track to outflank the British outpost. The corporal was reloading, closing the bolt as the clip fell away, firing. Smith glanced behind him over the two hundred yards of ground that lay between them and the dump, and saw a man standing in the gap in the wire and waving furiously. Taggart? Smith faced forward and found the line nearer. Had he hung on too long? Almost.

Blast whipped a hot breath past his face then the thump of an explosion slammed against his ears like a blow from an open hand. He spun around and saw the cloud of smoke and upthrown earth, the twisted rails. Carmichael's work. Even as he watched there was another explosion. And another. Every one left a crater, splintered sleepers and twisted lines. The railway to Gaza and Beersheba was severed for two hundred yards.

He shouted, "Cease fire! Retire! At the double!" He followed them out through the cactus, Buckley appeared alongside, and they were all out in the open and running for the dump. It was a long two hundred yards. Smith's legs felt like lead and there was a pain in his chest. He was aware that the Vickers at each end of the wood were firing now and loaded with tracer. Rifles blazed and he could see the men lying behind them, working the bolts. He stumbled through the gap in the wire and threw himself down.

He lay still a moment, winded. Taggart squatted on his heels behind the riflemen. He stared through the wire intently but spared a glance for Smith. "All right?"

He had to shout above the rattle of musketry. Smith lifted a hand. Taggart faced forward again. "I think it's time we left. We've got a tiger by the tail here. We've slowed 'em but they're still coming on."

Smith crouched beside him now, staring out at the open ground. The long line of Germans was gone, but rifle fire winked from where the survivors had found what cover there was in a fold of the ground or behind a hummock of sand. Smith's head turned, eyes seeking the line of the railway. Firing came from that direction too, and almost abreast of the dump.

Taggart said, "That's right. They're working down that flank. They're north, south and east of us. There's only our way out to the west left open and it's time we took it." He raised a whistle to his lips and blew one long blast. Both Vickers ceased firing and a moment later Smith saw their crews humping the guns back through the dump. Taggart's whistle shrilled again and the firing ceased in the line before him. Taggart's men were on their feet and scurrying back through the dump. Taggart turned on Smith and Buckley, "Come on!" The three of them ran after the soldiers, pounding between the net-draped heaps of supplies.

Smith almost fell over a man crouching with his head and shoulders under the netting. It was Carmichael, who was carefully pushing a matchhead into the end of a length of black safety fuse and rubbing the matchbox over it. The matchhead spurted flame and Carmichael tucked the fuse away under the netting and dragged a crate in front of it.

Smith ran on. They filed through gaps in the wire and were out of the wood and trotting across open ground. A hundred yards out they came on a straggling, well-spaced line where a platoon of the battalion lay, rifles covering the dump, a Vickers mounted at each end. The other soldiers kept running, headed for the train.

Smith and his two companions halted. Behind them Carmichael and his demolition gang were filtering through the trees and breaking into the open ground. As they came on, smoke wisped above the trees from the fires which had smouldered since the dump was taken. Carmichael halted, panting before Taggart, who asked, "All right?"

"Aye, sir, fine. I set the charges in the ammo mysel'. We've less than two minutes now. I think we should get out o' it."

Taggart watched the other men trotting towards the train in two lines. He answered Carmichael, "Too bloody true. When that lot goes up—" His whistle pierced the din again and they ran until they came on the flank of the second line. They flopped down behind a low dune and stared over the top of it. They could see men of the Afrika Legion scurrying in the dump now.

The ground lifted beneath them as a flash leaped up from the dump. The crash of the explosion drowned the firing; smoke and debris soared, and the dust boiled out towards them in a choking cloud. Through that fog of dust they saw Taggart climbing to his feet and heard his yell: "Fall back! Pass it on!"

As the swirl of red dust settled, the dump came into view, a smoking ruin of littered wreckage. No one moved, no one lived in that seared area of ground. But beyond it was more of the Afrika Legion and its reaction would be swift. They headed for the train at the run. The job was done. The Afrika Legion would be without supplies to prop up the Turks at Beersheba.

Now the battalion had to get out if it could.

The men were running ahead of Smith but stiffly, tiredly,

in two ragged lines, carrying their wounded. The farther line was almost to the train. Two trucks in the centre flew Red Cross flags from short poles. Smith thought he could see the blonde head of Adeline Brett in one of them. Two more Vickers were mounted, one in the first truck and one in the last.

The first line of men was climbing aboard the trucks now. Taggart was up with the second, urging them on and when Smith came up to him he reached out to shake Smith's shoulder. "It worked like a charm! We can't have more than a couple of dozen wounded. As I said, it's a miracle!"

A shell fell to the left of the train, two hundred yards away, hurling up rocks and making a small crater. Taggart swore. "There's a mortar somewhere in the trees!"

Smith headed towards the engine, Buckley following. The crew of the Vickers in the front truck were manhandling the gun around but suddenly another shell landed close by injuring two of them. The gun fell back into the truck and Edwards rose inside it, wrestling with Garrett, who had been set to guard him. Then Garrett slipped from sight and Edwards leaped over the side to the ground, rifle in one hand. He crouched there, lifting the rifle to his shoulder.

Smith halted and aimed the Webley, though it was a long shot for a pistol. "Drop it!" But Edwards only worked the bolt and Smith saw death looking at him out of Edwards's eyes. Then a rifle cracked at his side and Edwards pitched over.

Taggart panted, "It was him or us!" Smith knew that. His reason, always precarious, must finally have cracked. But it was a wretched end for so brilliant and unhappy a man. They left the dead man where he lay, the red dust blowing over him. Taggart bellowed to a group of his men who climbed into the truck. They passed down one of the Vickers' crew who was alive, though wounded, and Garrett. Across Garrett's belly a red stain was spreading. He looked up at Taggart grey-faced, and said bitterly, "When the machine-gunners got hit I took me eye off him for a second. Bastard had a knife."

"Never mind." Taggart raised his voice, "Get him to the ambulance truck!" But the man tending Garrett glanced up and shook his head. Garrett's eyes were staring sightlessly at the sky.

Smith stood with Buckley by the footplate. Charlie Golightly crouched in a corner with the shovel held up before his face. He shouted, "They're in the trees an' right close."

Smith could see figures in the wood two hundred yards or so on the far side of the engine. Probably the column marching from Lydda had arrived by now. A mortar shell landed, spattering the engine with stones. He glared at Golightly. *"Get on your feet!"*

He looked back along the train, saw the last men clambering into the open trucks. The riflemen in the trees were firing rapidly and some were advancing in short rushes, halting to fire and run on across the open ground. Smith swung back to Golightly, who had dragged himself to his feet, and said, "Drive it away!"

He ran to a truck flying a Red Cross flag, leaped up to hang on the side and peered in. Adeline Brett moved among the wounded and Smith shouted, "Keep your heads down!" He saw her turn, startled, then he dropped to the ground as the train jerked into motion.

The engine backed down past Smith and Buckley where they stood alone. Buckley tried to step aside but Smith snarled at him, "Get *on!*" He shoved Buckley up the ladder, grabbed at the hand-rail himself, missed, grabbed again and this time seized hold. After three long, leaping strides he jumped for the ladder, found it with one foot, swung wildly off-balance but then threw himself in.

There was a hand on the rail on the far side of the footplate. Then a head showed and another hand, this one pointing a pistol. Smith stared across at the dark face with its bar of black moustache. Golightly stood in the centre of the footplate, one hand on the regulating lever, the other gripping the shovel. Now he swung the shovel and the flat of its blade blotted out the face, the hand slipped from the rail and the pistol fired, kicking splinters from the wood piled at the rear of the footplate. The Turk disappeared.

Smith climbed to his feet shakily, moved cautiously to the side of the footplate and looked back along the rails. There were men swarming from the wood onto the track now, all of them small with distance and shrinking as the engine pulled away, the trucks ahead rocking and swaying. The enemy had been on the point of capturing the train and they had escaped only by seconds. But they still had a long way to go.

128

The sun would be well above the Hills of Judaea now but it was hidden by low-hanging clouds. They roared past the village of Beit Dejan and a Turkish patrol appeared from among the little houses to fire at the train, but harmlessly. Golightly laughed with a flush of false courage, feeling safe on his leaping footplate. But that firing was bad because it meant that word had gone ahead of them and the Turks at Jaffa would be waiting.

GOLIGHTLY shouted, "Stoke 'er, Mr. Buckley, if you please."

Buckley swung open the door and fed logs into the furnace. Ahead the track lifted to the crest of the hill where they had captured the train and there they would leave it. They were slowing now, the engine puffing short-windedly as it pulled up the slope.

Smith leaned out at the side of the footplate to peer forward past the swaying trucks. A tall man stood by the track, his slouch hat tipped forward. Smith said harshly, "Stop her!"

As the train clanked to a halt he jumped down and threw at Taggart, "Get them out and moving!" and ran forward.

Jackson asked, "Any luck?"

Smith nodded breathlessly, "The track and the dump."

Jackson whistled softly and his gaze went to where the battalion poured from the train. "I owe Taggart an apology."

He turned and walked with Smith at his side towards the point where the track curved to go down into Jaffa. "Just before it got light I occupied the crest."

Dust hung above the road out of Jaffa and under the dust four or five thousand yards away, was a fast-marching column of enemy infantry, an officer on horseback at their head. Jackson said laconically, "Somebody passed the word."

Smith remembered the Turks who had fired on the train at Beit Dejan. He turned to look back at the train where the men milled about, lifting down the wounded into Adeline Brett's little cart, which had been dragged from its hiding place in the orange groves. He could see her head and the big figure of Merryweather.

He said, "We can't stop to fight. We've got to get out quick, no long rearguard actions. But the wounded—we need time because of them." He knew what he was asking.

So did Jackson but he said only, "All right."

He strode into the grove past a big trooper who asked, "What's goin' on, Jacka?"

"Mounted action, that's what. Get your horse."

The horse-holders brought up the Walers, troopers swinging up into the saddles. One of them held a horse for Smith, who hesitated but saw no help for it and let another trooper boost him up into the saddle. He caught a glimpse of Buckley's face, worried, disbelieving and exasperated all at once. Then he grabbed at the reins and held on as his mount went with the others. Some-

where in the jostling throng of shifting, stamping horses Jackson shouted, "Remember, you jokers, it isn't a flamin' steeplechase!"

One of them grumbled, "Aw, give it a rest, Jacka."

The horses plunged forward. Jackson was in the lead, his horse stretching out into a gallop and the ragged line of ragged troopers tore howling after him. Smith was caught up in their madness. They seemed to gallop down a funnel leading them to the centre of the blue-grey enemy column and nothing else existed. The Turks were firing, he could see the muzzle-flashes of their rifles, but the rush

131

of the wind in his ears blotted out the reports and he only heard the whistling rip as the bullets sped past.

A man collapsed on the neck of his Waler but clung on. A horse plunged forward on its knees and rolled, throwing its rider over its head to sprawl in the dust. The column of Turks floated up towards Smith and now he could make out faces under the caps, fingers jerking at the bolts of rifles, all glimpsed across a shrinking strip of sand that the Walers gobbled up in seconds. And the charge struck home.

There was no bone-jarring impact, just a moment of slipping about precariously in the saddle as he reined in one-handed and snapped the trigger of the Webley at faces looming out of the fog of dust churned up by the horses' hooves. The Australians wheeled, and charged again, troopers firing the rifles one-handed, slashing with the barrel, clubbing with the butt.

The Webley was empty. The Waler surged under him, rode down a man who shrieked as he went under the hooves. Smith swung with the Webley at the face of another and he spun away. For a second he faced back up the hill, saw fallen horses, a trooper on foot wandering with his hands pressed to his head, the men from the train heading up towards the crest and the track to the Auja river.

Before him lay the plain where the Turks had stood. Some of them lay still, marking the line they had held, while the rest ran madly, Jackson and his troopers hunting them, firing, clubbing.

Jackson's voice bellowed, and the horsemen turned and trotted back to him. Smith realized slowly and with disbelief that he had been in a cavalry charge. It was ridiculous—he was a seaman and not even a halfway competent horseman. These men riding towards him now were the real thing, dirty and ragged, some with laughter on their brown faces, others silent and withdrawn. He thought them incredible. Already it was being said that this Anzac mounted force was the greatest cavalry in the history of the world.

He turned his horse and urged it back up the hill. Jackson and his troopers had cleared the way for the rest of them; there would be no rearguard action. But now they faced the long march back to the Auja. Smith was as weary as all of them were weary, but there could be no rest. Now it was a race. All surprise was gone and Edwards had said the Turkish regiment north of the Auja would come down like the hammers of hell. Edwards . . . the memory of his mad face still haunted Smith.

He marched with Taggart at the head of the column, Buckley two paces behind him. The Australians rode as front and rear-guards and flankers. Adeline Brett's cart was pulled along in the centre of the column, crammed with wounded but there were others who limped along with a man propping each side.

They were heading for the distant ridge, beyond which lay the Auja river and the sea. Smith turned his head to peer back at the column. For a moment he thought he saw a bird overhead but then it turned and he made out the biplane wings and the floats. It was a Short.

Another swung into sight behind it and the pair of them came charging along the column, roared low overhead and circled. Both Shorts carried bombs slung in the racks under their bellies and one was unmistakably Delilah, with little Maitland waving excitedly from the rear cockpit. Smith was glad that Pearce had not let him down but he wondered where the third Short was? Smith saw them straighten out ahead of the column and drop below the ridge, out of sight. In the silence after the engines' clamour he heard the distant crump of the bombs. Minutes later, there came the rattle of heavy rifle and machine-gun fire. He had lost his race, the Turks had come from the north to slam the door shut in his face.

He swallowed and ran forward as the shriek of a falling salvo of shells ripped the air ahead. Lieutenant Jameson stood on a crest and Smith laboured up to him and stopped, chest heaving. Before him the ground fell away to the river that lay under swirling, drifting smoke. Through it he saw the lighters beaching at the ford, the motorboat over by the far bank, and on the ridge beyond it, level with him, the sprawled figures of marines, rifles at their shoulders. *Dauntless* patrolled scarcely a mile offshore and the salvo had come from her. A light flickered rapidly just below the ridge, relaying to *Dauntless* her gunnery officer's orders for the shoot, bringing down the fire from *Dauntless* to lay a protective curtain ahead of the little party of marines.

Jameson was saying, "A Turkish patrol came down the coast from the north at first light to look for the break in the telephone wire and Brand took his marines across to the other side when the firing started."

The crest they were on was held only by the cutter's crew. Smith said, "Watch me. When I give you the sign you get out quick."

"Aye, aye, sir," answered Jameson and then asked, "What success, sir?"

Smith told him and the cutter's crew cheered.

The column came up. Smith knew they had only minutes because the regiment of Turks, despite the guns of *Dauntless*, would soon slip around Brand's thin line of marines and then only Jameson's men would stand between them and the lighters. He shouted to the battalion RSM, "Get 'em aboard anyhow, but as soon as you can!"

Smith stood on the crest with Taggart and watched the battalion pass, boots plodding wearily, eyes staring through the mask of red dust that coated them all. You could not order these men to double, it was a miracle they kept up the pace.

Adeline Brett's little wagon came up, dragged by a dozen men, the girl striding stiffly alongside, Charlie Golightly hobbling behind her. Now the rearguard of Jackson's troopers came up. All the time the shells from *Dauntless* howled in and burst, while the two Shorts trundled dangerously low on the far side of the river, their bombs all gone but the Lewis guns chattering.

Smith left Jameson's men to hold the rear, went down with Jackson and Taggart, hurrying after the column that waded the ford, stumbling and splashing out to the lighters and scrambling aboard. He went on past them, found his gunnery officer, Griffiths, and his signaller lying with Brand at the top of the far ridge and knelt beside them. Taggart and Jackson flanked him, crouched at his shoulder and behind them, down the slope, stood Buckley.

Griffiths rubbed a hand over cracked, dry lips and shouted above the rifle fire, "They can't cross the open ground but that scrub is swarming with them!" Beyond the ridge was a stretch of sandy plain but three hundred yards away, it ended in rolling scrub and cactus. Griffiths said, "They're working around to the right. Some of them are in that wood—" A salvo rushed overhead and burst a quarter-mile away to the right. Griffiths went on, "In a few minutes they'll be able to fire into the lighters and enfilade *us*."

A half-mile away the two Shorts came floating down to skim across the top of the scrub. Smith muttered, "They're desperately low. . . ." They were giving all they had, chancing too much. There were machine guns firing back at them, the lines of tracer sliding up, crisscrossing.

"They've done it two or three times in the last few minutes."

"They'll do it once too—" Smith bit off the rest of it. The leading Short had suddenly erupted in flames, tilted on one wing and slid away, down into the scrub. The smoke rolled black across the plain. Delilah was climbing and turning away inland.

Smith swore under his breath. Soon Turkish machine guns would be brought up to the edge of the scrub facing him, which already sparked with rifle flashes along its length. He turned to peer back at the ford. Two of the lighters were afloat and going stern-first towards the mouth of the river. The last horse was being hauled up the ramp of the fourth close by the shore. He ordered Brand, "Take your marines now."

Brand bawled at his men and led them down the slope at a run. As they splashed to the cutter, Smith stepped down the ridge out of sight of the Turks. He flagged his handkerchief over his head, saw an answering wave from the far crest and then Jameson and the cutter's crew spilling down towards the river.

He turned—and saw shells burst on the open beach in a close-packed line. As the dust blew away Griffiths said, "That's torn it. They've got a battery of field guns in action."

Smith rubbed at his face. "Take your signaller out now." He snatched a rifle and bandolier from the man and sprawled behind the crest, Jackson, Taggart and Buckley spaced out to his left. They opened fire, shooting rapidly into the scrub. The Turks had to believe the ridge was still held in strength long enough for Jameson and Brand to get their men into the boats.

The next shells came down just short of the ridge, raining pebbles on the four of them huddled down over their rifles. Smith twisted round to peer at the ford. Brand's men were already away, and Jameson's men were scrambling into the cutter. Griffiths was at the tiller of the motorboat. Smith shouted, "Right! Let's go!"

He pushed back from the crest but Buckley said, "Sir!" And

pointed. Smith's eyes followed the line of his outstretched finger and saw the far shore deserted except for Adeline Brett's wagon— and Adeline herself kneeling over a man's body.

Jackson said, "Why the hell doesn't she get out?"

Smith answered, knowing her, "She wouldn't leave him. The rest of you get down to Griffiths. I'll fetch her."

He ran down to the ford, waded across it and realized Taggart, Jackson and Buckley were with him. Jackson panted, "If she won't leave him, you'll need us."

They trotted stiffly to the wagon and now Smith saw it hid Charlie Golightly, legs sprawled, eyes closed, exhausted. The wounded man was the red-headed corporal, his face twisted in pain. Adeline Brett looked up at them, her face dirty, her hands filthy with blood and dust. She said hoarsely, "He'd crawled under the wagon. Nobody saw him except Charlie who came to help."

Smith thought Charlie was game enough but hardly able to help himself now, a sight too old for this. Jackson grabbed Charlie's arm, Taggart and Buckley lifted the corporal between them and Smith pulled Adeline to her feet. "They'll be firing down on us at any second!"

They started down to the ford, and waded out towards the motorboat. The sea washed up into their faces, then the motorboat slid down on them with hands reaching out to lift aboard the wounded corporal, grabbing at Smith and the others. He was last aboard and panted at Griffiths, "Get out!"

He saw Turks appear some four hundred yards away at the bend of the river but then the engine opened up and the boat surged seaward.

The men lay about the cutter and motorboat in slack exhaustion. Ahead, under a grey sky, were *Dauntless*, *Morning Star* and the four lighters, while *Blackbird* was hurrying up from the south. Smith thought it was a ramshackle little armada, thrown together to attempt a desperate enterprise, but they had done the job.

He said to Taggart who sat next to him in the sternsheets, "You must be proud of them."

Taggart nodded wearily. "I am. But they'll be split up after this." And when Smith looked the question at him: "Garrett is dead, so there's no more need for silence. . . . He shot the colonel back in Salonika—his brother had been killed in the attack there and when the colonel started bawling about cowardice Garrett coolly walked forward and fired three rounds, while we just gawped."

Taggart shook his head as if to shake off the memory. "I'd seen Garrett in action a few times. I suppose he was just a killer, and he and Edwards were a pair. The others protected him because they felt he did it for all of them—they were all guilty of wishing the colonel dead before he could be the death of every one of them. And me? Well, I didn't think Garrett deserved a firing squad after what he'd been through." He shifted on his seat. "If we get out of this I'll make a full report to Finlayson."

He rose awkwardly and moved away forward. Smith felt no outrage, and no surprise either . . . perhaps he had guessed the truth long before. Now he was weary to the bone, numb. Later he might consider the risks he had so boldly taken and they would cost him sleep, but now he did not care. He folded his arms tightly across his chest and watched the ships creep closer.

11 *Walküre*

Adeline Brett said, "I've had enough."

She had come aft. They were nearly at the ships now. She pushed at damp tendrils of hair that clung to her brow, raised her head to look at the lighters. Knowing Smith was watching her, she said, "There's plenty still to do—the wounded—and I'll do it. But afterwards—" She glanced sideways at him. "Garrett is dead."

Smith nodded. "I was there. And Taggart's just told me all about him. He's going to make a full report to Finlayson."

Adeline asked worriedly, "Will John get into trouble for hiding it all this time?"

Smith thought about it, watching Taggart and Jackson sitting shoulder to shoulder in companionable silence. He said, with relief, "I think he'll get away with it. After his part in this action they'll hush up the business of the colonel. Garrett is dead and there's no point in trying a dead man." His gaze shifted to Charlie Golightly where he lay in the bow, his bulk limp and drained by exhaustion. Charlie would get away with it, too, especially as Smith would recommend him for a decoration—the public did not like tarnished heroes so there would be no court martial for Charlie.

Tarnished heroes. . . . Edwards. Smith would tell Braddock and Finlayson the truth but his official report would say only that he was killed during the attack on Lydda. Edwards had found the Legion and more importantly its planned date of arrival in Beersheba. Also he had led them to Lydda. If anyone deserved a hero's laurels for his part in this operation it was Edwards.

Adeline Brett went on, "They'll break up the battalion now. I have money in Cairo and I'll rent a house there for a while. I'll see this war through to its end but just now I'd like to live a little." She paused, then said quietly, "Could you come with me?"

The question was unexpected but he needed no time to think. *Dauntless* would undoubtedly go into the dockyard for repairs and he would get leave. "I'd like to. Yes."

Dauntless was looming, the way coming off her as she stopped to pick up her boats. Her crew were lining the side and cheering. Smith saw Ackroyd out on the wing of the bridge, saw him take off his cap and wave it wildly, his Yorkshire stolidness cast aside.

SMITH CLIMBED to the bridge and leaned against the screen with head on his folded arms. He ached as if beaten all over and his eyes were rubbed raw by the dust. The breeze was chill, and now rain fell coldly. Yet still he felt full of hope.

He raised his head as Ackroyd said delightedly, "Terrific, sir! Shall I send a signal to the admiral now?"

Smith answered huskily, "Just send: 'Attack complete success. Dump destroyed, railway cut and Legion halted. Few casualties. Force re-embarked'!"

That was all Braddock and Finlayson wanted to know for the present. Braddock would have to be told, but not now, that Smith had flagrantly disobeyed orders and gambled on his own initiative —yet again. The old admiral's comments would be blistering but the thing was done and successful.

Ackroyd passed the message, turned back, "I must say I was surprised as well as relieved, sir, when I saw the troops coming off, that there were so many. I'd thought the casualty rate would be much higher."

Smith knew Braddock and Finlayson also would be relieved. The raid could have been a disaster. If the men had not been so brave, so well led. Taggart and Jackson. The Australians had got them in and got them out, but it was Taggart's battalion that had actually stopped the Afrika Legion in its tracks; while the Shorts and their crews, the guns of *Dauntless* and the parties ashore, all had played their part.

He said, "Maybe we were lucky." And: "Will someone fetch me a cup of coffee, please?"

He drank it standing on the bridge. His jaded mind was uneasy. Buckley stood at the back of the bridge, teeth showing white in a face smeared with dust and streaked with sweat runnels, grinning widely. The signal yeoman had shoved a mug into his hand, and Smith could smell the rum in it from six feet away. He wondered why he remained depressed with the open exuberance all around him. They were returning to Port Said and there would be leave then, with Adeline Brett in Cairo. But still he felt there was something he had overlooked, that had clamoured for his attention during the raid but had been lost in the press of events. . . .

Ackroyd said, "Here's a Short."

She came out of the coast, losing height steadily as she flew towards the group of ships. *Blackbird* was turning to make a lee for the Short, and they could see the mottled red skin of her. Smith said, "Ask *Blackbird* who's in Delilah?"

A pause as they watched the Short, then the signal yeoman reported, "Rogers and Maitland, sir."

As she came closer Ackroyd said uneasily, "Is Captain Webb going to swim for it again? That engine sounds a bit funny to me. I'm no engineer but—" His voice drifted away but Smith knew what he meant. Smith had heard Shorts flying often enough these last weeks to sense that the engine of Delilah had a different rhythm to it. He glanced quickly across at *Blackbird* and saw Pearce running across her bridge as the Short swung around the carrier, turning into the wind. The fitters and riggers in *Blackbird* were already over her side, balanced on her wide rubbing strake. They too knew there was something wrong.

Smith said, "Tell the motorboat to stand by."

Delilah came down, flying into the wind with her starboard wing tilted low but she straightened the instant before the big floats rubbed into the long, kicking waves. Rogers was slumped now and Maitland's white face was turned desperately towards the cruiser. The floats dug in and the Short settled, sat back on the tail float and the engine died. She was out in the open, rocking in the sea, and the wind must soon overturn her but the motorboat from *Dauntless* surged out to the seaplane and stopped under her nose. A man leaped onto a float and made fast a line that paid out as Delilah drifted rapidly downwind. He lifted a hand, and the motorboat forged ahead, towing the Short into *Blackbird*'s lee.

They were lowering Rogers down into the motorboat and young Maitland was climbing down after him. Smith said, "I want to talk to Maitland."

When they brought him to the bridge he was pale, but deliberately calm. He told Smith that, following Pearce's order, the three Shorts had flown to Lydda. "But we passed too close to that German anti-aircraft battery south of the station and they got Beckett. We saw them go down." He swallowed, "Anyway, Kirby and us pushed on—and the dump was burning like mad, sir! All the track was chewed up and there were two trains stopped on the line. We headed for the mouth of the Auja and that's when we saw you."

Smith nodded, and Maitland went on. "Well, we saw the Turks coming down towards the river so we dropped the bombs and then made a few passes over them. That's when Kirby caught it. There was a lot of machine-gun fire."

Smith nodded again, remembering, as he watched Maitland try to keep his thoughts in order. "So we cleared off and saw you all get away. Then Rogers shouted that we should have another look at Lydda. He said you'd want to know. The dump was still smoking and there were four trains stopped on the line, and the place was swarming with Germans." Smith thought there might be a dozen trains at least, halted on the line north of Lydda by now, the Afrika Legion stopped dead in its tracks.

Maitland took a breath. "So we started back, following the railway to Jaffa. We were at about seven hundred feet, but then the engine cut out. We glided down and it fired again when we were a couple of miles from the coast, but pretty low. There were some Turks by that little place Tel Aviv, and they fired up at us with rifles. Rogers was hit and a shot went through the radiator." He stopped for a moment, then finished, "That was rotten bad luck, sir, being hit by chaps with rifles."

Smith saw Ackroyd standing behind Maitland and shaking his head. Smith said, "You did very well. I'll send you back to *Blackbird* and you're to get some sleep. That's an order."

"Aye, aye, sir." And: "How is Rogers, sir?" Smith hesitated and Maitland turned and saw Ackroyd's face and said, "I see." He went miserably down to the boat that waited for him.

Ackroyd said, "The surgeon can't understand how Rogers got the thing down." He added bitterly, "But no matter what, Delilah *always* gets back."

The wounded had been hurriedly taken aboard *Dauntless* and *Blackbird* and Adeline Brett was below assisting Merryweather. The two ships then patrolled around *Morning Star* and the lighters as the tramp finished embarking the men of the battalion. When she finally signalled that she was ready to proceed the weather had worsened. The coast was still visible but clouds hung inland and their weeping was a grey curtain hiding the Hills of Judaea.

Smith went to his sea cabin at the back of the bridge as the convoy got under way, leaving the bridge to Ackroyd. Now he could and should sleep. But hardly had he sat on the edge of the bunk before boots pounded on the ladder to the bridge, and his cabin door burst open. Cherrett, breathless from his run from the wireless office aft, thrust out the signal and panted, "*Walküre*'s done it again, sir! She's out!"

Smith snatched the signal, saw it was from Braddock and started to read, unaware that he was shouldering past Cherrett. *Walküre* and the freighter *Friedrichsburg* were gone from the Gulf of Alexandretta. There was no sign of *Maroc* nor the US submarine-chaser except for some floating wreckage. *Dauntless* and *Blackbird* were ordered north-westward to take up a position between the gulf and Port Said. The French battleship *Océan* and the cruiser *Attack*, both only hours from Alexandretta now, would swing south-westward once they had cleared Cyprus.

Blindly, he climbed the ladder to the bridge. So it wasn't over. No Cairo, no leave, no Adeline. Clearly Braddock was sending Smith's force to act as a first line of defence for Port Said and the shipping lanes out of it. Braddock was concerned with convoys, so vulnerable with only elderly destroyers and armed yachts as escorts. *Attack* and the French battleship were more than a match for *Walküre* but she had too long a start on them. Why was the *Friedrichsburg* in company? She was not acting as her tender because with a best speed of no more than fifteen knots, she would slow down the big cruiser. So—was *Walküre* in fact an escort for the freighter?

Smith stared unseeingly past Ackroyd. During the raid he had suspected that he was overlooking something: now he had it! The Germans and Turks had difficulty in supplying their army by rail from Constantinople. Smith had told Finlayson that the Germans might find a way around this bottleneck. And so they had. Load a big, fast freighter with all the stores and ammunition that would take fifty trains and several weeks to move by rail, and send that ship on one swift passage to deliver her cargo to a port near the front line. To Haifa—*Friedrichsburg* could even lie off Jaffa while boats unloaded her under the protection of *Walküre*'s guns. The railway would then take her cargo to Beersheba and Gaza. Allenby was attacking in less than twenty-four hours. If he was stalled for even a day the results could be catastrophic.

But *Walküre* had not broken out of the Dardanelles only to run the blockade with one ship's cargo. She would have another task. . . . He realized Ackroyd and Henderson waited for him. Smith said, "Make to *Morning Star* and the lighters: 'Proceed to Deir el Belah independently.'" And, as the signal lamp flickered: "Pilot! A course for Alexandretta!"

Henderson blinked then strode quickly to the chartroom. He had seen the signal, had laid off the course for the position Braddock had ordered—but now Smith wanted a course for Alexandretta instead—Why?

Ackroyd was asking himself that same question, uneasy.

But Smith ordered, "Starboard ten! Steer nor'-nor' east. Revolutions for twenty knots. Pass that to *Blackbird*." *Dauntless* came around onto the new heading that was the reciprocal of *Walküre*'s course if she were bound for Jaffa. Smith told the signal yeoman, "Signal to Rear Admiral Braddock: 'Submit....'"

He had to word it carefully because if you act in contravention of an admiral's orders on your own initiative then you must be very tactful. Smith was only glad that the signal was to Braddock, who he thought would understand. He waited restlessly for an answer.

Braddock's reply only said, "Affirmative." Smith read the signal without change of expression, knowing he had to prove himself right or take the consequences. He returned to prowling about the bridge with his collar turned up against the rain and hands jammed in his pockets, trying to think ahead.

He asked *Blackbird* when a seaplane would be ready to fly and was told repairs to Delilah, the sole remaining aircraft, would take a minimum of six hours. Smith grunted and glanced at his watch. Six hours would be just good enough. If he had guessed correctly then in six hours he might have found *Walküre* unaided. But that was wildly optimistic: they would need the Short to search.

He clambered up onto his captain's chair and Buckley brought him a sandwich and a cup of coffee. . . .

A commotion woke him, jerking upright in the chair as Ackroyd said at his elbow, "Top reports a ship right ahead of us, sir!"

Smith climbed down from the chair and leaned against the screen, looked at his watch—three hours had passed—and growled, "Why did you let me sleep?"

"We've sighted nothing till now, sir." Ackroyd was undisturbed by Smith's censure and added frankly. "I thought you were due for some rest." Smith grunted reluctant agreement; he felt better for his uneasy dozing in the chair.

Ackroyd muttered, "She's not making any smoke, sir."

Smith made no comment. Ackroyd's implication was clear. *Walküre* was a coal-burning ship so that vessel ahead was not she. Then a report came down from the foretop: "She's bows-on but she could be that Yankee sub-chaser!"

No one spoke but a ripple of excitement ran through all of them on the bridge. Smith said, "Make the challenge."

The shutter on the searchlight clattered, then an answering light flickered on the horizon. The signal yeoman, telescope to his eye, called, "She's SC 101, sir!"

143

Smith took a breath. "Ask: 'Where is the enemy?'"

Again the light flickered and the signal yeoman read: "Enemy bears—" The signalman at his elbow wrote it down. Ackroyd grinned broadly, relieved that *Walküre* had not eluded them—but his grin slipped away as he saw his captain expressionless. Smith was translating the terse sentences into a mental picture of the ships ahead. Petersen said *Walküre* lay ten miles astern of his port quarter, speed fourteen knots. And the freighter *Friedrichsburg* was keeping station astern of *Walküre*.

Smith said, "Tell the Sparks: Wireless silence." And to the yeoman, "Make: 'Where is *Maroc*?'"

He was thinking quickly. *Walküre* would be leading *Friedrichsburg* because her captain would be expecting any trouble to come from ahead. He could not be aware of the chaser because, if he had been, he would not have tolerated her surveillance, would have sunk her. The chaser was petrol-engined, not making any smoke to give her away and the lookouts in *Dauntless* could only see her now because she was close. The same applied to the lookouts in *Walküre*. *Walküre* was twenty miles away from *Dauntless* and could not see her, nor hear her as long as *Dauntless*'s wireless was silent.

The yeoman was reading out the chaser's answers: "*Maroc* torpedoed by U-boat and blew up. U-boat sunk—" There was a growl of appreciation. "Submit—" Petersen submitted his opinion that *Walküre* had been ready with the freighter in the mouth of the gulf, waiting for the submarine to clear the way.

Smith agreed. "Make: 'Maintain observation of enemy but avoid action. Well done. Thank you.'" That was meagre payment for the chaser's part in this. She had somehow kept in front of and yet in sight of the big cruiser all through the day. And Petersen's cooperation had been, strictly speaking, a breach of neutrality. Smith's curt "Thank you" was the only official acknowledgment Petersen would ever get.

Smith went into the charthouse and peered at the chart. It would be suicide to meet *Walküre* head-on. But she must be stopped. *Friedrichsburg* was a part of the German plan to break Allenby's attack. The Afrika Legion was only delayed, and the supplies crammed into the freighter's holds could be crucial as the

campaign went on. The only cards he held were *Dauntless*'s
advantage in speed, and surprise. That was little enough. They
had saved him last time, but only just.

He pushed away from the chart and stepped out onto the bridge.
Ackroyd looked grimly expectant, young Bright was nervous and
excited. Smith said, "Make to *Blackbird. . . .*"

It was a long signal and he had to be careful in his phrasing.
There must be no mistake. At least, with Edwards dead, he no
longer had that nagging uncertainty about Pearce's actions. The
lamp flashed out to the carrier and from *Blackbird*'s bridge came
a flicker of acknowledgment, then she turned to port and headed
out to sea on a course almost due west. The chaser followed her.

Smith ordered, "Starboard ten! Steer oh-four-oh! Full ahead!"
And added: "General quarters!" Ackroyd punched the button and
the klaxons blared, calling the crew to their action stations. Then
he left the bridge to take command of damage control.

Dauntless turned to starboard and settled on the new course
that would take her to the coast, working up to her full speed. In
minutes the mountains of Lebanon loomed vague behind the curtain of rain but *Dauntless* held on until Smith ordered, "Port
ten! Steer three-five-oh!" *Dauntless* ran north close to the coast.

Smith shivered, cold in the battle-stained light drill uniform. In
the course of a day the summer had gone, the air was chill and the
rain whipped in on the wind of the ship's passage and dripped
from the peaks of their caps on the bridge. All of them looked out
on the port bow and beam now, glasses and telescopes trained out
to sea. As were the loaded guns.

The report came down from the control-top. "Smoke Red three-
oh!" The glasses and telescopes jerked around.

Jameson muttered, "I can just see something."

Smith grunted. There was a dark streak lying like a short pencil
stroke along the grey line of the seaward horizon. *Dauntless* held
on. She and the ships out there were on opposite and parallel
courses. As the distance between them shrank, as they came
almost opposite each other, the control-top reported: "Warship
hull-down! Red eight-oh! It's *Walküre*, sure enough . . . smoke
astern of her, a mile or more. . . . It's that big freighter, *Friedrichsburg*, all right!"

The lowering sun was hidden behind leaden clouds. What dirty light there was came from beyond the seaward horizon so that from *Dauntless*'s control-top the ships on that horizon stood out against it. While from *Walküre* and *Friedrichsburg* they would see only grey ocean and grey mountains as there was no light behind *Dauntless*.

Now was the time. He ordered, "Port ten! . . . Steer one-nine-oh!" There was a shifting on the bridge now, then a settling-down again as the ship's head came round. Now they were committed. *Dauntless* was making twenty-nine knots, headed towards the enemy. Smith cocked an ear to the ranges continually repeated from the rangetaker. They were ranging on to *Walküre*.

He said, "We'll engage *Friedrichsburg*."

Before that could be relayed to the gunnery officer he was himself reporting, "*Walküre* has hauled out of line and she's headed out to sea, course about southwest!"

Jameson said, "*Blackbird*, sir?"

Smith nodded. *Walküre* would be going after *Blackbird*, fifteen miles to the southwest and towards the sinking sun. *Blackbird* and the tiny submarine-chaser. The decoys.

Jameson muttered, "I hope Pearce is ready to run."

". . . Nine-five-oh-oh! . . ." The range to *Friedrichsburg* was below five miles now, and the big freighter maintained her course, passing distantly across the bow from starboard to port. Even from the bridge they could see the ten thousand tons of her now, her big derricks and the single funnel belching out smoke.

Jameson said, "They must all be blind aboard her."

Smith thought she should have seen *Dauntless* even though she was still four miles away and in bad light. But they were also astern of *Friedrichsburg*, and all eyes in the freighter would be drawn in the opposite direction, to where *Walküre* had gone.

"*Walküre*'s opened fire!" That came from the control-top but on the bridge also they had seen those distant flashes eight miles away, out on the far horizon.

A chorus of voices shouted, "She's turning!" They referred to the freighter, swinging out to starboard to run after *Walküre*. Some lookout had finally turned his gaze astern. The rangetaker chanted, "Seven thousand!"

They were close enough. Smith snapped. "Hard aport! Open fire!" And as *Dauntless* turned to head south the barrels of the guns trained out to starboard fired, shaking the bridge. *Friedrichsburg* was showing her stern to them now and Smith saw the salvo fall to starboard of her but close alongside. The light was poor but *Friedrichsburg* a huge target. Smith thought briefly that the same could be said of *Blackbird* with that huge hangar and she was under fire from *Walküre* now. The chaser he did not worry about. She was small, and could look after herself. But he hoped that his own attack on the freighter would soon bring *Walküre* hurrying back. He did not want *Blackbird* and her crew on his conscience.

Dauntless fired again and Bright shouted excitedly, "Hit her!" Water was hurled up close to the freighter but one shell burst inboard with a streaking flash. The guns were firing with the relentless rhythm of a trip-hammer, three rounds a minute from each gun and a good half scoring, crashing down through the thin decks to explode below, tearing out the heart of the ship.

At the end of a few minutes of that punishment she had three fires and smoke trailed from the length of her. Soon afterwards she swerved to port and her speed fell away. They watched the murderous pounding in silence on the bridge of *Dauntless* as she closed the freighter. Smith said, "Tell the torpedo-gunner to fire when he's ready."

Seconds later two torpedoes leaped from the tubes amidships and their tracks streaked out towards the freighter. The range was down to three thousand yards and the 6-inch guns still hammered.

Jameson said, "She hasn't struck." Smith knew he could not take this ship prisoner, not with *Walküre* only a scant few miles away. *Friedrichsburg* had to be sunk. But he admired the courage of the German crew and was not enjoying this.

Nor were the others on the bridge. A mutter ran through them as Henderson said, "God! She's blown up!" They saw debris flying into the sky and raining down while the ship listed, settling. That was when the torpedoes struck her, breath-held seconds between the two muffled explosions. They rumbled dully. Smith turned his ship to pass close across the bow of the blazing freighter. Almost immediately she lay over still further and smoke roared out of her. *Friedrichsburg* would sink in minutes.

He had stood with arms rested on the screen, watching stone-faced, but now he stirred. All through the action reports had been coming in: "*Walküre* firing. . . . *Walküre* ceased firing." And now "*Walküre* turning. Bears Red seven-five. Six miles." Smith walked out to the port wing of the bridge. He peered through the glasses, searching for the big German cruiser and found her, a tiny blip on that grey horizon. She was tearing back, too late, to the ship that she had thought safe astern of her as she steamed out to meet the threat from the southwest.

He ordered, "Steer northeast by north! Full ahead both!" That was a course to take *Dauntless* running away from *Walküre*. "Make a signal to the admiral. . . ." Now he could break wireless silence and report to Braddock.

Jameson said, "She's opened fire, sir."

Smith nodded. Huge shells were shrieking through the atmosphere towards *Dauntless*. But *Walküre*'s shooting would be largely based on guesswork. *Dauntless* was hardly a target at all, stern on and against the grey background of the coast. He was not surprised when the salvo fell half-mile astern.

Jameson said, "*Friedrichsburg* is going, sir!"

They could hardly see the big freighter now under the huge cloud of smoke that trailed from her, just the tilted masts which, as Smith watched, slipped from sight. He made out two boats pulling clear of the smoke so some few souls had survived the hail of fire that *Dauntless* had poured into their luckless ship.

He shifted the glasses until *Walküre* appeared in the distance. Another salvo from her plunged into the sea, still short by a quarter-mile or more. He wondered what her captain would do? Engage in a chase of *Dauntless*, that experience would have taught him he could not catch? Return to Alexandretta? But she would hardly have come this far solely to escort that one freighter, vital though her cargo might be.

"Control-top reports she's turning, sir." That was Jameson.

Smith answered, "Yes." He waited, as they were all waiting on the bridge, to see what *Walküre* would do now.

"Control-top reports she's steering southeast, sir."

If *Walküre* could see those two life boats, she was not going to try to pick up the survivors. That was only to be expected, while

148

Dauntless was in the vicinity. Smith knew now that she was headed for Gaza and Deir el Belah, to shell the shipping anchored off Allenby's forward base, and all the back area running up to Gaza and crowded with troops.

He ordered, "Port ten!" And: "Steer two-oh-oh!" *Dauntless* was now chasing after *Walküre* at full speed, headed a point or two to seaward of her. With *Blackbird* no longer a decoy he did not relish being trapped between her and the mountainous shore. *Blackbird* . . . he wondered briefly how Pearce had fared.

He dictated a signal to Braddock, reporting the survivors from *Friedrichsburg* he'd been forced to leave behind, giving *Walküre's* course and speed and what he believed were *Walküre's* intentions. Then he told Jameson, "I want the men fed. One man from each detachment to go to the galley to draw for the rest. We've got something like half an hour, I think." Provided *Walküre* kept her course till he caught up, and he was coldly certain that she would.

LOFTY WILLIAMS, the wireless telegraphist, found himself outside the galley alongside Buckley and said, "No orders come over the wireless but it looks like your bloke's going to have a go anyway."

Buckley shrugged, "He doesn't hang about waiting for orders."

"How d'ye reckon our chances?"

Buckley looked at him and said patiently, "You've seen this bloody big cruiser before, haven't you?"

"Cruiser! Jimmy-the-one calls her a pocket-sized battleship!" Ackroyd's description had stuck.

Buckley said, "Well, then?"

Lofty blinked at him, thought it over, then said, "Ah! Well."

Buckley nodded. "That's right. But I'll say this much: You'll have a better chance with Smith than with anybody else."

ON THE BRIDGE Jameson said, "Signal from the admiral, sir."

Smith read it, brief and to the point: "Engage the enemy." So Braddock also had seen the danger and had the courage to send that signal, knowing that a battle with *Walküre* must mean the destruction of *Dauntless*. But in that battle *Dauntless* might cripple *Walküre* so that she would be forced to abandon her mission. It was only a possibility, but *Dauntless* could not simply stand by while *Walküre* roared down on Deir el Belah. And the relieving ships, *Attack* and *Océan,* would not come up in time.

He asked, "What's her speed?"

Henderson answered, "She is making around fifteen knots."

But *Walküre* was capable of twenty-four knots, so why was she steaming comparatively easily now? Trouble with her engines? He walked out to the wing of the bridge and stared out at her. The ship was still just a speck off the port bow, but he watched her for a long time as they crept up on her.

Jameson came to stand at his shoulder. "Strange that she hasn't fired, sir. We're within range of her."

"Just." Smith answered absently, mind probing at the problem, seeking the reason for *Walküre*'s behaviour. He said, "Too far for good shooting in this light."

"Our guns can't reach her."

Not yet, thought Smith, but when they closed her. . . . The answer came to him then. *Walküre*'s captain knew that Smith dared not let him reach Deir el Belah without a fight, so he was waiting for *Dauntless* to try to close within range of her own 6-inch guns. Then she would make a sitting target. He had to settle with her so he would do it now, in the light of day, not risking a night action. And Smith dared not wait for the night either. If he lost *Walküre* in the darkness then with the dawn she would come roaring in on Deir el Belah. She had chosen the place and the time and Smith could do nothing but accept the challenge.

The crew of *Dauntless* had eaten and now they were at their action stations and ready to fight. On *Walküre*'s terms? Smith rubbed at his face. He had to do something to shorten the odds against them, could not throw them senselessly into the path of destruction. And what, he thought, of *Blackbird* and the sub-chaser? His orders had been, once the Germans had been drawn away, for them to circle out of range, and return to Deir el Belah. He could only pray that they had survived the first brief minutes of *Walküre*'s attack.

He turned and saw Jameson waiting for an answer. He forced a smile. "Pass the word for the men to rest at their action stations."

Jameson blinked. Why this delay? But Smith had turned away. Jameson answered, "Aye, aye, sir."

150

So they rested at the guns as *Dauntless* raced on at near thirty knots and they saw *Walküre* slide slowly down the port quarter until she was miles astern. They grumbled because of this stretching of their nerves, and looked up at the bridge where Smith stood out on the wing. "What the 'ell is he waiting for?"

Smith was working out a little problem in relative times and distances as he listened to the bearings and ranges monotonously repeated. He had the answer now, turned and walked back to the centre of the bridge. The bridge staff watched him come and Buckley, seeing the quick, restless stride, thought, "Here we go!"

Smith ordered, "Action stations! Make smoke!"

The wind was still out of the northwest. As the funnels began to belch out thick, oily smoke the wind rolled it down across the sea astern to drift out eastward and southward. Soon it had drifted far enough to hide *Walküre* from them. *Dauntless* maintained her course and her speed as the trail lengthened and spread astern of her. Smith joked, "A little of that goes a long way." That only brought tight smiles from one or two on the bridge. Smith supposed his own act did not fool them. Was it an act? No, the uneasiness, the tension had gone from him now, leaving only excitement.

He looked out at the smoke. Five minutes had laid a screen better than two miles long between him and *Walküre* and now *Dauntless* could achieve an element of surprise. "Hard astarboard!" She came around to run back along her wake. Now they were rushing down past the smoke that banked to starboard of them. Smith looked at his watch, a minute had passed.

"Starboard ten! Tell Guns to fire when he's ready!" *Dauntless* swerved into the smoke and it closed all around them. It caught at their throats and their eyes watered. But now the smoke was thinning, becoming patchy so that they caught glimpses of grey sky. *Walküre* would be waiting for them but her guns would not be laid on *Dauntless* until she appeared out of the smoke and that could be anywhere along its two mile length. That would give *Dauntless* some seconds of breathing space, all the surprise Smith could wring for her but it was better than none.

There was light ahead, patches of sea visible through the smoke. Bright shouted, "Fine on the port bow!"

Dauntless fired with the forward 6-inch, the only gun that would bear. Smith ordered, "Starboard ten!" Then, as the ship came broadside on so that both forward and aft guns would bear, "Meet her! Steer that!" Both 6-inch guns fired—and twenty seconds later they fired again.

Jameson said excitedly, "Caught her on the hop!"

"Starboard ten!" Smith watched the enemy as *Dauntless* headed back towards the smoke. *Walküre* had finally got her guns trained around and he saw the ripple of flame down her side, the wisping of smoke as the salvo was hurled at him. Also a yellow flash and a spurt of smoke in her stern.

He nodded as Jameson shouted, "That was a hit!" The 6-inch aft still fired as they rushed back into the smoke. *Walküre*'s salvo fell well astern in a close-packed line of waterspouts, then the gun fell silent as the smoke swirled around them, choking again, but nobody minded. The signal yeoman smiled wryly at young Bright who was laughing, excited, but Jameson said thoughtfully, "That salvo of theirs was well together."

"Port ten!" Smith's eyes were on his watch as *Dauntless* emerged on the seaward side of the smoke and turned to run south on her original course, still trailing smoke.

So for thirty seconds, then: "Port ten!" *Dauntless* plunged back into the smoke, tore through it and burst out into the open sea. *Walküre* had turned and was steering towards the long bank of smoke. This time both the 6-inch guns bore. They got off two salvoes before *Walküre* could reply and by then *Dauntless* was already heeling in the turn, spray bursting in a fine curtain over the bow, and the guns training around. They fired two more salvoes and the second scored, hitting *Walküre* amidships and right aft. As *Dauntless* rushed into the smoke the shells from *Walküre* plummeted close alongside in huge green towers of water.

They passed through the acrid pall into the grey light of the dying day. Smith did not want the range opening further because that was to *Walküre*'s advantage. "Starboard ten!" He sent *Dauntless* running northward with the smoke lying to starboard, until he ordered again, "Starboard ten!"

They were becoming used to the dive into the smoke now, though it was not so thick here so their emergence into the open came sooner. *Walküre* had turned and was heading south again, closing the range as *Dauntless* had done. Smith saw she still had a fire aft. As the 6-inch guns fired, the ripple of *Walküre*'s salvo ran along her side. Smith waited for the guns to fire again and, as the shudder of them laid *Dauntless* over, he ordered, "Starboard ten! Steer two-six-oh!" But as the stern began to swing the salvo from *Walküre* came in.

They did not hear it coming. There was only the shock of it, a glimpse of the sea lifting right under the bow and then a blinding light as the end shell of the salvo burst forward of the bridge. If her turn had been delayed for a second then *Dauntless* would have steamed under the whole salvo and probably that would have been the end of her. It was almost the end of Smith. He was lifted from his feet and hurled backwards. He felt the cushioning bodies beneath him as he hit the back of the bridge and then the air was agonizingly driven out of him as someone crashed onto his chest. He was still for only a second then shoved the man on top of him aside. It was Jameson, lifting a hand that dripped blood. Smith climbed to his feet and lurched to the front of the bridge.

He looked around him. The coxswain lay dead on the deck, but the quartermaster was now at the wheel and *Dauntless* was still turning in accordance with Smith's last order, onto the bearing that would take her back to the sheltering smoke. The quartermaster reported, "Course is two-six-oh, sir!"

There was not only the screening smoke ahead now. It poured also from the foredeck where the 6-inch lay askew on its mounting, its crew scattered around it. Smith looked out to starboard and saw *Walküre* fire again as there came the shudder and slam of the gun firing aft, the only 6-inch left to them. Smith told the quartermaster, "Keep her at that."

There were huge holes torn by ragged lumps of steel in the splinter mattresses around the bridge screen. But men from the heap of bodies at the back were pulling themselves upright and one by one the men were crawling to their feet and staggering back to their posts.

Ackroyd came on to the bridge and said hoarsely, "Forward 6-inch is a wreck. The fire is still burning but under control. How are things up here?"

Smith glanced around at the quartermaster at the wheel, at Henderson, Bright, Buckley. "We'll cope." He asked Jameson, "How's the hand?"

"I'll be all right, sir."

The smoke whipped around them now but *Dauntless* was hit again. It shook them on the bridge so they all staggered, and Smith saw the smoke and flames soaring aft. Almost immediately he felt the ship's speed fall away. He told Ackroyd, "Let me have a report as soon as you can." And said to Jameson, "Ask the chief as well."

Smith thought *Dauntless* could barely be making ten knots now as she limped away from the smoke that was shredding on the wind. But neither smoke nor poor visibility could hide *Dauntless* for long while the fire roared aft to mark her position for *Walküre's* guns, a pillar of flame bent by the wind of passage. Only distance would save her now.

He ordered changes of course to try to evade the plummeting shells that fell every thirty seconds. For a time he could not see the enemy ship and the salvoes screamed down as if simply hurled from the sky. Then Bright shouted, "Enemy Green one-oh-oh!"

Smith saw *Walküre* distantly off the starboard quarter, headed southward. No doubt her captain had deduced that if *Dauntless* had broken off the action she was probably too badly damaged to continue it. He would not engage in a pursuit drawing him northward because he had easier meat waiting for him in the south at Gaza and Deir el Belah. Smith watched *Walküre* bitterly as she drew farther and farther away, still firing from her after-turret.

The chief's voice came up the voicepipe from the engine room. "It's a right mess down here, sir. To start with—"

Smith cut in, "Details later, Chief, please. For now, what speed can you give us?"

"Maybe another couple of knots. It'll take a dockyard to—"

"I know nobody could do more than you, Chief. My thanks to all of you." Smith shut the cover on the voicepipe and wondered what it must be like for the chief, his engineers and stokers trapped far below deck when *Dauntless* was hit, expecting any moment that the engine room would become a flaming coffin.

Ackroyd reported over the voicepipe, "We took two hits aft, sir.

Luckily neither holed us below the waterline, but that's all the good news. The 6-inch is wrecked. So are the gig and the motor-boat, the 3-inch and some searchlights. And the starboard torpedo tubes; the training and firing gear is smashed to bits.''

These reports from the chief and the damage control officers meant that though *Dauntless* survived as a ship she was written off as a threat to *Walküre*. The shells continued to harass *Dauntless*, though *Walküre* herself disappeared. But finally the shells ceased screaming in and there were some minutes of blessed peace.

Ackroyd climbed onto the bridge, his face soot-blackened and his jacket burned down one sleeve. He reported huskily, ''Fire's out, sir.'' He looked at Smith, that look asking, ''What now?''

12 Make or Break

Dauntless was running northward. Smith ordered, ''Steer one-six-five!'' and Dauntless edged around onto the course that set her in hopeless pursuit of *Walküre*. They would never catch her.

The bridge had been hurriedly swept and swabbed, the debris cleared away. But as he looked along the length of *Dauntless* it hurt him to see the wreck the battle had made of her. He saw Bright, a small dishevelled figure, puffy-eyed with weariness, and thought Adeline Brett would mother the boy if she was there and give Smith the edge of her tongue because of him. That set him grinning and he called, ''Buckley! See if you can get us some cof-fee, please! I've still got the taste of that smoke in my mouth!''

His grin had an effect on them all and the bridge became a more cheerful place. He told himself that they had done all that men could. If anyone had failed it was himself. Now he must send a signal to Braddock telling him *Dauntless* was crippled and *Walküre* running loose, another repeating that to *Blackbird* and calling her to maintain radio silence and join him. And he must hope.

Dauntless crept southward. Smith stood pressed against the torn screen, chin rested on his folded arms and his face impassive. He pictured the anchorage at Deir el Belah, and the ships that in a few hours would be penned there under the guns of *Walküre;* while *Dauntless* limped southward and he stood helpless on her bridge.

THE REPORT came down from the control-top high above the bridge: "Ship bearing Red one-oh!"

Smith set the glasses to his eyes; every pair of glasses on the bridge was in use now.

Ackroyd said slowly, "I think—it's *Blackbird,* sir." So did Smith. The square boxy shape, even seen dimly through the rain, could not be *Walküre,* had to be the seaplane carrier. The lookout in the top confirmed it. "Ship is *Blackbird,* sir, and that sub-chaser is with her."

Thank God! Smith rubbed at his eyes and said, "Make to *Blackbird:* 'Where is the enemy?'" He waited while the searchlight's shutter clattered and *Dauntless* slowly closed the gap between her and *Blackbird,* saw the light blinking back her answer.

The signal yeoman reported, "Enemy not sighted, sir."

Ackroyd said softly, "*Hell!*" But it was everything that Smith had hoped for. The sea was huge and it was easy enough for two ships to pass without sighting each other. It was quiet on the bridge, they were waiting for Smith to make his decision, give his orders. He stared out across the sea as if looking for *Walküre,* and so he was but only with his mind's eye. Some might think she had a dozen courses to choose from, but Smith knew she was racing for Gaza and Deir el Belah.

He pushed away from the screen and shifted restlessly about the bridge, the others sliding unobtrusively out of his way. Then he swung on the signal yeoman. "Make to *Blackbird:* 'Is aircraft now available and pilot prepared for reconnaissance?'"

The searchlight clattered and Ackroyd said doubtfully, "It's foul weather for flying." Smith pushed past him into the charthouse and laid off a course. He stood still and looked at it a long moment then went out onto the bridge. The signal lamp was flashing aboard *Blackbird* and the signal yeoman read: "Affirmative. Pilot and observer ready to fly."

Smith said shortly, "Belay that! Tell him to load one big bomb —and I'm going as observer."

156

For a moment there was silence except for the clatter of the lamp then Ackroyd said, "Sir—" But there he stopped.

Smith stared out at the sea, the long waves and the spume whipped from the tops of them on the wind. "I want to see for myself." He was so tired. He had scarcely slept since long before the raid on Lydda. But he would send no one else on this flight.

"Maitland is a good observer, sir. He could do it."

"No."

"Any attempt to take off in this sea will be risky, sir—" Smith shook his head and Ackroyd stepped closer, lowered his voice. "You've done enough, sir! Too much!"

Bright said, "They're bringing out Delilah." That caused an uneasy stir on the bridge. The plane's reputation was not forgotten.

Smith ordered, "Call away my boat." He started towards the ladder, but Ackroyd clutched at his arm.

"That bloody thing has killed five men that we know of and damned near killed a few more! I'm not superstitious but there's something wrong about that Short. It's a bad luck—"

"Rubbish!" Smith pulled away and glowered at Ackroyd, saw Buckley hovering and about to back him up. "That's enough! God Almighty! I never heard anything like it!" For a moment he glared at them and they stared back woodenly. He rubbed at his face and told Ackroyd, "We'll fly a course of one-six-five degrees. Follow us and report to the admiral."

He ran down the ladder from the bridge, strode aft to where they were lowering the cutter, and in the waist he saw Adeline Brett. She stood amid the wreckage, huddled into a bridge-coat someone had lent her, and it hung to her ankles. He halted and stared at her white face, into the wide eyes that watched him. He remembered her cabin aboard *Morning Star*, and how he had held her, but now he could find nothing to say.

He turned away and went down into the cutter where Buckley sat in the sternsheets, the tiller under his arm. The sea threw them about as they made the crossing and he saw Buckley glancing sideways at him, knew he was thinking that the odds were against the Short getting off, that the wind and the sea would wreck it. As they ran alongside *Blackbird*, he saw the Short on its trolley outside the hangar. Its propeller was a spinning disc as the pilot warmed up the engine. A little crowd of riggers and fitters were holding it down against the tearing wind.

Smith climbed aboard and up to the observer's cockpit, seeing the single big bomb slung under the fuselage, a 264-pounder. He settled into the cockpit, pulling on the leather flying helmet and goggles he found on the seat. The pilot stood up to hook the derrick purchase onto the ring. It was Pearce, of course. Just as this was the sole remaining aircraft, so Pearce was the only surviving pilot. Smith flew with him in Delilah or not at all.

Chris turned, his face drawn and the eyes dark in their sockets. He shouted, "Course, sir?"

Smith peered at him, the driven rain cold on his cheeks. "Fly a mean course of one-six-five degrees." That meant Pearce would search in doglegs along that line. But they were not in the air yet. Smith said, "You know what I want you to do."

Pearce only nodded, turned back and dropped into his seat. He reached down and the engine cut out. The winch hammered, the hands stood back from Delilah and she lifted from the deck, swung jerkily on the wind as the derricks swung out, then plummeted towards the waves.

As the floats smacked into the sea Pearce opened the cock on the bottle of compressed air and the engine fired again. He yanked at the toggle and the derrick purchase snapped away. The note of the engine rose. The waves were huge and the wings rocked under the thrusting wind, the floats at the wingtips smashing into the sea. Pearce fought her into the wind with a burst of the throttle and kept her there. Smith could see the concentration on his face as his head turned. Now he looked back at Smith and shouted, "Ready?" He grinned recklessly and was, for a moment, the old Chris Pearce that Smith had first known.

Smith shouted back, "Right!" and Pearce swung away and opened the throttle. Delilah hammered across the rutted surface of the sea, bucking and rocking while the spray burst up from the floats and flailed over the open cockpits. Through the water that streamed across his goggles Smith saw Pearce shoving forward the big wheel on the control column and felt the tail float lift off. Delilah tried to slide sideways and one wing dipped, but Pearce

158

yanked her into the wind once more, straightened her up. He hauled back on the big wheel, and she lifted off.

Smith hardly dared to believe it. Delilah tilted and soared as the wind shook her, but they were airborne and climbing. He thought that only Pearce could have done it; Chris was the best pilot of them all. He peered down at the ships falling away below, the boot-shaped *Blackbird* with the patch on her side marked by the now new paint, *Dauntless* with her upper deck devastated.

Five minutes later they levelled off at a thousand feet, and Pearce started flying the doglegs of the search.

THERE WAS little daylight left, and they should turn back soon if they were to find *Blackbird* again. But Smith was certain *Walküre* lay ahead of them, would not turn back while there was yet light. He shifted in the cockpit, checked because for a moment he thought. . . .

He stood up and leaned to one side, pushing up the goggles. He tapped Pearce's shoulder and pointed to a patch of darkness in the murk ahead. Pearce nodded, eased the Short over a point or two and steadied it on the new course. *Was* it smoke? There was something . . . it was smoke . . . *and under it a ship!*

Pearce yelled, "That's her!"

Smith dropped back in his seat, switched on the wireless, unreeled the aerial furiously, then tapped out *Walküre*'s position and course as Pearce sent Delilah sliding down after the cruiser. Smith wondered if his signal was being received or whether they were out of range. He reeled in the aerial as Pearce glanced back at him and nodded, tight-lipped.

Pearce eased forward the wheel, Delilah's nose dipped and their dive steepened until Smith could see over Pearce and the upper wing to *Walküre* floating up towards them. They had been seen. Guns were flaming aboard the big cruiser and the Short lurched as a shell burst close, then steadied under Pearce's hands.

Walküre was big now and Smith saw there was damage amidships and aft and one gun pointed askew. She was huge! Pearce hauled back on the wheel and Delilah pulled out of the dive with her floats skimming the surface of the sea. They were under the traverse of the worst of *Walküre*'s guns. Smoke from *Walküre*'s funnels rolled down across the sea, half-hiding them for the crucial approach. But then they were through it, above it as Delilah climbed. She lurched again, side-slipped, then swept through a torrent of fire, low over *Walküre*'s stern. Smith remembered Pearce's harsh dictum: "To hit a ship under way you'd have to sit the Short on the funnel!"

Pearce did it.

The smoke-belching funnels loomed like towers as Delilah bucked wildly in the heat-laden air they streamed. Smith saw Pearce yank on the toggle release, felt the lift as the bomb fell away and a second later they were past *Walküre*, tearing away over open sea. He twisted round and saw the after of the two funnels topple and the smoke jetting, the wreckage soaring, felt and heard the explosion. *Walküre*'s guns were still firing. Delilah shook again and again, holes appeared in the fuselage and fabric streamed on the wind then tore away.

The Short was turning in a shallow bank to port. *Walküre* was far behind them but Smith saw she still poured out smoke and she was stopped. There was neither bow wave nor wake. *Walküre* lay dead on the sea.

He thumped Pearce on the shoulder and bawled, "You *got* her, Chris!" Pearce looked round and his teeth showed in a grin but then he turned back and briefly his head sagged, jerked up again to peer ahead. Smith shouted, "Chris! Are you all right?" Pearce nodded but he was lying. Smith could see the great holes torn around the pilot's cockpit. He shouted again, "Anything I can do?" This time Pearce shook his head. Slowly Smith wound out the aerial and switched on the wireless, tapped out that *Walküre* was hit and stopped and her position. That Delilah was returning. She droned on, shot through and tattered, over a darkening sea.

He was first to see the light that wavered on the horizon like a beckoning finger. He leaned forward to point it out to Pearce who nodded. They flew on towards the light and soon Smith made out through the rain and the darkness closing around them that it was a searchlight from *Dauntless*. *Blackbird* was alongside her and stopped to make a lee.

Pearce had shrunk down in his seat, but Smith grabbed his shoulders and hoisted him upright, held him there. Pearce turned

Delilah into the wind and brought her down until she skimmed
the tops of the waves then rubbed the floats into them, set her
down in a burst of spray. Smith's arms ached with holding Pearce
as the pilot worked the throttle and the Short swerved erratically
into *Blackbird*'s lee, turned too late and crumpled a wing against
the ship's side, despite the seamen on the rubbing strake striving
to boom her off. The engine cut out. Smith had to let go of Pearce
to crawl past him and grab at the heaving line, haul down the
block and hook on the Short. He turned then and saw Pearce collapsed in the cockpit. He reached down to lift his head.

Pearce said, "Good old Delilah."

Smith barely heard the whispered words, felt Pearce sag. The
winch hammered but as the wire tautened the ring on the Short's
centre-section tore loose. Smith realized that its retaining wires
must have been cut by shellfire, also that, with the Short not
secured, she would smash herself to pieces against *Blackbird*'s hull.

"Sir!"

He twisted around to see the cutter slipping in below him.
"Give me a hand here!" he croaked. "Mr. Pearce is hit!"

Two of the cutter's crew clawed their way up to him and
together they got Pearce down into the
boat as the sea pounded Delilah onto the
steel of the ship's side. The cutter
pulled back to *Dauntless* where
Merryweather waited, but Chris
Pearce died in Smith's arms
in the cutter.

Smith went to the
bridge and asked
Ackroyd, "You re-
ceived our signals?"

Ackroyd frowned.
"Signals? Only
one that said
Walküre was stopped
and you were on your
way back." So if they
had been shot out of

the sky as Pearce made his attack, then the cruiser's position would never have been reported. He looked across, saw the fitters trying to get lines around the damaged Short, and ordered Ackroyd, "Tell them to sink her." Then he added, "We haven't time." That was as explanation, and it was true. There were many who would be glad to see the last of Delilah, but it was the war, not Delilah, that had killed Chris Pearce. Delilah had found *Walküre* for them, in Pearce's hands had stopped her and then got them home. And Chris was dead.

He stirred uneasily, turned his back on Delilah as *Dauntless* got under way. It was true they could not waste a second rescuing a smashed seaplane—*Walküre* had been stopped but her engineers might get steam on her again. So *Dauntless* worked up to her pitiful best speed of twelve knots while *Blackbird* took up station to port and the little chaser to starboard. They went hunting *Walküre* in a creeping line.

Henderson, one eye on Smith propped against the bridge screen, said, "This is like shoving your head in the lion's mouth."

He was right.

DAUNTLESS rocked to a beam sea and the rain made worse the darkness of the night. Smith asked Jameson, "Torpedo gunner is ready?"

"Yes, sir."

"He fires on my order and not before. Tell him."

Because they would only get one chance.

Walküre, if she were still stopped, was somewhere close ahead of them. She still had teeth, more than enough to deal with this puny force of ships. Smith rubbed sore and aching eyes, set the glasses to them again. He picked out *Blackbird* under her smoke, then swept the glasses slowly through an arc across the bow of *Dauntless* and then on, seeking the chaser now. He only found her because he knew where to look. Low in the water as she was, only the broken water of her bow and the phosphorescence of her wake marked her.

Jameson said softly, "Hell of a game of blindman's buff."

Apart from her labouring engines the ship was eerily quiet, as if every man aboard her held his breath, waiting for the flash out in

162

the darkness and the shattering blow from the salvo that would follow if *Walküre* saw them first. . . .

The flash and the crash came as one and snapped their heads around.

"Chaser, sir!" That was Bright reporting. But all of them had seen the explosion to starboard. Was she hit? A heartbeat later a starshell burst ahead and to starboard. The chaser had not been hit but had fired her gun and the starshell lit *Walküre*.

"Starboard ten!" Smith gave the order as he saw *Walküre* was still stopped and a scant mile away. As the darkness rushed back to hide *Walküre* he ordered, "Steady! . . . Steer that!"

Beams of searchlights poked out from *Walküre* and fingered jerkily across the surface of the sea until one of them found the chaser. She was turning as she fired her little 3-inch again and a second starshell burst above *Walküre* as gun flashes prickled along the big cruiser's side. The fall of those shells hid the chaser in huge towers of water, and when these had fallen she was gone.

A gun cracked again to starboard and Jameson yelled, "The chaser ducked out of it! Bloody good, Petersen!"

The beams of light were searching frantically in a torn and empty sea. Smith's orders to both the chaser and *Blackbird* had been to draw the fire to give *Dauntless* a chance to close. As things had turned out Petersen had drawn the short straw because *Walküre* lay at his end of the line. They were certain to sink him in minutes—Smith knew that, but it was the only way he might win that one chance for *Dauntless*.

But *Walküre* was alive to the threat now. The searchlights were sweeping all around her, not just seeking the chaser. And this was no textbook torpedo attack by a destroyer hurtling in at thirty knots; this was a battered light cruiser limping to destruction. But they were closing. *Walküre* lay only a half-mile distant.

A beam flickered over *Dauntless* and on, wavered, returned and it lit them all on the bridge. Smith ordered, "Starboard ten!" and the bow started to swing. Flashes licked out at them from *Walküre* and a second later hell broke loose on *Dauntless*.

She rocked and shook through her frame as the shells hit her, flame spurted and splinters whirred. The tripod mast fell to hang against the starboard side with the control-top over the sea. Rigging collapsed across the bridge and a big double-pulley block felled Henderson. The top of the second funnel disappeared, blasted out of existence, and it seemed that the length of the upper deck was aflame. Smith was numbly aware that *Dauntless* was still turning, Jameson and Bright stood with him while Buckley stooped over Henderson. *Walküre* lay to port and she was so close the black bulk of her filled his vision. He croaked, "Fire torpedoes!" then lurched across to the port wing of the bridge to stare aft, squinting against the smoke and the glare of searchlight. He saw the gunner at the port tubes, saw one torpedo leap out into the sea, then the other. Guns flashed again on *Walküre* and he was thrown to the deck as the shells ripped into *Dauntless*.

She still turned. He pulled himself up by the screen, held on to it and stared across at *Walküre* as *Dauntless* slowly swung away so now the big cruiser was off the port quarter. At any second another broadside would come from her and *Dauntless* could not stand much more.

The sea lifted against *Walküre*'s side right under her bridge and a second later it spouted again below the solitary funnel the bomb had left her. The thumping explosions came to him across the sea dividing the ships, and the beams of the searchlights jerked away, wandering aimlessly about the sea as if the directing hands had been torn from them. The salvo did not come. *Walküre* was slipping astern of them now.

He shouted hoarsely, "Meet her! . . . Steer that!"

The searchlights went out and he peered blindly into the rain and the darkness that was broken by the yellow lick of the fires that roared around *Dauntless*. He was certain *Walküre* was finished but he had to be sure. While he listened to Ackroyd's damage report, the torpedo gunner and his crew were loading the tubes again.

When Ackroyd had finished Smith summed up for him: "So we're afloat and under way and that's the best you can say." Ackroyd nodded, the whites of his eyes gleaming through the grime. Smith said, "We'll attack again."

Dauntless turned and dragged herself once more towards her quarry, while Ackroyd's exhausted parties still fought the fires aft and in the smoke-filled inferno below. Ackroyd went down to that inferno but paused briefly at the door of the sick bay to shove his head in and ask, "How're things, Doc?"

Merryweather did not look up from the gash he was stitching, only jerked his head sideways indicating the crowded sick bay. He seemed to work in air made thick with the smell of blood and antiseptic. "As you see. What's happening?"

Ackroyd answered, "We're attacking again." He pushed away from the door and was gone to his duties.

Merryweather whispered, "My God!" His gaze fastened on Adeline Brett where she knelt on the deck, her quick fingers completing the dressing on a man's chest. He smiled down at her weakly and gratefully. She rose to her feet and drew the back of her hand across her brow.

Matthews, the cook, had brought in a man clutching a make-shift bandage about his leg and sat him against the bulkhead. As the cook made to leave Merryweather said, "Here, Matthews, take Miss Brett on deck and see her safe under cover."

Adeline protested. "Why? I'm perfectly all right. I—"

Merryweather cut her short. "Never mind what she says. Take her out of this if you have to carry her, and get some clean air into her lungs." To himself he added, "We'll need her again soon. Or she might get a chance in a boat or a life-raft."

The cook's hand encircled Adeline's arm and she had to go.

BLACKBIRD and the chaser were left astern; there was no point in exposing them again to *Walküre's* guns. Smith stared at the fires aboard the big cruiser as *Dauntless* crept towards her. He ordered, "Searchlight."

The beam swept out and edged along *Walküre's* length. She was listed to port and down by the head, already her deck forward was awash as far as the bridge. Boats were clustered at her side and filling with men, while other crowded boats pulled away from her. They were launching life-rafts. Smith said quietly, "Slow ahead both." *Dauntless* slowed until there was barely a ripple at her stern as she edged in towards *Walküre* and the boats.

Lofty Williams came from the wireless office aft, climbed the twisted ladder to the bridge and handed the signal to Smith. "From the admiral, sir."

Smith read it and lifted his eyes, saw them all watching him and said, "The Australians have taken Beersheba."

There was a moment of silence then Jameson said, without expression, "Oh, good."

It was not just good but tremendous news. This was the victory for which they had all suffered. General Allenby had secured the pivot on which he would turn to roll up the Gaza-Beersheba line, and maybe soon this war would end. Jameson and the others were just too benumbed to take it in. They would celebrate, but later.

They also had gained a victory. But they had paid an awful price. Smith looked from the blank, white face of the boy, Bright, aft along the torn length of *Dauntless*, then across to where *Blackbird* and the submarine-chaser were coming up out of the night. Men were on the decks staring silently at the stricken, sinking *Walküre*. There was no cheering. Adeline Brett stood, a small figure seen in the shifting light from the flames, the pale blur of her face turned up to the bridge.

Smith thought they had all paid. So long as he lived he would remember the red dust coating Taggart's battalion and the yelling madness of their night attack at Lydda, the roaring rush of the Australians' charge falling like a hammer on the Turks. The cold-blooded, calculating courage of Edwards, and Chris Pearce flying in at masthead height to ram the bomb into *Walküre*'s heart.

He had known from the start that this campaign would make or break him and he had not broken. He moved to his chair by the bridge screen and pulled himself stiffly up into it. "Make to *Blackbird* and the chaser: 'Stand by to recover survivors.'"

Buckley came with a blanket and hung it around his shoulders, but Smith did not notice as he hunched under the rain. *Dauntless* was not finished, nor was he.

AT FIVE P.M. on 31st October 1917, the 4th Brigade, Australian Light Horse captured the fortress of Beersheba with a cavalry charge, probably the greatest and last of them all.

And at noon on 11th December 1917, Allenby, the cavalry general, walked into Jerusalem, a conqueror going on foot like a penitent.

Alan Evans

Alan Evans's career with the Inland Revenue was being interrupted for just one day. It was a hectic day, too. On the morning we met, this popular author had just recorded an interview for Radio London's breakfast-time programme, and he was scheduled to take part in a book programme for the Forces Network in the afternoon. The publication of *Dauntless* has created enormous interest in the media, following the success of his two previous Great War sea adventure stories. But Alan Evans has no intention of allowing himself to be carried away by all this flattering attention. His regime will remain unchanged: each night he returns from the office, showers, has dinner with his family, and by eight o'clock is sitting at his desk. Then he writes until his patient wife comes into his den to stop him at ten o'clock, "or else I'd write all through the night," he says. "For me, writing is like an itch, and it won't go away!"

Soon he is off to Rome and Venice to carry out research for his next book, which is about the battle immortalized in Ernest Hemingway's classic *A Farewell to Arms*. Alan Evans's research is always meticulous. Before writing *Dauntless* he spent a week in Israel, where he walked every step of the route taken by Commander Smith during the raid on the ammunition dump, just to make sure that the raid would have worked. He discovered some interesting facts. For instance, although the railway that Smith and his crew so expertly disrupted in *Dauntless* did exist around that time, a short while later the Turks removed the tracks because they were needed elsewhere. His visit to Deir el Belah wasn't so necessary, however. "I had read the official history and the memoirs of many Australian cavalry men before my trip," he said. "Funnily enough, the town was exactly as I had imagined it."

The first books Alan Evans wrote were for children, and he would eventually like to return to writing children's stories. For the moment, however, he has enough ideas for Commander Smith's future to keep them both busy for a long while yet. C.C.

A CONDENSATION OF THE BOOK BY

Louis Charbonneau

Illustrated by Walter Rane

PUBLISHED BY DOUBLEDAY, NEW YORK

He had always known some people would be hurt . . . . It was inevitable, even necessary. Otherwise they would never be terrified enough to believe him . . . .

The city of Hollister is proud of the new central computer system that regulates all its public services—gas and electricity, traffic lights, fire alarms, hospital records—until an old man is found dead, victim of a computer "error". And that's only the beginning. Soon a string of computer-related disasters has the city stunned and cowering.

To Security Chief Michael Egan and his beautiful colleague Jennifer Tyson, what's happening is clear. Someone has penetrated the system and turned it to his own sinister ends. Who is this Intruder? And what else does he have in store?

Here is a chilling, informative novel of computer crime—a mind-boggling look at the potential for sabotage and blackmail that lurks within a modern computer system.

PART ONE
BREACH

ART Prochaska was baffled. He paid all his bills on time—always had—and he had paid his last utility bill promptly. It was that damned fool computer that got everything mixed up.

"I was in before," he said to the service representative on the phone, "and I talked to Mrs. Hemmings. She said I'd either get a new bill or the correction would be on my next billing."

"Mrs. Hemmings is on her break right now," the woman said stiffly. "If you'll hold on, I'll see if I can locate your file."

Snappish, Art Prochaska thought. Not like Mrs. Hemmings, who had been concerned and helpful when Art went in the first time to complain. He'd taken a liking to her right off. Reminded him a lot of Wilma. She wore the same little half glasses Wilma used for reading and her needlepoint. After studying the offending bill, Mrs. Hemmings had checked the file and agreed there was some mistake. Unaccountably Prochaska had been back-charged for service he had already paid for. Mrs. Hemmings explained that she could not make the correction herself; it wasn't done that simply anymore, because the computer handled all billing. One of the

171

young girls in back who were trained as operators on the computer would have to put in the correction.

Now, two weeks later, instead of a corrected bill, he had received a cutoff notice! The flat, impersonal, computerized note at the bottom of his bill read: NOTICE—DELINQUENT—SUBJECT TO SHUTOFF IF NOT PAID BY 05:00 PM JAN 28.

The deadline was today, and Prochaska had not even received the notice until the mail arrived, just after two.

The service representative came back on the line and said there did seem to be some confusion over Prochaska's bill. It would be better if he could come in.

"I can't come in this afternoon. My arthritis has been actin' up, and I can't drive, and there's nobody I can get to bring me in today. Listen, I don't want my power cut off without a by-your-leave. I always pay my bills. It's your mistake, not mine."

"There's no reason to get excited, Mr. Prochaska. No one's cutting you off. The computer sends out those notices automatically when payment isn't received. But I've talked to the computer operator. She tells me a correction was entered the last time you were in. For some reason that correction didn't get into the file at the Regional Data Center, which handles our billing now. I've put a note in your file, and an inspector will be out to check the readings at your house as soon as possible."

Somewhat mollified, Art Prochaska hung up. He hobbled into the kitchen, favoring his left hip, the one with the metal socket. That operation had not been entirely successful, leaving him in permanent pain. He rummaged among the dirty dishes beside the sink until he dug out a mug. He rinsed it out and poured coffee from the pot simmering on the stove. The brew was thick and black, left over from breakfast. He stood motionless for a moment, remembering the taste of Wilma's coffee, smooth and rich.

Shaking his head, he carried his mug into the living room, careless of the trail of spilled drops. Prochaska no longer noticed the patina of dust over everything, or the soiled sofa. At some point of past concern he had draped an old bedspread over his favorite chair. That was the most he would do. He settled into the chair with relief and glanced out the front window.

The house, at the edge of an older section of Hollister, New York, was set well back from the road, inconspicuous among the mature oak trees and evergreens that sheltered it. Few who drove by on the highway even noticed it. There were no close neighbors. The nearest was Mrs. Ringer, the one with all the dogs she was always turning loose to soil his lawn instead of her own. Not that the lawn amounted to much anymore. Last summer Evelyn's boy, Johnny, had done the yard a couple of times when they came over from Mount Washington for a visit. Prochaska smiled faintly at the memory of his grandson's short-lived enthusiasm for the chore. The smile faded. Evelyn didn't get over to Hollister much these days, or even telephone.

He felt a touch of cold. A storm was coming. Hell of a time to threaten cutting off a man's power, he thought, even someone who *hadn't* paid his bill. Art Prochaska prided himself on paying his debts. Except for the mortgage on the house, he and Wilma had tried to pay cash for what they needed. Of course, it had been different with the service station. You bought oil and gas on credit from the company, and you sold it on credit to most of your customers. There were days when he never took in any cash at all, when everything was on a credit card.

Six years had passed since Art sold the station. He'd been seventy then. Celebrating his retirement, he and Wilma had talked about buying a trailer maybe and traveling some. But within a year Wilma had died. Now he lived alone in the empty house. . . .

Art shook off the feeling of self-pity. Painfully he shuffled over to the television set and turned it on. He didn't always watch it, but he kept it on most of the time. It was company. Now, as he sat in the living room, ready to watch the five-o'clock news, the lamp beside his chair suddenly went out and the television picture receded to a pinpoint of light and vanished. Art Prochaska sat in winter gloom, shocked. In the sudden silence he could hear the rumbling of the furnace die away.

AROUND nine o'clock Art Prochaska dialed the phone number of his old friend Joe Peltier. Thinking how he would make a joke to Joe about the mix-up over his bill, he did not immediately notice that no dial sound or ringing was coming from the instrument. The line was dead. Prochaska felt a momentary alarm. It was a strange coincidence, the phone going out on the same night his power was cut off. But the wind was gusting and some lines must be down.

Standing in the dark, he felt the cold slowly penetrating the house. Early in the evening he had lit a fire in the fireplace, using up all the firewood. Now it was down to red-eye coals. In his bedroom there would be no heat at all.

Prochaska swore aloud in frustrated anger. Shortly after five, when the phone was still working, he had tried to call the power company. There had been no answer. That was one thing they did efficiently, he thought. They closed up right on time. And it was Friday. The offices would not open again until Monday.

He shivered, feeling the desolate loneliness of the empty house as he never had before. No. Someone would notice this compounding of error, he told himself. An inspector was coming out to the house, that woman had said. When would he come? Art could not remember exactly. Or was he afraid to face the truth that inspectors did not come on weekends?

By the next morning the house was gripped by cold as intense as that outside. There had been a heavy fall of snow during the night. Art Prochaska lay in bed, huddled under his covers, reluctant to rise. Movement was painful on the best of days. There was no special reason for him to get up today. No one depended on him. No one would come. After a while drowsiness overcame him, and he drifted in and out of sleep. The house cracked and snapped as the cold tightened its grip, but he did not stir.

When he came fully awake again, it was evening, dark. He knew that he should rouse himself, that it was in some way important to get up, but a great indifference had enveloped him.

The house in which he lived was soiled, neglected, shabby, he thought. It astonished him that he could see it now in the darkness with wonderful clarity, while still lying in his bed, as if he were able to leave his body and drift through the empty rooms like a ghost. He ought to tell someone about the power being out, the house unbearably cold. But he could not travel far on foot through heavy snow. The only person close enough was Mrs. Ringer, and she hadn't spoken to him since the last time he complained about her dogs. He could not go begging to her, even if he could get through the drifts.

174

At last he slept, and woke, and slept again, each time deeper. Each time it was a longer, harder climb out of the great dark trough into which he slipped, until the last time, when he had the sensation of letting go of something, falling back with a long, slow sigh.

LATE Monday night a sudden banging and crashing directly overhead drove Norma Hooper from her bed. She stood in the doorway of her bedroom, trembling. On the portable TV set, the eleven-o'clock news, which she had been watching, switched to a commercial. A diver dropped gracefully from a cliff into Acapulco Bay, wearing a Timex. As he struck the water, breaking glass exploded against the floor above Norma's ceiling.

She fled from the room. As she hurried to the front door of her apartment, something heavy—furniture?—overturned with a thud that shook the ceiling. With fumbling fingers Norma unlocked her door. The apartment manager's unit was directly across from hers. She knocked anxiously. There was no answer. While she stood uncertainly in the hallway, hugging her robe to her, a single cry of anguish came from the apartment above hers.

Then silence. What should she do?

Her fright was ebbing. All was quiet now upstairs, and she didn't like to make trouble. The occupant of 211 had never given any indication that he was a troublemaker, keeping to himself most of the time. She wondered what could have caused him such distress. In the cold hallway she shivered involuntarily and remembered the news item she had been listening to when the commotion broke out—a terrible story about an old man who had been found frozen to death in his own house on the outskirts of Hollister. The power company, it seemed, had mistakenly cut off his heat.

In the upstairs apartment he lay on the bed where he had flung himself, his rage momentarily spent. Terror still hovered in the dark corners of his mind. It was an accident, a freak accident. No one could have known the old man would actually freeze to death.

For one awful moment—listening to the news—he had seen everything collapsing around him, all because of a single miscal-

175

culation. As if he had built this towering work of genius—a pains-taking labor of years—only to make one clumsy amateur's mistake on the very eve of completing it.

As reason returned, the tenuous structure in his mind steadied. Arthur Prochaska's premature death changed nothing. He got up and set about cleaning up the living room. He had to have it straightened out before morning. Wouldn't do to let it be seen this way. The shards of broken glass, the pieces of a pottery ashtray, the wood chipped from a hurled chair were like small fragments of that imaginary tower. The rest would stand. It had been too carefully planned to be so easily brought down.

TUES FEB 1 / 07:30 AM

MICHAEL Egan had rented a small house at Lake Terry, twenty miles out of town. It was essentially a summer cottage, dependent on a Franklin stove for heat, which was probably why it had been available at a hundred dollars less than apartments in town. He had arrived after the start of the fall term at Hollister University to take up his new job, heading the security office of the Regional Data Center, which was housed on the university's campus.

The isolation of the cottage had appealed to him. Many of the homes around the lake were empty now, and he enjoyed the soli-tude. He told himself that the contrast with Los Angeles had much to do with his feelings. Los Angeles, and five years of fighting clogged freeways, angry streets and crowded restaurants.

Los Angeles, and Joan Wellman. He had been ready for a change, needed to be alone for a while.

Hollister University was situated at the northern rim of the city, six miles from the civic center. On Tuesday morning, as Egan turned into the parking lot reserved for data center employees, the eight-o'clock news came over his car radio. The lead story was local. An old man had been found dead in his unheated house yesterday, a victim of the latest storm.

Egan parked, cut the engine and sat unmoving. It was bad enough to be alone at thirty-five. To be alone when you were old . . . Egan had seen more than one man die during his tenure as an FBI man. But he had never hardened himself to it. Once a man

176

was dead—no matter what he had done—the sadness was always there. He opened the car door.

The new administration building was the pride of Hollister University, a naked tower of concrete and smoked glass, twelve stories high. It was flanked by two squat but otherwise matching cubes. The one on the south was the engineering college; its twin housed the Hollister Regional Data Center. The grouping formed the university's giant step into the future. Egan preferred the low, red brick buildings, most of them covered with ivy, which belonged to the university's past.

From his office in the data center Egan was able to survey the whole building by means of a bank of closed-circuit television screens—the computer room, surrounding corridors and all entrances and exits. The main security console also monitored environmental conditions, the functioning of machinery, and the alarm systems that warned of fire, electrical failure or an attempt at unauthorized intrusion anywhere in the building. Security officers watched the screens twenty-four hours a day.

The computer room itself was a cube within a cube. It was located in the middle of the building, isolated behind solid, windowless walls, buffered on the outside by offices, a tape library and service facilities. There had been a time when computer rooms were set proudly out in the lobby, on display behind glass walls. The turmoil of the 1960s changed that. At the height of the Vietnam crisis, bombs and other attacks had damaged computer centers at Fresno State, Boston University and the universities of Kansas and Wisconsin. The lesson had not been lost.

Access to the computer room of Hollister's Regional Data Center was through an anteroom called a mantrap. Programmers, operators and other authorized personnel opened the outer door into the "trap" by means of their personal ID cards, which bore both photo identification and a hidden magnetic strip. The code-operated lock on the second door could be opened only on signal from someone inside the computer room; it was under the control of the system itself. Anyone who entered the anteroom and was not cleared found himself trapped, unable to go forward or backward.

This morning, studying the computer room on the monitor screens, the rows of gleaming machines with their displays, their

177

keyboards and printout rolls and card decks, Egan felt out of his depth. After three months he was still an outsider at the Regional Data Center. Not only had he been hired from the outside to be the new security director, but he was not a computer man. More than once Egan had wondered why Del Thomas, the director of the RDC, had hired him. A recommendation from a well-placed former FBI friend did not seem enough.

Egan checked his desk calendar and saw that he had an appointment with Thomas at nine thirty to go over some security details.

IN THE director's office, Del Thomas had adopted a soothing tone that irritated the slim, dark-haired young woman facing him across the desk. "Calm down, Mrs. Tyson. There's no point in getting excited."

Jennifer Tyson was in charge of quality control—following up on errors—at the Regional Data Center. "But there is!" she said heatedly. "A man's dead!"

Thomas looked pained. "We can hardly be blamed for that."

"His heat was cut off," she said angrily. "He died because he was alone, and because the storm trapped him in that cold house. The computer cut him off!"

"Oh." Thomas leaned back in his chair as if he had been pushed. "Yes, I see what you mean. Field day for the media. It'll be on the nightly news, I suppose."

"That isn't what I meant—" She choked off the bitter retort. Del Thomas was not a man who tolerated criticism. She thought briefly of Robert Greiner, a former member of the RDC staff. Greiner had been a maverick who had made no attempt to conceal his dislike for Thomas. That, more than his tendency to work on his own schedule, independent of rules, had gotten him fired. Jenny went on more calmly. "You see, Mr. Thomas, it was a mistake. Prochaska had paid his bills. He was right up to date."

Now Del Thomas frowned. Bad enough for the news people to sensationalize an unfortunate incident. But the suggestion that there had been a computer error—oh, the press would love that! There had already been considerable resistance in Hollister to the rapidly expanding dependence upon the RDC to manage the city's life-support and governmental systems.

178

"How could that happen?" he demanded. "Why wasn't a proper correction made, Mrs. Tyson?"

"The correction was put through over two weeks ago. I checked this morning. Prochaska was billed the first week of January, but he didn't come in to complain until the fourteenth. There'd been an error on the data input from the power company, and he hadn't been credited with his previous payment. But the journal file shows that a correction was entered that day, January fourteenth."

Thomas stared at her as if she had announced the end of the world. "That's impossible!" he said. "Mrs. Tyson, what are you trying to say?"

"I'm saying that the corrected instructions were entered into the system." She paused a moment for effect before adding grimly, "The computer rejected them."

JUST as Michael Egan reached the door of Thomas' office it suddenly burst open. He grinned with pleasure at seeing Jennifer Tyson, but she swept past him and strode down the corridor, long legs scissoring under a trim gray skirt. Egan wondered what was wrong with her. Jenny Tyson had a quality of cool reserve, but she was invariably courteous. Egan had lately almost convinced himself that her casual smiles had become warmer, less impersonal. Oh well. He shrugged and went into the director's office.

For the next ten minutes Egan outlined his recently completed survey on computer security. Thomas listened pensively without comment, running a finger along one side and then the other of a neatly trimmed mustache. Egan was not sure he was listening.

A computer center, more than most other complex modern facilities, was vulnerable to natural hazards as well as physical attack. Fire, for instance, could be devastating. Heat alone could cause an entire system to crash. Egan remembered reading of an incident at Aqueduct Race Track when the failure of an air conditioner had caused the track's computer to go haywire, posting incorrect prices on the tote board and causing a small riot among angry bettors. Michael Egan's job was to make sure that such things didn't happen at the RDC—that the physical environment was kept stable, temperature-controlled, free from intrusion or attack. The one area which had caused Egan particular concern was the risk of fire. He turned to a discussion of that. "I don't like using carbon dioxide as an extinguisher," he said. "It's too dangerous."

"Oh?" Thomas had a habit of quizzically lifting one eyebrow. "It was approved by the local fire department."

"I know, but I think we can find something better."

"We can't use water," Thomas said. "When you add water from sprinklers to the high temperatures of a fire, you get both heat and humidity. Tapes disintegrate quickly with that combination."

"There's Halon 1301," Egan persisted. "It's a gas, just as effective as CO_2 and not nearly as dangerous."

"We've been through all this before you came, Egan. I understand there are problems with Halon, too. I really don't see why you object to the present system."

"It could kill people," Egan said bluntly. "That computer room is a closed environment. If anyone were trapped inside, the gas could kill them long before the fire would."

Thomas studied him in silence. He began to toy with his mustache again, plucking first at one side, then the other. His fingers were pale, the hands soft, like the man. Thomas was taller and bigger framed than Egan, but there was a prevailing impression of softness about him, as if there were no hard bone and muscle under the pale skin. "How long have you been with us, Egan? Three months, isn't it? Don't you think you should wait a bit before recommending major changes?"

"It wouldn't be all that major," Egan protested.

"Converting would cost money," Thomas said, coming to the bottom line. "We can't do everything we want, Egan. Let's sit on this one for a while, shall we?"

Lesson learned, Egan thought. Next time be better prepared to talk about money when you want to suggest a change. He could only hope there wouldn't be a fire inside that closed computer room before he got another chance to sell his recommendation.

AMONG other meetings taking place in Hollister Tuesday morning was one at the city morgue. Police Chief John Toland managed to get Leonard Hauss, the coroner, alone for a few minutes. "What do you figure, Doc?"

180

"There'll have to be an inquest, of course."

"I know that!"

Leonard Hauss studied Toland shrewdly. "I don't see any problems, John. There is one thing, though, in Officer Ramsey's report. He indicates a possibility that the telephone line to Prochaska's house was cut. What about that?"

"Nothing to it." Toland shifted the Browning belt slightly lower on his thick hard belly. "The line was down, but with the snow and ice we had all weekend, there were lines popping all over the place."

"Wouldn't a cut show up different?"

"Who'd want to cut the old guy's telephone wires?" Toland demanded impatiently. "Look, Leonard, let's not make a federal case out of this, huh? Reporters were already out there today."

"Okay, John. I see what you mean. This Prochaska case looks routine. Good enough?"

"Yeah. The guy got old and died."

JAMES Conway, Hollister's mayor for over three years, was intercepted by Kenny Nance, his press officer, as he left the parking lot behind city hall. "The vultures are waiting," Nance said. "This Prochaska thing looks like trouble. You want to sneak in the back way? I can hold those reporters off until we figure out an angle."

"No angles, Kenny," Conway said tersely. "Set up a short conference. And I'm not ready to start sneaking in the back way yet."

They entered the elevator together, two disparate figures, the mayor lean and cool, almost ascetic in appearance, Nance pudgy and rumpled, his fingers stained with nicotine. They had struck up an amicable relationship on Conway's first day in office, somewhat to Nance's surprise. He had not expected to like Conway. Now they were friends.

The reporters in Conway's outer office started hammering him with questions as soon as he appeared. The mayor waved them into his office and told them that frankly he had not received a detailed report on the incident.

"It was a computer error," one of the reporters pointed out. "Do you still feel the same about the data center after this?"

Although the question was loaded, Conway did not try to evade it. "Do you know how much local government spending is up in this country, Bob? Over one hundred and seventy-five percent in the last ten years. Finding ways to cut those costs and still provide services the people demand is our only chance to survive without a taxpayer revolution. The question isn't whether we should use computers or not; we *have* to use them. The question is how to use them safely and responsibly."

A young TV reporter cut in sharply. "The system wasn't used very safely for Prochaska."

"What apparently happened with Mr. Prochaska was, indirectly at least, the result of a billing error," Conway said soberly. "It's a terrible thing, but that kind of error didn't start with computers. As a matter of fact, we have a lot fewer errors now."

The rest of the questioning was friendly. After a few minutes Conway caught Nance's eye, and the public relations man moved in to herd the reporters out of the office. When the door closed behind them, Conway dropped into his ancient leather swivel chair, his expression somber. "Well, Kenny?"

"You said the right things."

"I wonder if Prochaska's daughter will think so."

"You have to worry about what fifty thousand voters think," Nance said reasonably.

Conway's answer was a sardonic glance. Nance shrugged. Sometimes he didn't quite know what to make of the man whose public image he so zealously guarded.

Thirty years in PR work had given Kenny Nance an unfaltering cynicism. Conway was too good to be true. Nance was still waiting for the young mayor to stumble. Sooner or later he would have to make a hard choice between the right thing and the politically expedient. When that moment came, Nance's hard-earned view of the human race would surely be vindicated.

"They'll keep asking about the computer system," Nance pointed out now. "And that's where you could get nailed bad. As far as the public is concerned, you're the one who piped us into the RDC, even though the project was on the boards when you took it up."

"Kenny, stop worrying about how I'm going to be nailed." Conway swung his chair around and gazed out the window.

Like many others, Hollister was a city in trouble. Conway wondered—not for the first time—how he would react if a genuine crisis came. There was the growing fuel shortage that no one wanted to admit was real—it would be worse next winter. City income was dwindling and its industrial base was quietly eroding. And now there was the shadowy figure of a lonely old man neglected by society. Arthur Prochaska might be the most damaging problem of all—because the computer center was involved.

People generally identified Conway with the RDC. When he was running for mayor, the nucleus of the system—created largely because of an unexpected bonanza of federal funds—was being used primarily as a toy by Hollister University. Conway recognized the potential of the data center and fought for the funds necessary to expand it. In spite of what had happened to Prochaska, Conway remained convinced that the conversion of many of the city's basic functions to computerized control was the one step that might keep Hollister a viable entity.

He broke the silence. "Nobody should die like that. I want to know why, Kenny."

"You want a fall guy?"

Conway's blue eyes turned cool. "Why should I want a fall guy?"

"I hear Councilman Burton is having his own press conference."

"So?"

"So he's the one guy on the council who fought hard against the data center. He's also the guy you whipped for mayor, in case you've forgotten. You don't think he's gonna pass up this chance to say I told you so, do you? Believe me, Your Honor, a lot of people don't like computers. They're afraid of them."

"When you call me Your Honor, Kenny, I really start worrying." Conway paused. "Why should people be afraid of computers? They're just machines."

Kenny Nance sighed. If James Conway had one weakness, it was an inability sometimes to understand the fear and insecurity that were the daily lot of almost everyone else. Conway had it all together. He was one of the youngest mayors around. He was married to a beautiful former model. He was cool and intelligent, and he had either forgotten or never known what it was like to be hanging on by your fingertips.

183

Nance said, "They aren't just any machines. They're machines that manipulate people's lives. They're part of big government and big business, all the things that are becoming so complex and remote that *people* don't mean anything anymore. Computers don't care; they can't. You can't argue with them or swear at them or make them listen to you when something goes wrong. They just keep giving you the same answer. They're another thing that says what happens now is beyond our control. This Prochaska incident, that's what it's gonna say to all those people."

Conway stared at him. "I knew there was some reason I kept you around, Kenny. Besides being my conscience." He gave Nance one of those quick, rare grins that had gone a long way toward getting him elected. "You afraid Burton's going to nail me?"

"He's gonna try."

At that moment, as Kenny Nance had predicted, Councilman Jay Burton was telling reporters, "This is just another example of what happens when government starts interfering too much in everyone's daily lives. It's a tragic thing. I would remind you that I always had serious doubts about this city's overdependence on the Regional Data Center, and I made those doubts very clear."

"Don't you use computers in your own business, Councilman?" a reporter asked.

"I do," Burton admitted. Owner of the Burton Trucking Company, he was a moderately wealthy man. "We use them for scheduling and accounting, the kind of things a computer does very well. But I'm not about to turn over the running of the company to a computer. The day that happens, it'll be a hot day in Hollister!"

Several of the listening journalists jumped on the phrase, scribbling it down. Given the current cold spell, it was as good a lead line as any.

TUES FEB 1 / 05:00 PM

FROM the office adjoining one of the laboratories in Hollister University's physics building Jennifer Tyson watched the department head, Dr. Linus Webster, talking with a young man who sat at the keyboard of the lab's minicomputer. The young man was a student assistant named George Devoto; Linus Webster was Jenny's father.

184

The small computer—a Digital Equipment Corporation PDP-11—was connected to the mainframe—the central computer—at the data center. With it Webster could now test mathematical theories in a fraction of the time once required. Problems that might have taken years for a team to resolve could be run through in days or even hours by one minimally trained assistant. Few revolutions were as significant.

Webster did not know Jenny was there. An aloof, brilliant and difficult man of sixty-two, he was tall and angular, with the tall man's bent shoulders exaggerated by age. He had been a remote figure to his only daughter throughout her childhood, a man who inspired awe rather than love. She still considered it astonishing that, after being on her own for eight years—married and living in another city—she was once again sharing the same roof with him. Even when her husband had been reported missing in action, his plane down somewhere over Vietnam, even when her mother had died, she hadn't come home. It was her father's recent heart attack that had brought her back to Hollister.

Jenny's father was not an easy man to live with. Often preoccupied with the problems of physics or mathematics, he treated any interruption as the intrusion of a fool. She had always thought her mother had been baffled and ultimately defeated by that irascible impatience. Jenny had been completely undone when her father broke down sobbing at her mother's funeral. She had realized then that she'd never really known him.

Now she poked her head into the lab. "Nearly ready, Dad?"

He waved a hand absently, not looking up. She heard him speak sharply to his assistant. "Do it right, George. A computer won't correct your errors, it will simply perpetuate them."

George Devoto was an odd one, she thought. Her father had a penchant for hiring the most unlikely assistants. He was never interested in what they looked like, how they dressed or cut their hair. All that mattered to him was that they be as intensely single-minded as he was. George Devoto seemed to qualify. Oh, that's right, she thought; he's coming to dinner on Friday! One of her father's unpredictable gestures, certain to lead to a small disaster.

While her father went to get his coat, she smiled brightly at Devoto. "I hope he's not keeping you working late again."

185

"No."

Witty exchange, she thought. "Did you get that apartment you wanted? Dad said you were moving in with someone closer to the campus." What kind of roommate had George Devoto found? she wondered idly.

"Yeah." He glared at her as if she had been spying on him.

"Well, I'm glad it worked out. We'll see you Friday, then."

"Yeah."

The young man stared after her as she left the office. He did not answer when she said good night. Friday evening was going to be a real delight.

When Jenny and her father reached the neat brick home they shared, Linus Webster went directly to his study, and Jenny brought him his ritual glass of wine.

"I've put a potato in the oven, and there's roast beef," she said. "I'm having dinner with Rob Greiner."

"Why didn't you tell me? I could have worked later."

"You work long enough hours. Besides, how would you have gotten home?" Webster no longer drove. He had had his heart attack while driving—and now found ways to avoid it.

"George could have driven me home."

"George has a car?"

"Yes, my dear, he's really quite normal."

"Well, he's not very sociable."

"I didn't hire him to be sociable. He's bright and diligent. Now run along and meet Robert. I'll be quite all right."

She went back to the kitchen, feeling vaguely guilty about leaving him to dine alone.

THE Mill, a huge two-story structure converted from an authentic old mill, was a favorite eating place for the university community. Jenny and Rob Greiner were at the bar, waiting for a table, when she recognized George Devoto's bearded face in the bar mirror. He was drifting along, searching for an empty stool, his eyes wary, as if he were afraid of being recognized. She turned around and said brightly, "Hello, George!"

He stared at her without speaking.

"Don't pretend you don't know me," she said, falling into the cajoling tone he unfailingly evoked in her. "I'll have to tell Dr. Webster where you spend your nights."

"I don't think he'd be interested," Devoto mumbled. He ducked his head in a nod and hurried on.

"Who was that?" Greiner asked.

"Dad's latest assistant. He came in the fall, about the time you left the data center."

"Why were you needling him?"

"I wasn't needling him," Jenny protested. "He's just hopeless when it comes to conversation. As a matter of fact, he's a lot like you when you want to be that way, except that I think he's really afraid of women." She groaned melodramatically. "And I have to go through my lively Jennifer act Friday night. Dad's asked him for dinner."

Greiner watched her intently, scowling under black brows. He had a beautiful scowl, she thought. He was a thin, elegant man, although he dressed in jeans and flowered shirts. With hair almost shoulder length, a Fu Manchu mustache and a small, untrimmed beard, he looked a little like Bob Dylan. Jenny suspected that if she had been a little younger, she might have had the crush on him that Greiner half expected.

"Why do you put yourself through that?" Greiner demanded. "You don't have to. Why don't you move out?"

"I can't. . . . Since Dad's heart attack—"

"Don't give me that."

She bristled. "I owe him something. He's my father."

"Nobody owes anybody anything! Haven't you learned that yet?" The remark was typical of Greiner, defiant and belligerent.

"I don't believe that. And what are we if we don't care anything about anyone but ourselves?"

"Listen, you've got to think of yourself first. It's like the beer people say, you only go around once in life, and you better grab all you can, because if you don't, you've thrown it all away."

Greiner's grin eased the sting of his words, but over dinner Jenny's thoughts kept returning to what he had said. There was only a limited truth in it. People did owe each other something. Even people whose connection was remote and accidental—like hers with Arthur Prochaska.

She waited until they were having coffee before she brought up the Prochaska incident. Greiner listened with an indifferent smile, but she knew that any computer problem interested him, even if the people involved did not. "So what do you think?" she prodded when he remained silent. "How come that correction was aborted?"

Greiner shrugged. "Let Del Thomas figure it out."

"Okay, so Thomas fired you and you'd like to see him hanging there, turning slowly in the wind. But look at it as my problem, not his."

Greiner frowned. Finally he said, "Somebody's being funny. Whoever it was won't admit it now—can't admit it. But that's what it looks like to me."

"Do you want to spell that out for a less devious mind?"

"Someone in the computer room was playing games. It's nothing new, it goes on all the time. But this time it boomeranged. Probably the old guy would've died anyway. But it looks like somebody fooled around with that billing program. Anyone in that room could've used your password and identification number—"

"But I haven't told anyone my identifier or my password!"

"You don't have to. I knew most of them myself, including yours. Some of those jokers can't remember their numbers. Look around. You'll find them taped right on the keyboards sometimes. And those that aren't, you can pick up by watching. Besides, there are ways to get information out of the system itself."

"But if someone made a change, there should be some kind of record. I can't find anything!"

"If it was done right, you wouldn't. Somebody could've put in a correction and instructed the computer to erase the fact that anything was done. Simple."

She was shaken. "Why would anyone do that? You're talking about people I know, Rob."

"I'm not asking you to believe me. I'm only telling you it could happen. Besides, whoever did it couldn't have known this old guy would freeze to death." He paused. "Have there been any other errors like the Prochaska bit?"

"No. . . . At least none that I know of."

"Then it was a one-shot deal. Whoever it was got his kicks, but he won't try it again after what happened. Or she won't."

"*She* won't!"

"Why not? It could've been anyone. Anyone at all. Even someone using one of the remote terminals, or even careful Carl."

"Carl MacAdam, Thomas' assistant? You've got to be kidding."

"Not in something like this. I'll admit MacAdam doesn't have a sense of humor, but it's still anybody's game." Greiner studied her speculatively. There was a glow about her, he thought, as if every other woman in the place had been somehow put on a dimmer switch and turned down. "What say we go back to my place?"

"We've been through that, Rob."

"What's wrong with me? I'm not exactly ugly."

She smiled wryly. "David was handsome, too."

"Okay, so your husband was posted missing in action. But don't give me that number again, I know it by heart."

"I doubt that. You don't have a heart. You've told me so yourself. All you've got is something inside your chest that pumps blood."

"Yes!" Greiner pounced on the point in triumph. "That's all I've got and it's all you've got. It's all anybody's got. That's what I've been trying to tell you."

She shook her head stubbornly. "It's not that simple, Rob. There's more to it than just grabbing what you can for yourself. Even that old man who died in his house last weekend because nobody cared. I owe *him!*"

"You're hopeless. I don't know why I don't give up on you."

"Maybe you feel you owe me something," she said with a laugh. Then she sobered quickly. "Will you do something for me, Rob, whether you owe it or not?"

His response was guarded. "Maybe."

"Think about this Prochaska thing. If it wasn't an insider, then what? What happened?"

He was silent a moment before he said grudgingly, "I'll think about it. For you. But that's all I'll do."

EDDIE Hamilton and Joe Martinez were having coffee in the cafeteria at Hollister County General Hospital. A premed student, Hamilton worked part time as a hospital orderly. Martinez, a dark, compact man with a handlebar mustache and glossy black hair, was an intern.

"There it is again," Martinez said, gazing out the front windows of the cafeteria.

"What?"

"That van in the doctors' parking lot. Nobody on the staff has a van like that, and it's taking up one of our parking spaces. I had to park in the visitors' lot tonight."

"So it's some guy whose wife's in the hospital," Hamilton suggested lightly. "What do you think he is—the mad bomber?"

"Okay, so I could be wrong." Martinez looked toward the elevators, impatience showing.

Hamilton shoved his empty cup away and glanced at his watch. "Gotta go push my broom. Isn't Maggie coming down?"

"She was going to try. She's not supposed to leave that computer terminal of hers, but this seems like the only chance we get to say hello. We might as well be on different planets."

"You won't be on nights forever," Hamilton said sympathetically. He scraped his chair back just as a young nurse stepped off the elevator. "I'll leave you two lovebirds."

Martinez's mood brightened as Maggie Henderson threaded her way among the tables. She slipped into the chair Hamilton had left, more breathless than her hasty elevator run from the sixth floor accounted for. "I can't stay," she murmured. "You know I'm not supposed to leave when Junior is running. . . ." She gazed into Martinez's soft brown eyes and felt her heart give a familiar lurch. For the next twenty minutes she did not think once of Junior, her unattended terminal.

The name was printed by hand on a strip of tape stuck to the terminal: Junior. The Intruder did not smile. The operator had neglected to log off again. That lapse had been helpful the first time he used this terminal to gain access to the Regional Data Center. All he'd had to do was resume transmission on the open line. He had acquired the operator's password and identification number simply by asking for a repeat of the previous transmission. The computer had not been programmed to suppress the password on retransmission, so he was no longer dependent on an open line.

He typed his write request on the keyboard. A reply appeared instantly on the cathode-ray tube display.

190

```
SYSTEM IN USE. YOUR SERVICE BEGINS IN 2 MINUTES
28 SECONDS. CURRENT SEQUENCE IS
1. HOLLISTER UNIVERSITY ADMISSIONS
2. CRTC
3. HOLLISTER COUNTY GENERAL HOSPITAL
```

The Intruder waited, third in line. His heartbeat quickened. He was in luck. Now he would be exploiting two important features of the Hollister system. First, the "systems status" program—a convenience to users which informed them who else was currently accessing the system and how long a wait there would be. This had given him valuable free information about what programs were running and for how long. Second, the memory space of the immediately preceding user was not automatically wiped out when he finished, and it was possible for the next user to read at least the last page of data just printed.

The Intruder asked for a repeat of his own write request. With it he also got what he wanted: a fragment of data from the CRTC, the city's Computer Regulated Traffic Control program.

WED FEB 2 / 08:00 AM

WEDNESDAY was the day Ralph Lambert was going to move up in the world. Banner Textiles was about to hire a new sales manager. He was convinced the preliminary interviews had gone well. Selling had made Lambert a shrewd judge of people's reactions, and he was sure that those who counted at Banner Textiles had been favorably impressed.

Banner had been running a background check on Lambert, of course. No well-run company hired anyone at an executive level without one. The Credit Bureau to see whether he was having money problems, the Medical Information Bureau, Dun & Bradstreet. Lambert knew exactly what kind of portrait would emerge. No serious debts, other than the mortgage on the new house on Sunset Circle Drive. Fifteen years with his last job. Married, with three children. A solid, dependable type.

As he ran this through his mind that morning to the comforting buzz of his shaver, he felt buoyant and eager. Banner had kept him

191

waiting for ten days since his interview with Lew Wallerstein, the company president. Then Bud Taylor, a golfing partner who had told Lambert about the opening, called to set up an appointment for one o'clock Wednesday. Lambert was certain Banner was going to offer him the job.

At noon the data center's cafeteria was crowded. Finding no familiar faces, Michael Egan took one of the small tables by the windows. A moment later he looked up to find Jennifer Tyson standing there. "Mind if I join you?"

"Are you kidding? It's one of my favorite fantasies."

She took the chair facing him, and they talked idly about the weather, the probability of more snow, the coffee. She was surprised to discover that he lived in relative seclusion at Lake Terry. The revelation caused her to examine him more closely.

Egan had a solid, athletic build, as might have been expected with his FBI background. When she bumped into him yesterday outside Del Thomas' office she had noticed that he was taller than he appeared at a distance, close to six feet. His hair was sandy, his eyes brown and steady.

She realized Egan was regarding her quizzically. "Congratulations, Mrs. Tyson," he said. "You haven't once asked me whether I spied on the Weathermen or taped a congressman's love nest."

"Do people usually ask those things?"

"It's fashionable right now. I am ex-FBI. They used to ask about Hoover. Today . . . let's say the image is a little soiled. But that's not what you wanted to talk to me about."

"Was I that obvious?" Measuring him as he talked, she realized that the eyes regarding her with such apparent candor actually revealed very little. He was a man firmly in control of himself, and this encouraged her. "You're right, there was something I wanted to ask. It has to do with security. That's why I picked on you."

"Ah well," he said with a mock sigh. "Maybe next time. . . ."

She did not smile. "Is there any chance that anyone could get into the RDC computer room who didn't belong there?"

"There's always a possibility, but I'd have to say no. For one thing, there's no way for an outsider to get in without going through the mantrap. You're held there until someone inside

192

authorizes your entry, and we keep a log on everyone who goes in or out. Anyone gaining access who isn't an employee is photographed. Those photos go on file."

"So there are some visitors."

"Yes. But there's always an escort. Usually Thomas' assistant, Carl MacAdam. And if he's tied up, someone else has the assignment." He paused. "There's a weakness in the system, by the way. We don't have much control over what goes on inside the computer room itself. Why do you ask?"

The abruptness of the question flustered her. She had known from the start that she couldn't give a plausible explanation for her uneasiness, and she didn't want to sound like a fool. Oh, never mind how you sound, she thought. And she told him about Art Prochaska. "The point is, that correction was put through, so there's no explanation for the fact that the man's service was cut off."

"Unless someone had unauthorized access to that file and countermanded the correction. Is that what you're saying?"

"Something like that."

"Have you talked to Thomas about it?"

A wry smile touched her lips. "He thinks someone made a mistake," she replied.

"What about the computer? It can make a mistake, surely."

Jenny Tyson shook her head. "No, computers literally can't. A programmer can write a bad program, an operator can make a mistake—even the engineers. But not the computer itself. If none of the people make an error, the right answers have to come out."

"You can have hardware failure, like overheating, for instance."

"Yes, that happens," Jenny admitted. "But the system is self-monitoring. It knows when there's a breakdown or malfunction. It will shut itself down or tell us something is wrong."

"And this time it tells you that nothing went wrong."

"That's right. I know what this all sounds like, Mr. Egan—"

"Michael."

"Michael." She smiled briefly. "I know what Mr. Thomas thinks. It sounds as if I'm trying to cover up. Errors happen all the time, but this time someone died because of a mistake. Quality control is what I'm there for, and it looks as if I fell down on my job and don't want to accept the blame. That isn't it, though. I checked back. I took a dump of the file, and that correction was put through properly. The right information went into the system, there was no breakdown, and the wrong answer came out. And that," she concluded, "is impossible."

Egan's gaze shifted away from hers. He doesn't believe me either, she thought, keenly disappointed.

"I heard about Prochaska," he said. "His funeral is tomorrow, I believe." Jenny was silent. "There's so much I don't know about computers," he went on. "Maybe we can help each other."

"Does that mean you're going to open a Prochaska file?"

Michael Egan smiled at her. "I already have," he said.

After Jenny had gone, Egan thought about her impression that someone might have tampered with Prochaska's utility bill. He didn't know enough about computers to evaluate her judgment—and that bothered him most.

Six months earlier Egan was still a special agent in the Los Angeles field office of the FBI. He had put in ten solid years with the bureau. Only after the Old Man died had he become aware of unsettling factors—infighting as a struggle developed between old-line Hoover men and a more independent faction. His faith in the bureau began to erode, and he realized it was time to leave. He still believed in what the bureau stood for, and he admired most of the men who were part of it. It was simply human after all. Like Hoover, it was fallible—and mortal.

He had picked a bad time for job hunting. The economy was down, and businessmen were uneasy about the future. When the job offer came from the Hollister data center—through the former FBI friend—he didn't hesitate to take it. He could handle paperwork and people, guard schedules and a budget. The computers were something else.

He wondered if he hadn't gotten in over his head.

```
DATE: 01/14/77 * TIME: 08:02 AM *
RDC/NO: L1279863 * B/D: 06/03/35 * NAME: LAMBERT
RALPH RICHARD
ADDR: 1431 SUNSET CIRCLE DR HOLLISTER 95260 *
LEGAL HISTORY:
DRUNK DRIVING VIOL/DATE: 01/02/72 *
```

```
CONV/DATE: 02/05/72
RECKLESS DRIVING VIOL/DATE: 05/11/73 *
CONV/DATE: 07/01/73
DRUNK DRIVING VIOL/DATE: 11/15/76 *
CONV/DATE: 12/17/76
DRUNK DRIVING VIOL/DATE: 01/01/77 * PEND
VEH/LIC: SOR 026
ACCIDENTS: 05/11/73 * 01/01/77 INJURIES 02
```

"What is this?" Ralph Lambert asked incredulously. "Some kind of a joke?"

"None of us are laughing, Ralph," Bud Taylor said. "It's plain enough. What made you think it wouldn't come out?"

Lambert stared at the computer printout Taylor had handed him. "Wait a minute—"

"No, you wait a minute." Taylor's expression was not friendly. "I stuck my neck out for you. You could've told *me*. We might have been able to handle it if you'd laid it right up front."

"Bud, will you listen to me? This is crazy. I've never had a drunk-driving charge in my life!"

"Oh, come off it," Taylor said disgustedly. "It's on the record."

"But it's not true!" Lambert was on his feet, his voice shaking with emotion. "Bud, you know me. Have you ever seen me really loaded? There's been some kind of a mix-up, a mistake."

"No mistake." But a crease of doubt appeared in Taylor's forehead. "You mean that, don't you?"

"Of course I mean it!" Lambert's anger was rapidly giving way to desperation. "Bud, this is my life we're talking about. Those court dates . . . I can prove I was never up on any of those charges."

"Now take it easy, Ralph. Sit down. Maybe there's still a chance. If you're telling me the truth—"

"I'm telling you the truth," Lambert said, suddenly exhausted.

"Well, I won't pretend this hasn't hurt. But Wallerstein's a reasonable man. Let me see what I can do."

Numbness crept over Ralph Lambert. Taylor would do his best, he knew. He had to; his own judgment was in question. But it was incredible, he thought. One machine error, one stupid mistake, and twenty years of hard work were wiped out. How could it happen?

AT TEN THIRTY-ONE that Wednesday night Maggie Henderson was typing updated file information on the keyboard of the remote terminal at Hollister County General Hospital. Most of it was routine medical histories, including socially pertinent records such as those involving communicable diseases. The computer system was programmed to delete all personally identifiable information and to pass the resulting statistical records along to the appropriate government agencies, such as the new National Medical Data Bank. Maggie paused in her keyboarding to glance at the clock. Joe would be in the cafeteria now, waiting for her.

She had told him that she might not be able to come down tonight. She couldn't keep stealing time from her work. This was the period assigned to her by the data center. The last time she hadn't even logged out, and the hospital would be charged for that computer time even though the terminal had not been active. But when she thought of Joe Martinez waiting for her, she knew it was no use. She had to see him. But at least this time she remembered to log out.

The Intruder tapped out his request for access to file number 382-ELC. Then he paused. The initials were a risk. Why did he take it? He shrugged off the question with arrogant confidence.

The file he had asked for was fictitious, but the computer system's response was automatic, and the Intruder waited while the system scanned its memory, searching for file 382-ELC. In seconds the response appeared on the video display.

```
FILE DOES NOT EXIST.
```

The Intruder responded politely.

```
SORRY, MY MISTAKE. PLEASE GIVE ME A DUMP OF
MY CORE FOR CORRECTION.
```

The dump—a printout of the entire hospital information program —followed almost immediately. Skimming the last readout quickly, he felt elation. This time he had panned gold. Unquestioning, the system had provided him with a record of its vain search through

196

*its memory for the "missing" file he had requested moments be-
fore. The random data vacuumed up in such a search was called
garbage, but the Intruder knew how much of value he could find
sifting through this rubbish. File locations. Data sequences. User
patterns. Even ID numbers.*

*Improvise, improvise. He would take what was open to him.
Introduce a change, steal a password, add false data, alter an
instruction. Hit them anywhere, everywhere, like dolphins butting
a shark until it became maddened, biting at its own flesh.*

THURS FEB 3 / 09:00 AM

THURSDAY morning Michael Egan had coffee and a Danish with
Tom Ames, security director for Hollister University and a retired
New York City cop. Although the RDC was responsible for its
own internal security and thus outside Ames's jurisdiction, Egan
made a point of getting together with him at least once a week.
The time might come when they would need each other. Right
now, the data center was the least of Ames's worries.

"Three rapes last month," Ames told Egan. "One a week up until
last week. The place is in an uproar."

"The same man, you think?"

"Looks like it."

"Why nothing last week? Lying low?"

"That's easy. He's home between terms, visiting the folks."

"That means you're thinking student."

"What else? It's someone who knows his way around here. I don't
have the manpower to police this whole campus, so I'm using
student escorts and patrols. No girl is supposed to go anywhere
alone." Ames sighed. "Not that that did the one girl any good. She
was grabbed in the hallway of her dormitory."

"In her own dormitory?" Egan asked in surprise.

"Yeah, he dragged her down to the basement."

"Where did he attack the other two?"

"One in the library, back in the stacks—that's always a security
problem area. And one right out in the open. He caught this girl,
a little thing who was too scared to scream, between buildings. It
was a quiet time of day, late afternoon, and he pulled her behind

197

those garages over in the southeast corner of the campus. He took a chance that time, doing it in broad daylight."

"Can't any of the victims give you a description?"

Ames shook his head. "Maybe the last one could, but she's too upset to talk about it. The one in the library was grabbed from behind, and he pulled her sweater up over her head. And the one in the dormitory didn't get a good look, because it happened too fast and he turned off the lights in the basement. All she knows is he wasn't very big and he had a beard." Ames handed Egan an artist's rendering of a young man with dark hair, black mustache and beard. The face resembled a thousand male students on campus.

"I'll keep this copy," Egan said. "He'll probably try again."

"Can't help himself, I suppose." Ames finished his coffee. "What about your office, Mike? Anything going on?"

"Nothing like your problem."

"I don't envy you your job, that's for sure. Those computers— we're all in there somewhere, aren't we? Every one of us." Ames shook his head. "At least I know what I'm dealing with."

THAT afternoon James Conway had a meeting with the Downtown Mall Committee, of which Councilman Jay Burton was a member. Burton was in a particularly belligerent mood and the conference disintegrated into a shouting match. Conway—over Burton's objections—adjourned the meeting. "What's eating him?" Conway grumbled afterward to Kenny Nance.

"Burton is just being Burton. Which means he's still running against you."

Conway shrugged irritably. Jay Burton was an annoyance, but he was not the real problem. "Did you check with the people at RDC about that Prochaska incident?"

"I talked to Del Thomas, the director. And the new security man, Egan. Thomas is a stuffed shirt, but Egan seems okay. From what I understand, it's hard to pin down who's to blame. Supposedly the right dope went into the computer. It just didn't come out right. They're trying to figure out why. Is it still bugging you?"

"Prochaska was buried this morning. That's bugging me."

"Why don't you take the night off?" Nance suggested. "Do whatever it is the Beautiful People do at home."

"Don't you start in on me."

Nance grinned. The citizens of Hollister took a certain pride in thinking of their mayor and his young wife as the city's Beautiful Couple. Although Conway was lean and intense, and stayed in shape, he was hardly beautiful. But Toni Conway was.

Nance said, "A woman who looks like Toni shouldn't be left alone too much."

"For once, Kenny, you've come up with a good idea."

Some hours later Conway remembered Nance's words as he looked into his wife's beautiful face, now half hidden by the spill of black hair. If this wasn't what the Beautiful People did at home, he thought, it would do for starters.

Languid in the aftermath of lovemaking, they relaxed in each other's arms, enjoying the simple warmth and closeness of their embrace. Idly Toni ran a fingertip across his lips, tracing their outline. "What if your constituents could see us now? What would your Mr. Burton do, do you suppose?"

"I wish you wouldn't tell him. Or anyone."

"Why not?"

"Because they're envious enough as it is. Especially Jay Burton. He's got an eye for the ladies, they tell me."

"Oh, does he? That sanctimonious fraud! He's got an eye for your computers, too."

Conway turned his head on the pillow to look at her closely. "They're not my computers. But what makes you say that?"

"I heard him on the news . . . talking about that old man who died over the weekend. He makes it sound as if it's all your doing."

"He's just a politician. It's strategy—part of the game."

The phone rang. For a moment they did not move. Calls at this hour usually meant trouble. Finally he wriggled out of her embrace, reached for the telephone.

Toni could hear the thin rasping of the voice on the line without being able to make out most of the words. The voice sounded agitated. She watched Conway's reaction. He seemed to turn into a statue carved in stone. "That's vicious," he said flatly.

Toni heard the caller say, "Yeah, I think somebody's out to get you."

"What are you going to do with it?" There was a short silence followed by a laconic answer. Conway said, "Thanks. I'd appreciate that."

When he hung up, Toni studied him worriedly. Without knowing why, she was frightened. She had never seen him look so cold and hard. "Who was that?" she asked nervously.

"A reporter from the *Times*." His glance was remote, impersonal. "Someone got hold of a criminal record and sent a copy to the *Times*. The man who called, Herb Greenberg—he's their political reporter—isn't going to use it, but he thought I ought to know about it. He's not sure whether anyone else got copies."

"But what does that have to do with you? Is it . . . is it someone on your staff?"

He stared at her without answering. If she touched his lips now with her fingertips, she thought, she would bruise her fingers.

"Who is it?" Toni demanded, her obscure fright expanding in her chest like a balloon. "Honey, what kind of criminal record?"

"It's a morals charge," Conway answered evasively.

"Jimmy! Is it someone I know? Tell me what's wrong!"

He regarded her for another moment before he shook his head curtly. She felt shut out, but she quickly reasoned that he was trying to shield her from something nasty—vicious, he had called it—and she accepted that.

A little later she slept, her head against his shoulder, unaware that he continued to lie rigid beside her, wide awake.

FRI FEB 4 / 08:00 AM

GRAYSON'S Department Store was a Hollister institution. Founded in 1910, it was a conservative, quality store, with much of its success attributable to the tenet that the customer is always right. If you bought something from Grayson's and were not happy with it, you could take it back, even a month later.

Laurence Grayson, grandson of the founder, was currently president. He had introduced a few changes, one of which was the installation of an IBM computer. Grayson's system had been programmed to handle almost all the operations of a large retail store. The billing procedure was now entirely automated, from the moment a customer's credit card was inserted into the terminal

200

at the sales register to the mailing of the monthly statement. Human handling of information was virtually eliminated.

That Friday the monthly statements went out as usual. It would be Monday before the first complaints began to come in.

JAMES Conway left for city hall shortly before eight. At the doorway, Toni, slender and vulnerable in her blue robe, lifted her mouth to his. He brushed her lips with his and turned away quickly. Driving downtown, Conway could not shake the image of Toni's lips reaching upward, a picture of innocence.

He remembered the first time he met her. At a party in Greenwich Village, although she seldom went out in those days, he later learned. She had been pale from overwork, and incredibly beautiful, as elegant and brittle as a piece of fine china. He had gravitated to her compulsively, wondering who she was, curious about her aloofness. A model, he was told. Antonia Wells. On a half dozen magazine covers that year. "An icicle," someone said. "You're wasting your time."

But they had talked, and Conway found that she was interested in politics and world events; her opinions were informed and thoughtful. Finally he had grinned at her. "And you were supposed to be the empty-headed mannequin," he said.

"Who told you that?" she retorted.

"It doesn't matter. Obviously they don't know you."

"Neither do you."

"No," Conway replied, "but I intend to."

Remembering that bold promise, Conway thought of Herb Greenberg's phone call, resisting it, not wanting to rehearse the details of the criminal history the reporter had read to him. But there was no escaping them—or the unanswered questions they raised about the woman who was now his wife.

Herb Greenberg, a sad-eyed man in his fifties, arrived at city hall shortly after one o'clock. When he was alone with the mayor, he silently handed over the manila envelope which had been delivered to his desk at the Hollister *Times*. Conway ripped it open, extracted a computerized printout and read it. When Conway looked up, Greenberg winced at the pain he saw in his eyes. "How did you get this?" the mayor asked.

"Came in the mail." Greenberg had a soft, gentle voice which had deceived countless people into underestimating him. "Addressed to me care of the *Times*, through the data center. Even my name and address were printed out by computer." He looked bemused. "I didn't know the computer knew me."

"You're a taxpayer," Conway said. "A homeowner, too. That's at least two files. You were in the census. You carry life and health insurance, which means you've been investigated."

"Some of the files you mention aren't local. You mean they're all accessible?"

"To an authorized person." Conway glanced at the printout again. "Criminal justice information is supposed to be limited to law-enforcement and government agencies, but in this state that can mean anyone authorized by local law. And his friends."

Greenberg considered this thoughtfully. "So if I had a criminal record, anyone with the right kind of clout could get it."

"Fact of life, Herb."

"One other thing," Greenberg said. "That data center wouldn't send out a criminal record report on its own. Someone had to order it up. Any idea who?"

"No."

Greenberg nodded. Conway hadn't asked him for anything. He liked that about the young mayor. Still, something else had to be said. "As I told you on the phone, I won't use it. Not unless . . ." He hesitated. It didn't come easy. "If it goes out to the other media, TV and all, we'll have to say something."

"You kept a copy, I suppose."

"I did, but nobody else has seen it, and nobody will."

At six o'clock, for the first time since the day began, Conway was alone. His glance went with reluctance to the telephone. Toni was expecting him to call. While he hesitated, Jerry Devine, the city comptroller, popped his head through the doorway. Did Conway have a couple of minutes?

Conway nodded. Devine was a small, neat man with a tendency to stutter when he was excited. He cleared his throat nervously. "We've got a p-problem. I d-d-don't quite know how to put this. . . . I mean, it doesn't make any sense. . . . You know the new s-solid-waste conversion plant is starting to pay for itself. We're t-taking something that was only an expense item and turning it into products, like the recycled paper. But there've been s-some foul-ups lately. The plant is ninety percent computerized—you have to control your temperature and humidity and pressure all the t-time, and the computer is perfect for monitoring the controls. . . ."

Conway shifted uneasily in his chair. "What's the problem?"

"Twice in the l-last week the paper line has acted up. It's programmed to turn out wrapping paper and it comes up with tissue. We're drowning in tissue paper we don't need."

Conway was silent, his sense of foreboding stronger. "The plant computer is linked with the Regional Data Center, isn't it?"

"That's right. The RDC keeps tabs on everything—inventories, orders, and so on."

Conway said thoughtfully, "Have these errors stopped?"

"Yes, but the funny thing is, nobody has been able to find out why these things happened. The system was instructed to do one thing, and it just did something else."

The mayor stared at him. The data center again.

After Devine left, Conway called in Kenny Nance. "You in a hurry to get home?"

"It's my night to watch Johnny Carson. Otherwise, nothing."

"There's something I want to talk about. Let's stop at the Mill—it's on the way."

In a secluded booth in a corner of the lounge, Kenny Nance puzzled over the abbreviated language in the computerized arrest record the mayor handed to him. What did you make of a line that said ARREST FOR POSSESSION NARC? Narcotics, obviously. But what kind? How much? Under what circumstances? And what of a line that read, almost prissily, ARREST MORALS CHG: CONTR TO DELINQ OF MINOR: CONC 07/05/73: PROBATION. And another: ARREST MANN ACT VIOL: 11/13/73: DISM LACK OF EVID.

"This last item shouldn't even be there," Nance pointed out. "There was an arrest, but it was dismissed. That could mean there wasn't enough evidence or the charge was phony."

"For God's sake, Kenny!"

Nance looked at Conway. He was jolted by what he saw. "Hey, wait a minute. You don't mean you buy all this?"

"What am I supposed to think? This isn't a fake document. It

204

came from New York State's Division of Criminal Justice Services—by way of our own data center."

Nance exploded. "Listen, you're married to Toni, I'm not—but I know this isn't her!"

The unexpected judgment caused Conway to sit back, staring at the pudgy man opposite him. "I don't want to believe it either," Conway said. "But—"

"*But!*" Nance's fair-haired boy had fallen short of expectations at last. "When did you learn about this?"

"Last night. Greenberg called me at home. He's the only one who has received this report as far as I know—yet."

"You should have told me this morning. Does Toni know?"

Conway shook his head. "No. . . . I couldn't tell her."

"Why not? She's your wife. You should have told her."

"She should have told *me!* Kenny, the woman in this record *was* found guilty."

"That can be checked. Chief Toland could run this through and get an answer in a hurry."

"No." Conway was emphatic. "I won't let him get hold of this."

"All right. I'll talk to Egan at the RDC. He's out of the FBI, so he should still have contacts there. He can check on this, and I think he'd keep his mouth shut."

"Get hold of him, Kenny." Conway slumped against the back of the booth, his expression haunted.

FRI FEB 4 / 07:00 PM

GEORGE Devoto was late arriving at Linus Webster's home for dinner that Friday night. The evening had turned bitter cold, with strong winds blowing the snow like icy sand. Devoto finally appeared at the door, bundled into a sheepskin-lined jacket, a knitted ski cap covering most of his face. Jennifer looked with surprise at the frost clinging to his eyelashes. A glance past him found no car in the drive. "You walked?" she asked incredulously.

Devoto stepped inside. "Walking's good for you."

"In this cold? Where is this apartment you've moved into?"

"A mile or so," Devoto said evasively. "Anyway, my roomie borrowed my wheels," he added reluctantly.

She wondered, with sudden amusement, if George Devoto's "roomie" was a girl. Did that explain his reticence?

The bearded guest was as laconic as usual through most of the meal, but he finally loosened up over dessert, and Jenny discovered that he was not without strong opinions. Most were standard student doctrine in the post-Watergate era. His scorn embraced Jews and Arabs in the Middle East, Catholics and Protestants in Northern Ireland, politicians and environmentalists in the United States. Big was definitely out—big oil, big business and even big unions.

"You make generalized judgments from too small a sampling," Linus Webster said. "That's unscientific, George."

Half smiling at her father's comment, Jenny asked Devoto what he thought of Jimmy Carter. He said he didn't think it made any difference who sat in the Oval Office. Jenny found herself defending Carter, although her own feelings about him were ambivalent. "A President can make himself felt," she said. "What about Carter giving amnesty to the draft evaders? No one else could do that."

Devoto stared at her. "How did you know?" he demanded abruptly.

"Know? Know what, George?"

"That I was one of them. A draft dodger."

"You were *what?*"

Devoto seemed pleased by the reaction he had produced.

"But . . . I never had any idea!" Jenny protested. "I wasn't thinking of you at all when I mentioned amnesty. Well, if you are . . . I mean, if you were, you *must* be grateful to Carter."

"I should be grateful for losing all those years out of my life?"

"Were you out of the country, George?" Linus Webster asked, his tone reflecting no surprise over Devoto's revelation.

"Most of the time, yeah. In Canada."

"Wasn't it dangerous for you to come back to this country early—before the amnesty?"

"Not so dangerous, Dr. Webster. They weren't really looking for me anymore."

Listening to them, Jenny for the first time felt sympathy for Devoto. "At least it's over now," she said.

"Yeah. But don't expect gratitude."

Devoto stayed a half hour after dinner, probably as a gesture of appeasement toward her father, Jenny thought. Then he struggled into his heavy jacket, pulled the brightly colored ski cap over his head and trudged off. Closing the door behind him, Jenny was aware of how much tension left the house with him, how charged with anger was the very atmosphere around him.

The Intruder glanced at his watch. Ten forty. Cutting it close. He scowled at the unexpected message from the main computer at the Regional Data Center.

```
UNAUTHORIZED REQUEST. PLEASE CONFIRM
IDENTIFICATION.
```

So terminal security had finally been tightened. Well, they had been slow enough to tumble to the possibility that someone was getting into the system between the lines. Now all the remote terminals would be closely monitored. But no one expected an intruder to have the proper password and user number. Smiling thinly, he typed out the numbers, then added:

```
ERROR ACKNOWLEDGED. END.
```

That admission, along with the proper credentials, might get by. It made his "unauthorized request"—he had tried to obtain more file data for the process control program of the city's solid-waste disposal plant—appear to be a routine operator error.

He had used this terminal for the last time. No matter. Over the past few weeks he had greatly expanded his knowledge of the system. He had already picked out his next point of entry.

AT TEN forty-five that Friday night Maggie Henderson reluctantly left the cafeteria and rode the elevator back up to the sixth floor. Her thoughts were with Joe Martinez as she walked past the nurses' station. The duty nurse had to call her name twice. "Maggie? Where did you come from? I could've sworn I just heard you typing away on the computer. It doesn't talk to itself, does it?"

"No. It's not a computer, anyway, it's a terminal. It prints out messages from the main computer. That must be what you heard."

Maggie hurried down the corridor. It was probably nothing to worry about, but she was remembering the extra time charges she had received this past month—three different occasions on which she could not account for activity at the terminal. She reached her office and flung the door open.

The room was empty. The terminal was silent. Her glance went quickly to the last printout. Anxiety coiled around her chest. No message had been printed out. The nurse had heard the typewriter clattering, but there was no new reading to account for it.

Someone had been at her terminal while she was gone.

SAT FEB 5 / 10:00 AM

KENNY Nance reached Egan by telephone at his cottage just after ten o'clock Saturday morning. Briefly Nance filled in the RDC's security director on the criminal record received by Herb Greenberg at the *Times*. Would Egan check it out? The mayor would consider it a personal favor. It would also be interesting to know who had ordered the record up. Naturally, under the circumstances, this inquiry was confidential.

After he had hung up, Egan sat at the shaky wicker desk that served as a telephone stand, staring out at the frozen lake. Another "error," he thought. Another odd, inexplicable event with an ugly twist, and connected somehow to the computer center.

Egan made a long-distance call to the nearest FBI field office. He identified himself, gave his phone number and hung up. A moment later the source of his call was confirmed when his phone rang. The agent in charge at the office, with whom Egan had once worked, was not available until Monday. Egan explained what he wanted and left a message asking the agent to call him.

He went to the kitchen, heated some soup and sat down with it at the wooden table. He thought about Hollister's relatively young mayor—Egan's own age. He had seen James Conway in town a couple of times, had noted pictures of his beautiful wife in the newspaper. A former model, he had read; she looked the part. He did not speculate over the truth of the criminal record; there seemed no reason to doubt it. What bothered Egan was how and why it had come out of the RDC.

208

He rinsed his bowl in the sink. While he was drying his hands on a paper towel he made his decision, and five minutes later he was nudging his Vega along the ice-coated road to the highway.

AT THE same time that Egan was driving in from the lake, Evelyn Burton, wife of Councilman Jay Burton, was enjoying her Weight Watchers lunch. Well, she thought, enjoying may not have been the precise word, but the results—she had lost fifteen pounds—were worth it.

She had married Jay Burton twenty-one years ago. She had borne and raised his children. She had loved him, and she still did. Now she was fighting to save her marriage. If that meant dieting, gym classes on Friday afternoons, changing her hair color, she was willing to do it—and more.

Not that Jay's skirt chasing was anything new. But this time was different. He was acting very strangely, refusing even to touch her. Sometimes when he had been playing around he was a more ardent lover than usual, as if to give the lie to any suspicions. Not this time. That frightened her. Perhaps this time it was serious.

Once again Evelyn thought of Terri Helms, that nineteen-year-old girl with the gorgeous figure Jay had hired. He needed her to sit out front at the main offices of the Burton Trucking Company and greet salesmen. At least that was what he said.

Lance, Evelyn's miniature poodle, set up a furious barking. Evelyn glanced at the kitchen clock. That would be the mailman. She went to the front door and retrieved two letters from the mailbox. Both were addressed to Jay, and the return address on one of them caught her eye. It was from Hollister County General Hospital, and it looked like a bill.

Evelyn Burton felt a chill. Neither she nor Jay had been to the hospital. Why would they be receiving a bill? Had Jay hidden something from her? Was he ill? Could that explain why . . . ?

She carried the envelope into the kitchen. There, feeling guilty, she held the envelope over the spout of the copper kettle. The water for her tea was still hot, and soon she had it steaming. She scalded her fingers before the glued flap of the envelope lifted.

The sheet of paper inside was a computer printout, with some unfamiliar abbreviations. But the gist of it was all too clear.

SOURCE: B BULLOCK: VD PROGRAM DIRECTOR COMMUNICABLE
DISEASE CENTER HOLLISTER GH PATIENT TREATED FOR
GONORRHEA * PENICILLIN DISCONTINUED 1/27/77 *
TREATMENT CONTINUING WITH TROBICIN. END.

For a long time Evelyn Burton sat still, her tea cold and forgotten. The patient's name and address were at the top of the printed sheet. She didn't know how or why the record had been sent to the house. It hardly mattered. What did matter was that the patient was Jay Randolph Burton.

THE Regional Data Center functioned around the clock, seven days a week, but weekend schedules were drastically reduced. There were only three people visible in the computer room when Egan arrived that Saturday afternoon. He sought out Ted Davis, an operator cleared for confidential files, and told him what he wanted. "That's heavy stuff," Davis said.

"It stays confidential."

"No kidding?" Davis said sardonically.

Five minutes later Egan had a copy of the printout of Toni Wells Conway's criminal history report, which Davis had found in a journal file produced on Wednesday last, the day the report was processed through the data center and sent to the *Times*. Egan had seen thousands like it while he was with the bureau, and he found nothing in it to make him doubt its authenticity.

Only one puzzle remained. Davis could find no record of anyone having requested the information from New York's Division of Criminal Justice—and nothing to justify sending the confidential information to a newspaperman. Egan hesitated a moment, then called Jennifer Tyson at her home.

"I know it's Saturday," he said, "but something's come up I thought you'd be interested in. It involves another computerized error."

"Not another one." Surprise became dismay.

"Yes. Well, it doesn't seem to be so much an error as an unauthorized use of information in linked data systems. I came into town to follow it up, and as long as I'm here, I thought I'd see if you were busy. If you're tied up, just say so."

He was struggling a bit, which made her smile. "As a matter of fact, I'm not."

"How about dinner, then?" Relief rang clear in Egan's voice. "You can look at it as a business dinner if you want. I really would like to pick your brains."

"I'd rather not look at it that way if you don't mind."

He laughed. "Okay. I'll come by and pick you up."

Shortly after six o'clock they were sitting in a booth at Lonnie's Grill, one of Jenny's favorite steak houses. Michael Egan was an easy man to be with, as she had observed before, and Jenny found herself relaxing and enjoying the good food.

Over a welcome after-dinner brandy, Egan brought up the puzzling criminal report that had been delivered to the *Times*, knowing he could trust Jenny's discretion. Shocked, she quickly matched that story with one of her own, involving a local businessman. An erroneous drunk-driving record had been sent to his prospective employers.

"You mean he didn't have a drunk-driving record?"

"That's right. When the query about him went through us, there was a false report generated. When it was checked directly through the police Teletype at the company's request, without going through the RDC, it turned out that he didn't have a drunk-driving record. What apparently happened is that two records requested through us at the same time were transposed. Maybe our mayor's wife's criminal history is false, too."

"It certainly seemed authentic." Egan shook his head. "Right now I don't know enough about those machines of yours, Jenny."

"I'm just an operator, Michael. I don't know the system inside out the way someone like Rob Greiner does."

"Greiner? I don't think I know him."

"He left the data center about the time you came. That is . . . he was fired. He didn't get along with Thomas."

"Friend of yours?" Egan's gaze was frankly curious.

"Yes." She let it go at that.

"Well, maybe you can fill in some of my blank spaces. If you don't mind being bored by obvious questions."

"You're not boring me, Michael."

Egan grinned. "Then the evening is already a success. Okay, you asked me the other day about recent visitors to the center. There haven't been any that can't be accounted for. So, either someone inside the center is playing games or there's been a series of improbable errors. Or someone outside has found a way to penetrate the system. I understand that's possible, but is it probable?"

"Not very." She wondered if she should tell him of Greiner's conviction that it was an insider. She decided not to. "Hypothetically, it could happen."

"Then let's make it a hypothesis. Someone has penetrated the system and is deliberately causing errors. How would he do it? Just how vulnerable is a system like the RDC?"

"It's not all that hard to get access through a remote terminal," Jenny answered slowly. "Although we have different levels of access. Some programs—like utility billings, for instance—aren't confidential. You wouldn't expect them to have any attraction for someone trying to circumvent the system. That's what's so crazy about Prochaska."

"Let me get this straight. If someone did penetrate the utility billings file, or another like it that's not considered sensitive, that wouldn't mean that he could get access to confidential files at the same time, right? Like criminal justice information."

"Right. Theoretically, that is. But a clever intruder might find a way to get into other files. We're a time-shared, on-line—"

"Hold it, whoa, whoa," he said in mock despair. "Would you mind leading me through that step by step?"

She smiled. "How did you get your job, anyway?"

"Well, between us, I think I was just what our mutual boss, Del Thomas, wanted. The way I read him, he has a very proprietary attitude toward his computers. He wants the center protected, but he doesn't want someone intruding too much on his terrain. So he looked around for a glorified door rattler, maybe an ex-cop. And he found me. Does that sound like Thomas or not?"

She had to admit that it did, although the admission made her uncomfortable. It seemed to say that Thomas wanted the internal security of the computer center to be completely under his control. And what did that mean when strange things started to happen?

"You were about to explain time-shared and on-line," he prompted.

212

She paused to take a sip of brandy while she organized her thoughts. "Okay. The more complicated a system is, the more vulnerable it becomes. The RDC is a time-shared system, which means that more than one user can be accessing the computer at the same time—literally sharing the time. The computer works so fast, it is able to handle scores of users more or less simultaneously. And it's an on-line system, so any input goes right into the system while the transaction takes place. Which also means that the *new* input can affect the transaction. Are you with me?"

"More or less." He smiled. It was, she thought, a nice smile whose progress you could follow from his eyes to his mouth.

"We also have all kinds of different programs," she went on, "that can be working at the same time, with different users and different levels of security. And all that is going on doesn't happen at the computer center. That's where the central processor is, and everything feeds through there, but there are remote terminals all over the city with some kind of access to the system over telecommunications lines."

"How does an outside user get access from his terminal?"

"All he does is dial in. He has to give his identity number—every user has one—and the password for the file he wants to do something with. Not every user is authorized to do the same things. Some have read-only access, which means they can get a display or printout of a file, but they can't do anything else. Or you might have authorization to add information to a file, but you can't read anything that's already in it. And so on, right on up to the user who has complete access to any file or even the whole system. Nobody on the outside has that level of privilege."

"How do you control who can do what?"

"The access codes—the personal identifiers and passwords. That's part of the internal security program for the system. If you call in, the system checks your identity number and your password against its authorization list to see what you're allowed to do. If you have those, you can get in. It's open sesame. You could even do it from a terminal outside the system."

Egan mulled this over. "In short," he said, "if I knew the password and identity number of an authorized user, and had access to his terminal, I could just call the computer, pretend to be that user and give the system instructions as to what I wanted to know or do. As long as those instructions fell within the user's legitimate activities, the computer would comply."

"Right. There's no way for a computer to distinguish a legitimate user from anyone else calling in from a remote terminal, as long as the inquirer has the right access information."

"Suppose someone managed to wiretap a telephone line going to a terminal—"

"I didn't say anything about wiretapping." She regarded him coolly. "I think you know more about this than you pretend."

"Not really, Jenny. Believe me." His glance was direct and sober. "Suppose our hypothetical intruder had access to a terminal," he went on. "How long would it take for him to do any damage?"

She laughed outright. "Fractions of a second."

Egan whistled soundlessly. "I never realized computers were that vulnerable."

"These things are possible, but that doesn't mean they've been happening at the RDC, Michael. And there are ways to prevent illegal access. Passwords are changed regularly, for instance. With some sensitive files, the computer might put any inquiry on hold while it printed out at the main console the fact that someone was calling for information. And the operator at the console would have to approve that action before it could take place."

Egan brooded over what Jenny had told him. "I can see what you mean about not expecting anyone to tamper with a utility bill. So that program wouldn't be secret. But criminal records are something else. They're confidential. Who would have access to them?"

"Besides law enforcement? I'm not sure. The city of Hollister is our biggest user by far. And if you have one person in city hall with the right authorization, and a remote terminal, you have the risk of others knowing the necessary access code. People are careless with passwords."

"So we're talking about any number of people outside the data center—and just about anyone on the inside," Egan said.

"Which means we're no closer to knowing what's been going on than before."

"Not quite true. I know one thing for sure that I didn't know before. If someone is tampering with the system in any of the ways we've been talking about, he's not your everyday man in the street. He's a computer specialist."

They were silent for a while, Egan pensive, Jenny Tyson momentarily talked out. She looked at Egan's hands. Square, strong, quiet. They betrayed no nervousness.

There had been little personal conversation, she reflected. No revelations. She still didn't know, for example, if he had ever been married, and if not, why not. Was the evening strictly business after all? Not that she cared, but— Okay. The truth was that Michael Egan had upset her preconceptions. The last kind of man for her to be drawn to was a law-and-order type. But for some reason she found Egan attractive in a way she had not experienced since . . . David. Jenny repressed a shiver. She wasn't ready for this yet. David might still be alive.

But she was not in love with David Tyson. That was over long before he went to Vietnam. Only the awful uncertainty about his survival had kept her tied to his memory and his name, wearing the M.I.A. bracelet on her wrist, a chain which kept her free of involvement. And free of risk.

"Take me home . . . Michael?"

"What? Oh, I'm sorry. I was chasing our phantom criminal."

She was silent in the car as he drove her home. When he pulled into her driveway she said, "Thanks for calling, Michael. That was nice." Then she had the door open and had disappeared up the short path before he could react.

Defeated, he sank back into his seat. He had thought things were going pretty well there for a while. What had he done to turn her off so completely?

SUN FEB 6 / 10:00 PM

JAMES and Toni Conway had gone up to Skull Mountain Saturday morning by train for a weekend of skiing. They were both exhausted after an afternoon on the slopes, and they went to bed early. Almost as soon as his head hit the pillow James Conway was asleep. When Sunday brought a freezing rain, they caught the afternoon train back to Hollister and arrived home tired and somewhat dispirited.

215

Conway was preoccupied, quiet and withdrawn, as he had been all weekend. Why? Toni wondered. Was it the Prochaska business? The fuel shortage? That strange phone call Thursday night?

She told him smilingly that she was going to bed. She could hear the television on when she slid, shivering, between the cold sheets. She waited for him. After a while the fear she had been trying to deny crept out of the shadows. Something was drastically wrong.

The phone call. It had all started with that call. Confronting a feeling of panic, Toni considered the depth of her dependency on him, her reliance on the certainty of his love.

She had grown up in Provo, Utah, convinced that she was both ugly and stupid, truths drummed into her by her mother. Betty Ann Wells took out the failure of her marriage on its only visible product—Toni's father had long ago departed. Her mother's harsh judgments were corroborated for Toni by the evidence of her mirror and her mediocre grades in school.

During her teens she took refuge in a cool indifference. Then, around her eighteenth year, something happened. A face that had been merely bony revealed an exotic angularity. Her skin was flawless, her eyes huge. Clothes fell beautifully around her slender body, and she moved with an unconscious grace.

A photographer spotted her by chance on her junior college campus. Three months after his camera clicked she was working in New York as a model, starting at a hundred dollars an hour. Her career, which lasted three years, still seemed a fantasy. She had come along, she reasoned, when odd-looking women were temporarily in vogue. At the peak of her brief career, when she was twenty-two, she met James Conway.

If Conway thought she was beautiful, it was a long time before he said so. He dug beneath the surface for her ideas and opinions and emotions, forcing her to articulate convictions she had never expressed. He was ten years older, and she quickly learned that he had an aggressive interest in politics. She was soon caught up in the fervor of his aspirations. He took such obvious pleasure in being with her that, for the first time in her life, she actually *felt* beautiful. What had changed him?

She lay in bed, frightened, a grown woman discovering that a lonely girl still lived inside her.

216

The Intruder watched the security patrol move away from him. Although the campus patrols were supposed to avoid any set pattern, he had observed a predictable routine in the coverage. No one would return to the science buildings for at least a half hour.

He crossed an open stretch of campus quickly and melted into the shadow of the chemistry building.

Security was nominal here. Researchers resented having their freedom of access restricted by alarms or monitored by hidden television cameras. Anyone with a key could simply walk in, and he had had his own key made to the building.

He moved purposefully down the stairs to the basement level. His goal was a junction box in a utility closet. He had found the box a month ago and had spent weeks secretly studying it, identifying the various lines and cables. It was one of several parallel junction boxes where communications lines terminated on their way to and from the remote terminals and the data center. He had no need of a wiretap, so long as he had access to the terminal at the hospital. That was no longer safe.

At the junction box he worked quickly, making two bridges. At one end was the drop for one of the city's remote terminals. At the other was the connection to the computer at the data center. And in the middle was a carefully selected telephone line to tap.

Any telephone repairman would instantly recognize the tampering, but the Intruder intended to use this tap for only a brief period. Even if it were found, he himself would not be in danger. There was no way the wiretap could point to him. The telephone line was not his.

He left the building the same way he had entered. He had been inside less than five minutes. He walked away with a savage grin.

THE only thing unusual about the beginning of that spring registration day at Hollister University was that all available parking spaces on campus were quickly filled. Cars spilled over onto neighboring streets in surprising numbers.

By ten o'clock harried clerks in the main assembly hall of the administration building were trying to cope with long lines of young people presenting their official permits to register. At ten fifteen, when the improbable lines reached all the way across the big hall and folded back on themselves, the counselors began pinning printed notices to a large bulletin board. A half circle of students quickly gathered before the board. "What's going on?" a girl asked. "Those are computer printouts of the class lists," a youth answered. "Those classes are filled up."

"How can they be full when so many of us haven't registered?"

Across the room at one of the registration tables, an embattled counselor tried to explain to a querulous registrant. "The computer processes the permits to register, and it takes class sizes into account. We don't accept more applicants than there is room for."

"Okay, so what about me, man?" A student waved a fistful of forms. "I was accepted. So how come you're tellin' me I'm not in?"

"It seems there's been some kind of mix-up . . . a computer error. We must have accepted too many applicants. I don't know how it could happen. . . ."

Some of the crowd around the bulletin board began stamping their feet. Others took it up. Through the din in the room an angry undercurrent was audible. A student at one of the registration tables began to shout, and the harassed counselor lost his temper and shouted back. A uniformed security guard trotted across the hall toward the commotion. When he reached the angry registrant he had to raise his voice to be heard. "What's the trouble here?"

The student, a sharp-faced young man, shouted shrilly, "Keep away from me!"

The security guard gripped the young man's arm. "Take it easy!" the guard barked.

"Easy!" The student wrenched his arm free. Angrily the guard

218

lunged after him. Suddenly there were other students around them pushing at the guard and yelling obscenities. He wore no gun, but he had a long club attached to his belt. The club slipped into his hand, and he swung it in a short, solid, backhand blow. . . . Two other security men closed in from opposite sides of the hall.

"Calm down, please!" The counselor tried vainly to make himself heard above the pandemonium.

Then a tall student with the build of an athlete slapped both hands under the rim of a registration table and heaved upward. The table flipped high. The counselor tried to dodge back out of the way, but he tripped against his chair and fell to the floor. Papers spilled everywhere.

At that moment Hollister University's security director was already alerting the adjoining data center. "Egan?" Tom Ames's voice was urgent over his two-way radio. "We've got a riot on our hands over here in the administration building."

"You need help?"

"You better keep your people where they are."

"How about the police?"

"They're on the way," Ames said. "This looks like some kind of computer foul-up, so they may come after you. Watch your doors."

Egan's security officer on the console that morning was a youngster named Riskind, one of the new breed of security people, with no practical law-enforcement experience. He was the first replacement Egan had hired, choosing him over a fifty-five-year-old retired police officer. Egan felt that if there was any place in security for someone young, quick reacting, flexible, it was a computer center at a university. This was as good a time as any to find out if he had made a good choice.

"Seal the computer room," he said. "Condition yellow."

"Yes, sir," Riskind said as he punched two buttons on his console. A program had been written for the computer, allowing it to take over complete access control during emergencies. The first button Riskind punched activated the automatic access-control system at stage yellow for the computer room. The second button automatically locked all the outer doors to the building. Both instructions were now subject to control only from the security console.

Watching the screen of the television camera that monitored the main lobby, Egan could see no trouble coming yet.

Del Thomas was on the intercom. "Egan, what's going on?"

"Trouble next door, Mr. Thomas. A student riot."

"Riot? Are you sure you're not overreacting?"

"Here they come, sir!" Riskind said.

"I'll get back to you," Egan snapped at Thomas.

His emergency team was already on its way to the lobby, responding to the yellow alert. "We'll go to red," Egan said to Riskind. "But let me clear the lobby first. I'm going up front." The youngster was okay, he thought. He had responded instantly to his orders, and hadn't asked a stupid question yet.

Egan reached the lobby just as a vanguard of students raced up the steps outside and piled against the outer doors. The doors were glass, but they were a half inch thick, reinforced with an inner layer of clear plastic. As the shouting mass of students surged against them, the doors held.

In the lobby, the receptionist was on her feet, gaping at the mob outside. "You'll be safer in the corridor," Egan told her calmly. "Go to red," he said to the desk guard, and the command was passed along to Riskind at the console. The doors separating the lobby from the interior of the building slid shut and locked.

As you moved inward in the computer center from the perimeter, you moved closer to the computer room—and security escalated. The corridor barriers were solid steel. If the mob did break through the main doors, they would get no farther.

Something flew out of the crowd and shattered against the thick glass. Egan watched the doors. It had not been a planned demonstration, he thought, or they would have been ready with something more than a beer bottle—a bomb or a Molotov cocktail.

Faced with the unyielding glass barriers, the crowd of students began to break up, first slowly, then in confusion, spilling down the steps. A police car raced into view and braked hard. Another appeared, its siren pealing.

Egan relaxed. "Back to stage yellow," he said to the guard, "but keep the front doors on manual. Nobody in or out without ID."

As quickly as it had started, it was over. A computer foul-up, Tom Ames had said. Could mean anything, but Egan had to know.

MINUTES LATER EGAN was leaving the administration building. The registrar had confirmed Ames's report that there had been a computer error. Instead of acceptances being mailed only to students who had been approved, every single applicant had been accepted—far more than could actually be registered.

Returning to the data center, Egan found two messages waiting, one from the FBI, the other from Jennifer Tyson. He put in a call first to the FBI field office. The agent in charge was friendly but seemed puzzled by Egan's query.

"You wanted the criminal history of Toni Conway, right? Maiden name Antonia Wells. Born Provo, Utah. Now married to your mayor in Hollister. That the lady?"

"Yes. What do you have?"

"Nothing," the FBI agent said.

"Are you sure?"

"Sure I'm sure. I ran the name through New York, and just out of curiosity through the National Crime Information Center in Washington. The lady is clean, Egan. Never been arrested, never been in jail. That what you wanted to hear?"

It was what the mayor would be glad to hear, Egan thought. After hanging up, he sat in thoughtful silence, trying to put a damper on his growing excitement. But a gut feeling was there, a conviction that he had locked on to something solid.

He called Jenny Tyson at her desk in the computer room. "I've been talking to the registrar. I think we can agree on what this new incident means."

"I'm sure, Michael, but they're working on it here now. Carl MacAdam and the others think it's probably a hardware problem, a breakdown somewhere. I don't."

"Neither do I. And I've got another reason." He told her about the FBI investigation. "It's definite. Toni Conway has no record."

"That's just like what happened to Mr. Lambert—the businessman I told you about." She paused. "The problem is here, Michael. At the center."

"Agreed. But we're going to have to convince Thomas. I'd like you to back me up when I go to him, Jenny."

"What are you going to tell him?"

"What we both know. That we've got an intruder."

PART TWO
TAKEOVER

ELINOR Crane received her bill from Grayson's Department Store on Monday, but she did not get around to opening it until the following day, when she sat down at her desk to catch up on a small pile of bills. The desk was a lovely fruitwood piece with an inset leather top and brushed-gold fixtures. She frowned at the Grayson bill. Really, it was hard to tell where money went nowadays. A hundred and forty-three dollars! What in heaven's name for?

She had been to Grayson's for the January white sale. And she had had to go in for a skin-care consultation. But that was all. Surely she hadn't spent nearly a hundred and fifty dollars. It was a shame they didn't send you copies of the sales slips anymore, just this computerized billing, and who could make sense of it?

Elinor sighed. Grayson's must be right, of course. Shaking her head, she wrote the check.

But at Grayson's accounting department, complaint calls were beginning to come in—irate customers insisting they had been billed for items they had never bought. By noon a report reached the supervisor in accounts receivable. Nearly a thousand of Grayson's customers had received wrong monthly statements. All the names were in the same alphabet group—*A* through *H*. This meant that the records all came from the same data file.

SHORTLY after three o'clock that afternoon Michael Egan and Jennifer Tyson emerged from Del Thomas' office.

"How about some coffee?" Egan suggested.

Tight-lipped, she glared at him. "He wasn't even *listening*. All he would say was that these incidents are being investigated by the proper people—*not* security—and that there's no evidence of a hypothetical intruder!"

"Maybe we didn't say the right things."

Her temper flared. "Don't be so reasonable. You don't even seem mad. You're just too rational for your own good, Mr. Egan."

"And you wear your heart on your sleeve, Mrs. Tyson."

222

There was silence for a moment. He touched her arm and steered her in the direction of the cafeteria. Seated at a table with a cup of coffee, she said, "I'm not sure I like that last remark."

"I didn't mean it the way it sounded." The comment, Egan realized, had seemed to go beyond the problem with Thomas.

Watching him, Jenny felt some of her anger evaporating. "I'm sorry. I make it sound as if you're to blame because Thomas is being so . . . protective."

"It's his territory. That makes it a natural reaction."

"Michael, the other night you said perhaps Thomas hired you *because* you didn't know anything about computers. You don't think— Could he have a special reason for not wanting a computer specialist around? I keep remembering that he got rid of Rob Greiner, too. He was our best systems analyst."

"Forget it. The RDC means too much to Thomas."

"But you've thought about it."

"It was one of the first questions I asked."

"What about me? Did you ever wonder about me?"

"I've asked myself a lot of questions about you, Jenny. That isn't one of them."

Okay, she thought, you were fishing and he told you what you wanted to hear. But she was pleased. Then he shattered her pleasure. "But I've been wondering about someone else. His name keeps coming up. You know who I mean, don't you?"

She knew instantly, but she still asked. "Who?"

"Rob Greiner."

GREINER moodily regarded the silent telephone on his desk, resenting it for failing to bring in any business. Immediately after he left the Regional Data Center there had been enough interest to convince him that he couldn't miss as a computer consultant. A lot of people in the industry thought well of him. Nobody knew more about computers than he did.

In the beginning he had done well enough. But the weather turned bad in December and interest in Greiner Consultants fell. In January the weather was even worse, and business was bad everywhere.

He remembered Jenny Tyson's plea for him to give some thought to the crisis at the Regional Data Center. If he had still been working at the RDC, *he* would have been assigned to dig into those so-called errors. The main processor there was his baby, a beautiful machine. He could respond to her every mood. He would not have tolerated anyone mistreating her.

The data center was one reason he had not left Hollister for good. Jenny Tyson was another. He was reluctant to sever his last connection with either. The truth was that he had been happy at the RDC. If he had been able to get along with Del Thomas, he would never have left.

But he simply couldn't do things Thomas' way. He liked to work unfettered, to keep things loose. Thomas was a tyrant for whom schedules mattered more than performance. When Greiner refused to toe the line, punch in and out, say "Yes, sir," he had to go.

The telephone rang. Greiner stared at the instrument without moving for a moment. Then he picked it up.

The call was from Grayson's Department Store. They had a problem in accounts receivable involving the computerized billing program. Was Greiner available? Immediately?

"Hell, yes," Greiner said, not bothering to dissemble.

"Could you come down to see us? That is, if you're not tied up."

"So I'll cut myself loose," Greiner said cheerfully.

At the dinner hour that evening the physics building was deserted. The Intruder waited until he was sure everyone had left, then let himself in.

His penetration of the RDC was entering a new phase.

While he had access to the terminal at the hospital he had found ways to exceed the operator's authorization, using her limited write-only access to browse; testing the responses he received from the central processor to his various probes. It was amazing how much you could accomplish simply by tricking the system into acting in your behalf. It was a very obedient servant. If you asked a logical question, it would seek to provide a logical answer.

Getting a page of the city's Computer Regulated Traffic Control program had admittedly been lucky. The page had been there for the asking, left behind by the previous user. And one thing had led to another. He now knew when the CRTC was updated each eve-

ning, and he had obtained the identity numbers for the program.

The system did not question him when he requested access with permission to write. He identified the page number he wanted and inserted a single, temporary change, effective immediately.

DICK Popolano had been out in the Humane Society truck most of Tuesday answering calls. The Hollister shelter was underbudgeted and understaffed; it was now after six, and Popolano, the animal regulation officer, was working on his own time. Wearily he checked his list. One more stop and that was it for the day.

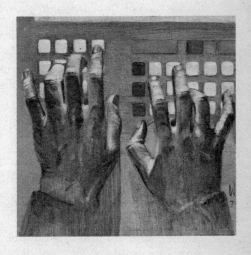

The dog was young, a collie cross. He greeted Dick like a long-lost friend. "I fed him," the woman said. She was gray-haired, and shivering as she stood in her doorway, anxious that Popolano would understand. "He's been hanging around here for three days. I'd keep him if I could, but the landlord doesn't allow dogs."

"I understand," Popolano said. Maybe this time it was the truth.

"Will you find a home for him, do you think? He would make somebody a wonderful dog."

"Somebody didn't think so," Popolano answered, suddenly impatient. Seeing the confusion on the woman's face, he regretted his lapse. "Don't worry," he said. "Someone's sure to like him and give him a home." If anyone came.

He went back to the truck, lifted the dog into a cage and secured the latch. The animal offered no resistance. Then Popolano swung the truck around and headed back across town toward the shelter. After a few blocks he cut over to Third Street, which was now one way and had regulated signals, part of the city's computer-controlled traffic program. If you drove a steady thirty miles an

225

hour, and if the traffic wasn't too heavy, you could make it all the way across town without stopping. Some of the streets were fairly clear of snow and ice, but there were still stretches of hardpack. The fewer times Popolano had to stop on treacherous surfaces, with a truckload of animals bouncing and sliding around in their cages behind him, the better he liked it.

THERE were six youngsters packed into the Saab. It was a venerable old three-cylinder put-put, built to accommodate four passengers. Bud Packer grinned as he skidded around the corner onto Hill Street, drifting into a slide but knowing the front-wheel drive would pull him out of it.

"Hey, man, you tryin' to cream us all?" Jack Hurley cried from the back seat. Bud Packer felt Julie Kramer's grip tighten on his arm in fright.

But the Saab predictably came out of the skid, and Bud's grin broadened. "You think that was scary?" he taunted Hurley over his shoulder. "Get ready for a toboggan ride!"

"Bud, no! Please!" Julie pleaded. But the others were laughing and jeering, and in the back seat Jean Towns was giggling—she was packed in with three guys.

The car picked up speed quickly going down the steep street, and even Bud Packer felt a thrill of risk. But he was a good driver. All he had to do was time the light at Renaldo. If he caught the green, he could also time the light at Third Street, coming out of the chute at the bottom of the hill.

Bud saw the light at Renaldo, just ahead, glowing red, but it turned.

He was doing fifty miles an hour when he went through the intersection, and if he held it just there, he would make the light at the bottom of the hill. Clear sailing all the way.

ON THIRD Street heading east, Dick Popolano was surprised when a traffic signal unexpectedly changed and he had to brake suddenly. What was going on? These lights were timed. Grumbling, he started up again when the signal turned green. He drove more cautiously, and sure enough, a couple of blocks farther on he was stopped by another light. The whole pattern seemed to be off.

When he approached Hill he was only doing twenty-five, but then the green light seemed to hold longer than usual and he saw that he was going to get lucky. He entered the intersection on the green, not even a warning yellow, but he waited until the last second to make sure before stepping on the accelerator.

He was cruising through on the green when he heard the high thin beeping of another car's horn.

The impact of the collision was like a bomb exploding. An instant later there was a second explosion and a geyser of flame lit up the intersection like hellish day. The Saab, its front end crushed and the engine driven back into the passenger compartment, bounced off the truck's side, careened across the intersection, hit the curb and flipped over. The truck veered left, out of control, piled into a brick wall and burst into flames.

After a brief eruption of chaotic sound there was an interval of awful silence. Then small sounds were heard. A girl, Julie Kramer, lay on the sidewalk, moaning. She had been thrown clear when the passenger door of the Saab burst open. One other person in the crowded small car was alive. Miraculously Jack Hurley had been ejected from the back seat. He sobbed uncontrollably, sitting on the curb, staring at the ball of fire enveloping the cab of the truck. Dick Popolano was pinned inside, impaled on the steering column.

In less than a minute the first police car arrived. As the doors fell open, a dog yelped and dodged away. It started up the street, limping badly, glancing back once over its shoulder. Looked like a collie, thought one of the officers. It kept on running.

The brake marks on the slick pavement told the story. It was confirmed by Jack Hurley. The driver of the Saab, he said, had tried to brake at the last minute, but he was traveling at fifty miles an hour on the icy street. The traffic light, Jack Hurley repeated over and over, had not changed when it was supposed to.

WED FEB 9 / 10:00 AM

BY THE time the mayor got to his office Wednesday morning a full report on the problem with the Computer Regulated Traffic Control program was on his desk. Between six and seven o'clock Tuesday evening there had been fourteen accidents in one grid of

the traffic-program pattern, the grid which included Third and Hill streets. It was not clear exactly what had happened. The traffic signals had continued to function, but their timing had been scrambled.

Conway read the report through a second time before he reached for the mug of coffee on his desk and looked up at Kenny Nance. "What's happening, Kenny? What's going on?"

"Don't ask me to figure out the Regional Data Center."

"I smell real trouble." Conway punched through to his secretary. "Get me Del Thomas at the data center." The call came through almost immediately. "Thomas? This is the mayor. What the hell happened last night?"

"We're investigating it, sir, I can assure you," Thomas said stiffly. "The system is working fine now."

"Can you also assure me it'll be working fine at six o'clock tonight? And tomorrow night?"

"We're doing the best we can." Thomas was on the defensive.

"Is that what I'm supposed to tell the parents of those four young people who were killed last night? For God's sake, Thomas, how could that traffic program be changed without anyone over there knowing?"

"We're . . . trying to find out. Of course, we could shut down completely. Then we could go through the whole system."

"And just how would the city function while you do that?"

Thomas had no answer. We can't go back, Conway thought. We're committed to the data system. For utilities. Traffic. Fire- and police-response systems. Supplies, inventories, payrolls. The system now controlled the very life of the city.

It was time to let up on Thomas a little, Conway decided. The man was fraying around the edges, and panic wouldn't help. "Del, listen, I want to know what you find out as soon as you have anything. Meanwhile, if you get any reporters around there, you can confirm a temporary problem in traffic control last night, but everything is functioning normally now. That's the key word. Normal. Understood?"

"Of course." Thomas rang off with relief, and Conway turned to stare at Kenny Nance. "Well?"

"You've got no other way to go."

Conway sighed. He could not shake off a feeling of foreboding. Too many unexplained errors. Too many bizarre incidents, like Toni's supposed criminal record. No real harm done there, thank God, but how could such a thing happen? "Kenny," he said, "you remember that quote from Thomas Paine I used in the speech when we took office?"

"I remember: 'We have it in our power to build the world all over again.' I liked it."

"It could go the other way. We could tear it down overnight, without even knowing what went wrong."

Meanwhile, at the Regional Data Center's security office that morning, Egan was briefing Riskind. The young security officer said, "You really think something funny is going on in the computer room? That it's one of our own people?"

"I'm not assuming anything, but it's a possibility. I just have a gut feeling that we're not dealing with a series of machine errors. We're dealing with an individual, and one of the first steps is to clear innocent people. That's really what you'll be doing with these background investigations. I hope we don't find anything wrong, but we have to look."

On Egan's instructions Riskind had compiled a list of all present and recent RDC employees, going back twelve months. No one was excepted—not even Del Thomas.

"Everyone at the center was screened when he was hired," Egan said, "but those checks were routine. I want a closer look. I want you to talk to someone who knew each of these people at his last place of employment."

"It's a long list," Riskind said.

"And it's only the beginning. Now you see what being an investigator is all about."

When Riskind left, Egan pondered what he was doing. Del Thomas would hit the roof if he found out. So why was he sticking his neck out? He thought about his brief conversation with Carl MacAdam, Thomas' bright young assistant. He knew he was putting MacAdam on the spot when he approached him, but it had seemed worth a try.

"You have to understand something, Egan," MacAdam had said carefully. "Del Thomas is an excellent administrator. But he doesn't get involved in the technical end of things anymore."

"What does that mean exactly, Carl? Are you telling me he's out of touch?"

"It means he's able to get things done—through others. That's what he's here for. He doesn't have to do all the work himself."

"Does he know this system and what can go wrong with it? That's what I really need to know. We have a conflict—"

"I know about your argument with Thomas." MacAdam would not be stampeded. A slender, handsome young man with a full head of blond curls, he seemed more mature than his youthful looks suggested. Like Thomas, he wore a mustache, but unlike the director, he never seemed to touch it. MacAdam was not a nervous man, Egan thought. He was very sure of himself. Cool.

"Then you know about the problems that are bothering me."

MacAdam did not answer him directly. Instead he said, "Thomas was a top designer in the early days. On first- and second-generation systems he built a national reputation. But you don't stay at one level, Egan. You move up if you're good enough."

"That's twenty years ago, if I've got my timetable straight. A lot has happened in your field in twenty years."

MacAdam's gaze was bland. "The machines got smaller and faster."

"Look, Carl, something's going on here, and Thomas won't admit it. You're closer to the technical side of things. You must know what's happening. If you talked to him—"

"You're asking me to do something I can't do."

"But if there is an intruder . . ." Egan paused. MacAdam was obviously loyal. Thomas was the man who had hired him and made him an assistant, the man who could help him climb the corporate ladder. MacAdam struck Egan as a young man in a hurry. Changing his tack, Egan said, "If this trouble is real, you're not doing Thomas any favors by ignoring it."

"We're looking into it. If we find anything, you'll know it."

"Who'll tell me?" Egan asked dryly. "You or Thomas?"

MacAdam smiled thinly. "Thomas calls the shots, Egan. That's the way it is."

MacAdam was a realist, thought Egan. Why not emulate him and play it safe? He shook himself. He could not ignore his job, no matter what the personal risks. The Regional Data Center, in his opinion, was in trouble. It was under siege, as surely as if a terrorist were inside the computer room with a gun.

THAT evening after supper Rob Greiner drove to the Webster house. It surprised him to realize that the last time he had dropped by to see Jenny without an invitation was during the holidays. They had been closer when they were both working for the data center.

Jenny Tyson looked startled when she opened the door. "Rob? For heaven's sake, come in!" She led him to the den, where she and Webster had been having coffee.

"What have you been up to, Rob?" Webster asked. "How's the consulting business?"

"It hasn't gotten any better. What about your own project, sir?" Linus Webster was one of the few men alive Greiner could address as "sir" without resentment. "Have you finished your model?"

"Hardly finished, but progressing, Rob. Progressing."

Linus Webster's current project involved designing a new mathematical model of the giant electrical grid complex interconnecting the various power sources around the country, for which the physics professor had received government grants as well as a contract with the power industry. The problem had always interested Greiner because of its inevitable dependence on electronic data processing. Without computers, Webster would have been working a lifetime on the difficult equations alone.

While Webster and Greiner talked about the model, Jenny wondered what had brought Greiner here tonight. Had he come up with some thoughts on the data center's series of mishaps?

"I've been doing some consulting work at Grayson's, Jenny," he said, turning to her. "They've been having problems."

"Oh? What kind of problems?"

"First you tell me what's been happening over at your place. More of the same, I hear."

Jenny nodded glumly. She mentioned the riot, and the erroneous criminal record attributed to the mayor's wife. Then she explained about the temporary failure in the traffic-control program the night before, resulting in a rash of accidents.

"I read about the massacre on Hill Street. There wasn't anything in the paper about the traffic signals not working."

"The signals were working. They just weren't on the regular pattern."

"My dear, you didn't say anything about that before!" Linus Webster exclaimed.

"I thought you had enough on your mind, Dad."

"Too much to care about what has been troubling you?"

She looked at him in surprise. "I didn't mean that. Anyway, we're not supposed to talk about what's been happening outside the center."

"Del Thomas' edict?" Greiner guessed.

"Naturally."

"What's being done? What does Thomas say?" Rob asked.

"He still insists that it's a hardware malfunction. Michael and I have tried to make him see—"

"Michael?"

"Michael Egan, the new security director."

"Oh, yeah," Greiner said dryly. "Michael."

"Don't be silly, Rob," she said, but there was color in her cheeks. "Anyway, Thomas doesn't want any interference. He has to do it his way."

"That sounds familiar." Greiner regarded her thoughtfully. "I wonder— I told you Grayson's had a problem."

"They've had something like these other incidents?"

Greiner explained what had happened at the store. Nearly a thousand charge customers' records, all stored on the same magnetic disk, had been scrambled. "The way they use it, it's a primitive system," Greiner said. "Like a glorified adding machine. And there's no real security."

"But surely the mix-up was coincidence," Linus Webster broke in. "Isn't Grayson's system autonomous? You can't link the two problems just because they happened about the same time."

"Grayson's has its own system," Greiner agreed. "And errors in computers aren't so rare that you couldn't have two systems running into problems at the same time. Still . . ."

"Why don't you talk to Thomas about this?" Jenny urged.

"He doesn't give a damn what I think," Greiner said, savoring his bitterness, then relenting. "But just for you, Jenny, I'll let you know what I come up with at Grayson's. At least I can shut their whole system down temporarily if I have to."

"Why can't they do that at the center?" Webster asked. "That sounds like the only sensible thing to do."

Greiner shook his head. "It's a unique system. The computer was built for the RDC, and there's no backup. They're working on a companion system, but they don't have it yet." He paused, looking at Jenny soberly. "You want to know what I think. Well, I've stopped thinking it's someone on the inside. This isn't fun and games. You've got an intruder from the outside. And whoever it is *knows* you can't shut down!"

Returning to his apartment, he hastily collected what he needed for this night's mission. On his way out again, he had reached the foot of the stairs when the door on his right suddenly opened and Norma Hooper emerged from her apartment. They both stopped. Why was she staring at him that way? Did she guess? Could she read the truth in his eyes?

Angrily he shook off the impression. He took the last step down that brought him face to face with her, and forced a smile, "Evening, Miss Hooper. Going out?"

"Well, I . . . I was just . . ."

She was frightened. Of him? Or of the world in general? There was a pinched quality to her, not only in the tight, anxious eyes but in her body. He had often seen her walking along the side-walk with her minced, careful steps. Had she ever known any intimacy? Had she ever made love? It seemed absurdly unlikely. There would have been some mark, some evidence of softening.

Another spasm of anger, but this time he looked away in time, hiding it. Hiding, too, the tears. Oh, my God, he thought, seven years and I still can't bear thinking about her that way. I still remember every minute of it, everything about her, everything that happened.

His voice was calm. "Can I give you a ride?"

"No . . . no, thank you. I like to walk."

She turned hastily, opened the front door and fled. No, he thought, she had seen nothing in his eyes. Love was impossible to conceal, but hatred was easier to dissemble, and he had had years of practice. Even murder could hide behind a smile.

It was the first time he had allowed the word to surface in his mind, but he did not flinch from it. He had not planned or directly caused those joyriding kids to crash. He had only made it possible. And he had always known some people would be hurt as he carried out his plan. It was inevitable, even necessary. Otherwise they would never be terrified enough to believe him. They had brought it all on themselves. No one was innocent.

HENRY Adams High School in Hollister consisted of a solid old brick structure and two "temporary" frame buildings which had been in use for the past fifteen years. On Wednesday night a wastebasket had been overturned in a first-floor classroom of one of the buildings and the pile of debris soaked with gasoline.

A long piece of string stretched across the floor from the debris to the door, where one end of the string burned slowly. At the other end, where the string reached the trash, it was tied around the middle of a bulging letter-sized envelope, dividing it into two parts, each containing a separate chemical element. The improvised fuse took nearly fifteen minutes to reach the envelope. When the pressure around the center of the envelope was released as the string burned away, the two chemicals were allowed to come together.

There was a small explosion, followed almost instantaneously by a fiery blast as the saturated pile of debris burst into flames. The flare-up gave the fire a strong start before enough heat reached the detector on the ceiling to trigger the alarm.

Although the city of Hollister now had a computerized fire-response program, the alarm at Henry Adams High was a local bell. With a custodian living in a mobile home just beyond the football field, the school board had voted against the extra expense of a direct connection to the fire department's communications center.

The hammering of the bell brought the elderly custodian running. He had to cover the length of the snow-covered football field, puffing and laboring, before he could see the fire. Then he ran all the way back to the trailer and grabbed the phone.

This time he used the wiretap.

System hackers had all kinds of fun and games, most of which were well known to the computer science students he had cultivated. A brilliant, reckless student named Olsen had explained how a piggyback entry worked. "It's simple. You insert another computer into a communications line between a remote terminal and the mainframe computer. You have your minicomputer, or whatever you're using, fool the remote operator into thinking that he's communicating with the central processor. You acknowledge his access and accept his message. Maybe you confirm it and wait until he logs off. If you want to, you can change messages. What you do essentially is ride piggyback on the remote user's communication. Of course, you've got to have some equipment to bring it off, and you've got to tap the line."

The message from the remote terminal operator at the fire department communications center to the Regional Data Center was sent at nine thirteen p.m., addressed to the automated fire-response program.

The Intruder intercepted the message. Playing the role of the central processor, he acknowledged the message, using the physics laboratory minicomputer. The message reported a fire at the Henry Adams High School at 1313 McKinney Road in Fire Zone 6. The computer program was designed to route available units to the fire area.

When the operator signed off, the Intruder transmitted the message to the RDC, using the same entry code he had just received. He made only two small changes. The address became 3113 McKinney Road in Fire Zone 9. Any inspection of the log later would reveal only a transposition of numbers in one instance, a common error in the other.

MICHAEL Egan seldom received telephone calls, but that night the phone rang twice in the cottage at Lake Terry.

The first caller, from California, was Joan Wellman. She had phoned once before since he left Los Angeles, to wish him a Happy New Year. He had not called her, and she reminded him of it. "Still pouting?" she asked.

He smiled at the phone. "You still don't understand."

236

"But of course I do. You're the one who doesn't understand." It was an old, pointless argument. He did not pick up his cue, so she said, "You were right about Howard. He's . . . moved out."

"I'm sorry."

"Why should you be?" She laughed brightly.

Egan said nothing to that. It was Howard who had brought matters to a head between Joan and himself. They had gone together three years, and Egan had taken it for granted that they would be married. But for someone trained in investigation, he had not been very observant. He was the last to find out about her affair with Howard Simpson, among others. Egan had felt stupid and angry and betrayed.

"Anyway," Joan went on, her tone wistful, "I'd like to see you, Michael. I'm going to be in New York next month. That wouldn't be so far for you to come, would it?" She wanted to meet him on her own ground, Egan thought. She had dazzled him once and she wanted to do it again. He discovered that he could smile about it.

"Call me," he said. "If I can get away, I will."

Moments later she rang off, and Egan examined the fact that he no longer felt anger when he heard her voice, nor much of anything else. He was pleased with himself.

The second telephone call, which woke him shortly before midnight, was from Mayor Conway.

"Sorry to call at this hour," the mayor said, "but can you meet me at my office at seven tomorrow morning?"

"Certainly, sir," Egan answered. Conway didn't waste words, he thought.

"Good." The mayor sounded as if he were going to hang up, and Egan spoke quickly. "Has something happened?"

There was a brief pause before Conway said, "We've had another foul-up in one of the city's computer programs." Tersely he explained about the school fire and the routing of responding apparatus to the wrong location. The units had been delayed over a half hour getting to the scene of the fire. "I've talked to your director, Del Thomas," Conway went on, "and he seems unconvinced that these incidents are being deliberately caused. Kenny Nance tells me you don't agree. Is that correct?"

Egan had told Nance his suspicions after turning up the information about Toni Conway's false criminal record. Now, although he knew Del Thomas wouldn't like it, he did not hesitate.

"Yes, that's right. I think there's an intruder."

A silence. "An intruder?"

"Yes, sir."

"I almost wish I hadn't asked." Conway gave a short, mirthless laugh. "See you at seven in my office."

He hung up, and Egan lay down on the bed, his thoughts tracking back over the incidents of the past ten days. The Intruder was not yet visible, but he was there.

At first he had been flexing his muscles. Arthur Prochaska's death must have been an accident. The other early tricks had been almost playful, malicious games. That had changed. Now the Intruder had blood on his hands.

THURS FEB 10 / 07:00 AM

EGAN found James Conway waiting for him in his office. "Glad you could come, Egan. You know Kenny Nance, don't you?"

Egan greeted the amiable press aide. Then Conway asked, "Have you given some thought to what I told you last night?"

Egan nodded. "It fits the pattern."

Conway eyed the other man sharply. "You still think an intruder is responsible?"

Conway liked to challenge people, Egan thought. "I'm sure of it. I'm no computer expert, but I'd stake my job on the fact that we're dealing with one man—a new kind of computer criminal."

"You may be risking just that. Your boss should be here in a few minutes, and he doesn't agree with you." Conway did not give him time to dwell on the news of Thomas' imminent arrival. "Suppose you're right, Egan, and there is an intruder. Do you think he meant to harm anyone last night? Before you answer, I should tell you the preliminary indication is arson."

"A couple of days ago I'd have said no," Egan answered thoughtfully. "But people died when that traffic-control pattern was changed—and the Intruder still went ahead with last night's fire." He paused, troubled. "You said arson."

"Yes, that's what it looks like."

238

"That makes this incident different from all the others," Egan observed. "Arson means he was there, at that school, lighting a match. It's a different kind of crime."

"Yes, but what about the fire-response system malfunctioning? That's another computer problem."

"I know, and that convinces me the fire is the work of the same man. Maybe starting it was the only way he could get the results he wanted. Either that, or he could be going into a new phase. I don't pretend to understand his motives. But whatever he was after in the beginning may be changing." Egan paused. "He's getting arrogant. He doesn't care if we know he's there. I get the feeling"—Conway and Nance both stared at him in silence—"that this whole thing has been orchestrated. And what's happened so far may be a picnic compared to what's ahead."

IN ADDITION to Del Thomas and Carl MacAdam from the RDC, Police Chief John Toland also arrived for the mayor's early morning council of war. Thomas' face reddened as he listened to Conway's summary of the computer-related problems of the past two weeks. When Conway mentioned the possibility of an intruder, Thomas interrupted angrily. "We are investigating these problems. Ask Carl here." But Thomas did not give his quiet assistant time to answer. "And there simply isn't any evidence that anyone has penetrated the system."

"Looks to me like we don't have evidence of anything," Chief Toland said. "All we have here is a handful of errors coming out of these computers. There's nothing so unusual about it. It looks to me like the whole country's conspiracy-happy—no offense, Your Honor, but that's the way I see it."

A surprised silence greeted Toland's comments. Egan wondered if the chief had his back up because the mayor had bypassed him in checking on his wife's supposed criminal record.

"I don't think anyone is suggesting a conspiracy," Conway said at last. "But there seems to be enough to justify an investigation."

Del Thomas tugged furiously at one end of his mustache. "It's an internal RDC problem," he said. "We'll investigate the computer system ourselves. We're the only ones who *can* do it."

"That's not good enough." Conway's gaze was a cool challenge.

"No offense, as our police chief says, but we can't wait while you go through the system looking for a hardware or software problem that may not exist. Egan tells me he's started a personnel investigation. I want that to go ahead as quickly as possible." A raised palm warded off Thomas' protest. "I'm not accusing anyone at the data center of anything—yet. But there doesn't seem to be much doubt that someone who has access to the computer system would be the most likely candidate." He looked suddenly at Carl MacAdam. "What are you doing at the RDC?"

MacAdam hesitated, cleared his throat, glanced at Thomas, who nodded. A loyal man, Egan thought—or just a cautious one. He would say what Thomas wanted him to say and, unless something jumped up and bit him, he would find what Thomas wanted him to find. "We're going through the programs where there's been a problem," MacAdam said. "You know, of course, that logging every activity that takes place in a system as big as this one is complex and, well, expensive. So what we've had in the past has been selective logging—what we call measurement logs—that tells us when there's any significant departure from normal activity."

"Spot checking," Conway suggested.

"Well, yes, you could call it that. But what we're doing now is complete logging of every transaction. We're noting every mismatch of identification, every mistake in the use of passwords, every unauthorized request for data or processing. Most of those are simple user errors, understand. They don't mean someone is penetrating the system. But at least we'll have a record."

"What you're saying is, even if there has been penetration of the computer system in the past, it couldn't happen now?"

"Not without our knowing it. Unless, of course . . ." MacAdam paused, glancing at Thomas as if seeking a cue.

"Unless what?" Conway snapped.

"Well, unless the operating system itself has been penetrated."

Conway said slowly, "Is that possible?"

Del Thomas intervened. "Of course it's possible," he said testily. "Almost anything is."

"Let me ask something else," Conway said. "If the operating system has been penetrated, is there anything we can do?"

Thomas hesitated, seemingly reluctant to answer. Finally he

240

said, "We have a fresh, verified copy of the operating system we keep to fall back on. It's under double lock—no one person can open the safe—so there's no way it could have been tampered with. We can't afford to shut down the system for long, but we might be able to shut down long enough to load the new copy of the operating system. We'd lock out all the terminals and peripheral equipment, then reconnect them one by one after they're checked out."

"Del, that's perfect!" Conway exclaimed. "How long would it take? When could you do it?"

Del Thomas appeared unhappy. He glared at MacAdam, as if blaming him for bringing up the possibility of a compromised operating system. At last he said, "We can work tonight, loading the fresh system. And this is a three-day holiday weekend coming up, so traffic will be light. We might be able to be back in full operation by Monday."

Conway grinned, more relaxed than he had been since the meeting began. "Do it, Del. Right away. If there is an intruder, and he tries anything else, he'll be in for a surprise!"

LATE that afternoon Herb Greenberg was at work at the *Times* when a copyboy came to his desk. "Mr. Greenberg? There's a lady to see you." The boy grinned. "And I mean, dream stuff."

She was waiting in the reception area by the elevators. Greenberg recognized her instantly. "Mrs. Conway!"

"You're Mr. Greenberg?"

"That's right. What can I do for you?"

"My husband says you can be trusted."

Greenberg smiled. "That's nice to hear."

She glanced around the reception room. "Is there someplace we can talk?"

"We can go back to my desk." She followed him there and perched gracefully on the edge of a wooden chair he pulled up for her. "What is it, Mrs. Conway?" he asked gently.

Her eyes met his, searching. Seemingly satisfied, she did not hedge. "I'd like to see that arrest record that was sent to you—the one that was supposed to be about me."

"Well, I don't know. . . . The mayor told you about it?"

"Yes. But he . . . he was so angry that he destroyed his copy.

241

He never showed it to me, and he couldn't recall the details."

"Maybe that's best, Mrs. Conway."

She smiled. "Wouldn't you be curious, Mr. Greenberg, if something like that was said about you?"

"I suppose I would."

"I told Jim I was going to ask you about it. Did you destroy your copy, too, Mr. Greenberg?"

He hesitated an instant too long, and he saw that she knew it. She was quick. Cool and quick. Greenberg felt himself on the spot.

"It's important, Mr. Greenberg. If I'm going to defend myself against such accusations, I need to know what was said."

"You don't have to defend yourself, Mrs. Conway. Nobody believed that report."

"Then there's no harm in my seeing it, is there?"

Reluctantly Greenberg nodded. He knew exactly where it was, in a folder at the back of his file drawer. He retrieved it and handed it to her. He watched her eyes shift as she read, saw them widen slightly. Then she folded it up. "May I have this?"

"Let me get rid of it, Mrs. Conway."

She did not protest. When she handed it back to him he thought her fingers trembled slightly. But she was smiling at him. She stood. "Thank you, Mr. Greenberg. I can find my way out." Then she was gone, followed by every pair of eyes in the city room.

Later in the day James Conway tried to call Toni from the office to say he would be delayed. Surprisingly there was no answer. When he finally arrived home the garage was empty and the house was silent. Puzzled, he checked the kitchen, thinking she might have run out to the store. But there was no evidence of meal preparations. Where was she?

He found the note in their upstairs bedroom, propped up on the dresser before their wedding photograph. It read:

Dearest Jim,

I'm sorry to do this, but I don't know any other way. I went to see Mr. Greenberg today and he showed me a copy of that sick report that was supposed to be about me. Don't blame him—I told him you said it was all right. Now I understand what's been going on. I see that you had a problem, believing all those things about

242

me. This past weekend you got over it, sort of, and I appreciate it, but you didn't really come on like gangbusters either, so I guess you were still a little turned off. So you see, I've got to think this out by myself. I can't do it here. I wish you had asked me straight out, but like you say, wishes don't build bridges. Please don't try to find me. I just have to work this out by myself, to see where we are.

Love,

Toni

Conway sat on the edge of the bed, feeling the hurt behind the words, bleakly observing the signs of her hasty departure: the open dresser drawers, the slack suit on the closet floor, where it had fallen from a hanger. How could he have believed that filth about her even for a moment?

He rose, answering the impulse to pursue her. But that was not what she wanted. Or needed. He was thinking of himself, *his* need. Hers was to be alone. He could only wait. Wait and wonder when, or even if, she would be back.

FRI FEB 11 / 01:00 PM

BECAUSE Friday was the designated Lincoln's Birthday holiday, Jenny Tyson was at home when Rob Greiner phoned around one o'clock. "Did you know about it?" he demanded. "Did good old Michael Egan brief you?"

"Brief me on what? What are you talking about, Rob?"

He told her in blunt, angry terms. That morning, when he returned to his apartment after breakfast, a police squad car had been parked outside. Two officers followed Greiner into the building. "Police Chief John Storm Trooper Toland wanted to talk to me, they said. I wasn't exactly arrested. But they made it damned clear I was to go with them for questioning about what's been happening at the data center."

"I don't understand," Jenny said. "Why would Chief Toland pick on you?"

"That's easy. He got my name from somebody. And there's one person who'd be quick to feed me to the pigs, who really might believe I'd rip off the system."

"Del Thomas," she said. Of course. Thomas had never forgiven Greiner for the way he told him off when he was fired, which was ironic, for Del Thomas had once seemed indulgent toward Greiner's maverick ways. When Thomas' attitude changed, Greiner had insisted that someone—he never said who—had sabotaged his standing with the RDC's director.

"That's right," Greiner said. "It had to be Thomas feeding garbage to Toland." He paused. "I never really thought you were in on it. Although I'm not sure about your Michael."

"He's not *my* Michael. We just happen to agree on what's been happening at the center, that's all."

"Yeah, sure. Listen, hon, if you don't know yet how your voice changes when you talk about him, don't expect me to tell you."

Dismayed, she felt an immediate impulse to deny what he was implying. Did Egan find her equally transparent? There was silence, and then Greiner added, "I don't know him—I don't even want to know him—but he's a lucky man."

"Rob, I want you to talk to Michael."

Greiner snorted. "We've got nothing to talk about. What do you want us to do—compare notes?"

"Don't be nasty. I want you to talk to him about the computer system. You can help, Rob—I know you can!"

His tone flat and final, Greiner said, "After what Thomas pulled, I hope they never find out who's been screwing up the system."

When Greiner hung up, Jenny immediately tried to reach Egan. He did not answer his home phone, and when she called the data center, the officer on duty could not tell her where to reach him. He had left before noon.

"Well, if he checks in, just . . . tell him I called."

ALTHOUGH Friday was a holiday, George Devoto went, as usual, to the physics laboratory. "I thought you might be testing the model this afternoon," he said to Linus Webster when he got there. "I mean, now that everything's ready."

"No, George. The data center people disconnected all terminals last night."

"Disconnected?"

"It's a temporary thing." Webster reminded himself that he had

244

promised Jenny he would be circumspect about what was happening at the RDC. "Some kind of audit, I suppose. We'll be put back on-line, of course, but probably not before Monday."

"Yeah, well . . . I'd just like to see how the program works."

Webster gave his young assistant a distracted smile. "Impatient, George? Don't worry about your program. I'll start challenging the model with actual problems from the power companies Monday morning. We'll be able to observe a more valid pattern if we begin with the first day of a normal week."

George Devoto did not respond. His disappointment was plain.

SAT FEB 12 / 03:00 PM

HALFWAY to the lake that Saturday afternoon Jennifer Tyson began to admit her misgivings. Obviously Michael Egan hadn't gotten the message she left at the data center, and she had telephoned his cottage several times that morning, too, without success. Finally she had called the operator and learned that the line was down. Of course, he might be out of town. Doing what? Pursuing his investigations? Or something more personal?

Stop it, she admonished herself. The important thing is that you talk to him as soon as possible. He would want to know what Del Thomas and the police chief were up to. Lake Terry was not all that far. The threatened new storm had not yet materialized. If Egan weren't there, she would have had a pleasant drive.

And if he were there, what? she asked herself, fighting the wheel as a vicious gust of wind rocked the car. Snow was beginning to come down now, as if the storm had waited only long enough for her to get out on the road. What was she going to say when she pulled up at Egan's cottage in the middle of a blizzard? She ought to turn back. Coming out had been foolhardy.

But then the road leading to the lake appeared on her left, the sign almost completely obscured by the driving snow. After an instant's hesitation she found herself turning onto it.

Out of the white gloom a small house appeared, half hidden by trees. She pulled up in a gravel driveway, and then she saw him—first at a window, then bounding down the steps. Opening the car door, he switched off the ignition. "You've got to be crazy, coming out in this!" he exclaimed. "But I'm glad you did." In that moment her nervousness vanished.

Inside the cottage, the Franklin stove glowed cheerfully. "Looks like you're stuck for a while," Egan said with a grin. "I'm happy to report there are two steaks in the fridge."

"Oh, no—"

"Oh, yes," he said firmly. "You're not going back until the snow stops. How about some wine?"

"Well . . ." Her glowing smile contradicted the hesitation.

She told Egan about Greiner's angry phone call, and Egan surprised her by saying he hoped to enlist Greiner's help himself—he had had Greiner's background cleared through an old buddy in the regional FBI office. "That's where I was yesterday," he said. Jenny wasn't very sanguine about the chances of getting Greiner to cooperate, but she agreed that it was worth a try.

"How was it to be back in the familiar bureau setting?" Jenny asked. "Did you feel you'd ever want to go back there?"

"No—that's over."

"I don't know," she mused. "You being with the FBI so long. It's as if you'd been a priest or a clergyman—"

Egan's reaction was quick. "Spoken like a true media follower."

"What's that supposed to mean?" She bridled resentfully.

"How much do you really know about the bureau? I mean, besides Efrem Zimbalist on TV? Television's version of the FBI was a comic strip, but it was good PR. That's why the Old Man loved it. But the current witch-hunt—this exaggerated cynicism about the FBI and the CIA is just as silly, just as unrealistic."

She regarded him with a tolerant smile. She said, "It really bothers you, doesn't it? All the criticism."

"I was part of the bureau for ten years, and I still believe in what we were trying to do."

"And what was that?"

He hesitated. "To . . . control the predators. At least to build a few fences around them."

"You know what you are, Michael Egan? You're a genuine, four-cornered square."

"So are you." He said it with a smile.

"Now you're just trying to get even."

"No. I simply get a different reading on what a square is. Most of this country is square, and that includes much of what's good about it. It's the squares who join the FBI, you're right about that. A lot of them go to church on Sunday and most of them vote in the elections. They also join the army when the country's at war. Arlington cemetery is full of squares."

"You said I was a square. Well . . . I wouldn't have fought in Vietnam."

"Vietnam was a problem for squares and nonsquares," Egan agreed. "But let's get back to you. Squares have a respect for tradition, for life, liberty, property. You work for a living. You've come home to stay with your father because he needs you. You worry about another old man you never even knew. Very square."

Jenny was silent. She thought of herself as liberal, not square. But she *had* come home when her father was ill. And she couldn't accept Rob Greiner's argument that nobody owed anyone anything. "There's one thing you don't know about me," she said finally. "I walked out on a man who was on his way to Vietnam. A true square would have stuck it out, wouldn't she?"

"Do you want to talk about it?"

"No."

"Then tell me something else about you."

She smiled, then laughed outright. "Well, I did grow up in a square box—Mount Airy, Pennsylvania. That was before my father got a professorship at Purdue. I was runner-up for homecoming queen. How's that for traditional values?"

She paused, embarrassed. "Why am I telling you all this?" The gay humor faded from her eyes. But she continued. "That was the good part. I got married when I was a junior in college. It was one of those *in* weddings of the sixties. We read poetry to each other, and my best friend played the guitar. I thought everything was going to be as beautiful as that day."

She realized she was doing exactly what she had said she didn't want to do, bringing the conversation back to herself and David. Then she found herself talking about the marriage that began to come apart and what that failure did to her. About David's enlistment in the air force. About the quarreling and the separation before he went to Southeast Asia. She did not go through with the

247

divorce only because it didn't seem right while he was fighting in a war. And when his plane was reported down she had felt obliged to wait. And wait. . . .

She wanted Michael Egan to understand, but she was also releasing something she had kept penned up for far too long. David Tyson was dead—she had known it for a long time—but the hurt of her life with him had not yet healed.

"David looked so simple on the outside. He was a scratch golfer and the best halfback on the football team and all the rest of it. He expected a kind of hero worship." She paused. "He really felt justified in having other women. They gave him something I didn't, he was happy to tell me when the big blowup came. They were grateful. And I'm not surprised. He was a beautiful man to look at, and for a lot of women that must be enough."

She punched a sofa pillow into shape and crossed the room to the front windows, where she stood looking out at the blind white landscape. Egan watched her, resisting the urge to go to her, turn her around and comfort her as one would a distressed child. She was not a child, and she was not ready to be comforted.

Jenny glanced back at him. "Shall I continue?"

"You stopped because you were getting angry. You don't have to go on, but I think it's something you want to say."

She looked at him closely, surprised by his perception. "The terrible thing was that for a long time I believed there was something wrong with *me*. David said I was frigid, so that meant I was. A cold woman. I was sure it must be true or I wouldn't feel the way I did whenever he touched me." She stopped again, staring intently at Egan. Am I putting you off, darling? she thought. Startled, she wondered when was the last time she had thought of anyone as darling. Slowly, nervously, she said, "It took me a long time to start believing in myself. I'm on nice solid ground now, Michael Egan. I'm not sure I want to try the swamp again."

"But you can't stay in one place, Jenny. Sooner or later you have to find out if there's solid ground on the other side of the swamp."

"Oh, that's clever, Mr. Egan."

"I'm not trying to be. I think what I want to say is . . . we're both old enough to take our time, not to rush things. All you really have to do is take one step at a time."

248

She was silent, studying him gravely. And he realized that it was time to stop talking. He went to her and put his hands on her shoulders and pulled her close. For a long moment he looked into her eyes. Then he kissed the lids, one by one. Touched her nose with the tip of his finger. When he kissed her she pressed her body against him. Then she pulled away, smiling too brightly. "Didn't you say something about a couple of steaks?"

"Are you sure that's what you want?"

"Yes . . . please, Michael. I need . . . time."

"We've got all the time in the world," he said gently.

SUN FEB 13 / 08:00 PM

SUNDAY night the staccato clatter of a snowplow could be heard on the Hollister University campus as the maintenance crew worked to clear the walks for the opening day of classes Monday morning. George Devoto listened nervously to the coughing engine in the distance, wondering if it might come back.

The girl was hurrying along the path at the front of the chemistry building, keeping to the freshly cleared walkways. She was nervous about being out alone at night, and she walked rapidly.

He stepped in front of her at the corner of the building. Her eyes widened. He could see little else. She had a scarf over the lower half of her face for protection against the cold. She could see no more of him; his ski mask covered most of his face, with holes only for mouth and eyes. He raised his hand in casual greeting and stepped toward her. It was a mistake. Because of the knitted mask she could not see his smile.

The girl screamed.

He tried to reach her and clap a hand over her mouth, but she stumbled back. "No—stay away from me!" Her hand clutched at her throat, found the whistle she had worn around her neck since the rape scare started. She blew it frantically. The piercing blast shivered along Devoto's nerve endings, pulsated in his brain. He turned and ran.

The shrilling of the whistle pursued him. He cut to his left across an open area. The deep snow slowed his flight as the whistle gave way to a deeper cry—the patrol car's siren. Damn her! If she was so scared, what was she doing out at night alone? She was asking for it!

He reached a shoveled path and sobbed aloud with relief. He had a good head start. Now he would leave no tracks to follow. He turned right toward the dorms, which were visible ahead. He had parked his van behind one of the men's dormitories because it was inconspicuous there, buffered by several other cars.

He heard a shout. "He's heading for the dorms!"

He stopped. The yell had come from the top of a rise ahead of him. Frantically he looked around. A big oak loomed over the path. He jumped as far as he could from the walk into the oak's shadow, so that he would leave no tracks in the snow. Then he fell against the thick trunk, trembling. From his patch of dark shadow he saw figures blundering across the top of the rise. His way to the dorms was blocked. He could not reach his van. He was cut off.

Two new figures pushed through the drifts, heading straight toward him. They were students, not guards, but he had no doubt they were after him. He did not move. Even his heart seemed to stop. Breathing heavily, the two students reached the narrow path and ran past the oak tree. They did not even glance toward him. When they were far enough away, he stepped out onto the path again and turned in his own tracks. The one place they would never look for him was back by the science buildings.

The slope seemed steeper now, the snow deeper. Near the crest of the rise he slipped, clawed wildly at the air and fell. For a moment he was tempted to lie where he was. He was exhausted. Not simply tired of this night's running but of all the years of yearning and angry frustration, rooted in his anxious failure with women. Damn them! They were all the same. They teased you, flaunted their sex, and then when you were ready to give them what they asked for they suddenly protested. Or screamed. Or, worst of all, laughed. Rage drove him to his feet.

The physics building was directly ahead. He started toward it and heard shouting again, closer. "Back this way! He's turned back!" And then, shrill, "There he is!"

He did not stop to look. He ran around the dark old building to the side entrance. He had the key ring in his hand. He knew the feel of the office key—he used it almost every day.

His pursuers were tumbling around a corner of the building as he ducked inside. He took the stairs three at a time and was fumbling with the lock of the office door when he heard them on the stairs behind him. He slipped into the dark office and carefully shut the door. The lock closed behind him with a tiny snap. Then he stood motionless in the darkness, his chest heaving, his legs trembling.

The office door shook as a hand rattled the knob. George Devoto waited, but nothing more happened. The student patrol would not have office keys. A moment later another doorknob rattled, then another farther away. They were checking every door along the corridor to make certain none had been left unlocked, providing a hiding place for the fleeing rapist. It did not occur to them that he might belong here in this particular office and laboratory.

After a while there was silence. He did not completely trust it. Nor did he trust his legs to carry him out of the building. He could outwait them—until morning if he had to, when Dr. Webster would find him early at his desk.

He retreated from the office into the main laboratory. In the darkness, he moved easily around familiar sinks and racks. He stopped near the lab's computer, puzzled. Enough light filtered from the windows for him to see that some copy had been printed out, a record of the last activity.

George Devoto frowned. Picking up the printout, he peered at it closely and recognized the program for Linus Webster's power-usage model. Devoto had prepared it himself and had had it ready Friday afternoon. But he had not run it through. There should not have been a printout.

And something about the pattern of the program puzzled him, something unfamiliar. It was the same, and yet . . .

He lifted his eyes from the paper, and his nostrils flared as he detected an alien smell. Cigarette smoke. Dr. Webster didn't allow anyone to smoke in the physics laboratories. No one on the staff would have dared to smoke here, even alone at night. Someone else was here. He heard something then, on the far side of the room, faint sounds moving away from him toward the office. He thought he saw a shadow in the doorway.

Light burst abruptly in the office. The outer door slammed open, and someone shouted urgently, "Here he is! In here! He's hiding in the lab!"

In seconds heavy steps pounded along the corridor. There was a rush of activity in the office. George Devoto stood helpless, immobilized by shock and confusion. Who had been here in the lab? What was he doing here?

The laboratory lights bathed him in their full glare—a trembling figure still wearing his heavy coat, his ski mask. There was no escape. Devoto stared at the grim faces of the student patrol as they crowded into the lab. Behind them, in the outer office, a figure slipped into the corridor, his back visible for only an instant before he was gone.

A knot of students had gathered outside the physics building. "Did you catch him?" one of them asked. He nodded. They thought he was part of the patrol.

Unhurried now, he walked away from the building. Poor George, he thought without emotion. Poor, dumb, angry George. So angry, and yet so eager to share that anger with someone who gave him half a chance, so ready to let his shallow rage spill out.

The Intruder had listened while George talked, encouraging him, even asking questions about his work in the physics lab, the computer he used, the project Professor Webster was working on. George told him everything. All he had to know.

And more. One night he had seen the blood on George's trousers when he returned to the apartment they had lately shared. The next morning there was news of another coed attacked. George had been oddly relieved that someone knew. He had needed the catharsis of confession.

If only George had not picked tonight for another of his escapades! Or if, on this night of all nights, he had sought some other place to hide when he was pursued! Taking refuge in the physics laboratory, Devoto had almost discovered him. There in the lab by means of the copy he had made of George's key. Accessing the computer through George's identity number. Tampering with George's program. There had been nothing he could do but give the alarm. . . .

At the edge of the campus the Intruder lingered. He had not

253

had time to retrieve the program printout when he was interrupted by Devoto's sudden arrival. Would he dare risk returning to the laboratory, even when activity around the building ceased? No. Someone might still be there.

Would Dr. Webster question the printout in the morning—detect the one small variation the Intruder had inserted in the instructions? Would he recheck the program before running it through the computer at the data center?

The risk seemed minimal. George had said the physicist seldom checked on his work anymore, as long as he stayed within the narrow limits assigned to him. It was this assurance that had emboldened the Intruder to act.

He had always planned to use a Trojan horse if the opportunity could be found. He had needed access to a computer interfaced with the RDC. He had needed an innocuous piece of software, a frequently used program that would not be questioned. The routine program prepared for the series of challenges that would be made against Linus Webster's mathematical model of power usage seemed perfect. That program waited now in the minicomputer's memory bank, ready to run. The Intruder had simply replaced George Devoto's version with his own: They were identical except for one small change, a Trojan horse whose trapdoor would open only when the program ran. And as soon as that happened, the secret instruction would self-destruct, erasing all evidence that it had ever existed.

The Intruder himself could not transfer the booby-trapped program to the RDC's main computer. George Devoto had not had that authority. Only Webster could do it. When he did, the program would be activated at his level of access—privilege mode, the highest level offered to any RDC user. There the trapdoor would open, allowing the Intruder to penetrate the heart of the system at last.

He shivered, not with cold. It would happen Monday. George Devoto had said that Webster would begin to run his tests then. It seemed unlikely that the shocking news awaiting him about his young assistant would delay his schedule.

Monday. He had waited seven years. He could wait one more day. . . .

THROUGHOUT Monday morning Linus Webster received a flow of data on energy usage from the Atomic Energy Commission, Consolidated Edison and other public utilities participating in his research. Now it was time to challenge his model with real problems—a brownout in Lansing, Michigan; an explosion knocking out a utility tower in Berkeley, California; another blizzard sweeping the Rockies—all occurring on the same morning and making demands on the nation's interdependent power system.

Locked in concentration on his project, Webster was unaware of the rumors penetrating every corner of the campus—rumors about his assistant, George Devoto. Webster was aware only that Devoto had not shown up for work. Considering his eagerness on Friday to try out the test program, his absence was strange. Checking the lab computer, Webster discovered that Devoto had, in fact, verified the program in hard copy; a printout was there.

By eleven thirty, disgruntled, Webster gave up on his assistant for the day, and at eleven thirty-three he accessed the RDC's computer in privilege mode. The system identified and cleared him. Webster immediately activated the test program George Devoto had been working on. The program went into its routine without a flaw. Unnoticed, the Trojan horse ran.

TUESDAY was payday for all city employees, and Kenny Nance's check was fifty dollars short. Grinning, he carried the check into James Conway's office. "Okay," he said, "I know we've got budget problems, but why start with me?"

The expression on Conway's face stopped him. "It isn't only you, Kenny. It's every employee on the city payroll."

The pattern was clearer by Tuesday afternoon when Del Thomas, white-faced, arrived at the mayor's office. A dump had been taken of the computerized payroll program which had run Monday night. Buried in the program was an instruction directing the system to divert fifty dollars from each paycheck to accounts at three different local banks. Surprisingly there had been no effort to hide the transfer of funds. The accounts had been opened recently in three names: Anderson, Benson and Cole.

"What about the money in those accounts?" Conway said.

Thomas floundered. "It...it hasn't been touched."

Conway let him squirm a moment. "Don't you have any idea how this instruction got into the system? Or when?"

"No." The response was barely audible.

"Could it have happened before you shut down last Thursday? Before you put in your so-called clean operating system?"

"My people say no. After the new operating system was put in, we checked out each program before it was reactivated. That includes the payroll program."

"What you're saying is, since you shut down and started up again with a clean system, the Intruder has penetrated it again."

The RDC's director nodded reluctantly.

"Why were you able to find his instruction so easily? Every other stunt he's pulled, you couldn't find out how he did it. But this one pops out of the machine the first time you ask. That tells us something, doesn't it?"

"I ... I'm not sure." Thomas was afraid to commit himself.

"He wanted us to find it," Conway said. "He never intended to withdraw that money. He's just letting us know he can do anything he wants with the system."

The first direct message from the Intruder, shortly before four o'clock that afternoon, confirmed Conway's fear. Addressed to James Conway, Mayor, and labeled TOP SECRET, it appeared only on the terminal in Del Thomas' office at the Regional Data Center and was displayed only once, briefly. A hard-copy printout followed immediately. It read:

```
DEMAND IS MADE UPON THE CITY OF HOLLISTER
FOR PAYMENT OF INJURIES IN THE AMOUNT OF
$5 MILLION—REPEAT $5 MILLION.
INSTRUCTIONS TO FOLLOW. END.
```

A second message was shorter and was accompanied by a simultaneous system crash, which shut down all activity at the data center for one minute with the exception of the terminal in Thomas'

256

office. The shutdown began at four o'clock. At 04:01:01 the system began to function normally again, to the buzzing confusion of the programmers and operators on duty.

Thomas called MacAdam into his office when the second message appeared on the screen. They stared numbly at the repeated communication. It said:

```
THE SYSTEM IS MINE
THE SYSTEM IS MINE
THE SYSTEM IS MINE
THE SYSTEM IS MINE
```

PART THREE
MATCH

WED FEB 16 / 08:00 AM

EARLY Wednesday morning Egan met with Tom Ames in the campus security chief's office and filled in the burly ex-cop on the events culminating in the Intruder's takeover of the RDC.

"What can I do?" Ames asked.

"I need extra legs," Egan said. "One of the ways to penetrate a computer system is a wiretap. That means getting at actual communications lines, or using equipment to pick signals out of the air from communications lines or from computers themselves."

"Sounds far out."

"I think it is in this case, but only because he'd have to be more visible than he's been. We're talking about several weeks at least. It'd be hard for a truck full of gear to go unnoticed around here for that long."

"How about one of those painted-up student vans?" Ames said. "I can check that out. What else?"

"I've got a chart of communications lines feeding into the data center. I need a manual search made of every junction box on this campus, for any sign of a wiretap. I'm told there's a way to insert another computer into a line so you wouldn't know it was there. That's the kind of thing I'm looking for."

"Okay," Ames said dubiously. "That it?"

Egan hesitated. This was what he really wanted. "I need names," he said. "Student names, addresses, records, identifying data. Plus faculty, administrators and anyone else who's been around this campus recently."

"What are you looking for?"

"I'm not sure," Egan admitted. "But I'll know if I find it."

A message from Del Thomas was waiting on Egan's desk when he returned to his office, and Egan called him immediately. "We've got something for you," Thomas said tersely. "I'm tied up for the next hour. MacAdam will fill you in."

Carl MacAdam was expecting him, but he betrayed no excitement as he waved Egan to a chair. His office was like the man—cool, spartan, efficient—the top of the desk almost bare.

"I hope you've got something good," Egan said. "I could use some good news about now."

MacAdam lifted his shoulders in a deprecatory shrug. He gave the impression that the problem of the Intruder was simply another vexing programming error. He began with a brief authoritative explanation. "There are checkpoints in computerized data files. These are created so that if there is an error or a security violation to be checked out, it isn't necessary to go through the entire file from the beginning. It's possible to fall back to the nearest checkpoint, since we know that all the data up to that point are uncorrupted." He raised an eyebrow questioningly.

"I'm with you so far," Egan said.

"Some of the errors we're now attributing to this Intruder had to do with information from other data banks," MacAdam went on. "Or misinformation in the case of the criminal histories attributed to Ralph Lambert and Mrs. Conway. There is authority in the system to request such information. The city, for example, can get arrest records on its job applicants even though those records are denied to the private sector."

Egan nodded. The ready accessibility of data in the criminal justice system explained how the Intruder had made erroneous transcripts appear so authentic. They were. The records simply belonged to two other people, not to Lambert or Toni Conway.

"Unfortunately we still don't know how he did it," MacAdam admitted. "The Intruder succeeded in suppressing any evidence of his manipulations that we could find. But by falling back to check-

258

points in one particular file, it has been possible to establish that Hollister University's administrative program had been penetrated on the night of Thursday, December 16, when the letters of acceptance for spring registration were processed. The names of all applicants were already in the computer. We can pinpoint the time of penetration because the input—which listed the successful applicants—wasn't completed until late Thursday afternoon, around five o'clock. The automated processing of the form letters and the confirmation punch cards was done after that."

He paused, enjoying Egan's eager attention. "That volume of typing takes time, even for a computer, so it was scheduled when other activity was light. So what we now know is this: sometime between five o'clock in the afternoon and midnight of December 16, the system was induced to accept every application on file, rather than only those that had been approved."

MacAdam picked up several sheets of paper, tapped them neatly into line and handed them to Egan. "If you'll study these transcripts, you'll see what else we have. We checked the five-to-midnight record of usage for that date at every terminal. Then we compared those usage records with normal activity at each terminal over the last two months. We did find unusual activity at one terminal—excessive user time-outs and a higher than normal error rate, always occurring at night. You'll find it all here, including the last record of an unauthorized request on Friday, February 4. There's been nothing unusual from that terminal since."

"Where is this terminal?" Egan asked.

"At Hollister County General Hospital."

MAGGIE Henderson, the night operator at the hospital terminal, did not come on duty until four in the afternoon. Egan obtained her name and address from the hospital administrator's office. She shared an apartment with one of the hospital's interns.

The young man who opened the door was swarthy and black-haired. He was not yet thirty, Egan guessed, but he had tired eyes.

"Mr. Martinez?"

"Whatever it is, we're not buying."

"I'm not selling. Is Miss Henderson in? It's important that I talk to her." Egan fished out his ID card.

259

"Joe? Who is it?" a woman called out.

Martinez gave ground grudgingly as Egan entered the room. He seemed uncertain of his role.

The young woman was tall and leggy, with a full, soft mouth and suddenly frightened eyes. "He's from the RDC," Martinez said tersely. It was meant to be a warning.

"Oh no! Joe, I told you—" She broke off, staring at Egan. "You know, don't you?"

"Suppose you tell me," said Egan. He smiled, trying to put her more at ease. "Is that coffee I smell?"

"Yes . . . uh . . . would you like a cup?"

Over coffee she opened up. She had known all along, she said, that sooner or later the RDC would find out that she had been careless about terminal security.

"Did you suspect someone else might be using the terminal?"

"Yes . . . but I couldn't see why."

"Couldn't medical records be stolen?"

"Yes, but what use would they be to anyone?"

Egan did not tell her that a great many people might find medical data useful—insurance and credit companies, employers, friends and enemies of the individual about whom the reports were made. "Why didn't you report your suspicions?" he asked.

"I . . . I was afraid of losing my job."

Egan nodded. She wasn't guilty of anything worse than carelessness, he thought, and her confession did not bring him any closer to the Intruder, except to confirm that he had probably used the hospital's terminal to gain access to the data center.

"Can you give me any idea who might have been able to make use of the terminal without your knowledge?"

Mutely Maggie Henderson shook her head. There was little more for Egan to learn. And now he had to consider the entire population of a busy county hospital among his suspects.

But how could the Intruder have known that Maggie's terminal was sometimes left unattended? Perhaps, as Egan had suggested to Tom Ames, he might have parked a well-equipped van in the parking lot and picked up signals emanating from the terminal simply by listening. But then again, no firsthand observation would have been necessary if the Intruder was an insider at the

260

data center, someone able to examine records of transactions from various remote terminals. He might have found evidence of repeated gaps in nightly transmissions, suggesting that the terminal was unattended. Egan shook his head in frustration. Too many possibilities were still open. The Intruder had everything going for him—including time.

ALL Wednesday morning Mayor Conway's outer office had been crowded. A lawyer representing one of the victims of the Hill Street accident was threatening to sue the city. A member of the school board was irate over the fire department's failure to save many of the classrooms at Henry Adams High. Skeptical reporters were seeking answers to spreading rumors about problems at the data center. The city was uneasy, Conway thought. An invisible and random threat was always the most frightening. Like a plague that selected its victims unpredictably. The Intruder had brought that kind of fear to the city.

Conway gazed out the window, brooding—and thought of Toni. Where was she? He wondered if he should ask Nance to trace her. He only wanted to know that she was okay. But at the same time he couldn't risk having her think she was being watched. That might be the last straw. He knew he had let her down.

In some ways she was naïve for her years. She had stepped from childhood into marriage, with a brief episode in between when she wore beautiful clothes and everyone admired her. She had believed in him with an innocent faith he had failed to return. What scared him was that she might just say to hell with it.

He shook himself. He was still mayor, and if anything, his city was in worse trouble than he was. The Intruder had brought the crisis Conway had always wondered about. Now that it was here he was still unsure of himself. Events—public or private—could not always be manipulated. Neither his marriage nor the fate of Hollister was under his control. In each case, someone else was in command.

At noon the mayor's emergency task force met in the private banquet room of a bar and grill two blocks from city hall. The group included Jay Burton of the city council; Jerry Devine, the comptroller; Keith Simpson of the Merchants Bank; Laurence

Grayson of Grayson's Department Store; and Michael Egan from the data center's security office, who had just finished conferring in low tones with a heavyset, quick-eyed field agent from the FBI. The noon hour had been chosen to give the meeting the appearance of a routine business luncheon.

"I don't quite understand why you wanted me here, Mr. Conway," Laurence Grayson said.

"You will," Conway assured him.

For ten minutes, calmly and quietly, Conway addressed the meeting, outlining the Intruder's bizarre campaign against the city. After the first few minutes, he spoke into an awed silence. No one was eating. Conway's last words repeated the ransom demand. "He wants five million dollars."

"It's outrageous!" Burton shouted. "This is your doing, Conway—you and your computer system!"

"W-we can't p-p-pay," Jerry Devine said, shocked into stuttering. "It would b-bankrupt us."

"Can't you shut the system down?" Laurence Grayson asked.

"That's right!" Burton cried. "Shut down. Turn off the faucets. Then let him sing for his money."

Conway checked an impatient retort. He had not wanted to bring Burton in on this meeting. But whatever decision was made, Conway would need the support of the city council. "We can't shut down without making the situation public," he pointed out. "And that would be like shouting 'Fire!' in a theater. Secondly, the Intruder has threatened to wipe out our entire software system —the operating system for the RDC and all of our programs and files—if we attempt to shut down. Even if we could reconstruct all the data, which is questionable, the time and costs involved would be catastrophic."

"Can he wipe out the system just like that?" the banker, Keith Simpson, inquired.

"He can if he's in complete control," Laurence Grayson said. He was more familiar than the others with computer technology. "What about cutting off power to the RDC?"

"We thought of that," Conway answered. "Unfortunately there's no way we could cut off the power without the Intruder discovering it. He may even have programmed the system to self-destruct

262

if its power is interrupted. In any event, cutting it off would leave us with the same problems we'd have in shutting down." Conway could sense the dismay among his listeners as the gravity of the situation became clear.

"We'll have to pay," Grayson said. "Under the circumstances, I'd say he's letting us off cheap."

"Cheap!" Jerry Devine protested. "You call five million dollars cheap?"

"Stop and think for a minute what he can do," the store owner explained. "What if he shut down the fire and traffic programs completely? What if he decided to scramble property and tax records? What I'm saying is, this Intruder hasn't even scratched the surface of the chaos he can produce in this city."

"Yes," Conway said slowly, "and he can always increase his demands, like any other blackmailer. What we're doing is buying time until we can catch him."

"Catch him!" exclaimed Keith Simpson. "Is that still possible?"

"It's a long shot, but we haven't given up. Chief Toland is working on it, and the FBI is cooperating." Conway turned to Egan with an expression of confidence he was far from feeling. "Mr. Egan is the new security director at the RDC. He's working on a plan to try to identify the Intruder. Would you tell them what you have in mind, Mike?"

"What I have in mind," Egan began, "is simply to use computers, the Intruder's own weapon, against him. To do that I need access to a computer system that can be divorced completely from the data center. And I need a computer expert to work with me. In a nutshell, we're going to try a nationwide search for information that will connect this man with Hollister. I'm talking about a computer search, inquiries against every data system that could possibly provide us with some kind of a clue."

"It's a long shot, all right," Laurence Grayson said. "Do you have your expert?"

"The man I have in mind is a local consultant who used to work at the center. His name is Greiner. I believe he's already working on your problem at Grayson's."

"And do you have a computer system in mind?"

"Yes, sir. Your system at the store."

For a moment Hollister's leading retail merchant was silent. Then he nodded. "You've got it."

"Thank you, Laurence," said Conway quickly. "Now you know why I asked you to be here."

There was a sober silence in the room.

"You'll make arrangements to pay, then?" the FBI man asked quietly. It was the first time he had spoken.

Conway hesitated. "The city attorney tells me I have a fairly broad authority to use the emergency fund in a crisis. But I don't know how the city council would feel. . . ."

Everyone looked at Jay Burton. The councilman stared at Conway with hostility, but there was something else in his eyes, an uneasiness beyond anger.

"He could ruin us," Burton said in a low voice. "There was something mailed to my house. A . . . a medical report. I don't need to go into what was in it except that it was . . . embarrassing. And it came out of the RDC. You can add that to your list of the Intruder's tricks," he added bitterly. "You got us into this, Conway. Now you're going to have to buy us out."

Conway cleared his throat. "It's settled, then." He turned to Michael Egan. "You may be our only hope, Mike. You'd better get started."

THE movers arrived at Norma Hooper's apartment building Wednesday afternoon. The building manager had protested when she told him she was moving out. There was no reason to go, he had insisted. Neither he nor the regular occupant of 211 could be blamed for the actions of some loony. "He told me he got this George Devoto's name from the university bulletin board just last month. How could he have known?" Anyway, Devoto was now in jail—and even if he got out, he would never move back into this building.

Norma didn't really want to leave. She had lived in this apartment for nearly five years, and it was home. But she couldn't sleep at night. She found herself listening to the sounds from the upstairs apartment, which could often be heard late at night. She would never relax until she got away from this place whose common roof she had unwittingly shared with a rapist.

THEY WERE LIKE animals strange to each other, Egan thought, unexpectedly penned inside a cage, circling each other warily. The cage was the computer-terminal room on the sixth floor of Grayson's Department Store. Communications lines linked the computer directly with the telephone company's central station. Those lines were now being monitored against wiretapping.

"You talked to the mayor?" Egan asked Rob Greiner. "You'll cooperate?"

"I said I'd listen. The city's paying me if I take the job. So what is this bright idea?"

"I'm not a computer man," Egan began, "but I know some of the ways data systems can be used. I was with the FBI—"

"One of my favorite teams."

Egan let the sarcasm go by. "My point is that most cases are solved by running down information that is already on record."

"I don't get it. How do we run down records on somebody we don't know anything about?"

"We use this country's data banks. And we look for a match. That's what you call it, isn't it? When you can pair off different facts or link sets of data?"

"Yeah. But a match is like a love affair. It takes two. You don't know a thing about this Intruder."

"We know a little. We've got a connection with Hollister, probably sometime in the past. We've got an 'injury' of some kind—that's what the Intruder called it—and we have what amounts to a vendetta against this city because of that injury. It must have been something important enough to be noticed. So we start looking in local records—births, deaths, marriages, divorces."

"You're forgetting something. Those are in the RDC now. And your boy would know it if you started digging."

"I'm aware of that, so the FBI will be working with the local police on a manual search of all local records."

Greiner frowned. "You still need a name to start with. It took your FBI a year to find Patty Hearst, and they *knew* who she was."

"I know it won't be easy. Anyway, my guess is the Intruder would anticipate a local search and cover himself. So we start looking elsewhere. We know that he knows computers well; he has to have studied computer technology somewhere. That adds another factor.

Now we have three things: a connection with Hollister, a grievance and a computer background. As for names," Egan went on, "we have a lot of those. Too many. There are the RDC people, for instance. I have security files on all of them, and recent background checks on most. Then there are the students at the university with computer studies in their records. And there are the victims, all those who've been affected by what the Intruder has done up to now. Maybe all of them weren't random victims."

"You're really grabbing at straws."

Egan shrugged irritably. "Maybe. But it's worth trying. People think they don't leave any traces of themselves, but they do—wherever they go, whatever they do. This country is a maze of record systems. On the state level, there are driving records, criminal records, labor records, tax files. This state has a centralized student information system on computer, and so do many others. When you move up to the federal government, there are hundreds of data banks. The U.S. Office of Education has a migrant student record system. The Department of Justice has a civil disturbance file and an interdepartmental intelligence unit. Then there are military service records, the FBI, the Internal Revenue—"

"Hold it!" Greiner protested. "Okay, I get your point."

"The kind of search I'm talking about wouldn't even have been possible a few years ago. I'm talking about a national search, Greiner. Every data bank we can query. How long does it take a computer to search its own files, anyway?"

"Depends. If the data's on-line, not long. A medium-sized computer can execute about a million instructions in one second." Egan sensed an alertness in Greiner which had not been there a few minutes ago. That was important. If he saw it as a challenge, Rob Greiner going one-on-one against the Intruder in a test of wit and skill, he would give it his best shot.

"What you want is a profile of this whole case," Greiner said slowly. "Everything we know about this Intruder, what he's done and who he's done it to. And you want me to search the whole country's data files for some kind of match?"

"That's it."

"Crazy," Greiner said. Abruptly he smiled. "I wonder if he's thought of it. If I set out to terrorize a whole town and rip off five

266

million dollars, I'd use an assumed identity. And I'd have erased Robert Greiner from the records."

"This whole idea is based on the fact that he couldn't remove every trace."

"Yeah. He probably couldn't get into some systems. The security gets tight in those big government files. By the way, how do *we* get into them?"

"Some will do their own searching, if they give us anything at all. Some may just say no. But this is a local government problem, which will get us cooperation in most areas. And we can also get some clearances through the FBI."

"You've thought about this," the other man said grudgingly.

Egan smiled. It had been a small skirmish, he thought, but an important one to win. Greiner was committed. "How long will it take to profile all the information we have?"

Greiner shrugged. "Any way of cutting down the roster? Incidentally, we can't go after the university records. They're in the RDC's files, too."

"I've got student names already," Egan said without explanation, thankful that Tom Ames had done his work quickly. "We can narrow the list down. We're probably looking for a man, for instance. Very few wiretappers and arsonists are women."

"Okay." There was a new urgency in Greiner's voice. "Break down your lists—and give me some priorities. What's the most important set of names or facts, what comes second, and so on."

SHORTLY after five Mayor Conway arrived at the data center. Del Thomas escorted him to his office. "I'm sorry to bring you over here," Thomas explained agitatedly, "but the . . . the Intruder insists that from now on he will communicate with you and no one else. I am to . . . push the buttons," he added morosely.

At right angles to the director's desk was a console housing a small unit of the computer system with an input keyboard and a video display panel. "We're to let him know when you've arrived," Thomas said. He typed rapidly on the keyboard, and the words appeared on the cathode-ray tube display.

MAYOR CONWAY IS READY TO RECEIVE YOUR MESSAGE.

Seconds later an answering message moved across the screen.

```
YOU ARE LATE MAYOR CONWAY. DO NOT DO
IT AGAIN. IN FUTURE YOU WILL HOLD YOURSELF
READY TO RECEIVE INSTRUCTIONS ON THIS UNIT.
HAVE YOU MADE ARRANGEMENTS FOR PAYMENT
OF THE $5 MILLION SETTLEMENT?
```

Conway tried to find emotion in the electronic display. There was a humorless arrogance, to be sure. A trace of bravado: he was young. Putting a mayor through his paces was new to him. But there was something else behind the impersonal electronic images on the screen. Impatience. Edginess. Was he not quite as sure of himself as his performance these past weeks indicated? Or was something else disturbing him?

Conway looked at Thomas. "Tell him I'm working on it, and I must have approval of the city council."

The Intruder's response to Conway's message was immediate.

```
DELAY IS UNACCEPTABLE.
YOU HAVE EXACTLY 48 HOURS TO
COMPLETE ARRANGEMENTS FOR PAYMENT. MONEY
WILL BE HELD IN MERCHANTS BANK CITY ACCOUNT
WITH AUTHORIZATION FOR WIRE TRANSFER AS
DIRECTED AFTER 05:00 PM FRIDAY. YOU WILL
STAND BY TO RECEIVE FINAL INSTRUCTIONS
AT THIS HOUR TOMORROW. END.
```

The display screen went blank. Conway stared at the empty screen, feeling a helpless frustration. Wire transfer, he thought. Not cash that could be marked or traced. Something invisible: an electronic funds transfer, an exchange of information between two or more computers. Instant transfer from Hollister to a private numbered account in a bank anywhere in the world.

The moving van was pulling away from the apartment building as the Intruder drove up. He watched it lumber around the corner, heading north. He was feeling depressed now, like someone com-

*ing down from a high. He had been exhilarated when he had
Mayor Conway dancing at the end of his line. Now there was an
awful letdown.*

As the time drew near, rage was never far away.

*Entering the building, he saw that Norma Hooper's door was
open, and he stood for a moment, staring into the empty room. So
the timid Miss Hooper was running away. For a moment it seemed
as if her flight were a personal insult, for which she must be punished. He had done nothing to harm her.*

*He wondered if Norma Hooper had fled because of what she
had learned about George Devoto, so briefly her neighbor, or because she had sensed that a greater danger still lived less than ten
feet away, directly overhead?*

*He went up to his apartment. Angrily he stomped across the floor,
on the chance that Norma Hooper had lingered, packing her souvenirs of an unlived life. Why did she make him so angry? Because
of the reminder of that other life so pathetically wasted?*

*He lost minutes to his rage, so indistinguishable now from his
grief. Then he remembered the scene he had played out with
Mayor Conway, and there was a renewed surge of elation.*

"IF YOU keep buying me dinners," Jenny Tyson said, "I'm going
to feel obligated."

"That's the idea," Egan said amiably.

It was after nine o'clock, Wednesday evening, and they were
finishing off a hamburger and fries at the local fast-food outlet.
Jenny looked down at her paper coffee cup. "Do you still hear from
her, Michael?"

"Who?"

"You know who. Miss California. The woman you left behind."

"How do you know there was one?"

"I'm psychic, didn't I tell you? You're not being fair, you know.
Here I went through my whole true-confessions number Saturday,
and you haven't told me a thing about her." She hesitated. "Are you
still in love with her? Is that why you don't talk about it?"

Egan was instantly sobered. "It's been over a long time. As far
as being in love goes—really being in love—I think I'm only beginning to get an idea what that might be."

She didn't care then if he never talked about Miss California, but he did. "There isn't much to tell," he said, and proceeded to tell her about Joan Wellman.

He told the story unembellished, as if he were giving a deposition. The truth, the whole truth, and nothing but the truth.

"I was just one of her display pieces," he said finally. "The FBI man. There was also the actor, the stockbroker, the yachtsman . . . you name it. So I discovered during one memorable argument. I think I might have stayed angry longer if it had been only the stockbroker. But you can't stay mad or jealous when you find out you were something like part of a chain letter."

"Ummm." Jenny decided she had heard enough about Joan Wellman, her Mercedes and her chain of admirers. But this resolution had hardly formed before the next question popped out, unbidden. "Does she still phone?"

"No."

"A little too much hesitation there, Egan." Oh, wrong, wrong! She was coming on like a shrew. But she couldn't stop herself. "Is she still important, Michael?"

"No—you are. Jenny . . . forget about her. She belongs to another world. Not even a very important one."

"Are you kidding? Forget about her? I can't even handle a dead husband, much less a live Miss Sunkist." She stopped. "I said it, didn't I? About David."

"Loud and clear. He *is* dead, Jenny. And it wasn't your doing. He was where he chose to be, from what you told me."

"I know, I know." She sighed. "We've got a problem."

"I don't think so."

"What do you know?" Her eyes were full on him, and she said quietly, "I'm in love with you."

There was a long moment before Egan said, "It's about time you admitted it. And I thought you were such a cool lady."

"Think again, sir."

They grinned at each other foolishly. At last Egan said, "Our timing is lousy. I've got to get those lists of names to Greiner."

"Don't apologize," she said. "Michael, darling—I'm the one who got you into this thing, remember? I'm the girl who suggested there was an intruder." The glow of the past few moments remained,

270

but she became thoughtful. "You and Greiner—it surprised me when you decided to use Rob. I thought you suspected him."

"I haven't ruled him out completely. But if you suspect someone in a situation like this, you're better off having him where you can watch him. Anyway, I don't think he's the Intruder. Whoever the Intruder is, he's someone you don't notice much, because he's not what he seems to be. Greiner is just too conspicuous."

"Do you think you have any real chance of identifying him through the data banks?"

"It seems like a good idea, but—" Egan suddenly threw up his hands. "What's wrong with me? Jenny—you can speed things up! You could work with Greiner. That is, if you don't mind going without much sleep for the next two days."

"You know I don't," she said eagerly.

"I'll get Thomas to lend you to us. He won't object. I've got a lot of clout right now—five million dollars' worth."

"Five million dollars," Jenny said with a kind of awe. "Is that what he was after all along?"

The question had been on Egan's mind ever since the Intruder's ransom demand. Motive was a crucial factor in any crime. "I think the money is only part of it," he said finally. "Whatever it was that happened—whatever he blames Hollister for—means more to him than the money. At least it did in the beginning. . . ."

After driving Jenny home, Egan returned to the data center to set some priorities on his lists of names. It was midnight when he dropped them off at Grayson's. "I'll be back in the morning," he told Greiner. "With some help for you."

"I don't need any help," said Greiner quickly.

"You've got a lot of names to go through and we have less than forty-eight hours. That's the deadline he's given the mayor. Besides, I think you can work with this person. Jenny Tyson."

Greiner broke off his protest. He stared at Egan for a moment in silence, then said, "Why are you so hot on catching this guy?"

"It's my job. Besides, in my book he's a murderer."

"Maybe he didn't mean for anyone to get hurt."

"That's one of the problems with crime. You think you can contain it. You can't. You're going to rob a bank, say, and all you want to do is scare the folks into following orders. Then a little old lady

271

walks in when she isn't supposed to, somebody gets excited, and a few people get shot. There's no such thing as a harmless crime."

"Hmmm. All right, Egan. I've got one more question for you. How come the Intruder's giving the mayor forty-eight hours to come up with the money? Have you wondered about that?"

"Maybe he thinks it will take that long for Conway to get authorization and set up the payment."

"Uh-uh. He's not doing the city any favors. He's got his own reason for stalling. You better try to figure out what it is, Egan, because I think he's got something else up his sleeve."

BY LATE Thursday the responses to the computer search for the Intruder were beginning to pile up in long ribbons of white printout paper on the floor at Grayson's. For each of the names on Egan's lists a punch card had been prepared—Jenny Tyson's assignment—and fed into the computer. For each name the same questions had to be asked. The most time-consuming task had been getting the known information organized, programmed for the computer and punched onto the cards.

The search itself within any particular data base would be simpler. The repetition of simple steps over and over with dazzling speed was precisely what computers did best. For any computer to search its memory and pick out data matching people with certain keys—Hollister, computer education, injury or accident—was a swift and simple procedure.

The computer search had begun with other city, county and state record systems—including motor vehicle departments, medical and insurance records, and criminal history files in each state. Names of individuals had been checked against the cities they had lived in, the schools they had attended, the organizations they had belonged to. One student at Hollister University had sixteen unpaid traffic tickets. Several had been arrested for minor offenses. Every incident reported, every match recorded for every name, had had to be examined, but not one had suggested a motive for the Intruder's vendetta or a clue to his identity.

The search had then turned to national data banks. Some were huge—the Social Security Administration alone had over a hundred and fifty million citizens listed. The Veterans Administration and the Department of Defense had data banks almost as large.

Credit agencies were being queried when Egan left the terminal room for a smoke in the adjoining office. His reflection brooded at him from the window as he stared out at the darkening city. Another reflection appeared behind him and he turned quickly. "Getting discouraged?" Jenny asked.

"Let's say I'm not exactly encouraged."

"We've still got a long way to go."

"And we have less than twenty-four hours."

"That's a lot of time for a computer," she said.

The Intruder walked rapidly away from the physics building. Lights were on in the laboratory on the second floor, and someone appeared briefly in one of the windows. He had a plan for such a contingency.

Now that he had established full communication with the RDC's computer, he had been able to adapt a portable, hand-held terminal for direct input to the main processor. He preferred the greater

flexibility of the laboratory's minicomputer, but for tonight's message the portable terminal would be adequate. He wanted only to give the mayor his final warning.

His hand closed around the emergency terminal in his coat pocket—a tiny keyboard with a slightly elongated miniature display panel.

Two blocks from the campus he found what he was looking for—two public phone booths outside a gas station which had closed early for the night. Both phones had Touch-Tone dials.

He stepped into one of the

booths and closed the door. It took him only a few seconds to hook up the portable terminal to the telephone. Then he dialed the RDC.

His first message, again received in Del Thomas' office, directed Mayor Conway to be present in the computer room at the RDC the next day, Friday, from five o'clock on. The room was to be cleared of all personnel; Conway would wait there, with only one designated operator in the room with him.

Prior to five o'clock Conway was to have completed all arrangements for the transfer of funds. He was to be on hand to authorize the payment, the operator to carry out instructions as they were received from the Intruder. No one else was to be present. Not only the computer room but the entire data center was to be cleared.

"That's preposterous," Del Thomas objected. "I won't leave—"

"The whole thing's preposterous," Conway cut him off. "But we'll do what he says. We have no choice."

The second message was briefer. It said:

```
ADDITIONAL DEMONSTRATION OF WHAT WILL
HAPPEN IF MY ORDERS ARE NOT OBEYED
WILL BE PROVIDED WITHIN THE HOUR. END.
```

For the next hour an atmosphere of tension pervaded Del Thomas' office. There was little discussion. Six o'clock came and went. Nothing happened. Conway broke a long silence. "Any guesses on what that last threat meant? Why haven't we heard anything?"

"It's possible," Thomas suggested, "that he's failed. That he can't do everything he claims."

Conway stared at him bleakly. "He can do enough. We probably haven't had time to get word of this next disaster."

The call came at six thirty—from Kenny Nance. Conway took the phone, and his face drained of color as he listened. "The bastard!" he said hoarsely. Conway hung up and stood for several seconds in silence. When he spoke his voice was dull. "He cut off the power to the county hospital," he said. "Five minutes ago."

Four hours after receiving Nance's call, Mayor Conway turned into the driveway of his home. The hospital was running on emergency power. The scene there was one of confusion and anxiety, improvised heroics in the emergency room, frightened relatives and patients—and questions Conway could not answer.

His exhaustion was more than fatigue. Defeat was the crusher. Knowing you were beaten and there wasn't a thing you could do about it. Suddenly his head snapped up. He was still sitting in the car, and he had been slow to react to an ordinary fact that was not ordinary now. Lights were on in the house. Downstairs in the den, the kitchen. The porch light, too. And upstairs, light shone in the windows of the front bedroom.

Conway tumbled out of the car, weary lethargy falling away. He was calling out before he reached the front door and threw it open. "Toni? I can't believe it. Toni, where are you?"

She ran out of the bedroom and stopped, one hand on the banister, the other holding her robe together in front. "You're back," he said, his voice threatening to break. She nodded.

He went up the stairs slowly, with an instinctive need for caution. At the top he paused, facing her. Her robe, the combed-out hair suggested she was back to stay. But there was a gravity in her eyes that left him uncertain. "Why did you come back?" he asked.

"I belong here."

"Yes," he said happily. "You do."

"As long as you feel the same way."

"I love you, Toni—I have from the first night we met. I would love you even if the rubbish in that report had been true."

"You weren't so sure about that at first."

"I am now."

She studied him intently, the grave expression still in her eyes. Conway realized that, whether it had been happening all along or had occurred overnight, his beautiful child bride had grown up.

"I had to work things out," she said finally. "How I really felt."

"And did you?"

She smiled. And there was no hesitation as she came to him.

In the small office adjoining the computer room at Grayson's, Greiner shook Egan awake. "Egan. There's a message for us."

It was at the top of the printout roll in the next room.

```
YOU ARE WASTING YOUR TIME. THE MAN
YOU ARE SEARCHING FOR NO LONGER EXISTS.
DISCONTINUE YOUR SEARCH OR ACCEPT
THE CONSEQUENCES. END.
```

"How did he get into Grayson's system to deliver that message?" Egan demanded. "And how did he find out what we're doing?"

Greiner gave a snort of disgust. "Up until the last few days, getting into this system would have been easy. And he could've planted an instruction that lets him dial in anytime he wants."

"Why didn't he go on using this system?"

"He wanted to get at the city, not Grayson's. To do that he had to penetrate the RDC. I'd say our Intruder was curious, made a quick probe or two, and found out we had a private show going up here. He couldn't know much more than that. Grayson's people are running a very tight ship now, monitoring all activity."

"He knows we're looking for him."

"He knew that anyway."

Egan nodded slowly, his anger under control.

"What about his warning?" Greiner nodded toward the printout. "Discontinue your search or accept the consequences."

"Forget it," Egan said.

"Yeah? Maybe the mayor wouldn't agree."

"The Intruder's not going to do anything to jeopardize his plans because of us," Egan said flatly. "He's too close to getting what he wants. Besides, he probably has a good idea that we *are* wasting our time. You said it yourself; he's only confirming it. He's living under another identity now. That's the only thing his message can mean. The man we're looking for doesn't exist anymore."

"So you're not even going to tell Conway."

Egan's gaze was level and hard. "That's right."

EGAN had slept on a cot in the lounge of the campus security department. He was awake when Tom Ames arrived in the morning. "I think we found where your wiretap *was*," Ames said. "The telephone company guy says a tap was put on a junction box in the

276

basement of the chemistry building, wired into the RDC line, but it's gone now. Sorry, Mike—it doesn't help much."

"It tells us that he was on this campus and knew his way around."

"Any luck with the computer checks?" Ames asked.

Egan shook his head. "We're running out of throws of the dice."

"It's gonna go down tonight, then, just the way this Intruder called it."

"Looks like it. You'll have your people ready? It's been agreed we won't have police on campus. They'd be too conspicuous."

"We'll be ready," Ames said.

Egan nodded. "I've got to make a call," he said. "Then I guess I'd better find a razor to borrow."

Jenny Tyson was having breakfast with her father when Egan called. Returning to the kitchen after talking with him, she dropped into a chair beside her father and yawned. "You've hardly been getting any sleep," Linus Webster said.

"I'll have plenty of time for sleep after tonight." She had told her father of the Intruder's ultimatum, with Michael Egan's sanction.

"You're sure that will be the end of it?"

"Michael thinks so."

"Ah, yes . . . that was Michael on the phone just now?"

"He called to tell me the brownout still has the hospital on emergency power."

Webster looked thoughtful. He sipped his coffee slowly. "Curious," he said after a while. "Your Intruder shows a remarkable knowledge of the power grids. To arrange a selective blackout in that way. It's a very complex system."

"Not for a computer, surely."

"No. . . ."

"What's on your mind? What are you thinking?"

He shook his head. "Nothing that would help you, I'm afraid." He glanced at his daughter fondly. "Isn't it about time I met this young man of yours?"

She laughed, struck by his old-fashioned tone. "You will, as soon as this is over. I think you'll like Michael."

"I expect I will. I enjoyed David, for that matter. But he was not the right man for you. It's time you married again, my dear."

She laughed again, nervously this time.

"That bracelet you wear . . . isn't it time you put it away?"

She stared down at the bracelet, turning her wrist so that she could read the engraved lettering. DAVID TYSON MISSING IN ACTION. She wondered how her wrist would feel without it.

IN ORLANDO, Florida, that morning Rick Harmon, a data processor at the national headquarters for Credit Systems, Inc., went directly to his console. The day before, he had been working on a long inquiry from Grayson's Department Store in Hollister, and the rest of the job was still waiting for him. Harmon felt a bite of irritation. What did they think Credit Systems was running? He didn't like the idea of a wholesale inquiry, even though Grayson's had heavy backing from the city of Hollister. And the FBI.

There were more than two hundred and fifty names in the Hollister inquiry, with a check request going back as far as Credit Systems' files permitted. The whole thing was taking a long time, even at the speed with which the computer read.

By ten forty-two that morning Harmon had completed the last inquiry. And all of it for nothing. Two-thirds of the names were students, most of whom didn't even have credit records. There were several car repossessions, one bankruptcy and the usual number of slow payers. But nothing out of the ordinary. Rick Harmon called up Grayson's computer, using the prearranged code, and an instant later the data was flowing north. Job finished.

Back at his desk he hesitated. Something was nagging him. Something about Hollister and Grayson's Department Store. Then he remembered. He put through a call to the auxiliary facility in Tampa which housed the backup files for Credit Systems. As a precaution against disaster, such as a fire or a hurricane, backup data was stored in a different city.

"Janice? This is Rick Harmon. Listen, I'm sending over a bunch of names. You should have them coming out of the machine in a couple of minutes. I figured I'd better tell you before you started screaming. It's a lot of names."

"What's it all about?"

"I don't know exactly, but . . . a few weeks ago I had a series of inquiries from Grayson's Department Store up in Hollister. They're one of our big subscribers. Routine stuff, but I remember thinking the operator up there was calling in more than usual. I mean, he'd call in for one check, and a half hour later he'd be back. It was like he was trying to find out how our system responded."

"So what?" Janice asked coolly.

"It just seems funny to me, is all. And the Hollister people are looking for something important. I want you to run the names against the backup files to see if there are any unusual intersects. Let me know if you stumble onto anything, okay? Give it priority. This is an urgent special request."

"Isn't everything?" Janice said.

THAT morning Conway had arranged for the ransom demanded by the Intruder to be ready for transfer at the Merchants Bank. Shortly after two o'clock he left his office and drove slowly over to Grayson's, to talk to the search team there. In less than three hours he was to be in the computer room at the data center.

No one at Grayson's was able to offer a reason for Conway to change his mind about making payment tonight as demanded. But Michael Egan stubbornly objected to Conway's willingness to appear in the computer room himself. "It's not a good idea," Egan argued.

"It's not my idea," Conway said. "It's an order."

"Why has he waited until tonight?" Egan said, with a glance of acknowledgment at Greiner. "Why not last night, for instance?"

"You have an explanation?"

"Maybe. For one thing, he means to have the five million dollars transferred through the interbank wire network. He needs someone in a position of authority to get the money out of Merchants Bank. But once that's done, he can have that money routed halfway around the world. The money doesn't move; all that happens is that one bank's computer records a loss and another bank's computer records a credit for the same amount. And there's a good reason for doing this Friday night after five o'clock."

"The banks are closed," Conway said.

"Officially they're closed, but actually a lot of banking activity goes on during those hours. Wherever that money ends up— Switzerland, Argentina, Hong Kong, wherever—the Intruder means to be there to get it. The way he's got this set up, he'll have

279

the whole weekend to get a running start." Egan paused. "Do you see what's bothering me, Mr. Conway?"

"I'm not sure I do. . . ."

"What about the two people who are in that computer room helping him transfer the money? If they know what he's doing, if they're able to follow the money trail, then the Intruder can't show up to collect. We'd be waiting for him."

"We might not be able to keep track of what he does."

"Can he be certain of that? Even though he's in control of the transaction? I'm not sure he'd take that chance."

"What exactly are you driving at, Egan?"

"Whoever goes into that computer room tonight has to be a hostage. The Intruder wants to disappear forever—with the money. He might have started out on this escapade to get even for something, but that isn't enough now. He wants the money, too."

"I'm still not clear—"

"And there's something else," Egan went on stubbornly. "Why did he insist on you being there? You could give the authorization without being in the computer room."

"All right, why?"

"Because you're the mayor of Hollister. You represent this city. And that's also why you shouldn't go into that room. Whoever handles that money transfer can't be allowed to talk."

"Killing two birds with one stone!" Rob Greiner interjected. "I like it, Egan. You're making sense."

There was a prickly silence. "What could he do to us?" Conway asked finally.

"I don't know," Egan admitted. "But he does. Call his bluff. Tell him you'll pay, but not that way."

Conway slowly shook his head. "He won't go for it," the mayor said. "He doesn't have to. And I can't take a chance on what else he might do to this city."

"Whoever walks in there with you will be running the same risk you are," Egan pointed out.

"I understand that. I can't order anyone else to do it."

"You don't have to," Rob Greiner said. The others looked at him in surprise. "If there's anybody who knows that system better than this Intruder, it's me. And if there's anyone who can figure out a way to beat him at his own game, that's me. If I'm in there, I can get at the hardware itself. And maybe—"

"Maybe what?" Conway demanded. "What are you thinking?"

Greiner regarded the mayor with cool arrogance. "Do I go with you or not?"

"Someone has to," Conway said after a moment. "It has to be a volunteer, so it might as well be you. But I don't want you to try anything that will set this man off. That's an order."

"Stop worrying," Greiner said. "I haven't even said there's anything I can do for sure, only that I'd like to have a look."

"All right. We go in at five," Conway said.

"Give me an extra half hour," Greiner said quickly. "See if you can shut down the center by four thirty, and get me in there with nobody else around. We may not have any time after five."

Michael Egan felt a momentary uneasiness, remembering his earlier suspicion that Greiner himself might be the Intruder. What better way to complete his coup than to carry out the last phase himself? But he had to go along with his instinct. "Give him the time, Mr. Conway," he urged. "It may be the only chance we have."

In Orlando, Rick Harmon answered the call from Tampa. "Who did you say is calling?" he asked.

"Janice," the voice said tartly. "Don't tell me you've forgotten your high-priority urgent special request."

"Janice, would I forget you? Did you find anything?"

"Well, one of those names did show up in a file." She read him the brief record. "Notice something funny?"

"What's that?" Harmon asked, while his mind probed the fact that there was a record in the backup file that was not in the main tape library. One was an *exact* duplicate of the other. He thought about all those inquiries from Grayson's a few weeks ago. Had someone used them to get into the files to *remove* a record?

"The date," Janice said. "February 18, 1970. That's today's date, exactly seven years ago."

"So it is," Harmon said.

"So seven years is our time limit, right?"

"Yeah, right." Derogatory information was retained by law for seven years, after which the file was destroyed.

"We're just getting ready to update," Janice said. "If you had called for that information next week, it wouldn't be there."

"That's a funny coincidence, all right. Listen, Janice, thanks a lot." Harmon hung up. He stared at the information he had scribbled down. It didn't look like much. Still . . . you never knew.

"Edward Lee Craddock?" Michael Egan said into the phone.

"That's the name," Rick Harmon answered. "And like I said, it was seven years ago. I mean, to the day! February 18, 1970."

Egan stared at Jenny Tyson, his face mirroring elation and disbelief. "Mr. Harmon, will you go over that again? From the top."

"He was on a Stop Credit Bulletin," the bright, sunshiny voice from Florida said. "He was twenty-one years old and AWOL from Fort Benning, a deserter. Born in Detroit. It looks like he was trying to get to Canada on a credit card. He kept using this oil company card all the way from Georgia on up north where you-all are, and nobody caught it in time. The oil company puts out a Stop Credit Bulletin on bad cards, and they pay a ten-dollar reward for cards that are picked up. Well, this gas station near Hollister, the owner checked the bulletin when this kid tried to use the card to buy some gas. He picked up the card and held it. This Craddock lost his card, and he didn't get any gas either. The station owner turned the card in later and got his ten bucks. I thought it might be important, Mr. Egan, because that station owner was on your list. His name was Prochaska—Arthur J. Prochaska."

"My God!" Egan breathed.

"Listen," Rick Harmon said. "You're lucky to get this. It wasn't in our regular file, but I checked the backup in Tampa on a hunch, and it was there." He paused. "I think someone got in and erased the primary record. Which sounds like Craddock to me."

"Do your records show any personal information on Craddock?"

"Only that he was married and his wife was pregnant."

Rob Greiner had been in the RDC computer room since four thirty and had missed the call from Florida to the task force at Grayson's. The regular staff had been sent home, the center virtually shut down, when the buzzer sounded. Looking up, Greiner saw Mayor Conway standing in the mantrap. Greiner punched

282

the code that operated the inner door, and it opened instantly.

"We've got a match!" Conway shouted. "Egan's done it!"

Conway recounted what Egan had told him about the call from Orlando. "I still don't know how it all ties up," Conway concluded, "but that old man froze in his house because of a computer foul-up on his utility bill. That can't be a coincidence."

"No," Greiner agreed. "But nobody waits seven years to get even for not being able to buy some gas."

"I know. There has to be more to it, but at least we have a real identity. It shouldn't take long to pin down who he is."

"I wouldn't count on it," Greiner said. "You say Craddock got into Credit Systems' files to erase his record. He slipped up on the backup file, but now we know he's been busy making sure he doesn't exist on record."

Conway's elation died. Knowing the Intruder's real name might eventually expose him—but not soon enough. "Could he really have created an identity we couldn't penetrate? Is that possible?"

Greiner shrugged. "I could. Pick a town where the vital statistics are in a data bank and he could be born again, with a new name. You'd have to do a lot of scratching before you'd find out if somebody's loving mom and dad only exist on a piece of tape. And once you get data like that on file, you can build everything else from it—Social Security number, driver's license, the whole bit." Greiner paused. "Yeah, he could be hard to find. He just forgot that backup file. You better hope that wasn't the only mistake he made." Another pause. "I wish I knew how he did that."

"What?"

"I didn't find any extra activity between Grayson's and Credit Systems. I looked for stuff like that when I checked out Grayson's system. There should have been extra line charges, higher billings from CS. There weren't."

Conway felt thoroughly deflated. He glanced at the digital clock on one of the consoles. Five minutes to deadline.

"Well," Greiner said, "what are we gonna do?"

There was a gleam in Greiner's eyes that made Conway look at him narrowly. "Greiner, have you come up with something? Have you found a way to cut him off?"

"No, but I got in there." He looked at the processor. "She's got holes in her. Every system does. And if you can find the holes, you can get into a file and change it, just like your Intruder."

"If he's as smart as he seems, he'll know what you've done!"

"Give me credit," Greiner snapped back. "Look, I'll make it simple. If you know a system well enough—and I do—you can make it work for you. I figure Craddock will be looking for trouble; he'll expect us to try something. So he'll be making a sweep, sending out test signals to search for any changes we might make. But you can also beat that. You can put in what's called a user-controllable change. It answers only to the user. No matter what test he runs, what you've done won't show up. You can make your little piece of business play possum, understand?"

"I think so," Conway said slowly. "What did you do?"

"I figure the one thing he doesn't want us to do is follow the money trail. He'll suppress any printout, and he'll write over the instructions so there's no afterimage we can read later on." Greiner paused, and now the gleam in his eyes was unmistakable. "I just set it up so he'll leave us some tracks, that's all."

LINUS Webster closed the laboratory early. Because Jenny had been uncertain about getting away in time to pick him up, he had made arrangements with Barry Westfield, a young professor in the department, to give him a ride home. Westfield was ready to leave when Webster stopped by his office.

"All set, Doctor? Be with you in a minute."

Linus Webster came to a sudden decision. "That won't be necessary, Barry. My daughter is picking me up after all. So I won't have to bother you."

"No bother, Dr. Webster," the younger man said cheerfully. "Is she meeting you in the parking lot? I'll walk out with you."

He never seemed to be tired, Webster thought, unable to control a slight resentment. One of the problems with growing old was that it was no longer possible to shrug off fatigue. He wondered for a moment how he actually was going to get home. Then he dismissed the thought irritably.

The two men parted near the parking area. Killing time, Webster had a cup of coffee at the student cafeteria. Then he left and slowly retraced his steps.

The physics building was silent as he entered. It was nearly five on a Friday night, and even the dedicated people were anxious to leave. He saw no one as he climbed the stairs to the second floor. The office was dark. Through the frosted glass he could see the glow from the laboratory beyond. He let himself in.

A young man was on the far side of the lab, bent over the minicomputer. His expression was startled as he saw the old man standing in the doorway; his eyes darted anxiously this way and that, as if searching for a way to run. But then his eyes riveted on the physicist, and Webster saw their expression harden.

Webster had known him on sight—at least by the name under which he had masqueraded in Hollister. But the hunch which had brought the physicist back to his laboratory tonight also suggested another name. "You must be Eddie," Linus Webster said.

FRI FEB 18 / 05:00 PM

Now THERE was only one name to match in the labyrinth of data banks: Edward Lee Craddock. At Grayson's, an open line had been set up to the regional FBI office, and Egan had been on the phone constantly. Jenny Tyson was at the computer terminal, sending out requests for data on Craddock to the sources previously queried. Nothing turned up. No Edward Lee Craddock, aged twenty-one in 1970, could be found.

According to Credit Systems, Craddock had come from Detroit. But, as far as Detroit's records were concerned, Edward Lee Craddock had not been born there, he had not attended school or been a truant, he had never been on welfare. He had had no car or driver's license. On record, he did not exist.

Egan appeared in the doorway connecting the two search rooms. "There's nothing on him. Not word one. I can't believe it."

"It's exactly what he told you he'd done," Jenny pointed out.

"I know." Egan scowled pensively. "The irony is that he never could have pulled all this off if we were still using old-fashioned manual records." Egan paused as a new thought struck him. "He's had a lot of time since 1970 to set up his dirty tricks. Where's he been all this time?"

"Canada? Maybe we should be making some inquiries there."

285

"Let's get the FBI on that. They can use their clout with the Royal Canadian Mounties. The fact that Craddock was on the run, a deserter from the army, is still the best lead we have."

At that moment the phone in the computer room rang. Jenny scooped it up, listened briefly, then held it out. "It's Herb Greenberg," she said. "From the *Times*." Later Egan remembered looking at his watch just before he took the phone. It was one minute past five. He wondered what was happening at the RDC.

THE Intruder regarded Linus Webster coolly. He felt quite calm. "Why did you call me Eddie?" he asked.

"George Devoto used the name once, talking about his new roommate. Then he acted as if he wanted to bite his tongue. At the time, I never thought much about it. Why was George worried? Is Eddie your real name?" When the young man did not reply, Webster speculated aloud. "I know about George being a draft evader. He was quite bitter about it. I suppose that's where he knew you before—in Canada?"

"If you think George knew about what I've been doing, you're crazy."

"But you used him. You dealt badly with a friend."

"I wasn't hurting him—he did that to himself."

Linus Webster shook his head in self-deprecation. "I should have suspected. But I didn't. It was that interference with the hospital's power supply that made me wonder. Today I did something I should have done before. I examined the program George worked on for me." The old man paused. "You used my computer and my program to take over the RDC."

"If it hadn't been your program, it would've been someone else's. But if you guessed what happened, why did you come back here alone?"

"Curiosity, I'm afraid. A weakness of my profession."

"Have you told anyone else?"

The old man smiled at the transparent motive behind the question. "Scientists don't publicize their guesses."

The younger man was silent for a long moment before he said, "It doesn't matter. I have no reason to harm you."

Hearing the lie, Linus Webster felt an infinite weariness. He

286

sank onto a stool, wondering if he should take one of his pills. Ordinarily he was able to get by on two a day, but he carried a pillbox in case of sudden stress. He decided to wait. He had less to fear from his heart than from this young man.

"Why did you take over the computer, Eddie?" he asked. "You must have had a strong motivation. It wasn't only money, was it? I can hardly believe that."

The Intruder laughed, but Webster caught the young man's uneasiness. "I want the money because that's the only way you can really hurt them. I'm going to make them bleed money, because that's getting them where they live."

The old man nodded, as if this were a sensible explanation. "It's time you told someone why you find it necessary to punish this city. Don't you want someone to know? It was something that happened a long time ago?" he prompted.

"Yes. Seven years—" The Intruder broke off, suspicion flaring. "Why are you asking so many questions?"

"I'd like to understand. Perhaps even help."

"No one can help. Not now. And you wouldn't understand."

"Try me."

The younger man was silent, struggling with himself. He discovered to his own surprise that he did want someone to know— even if Webster could not be allowed to carry the knowledge away. "They killed her," he said, the words almost inaudible.

"Killed whom, Eddie?"

"My wife! Mary Jane, and . . . and . . ."

Webster's chest contracted painfully. He took a careful breath. "Who did? What are you trying to say?"

"This city—these people—all of them!" Eddie cried. "No one cared—no one would do anything to help! They let her die. And now they're paying for it! Yes, I used your program. George Devoto didn't know, but he almost caught me out. I was here last Sunday night when George tried to hide. I'd been working on his program. I had to give him away. I didn't want to hurt him. He wasn't to blame!"

"The others you've hurt," Webster said softly, "weren't to blame either, surely, for something that happened seven years ago."

"How do you know? You don't know anything!"

"Then tell me!" Webster thundered, the words a command. "For heaven's sake, man, you must tell someone."

Staring at him, startled, the Intruder knew that the old man was right.

"You called in a while ago about this Craddock?" Herb Greenberg said from his desk at the Hollister *Times*.

"What have you got?" Egan asked eagerly.

"With a name and a date to go by, it was easy," Greenberg said. "I looked for something on Craddock for this date back in 1970. I found it in the obits the next day." Egan held his breath.

"The death of one Mary Jane Craddock and a baby, unnamed, on February 18, 1970. Survived by husband, Edward Lee Craddock." Greenberg paused. "It's not much."

"It's a lot more than you think, Herb."

Greenberg was silent a moment before he said, "I guess you have your motive now."

"I guess you're right," Egan said. But as he pressed the disconnect button, he wondered what, exactly, Arthur J. Prochaska's pickup of a credit card had to do with the death of Mary Jane Craddock and her baby.

When the line was clear Egan placed a call to the county hospital's security office. The records were in manual files in the basement, under lock and key. The Craddock file was intact.

"The infant strangled on the umbilical cord," the security man said briskly. "The fetus blocked the passage from the womb, and there was catastrophic hemorrhaging by the mother. Delay in treating a case like that can be fatal, and this time it was."

"I'd like a copy of that record," Egan said. So that was what happened to Edward Lee Craddock's wife and his unborn child.

THE Intruder had turned off all the lights in the physics laboratory except those in the alcove that housed the minicomputer. Feeling the cold and listening to the silence that pervaded the empty halls, Webster had a sense of his isolation.

The Intruder spoke of a lonelier, embittered exile that would never end. "All I wanted was a can of gas," he said. "We ran out on the highway just outside of town. I thought I had enough

288

to get into Hollister, but we didn't make it. It was cold and snowing, and I didn't want her to have to walk, with the baby due any time, so I had to leave her in the car." He paused for a long time. Webster said nothing. "She was all right when I left her. I walked back about a half mile to where I'd seen this gas station, because it was one I had a credit card for. We were out of money. Flat broke. I had spent our last dime on a candy bar for Mary's lunch." He faltered, his features contorted. "This old man was there alone. He was suspicious right off. I had long hair and a beard, and I must've seemed dangerous to him. 'I don't give credit to hippies,' he said. I told him I had a credit card. He took the card and told me I could fill up a can of gas. Then he went into the station, and when he came out he was holding a shotgun. He pointed it at me and said, 'You can leave the gas right there.' He told me my card was on a pickup list, and if I wasn't on my way in ten seconds, he'd call the police.

"I tried to tell him that Mary Jane was in the car, waiting, and that she was pregnant and I had to get her to the hospital. He said I was lying." Anger soured the Intruder's mouth. "I should have gone for him right then, but he looked like he really *wanted* to use that shotgun."

"What happened to your wife?" Webster prompted.

"What happened?" Wildness flamed in Eddie's eyes, then faded. He told the rest of the story in a dead monotone. "When I got back to the car there was already a lot of bleeding, and she kept begging me to get her to the hospital. 'Hurry!' she kept saying. 'Hurry!' But we had to walk, and all these cars kept driving by us, all heading into Hollister. After a while I had to carry her. I tried to get someone to stop. No one stopped. Nobody. All those good citizens of this wonderful city drove right past us.

"We were almost to the hospital when an ambulance pulled up. The blood was running down my legs, and they must have seen the red tracks in the snow. They took us to the hospital, and she was screaming when they took her inside. But it was too late. . . ."

Linus Webster lifted a trembling hand in protest.

"I swore I'd come back," Eddie said in the same flat tone. "When I was ready, I'd come back and make them pay—all the upright citizens of this fine city who let her die."

"You waited all those years."

"I had to get out of the country!" Anger flared. "They weren't finished with me. My wife and baby weren't enough, they wanted *my* life, too! So all I could do was wait and think about how I would pay them back. I had plenty of time to think."

Seven years, Webster thought. For the grieving young husband, seven years of brooding, plotting, scheming, keeping alive his anguish by making it the center of his life. There was a madness in that prolonged nurturing of vengeance.

"What made you think of using the computer system against the city?" Webster asked quietly.

"They used it against me—why shouldn't I use it against them? I didn't know how at first, but I knew there had to be a way. I knew a little about computers, but I started learning everything I could, taking courses. Then, about three years ago, I was sitting in this coffee shop in Montreal, reading a magazine story about cities setting up computer systems, and the name jumped right out at

me: Hollister! The story said Hollister would have this marvelous total-information system that would control all the city's vital functions. I knew that was what I needed the minute I read it. It was better than any bomb. I didn't want to just blow up a building. People did it to Mary Jane. It was people who had to pay. Like Prochaska, who wouldn't believe me."

"Prochaska? The man who froze to death . . . he was the one."

"He got off too easy," Eddie said bitterly. "You know what I had planned for him? I was going to doctor his credit, ruin him, make him see what it was like to beg for a can of gas. But would you believe it? He didn't have any credit. That stupid old man always paid cash for everything! I had to find something he couldn't pay cash for—like his utilities. So I worked it out to cut off his power. I cut his telephone line, too. But I didn't want him to die then—not so easy! I wanted to make it last—"

Abruptly the young man broke off. He said, "You think you're very clever, don't you, Professor? Making me talk like this."

Webster shook his head. "You needed someone to talk to."

"I don't need you. I don't need anyone—not anymore. She was the only one I needed. She was the only one who ever cared."

"What about your parents?"

"You're beautiful, Professor, you really are." Eddie laughed without mirth. "You want to talk to me about parents? My old man would've turned me in if I'd gone home when I was underground. When I was kicked out of school for protesting that whole Vietnam scene, he was so uptight he wanted to disown me, so I beat him to it. I disowned *him!* I don't have any parents. They don't exist." He leaned closer to the physicist. "Remember, I told you I was broke that day seven years ago. Well, I took a chance the day before and wired them for money. But I had a hunch, and I waited across the street from that Western Union station. Do you know who showed up? The FBI!"

"Maybe they intercepted the telegram."

"Maybe. And maybe somebody told them." Eddie shrugged, as if it were no longer important. "Mary was the only one who never lied to me. I let them draft me because of her. She thought it was honor and duty, God and country. I tried it, man, I just couldn't handle it. Did you ever have anyone tell you how you're supposed to stick a bayonet inside somebody's guts and rip him up? They wanted me to practice it!"

Webster felt another constriction in his chest. The young man's pain was like his own. He said, "Yet you would risk lives now—"

"Shut up!" Eddie screamed. "It's not the same. This is *punishment.* I loved her, do you hear me? And this city took her away from me!" He struggled for control. "Do you know what this sick society says is good? Good is what makes you feel good. Well, it makes me feel good to make this city bleed."

"They'll find you, Eddie. It's only a matter of time."

"How? Because you'll tell them?" Eddie's stare was pitiless. "No. I didn't ask you to come here. But you're here now, and you won't tell anyone anything." He turned toward the minicomputer. "Just stay where you are, old man. You can watch until I'm finished." He grinned savagely.

"What are you going to do?"

"Watch, Professor. Just watch."

Edward Lee Craddock no longer existed.

Except in a backup credit file maintained by Credit Systems, Inc., in Tampa, Florida.

Except in a dusty obituary file in the Hollister *Times*.

Except in the archives of the Department of Defense, at Fort Holabird, Maryland.

At Grayson's, Jenny Tyson had been trying to reach her father. There was no answer at home. She had dialed his office and waited for a full dozen rings. She was looking up Barry Westfield's number when she heard Michael Egan's triumphant shout.

"We've got him!" he cried exultantly as he came in. "That was Defense finally coming through—all we needed was Craddock's real name. The DOD has his discharge record. He's a 669—that means dropped from the rolls, AWOL, desertion."

"So he wasn't able to erase himself completely after all."

"He probably tried," Egan said. "But that DOD center has to be one of the toughest places in the world to get into for information. And he probably thought we'd never learn his name."

"But Michael, we still don't know what he looks like—we don't know who he is now."

"I know. But once you have the basic identification, you've got case files to dip into—manual files. Craddock was army—and a deserter. They should have a file on him, with all kinds of physical ID." He paused. "But you're right. Until we get fingerprints or a photo, we don't have a match. And we're running out of time."

Close, Jenny thought, but still no cigar. "I wonder why he left those hospital records intact?" she said. "You'd think—"

"They were locked up."

"But he went to such elaborate lengths to erase himself. And we know he was in the hospital and used their terminal."

"I think I understand that," Egan said thoughtfully. "What happened at the hospital is what this whole affair is all about. It started there. Psychologically, he may have found it impossible to destroy the only proof that his child ever existed—and the documentation of his wife's death. Besides, if we hadn't stumbled onto that Credit Systems match, the hospital records would have been no threat to him at all. They could have remained there forever, a record that justified everything he did here in Hollister."

"In his eyes."

"That's the way we all see things."

IN THE computer room at the Regional Data Center, Mayor Conway asked, "Why haven't we heard from him? He instructed me to be here at five. Something must be wrong. Maybe he knows what you've been up to."

Greiner shook his head, arrogantly confident. "He may be looking, but he won't find anything. Take it easy, Mr. Mayor. You'll hear from him soon enough. I wouldn't be so anxious."

The computer staff of the Merchants Bank had worked out the method for transferring the funds. The Intruder could not be permitted direct access to the interbank wire network. Instead, he was to transmit his instructions to Greiner, who would then key in the required access code. A one-time-only code would deny the Intruder the ability to repeat the performance on his own.

Conway had expressed doubt that the Intruder would accept the arrangement. "He's got nothing to lose," Greiner pointed out. "We complete the transaction for him, but he's in control of our system, so he can monitor everything that's done. And he can suppress any printout. There's no permanent record. He doesn't need one. All that matters to him is where the money ends up."

Suddenly there was a clattering at the main console. The Intruder's instructions, when they finally appeared on the screen, came in quick flurries, sometimes followed by pauses of several minutes. Keith Simpson had provided Conway with a list of current numbers for major U.S. banks, and Conway recognized several of them in the early messages as they appeared briefly on the video display. Following the Intruder's orders, Greiner moved the five-million-dollar ransom from the Merchants Bank in Hollister to a numbered account at a New York bank. From there it was transferred to Chicago, back to New York, and on to Atlanta. After that, Conway lost track.

"Won't the interbank system's computers question all this activity?" he asked during one of the lulls.

Greiner shrugged. "Any human being would question such

294

erratic moves, but not a computer. To the computer there's nothing illogical whatever about transferring money electronically. Not just once, but a hundred times, ad infinitum. The hundredth transfer is just as logical as the first."

There was another burst of activity. Greiner repeated the Intruder's instructions. Another silence followed. "Where is the money now?" Conway said after a moment.

"Overseas, I suppose. Switzerland? Luxembourg?" Greiner chuckled. "Only the Shadow knows."

"Greiner, this isn't funny! What did you do to this machine before I got here? Is that money lost or not?"

Greiner's gaze was cool. "Take it easy, Conway. The game isn't over. Let's just play it out."

Conway sagged into a chair. He was out of the action. From now on the game was between Greiner and the Intruder.

"Justice turned up a file on him," Egan was saying. "Not only as a deserter but as a student activist. Seems he took part in an occupation of a computer center at the University of Michigan in '69—which tells us he knew something about computers way back then—" He broke off. "What's wrong, Jenny?"

She was putting on her coat. She was genuinely worried. No one had answered any of her calls. "I don't know, Michael. I can't raise Dad anywhere. And I have a . . . a funny feeling about it."

"Wasn't he getting a ride from another professor? They're probably visiting."

"I know, that's probably it, but I just have to make sure. Barry Westfield's number is unlisted, but it should be in Dad's black book at home. You don't need me here now. I'll feel better when I find out where he is, that's all."

Egan was sure that she was alarmed for no cause, but he could see she was uneasy. He took her by the shoulders and kissed her gently. "Go on home. There's not much either of us can do here until we get some physical ID on Craddock. We'll talk later."

There had been silence for several minutes in the physics laboratory since the last time the phone had rung. Watching the young man he knew now as Eddie, Linus Webster considered making a run for it. But he decided his chance of success was very slight.

There had been several long periods of inactivity between Eddie's transmissions to the RDC. But the current delay seemed longer than the others. Why was he taking so long? Webster wondered. Eddie turned to stare at him. "It's done," he said in a matter-of-fact tone. "Can you believe it? Five million dollars! And it's out of their reach forever!"

"Let them go, then," Webster said. "Tell the mayor it's over."

Slowly Eddie shook his head. "Uh-uh. You think I don't know they're trying to trick me? Greiner knows the system inside out. So what's he been doing there all this time? He's probably set it up so that he has a record of everything I've done, even though I stopped any printout." The young man flushed angrily. "But it doesn't matter. You see, they're like you. They know too much."

"I couldn't tell anyone where the money is," Webster said.

"No, but you can identify *me*."

"I see." Webster smiled mockingly. "What do you propose to do with me? Choke me to death—in memory of your wife?"

"Shut up!" Eddie came to his feet. "There are other ways."

"Oh, there are many. But murder isn't the same as pushing a key on a keyboard. It's more like using . . . a bayonet. I wonder if you have the stomach for it, Eddie. And how are you going to harm the mayor and Greiner in the computer room? You can't possibly go there."

"I don't have to," the young man said harshly. "All I had to do was push one of those keys, Dr. Webster. And it's already pushed. You understand now? It's already programmed to happen just when I want it to!" He was glad Webster was there, a witness to this moment. But he felt his brief euphoria beginning to fade. He was conscious of the time—of the minutes ticking closer to that unbearable reminder of what had happened on this night seven years ago.

"On your feet, Professor," he said coldly. "I don't have to choke you to death. You've got a bad heart, right? I saw you fingering those pills a while ago." As he spoke, he moved quickly, blocking Webster's hasty grab. His hand snaked into the old man's pocket and emerged with a small pillbox. "I'll just keep these, Dr. Webster, while you and I go for a nice long run."

THE LAST MESSAGE from the Intruder remained on the video display in the data center:

```
THANKS A MILLION, MR. MAYOR. MAKE
THAT FIVE MILLION. END OF MESSAGE.
```

"So he's got away with it," Conway said after a moment. He shook his head. "But it isn't like him to end it this way. He should be making a grand gesture, something dramatic. His whole performance has been theatrical. Why be different at the last?"

"I don't know, but let's work it out later," Greiner said. "Right now I'd like to get out of here. There's something creepy about this place tonight. And don't worry about the money, Conway. I know how to follow where it went. I asked Baby here to store a repeat of our friend's transactions where he couldn't find it or even know it was there."

"You like being onstage yourself, Greiner."

"Doesn't everybody? Come on, Mayor, I'll open the door."

Conway nodded. He, too, felt uneasy in the isolation of the computer room, in the heart of the empty building. At the door he looked back, puzzled. "Open the door, Greiner—"

He saw that Greiner's face had turned pale. "I already keyed the exit code," Greiner said slowly. "It doesn't work. He's changed the code that opens the doors."

Greiner's glance darted across the room to the heavy fire door—it could only be opened from inside. "Let's get out of here!"

He reached the door ahead of Conway and shoved down on the panic bar. The bar moved less than an inch, and the door didn't budge. Greiner stared at it, breathing hard.

"The door's jammed—he must have done that earlier. I should've guessed! He knew what I was up to here, and he didn't care! He knew it wouldn't make any difference!"

"Greiner, make some sense! What can he do to us now?"

"He's already done it." Greiner slowly surveyed the computer room. His eyes settled on the small, unobtrusive vents in the ceiling, openings for the automated fire-extinguishing system. He spoke quite calmly. "Don't you see it, Conway? We were never supposed to get out of this room. We're trapped!"

EGAN TOOK JENNY Tyson's phone call. "Michael, he's not here! And I just talked to Dr. Westfield. Dad's not with him. Dr. Westfield said Dad told him I was going to pick him up. He knew that wasn't true, Michael—why would he say it?"

"Maybe he forgot."

"No. He acts absentminded, but he's not, really. And there's something else. This morning he was curious about that power failure at the hospital. When I asked him why, he put me off."

"What does that have to do with—"

"That's what Dad's been working on for the past year. He uses the laboratory computer to communicate with the RDC, working out power-usage problems. I know this sounds crazy, but what if the Intruder has been using the lab computer the same way he used the terminal at the hospital? And what if Dad went back there tonight to find out?"

Egan felt a chill. "Don't start jumping to conclusions."

"There's information about local power grids in Dad's files. And the Intruder managed to shut off power to the hospital. I think that's what had Dad wondering this morning. And he lied to Dr. Westfield about the ride. He was staying behind, Michael. He's still at the university, but his phone doesn't answer."

Egan cut in. "I'm on my way there, Jenny. Don't worry."

"Michael, hurry! I'll meet you there!"

FRI FEB 18 / 06:00 PM

"KEEP moving, Professor!"

Eddie shoved Linus Webster ahead of him, forcing him into an awkward, stumbling run. The physicist tried to pull free, but Eddie was younger, bigger and surprisingly strong. "We'll be seen," Webster gasped. "Don't be foolish, Eddie."

"A couple of joggers? Who'll care?"

Webster's heart was laboring, and there were darts of pain in his left arm. How long before the seizure? When they left the physics building Webster had been convinced that someone would see them—a guard, a student, another teacher—and Webster could call for help. But there had been no one on the paths outside. Then Eddie had struck out across campus, alternately dragging

298

and prodding Webster through deep snow until the huge bulk of the football stadium loomed above them.

The stadium dominated the recreation complex along the west side of the campus. It was dark and deserted, but the gates had been left open for joggers, and the track that circled the field had been cleared. Linus Webster and Eddie were alone on the track, shielded from the rest of the campus by the high stadium walls.

Webster fell heavily. There was constant pain now, a tightening band around his chest. Eddie picked him up and urged him on roughly. Webster's anger overrode the pain. "Did you bully her, too, Eddie? When you made her walk to the hospital?"

The young man's stride broke. Seeing the shock on his face, Webster knew that he had struck a vulnerable spot. Eddie also had his point of pain. Webster pulled up, forcing him to stop. "Were you angry with her, Eddie? Yelling at her? What's the matter—*did she fall, too?*"

"Shut up!"

They confronted each other on the empty track. Linus Webster bent over the pain that enveloped his chest, hugging his body. It was hard to talk, but he knew he had to keep Eddie off-balance.

"What about running out of gas, Eddie? Whose fault was that? And why were you there on the road that night when she should have been at a hospital?" The young man seemed paralyzed, and there was torment in his eyes. Relentlessly Webster kept on. "Are you punishing us because you've been blaming yourself for seven years, punishing yourself?"

"No! No, you're wrong—"

"Did she want you to run out on everything, Eddie?" He read the answer in the young man's anguish. "Did she want to run away? To escape to Canada? Or did she want you to stay and face up to what you believed in? Dear God, that's it, isn't it? She never wanted you to desert—"

With a scream Eddie hurled himself at the older man.

JENNY Tyson raced recklessly over the frozen streets to the university campus. The parking lot nearest the physics building was empty. Finding the building entrance unlocked, she went straight to the second floor. The door to Linus Webster's office was open.

The lab was dark except for one small area around the computer.

"Dad?" she called out. "Are you there?" Silence.

The door left open, lights on at the computer. He would never have gone of his own volition without locking up. Her thoughts were clear and logical—a barrier erected against her unreasoning fear. He might still be in the building, she told herself. She was only guessing about the connection with Craddock.

But she had not been wrong. The cigarette smoke that still hung in the air confirmed her guess. Near the computer she found several butts on the floor. In panic she ran out of the building.

Once outside, she had no idea which way to turn. The walks were clear of snow, revealing no tracks. Where was Michael—what was keeping him? She circled the building, away from the parking lots to the east, because she had just come from that direction. Near the side exit on the west side she found fresh tracks leaving the walk, breaking a path in the deep snow. The tracks were uneven, as if someone had been dragged along, his feet resisting.

She followed the path, her heart beating rapidly. Her father and Craddock—he must have gone back to the lab *expecting* to find Craddock there.

The trail ended at an entrance to the football stadium. Jenny was standing still, her despairing glance finding no trace in either direction, when she heard a cry of pain or rage.

The Intruder rolled with the old man off the cinder track into a bank of snow. His bulky jacket was cumbersome, and in his anguish he struck out blindly. Webster's heavy clothes protected him—the Intruder's fists glanced off a padded shoulder, an upraised arm. One blow skidded off Webster's jaw.

The old man's tenacious resistance surprised him. As his wild rage ebbed, the Intruder's head began to clear. Get him on his feet, he thought. Run him into the ground. He caught hold of Webster's lapels and lifted him. A woman screamed. Looking up, the Intruder saw that the woman was already through the gates at the end of the stadium. "Craddock, stop!" she cried.

It was the name that panicked him. His name! There was no way she could know it. He had buried the name as he had buried everything else that mattered in his past.

"Craddock!"

The name broke his rage. The woman was still some distance away, but he recognized her—Webster's daughter! How did she know? He shoved the elderly physicist away, but suddenly their roles were reversed. Now Webster clung to him, refusing to let go. The Intruder twisted and pulled, but the old man hung on, his breath rasping. Webster fell to his knees, but his hands still clutched at the young man's legs.

The girl was close. In desperation the Intruder dug into his coat pocket. He pulled out the portable terminal he carried there and clubbed Webster viciously on the head. With a soft moan the old man fell away.

Jenny Tyson was almost on top of them now. The Intruder plunged through the snow to the grandstand, leaped a low railing and scrambled up the steps. At the mouth of the nearest tunnel he looked back. The woman had dropped to her knees beside the fallen scientist. Her face lifted toward the young man. Once more she screamed his name. "Craddock—you're finished now!"

The Intruder ran down the tunnel and disappeared into the bowels of the stadium.

ALERTED by a call from Tom Ames on his two-way car radio, Egan drove directly to the campus security office. Webster lay on a stretcher, which had been placed on a cot. His face was white, its parchment color accentuated by the bloody mass of a deep bruise on his temple. But he was alive.

Egan looked compassionately at Jenny. She seemed calmer than she had when he had entered the office, as if she was reassured by his presence. "The ambulance should be here any minute," she said. "Mr. Ames and one of his men brought Dad here." Briefly she told Egan of tracking her father and the Intruder to the stadium.

"What was he doing? Why did he take him there?"

"He was trying to kill him! They were running around the track!" She smiled a bitter smile. "Obviously he knew about Dad's heart. What he didn't know was that Dad's doctor believes in having his heart patients take up jogging."

Egan heard the rising wail of the ambulance siren. He glanced again at Linus Webster. His lips tightened angrily. One more victim, the first the Intruder had actually struck with his own hand.

"I'll be going to the hospital with him," Jenny said. When he looked into her eyes he found a flashing light that matched his own anger. "Find Craddock, Michael. You've got to stop him."

"Don't worry, we will."

The ambulance pulled up. Jenny watched as two white-coated young medics hurried inside and began working over her father. When they carried him out on the stretcher, she followed. At the door Egan caught her arm. "One last thing—did you get close enough to Craddock to recognize him?"

She shook her head. "It was too dark."

"And your father? Did he—"

"He was unconscious when I got to him." She broke away with a sob and stepped into the back of the ambulance.

Egan had intended to join the hunt across the campus. But suddenly he knew that Edward Craddock would not be found hiding behind a bush or in a darkened entry. Craddock knew he had been identified. That meant he knew the game was lost. He was no longer running.

It was all coming down around him, the intricately balanced edifice he had so painstakingly constructed for so long. Somewhere he had missed some necessary point of stress, some needed support. What had he forgotten? How had they identified him?

In the empty field house near the stadium he found a Touch-Tone telephone. He attached his portable terminal and dialed into the RDC. He had instructed the system to seal the building after Conway and Greiner were inside and the rest of the center was cleared. Now he wanted the lobby entrance opened.

He felt emotionally empty. Out of the blue he thought of the moment he had left home for the last time. When he had banged the door shut on his father, a man as rigid and fearful of change as Arthur Prochaska, he had felt a momentary elation. Then, with shocking suddenness, had come this awful feeling of emptiness, of being gutted like a fish. . . .

He shook himself, shedding the memory. He had got over the loss then. He could survive it now.

302

His message completed, he lurched out of the telephone booth. Moments later the data center loomed in front of him. He dragged himself up the steps. In the shadowed reaches of the campus the guards were searching for him, but no one challenged him now. The doors parted for him. Entering the lobby, he felt lighter, freer. Here in the data center he was in command.

He turned quickly into the main corridor. He was eager to view the computer center—and the two men trapped inside. The monument he had built was collapsing, and it would bury him—but not him alone.

He glanced at his watch anxiously. He was still on time. He had done that much for her, at least, his beloved Mary Jane. He had made it possible for her to play a role in his final act of vengeance. "I'll set the time by you," he had promised her in the endless dialogue that was part of the endless fantasy that kept her alive. "So they'll never forget why I had to do it."

He started down the corridor. Flight was useless now. All that was left to him was to view the climax of all his planning. He would bear witness. That old professor was wrong. He could do more than push a button from a distance.

He was almost at his goal when he heard a footstep far behind him. He turned quickly. Michael Egan stood in the entry between corridor and lobby. "Stop right there, Craddock," the security man called out.

The Intruder broke into a run. The office he sought was close. He would lock himself in just long enough— He stopped. Other footsteps pounded along the corridor ahead of him. A uniformed security guard bolted around a corner. His way was blocked. The guard tried to stop, skidded on the tiled floor and crashed into the wall. The gun he was carrying nearly slipped from his grasp.

The Intruder swung back toward Egan. The portable terminal he still carried was in his hand, its elongated miniature display panel jutting out. He raised it as if to show it to Egan. "It isn't over—" he cried.

Egan shouted, "Riskind, no!"

The Intruder heard the shot, amplified a hundred times in the smooth tunnel of the corridor. Its force lifted him up and threw him forward.

He knew what was happening then.

What had he forgotten? he wondered as the structure of his terrible dream collapsed around him. *What had gone wrong?*

"I THOUGHT it was a gun," Riskind kept saying. "I thought it was a gun!"

Egan could not answer him. Kneeling beside Craddock's body, he could not bring himself to look up at Riskind. It was not the young officer's fault, he told himself; it was his. He had put the gun in Riskind's hand. Well meaning, he had chosen youth, flexibility and quickness over age, rigidity and experience. And perhaps an argument could still be made that he was right.

But because he had made that choice, the Intruder was dead.

The whole case fell into a pattern, Egan thought bitterly. We put new and unfamiliar tools in the hands of people not yet skilled enough in using them. Tools that were also weapons. His mistake was the same as Mayor Conway's—the mistake the city of Hollister itself had made. Egan had an exaggerated vision of a world shaped by well-intentioned fools, each destroying what he had sought to build. Mayor Conway and his data center. Michael Egan and his youth movement. And Edward Lee Craddock. . . .

He stared down at the man he had known as Carl MacAdam.

Riskind brought him back to reality. "I don't understand," the young man said. There were tears in his eyes. "He could never have gotten away with it. If he planned on disappearing, we'd have known it was him then. As soon as he showed up missing!"

"Would it have done us any good? I doubt it, Riskind. Not without his real identity. We would have been searching the world over for Carl MacAdam, and he would have ceased to exist. Edward Lee Craddock would have been home free."

There was a pause before Riskind said, "What did he mean? The last thing he said was 'It isn't over.' What did he mean?"

In the next moment the silence of the empty building was shattered by the hammering squawk of the fire alarm. Simultaneously Egan remembered that the building was not empty—and he thought of the extinguishing agent he had wanted to change, the deadly carbon dioxide, flooding the computer room.

"He meant just that." Egan jumped to his feet. "It isn't over!"

AT THE console in the security office Egan spoke over the intercom to Mayor Conway and Rob Greiner. He told them tersely that Craddock—Carl MacAdam—was dead. Then he asked Greiner one question. "Was MacAdam the one you suspected of getting you fired?"

"Yes." Greiner scowled. "So that's how he got into Credit Systems without leaving any trace at Grayson's. All he did there was get a code he wanted and scramble some records as a calling card. He must've done everything else through the RDC."

Egan nodded. MacAdam had probably also been instrumental in his own hiring—a security "expert" who knew little about computers. He said, "All that's left is to get you two out of there."

"How much time do we have?" Conway spoke calmly over the clamor of the fire alarm. On the monitor screen Egan could see the tension etched clearly in the mayor's face.

Egan glanced at the countdown dial on the console. To allow for evacuation there was a five-minute delay between the first alarm and the release of the extinguishing gas. "Less than four minutes. We're trying to break in now. But this place wasn't built to be broken into easily—"

"Didn't Craddock say anything about those locked doors, Egan?" Greiner interrupted. "No last-minute confession?"

"Nothing. But I do think Craddock could've opened those doors if he'd wanted to. He had obviously changed the code, but he was still carrying a portable terminal. Maybe he would have opened the doors if he'd had time. . . ." Egan shook off the speculation. "The problem is finding that new code. The last couple of days I've kept asking myself why he was waiting for Friday night. Why not Tuesday, Wednesday, Thursday? He was in complete control then. I think he wanted the weekend to get clear, but that's not reason enough to risk waiting until tonight. I think he *had* to wait until tonight."

"Why?" Greiner demanded impatiently.

Egan checked the countdown time. Under three minutes now. "His wife died on this date seven years ago. It was a fixation with him. He timed everything tonight to match what happened then.

I know this is guesswork, Greiner, but we don't have anything else. Have you tried to break that code?"

"What do you think I've been doing the last thirty minutes? He could have used anything—random numbers."

"No, he wouldn't," Egan said. "Not him. Why wouldn't he have used what was so important to him? The date and time it happened seven years ago! Feed that to the computer, Greiner!"

"What was the time?"

"I don't know—but it was at night."

"Never mind, never mind." Greiner was already at the keyboard of the main console. "Let's have Big Bertha run through the numbers. She's good at that."

"You've got two minutes," Egan said.

They were the longest two minutes of his life. He watched Greiner frantically keying the computer, feeding in the latest possible code, setting up the variable sequences. The computer was capable of about a million separate calculations per second, but Greiner's work at the keyboard seemed agonizingly slow.

Then Greiner slumped back in his chair, his part finished.

The last minute ticked away.

At six thirty p.m. the harsh ringing of the alarm was abruptly stilled. Michael Egan stared helplessly at the two men locked in the computer room, knowing that the overhead vents were now opening, releasing their smothering gases.

The cathode-ray tube display at the console beside the main processor was already beginning to be obscured by a dense white cloud of gas when a single sequence of numbers marched across the screen:

02 18 70 06:31

Conway and Greiner bolted toward the mantrap. The door was opening.

Egan was shaking with relief as he flipped on the intercom. "Break off and pull back," he said to the security crew who were attempting to break into the computer room from the media library. "Clear the building—it's all over!"

As he rose, his glance went once more to the display in the computer room. The screen was almost completely hidden by the gas that filled the room, but the numbers still glowed, dimly visible: the code that recorded the month, day, year, hour and minute when Mary Jane Craddock died.

SHORTLY before midnight it began to snow. Egan and Jenny ran through white flurries from the hospital exit to his Vega.

He drove back toward Hollister University, where Jenny's car had been left when she rode in the ambulance carrying her father. Egan glanced at her. "He's going to be fine," he said.

"Yes, I think so. MacAdam underestimated him." There was a moment's silence. "I never would have guessed it was MacAdam."

"Maybe that's one reason I should have suspected him. He had a way of disappearing into the woodwork."

"That could apply to a dozen people or more, not just Mac."

"There were other things. . . ."

"Name some others," Jenny said.

"Well, for one, MacAdam was involved in the internal RDC search for evidence of any intrusion. But what he came up with was always too little and too late. Then there was the way the Intruder always seemed able to keep a step ahead of any attempt to stop his penetrations. Take tonight, the way he set things up, insisting that the data center be completely evacuated. That accomplished several things for him, but one was that it wasn't necessary for Carl MacAdam to explain why he wasn't there." He paused, braking cautiously at a crossroad. "All of that suggested someone on the inside. We just didn't believe it."

"Why didn't he simply work from inside? Why go to all the trouble of wiretapping and using outside terminals?"

"It had to seem like an outsider for him to escape closer scrutiny. Instead of looking at a couple dozen people, we had to consider hundreds. That was really the key. That threw us all off."

Egan turned onto the campus, driving slowly. Fatigue had settled behind his shoulder blades, and he felt a weary letdown.

"I have one more question," Jenny persisted. "How did MacAdam get through your background check of all the RDC people?"

"Riskind did look into Carl MacAdam's background," Egan admitted. "Everything checked out. A degree from Boston University, a clean record with a big software firm. He planted that information in computerized files. And it looked authentic enough to fool Riskind. I can't really blame him."

He frowned. "There was one other thing. It even jarred me a little at the time, but I let it slip by. It was during the first emergency meeting that I sat in on. MacAdam was there, and he let drop the possibility that the whole operating system had been corrupted. That forced Thomas to admit to the mayor that there was a clean, uncorrupted copy of the data center's operating system under lock and key. That was the system's safe fallback position. Once that was taken out and loaded, all the Intruder had to do was complete his takeover, and the data center was his. Thomas didn't want to use the backup system, and I noticed that. I didn't pay enough attention to the maneuver that forced his hand."

Jenny sighed then, accepting the inevitable. "I'll never get over being surprised."

Egan did not answer. Ahead of them the modern administration building rose into a blurred midnight sky. Egan drove past the Regional Data Center, glancing thoughtfully at the lighted lobby. A moment later he turned into the parking area behind the physics building. Jenny's car stood alone in the lot.

She sat up suddenly. "What are we doing here?"

"Your car," Egan said.

"We don't need more than one car tonight, do we?"

Egan stared at her. The heavy feeling of fatigue lifted magically. "I guess we don't," he said, smiling slowly.

She leaned against him, relaxed and sure. "My place is closer," she said.

Louis Charbonneau

Louis Charbonneau, who originally came from the mid-west of the United States, now lives in Pasadena, California. When not writing, he is the managing editor for a publisher specializing in books about criminal justice and security. Working recently on a manuscript dealing with computer systems, he was impressed by the vast amounts of confidential information stored in large data banks—and the easy availability of that information.

"The number of unauthorized persons browsing through the federal data banks alone is alarming." Charbonneau says. "Agencies like Social Security and Medicare, to take only two examples, are full of sensitive information, but they do not meet even minimum standards for protecting their records." However, the dangers have begun to be recognized, the author points out, and Congress is now considering legislation that will reform the system and better protect the privacy of American citizens.

Fortunately, no such massive invasion as *Intruder* depicts has yet occurred in any city that uses computers to manage its affairs. But all the varieties of manipulation in the novel are real; they have actually happened somewhere, using the methods Charbonneau describes.

In *Intruder* the vivid episode of the stray collie and the kindhearted dog warden reflects Charbonneau's strong interest in dogs and their welfare. He and his wife Hilda once bred championship poodles, and now Hilda works as a volunteer for the Pasadena Humane Society. The couple often take in strays until homes can be found for them. "Hilda's on the Poodle Squad," her husband explains. "When a poodle's turned in, they don't even call us. They just bring it over. I had a lot more to say in the book about people who abandon dogs, but my editor made me take it out," he adds, smiling.

Going Wild

a condensation of the book by

David Taylor

ILLUSTRATED BY JACK McCARTHY
PUBLISHED BY ALLEN & UNWIN

Just imagine going swimming with a killer whale,
coping with escaped rattlesnakes in the middle of
Manchester or recapturing adventurous monkeys.
It's all in a day's work for Dr. David Taylor,
zoo vet. Little black bag in hand, he flies all over
the world as a specialist in the diseases of exotic
animals; and his motto, appropriately enough, is
"Have dart gun, will travel".

Going Wild is the account of Taylor's struggle to
set up an independent practice and the adventures
which follow—sometimes hilarious, sometimes
dangerous, always fascinating. His patients range
from a giraffe with a broken leg to a near-blind
zebra foal, and each case poses its own special
problems. Will a killer whale take injections as
placidly as an elephant will? How much
tranquillizer will calm down an over-excited wallaby?
The intrepid zoo vet's successes and failures are
delightfully described, with humour and above all
with compassion.

Chapter One

IT MIGHT have been a scene from a war film: I was John Wayne with an M16 carbine crouched at the open door of a helicopter gunship as it whirled low over the bush. Not quite, but I was hanging from my straps with my eye jammed to the sights of a rifle. I had drawn a shaky bead on something on the sunbaked ground forty feet below.

"Right ho, Doc, let her have it!" shouted the pilot, levelling the chopper out.

I squeezed the trigger gently. There was an almost inaudible crack and a spot of blue suddenly appeared on the offside haunch of the zebra mare galloping flat out through grass dark with our insect-like shadow and pressed flat by our rushing wind.

"Got her!" I bellowed, and we curved abruptly so that my doorway was full of the rich blue of the African sky. A minute later we settled down onto the scrubland in a cloud of yellow dust. Not far away the zebra mare was buckling at the knees, nostrils flared, eyes unseeing. Tidily she collapsed and rolled onto her side. Louie, the pilot, was already giving directions over the radio that would bring

313

the boys in the truck over to us, while I ducked under the slowing rotor blades and ran towards the zebra.

Not a war film, not hunting even, at least not of the killing sort. I am a veterinary surgeon, and I specialize in zoo work and wild animals. I was in East Africa on the Kenya–Tanzania border, collecting a group of zebras for Mr. van den Baars, a Dutch animal dealer and one of my best customers. Instead of the pole and lasso handling from a pursuing truck, we were trying out the more sophisticated technique of air-to-ground missiles: blue tufted flying syringes fired from a dart rifle and loaded with etorphine, a powerful, reversible anaesthetic.

It had been a very successful week, with thirty zebra captured, no deaths, no fractures, and no men injured. It had also been a tremendously good time, with cold beer at the Nairobi Hilton every evening and slivers of roast lamb eaten before sunrise with Masai herdsmen beside one of their lonely circular corrals of thorns.

When the truck rolled up quarter of an hour later, the sleeping zebra was lifted easily by half a dozen cheerful Africans into a wooden crate. Just before shutting her in, I injected a syringeful of antidote into her jugular vein. She would be on her feet within minutes. Later in the day all the zebras would be on their way via Nairobi to quarantine in Mombasa, and after a couple of months there they would make the three-week journey by sea to Rotterdam. The mare was the last of the consignment.

Louie, a young white Kenyan with skin like burnished bronze, sat in the shade of his chopper with a grin on his face. He squinted after the dust cloud that was the wagon bouncing its way back to Nairobi and unscrewed a bottle of pomegranate juice.

"Well, Dave, I fancy all is hunky-dory," he said, with his rather old-fashioned turn of phrase. "What do you want to do for the rest of the day? We might go for a spin and get a peek at some of those poacher johnnies."

Elephant poaching was rife. We had dropped down a few days earlier beside the bloated corpse of a big bull that had died slowly from a gut shot. His tusks had been hacked from him while he lay dying and would by now be on their way to the Nairobi dealers who would turn them into souvenirs for tourists. Yes, I would dearly like to come across poachers in action, even though they were reputed to be hard cases who would exchange fire with police and game wardens and pump rifle slugs at intruding whirly-birds like ours.

The engine thumped into life, and soon we were scything through the air, our skids almost touching the tops of the acacia trees. There was not much life about: a small cluster of elephants sheltering from the midday sun, a lone warthog scooting angrily from a mud-bank, a clay-red Masai in a ragged shawl leaning against the trunk of a baobab with the elegance of a Roman senator.

"I can remember when the game hereabouts was thick as locusts," shouted Louie, "but look at it now. Over-hunting, poaching, indiscriminate burning of tree cover. It's a bally shame."

I looked down as we passed over a handful of zebras trotting apprehensively beneath our shadow.

"Some poppets among that lot," bellowed my pilot. "Still, we've got our quota." He pulled the helicopter round into a tight circle and we ran back to look at the zebras head-on.

The lead stallion had had enough of this uncomfortable aerial attention. He wheeled about and broke into a fast gallop, the rest of the herd keeping up with him. There were ten altogether, including three young foals. We followed, hovering, as they raced along. There were trees ahead, leafless, twisted skeletons of acacia killed by a grass fire. As the zebras charged towards the trees they split into two groups to pass the gnarled white trunks. Once beyond the trees, they re-united into a compact band—except for one of the foals. From above we saw it gallop full tilt towards one of the acacias, then slam hard and unswerving into the bleached wood. It fell instantly as if pole-axed.

"Land!" I yelled, but Louie was already closing the throttle. He touched down light as a feather. The zebra herd had disappeared as we both ran across to the little body lying beneath the tree.

I knelt down and put my hand flat on the foal's chest. It was alive, the heart thumping under my palm. I raised its head and pressed cautiously over the head bones, but there was no detectable fracture. It was a youngster of around three weeks, concussed, out for the count.

"Darn queer how it ran slap bang into the tree," mused Louie.

I lifted first one eyelid then the other to test the corneal reflex. "Just look at that!" I exclaimed, pointing to the eyes. "There's your answer."

Louie bent close as I indicated the blue-white spots deep within each of the eyeballs. They were cataracts. The baby zebra was as blind as a bat.

"Get my gear, please," I said, as the foal began to come round, and Louie loped back to the helicopter for the workman's toolbox in which I carry a full set of emergency equipment when on safari— whether in Africa or on English moorland. I gave the foal an injection of valium and betamethasone. We sat on the baking ground, watching as it wobbled into a sitting position.

"What are we going to do with the little blighter?" asked Louie. That was indeed a poser. It was amazing that the animal had survived so long. I assumed that the cataracts were congenital, present at birth. The foal's dam must have taken good care of it, keeping a watchful eye to see that it did not stray too far from her side. It must have used touch and smell to feed, and hearing to move when the others did. But its future in the bush was sure to be brief. It would be taken by a hunting dog, hyena or lion, drowned at a waterhole, or break its neck by falling into a dry riverbed. Life in the bush is devoid of pity and only the fittest survive.

Louie and I both knew this, and we also knew we had to make a decision on the wild animal's behalf. Let it go? Maybe it would be found again by the herd. Kill it? I had a bottle of barbiturate in the box. I looked again at the unseeing eyes. A sunbeam caught one of the pupils and it narrowed fractionally. There was a faint light reflex then, which meant that a normal retina probably lay behind the opaque lens.

I made up my mind. We would take it back with us. Louie helped me carry the foal to the helicopter. "What are you going to do with him, old boy?"

That I was not clear about. Get him back to Nairobi first of all. Then what? He could be artificially reared easily enough on cow's milk diluted with lime water and sweetened with lactose: I had done it several times at zoos in England. But what about the eyes?

When I was in general practice I had taken a special interest in ophthalmology, done a post-graduate course in eye surgery at Manchester Royal Infirmary and extracted a number of cataractous eye lenses from domestic dogs. But I had never tackled a single case in a zoo animal, and I thought about operating on the zebra as we whirled towards the outskirts of Nairobi. Maybe van den Baars would accept the youngster if the operation went well, and Louie offered to keep it on his big farm meanwhile. I decided that if the Dutch dealer would agree to have the foal added to his shipment, I would operate and the little animal could go down to Mombasa after a week or two. I would only be in Kenya for another fourteen days, so I would have to get cracking immediately. After I left, maybe one of the local veterinarians would keep an eye on the patient—if the surgery was successful.

Back at base, Louie arranged the quartering of the foal in a cool loosebox at his farm while I went to phone van den Baars. As I had anticipated, the bluff Dutchman was pleased with the success of our helicopter hunt and readily agreed to take a chance on the little fellow. Now I could make arrangements for the operation, although the prospect made my spine tingle with a mixture of fear and excitement.

When I went back to the loosebox, a young Kikuyu with buck teeth and a smile from ear to ear was leaning over the half-door, looking at the foal. The animal was on its feet and wandering dreamily about.

"*Jambo*, Doctor," said the African. "I am Augustine. Mr. Louie says I am to help look after the young one."

"Have you taken care of young stock before, Augustine?"

"Yessir. Waterbuck, impala, leopards, many things."

"You'll do excellently. Now please make up a feed for it like this." I gave him instructions, and Augustine bottled the milk mixture into the foal with firm yet gentle expertise. It looked as if the baby—we decided to call him Tatu, Swahili for "three", because he had three black spots on his forehead—had found a capable foster parent.

I then took Augustine's place at the half-door, and watched the little zebra walk smack into a wall. He was moving so slowly he came to no harm, but it was clear that I would have to operate within forty-eight hours. First I wanted him to get over his shaking-up in the bush, and I also needed the time to dilate his pupils as much as possible with atropine ointment to give me a wide opening to approach the lenses.

Louie and I drove into the city. Although I had my toolbox of basic surgical instruments, they were not suitable for eye work. I needed special scalpels, needles and silk thread. Our first stop was the main hospital where I explained my problem to the consultant ophthalmologist, a pawky Scotsman with a broad Glaswegian accent.

"'Fraid there'd be the dickens of a row if I was caught lending out the theatre equipment," said the surgeon, "but what I can do is let ye use my old field kit. It's a bit antiquated but ye should be all right."

He produced his set of instruments. They were collector's items: ivory-handled, thin-bladed cataract knives, and tiny needle-holders. They lay in padded velvet within a brass-inlaid mahogany box.

"Take them and welcome. Hope ye're successful," he said.

Next I called on a veterinarian who had a sizeable horse practice around Nairobi. He willingly agreed to watch over Tatu's post-operative care when I went on my way.

All was arranged. Now all I needed was a large helping of luck—and no nasty surprises lurking in a zebra's eye to booby-trap me on what was, as far as I could tell, the first cataract operation on the species.

Two days later, Tatu was strong and lively. His pupils were nicely dilated. I decided to operate in the cool of the day before the flies clocked on. With Augustine and Louie each holding one end of Tatu, I slowly injected a dose of xylazine solution into his jugular. After three minutes he was sleeping soundly and I dropped local anaesthetic copiously into each eye. Then we lifted the foal onto a table set up outside his loosebox. The light from a pink and silver sky was good.

Many folk imagine the eye to be a terribly frail organ that must be handled like a soap bubble. In fact it is a tough and resourceful piece of equipment that can be tackled surgically with the same

318

Going Wild

basic techniques of cutting and stitching which are employed on
humbler parts of the body.

One cut opened the transparent and remarkably thick cornea
along one-third of its circumference. Now for the tricky bit. The
lens lies behind the pupil, suspended on tough strands of rubbery
jelly. First I had to get a grip on the lens, which I managed with
the help of a small rubber bulb attached to a metal pipe which
stuck to the lens by suction pressure. Now to free the lens. I
wiggled it very gently. It did not want to break free from its
strands, so I would have to try dissolving the attachments with an
enzyme. I injected a little of the chemical around the lens, then
waited for five minutes. Then the wiggling again. Marvellous! The
enzyme had done its work, the lens came free and I lifted it out of
the eye on the end of my suction tube.

Anxiously, I looked into the completely bloodless wound in the
eye. I was relieved to see that the thick jelly behind the lens had
not tried to follow the lens out—a crucial matter. Now all that was
left was to stitch the corneal incision with silk. The collapsed front
of the eyeball would quickly fill up with water again if I made a
watertight seal. In twenty minutes it was over. One eye done with
no signs of trouble, now for the other.

We gently turned Tatu over and I began all over again. Augustine
watched, wide-eyed. Every half minute Louie dropped sterile saline
into the foal's eye to keep it from drying up. The second eye went
as well as the first had done. An hour and a half after I had knocked
him out, Tatu was cataract-free.

"Whizzo, old boy," crowed Louie, as I plastered antibiotic cream
into both eyes before we carried the unconscious foal back into the
loosebox.

"Let's wait and see how he looks tomorrow before we start
getting excited," I said. "Meanwhile keep him in the dark."

Next day it was raining heavily when I went to look at Tatu's
eyes. Augustine was standing outside the loosebox looking drenched
and very miserable.

"Good morning, Doctor," he said as I came up to him. "Before
you go in—" he cast his eyes down and I saw that there were tears
as well as rain running down his face "—I have unfortunate news."

My stomach turned over. "What is it?" I asked, not daring to open the half-door.

The African kept his head down and spoke softly. "I think, Doctor, that all was in vain. The cataract is back, worse than before, in both eyes. I have seen it when I fed him this morning."

I flung open the half-door and looked inside. Tatu was standing there quietly. When Augustine had backed the foal into a corner I went in and took out my pencil torch. The narrow beam of light played over Tatu's eyes. True enough, they were blue-white again, all over; it was impossible to see into their depths. There was no sign of blood and the eyeballs had plumped up to their original shape. First class!

I slapped Augustine hard on the back. "That's not the cataract back," I said. "Without lenses you can't get cataracts. The haziness of the cornea is quite natural after it's been interfered with. It will clear gradually over the next week or so."

Augustine looked up at me and the ear-to-ear grin reappeared. More tears—of relief—trickled down his cheeks.

"Now go and get dried," I ordered.

As the days passed, Augustine fed the foal, put cream in his eyes and generally fussed over him. The animal was taming surprisingly quickly. Each day I looked at the patient, and slowly the opacity of the cornea began to clear without any sign of infection. By the fifth day I got my first glimpse of the deepest part of the eye, the retina. It looked good, but I kept the pupils dilated with atropine and would not let the zebra be exposed to anything but the dimmest light. The acid test would come when I took out the stitches on the tenth day. Until then I had the other animals to blood sample and see loaded for Mombasa.

Just before sun-up on the tenth day, when the air was heavy with the perfume of frangipani blossom, Augustine brought Tatu out onto the hard ground. I gave him a knock-out injection of etorphine and when he was unconscious I squinted into his eyes through my ophthalmoscope.

The interior of both eyes looked fine and the pupil constricted slightly as the light from the instrument hit the back of the eye— very good! There was still a fuzzy line of blue-grey where the eyes had been cut, but that should soon vanish after the stitches were gone. With forceps and scissors I picked up the knots of silk, cut them and pulled the sutures out. A shot of antidote and Tatu was back on his feet in five minutes.

Now for the test. There was an empty corral nearby. "Put him in there," I said to Augustine. "Let him go and we'll watch."

The little foal was pushed through the gate, then Louie, Augustine and I sat on top of the fence anxiously observing his movements. There were adult zebras in the enclosure next to Tatu's and he could hear and smell them. He seemed to be looking in their direction and when I called out loudly, he turned his head towards the sound. He was looking at me, wasn't he? Or was it just reaction to the noise? Tatu skipped a few steps, then he stood still, little nostrils distended, sniffing the morning air.

Suddenly, the first fiery ray of the rising sun cleared the ground to the east. It flashed through the limpid air, a bolt of gold which spread over Tatu's left side. Then, to my spellbound delight, the little foal turned his head to look at the flash. He blinked, dazzled.

"He can see, he can see!" cried Augustine.

Louie whooped, while I scrambled exultantly down from the fence. Augustine was still yelling, "He can see," as I went cautiously towards the foal to make sure. Tatu dodged out of my way, pranced towards the fence and quite definitely checked when he came within two feet of the wood. Then he turned nimbly away. I was convinced. Probably Tatu's vision was only fuzzy, for without a lens the eye cannot focus and in the wild he would still be greatly handicapped, but in a zoo or safari park he would be as good as the next little zebra.

For the first and only time in my life so far I had champagne for breakfast. Louie cracked a bottle of Mumm and by nine o'clock we were definitely tipsy.

With Tatu's eyes looking good, I prepared to leave Kenya. Louie arranged for Augustine to go with the foal down to Mombasa when the time came and to stay with him until he was shipped. On board ship there would be an experienced man from van den Baars's organization to take over.

"See you in Rotterdam, young feller," I said, as I took one last look at the zebra and waved my ophthalmoscope in front of him.

He did not answer with words of course, but he said all I wanted to know by following my moving hand with his large, brown, shining eyes.

Chapter Two

IT WAS IN 1968 that I had taken the plunge and set up on my own as the world's sole independent, full-time veterinarian for zoo animals and other wild, exotic creatures.

For the previous dozen years, as part of a general veterinary practice in Rochdale, an unexotic cotton-mill town in drizzly north-west England, I had been gradually expanding my wild animal work there, especially my wife Shelagh, but also our two young had taken over the veterinary care of the animals at Belle Vue, the Manchester city zoo where I had taken my first steps in wild animal medicine. My family had often found themselves involved in my work there, especially my wife Shelagh, but also our two young daughters, nine-year-old Stephanie and five-year-old Lindsey. I had travelled increasingly to patients all over the world, and gained my fellowship of the Royal College of Veterinary Surgeons in the specialized area of zoo primate diseases.

During those years I had not only been backed up by my partner, Norman Whittle, but I had been able to fall back on cattle, dogs and cats when ailing armadillos and infirm elephants were hard to come by, and there had been a secure, regular income from the practice in the cobbled streets of Rochdale and its surrounding rain-swept Pennine farms. Now all my connections with my old practice had been severed. A legal document dissolving my partnership with Norman had been drawn up and I was forbidden to treat anything other than exotic species within a ten-mile radius of Rochdale Town Hall.

I did not at first find the start of my new venture very encouraging, and sat in our old farmhouse on the outskirts of the town waiting for the telephone to ring. It often did ring, but invariably the caller was someone with a horse, a cat, a cow, or something else that did not fall into my new province. I knew that there were parrots and bushbabies and snakes and monkeys around, for I had treated many of them in my old practice, but where were they now? Professionally prevented from advertising my presence as a zoo vet, I sat in the white-tiled farmhouse dairy that Shelagh had converted into an office, and began to consider whether my planned exotic animal practice was not only invisible but illusory.

Soon, however, autumn was upon us. In Manchester this was the time for smog, that sulphurous yellow blend of water vapour and industrial smoke. Smog time was always busy for the veterinarian of a city zoo, and I was still responsible for Belle Vue zoo. As October came round, cases of disease among the animals at Belle Vue began to soar. Peacocks hacked away like chain-smokers, tigers heaved their chests asthmatically, and chimpanzees wiped running eyes and nostrils with the backs of hairy hands. And animals died. Some, experiencing these weather conditions for the first time, died quickly from pneumonia. Others, the time-servers, finally gave up the struggle against fibrous lungs and chronically enlarged hearts and wheezed their last. In the bodies of big cats, rhinoceroses, apes and the like, I saw all the postmortem signs associated with old human city dwellers.

The leaves fell early that year and were whisked away by the moist wind, and ice silvered the bare trees in Belle Vue's Victorian gardens. What was more, as if Matt Kelly, the zoo's Irish head keeper, was not busy enough breaking the ice on moated paddocks to prevent inmates walking out, there was a positive epidemic of animals going "over the wall". The keepers had neglected to re-clip the flight feathers of the flamingoes at six-monthly intervals, and on a windy day a gang of the gorgeous birds took off and cleared the zoo walls, never to be seen again.

With even less chance of survival, unless they could reach some centrally-heated building, seven young rattlesnakes set forth from the reptile house one day after sneaking through a broken pane of glass. The keeper in charge decided to keep quiet about it in the hope that either they would turn up or the low temperatures outside would finish the little wanderers off and so remove any threat to the local population. If it were known that such creatures were on the loose, he could foresee the zoo director giving him the boot.

The keeper tried to conceal his loss by stuffing rocks and vegetation into the rattlesnake vivarium, so that what had been a fair simulation of the dry, sun-baked environment of a Californian rattler, with coiled serpents easily seen against a sandstone background, was transformed into a dripping, dense and inappropriate jungle, in which the rattlesnakes could rarely be glimpsed, let alone counted.

This trick worked until two little girls, coming through the main gates on their way to the fairground, came across a pretty, if rather sluggish, little snake wearily making in the general direction of the bus stop. They were relieved to see that it had not got a V-mark behind its head—they had been learning about Britain's only poisonous snake, the adder, at natural history lessons—picked it up and popped it into a bag. Their brother would just love to have a grass snake as a pet.

Later that day, back at home, Dad wound the little snake round his fingers, remarking how the warmth was making the little fellow much more agile and alert. Then he noticed the curious rings of loosely jointed dried skin at the tail. Something worried him about

324

those rings and he reached for a copy of *Pears Cyclopaedia*. Two minutes later he dashed to phone the police.

Matt Kelly, the head keeper, was the one who had to clear the mess up, calm down the family, defuse the concern of the constabulary and divert the press with blarney. He then fired the reptile keeper.

To add still more to our troubles that autumn, the numbers of animals being purloined rose dramatically. All zoos have stock stolen from time to time: a guinea-pig or two from the Pets' Corner, tortoises from the reptile house, birds, particularly parrots and cockatoos, and a variety of small mammals. That autumn saw some sizeable creatures disappear.

One almost had to admire the thieves who got clean away with an irascible five-foot alligator in broad daylight, while the two little urchins who were collared half a mile from the zoo, breathlessly lugging home a trio of outraged coatimundi bundled inside a sack, must otherwise have led sainted lives not to have been severely injured by the hard-biting beasts.

Matt Kelly had hardly finished giving the crestfallen young culprits a lecture when he was summoned to another scene of missing animals. Two valuable De Brazza monkeys had vanished and the monkey keeper was certain that they had been stolen. A party of noisy schoolchildren had been round just before they had gone. Matt quickly inspected the cage; just possibly someone could have forced apart the vertical wires that formed the front. But how could anyone have grabbed hold of a big, tough species that could bite harder than a dog.

Matt rushed off to the car park with the monkey keeper. They were too late; the school party's coach had gone. The school headmaster was contacted, but the pair of monkeys, to my mind the most attractive of all primate species with their olive coat, brown and white face and goatee beard, were not forthcoming. Matt cursed and worried. Both of us could imagine the two monkeys stuffed into a dark, cramped rabbit hutch somewhere and pressed to take a diet of sweets and peanuts.

The next crisis of that eventful autumn for Belle Vue was not long in coming. Someone was pinching food. Fruit and vegetables were being stolen, particularly from the great-ape house, the modern, self-contained unit which housed the chimpanzees, orangutangs and gorillas.

Len, the senior great-ape keeper, was up in arms about it. Food pilfering by keepers is an unpleasant but not uncommon problem facing all zoos, but a particularly severe outbreak at Belle Vue a few years earlier had led to the most rigid controls being imposed there. Ration sheets were printed for each species, and a cook dispensed all the food to the keepers.

I discussed this latest problem with Len and Matt Kelly. "Whoever's doing it, they're damned sharp at it," said Len, as he told us how some "hands" of bananas had vanished during the tea break. "Funny thing is, I didn't pass any keepers on my way back from the cafeteria."

The great-ape house stood apart from the other units, so anyone entering or leaving the house would have had to cross open ground. The nearest unit was the Pets' Corner, but Matt found nothing there to incriminate anybody—no banana skins in the dustbin, nothing secreted in the staff restroom.

Two weeks passed. Each day one section or another reported food losses—apples here, tomatoes there, but always Len's great-ape house was hardest hit.

Then came the nastiness. First to go was a fountain pen, then a cigarette lighter and a packet of cheroots. Len was furious, but there was nothing to be done except to keep a sharp eye open.

"Oi'll have him. Oi'll catch him with the stuff on him one of these foine days," proclaimed Matt after Len's lunch, a packet of sandwiches, vanished into thin air. "Oi think the bloighter's havin' us on, teasin' us."

The crime wave grew, and night attacks became more frequent than ones during the day. The fact that there was no forcing of locks or windows anywhere confirmed our suspicions that a keeper with a key was behind it all.

The real malevolence seemed to be aimed at the unfortunate Len. "This kleptomaniac has a grudge against me," he moaned bitterly. "It can only be a keeper who thinks I've done wrong by him."

326

"Why, what's he done now?" I asked.

Len drew in a great breath and then spat out the words with ripe indignation. "Crapped in my tea and taken my *Daily Mirror*!"

I cleared my throat as I tried not to laugh. "Could it not have been, say, chimpanzee or orangutang excrement?" The great apes generally are enthusiastic and skilled throwers of faecal matter.

Len sniffed. "It could not have been put there by apes," he said. "None were loose. The cup and the table it was on are twenty feet or more away from the nearest animals. The only animal that could have had access to my tea was human!"

The deed had been done while Len was feeding his animals elsewhere in the ape house with the outside door to the passageway leading to his room locked, and an inside catch secured. Even if the culprit had a key, it would have been useless with the catch down. The only logical answer was that the villain had been in the house all the time.

I decided to look again at the scene of the crime. Len's room was a bare, smooth-walled place with an empty isolation cage against one wall, and a single door. High on the wall facing the door was a window that flapped back on runners, leaving an opening too small for a human to climb through. Just possibly someone could throw objects from the outside up and over the window when it was open, but aiming would be impossible. I looked up at the ceiling and at the large, galvanized central heating duct which ran across the width of the room. Then I noticed something. The vent for warm air was a slotted grille in the duct, and it was situated directly over the table.

The great-ape house's revolutionary system of channelling warm air to all the exhibits through the galvanized ducting had proved very successful until it was found that thick growths of mould had begun to sprout on the inside of the metal tube, encouraged by the warm, moist air. I had managed to solve the problem by getting Len to spray a non-toxic fungicide into the airstream once a week. Every few yards along the ducting there was a manhole covered by a disc of metal that was secured by two wing-nuts. The manhole in Len's room was firmly sealed. I walked back down the passageway and looked up at the ducting. Another manhole, sealed, then another, its covering plate slightly askew. Halfway down the passage was one manhole where the cover was completely off. I looked up at a round black hole from which a draught of warm air blew gently down.

"Get a stepladder and a torch, Len," I said. "I'm going to have a look up there."

I climbed up to the hole and got my head and one arm into it. I switched on the torch and shone it down to my left. An empty black tunnel, dusty but no longer choked with mould, stretched down to the end of the house. Wriggling round, I pointed the torch down the ducting extending over Len's room.

"Gotcha!" I said quietly.

"Who's up there? Let me get at 'em," shouted Len, rushing forward to take my place. There was a silence, then his wrath turned to chuckles. The torch beam shone on a colourful, twinkling tableau at the far end of the ducting, a cross between Fagin's den and Aladdin's cave.

There, blinking in the beam of light, caught red-handed with apprehension written all over their faces, skulked the two missing De Brazza monkeys. They crouched on a bed of paper, shredded cheroots, dried vegetable peel and nutshells, surrounded by fruit of every kind. Bags of nuts, dog biscuits and bars of stolen chocolate were near at hand. Amid the debris the polished metal of a lighter and a fountain pen glinted.

The episode drew to a swift close. The De Brazzas were injected by dart pistol with a quick-acting anaesthetic, and when they were unconscious I raked them back to the manhole using a shepherd's crook lashed to a long pole. When Len cleared out the den in the ducting, he found the total weight of the cache of food and other items was seventy-eight pounds.

I was surprised that Len had not heard any noises in the duct above his room, but he had noticed nothing apart from the gentle scurry of mice. We could only assume that the monkeys, like prisoners of war on the run, had lain motionless amid their booty as long as the "enemy" was present below. It was surely accidental that they had fouled Len's tea in obeying a call of nature close to the air vent. At night they must have dropped from the manhole, moved up the passageway to Len's room and left the house through the gap in his window. From there it would be easy to enter almost any other building in the zoo through holes, skylights or broken windows. De Brazzas have a distinguished, aristocratic countenance and, loping over the flower beds with armfuls of edible swag, they would have been the nearest thing in the monkey world to Raffles and Bunny.

Chapter Three

MY NEW LIFE had its minor compensations; for one thing, night calls became few and far between. General practice had been teeming with dogs run over just as the pubs closed, cats that threw fits in the early hours and, of course, farm visits. But zoo animals are locked up in the evening and rarely looked at during the next twelve hours. Unless an already sick individual needs attention or an important birth is anticipated, ailments and accidents that happen in the hours of darkness are not discovered until the keepers clock on in the morning.

As a result, my glummest hour of the day now became that between 7:30 and 8:30 a.m. It is still so. As like as not, a shrill telephone bell at this hour heralds tidings of a warm corpse discovered when the animal house was opened up. If I can finish off my scrambled eggs and coffee and launch a sally at the *Daily Telegraph* crossword without the phone putting paid to these bastions of my day, you can be absolutely certain that the birds and beasts at zoological collections dotted all over Europe have passed a peaceful night.

It was a dreaded breakfast phone call, one bitter January morning, which summoned me urgently to Belle Vue. The twenty giraffes in the quarantine premises were in trouble, and four of them were doing the most sinister thing a giraffe can do: lying down and not getting up. It was the simplest but deadliest of symptoms, and Matt Kelly had often told me when I was a student, "Boyo, if a giraffe goes down, it never gets up!" I had seen giraffes recover after being down, but he was as near right as made no difference.

The giraffes in question were new arrivals into the country and, though they did not actually belong to Belle Vue, they were being quarantined there in two red-walled blockhouses. Once the giraffes had finished the quarantine period, the dealer who had rented the accommodation from the zoo would sell the animals to collections all over Great Britain. They had arrived in Manchester on a foggy October day, having been in the heat of Mombasa three weeks before. No one in their right mind brings African fauna into Britain after September, but the cut-price East German freighter booked to carry them had been delayed in setting sail and, as usual where commercial interests are involved, time is big money. To winter the giraffes in Africa would entail considerable expense and so someone gambled—with the animals' lives. Feed had run short on the long journey, and so the giraffes had lost some of their protective layers of fat.

I drove up to the quarantine area and joined Ray Legge, the zoo director, and Matt Kelly, in one of the blockhouses. Two giraffes were lying on the straw, surrounded by a forest of legs. Their companions stood looking lugubriously down at them. It was freezing hard outside; there had been a power cut during the early morning and the temperature in the house had plummeted. The picture was the same in the other blockhouse, where another couple of animals lay limply on the ground.

I examined the recumbent giraffes. They looked sleepy, with drooping upper eyelids, their pulses were abnormally slow, their ears flopped like spaniels' and they made no effort to rise. Their temperatures were way below normal at the mid-nineties Fahrenheit. While I cautiously worked over my patients I kept a wary eye open for the flailing kick of one of the nervous beasts who towered above me, silently supervising the examination; if the standing animals panicked and began to mill around in the confined space, I would be pounded into the ground in an instant.

There was no evidence of infection, and I had no doubt that I was handling my first cases of hypothermia—chilling, or exposure—in giraffes. Manchester's winter frosts and bitter winds had gripped these unacclimatized creatures. If only they had had an English summer to give them time to adjust, to grow longer coats, to store up fat.

"What do you think?" asked Ray anxiously. "The emergency hot-air blowers are being brought over this minute. Is there anything else to be done?"

In general practice, I had brought round cows dragged out of icy reservoirs by vigorous, commonsense treatment. I decided to try the methods that had proved successful in domesticated animals, since there seemed no reason why they should not work just as well on giraffes.

"Blankets, more straw, some clean yard brushes, two bottles of good rum from the bar," I ordered. "While you're getting that, I'll give some injections."

The droopiness and slow hearts of the animals worried me. Circulation seemed to be failing and the extremities were icy. I took some bottles of circulatory stimulants out of my bag; to get maximum effect I would shoot them straight into a vein.

Finding the jugular of giraffes is dead easy when they are lying down. I knelt by the first animal's chest; the giraffe did not seem to notice the needle and soon the stimulant liquids had all swirled into its bloodstream. I kept a hand on its pulse and listened to the mighty heart through my stethoscope. After a few seconds I felt the pumping action increase in speed and volume, but the effect seemed to fade rapidly.

331

As I completed the injections, Matt and Ray arrived with the equipment I had asked for.

"Right," I said. "Now pour some of the rum over the legs and hindquarters and start brushing it in vigorously. Make sure your movements are all upwards towards the heart."

Matt shook his head sadly as he splashed the rich liquor over the first animal. "Can oi have a pull too, Doctor?" he asked.

"Yes—when they're on their feet and not before," I answered with a grin.

They both worked away at the rough massage while I set about giving inner warmth to the nearest giraffe. Holding the animal's muzzle under one arm was not difficult; it seemed too weak to struggle. With my other hand I carefully pushed the neck of the other rum bottle between its lips and let the alcohol slip over the back of its tongue. When a quarter of a bottle had disappeared I moved on to the next patient. I kept checking circulation, but there was little sign of improvement.

When Ray and Matt had worked up a good sweat brushing the animals' legs, we covered the recumbent beasts with a loose sprinkling of straw and then laid blankets over the top. The air spaces supported by the straw between the giraffes' skin and the blankets would make a warm, insulating layer. If these animals reacted like bullocks, they would be chirpy and as warm as toast in no time—*if* they reacted like bullocks.

We went for a cup of coffee in Ray's bungalow and discussed ways of combating future power failures. An hour later I returned to the giraffes and was horrified to find that there were now three animals down in the first blockhouse and five in the other. The ones I had already treated were worse, if anything, and the newly prostrate beasts were showing the identical signs of failing circulation and drowsiness. By now I was thoroughly alarmed, Ray was as white as a sheet with worry and Matt was muttering colourful Irish imprecations under his breath.

"It's like oi've told ye," opined the head keeper, nodding grimly. "Giraffes never get up!"

The two of them set to work rubbing and brushing with further supplies of rum, while I tried anti-shock drugs, filling giant 60-cc syringes with cortisone and anti-histamine solutions and jabbing clammy buttocks. The air blowers were pumping hot air into the buildings in gusts that swirled about us. Surely, if only the giraffes would hang in there for a little while longer, they would feel the rosy glow of vitality.

Not so. As we stood and watched, first one and then another adopted a posture of the head and neck that I knew to be a precursor of death. Curling their necks round and tucking them into their sides, they gazed with half-shut eyes at their rear ends. I was almost desperate, but I had a few shots left in my locker. I sent for glucose powder, dissolved it half a pound at a time in hot water and bottled it into the giraffes as another source of calories. When that failed I transfused dextrose solution into the jugular, using Matt and Ray standing on chairs, their arms outstretched painfully high above their heads for long periods, as holders for the slow-dripping bottles.

But no matter what we did, the eight prostrate giraffes were slipping inexorably away. Nothing had the slightest effect. One animal quietly died, then a second and a third. Night came and another morning and the three of us worked on without sleep, moving from one blockhouse to the other, going through the motions of rubbing and injecting but knowing that all was in vain. That afternoon the last of the recumbent giraffes died. Not one of them showed any pathological abnormality when I wearily tackled the huge task of autopsying them, alone in a cold and windy yard. The twelve remaining animals were given supplements of glucose in their drinking water; it was the best I could do.

Exhausted and demoralized, I set out at last for home. All our efforts had proved utterly impotent and eight giraffes out of twenty had been lost.

DURING THE NEXT few days I was not called out anywhere. I had plenty of time to sit in my favourite room of our Jacobean farmhouse. It had windows piercing the thick stone walls on three sides and overlooking a raised garden where rhododendrons and roses crowded round a little pool which I had installed and stocked with frogs and ramshorn snails. Sprawled on the couch, I immersed myself in baroque music which, combined with the peaceful surroundings, was an unfailing washer-away of depression.

The room was my think-tank, too, and there I ruminated for a long time over the giraffes. As far as I could learn, no one had reported dealing with hypothermia in the species before. I was puzzled by the lack of response to normally effective stimulant techniques: it was as if the circulation system of these animals, which we knew to be specially adapted to forcing blood up and down long legs and necks, collapsed remarkably quickly.

I felt a gnawing sense of guilt on several levels. First, I had to face the fact that my treatment had met with a complete lack of success. Had I missed something in the therapy? Then, at another level, I pondered over my position as someone working for an organization that did irresponsible things like letting giraffes get cold. I had not personally given the OK to load the animals onto the boat in Mombasa, nor had I selected the blockhouses as quarters for the new arrivals, but I was part of the business that made cash out of captive animals. At yet another level, I questioned once again whether I, as a human being, had any right to assist in the bringing of wild creatures forcibly out of their rightful habitats. I was glib with plausible justifications: education, scientific study, conservation, enrichment of the lives of those who cannot afford to travel to the Serengeti or Galapagos. But such sophistries neglected the moral argument, and that was the one that tugged and still tugs.

MY NEXT GIRAFFE CASE came up when I was attending an aquatic mammals conference in Harderwijk, a little Dutch seaside resort which boasts one of the finest marinelands outside the United States. I missed the end of that conference, because Shelagh phoned my hotel with news of an accident at Belle Vue. Pedro, the smallest of the zoo's bull giraffes, had been wounded in the neck. He was eating and drinking all right, but dribbles of food and water were running out of the wound when he did so. I took a taxi to Schiphol airport and caught the next plane back to Manchester.

It was past midnight when I met Matt Kelly outside the darkened giraffe house. "Looks nasty to me," he said, clicking his teeth. "We'll have to be careful puttin' the loights on," he added.

When zoo animals are put down for the night, they expect to be left undisturbed. Suddenly breaking the routine by switching on lights can startle the resting inhabitants, sometimes with disastrous results. After "lights out" you go back into an animal house very carefully.

Before opening the door, Matt began to talk just loud enough to be heard inside. Gradually he increased the volume, whistled a bit, tapped on the woodwork and finally turned the knob. Very slowly pushing the door open, he addressed the animals, which were pulling themselves to their feet and flaring their nostrils in the blackness. "There, there. How're ye doin', me beauties? Oi'm sorry to be disturbin' ye." He switched on the lights one by one. We moved unhurriedly into the house, billing and cooing softly towards the knots of zebra, giraffe and wildebeest that stood alertly, all with eyes upon us and ears pricked. After a few moments inspecting us, the animals relaxed: there was no mistaking the familiar, friendly tones of the head keeper.

Pedro, the giraffe, was standing in a corner. He seemed unconcerned about the ugly, six-inch-long tear, caked with blood, in the left side of his neck.

"How did it happen, Matt?" I asked.

"We're not too sure, but it looks as if he got his muzzle jammed in one of them water bowls up high on the wall, panicked and crashed against the iron hayrack. It came away from the wall and a bracket went through his throat."

Matt pulled an apple out of his coat pocket and offered it to the giraffe, who took it willingly. Pedro chewed it, drooling saliva down onto us, and swallowed. We watched the sinuous waves of the gullet muscles carrying the mashed-up apple towards the stomach. As the waves reached the neck wound, a pink finger of foam welled out of the bloody hole and then, to my horror, soggy pieces of apple pulp emerged and dropped onto the straw-covered floor.

"Bejasus!" exclaimed Matt.

There was no doubt that Pedro had punctured his gullet, a rare and serious injury, particularly in an animal like a giraffe.

There was nothing to be done that night apart from shooting some penicillin into him. The formidable prospect of trying to close the wound would have to wait until daylight. I drove home to Rochdale with my head full of questions. How to lay hands on the beast? What type of anaesthetic to use on the most notoriously unpredictable of zoological patients? The operation itself: repairing such a wound might present problems never encountered in the day-to-day cobbling together of skin and muscle injuries. Giraffe again, I thought. One of the most difficult of all zoo species to treat, and one which seemed lately to be needing a lot of my help—such help as I could give.

AS I ARRIVED at Belle Vue next morning I was no nearer finding the answers which had haunted me all night. Matt was already in the giraffe house, looking worriedly at Pedro, whose appearance had altered distinctly in the past six hours.

"Would ye look at that, Doctor," said the head keeper, pointing. "He's gettin' fatter somehow."

Sure enough, Pedro did look plumper. It was not that he was bloated with excess food, but there was no question that his neck, chest and forelegs were fatter. Ominously, the giraffe had stopped eating and was looking depressed and miserable. Sticky froth had made a trail down his neck from the wound.

"I'll need to examine him, Matt," I said, "but how?" There was at that time no proven reliable anaesthetic for giraffes.

"What d'ye want to do exactly?" Matt asked.

"First, I'd like to feel him to see why he's so much bigger than last night, then if possible, to get a finger into that neck wound."

"It's goin' to be tricky. Let's try a door and some straw bales." He shouted to a bunch of keepers, "Lift the elephant house door off its hinges, and look sharp about it!" The elephants were already outside for the day and had no need of their night-house door.

After a few minutes the keepers tottered into the giraffe house, straining under the weight of the massive, iron-studded door. The idea now was to take it into the giraffes' quarters, and then gradually press Pedro against a wall by using the door as a portable barrier.

All went well at first as the door was introduced quietly and slowly. Then Pedro began to pace about nervously as the men under Matt's command advanced, carrying the door in an upright position. At least if the giraffe lashed out with one of his feet to deliver the powerful blows that can brain a charging lion, the solid wood should afford the keepers some protection. Gently cornered at last and unable to turn round, Pedro began to "stargaze"— holding his head up so that his chin pointed directly at the ceiling— a sign of profound mental agitation. I told the men not to press the door actually onto the animal, for under such circumstances Pedro might try to climb the wall or throw a limb over the door. Such displays always ended in torn muscles, fractures or even worse.

Matt piled up some bales of straw on our side of the door and I gingerly climbed up them. Now I was high enough to put my arm over the top of the door and do a bit of prodding around. I lightly stroked Pedro's neck. He swung his head to and fro and then lunged down awkwardly, trying to butt me with the hard pegs on his head. "Coosh, coosh, boy," I murmured.

Pedro became accustomed to my touch on his skin, which flickered and jumped beneath my fingers. I prodded carefully. Scrunch! Scrunch! It was just like pressing shredded cellophane— I could hear as well as feel the crackling beneath the skin. This was not fat, nor the soggy fluid of dropsy. It was gas, gas collecting in thousands of bubbles under the animal's hide and puffing him up like the Michelin man. If the gas was being produced by bacteria, Pedro really was in trouble: gas gangrene is usually lethal. But somehow he did not look poorly enough for that. I looked at the neck wound and listened intently. As Pedro moved his head about I could hear the faintest sucking sound. A bubble of serum would appear at the hole, swell, shrink and vanish. That was it: movement of the neck was drawing air in through the wound, which acted as a valve. Once inside, the air was gradually working its way through the subcutaneous tissue. Another day or two of this and Pedro could be like a zeppelin right down to his hind feet.

The operation to repair the gullet and close the overlying tissue would put a stop to all that. As long as I continued to provide anti-biotic protection, the air under the skin would be absorbed by the blood capillaries and harmlessly dispersed. I moved my fingers up towards the wound and delicately pushed my index finger into the

337

ragged hole. Pedro swayed about. I swayed with him, letting my hand ride with his neck. I felt my finger pass through a thin layer of split muscle and slip on the smooth lining of the gullet. The gap in its wall was as big as a plum.

Suddenly Pedro had had enough. Kicking mightily sideways he connected with the door with a crash that shook the building. The heavy slab of wood fell away from him, taking me and my pile of straw bales with it. A yelling, struggling heap of keepers, plus one startled veterinarian, saw the great door come toppling down onto them. Only Matt Kelly had managed to skip out of the way. Luckily the straw bales in which we were tangled took much of the impact and saved us from being utterly flattened, but even so the accident resulted in a broken collar bone and a bloody nose for one of the keepers, and made my ear swell up like a tomato.

As the wounded keeper was borne off I told Matt to prepare for an operation. At that time few attempts had been made to anaesthetize giraffes, and those who had tried had found grave difficulties in coping with the tall beast: its peculiar circulation system seemed to distribute anaesthetics in an unpredictable way. Slowly induced anaesthesia resulted in dizziness, panic and awful accidents, while fast knock-out shots brought the animal crashing straight down from its height of seventeen or eighteen feet. In the rare cases where the operation was completed satisfactorily, a giraffe might well refuse to get up on its feet ever again, or else develop a grotesquely twisted neck. Zoo vets had one recurring nightmare: that a giraffe might need surgery.

I had not wanted to use an anaesthetic just to examine Pedro, but for the operation on his throat I reckoned that the best and safest thing to do was to use acepromazine, a sedative made for farm and domestic animals which leaves the animal standing but relaxed and uncaring. I would put the patient behind the door again and then numb the operation site with local anaesthetic.

Even with the decision about the anaesthetic resolved, there were still the surgical problems. I had never operated on a mammal's gullet, but left untreated the hole would never heal. I would have to close it with special stitches that rolled the wound edges inwards, so that the mucous membrane lining the tube could knit together, and I must not cause an obstruction to swallowing by narrowing the tube too much. The rest, closing the muscle and skin, and thus putting an end to the air-sucking, would be simple.

The first step was to give the sedative. As usual, I worked out the dose by estimating the patient's weight. Then I assembled one of the aluminium flying darts with its ingenious, explosive-activated plunger and selected a needle appropriate for the buttocks of an adult giraffe. Finally, I charged the dart with the calculated volume of acepromazine, a beautiful golden-coloured liquid. With a soft "phut", the dart flew from my gas pistol and homed perfectly into the giraffe's rump. So fast and surely do these devices travel that there is far less sensation for the recipient than there would be if a hypodermic needle were punched in manually. Pedro seemed unaware that he had been slipped a Mickey Finn.

I looked at my watch. Usually the first signs of drowsiness appear after five minutes or so. We all waited.

Six minutes went by. The giraffe started to droop his upper eye-lids, and his muscles visibly relaxed.

"Get the door, lads," I said, "and approach him nice and easy." As I spoke, Pedro gave a great sigh, keeled over as if struck by invisible lightning, and crashed onto the thick straw. I was stunned. The giraffe lay flat out, legs flailing and eyes rolling wildly.

Matt and I dashed over, and I put my ear to his chest, listening to the slow thud of the mighty heart.

"Get up, Pedro, get up!" yelled Matt, as I felt for the giraffe's femoral artery. The pulse was soft and weakening.

"Come on, everyone, hold his head up!" I shouted, and the keepers crowded round. "Head up at all costs," I repeated, and rummaged in my bag for syringes and needles.

Thoughts whirled through my mind. Certainly I had taken the correct drug from the correct bottle. It could only be a side-effect of the acepromazine: it was recognized that one effect of the chemical was to lower the blood pressure. Yet we had all agreed that he weighed around sixteen hundredweight, and I had given 5 cc's, a low to moderate amount.

Matt and his men pushed the now unconscious giraffe into some semblance of a normal sitting position, with the head propped on one fellow's shoulders. I bent to pick up a syringe and heard Matt's words as if in a dream. "He's gone, Doctor," he said quietly.

I went over to the giraffe, jammed my head against the warm chest and listened. Matt was right. Pedro had died. Just like that. The acepromazine had over-expanded the blood vessels, Pedro's blood pressure had plummeted and his vital brain cells had been starved of circulating oxygen. "Damnation," muttered Matt. The men all stood back and let the giraffe's body slip onto its side.

"Unpredictable things, giraffes. Bloody terrible to treat," I said. It sounded like an apology.

No one said anything further as we collected our gear. Matt left silently to phone the knackerman.

I drove home in despair. I went to my office to sit and think, go over all the possibilities, to try to get an inkling of what had gone wrong. The thought that one day there would be another giraffe case was like iced water in my brain.

Shelagh brought me a cup of tea. "Come on," she said. "The cup that cheers. By the way, there's been a veterinary student on the phone a couple of times. He wants to know something about lobsters. His name's Greenwood, Andrew Greenwood."

"You can tell him what he can do with his lobsters, love," I replied, and stared unseeing out of the window. The gangling, long-necked creature that the ancients had called a camel-leopard, *Giraffa camelopardalis*, was becoming my jinx.

ON THE WAY to Harderwijk for the conference which Pedro's accident interrupted, my old friend Mr. van den Baars had invited me to Rotterdam to look over a mixed bunch of animals which had just arrived from East Africa. One of his keepers took me round the live cargo: giraffes, antelopes, a hippo and zebras.

"You should be interested in this one," the keeper said, pointing to one slatted crate. "It's a young zebra."

My heart leaped as I looked inside. A beautiful, nine-month-old zebra colt was looking directly towards me with his ears pricked forwards and his eyes glistening like cobs of coal. There were three spots on his forehead. It was Tatu!

I was ecstatic. Tatu had survived. Blind and concussed in the heat of the bush eight months before, he was now a stroppy individual with glancing, arrogant eyes.

"Spirited little devil," said the attendant. "He kicks and bites as soon as look at you."

"But does he look?" I asked. "You've not seen him bump into things, have you?"

"Definitely not," came the emphatic reply. "See this blue dent in my wrist? That's where he grabbed me a couple of weeks ago when I was mucking out. He saw all right."

I was content. No doubt Tatu could have done better with a pair of bifocals or even contact lenses if such things had existed for wild animals, but he was biting folk accurately enough. That was just what I wanted to hear.

Chapter Four

PEDRO'S DEATH had driven all thoughts of Tatu from my mind, and it was only some days later that I remembered to tell Shelagh about my reunion with the young zebra. She was thrilled.

"What's for dinner?" I asked when I had finished my tale.

"Can't you smell it?" Shelagh replied. "It's mackerel today."

341

"Fine by me," I said. It was true there was a strong fishy smell.

"And it's mackerel tomorrow, and the day after and Friday, Saturday, Sunday . . ."

"Whoa! Hold on!" I interrupted. "What are you going on about?"

"Mackerel—twenty stone of it. It arrived on the front doorstep this morning, sent by Pentland Hick of Flamingo Park. He wants you to check its quality. He's bought a killer whale in Seattle and hopes to fly it over in two or three weeks, so he's been talking to merchants at Billingsgate about fish supplies."

A killer whale! Determined to make his Flamingo Park Zoo in Yorkshire the finest in England, Pentland Hick had built one of the country's first dolphinaria and had become fascinated by the cetaceans—whales, dolphins, porpoises and the like. The marineland at Harderwijk had had the first killer whale in Europe a few months previously, but it had not survived long before dying of a brain haemorrhage. Now with any luck I was actually going to touch one of the most awesome marine mammals, probably handle its medical problems.

A frisson of excitement ran down my spine as I thought about it. My first contact with Flamingo Park had involved capturing an escaped nilgai antelope for them. Since then I had gradually seen more and more of Hick's growing empire of animals. I telephoned him immediately.

"Yes," he said, in his deceptively soft and sleepy voice, "I'd like you to go to Seattle next month. Bring back a killer whale. Think about it. Talk to the Americans by phone. But remember—" his voice took on the menacing tones of the Godfather "—nothing, but nothing, must go wrong, David."

My contemplation of this momentous news was interrupted by Shelagh's more mundane but highly pressing problems as owner of twenty stone of mackerel, a fish renowned for its lack of keeping quality. It was all over the kitchen, filling the sinks. My daughters, Stephanie and Lindsey, peered somewhat mournfully from behind a stack of fish boxes which we had to climb over to get out of the kitchen.

"Lancastrians don't seem to eat mackerel," Shelagh complained.

"I've managed to give away about ten pounds, but look at the rest! What are we going to do with them before the house stinks of rotting fish?"

For the moment, though, they were beautiful fresh fish, youngsters about seven inches long. I inspected a selection, checking gills, eyes, skin, oil content, smell, parasite load, muscle firmness; they were perfect. It seemed safe to order for the new whale, but just in case there were invisible bugs in the fish I took samples for bacteriological culture and for analysis for heavy metals, an increasing worry as the seas become polluted by man and his industries.

That evening I was to be found bearing unsolicited fishy gifts wrapped in newspaper to friends and even mere nodding acquaintances all over Rochdale, and for the next week my enthusiasm for cooking was put to the test as I experimented with the mackerel. We had it boiled, with white wine sauce, barbecued, as kedgeree. We had it in cider, with cucumber, and with tomato. With the groans of the family in my ears as I brought in my *pièce de résistance*—curried mackerel—I began to doubt a killer whale's famed intelligence; after all, he would swallow a hundredweight of this stuff, day in and day out—and raw, without the benefit of my sauces!

A FEW WEEKS later, I was sitting in a restaurant on the Seattle seafront, chewing broiled lobster and outsize oysters. Through the window I could see below me the round metal pools of the Seattle Aquarium. Floating motionless in the one nearest to me, eleven feet long with oil-smooth, jet-black skin and crisp, snow-white markings, was the young killer whale I had come for. He was a perfect specimen, about two-and-a-half years old, with the teeth at the front of his jaws only just beginning to push through the gums. I was stoking up for the two-day journey to Flamingo Park. He was fasting; whales and dolphins never travel on full stomachs.

Don Goldsberry and Ted Griffin, the two owners of the aquarium, were the pioneers of killer-whale catching. Using a mile of stainless steel netting, they trapped the powerful and sharp-witted whales in Puget Sound. Goldsberry, Griffin and their veterinarian, Bill Klontz, were the experts at what was a fairly new game. All I was supposed to do was watch and listen and learn.

The first of their killers had been given the Eskimo name of "Namu", and they had a few appropriate, noble-sounding suggestions for my little fellow.

"Sorry," I said, "Pentland Hick has already decided he is to be called Cuddles."

The Americans did not like it. I hated it. But Hick was a shrewd entrepreneur with an eye to publicity: "A fierce hunter of the oceans with a soft and winsome name. It's a good gimmick," he reasoned. He was right.

Goldsberry and Griffin gave me a long list of dos and don'ts concerning the whale, all of which I meticulously noted down. "If his dorsal fin flops over he's short of sweet water;" "Use a three-inch needle if you have to inject him;" "A shot of penicillin before he travels is all he needs;" "Eggs are bad for him;" "Sugar and glucose aren't absorbed by his gut and may do him harm;" "If he falls ill give him a quart of Maalox and fly us over."

As the practical study of larger cetaceans in captivity had not even begun in Britain, it was prudent to go along with the instructions that accompanied the goods, not least because Pentland Hick had paid fifteen thousand dollars for Cuddles. It would be two years or more before we realized that the Seattle team knew little more about the care and treatment of these complicated marine animals than we did.

Next day Cuddles's long journey began. A padded hammock with holes for his eyes and flippers was slipped under him as he floated in three feet of water. He did not fight or complain as a crane picked him, dripping, out of the pool and lowered the hammock gently into a framework of tubular steel. At last I got a chance to touch him. It was a wonderful experience. As I leaned over the placid beast, he exhaled with a soft roar: a blast of hot air, carrying a not unpleasant, cow-like smell, hit me in the face. I revelled in the sensuous delight of passing my fingers over his skin. It was polished, very finely grooved and had the consistency of hard india rubber. It was soft and cool under his axillas, like sheet-steel across the blade of his tail-fluke and warm as toast on his forehead, or

344

melon. I climbed down and looked through the holes in the hammock. I waggled the paddle-like flippers and tried to trace the outlines of the bones within. Then I peered close to one large round brown eye. The chocolate-coloured iris rolled slightly and fixed on me. He was looking at me. I stroked the nearby flipper and whistled.

To my utter delight, the eye remained gazing at me and a squeaky, high-pitched chirruping was squeezed out of the blow-hole on top of Cuddles's head. I whistled again. The whale chirp-chirped in turn. He was answering me. That first moment when I came eyeball to eyeball and conversed with a Lord of the Sea, as the Eskimos call this magnificent beast, was one of the most moving of my life. Quite inexplicably, a bond had been forged between the whale and me.

I was allowed to help in coating every inch of Cuddles's body with thick lanolin grease. This would stop the delicate skin drying out and cracking. Next, towels were spread along his back and smoothed to get rid of air-bubbles that could "burn" the skin during the long journey. After that, hundredweights of crushed ice were sprinkled on and around the whale. The entire framework was shrouded in plastic sheeting and a water-spraying system of pipes, pumps and electric batteries was set up. The animal would go all the way sticky, wet and cold to avoid the killer's principal enemy, the risk of internal overheating.

We set out for the airport by road, on the back of a long low-loader. In the freight hold of the TWA jet freighter purposely kept at 1°C to help keep the whale cool, it was no fun clambering over his framework for a solid twelve hours. Goldsberry, Griffin and I had to keep a constant watch for "bedsores" that can end in death from toxic gangrene, for blobs of lanolin melting and running into the blowhole, for shifting towels that could be sucked in by one powerful inhalation of the whale's breath. The water sprays had to be kept going, and, most important of all, the whale had to be constantly reassured. Stroking his forehead, whistling to him, or just talking nonsense into his pinhead-sized but highly sensitive ear—it did not matter what, as long as we kept doing it, hour after hour. I had brought my *Collected Poems* of John Betjeman with me, a constant companion on my travels, and I passed the time on my spells of duty at the head end by reading aloud to Cuddles from the book.

Arriving at London Airport, we passed smoothly through Customs, and the whale's inspection by the government vet. After a six-hour road journey up into the northeast of England, where Flamingo Park lies in the sleepy village of Kirkby Misperton, the whale was unloaded and hoisted above the floodlit figure-of-eight pool that was to be his new home. Gently he was lowered into the icy-cold water where several of us were waiting in wet suits to release him from his hammock. My tiredness was forgotten as the canvas fell away. Heart in mouth I waited, bobbing by Cuddles's side. If he had become stiff and could not flex his tail-flukes, if he sank out of control, or if he listed because of a congested lung, we would have little chance of manhandling his great bulk in the deep pool. I saw that the two Americans were looking tense, too.

For a second Cuddles hung in the water. Lazily he raised his great tail. Its powerful upbeat thrust the water into foaming furrows and his torpedo body glided gently forwards into the centre of the pool. Goldsberry called for a mackerel and threw it a couple of yards ahead of the whale. It sank in a flickering spiral through the blue water. Instantly Cuddles saw it, blew out a broad plume of water droplets and dived. Half-turning gracefully ten feet down, he opened his mouth a mere inch or two, sucked and the mackerel shot in. Then he rose to the surface, floated vertically with his head well clear of the water and opened his jaws wide. For the first time I saw the salmon-pink expanse of Cuddles's unmistakable grin.

Half an hour later, this untrained animal that had roamed the north Pacific only one month before, that had raided fishing nets, murdered great whales, out-run and out-thought sharks and sea-lions and dolphins, this grinning, cuddly Cuddles with the appealing chirrup, began playing with a floating beach ball.

DURING THE following weeks the killer whale settled down admirably in his new home. Every few days I made the 200-mile round trip over the hills from Rochdale, through Leeds and York and across the Vale of Pickering, to see that all was going well. This usually entailed swimming with Cuddles in his pool of artificial

346

seawater. In a wet suit and face mask I inspected his ventral surface underwater; it would be several months before he was trained to roll over on command so that his tummy could be viewed and prodded from dry land.

Underwater, too, I had a chance of catching, for parasite analysis, a sample of his faecal matter before it dispersed irretrievably in his wake. Even so humble a task as collecting droppings from these remarkable creatures presented quite special complications, as the whale, ever curious about my ungainly submarine antics buffeted me with his round nose.

Giving injections was another poser. Asian flu swept through the human population of Britain shortly after Cuddles's arrival and, on learning that the influenza virus could attack cetaceans, I had to think of some way of jabbing Cuddles with flu vaccine. In the early days we had no special slinging device for "dry-docking" the whale; and emptying the 300,000-gallon pool except for serious emergencies just was not on. For one thing, artificial seawater is expensive to make up. For another, the local river authority did not take kindly to so vast a quantity of brine passing into their waterways, as the salt injures freshwater river life and could poison vegetation along the banks. On top of these problems, pools like the one at Flamingo Park, built in sandy soil with a high water table, would often collapse inwards when the enormous outward pressure of their contents was removed.

Cuddles had behaved like a playful, amenable child so far. He doted on humans, craved their attention and was impeccably well-mannered. Pondering the problem of the flu vaccination, I decided to try simply swimming up to him in the water and slapping a needle in. I was a dab hand at doing this sort of thing with large land animals. Take an elephant: thump his buttocks hard with your clenched fist two or three times so that he knows you are there and is accustomed to what is, to him, a friendly pat on his inch-thick skin. Then, with the fourth thump flick forward the wide-bore hypodermic needle that you have concealed in the palm of your hand. Slap goes your fist for the fifth time and the needle zooms to the hilt right through the tough grey leather: the elephant does not feel a thing.

347

I looked at the whale contentedly basking on the surface after a snack of twenty pounds of mackerel and I reckoned there was a good chance of doing it the same way with him. The press were going to take pictures of the inoculation, and I came forth from the dressing room wearing a frogman outfit with a disinfectant aerosol in one hand and a syringe fitted with a ten-inch needle in the other. With the panache of a commando off to plant limpet mines on the *Tirpitz*, I somersaulted backwards into the pool. This flashy entrance was then followed by a more feeble dog-paddle towards my prey. As I arrived at Cuddles's glistening hull, he tolerantly rolled a liquid brown eye at me and gave me the salmon-pink grin. The sloping rows of conical white teeth sparkled.

I selected a spot on the top of the killer's back at the base of the dorsal fin, sprayed the area with disinfectant and then threw the can away from me. Cuddles was most intrigued. Only his big eye moved, following my every movement. I balanced myself in the water and raised the syringe high in the air. Then with my free hand I slapped at the disinfected spot, One, two, three. "What *is* the lad up to?" I could imagine the whale musing good-humouredly. Four, five—down came the syringe, straight as an arrow, and at exactly the same instant I had the impression that someone had dropped an atom bomb on the pool: the entire three million pounds of water beneath me seemed to levitate itself, and I felt I had been transported into a giant washing machine. Arms and legs flailing, I was sucked down in a maelstrom of foaming water. What looked like a nuclear submarine with a full-open throttle was tearing round me. My lungs were bursting, and my shins had received an excruciating blow. A half-drowned veterinarian was hauled miserably over the edge of the pool and lay coughing up salt water in a very un-commando-like fashion at the feet of the pressmen, who found it all very interesting.

Apparently as soon as the needle had touched the whale, he had launched himself forward with full, fast beats of his flukes. The entire muscle strength of a cetacean's body is concentrated on the hinge of the tail. The energy contained in this highly efficient propeller is enough to storm-toss incredible volumes of water in the twinkling of an eye. I had been the centre of such an instant storm and the painful bruising of my shins had been caused by the tip of a flipper grazing by.

Half an hour and a stiff shot of brandy later, I felt ready to try again. I was loath to use the dart gun, since I was afraid that the wide bore might carry unsterile water into the tissues. The question of needle length interested me. It was generally assumed that a long one that could reach beyond the thick blubber layer was essential: everyone talked as if the blubber was inert stuff, without blood vessels that could circulate drugs and vaccines. But even fatty tissue must have blood to remain alive, and I decided to try a shallow injection method on Cuddles. I telephoned a friend at a Leeds University dental clinic, and a car was sent over with what I wanted: the needle-less gun that fires liquids at high velocity into human gums or skin. It was the instrument being developed for mass vaccination against cholera, typhoid, polio and so on.

Now the intrepid frogman re-entered the water carrying the vaccine gun. Once more Cuddles was resting and gave no sign as I approached that only a couple of hours before I had tried to harpoon him. Again he grinned disarmingly as I raised the gun and drew in a big breath. If the typhoon struck, I was determined to keep my mouth shut this time, no matter what.

I pulled the trigger. There was a sharp crack. Cuddles grinned benevolently again and did not move an inch: he was vaccinated and had not felt a thing. Now all I had to do was wait and hope that the inoculation was effective, as one of my problems had been to discover the correct dose of vaccine for a killer whale. With most vaccines it is by no means safe to give, say, six times the amount of vaccine to an individual who weighs six times the average for any particular dosage. In the end I had decided to give Cuddles three times the human dose of flu vaccine and then take blood after a couple of weeks, when a dry dock would be ready. I would check the level of flu antibodies and give bigger booster shots if necessary.

I was quite pleased as I struggled out of the pool for the second time that day. One way or another, I had injected my first real live killer whale. By the time I had showered and got into warm clothing once more, everyone had gone from the dolphinarium except one fellow, whom I took to be the last of the press. He stood at the water's edge, looking down intently at the whale, a camera slung from his neck and his pockets bristling with notebooks. "Get what you want?" I asked.

"Oh yes, very much so," came the reply. "By the way, I'm Andrew Greenwood. I spoke to your wife a few months back. Lobsters—remember?"

"How did you know I was working on the whale today?" I asked.

He grinned. "I drop a keeper in the bird section a packet of fags every week to keep me informed."

His nerve appealed to me. "Come and have a spot of lunch and tell me all about your lobsters," I said.

Andrew barely touched the meal, he spent so much time enthusing over his determination to practise with zoo animals once he had qualified at Cambridge. Earnestly, he told me about his research. "You may well know of the significance of lobster blood serum in identifying a certain type of human haemophilia," he began. "It's a very rare condition, and only about eight cases have been reported so far, but Manchester Royal Infirmary are working on a test for the disease. That test relies on a supply of lobster serum."

"Quite. To detect the missing clotting factor in the human blood," I said, nodding sagely but not knowing the faintest thing about the role of a crustacean in such obscure areas of medicine.

The intent young student appeared to think that I knew all about the matter. "So I've been asked to supply the laboratory at Manchester with lobster serum and I came to you, Dr. Taylor, for advice on taking blood from lobsters."

It was flattering, of course, but I had no idea where to begin finding veins on such an armour-plated creature.

"I'm afraid I can't help you," I confessed. "Lobsters don't fall sick very often these days."

Andrew Greenwood seemed disappointed. "There must be a way of sampling a lobster without doing it like the Dutch scientists do— simply chopping off a claw and letting the poor thing bleed into a jar," he said.

I liked his attitude. Andrew seemed a promising sort of bloke, and I had the feeling that he was not the type to let it rest at that.

350

When we parted he promised to contact me and keep me informed of his progress, and I was impressed when, three or four weeks later, he proudly appeared at my home in Rochdale carrying a little tube of pale blue liquid. He had studied the architecture of the crusty old lobster and had found a particular soft spot where a needle can be inserted and blood drawn off without hurting the creature in any way. It was his unusual début in the world of wild animal surgery.

Chapter Five

IN THE EARLY MONTHS of 1970, I was happy to realize that my practice was becoming busier and busier. I had been on my own for eighteen months, and it seemed that the venture might have turned the corner. Cuddles occupied a good deal of my time, of course: like any infant, he had teething pain as more of his ivory fangs came through his gums, but I soothed his mouth with vast quantities of babies' teething jelly held on by water-resistant denture paste. That winter was quite eventful elsewhere, too, which was why I came to be sitting on a Derbyshire hillside one freezing afternoon, cradling my dart rifle.

Whereas America has its Big-foot and the Himalayas their Yeti, not forgetting Scotland's "Nessie", the English have to make do with the more mundane monsters which are reported every six months or so in the newspapers and are usually identified as pumas or lions. Regularly these large felines are spotted by ostensibly sober members of the community, and I often marvel at the certainty with which folk whose knowledge of the jungle is minimal will cry wolf (or tiger, or puma) when a twitching brown tail is spied vanishing into a thicket three hundred yards away.

The "puma" which surfaced that January in Derbyshire, fifty miles south of Rochdale, was bothering the inhabitants of a little town set on a hillside criss-crossed with limestone walls. The beast had been seen by the schoolmaster, several farmers and various other people. It was exactly three feet to eight feet long, a minimum of four feet to six feet high at the shoulder and was variously black, dark brown, gingery and light yellow. I was asked to go over with a dart rifle and join in a concerted hunt by police, RSPCA men, journalists and small boys.

I looked forward to a leisurely stroll over fine countryside, and was confident that I would end up by feeling as fit as a fiddle and without having seen anything more wild than a hare. There are, however, wild wallabies living and breeding successfully in the Derbyshire heather; they are rarely spotted but I reckoned that the "puma", if it existed at all, was probably one of them.

The local village constable organized the sweep of the countryside very efficiently. He had plotted the most recent sightings and when I arrived was distributing walkie-talkies, maps and thermos flasks of tea. He lined us up and announced the Orders of the Day as if he was sending us in after Bonnie and Clyde. Off we set, and I soon found myself alone on the hillside, pushing through beds of dripping bracken with the wind making my cheeks tingle. When I was almost at the top of the main ridge and could look down at the streets of glistening grey slate roofs, I was told over the walkie-talkie to find a sheltered spot by one of the moorland walls and wait. The constable had deployed his posse in a circle enclosing hundreds of acres. I was the centre point of that circle and the order to beat inwards would now be given.

Squatting down out of the wind, I could not see any of the other searchers although I could hear the constable chivvying his right and left flank. Then, suddenly I heard my name called urgently over the walkie-talkie. I took in the astounding message that came crackling over the air in the constable's excited voice: "Dr. Taylor, hold your position. Animal sighted coming in your direction."

352

I looked hurriedly around and pressed in against the dry-stone wall. My heart began to beat rapidly with excitement. I carefully checked that the safety catch on the dart gun was securely in the "off" position. There was a new compressed-air cylinder in the chamber and a syringe loaded with enough phencyclidine to clobber a grizzly bear.

The walkie-talkie crackled again. "Dr. Taylor, keep down. Animal seen still coming your way, approximately quarter of a mile from you. Other side of your wall. Running at present time parallel to wall."

At this point I felt a trifle apprehensive: if they had been able to identify the creature, they hadn't bothered to tell me. I had tangled with big cats many times in zoos and in Africa, but under controlled conditions, and the difficulty I faced now was knowing when to stand up and look over the wall. Too soon or too late could obviously be disastrous, and the wall was too well built to have any chinks in it. The trusty constable solved the problem almost at once. "Dr. Taylor, Dr. Taylor, animal now one hundred yards approximately to your left. Still running parallel to wall."

My mind raced. I would have only a few seconds in which to stand up, aim and fire. I had fitted my shortest barbed needle, so that no matter what the creature or where I hit it, there was the smallest risk of the needle entering a major body cavity. I would swing the gun round with the movement of the animal, assuming it was still running.

I stood up and rammed my rifle over the wall. Twenty feet away, slightly to my left and going at a steady pace, loped a tawny creature which at first sight looked dramatically like the Hound of the Baskervilles. The beast that had been blamed in the locality for every sort of misdeed was a lanky Great Dane. Looking closer, I saw it was in terrible shape. Scurfy skin was stretched tight over its prominent skeleton, its sides were disfigured with numerous red scars and wounds, and the eyes were sunken and desperate. It was an animal that must have been out on the run for months, and it was easy to see from the slight sway of its hindquarters that it was coming to the end of the road.

All the same, my sudden emergence like a jack-in-the-box

produced a surge of alarm and determination in the dog. Its eyes bulged with the effort as it strained for more speed and veered away from me. I looked down the gun barrel, made my split-second assessment of wind and likely trajectory and fired. The dart flew strong and straight—straight over the back of the Great Dane. It thwacked impotently into a tussock fifteen yards away, the dog vanished over a rise in the ground and I shouted unrepeatable oaths after it. You never get a second chance in such cases.

It was a very subdued marksman who shortly afterwards explained to the constable and his troops what had happened. They took it very politely and we started another, rather half-hearted hunt. By late afternoon we were about to call it a day when an amazing piece of good news came up from the town: the Great Dane had dashed into a timber yard and someone had closed the gates. It was holed up behind a pile of wood and was in a mean mood.

Somewhat cheered by this turn of events, I went down to the yard. Distressed and terrified, the animal was snarling and snapping in earnest, and no one dared go near it. There was no way I could find to get a shot at the dog other than from directly in front, and I was afraid that the dart might hit the head. I sent a boy to the nearest butcher's shop for a pound of sausages. When he came back with them I threw a couple to the dog, which swallowed them ravenously. Next I took a third sausage and injected into it a quantity of powerful narcotic with no smell and no taste. I tossed the morsel to the wild-eyed dog. One gulp and it was gone. In eight minutes the poor creature was sound asleep and I could approach him to make a thorough examination. He must have been straying for a very long time and was suffering from malnutrition, multiple wounds, a grass seed embedded in the cornea of one eye and a tumour on the breast.

The owner was never traced but the story ended happily. I arranged with a colleague to hospitalize the wanderer, operate on his eye, remove the breast growth and generally tack him together. A good home was found for him by the RSPCA, and when I saw him a month later he had become plump, glossy and relaxed on an intensive diet of steak, eggs and milk. And the would-be "puma" nearly licked my hand off.

THE FAMILY SAT at breakfast. I had just taken the first call of the day and it had produced an instant cloud over the grilled kippers and marmalade toast. "Doesn't Daddy look grumpy all of a sudden?" piped Stephanie as I pushed away my plate. "What's up, Doc?" The girls chuckled happily.

Shelagh knew instinctively what was likely to have made my face so bleak. She frowned at the children and shook her head. "What was it, love?" she asked quietly. "Giraffe trouble?"

I nodded as I put on my coat and picked up my instrument bag. "Yes," I said, "at Flamingo Park. A young giraffe's been beaten up by an ostrich. It might be a broken leg."

Giraffe surgery was really beginning to prey on my mind. Since the death of Pedro, I had noticed the quickening of my pulse when the phone rang and a voice brought tidings of sickness or accident in some member of this particular species. If the complaint seemed to be essentially a medical one my heart rate returned quickly to normal; it was the surgical side of this beast that was making me lose my nerve.

I had seen the results of a furious attack by red-neck ostriches on zebras and giraffes before. Flailing their powerful legs, beaks agape and stubby wings jutting out like ragged flags, they had snapped limbs, broken skulls and stoved in chests. This time the curator had talked of a six-month-old giraffe with a hind leg that dangled and would not bear weight. Dear God, let it be severe muscle bruising! I had some marvellous drugs in my bag for such conditions, which could be administered without anaesthetic. By the time I turned into the gates of the park I had quite convinced myself that I was going to face a simple case of severe bruising.

One glance at the giraffe with its swinging hind leg quickly put me straight. I felt slightly sick as I stood and watched the calf, a male, lurch gracefully on three legs. The femur—the thigh-bone— was broken, although the blow from the ostrich's horny foot had not left so much as a scratch on the skin's surface.

Frank, the curator, was impatient for my decision. He had hand-reared the youngster himself when its mother had refused to stand for her offspring to suckle. "What about it, then, Doctor?" he asked. "Plaster of Paris?"

I shook my head slowly. "No chance. If the break had been lower down the leg, maybe. But with high fractures in the femur there's too much ham muscle round the site. The plaster can't hold the bone pieces firmly." I took a deep breath. "I'll have to pin the leg with a vitallium spike. Maybe screw a plate on as well. I can't say more for sure till I open up the leg to look."

Frank managed a tight smile. "Great, Doctor."

While Frank and his keepers prepared ropes, straw, water and all the other things necessary for surgery, I turned my attention to the old bugbear of anaesthetic. Should I pre-medicate with valium instead of acepromazine to avoid the blood pressure effects which had killed poor Pedro? Then what? A touch of xylazine as a tranquillizer with a final knock-out shot of etorphine? I pondered. If the broken ends of bone had overlapped I would have to use brute force to re-position them. I settled for the valium, xylazine and etorphine cocktail.

When all was ready the giraffe, calm as a child's pony, was coaxed into a narrow, high-sided box. Before starting, I listened to its heart through my stethoscope. It was bounding but I could not detect any abnormalities. The animal accepted slivers of apple from Frank while I began the injections into its neck muscles. I worked like a zombie. I could hear nothing but the breathing of the animal, the tap of its hooves against the woodwork, the dull rush of blood in the centre of my head.

After the valium the calf soon became droopy with half-closed eyes; the xylazine settled it down gently onto its knees in the straw. Now to bring oblivion down onto the gentle creature. The door of the box was lifted and I squeezed inside. The giraffe's pulse was reasonably regular. Quickly I injected a small dose of etorphine into the neck. Once flat out, the giraffe would be hauled out of the box by Frank's keepers and I could work in the open.

Again I put my stethoscope to the rib cage. "Lub-dup, lub-dup, lub-dup." All sounded well. "Lub-dup, lub-dup, lub-lub-lub-dup."

What was that?

I instantly began to sweat. One hand still on the stethoscope, I groped with the other beneath the animal's groin to take the pulse in the femoral artery. It was hard to find, the sound coming through my ivory earpieces seemed softer now, and the breathing was barely detectable. I fought down panic. "My bag—quick," I hissed to the curator who crouched behind me. "He's collapsing."

It took me a few seconds to load a syringe with a circulation booster and an antidote to the etorphine. Thank God giraffes have jugulars like drainpipes, I thought, as the drugs shot into the bloodstream. "Lub-dup, lub-lub . . . lub . . . lub . . . lu-u-b. . . ."

I could not believe it. There was no more sound.

"I'm afraid that he's dead," I said bluntly. "And I haven't got a clue why."

I DECIDED TO do an immediate post-mortem on the young giraffe. The scalpel revealed white, dry areas of tissue scattered throughout many of the muscles of the body and most significantly in the thick muscular wall of the heart. It was unmistakably "white muscle disease", which I had often seen in calves and even wallabies and pelicans, but it was the first time I had come across it in a giraffe. The diseased heart had simply failed when the added stress of anaesthesia had been loaded onto it. But it was little consolation for Frank as I explained that the animal's days had been numbered anyway. "Irreversible change caused by a deficiency of a chemical called selenium in the fodder and herbage," I said. "I'll take some samples of soil and hay for analysis."

So it turned out: there were barely two parts in ten million of selenium in the soil and even less in the fodder. Selenium is a rare element, named after the Greek word for "moon", but to giraffes the presence or absence of it in their environment can be a matter of life or death. A mere five parts in ten million of the strange "moonstone" could have been enough to save the giraffe.

That evening Shelagh listened as I cursed the day I had ever decided to specialize in exotic animals. "I'm beginning to think that I'm a positive menace where giraffes are concerned. Cats and dogs, pigs and ponies—they're more my measure. Bring back the budgies and moggies."

"Do you really mean that?" Shelagh asked quietly after a moment's silence. She smiled gently and fixed me with unblinking green eyes.

"Er, no," I said.

"I'll get you a cup of tea while you work out a dose for supplementing the other giraffes with selenium," said Shelagh, rising to her feet.

MIRACULOUSLY, IT WAS NOW, despite this latest giraffe débâcle, that Pentland Hick of Flamingo Park made me an amazing offer. Frank, the curator, was leaving. Would I go to live at Flamingo Park and take the position of curator and group veterinary officer? Hick said I could retain an essential degree of independence, visit Belle Vue regularly, go out to other exotic animal clients if they called, and use all the facilities of the operating room he was building for my use at Flamingo Park. More, he would pay for me to travel around the world, studying wild animals and visiting other zoos and animal dealers. I would have to live a bachelor life in a caravan on the site in a peaceful corner of the park, but Shelagh and the girls would join me at weekends. The offer was a unique one and without hesitation I accepted: few zoo veterinarians have any experience of the other side of the fence, of general keeping and management, yet they can never be fully efficient without it. It was to prove a watershed in my life.

Flamingo Park Zoo was built round an early Victorian manor house and occupied the house itself, the grounds and two or three outlying farms. The house and lake stood at the top of a rise, from which the ground sloped away to a stream and the caravan site. Across the Vale of Pickering, the hazy line of the North Yorkshire moors stretched across the horizon.

My first days as curator were highly discouraging. There was far more than I had ever imagined to running a zoo with a couple of dozen keepers and hundreds of assorted animals, not to mention the thousands of human varieties that arrived by car and coach each week. Headline-grabbing surgery on cute zoo inmates, the occasional dramatic intervention and the midnight emergency were not as central to my life from now on as keeping the drains unblocked and dealing with grumbles from visitors about catering, lost boys, too few lavatories, spectacles snatched by monkeys and coats ruined by wet paint.

I soon found caravan life too spartan for my tastes. Days that had started with one of Shelagh's fine breakfasts and time for a stab at the *Daily Telegraph* crossword in front of the log fire were replaced by the miseries of tea stewed over a calor-gas heater, cold baked beans and no morning paper. An unusually depressing spring, with icy winds and snow right through till May, turned the land round the caravan into a gumboot-removing quagmire.

Despite all this, I soldiered on. I had the animals, and for the first time in my life they were all under my care and not just with respect to veterinary matters. Want to hire an elephant for a store opening in Leeds? I was the chap who organized everything. The rewards for putting up with the mud and the baked beans were the opportunities to touch, see, smell and just be with a whole variety of animals all day long.

Everyone taught me something. I was initiated into the highly complex business of water treatment and filtration by the dolphinarium staff. Violet, the head of the animal food kitchen, showed me how to present acceptable and appetizing meals to some of the rare animals like lesser pandas, pangolins and Gambian pouched rats.

Most of all, the animals were always instructing me. Mangrove snakes went into convulsions when I experimented with what I had thought was a safe anti-tick aerosol. The great elephant seal demonstrated the uselessness of a dart gun on him even at point-blank range: the near-liquid blubber in this species absorbs the shock of the syringe impact, and the charge that actually pushes the injection in does not detonate. Tigers, camels, elephants, cockatoos and kangaroos taught me respect for the way they insisted on certain standards in the daily routines of cleaning, feeding and general maintenance. Break the routine, disturb their ordered lives, be brusque or absent-minded and they meted out punishment. I was learning the hard way, but I was learning fast.

WITH THE ARRIVAL OF summer, caravan life at Flamingo Park became less stark and Shelagh and the girls drove over at the weekends.

Cuddles had by this time settled down wonderfully at Flamingo

359

Park. The flu vaccine worked and no booster shots were needed. He was devoted to the American girl whale-trainer, Jerry Watmore, who had come over from the USA to school him, and he was eating like a horse. A whale sling that could be run over the pool on massive steel beams had proved a success, and Cuddles had swum into it at our first attempt. Blood sampling and health inspections were easy and quick, and the only problem was to persuade the whale to back off out of the sling when the examination or whatever was over. He loved this giant doctor's couch.

I fussed over every little ailment, real or imagined, that beset Cuddles. Slight cracking of the skin in the corners of his mouth? I had read of scurvy, the disease that was once the bane of mariners, cropping up in whales, so I trebled his daily dose of vitamin C. A small spongy wart on his dorsal fin? Into the sling, a shot of local anaesthetic and off it came.

I was beginning to get the "feel" of this animal. Every time I visited I swam with him for a few minutes. He adored having his tummy scratched and lightly kicked by my flippered feet as he hugged me between his flippers.

Cuddles was as good-natured with Shelagh and the girls as he was with me, and we would all swim with him. This gave Stephanie and Lindsey something of an advantage when talk among their school friends turned to dogs, cats and other more mundane pets.

There was a lot of animal training going on in the park. Sharp-eyed macaws played pontoon with members of the public and always won. Their opponents never realized that the crusty-natured birds had been trained to spot marked cards which bore minute black dots on their reverse side. I learned how easy it is to train dolphins and I also spent long hours watching Jerry Watmore turning Cuddles into a star performer. When she had given him a full repertoire of jumps, rolls, handshakes and tricks of all kinds, she handed Cuddles's presentation over to a young English boy who had the makings of a marine mammal trainer. Cuddles liked him and appointed him one of the select coterie, which included myself, who were allowed to ride round the pool sitting on his back either in front of the dorsal fin or, should one prefer a more exciting, bumpy journey, perched directly behind it.

Cuddles was like a lamb—but the public did not know that. The very name, killer whale, the vague recollection of stories by polar explorers of how these creatures had lunged up onto ice floes in pursuit of human prey, the way whaling fleets detested marauders who blatantly freebooted among the coveted blue and fin whale herds, memories of old seafarers who had seen the sea turn red as packs of distinctively marked assassins slaughtered whole dolphin schools—all this patchwork of myth and folk memory made a reputation for his kind of which Cuddles, as he basked in his pool with his belly full of prime herring, was quite unaware. He liked people and seemed to try to reach out mentally towards them, but there was a chasm of incomprehension between them: people thrilled and admired and shrank back as they looked down at him.

Martin Padley, the head of the dolphinarium, and I did not include ourselves among these landlubbers. With much delight and more than a touch of exhibitionism we continued to swim daily with the whale.

The crowds thought us daring, but, in fact, I had never felt safer. I had been frightened by horses that lashed out with both hind feet at the slightest touch, cornered by hysterical Alsatians, and forced to back down by bloody-minded alligators. But Cuddles I knew instinctively to be benevolent. It was in his eyes, the carefully measured pressure of his jaws on my hand or leg, the squeeze of his flippers round my trunk, his very presence. Looking through the literature, I could find no authenticated cases where killer whales had been proved to attack humans. The polar explorers' story of the animals breaking a pathway through ice to reach them did not end in actual assault and was, I believe, more probably just sheer curiosity on the whales' part. Americans had already swum among schools of wild killers and come to no harm.

Scientifically, we were convinced that unlike the dim-witted and primitive shark which will snap at anything, the highly sophisticated whale does not do anything without thinking first. It is equipped with sonar that can not only judge ranges but identify the nature of objects with a precision far beyond the capabilities of man-made devices: in pitch-black water it can distinguish between one kind of fish and another and even read the emotions of another of its species by "looking" into the skull sinuses to detect internal blushing. It has an intricate communications system that uses unjammable codes, and eyes that see well above and below the surface. It seizes only what it wants to seize, never attacks blindly. And whereas it counts dolphins, seals, fish, squid and, no doubt, ships as familiar inhabitants of its environment to be eaten, hunted, or avoided in the natural order of things, free-swimming, awkward humans are outsiders and of less significance than a clump of floating seaweed. Killer whales do not waste time on seaweed, so we romped with Cuddles in the water during his first year without qualms. The whale treated each and every playmate considerately and benignly.

I had, however, overlooked one important fact. Bright as they are, killer whales are not omniscient. Wise in the ways of the deep waters, they know nothing of fellow mammals who stayed on land when they, aeons ago, went back to the seas. They assume that all creatures can survive in a liquid world. Watching, touching me, Cuddles must have assumed too much.

I imagine he was impressed by the way in which so clumsy a beast could evidently hunt, somehow coming up with an inexhaustible supply of herring and mackerel. In my bathing trunks I showed no sign of possessing much in the way of weapons and my feet seemed very inferior to flippers and flukes. Still, the proof of the pudding was in the eating, and I appeared to be good at catching fish.

The crunch came when Cuddles assumed that I was good at something else. Killers can hold their breath underwater for more than a quarter of an hour. While it is true that a man has stayed under without special gear for $13\frac{3}{4}$ minutes, most homo sapiens have a far lower limit of endurance.

Cuddles could not be expected to know this when we began a new game one rainy morning after I had dived into his pool for our regular daily mixture of fun and veterinary checks, while Martin and his trainers prepared the whale's food downstairs in the fish kitchen.

It all developed out of something we had enjoyed many times before. Cuddles would push me round the pool with the point of

362

his snout, and I was expected to tickle his throat with my toes as he propelled me backwards through the water. Sometimes he would angle me down a bit and we would take a quick swoop towards the pool bottom, then up he would soar, balancing me perfectly as I crashed through the surface in a welter of foam.

This morning Cuddles decided on a further variation. He would push me as usual, then he would stop abruptly. I quickly caught on that I was supposed to flounder away, and when I was a few yards off he would come after me and gently pick me up once more on the tip of his snout. It was a sort of tag. Cuddles enjoyed the competitive aspect of the new game immensely. He would roll slightly to one side and watch me make off with the glint of an excited puppy in his eye.

I did quite well and on the odd occasion almost managed to side-slip when he took up the pursuit, which is not to be sniffed at when you realize that killers can turn on a sixpence and use their great tail-flukes to brake to a dead halt from sixty miles per hour in a second.

Cuddles thought it was all a marvellous wheeze. He began to come in twisting like a snake so that I could not see him for foam, or climbing up like a fighter plane to intercept me at my blind spot, below and behind. Always his final attack was gentle; I felt the round, warm smoothness of his muzzle press into me and I knew I had been caught again.

Next I tried deflecting his muzzle at the last moment by pushing him off with a hand so that he cruised by me. That, and a kick back with one foot pressed against his side, and I was away. Cuddles squealed contentedly and turned to follow me. Before my fingers could touch him, he stopped dead, sank vertically a few inches and zoomed in for my stomach. With consummate ease he made contact, and to secure his hold dived slowly at a shallow angle. Holding my breath I went down, expecting any second to be taken up to the surface as usual for the next round.

But no. With a soft thwack, my back was flattened against the wall of the pool. Not painfully—Cuddles was far too careful with folk to act roughly. He simply pressed me against the concrete. I could almost hear him clicking through the water, "Now, old friend, get out of this one if you can!" All of which was good, healthy fun—except that we were four feet under water. He could hold his breath for fifteen minutes and I knew it. I might manage two at a pinch, and he did *not* know it.

I pushed. Cuddles increased the pressure just enough by the minutest vibration of his tail-fluke. I wriggled, tried to squeeze sideways, thumped on his forehead. Cuddles did just enough to make sure I was fixed. My wriggles and thumps no doubt showed how much I was enjoying myself.

Fear swept through me. My lungs were ready to explode. I must breathe, even if it was only one last inhalation of sparkling blue water. I remember the resentment I felt at dying accidentally, the ridiculousness of it all. As my fear turned to terror and my resentment to despair, Cuddles remained motionless, holding me as surely as a pin transfixes a butterfly in its glass case.

The haze of green and blue, the dancing white bubbles, the black fuzz of the whale's head were beginning to spin when I heard through the rising roar in my ears a far-off whistle. Instantly the pressure on my stomach disappeared and I felt my hair grabbed painfully: the next moment my head was above water and I was pulling in chest-fulls of precious air. Martin was kneeling on the poolside, holding me up by my hair while Cuddles was floating a few feet away with his eyes fixed on the gleaming bucket by Martin's side.

By good fortune the head trainer had come up with the first fish of the day at exactly the right moment. He had taken in the situation immediately and blown his whistle to give the "come and get it" signal to the whale, who had at once left our deadly game and gone to breakfast.

Martin helped me out. When I had got my nerves under control I issued an instruction that no one was to swim alone with Cuddles ever again. Killers may not attack human beings but I knew now how easily they could kill accidentally.

Things were never the same again. Children were no longer invited to have a dip with the genial giant, and when we went in there was always someone on the side with a whistle and a bucket of fish, just in case. We found out that some of the American marinelands always had a baseball bat on hand when their killers were being ridden. They did not like talking about it, but it was plain that other folk had had their doubts about the safety of these whales.

Before long it was Martin's turn to revise his ideas about our cuddly Cuddles.

"I can't put my finger on it," he said to me one day after swimming with the whale, "but I don't feel as secure with him any more."

We discussed it, but could not arrive at any precise reason for his apprehension.

Then Cuddles developed a fetish for rubber flippers. First he started refusing to release the grip of his teeth on the webbed footwear of a diver in his pool. Quickly this worsened to the point where he was obsessed with the things and, with a jerk of his head, would wrench the flipper off. His pursuit became keen to the point where he would surge up and snatch them as the swimmer scrambled over the pool edge. Martin's fears deepened, but we decided to continue swimming with the whale whenever necessary for veterinary inspections and for cleaning and maintaining the pool.

The next stage was more serious. Like an underwater commando, Cuddles would neatly break the air-pipe of a diver's scuba gear, forcing him to surface rapidly. We stopped the use of scuba gear unless absolutely essential and made do with masks and snorkels. Cuddles soon found he could rip the masks off, breaking the rubber retaining bands with ease.

Finally, Martin walked dripping into my office with his wet suit in tatters. There were blue weals on his skin below long tears that had shredded the rubber. He looked pale and grim.

"I went in to seal a leaking window," he said, shivering. "Cuddles came up like an express train and tried to rip my wet suit off. His teeth bruised me for the first time. I can tell you, I was bloody scared."

So our salad days were over and swimming with Cuddles came to an end. On special occasions when we had to go into the water, we wore bathing trunks and hung protective nylon netting between us and him. I believe that the wet suits were the key to the problem. In them men became sleek and shiny like sealions, and maybe awakened memories in Cuddles's subconscious of those fin-footed creatures which, while able to dart like arrows through the dark water, are not able to out-manoeuvre the killer whales who find them such tasty morsels.

Chapter Six

THE FOLLOWING summer was exceptionally busy. It was the height of the craze to open safari parks, following the lead of places like Woburn and Longleat. Every duke or earl was scattering lions and giraffes around the Nash terraces and along the rosewalks.

The safari parks undoubtedly saved a number of aristocratic residences and contributed a great deal to our knowledge of keeping wild animals in captivity. Jimmy Chipperfield showed at Longleat, Woburn and elsewhere that properly acclimatized tropical mammals, with their built-in heat-regulating systems, could prosper in the depths of an English winter. Town folk got a taste of the African bush without driving far from London or Liverpool. Species such as the cheetah, notoriously difficult to breed in traditional zoos, began to reproduce at an increasing rate.

There were problems, however. The wide open, grassy spaces of the parks, with an abundance of food lying around, encouraged rodents and other pests to move in and import troublesome diseases, and the animals were not as easily inspected as in the closer confines of a zoo.

Not all of the problems were purely veterinary ones. The controlling of social groups of creatures like lions, zebras and baboons in extensive parkland presented many challenges for the pioneers. I found myself one of those pioneers when, through my connections with the Smart circus family, I became involved in helping them to set up a safari park at one of the finest sites in Britain, on a hillside looking towards Windsor Castle.

Baboon reserves are certainly one of the most entertaining features of a safari park, and the baboons were some of the first animals to take up residence at Windsor. They gave us a heap of headaches in the early days, mainly because of their obsession with escape. Compared to baboons, prisoners of war with their wooden horses and other feats of mental and physical ingenuity were mere beginners. If they could talk, some of the baboons I know and respect, with names like Scarface, Tin-Ribs, Wart and Squint, could confidently drawl, "The gaol hasn't been built that can hold me!" and mean it. At Windsor the baboons were originally corralled by a high wire fence with a sheet of smooth, slippery plastic on the top: the idea was that they could not get a grip on the plastic. The baboons solved this minor problem by climbing up the wire until they reached the bottom of the plastic sheet and then, like a troupe of circus acrobats, forming a baboon pyramid to by-pass the puerile device. Sitting on the top edge of the fence, the first escapers would then reach down and give a hand up to their mates who had been the sturdy-shouldered base of the pyramid.

To make the baboon pyramids unstable and unworkable, we stepped the plastic sheet inwards a foot or so from the fence. Back went the baboons to the secret drawingboard. The next schemes involved either unpicking the slippery green sheet with persistent patience, or mounting diversionary attacks on the Alsatian dog that guarded the gate to the reserve whilst the main bunch of escapers slipped out on his blind side.

In the end the Windsor baboons opted for a peaceful life within their compound, mainly because their successful break-outs led either into the tiger reserve, where they got the fright of their lives, or into less lethal parts of the park where meal tickets were hard to come by. Also there were lots of fun things to do inside, like dismantling cars: the baboons could take the trimmings off a moving car far quicker than any production line worker could put them on. It was not as if the animals wanted to do anything useful with the articles that they stole. They just collected them for collecting's sake.

I knew where to find the looted bits of cars. Along with the baboons in the reserve at Windsor lived a lugubrious coven of Egyptian vultures. These harpies were remarkably diligent in building nests, not nests of twigs in the approved ornithological manner, but jazzy, glittering, pop-art bowers, lattice-work constructions made from windscreen wipers and radio aerials gathered from the ground after the baboons had knocked off for the day.

At a safari park which I visited in Spain, the wire fence of the baboon reserve was topped not by slippery plastic but by a strand of electrified wire of the sort used to corral cattle. Here the baboon POWs adopted a method of escape which might have been copied from the way soldiers are supposed to deal with barbed-wire barricades. One individual would fling himself onto the wire and lie there, twitching and jerking, whilst the others would quickly scurry over the bridge made by his gallant little body. When all had gone, he would drop back exhausted. It would be his turn to go out with the next batch, when someone else would act as the insulator.

I also went to the beautiful zoo at Kolmården, on the Baltic coast of Sweden, to study their well-built baboon compound. High fences with their top sections angled inwards, deep foundations to thwart tunnellers, electrified mats at the exits and entrances—this was surely a maximum security unit. But they said that about Colditz.

Beyond the baboon compound was a lovely wooded reserve of pine trees in which a number of bears ambled about. The ground was covered with delicious pine kernels. The baboons could see and smell the tantalizing morsels through the wire, but how were they to get at them? First they tried sneaking along beside a car, keeping the vehicle between themselves and the guards and then, as the car reached the electrified mat, jumping up, holding onto a door handle and keeping their feet clear of the ground until they were safely through. Using a pair of guards, one at each side of the mat, soon put a stop to that. The Escape Committee put their heads together. As a coach approached the exit gate, the baboons would nip smartly between its wheels and latch onto the chassis. Out went the coach with its stowaways, who dropped from the undercarriage like autumn leaves when they reached the pine trees. The answer to that one was to equip the guards with angled mirrors on the end of long poles. Before each coach left the reserve they inspected its underside carefully for contraband apes, just like the stony-faced East German border guards at Checkpoint Charlie.

Unlike the prisoners of Colditz, the baboons do not need to fudge the numbers at roll call to give fugitive comrades time to get well clear of the camp. Keepers and curators do make regular checks of the stock list, but the shifting bands of baboons in a spacious reserve are as uncountable as a flock of sparrows. So some who "make it" are not missed for a long time and their disappearance can remain permanently undiscovered as numbers are built up by breeding or as the keeping staff change. I know one deep English wood of birch and fir trees, fringed with palisades of brambles and wild roses that are heavy with juicy hips and blackberries in the late summer. Its inner fastnesses are carpeted from June with succulent red-cap boletus mushrooms, and blewits can be found even in the first frost. Shallow, reedy pools tremble as water beetles, caddisflies, water snails and frogs go about their business. In the depths of that wood live at least three baboons with long and glossy coats. They supplement the harvest of food which each season naturally brings with occasional forays for eggs, vegetables and discarded goodies from the gardens of cottages just outside the wood.

There was another baboon in the fugitive band but she was caught in an illegal gin-trap and died miserably. I was brought her mutilated corpse, and at autopsy I found the pieces of insect carapaces, seed husks, toadstool stems and bone fragments from small creatures that revealed how she and her comrades feasted in their woodland territory. And there is an abandoned badger sett, where the gang holes up, dry and snug, during winter.

I would not reveal the location of these English baboons for a king's ransom; like slaves in ancient Rome, these doughty creatures have earned their freedom.

ALTHOUGH MY BABOON friends at Windsor and Belle Vue did not pose any exceptional veterinary problems for me, I did meet a certain baboon, named Wunn, who had had a whole bundle of surgical problems heaped on his little shoulders by mankind. Wunn was an experimental baboon in a university laboratory involved in advanced transplant research.

After being captured as a youngster in Africa, Wunn knew no home other than a small galvanized box with a metal grille at the front, one of many identical one-man cells that stood in rows in an antiseptic, green-tiled room. He grew well enough on a scientifically perfect but unutterably boring diet of monkey pellets with the occasional half-orange and, when his turn came around, was experimented upon. Bits were taken out and put back in, plastic tubes were inserted to replace portions of his natural ones, miniature electronic gadgets were buried in his flesh to record this and that and always he was being sampled—a biopsy today, blood tomorrow, urine catheter the day after. For years Wunn bore it all stoically and displayed a gentle and warm nature towards the laboratory staff.

Eventually the series of experiments on Wunn came to an end, and there was only one remaining thing for him: death. According to the strict vivisection laws which operate in Great Britain, a laboratory animal which has played its part in a series of experiments must be put to sleep.

The girl laboratory technicians who had worked with Wunn had become particularly attached to the sweet-natured baboon. With the tacit approval of the surgeons involved, they contacted me. Could I find a zoo where Wunn might for the first time in his life rattle about with a troupe of other baboons just like baboons are supposed to do? I was all for it, but there was one possible snag: baboons live in strictly organized social communities where everyone knows his place. Singleton strangers are rarely tolerated and at worst are beaten up and driven off or killed.

Windsor Safari Park agreed to accept Wunn, and we decided to put him first in the baboon reserve in a cage normally used by nursing mothers. Wunn could see and be seen by the other animals but was protected from them by the wire. They became used to his presence and his smell. But what would happen when the new-comer was eventually let out into the main bunch? When should we try it? I knew that if I saw Wunn at the receiving end of a lot of punishment from the other adult males, I would have to put him painlessly to sleep.

After Wunn had spent three weeks in his separate cage, I decided to release him. My heart was in my mouth as Wunn shuffled out into the grassy reserve. Now for it, I thought. Wunn went a few yards, sat down and blinked towards the sunlight. He picked idly at the funny but tasty green matting on which he was sitting. Slowly, nonchalantly, the baboons began to gather round him. To my surprise, instead of marching up to him and demanding to see his credentials, they drifted up in twos and threes diffidently and almost respectfully. The first individuals to come right up to Wunn were the young baboons. Within minutes, one or two of the smallest were climbing over his hairy mane as if he were their long-lost favourite uncle.

We were overjoyed. So far, so very good. After the kids, one of the dominant male baboons cautiously approached the stranger, sniffed at him from a couple of feet away and then walked off unconcernedly. Wunn gazed benignly after him. I had already noticed that Wunn's testicles were abnormally small, probably because of his lifetime of acting as a surgical swap-shop. Perhaps he did not give off enough of the masculine scent to provoke the males; if so, I thanked God he was so poorly endowed. A few of the females came closer and gave Wunn the once-over, but from their reaction they did not seem interested, and the main group moved off. It was all going far better than I could ever have hoped. Wunn was left peacefully alone to begin doing amazing, novel things like sticking a finger into the soil or finding his first discarded wind-screen wiper.

Not once in the days that followed did we see Wunn get into trouble. The kids liked him and a gang of them were constantly in attendance. The women continued not to be turned on by his charm, and the leaders of the pack ignored him. Gradually, as the months passed, Wunn was absorbed into the troupe, but he still seems one apart, with no precise place in the hierarchy. The important thing is that he enjoys the sunshine and the rain, climbing over the rocks, taking handfuls of warm meat and vegetable stew in the winter and riding round the reserve on car bonnets during the summer. Two recent events have given me the utmost pleasure: Wunn has acquired a timid and devoted lady companion who grooms him whenever he feels lordly; and I have watched him deftly steal the chromium-plated wheel-trim from a coach—a coach carrying a visiting party of eminent surgeons.

Chapter Seven

IT WAS AT WINDSOR that summer that I was approached by "Mac" McNab, the head keeper there, a plump, genial individual. "We're going wallaby catching," he announced. "Do you know much about them?"

The honest answer was "No"; I had already found these mini-kangaroos from down under to be uncooperative in responding to medical ministrations. With the aid of a certain brand of mint which these animals adore, I had been able to come into contact with the timid marsupials from time to time but had found the early diagnosis and effective treatments to their ailments difficult.

"Not really, Mac," I told him, "but I'd dearly love to come on the catching."

"Right," he replied. "We're going down to Hampshire. Leonard's Leap, a private estate, has a surplus of the little beauties. We've got to grab them ourselves, though. It'd be best if you came along in case they need doping."

Although McNab's words made it sound as if I were a key member of the hunting team, I had a feeling that I was being invited more as a professional scapegoat than as an insurance against mishap. My old partner in general practice, Norman Whittle, had warned me early in our days together of how often the zoo vet finds himself playing this role.

With an assortment of wooden crates and three vehicles we set out from Windsor and drove down to Hampshire. The Leonard's Leap estate is buried deep in the countryside, a network of small valleys thickly scattered with large rhododendron bushes. These bushes had dry and hollow centres where the wallabies could be found, snugly holed up and proof against the elements. All that McNab, I and the keepers had to do was to chase the wallabies out into a funnel-shaped trap which the estate gardeners had made with wire-netting at the head of one valley.

All through that hot afternoon we panted and puffed, running up and down the grassy slopes, crashing through bushes and hurling ourselves in futile rugby tackles at the lithe, grey-brown bundles of fur that sprang silently over the ground as we approached. By late afternoon we had at last bagged our quota. Although not as worn out as we were, the wallabies had begun to pant and their heart rates were almost too rapid to count. I decided to give each animal a shot of tranquilliser before crating it so that it would be able to relax on the long journey home.

McNab held the wallabies by the base of the tail while I gave the injection and checked to see how many of the females were carrying babies or "joeys".

Of the twelve wallabies we had caught, ten were females and eight of them had sausage-sized infants firmly attached to the milk teats in their warm pouches. Safely on board the vans, the animals settled down quickly and without fuss in their boxes. I felt confident that my little drop of tranquillizer had set a seal of professionalism on the proceedings. Get this load back alive and well, and McNab would undoubtedly appreciate the virtues of modern veterinary science in the zoo field.

Back at Windsor, as the light began to fade, the wallabies were released into their grassy paddock. Ten, eleven, twelve: I counted them out. They were all looking fit, and immediately began jumping nervously along the perimeter of their new compound and glanced with darting dark eyes at all the strange surroundings. McNab and I watched them, but suddenly he cursed and leaned forward.

As the wallabies hopped, wriggling pink lumps fell onto the ground from the pouches of some of them. Within a minute or two, eight helpless baby wallabies, still with the foetal appearance of marsupial young who spend the latter half of "pregnancy" in the pouch, were blindly writhing on the grass.

"Jeez, will ye look at that!" exclaimed McNab. "Every mother's lost her young 'un! Why d'you think that could have happened?"

Quickly but carefully, we began to collect the hairless infants. Suddenly the answer came to me: my wretched tranquillizer. It had done the trick all right on the mothers during the journey, but a proportion of it must have passed from their blood into their milk. Taken in by the babies, it had made them slightly drowsy and, when their mothers were released at the park and began to leap about, they had lost their hold on the teat and had been thrown out. I had given them each an indirect Mickey Finn.

I explained my theory to McNab, who nodded grimly. "Hrrumph. Never did like the idea of all these new-fangled chemicals. Far too much of it," he growled.

His opinion had been confirmed, but there was no time for further recriminations. Something had to be done—fast. The awful thing was that all the babies looked alike: there was just no way we could tell which infant fell from which pouch, but back into someone's pouch each would have to go. McNab called in some keepers and the job of re-catching the wallabies began. Carefully, I stuck a couple of fingers into the pouch of each female. If I found a damp teat from which a drop of milk could be drawn, I plugged on one of the rudely evicted innocents.

Back in the security of a pouch, each joey latched firmly onto its teat and snuggled down, but the chances that I had paired the right mother and offspring in each of the eight cases was something like one in five thousand. What if wallabies were like many other mammals and identified their own babies by scent, rejecting all imposters? In that case there would be de-pouched youngsters on the ground again in a little while and the deadly game of snap, using flesh and blood creatures instead of cards, would have to be played over and over again.

"Let's put them all in the night-house now," I suggested to McNab. "That way, at least they won't be bouncing around and it will give more time for any tranquillizer still in their systems to wear off."

He agreed, and we released the nursing mothers into their indoor quarters.

After a sleepless night I went down to the safari park early. My heart was bounding as I went to the wallaby night-house and opened the sliding door an inch. Peeping in with my stomach anxiously churning, I scanned every inch of the sawdusted floor. I strained my eyes till their muscles ached, but there was not a joey in sight.

Only then did I raise my head a little to look at the crouching wallabies. McNab and the rest of the staff would not be in for another hour. All twelve of them seemed in good order, but there was no way of knowing how things were going in their pouches. Maybe the flattened corpse of a joey was underneath one of them or hidden under a layer of bedding.

I pulled the door right open and gently shooed the animals out onto the grass. On hands and knees I meticulously picked through the sawdust, the bedding and the droppings, sweeping clear every inch of the floor with my bare hands. Saints be praised! Not one single baby could I find.

I went outside and watched the wallabies moving about, busily cropping the short grass. All seemed perfect. I hurried off to see if Mac was in yet and to give him the good news.

In the days that followed, it gradually became obvious that all eight babies were none the worse for mum-swapping, and after a few weeks furry brown heads began to peep out of the pouches on sunny days.

"Well, Mac," I said, when it was clear that the wallabies were out of danger, "it seems that they must be very tolerant creatures. One kid's as good as the next to those little ladies."

"Yes," he murmured, "but no thanks to your tranquillizers, David. How many millions of years have wallabies been happily bringing up their young without 'em?"

He had a point, but it struck me nonetheless how generally accepted on the zoo scene the veterinarian had become. Most zoo men appreciated well enough how veterinary science could make their jobs easier and raise the standard of zoo care by improving the health, diet, breeding and day-to-day welfare of the animals. I thought back to my early days at Belle Vue, when I despaired of my medical knowledge ever matching the wisdom and experience of Matt Kelly, or of showing him that modern drugs and other developments could go hand in hand with his innate animal-craft. Now even Kelly and McNab would grudgingly admit that perhaps my potions, flying darts, autopsies and analysing did have something to offer.

THAT SUMMER Andrew Greenwood took his final examinations at Cambridge and in June he telephoned to say that he had qualified. He was now a fully fledged Member of the Royal College of Veterinary Surgeons. After congratulating him, I asked about the future.

"I'm going to stay on in Professor Harrison's department at Cambridge and do some research in diving animals. But I'll be able to help you out, do locums when you're away, that sort of thing."

"What diving animals will you be working on?" I asked. "Seals, dolphins?"

"Nothing so grand," came the reply. "I've got a research grant from the Royal Navy and they do their diving experiments with far more prosaic species."

"Such as what?"

"Would you believe, goats? Goats that get the 'bends'."

Over dinner that evening I said to Shelagh, "Pity about Andrew. What a waste of a good man. Research! Goats! And I thought he had the makings of a first-class zoo vet." Thoughtfully, I stabbed at a potato.

MY VISITS TO cases outside Flamingo Park had meanwhile become steadily more frequent. Pentland Hick was very patient; sometimes I would be gone for two weeks at a time. I was driving 70,000 miles a year, flying four times as far and becoming accustomed to sleeping by the roadside in my car. Rochdale to Stirling to London and back to Rochdale all in one day by road was nothing abnormal: 850 miles, virtually non-stop, between a sick dolphin in Scotland and a dying sealion in southern England. It was a cracking pace that was required, manning a practice that had grown to be almost a thousand miles square.

I saw Rochdale and my family less and less and I formed the opinion that being a peripatetic, single-handed zoo vet is ideally work for a bachelor. I sympathized with Shelagh when I rang her from a hotel bar in San Diego or Nassau. She was at home, coping with worried owners of parrots and gerbils fretfully awaiting my return, bringing up the girls and keeping the house together in the rainy northwest, while I was grumbling about being delayed for an extra day on Grand Bahama Island. I remember telephoning one time to find her coping with a typical list of problems: she had passed a falcon with what sounded like severe respiratory trouble over to Andrew, put a stitch in a hedghog and been over to Oldham to console a distraught old lady whose even more ancient Patas monkey had collapsed suddenly and died. There had been trouble with a bison at Belle Vue; she had asked my old partner, Norman Whittle, to go and see it.

"One of these days you're going to have to get a partner in the zoo business," she said. "What happens if there's a really serious emergency while you're off on one of your trips?"

It was good to know that she was looking after things, but she was right. Not only was the practice keeping me fully stretched, but at this rate there would soon be enough work for a partner who could also cover for me when I was away and so take some of the pressure which I was unfairly loading onto Shelagh. But one thing I was certain of: nothing, but nothing, would tear me away from exotic animals in a million years.

After a year and a half at Flamingo Park, I decided the time had come to return to full independence: there was an abundance of cases and little likelihood that I might have to sit at home waiting for the telephone to ring. I was not sorry to leave. Pentland Hick had sold his zoo empire and, as happened in so many similar cases around that time, the big public company moved in. Anxious to diversify into what they believed to be a lucrative sector, these experts in bingo, catering and discos looked at animal collections and assessed them like banks of one-armed bandits. Targets, budgets, productivity were words bandied about when animal diets were adjusted to suit the changing seasons or repairs to houses had to be made.

Cuddles the whale suffered a grave attack of intestinal ulceration with massive bleeding, but after intensive treatment he rallied and pulled round.

Against my advice, Cuddles was moved shortly afterwards to Dudley Zoo in Worcestershire, where he was put on show in a hurriedly adapted pool. He proved a great attraction, but the writing was indelibly on the wall: from now on, commercial considerations took pride of place, even where the health of a very valuable animal was at stake. I continued to act as Cuddles's doctor until 1973.

Then, whilst I was on a visit to Communist China, Cuddles mysteriously broke a rib, developed an abscess at the site of the fracture which sent seeds to infect his brain. He died within three or four days of falling ill. Having been in at his beginning, I was heart-broken not to have been on hand when he was finally up against it.

MY LIFE AS A vagrant veterinarian-in-a-suitcase suited me, except for the fact that I was seeing Shelagh and the girls but rarely. Also, I still had this "thing" about doping giraffes. I consoled myself with the thought that with a little bit of luck I might be able to keep

378

dodging the issue, though deep down I knew that one day I was going to have to anaesthetize another giraffe.

So the familiar butterfly sensation started in my stomach when Matt Kelly telephoned from Belle Vue, which still provided a good proportion of my cases. The head keeper sounded concerned but hardly panicky. "Oi've got a giraffe with a tomato stuck in its gob," he told me. "Strange thing is, it's not causin' her trouble. Mebbe it's caught on a tooth. The keeper thinks he got a glimpse of it two days ago."

If it was a tomato, it should not take long before the squashy fruit disintegrated without causing any further trouble. Still, it sounded a rum story and I promised to go straight over, though I reckoned it unlikely that I would have to do much else but mutter a few reassuring words and let time do the rest.

Molly was a lovely specimen of Masai giraffe and had already produced three healthy calves. Standing looking up at her, I could see a red sphere protruding from the right-hand corner of her lips. It was smooth and shiny and looked at first glance like a tomato but, encapsulated in a fold of gum tissue that had grown big enough to flop out of the animal's mouth, the spherical object was without doubt a cyst or a tumour. The giraffe would not be able to feel any pain from the lump and it had not grown enough to interfere seriously with her feeding.

"What d'ye think, Doctor?" asked Matt, after giving me a few minutes to ruminate while the butterflies in my stomach became bat-sized.

"A growth, Matt. It's probably been hidden in there for quite some time, but it's not causing any problems yet. Let's wait and see first."

There were two chances that I might be really lucky. If it was a saliva-duct cyst it might burst or subside spontaneously. If it was a papilloma, it might drop off like a wart on a human hand.

"I'll have a look at it in a couple of weeks," I said, as we went out of the house.

Two weeks later, the tomato had grown into an apple. Its presence was beginning to irritate the giraffe as she ate, and there was not the slightest sign of bursting or separation. I stood on step-

379

ladders to try and touch the thing, but Molly swung her head as I approached and sent me tumbling down onto the straw.

Picking myself up, I said the words that sounded in my head like a death warrant. "There's nothing for it. I'll have to take it off—under general anaesthesia."

I arranged the operation for the next day. Andrew was still messing about with goats, but was always ready and eager to do work for me when asked. I gave him a call and explained the position.

"We'll put her under," I said, "then I'll get the surgical side over as quick as possible while you keep an eye on her system reactions. Then we'll pull out all the stops to reverse her." We talked for a long time about what drugs to use and how we might approach the difficulties that we felt sure were associated with the giraffe's peculiar blood circulation to the head and neck.

"This fainting under tranquillizing is the problem," said Andrew. "If they do that, everybody rushes around trying to hold their heads up in a 'normal' posture; it strikes me that's just the wrong thing to do. The beast should be laid flat and given deeper anaesthetic at such times."

It made sense physiologically, I saw, although I had made the Belle Vue keepers hold Pedro's head up when he fainted. We would try it Andrew's way and, as well as using etorphine and xylazine, would experiment with Dopram, a new American drug that counteracts the respiratory depression caused by narcotics. Our armoury of drugs was increasing every day.

Next morning we all assembled at Belle Vue. Matt was organizing his keepers and looking very apprehensive. The giraffe keeper was truculent and pale-faced. I tried not to let my own trepidation show, but I suspect I failed.

When everything was ready we began. First a small dose of xylazine was injected into Molly's shoulder and then, when she went drowsy, I jabbed the etorphine into her jugular vein. She went down onto the thick bed of straw and, while Andrew was still attaching the electrocardiograph leads and administering the Dopram, I splashed iodine over the operation site and grabbed the lump. A glance showed me that it was a benign tumour. With all my attention fixed on the edge of my scalpel blade as it swept round

380

the base of the tumour, I worked as if it were a small time-bomb. It fell free. Blood welled up. I punched a gauze swab into the wound and then clipped off the main blood vessel. One, two, three, four—I slapped in the sutures and knotted them furiously. Swab again. No blood ooze. Done. It had taken about two minutes.

"Right, Andrew," I said, louder than I intended. "Bring her round."

Andrew moved to the animal's neck and shot the syringeful of blue antidote into her vein. Almost at once, Molly gave a great sigh and blinked. She was coming round. If we were in for trouble, this was where we would run into it.

"Keep her head down until we give the word," I instructed our helpers.

Andrew gave Molly more Dopram. He pressed the button on the electrocardiograph and coils of paper bearing the characteristic tracings were spewed out. He disconnected the leads and bent over the giraffe's heaving chest with his stethoscope.

"How's it going?" I asked.

He gave me the thumbs-up.

I asked three keepers to sit on her head and neck while Andrew stayed at her chest. I looked at my watch. After five minutes, Molly was obviously very conscious and wondering why she had three heavy men pressing down on her. I slipped a final two millilitres of antidote under her skin to guard against any anaesthetic that had still not been neutralized.

At last I took the bit between my teeth. "Everybody off," I shouted. "Stand clear!"

The men jumped to their feet and we all moved smartly back. Molly lifted her neck, looked round at us and slowly fanned her long, glamorous eyelashes. Effortlessly, she gathered her legs under her and stood up.

I bit my lower lip till it bled. Molly walked slowly over to her feed-trough high on the wall and cast a liquid eye over the pile of fresh fruit, corn and celery that Matt had prepared. Then she curled out her grey tongue and began to eat avidly.

No one spoke until Molly had emptied the trough and was looking round for dessert.

I cleared my throat. "Er, I think, gentlemen, she's going to be OK. Thank you very much. One stays with her. The rest come and have a beer."

Andrew grinned. "We've cracked it," he said.

It certainly looked so. "Look here," I said to him, as we walked over to the dispensary to wash up, "why don't you pack up this research business and come into partnership with me? Do some real work."

He answered immediately. "Of course I will. I wondered when you were going to suggest it."

Molly was to be the last case I treated as a solo zoo vet. We were on our way.

David Taylor

David Taylor decided he wanted to be a vet "at about the age of two"—and not much later determined to specialize in wild animals. As a schoolboy he took a keen interest in "everything that flew, swam, crept or crawled," and his earliest cases were the sheep that wandered the moors of his native Yorkshire. Dr. Taylor's *official* veterinary career began in 1957 after a year's research at Glasgow University. It was an ideal time to start out, he recalls: until that time zoo medicine had remained a largely undeveloped science, but suddenly the invention of the dart gun and a whole range of drugs "really brought veterinary surgery into the twentieth century." Taylor is proud to have taken part himself in pioneering new methods of treating animals.

Belle Vue Zoo in Manchester was Taylor's first big client and he has never looked back. When the first marinelands were opened he went to the US navy to learn all he could about marine mammals—and now dolphins, whales and sea lions have become something of a speciality. Since setting up on his own, Taylor travels to zoos and safari parks all over the world, and he's in constant demand: for he and his partner Andrew Greenwood are the only independent travelling zoo vets outside America. "Three American vets cover the United States and Japan," says Taylor. "We cover the rest of the world—from Greenland to Hong Kong!"

So it's no surprise that the telephone is constantly ringing in Taylor's Surrey home. At the start of a typical week, he was just off to see some ailing elephants in Germany; next stop would be Madrid (where the Chinese pandas are very special patients), then on to Houston, Texas, to pick up some dolphins wanted for a British television programme. A normal season might include a stint in Abu Dhabi zoo and a journey to Iceland to help with the capture and transportation of young killer whales.

Amazingly, Taylor still finds time to write: he's just finished a series of books on the care of domestic animals. Nor do letters from schoolboys with blind terrapins or lame rabbits go unanswered. "It doesn't matter what the animal is worth in financial terms," David Taylor says. "If I can help it, I will."

Dinah, Blow Your Horn

A CONDENSATION OF THE BOOK BY

JACK BICKHAM

ILLUSTRATED BY TED LEWIN

PUBLISHED BY ROBERT HALE

I've been workin' on the railroad
All the livelong day;
I've been workin' on the railroad
Just to pass the time away.
Don't you hear the whistle blowin'?
Rise up so early in the morn.
Don't you hear the captain shoutin':
Dinah, blow your horn.

In the town of Preacherville the railroad workers struggle to organize as company police patrol the streets with guns and clubs. Fear hangs in the air, and even thirteen-year-old Bobby Keller feels it. Then it creeps into his home, to menace Bobby's faith in his father . . . and in himself. Nothing seems safe except the boy's love for his pet pigeon and his attachment to Flanagan, the warmhearted old telegrapher who lives next door. But even they are imperilled—until Bobby concocts a daring scheme that just might save them all.

One

I know we were poor that spring so long ago when we moved to the hill country, but the feeling that overwhelmed me on the day of our arrival was sheer excitement. We were starting a great adventure.

My parents had been forced to leave almost everything behind in making this move. Even I had had to take losses, including my handful of books, my bulldog, Danger, and my little flock of pigeons. But my father had told us many times—as if to convince himself—that one went where the railroad ordered, and a man who had lost a hand in an accident was lucky to find any kind of work.

We were nearing our destination now, the train chuffing up the valley on a high embankment overlooking the river. The angle of the sun made the world beyond the window a charcoal drawing: river a gleaming black, trees on the far hillside vertical slashes of gray. But it was warm today. Spring was near. I had my window of the day coach open so I could hang out and look down the curving line of cars toward the engine throwing up its cloud of smoke and fine cinders.

"Bobby," my mother said sharply, "get your head back in. You'll catch your death!"

"Mom, I want to see everything!"

"Robert," my father said sternly.

I obeyed. My parents faced me on their hard leather seat, two slender people, blond, rumpled from the long ride. Beside me were my two younger sisters, Mary Eleanor, nine, and Rachel, six. Both were sleeping, Rachel with her thumb in her mouth.

Our car was less than half filled with passengers. There were two old people a few seats ahead, and a scattering of salesmen. All the way to the front were two beefy men in dark suits who interested me intensely. They had not removed their bowlers despite the heat, and I had not seen them speak or move significantly since they had boarded the train the night before at Cincinnati. But whenever I had moved past them to go to the rest room, their eyes had followed me like ball bearings.

"Now, when we get to Preacherville," my mother lectured me, "I want you to take Rachel's hand and not let go for an instant." She raised a slender hand to brush back a strand of golden hair that had escaped her bonnet, and in that instant she looked much younger, a beautiful girl with her pale hair and blue eyes, despite the lines of worry and fatigue. "Preacherville," she told me, "is not a small town like Henryetta. And there's all the trouble. I expect you to help watch over your sisters."

My father had had his eyes closed. He now opened them. "There's not going to be any trouble, Alma. The H&O has the situation in hand. Everything will be fine."

My mother nodded, although the worry was clear in her eyes.

"And I'll hang on to Rachel," I added. "In case some striker tries to grab her."

My mother said, "Don't talk about strikers."

"Those stories are exaggerated," my father said.

"How about the two guards sitting up in front, then?"

"You don't know they're guards, Bobby."

"They might even be Hobart-Grimes," I said, tossing out the name of the infamous private detective agency that, it was said, railroads used in the worst of times.

My father leaned toward me, anger in his eyes. "I don't want to hear any more of that talk. Do you understand?" He tapped my knee with the stub of his right wrist for emphasis.

I nodded, suppressing an involuntary shudder. It had been a year

388

since my father, a yardman for the Harristown & Ohio Railroad Company, had been examining a faulty car coupler in Henryetta. He had moved his lantern to get better illumination, and the engineer on the switcher up the track had misinterpreted the movement as a signal to back up. The cars had jolted without warning, slamming the steel fittings together on my father's wrist and hand. He had managed to make a tourniquet with his belt and stagger back to the yard office. The doctors had amputated at the wrist and then pulled him through an infection. But he was still very thin and not at all well.

In all this time I should have become accustomed to the stump. But when he touched me with it, as he had just done, something primitive made me shudder. I considered this a flaw in my love for him, as well as in my character, and hated it.

The train slowed, but we were still out in the country. I decided a trip to the rest room was in order. Crawling over my sisters, I made my way up the aisle. The eyes of the two beefy men swiveled in unison as I entered the small compartment. When I came out, they swiveled again. I started to walk past their seats, but my curiosity was too much. I stopped and stared back at the men. Their expressions did not change, but I thought I saw surprise in their eyes. "What are you guys?" I asked. "Hobart-Grimes, or what?"

The nearer man blinked. "Beat it, sonny."

"You figure there's going to be some kind of trouble?"

The other man scowled. "We said beat it."

"Could I see your guns?"

The door opened behind me. Through the rush of noise and sooty wind came Mr. Stein, the conductor. He was a jolly fat man who had been nice to us. When he saw me standing there, however, his face tightened with alarm. He grabbed me by the shoulders. "Here, now. Let's not be bothering these gentlemen!" He propelled me back down the aisle to my parents.

"What was he doing?" my mother asked, as I took my seat.

"Well, he was talking to the . . . uh . . . gentlemen up front."

"Oh, good heavens," my mother breathed.

"All I asked them was if they're Hobart-Grimes!"

"Bobby," my father said, tapping me again, "you're a lot

brighter than most boys. We try to make allowances for that mind of yours. But don't you know you could cause trouble? We're new here. I'm on trial. We're *all* on trial, in a way."

"Yes, sir," I said.

He sighed and looked up at Mr. Stein. "Thank you."

"No harm done," Stein said. "And I wouldn't worry, folks. Preacherville is a railroad town. It's one big happy family most of the time." As if to change the subject, he removed his large silver watch from his vest pocket and popped open the cover.

My father also consulted his watch. "Are we on time?"

"Right on time." Stein smiled.

"Right on time," my father repeated with quiet pride.

THE TRAIN MOVED into Preacherville. We passed the yards, with their gleaming confusion of tracks, and rows of small houses. Then I spied the cluster of larger buildings that was the business section. The train groaned to a halt near the center of the platform.

In the aisle, my father got one suitcase in his hand and another under his stubbed arm. My mother was also loaded down. Mary Eleanor helped, wide-eyed with excitement. Rachel pretended to sleep on. "You'll have to carry her, Bobby," my father said.

I obeyed, but thought Rachel was faking. She did things like that.

Out on the platform it was sooty, and crowded with porters and scurrying passengers. "Do we have everything?" my mother asked. "Mary Eleanor, put that small blue bag down. Bobby, you'll have to carry it. Mary Eleanor, take this food basket before I drop it."

As Mary Eleanor put the bag down, my father turned quickly, bumping me. I saw an intent look on his face. Forgetting the bag, I turned in the direction he was looking.

Down in front of the next car, talking to a porter, were two gray-haired businessmen surrounded by their luggage. The larger man was rotund, wearing a long black cape with crimson lining. As he gestured toward the depot, the pale sunlight glinted off a huge diamond ring.

"Good Lord," my father almost whispered. "That's Nathaniel Harris!"

"Who?" my mother gasped.

"Mr. Harris—the owner of the company!" My father glanced around. "But where is the welcoming committee? Someone has made a terrible mistake. Wait here," he said, and hurried down the platform.

We stood watching him. As he approached the two businessmen, my father snatched off his cap. It was clear that he spoke with the utmost deference. Nathaniel Harris studied him, frowning a bit. Then he extended his hand. My father started to offer his stump, remembered, and extended his left hand. They shook awkwardly. Harris said something and my father replied animatedly, pointing toward us. Harris looked our way and then the three men started walking toward us.

"Oh, no," my mother murmured. "I look a fright." She glanced at us with stricken eyes. "Mary Eleanor, wipe that candy off your face. Rachel, wake up!" She licked her fingers and dabbed at my hair. "Bobby, mind your manners now!"

I pulled back in disgust at her panic, and simultaneously Rachel began to wiggle, demanding to be freed. I put her down with pleasure and tried to curb my resentment. It had cut deep, that instant of seeing my father snatch off his cap and practically bow. And now my mother was all atwitter, making a fool of herself.

My father reached us. "Alma," he said breathlessly, his face shining, "may I present Mr. Nathaniel Harris and his associate, Mr. Leonard Nelson. Gentlemen, this is my family—my wife, Alma, and my children, Bobby, Mary Eleanor, and Rachel."

My mother extended her hand. "It's *such* a pleasure, Mr. Harris!"

"Bobby," my father said, "run into the depot master's office. Tell him Mr. Harris is here."

Nathaniel Harris relinquished my mother's hand and chuckled. "No hurry, Keller. This was our intention, to arrive unannounced and look about on our own."

I hesitated, but my father shot me a look that said life and death depended on my obeying his order. Dodging porters and passengers, I rushed into the depot toward a sign saying OFFICE. Inside, a man was sitting behind a desk littered with schedules and ledger books. The desk had a sign on it that said MANAGER.

"Listen—" I gasped.

"What do you want, boy?" he snapped, looking up from his paperwork.

"My father told me to tell you—"

"This is a private office! Now you just—"

"Nathaniel Harris is out there on the platform!"

The manager's jaw dropped and his metal-framed spectacles almost slipped off his nose. "What?"

"He's out there!" I panted, caught up in the drama. "He came in on the noon special and no one is meeting him and—"

The manager stood, whipped off his glasses, and looked out the window. Grabbing the telephone, he began banging the hook up and down. "Get me South Yards, emergency!"

My duty done, I went back outside at a more leisurely pace. Mr. Harris and Mr. Nelson were still standing there with my family, talking for all the world as if everyone were equal.

"Ordinarily we use my private car," Nathaniel Harris was saying. "But you must know, Keller, that there have been serious labor problems in the industry in the past year."

"I know," my father said, in a tone of deep regret.

"I'll not pretend that the H&O has been without its share of those problems," Harris added. "By riding under an assumed name, in a public car just like everyone else, I have a fine opportunity to experience the rails like common folk."

"I see," my father said. "But don't employees recognize you, sir? You're a very famous man, one of the greats of railroading!"

Harris smiled. "Yes. But sometimes I travel for many miles without being recognized. That's always a pleasure. You probably do not realize what a trial it is, being famous. Be glad for your more humble standing. It gives you freedoms men like myself can never enjoy."

"I can see that, sir," my father said. He looked as if he were actually feeling sorry for poor rich Nathaniel Harris.

Harris turned and tousled his fingers through my hair. "And how are you, youngster? What's the name again?"

"His name is Robert Joseph," my mother said.

"Bobby," I snapped.

"Bobby, is it?" Harris grinned. "And how old are you, Bobby?"

392

"Thirteen," I said. My parents were both giving me the eagle eye. Watch your manners!

"And what," Nathaniel Harris went on, "do you want to be when you grow up, Bobby?"

"I don't know yet, sir," I said honestly.

"Think you'd like to be an engineer, drive one of the big rigs?"

"No, sir. I don't want to work in railroading."

"Bobby!" my mother said, as if I had blasphemed.

But Nathaniel Harris was watching me with keen interest. "You don't like railroading?"

"I like it," I told him. "I like trains. But I don't want to work for somebody else all my life."

Harris chuckled and nudged Mr. Nelson, whose gold teeth were showing. "If you work hard enough, you can own a railroad someday yourself."

"I wouldn't mind owning one," I admitted.

"Well, then, work hard and save your money."

"How much does a railroad like the H&O cost?" I asked, interested.

"Bobby, mind your manners," my father said quietly.

"No, Keller," Harris said. "I like this lad's spunk! I tell you, Bobby, a railroad like the H&O is a multimillion-dollar enterprise!"

"Well, I don't think it's too practical, then, what you said about working hard and saving my money. Even if a railroad only cost *one* million, at six dollars a week, even if I could save half of it, it would take me, uh . . . three hundred and thirty thousand weeks to save enough. By that time I would be . . . uh . . . oh, I would be dead for a million years."

My parents looked horrified, but Nathaniel Harris guffawed. "How did you figure that out so fast?" he asked.

"I ciphered it rough in my head."

His eyes widened. Then he reached over and tousled me again. "I like you, youngster. You've got a head on your shoulders!"

At that moment a small, dark-haired, intense-eyed man rushed up, his coat and vest flapping open behind him, tailed by two larger men. "Mr. Harris! It's good to see you again, sir!"

Harris shook hands. "Glad to see you, Jones. I was just talking

393

with Keller, here, and his family. Keller, meet Bill Jones. He's our superintendent here, which makes him your boss."

My father started to extend his hand, but Jones kept bright black eyes on Mr. Harris. "If we had known you were on the noon train, Mr. Harris, we could have had a proper welcome."

"No need, Jones. Just a brief fact-finding visit."

"Well." Jones appeared at a loss. "I can get a carriage to take you to your office."

"That will be fine," Harris said. He turned to me a moment. "I like your spunk, youngster. If you ever change your mind and want a job, or if I can ever do anything for you, just send me a letter or a telegram at the home office. Agreed?"

"Yes, sir," I said. "But I don't aim to change my mind."

Harris guffawed again and turned to walk away.

My father tentatively touched Mr. Jones's sleeve. "Mr. Jones? I'm Ned Keller, assigned to track maintenance office, and—"

"Not now, Keller," Jones snapped. "Report to the office. I'll talk to you later." With a curt nod to my mother, he left with the others.

My father watched them out of sight. "Imagine that. *We* met Nathaniel Harris. Can you believe it, Alma?"

My mother's face was pink with excitement. "He talked to us just like ordinary people would."

"That's part of what makes the H&O great," my father said with feeling. He paused, then held up his stump for all of us to see. "The H&O was training me to be a conductor someday, or a yard foreman. I can't do any of those jobs with *this*. They could have just put me out. But they're giving me this chance in the office. That shows how great the H&O is. We owe them a lot."

Outside the depot we had to wait for a streetcar. I spied Mr. Harris and some other men seated in a carriage out in front, as if they were waiting for something. I did not see Mr. Jones and concluded they were waiting for him. What most caught my eye, however, was a group of eight or nine men across the street— workers, by their dress—walking up and down with signs. FAIR WAGE, one said. UNION IS STRENGTH, said another. H&O UNFAIR, read a third. The men were ragged, unshaved, morosely silent.

"Are they strikers?" I asked my father. I had never seen strikers.

"No, son," he said. "They're scum—wildcatters."

"What is that?"

"Troublemakers. They're trying to start a strike, trying to get everyone into a union. It doesn't concern us. Come on, now, gather up the bags, everybody. Here comes the streetcar."

"The blue bag," my mother said. "Where's the small blue bag?"

I had left it on the platform in all the excitement. "I'll go get it!" I said, and ran across the street. Dashing out onto the platform, I found the bag and bent to retrieve it. As I did so, I heard a familiar voice on the other side of a loaded baggage cart.

"But I didn't know who he was! His ticket didn't show that name!"

I peered around the corner of the cart and saw Mr. Stein, our train conductor, facing the cold-eyed Mr. Jones. Jolly Mr. Stein was without color, his eyes wide, his lips trembling.

"You *should* have known," Jones was telling the conductor. "It's your business to recognize important people. If I hadn't been here in the yards, he might have wandered all over the place before we showed enough sense to greet him. You're suspended, Stein."

Mr. Stein's mouth gaped. I had never seen that kind of fear before. "Suspended? Oh, no! Please, sir, I—"

"Two weeks without pay," Jones said. "Effective tonight at midnight."

Mr. Stein's eyes filled and I had the horrible feeling he was going to cry. He said nothing, just stood there, staring at the smaller man.

I turned and ran for the streetcar. I got there just in time. On board, we all had seats together, my father and I side by side on a wicker bench. "It's a nice little city," he told me, his eyes keen with excitement as he peered out at the strange buildings and streets. "We're going to do fine here."

I had no idea what to say to this man I loved so much. I wondered if there were times when he had to stand in front of a Mr. Jones, tears in his eyes, taking it. I hoped it never had happened, and never would.

MY FATHER deposited us in a room in a dingy brick hotel and hurried off to report to the central offices of the Harristown & Ohio Railroad Company. My mother took Mary Eleanor and Rachel down the hall to the bathroom to be cleaned up, and I stood in the open window and looked down at the street. Preacherville was much bigger than Henryetta, and the leaden sky depressed me. By leaning out, I could just see the plumes of gray smoke issuing upward from the yards well to the south.

"Bobby, get back in here before you fall!" Mother said sharply, returning with the girls. Although they looked fresher, my mother had the same gray fatigue in her face, and I didn't argue. She led my sisters to the bed. "Now lie down and take a good rest. We're all tired."

"Momma, I'm hungry," Rachel said.

Mother's lips pinched. "Do you want a glass of water?"

"I'm *hungry!*"

With a sigh, Mother dug into the wicker food basket. We had eaten out of that basket for more than a day, and there wasn't much left, but she came up with a part of a jelly sandwich. Rachel took it eagerly, lay down with it clutched to her chest, and immediately went to sleep.

Mary Eleanor, bouncing on the bed, chirped, "When will Daddy be back, Momma?"

"I don't know, Mary Eleanor. As soon as he can, I expect."

"When are we going to find out where we live?"

"When he gets back, I hope. There are company houses for office employees, you remember."

"When will our things get here?"

"I don't know. I imagine it will be a day or two."

"What will we do till our beds and everything get here?"

Mother set her lips. "We'll just do our best, Mary Eleanor."

We waited more than three hours, and then in the gloomy afternoon my father came back. I was at the window and saw him coming across the street on foot, head down, his shoulders bowed. Looking up, he spied me and instantly underwent a complete transformation. His shoulders squared. His step became jaunty, and he raised a hand in a perky salute. A moment later he was back with us in the room.

"Everything is going to be just fine," he said, holding my mother's hand. "I already like the people I'll be working with, and

396

my salary of six dollars a week starts tomorrow morning. And our house is ready for us. Number Four B, North Branch Road. We take the streetcar north to the end, and it's not a bad walk out from there." He grinned at me, but I saw the nervousness in his eyes.

"Can we get in?" Mother asked. "Will there be anyplace to sleep?"

"Everything will be fine, Alma. They sent someone out to unlock the doors. They say the house is partially furnished, so we'll be fine!"

"We'll have to buy some groceries."

"Well," my father said, "there's a company store less than a mile from the place, where we can get anything we need, I'm sure."

"It might be cheaper in town here."

My father frowned. "Well, Alma, we'll really need to . . . be sort of careful for a while yet . . . until I get a paycheck."

She stared blankly. "We still have what we saved back."

"Well . . . we have some of it. See, I had to put down a deposit on the house rent."

"A deposit! How much?"

"It was eleven dollars. But—"

"*Eleven!* Half our—"

"We get four of it back after three months, Alma. It's like money in the bank."

"How can we buy enough food?"

"Well, there's credit at the company store—"

"Never! We'll never do credit, Ned. I told you that. We'll never be in debt like that again."

"What if we have no choice?" he asked sharply, losing his temper.

Tears filled her eyes as she stood facing him. With a murmur of regret, he took her into his arms and held her. I turned to the window, pretending not to see.

THE NORTHERN END of the streetcar line was already in the country. The road became dirt not far beyond. It wound through a creek bottom and brushy woods, then up to higher ground and around a small hill. Beyond the hill was a long, narrow valley, some of the land in farms.

There was a row of houses not much farther on, with scattered outbuildings. Evidently they had once been individual farmhouses that had been bought up by the railroad. There was a crossroad, then, and our house was another half mile on. Behind a broken wooden fence, the two-story white frame structure looked deserted across its yard of winter-brown weeds. But it had a front porch and was really much nicer than some of the homes we had passed. It had an outhouse, a well house, a small but sturdy-looking barn, and beyond it a tiny creek.

My father opened the gate, which fell off its hinges. He set it against the fence post and led us up to the house. Piling our things on the porch, we went inside. It was big and empty and dusty, with pasteboard at some of the windows that had been broken. In one room we found several straight chairs, a table with a leg missing, and a stack of straw mattresses. Our voices echoed as we made discoveries.

First upstairs, I found three bedrooms. The back one, the smallest, I knew at once to be mine. Going to the dusty window, I heaved at it. It slid upward with a bang, loose in the frame. From the rear porch a dozen or more fluttering pairs of wings startled me. They were pigeons that had been sitting on the back roof. Now they wheeled above the treetops in loose formation, then swooped toward the barn and lit on the roof, one after another. Some were white, others gray blue.

I started to turn and yell "Dad"—and almost bumped into him.

He grinned and hugged me. "I'm right here, sport."

"Do you see? Pigeons! I bet they're nesting in the barn!"

My father stooped to look from the window at my level, his arm still around me, his eyes glad. "That's great, son, isn't it?"

In Henryetta there had always been pigeons around the house and shed. My mother had never let me befriend them, but I had had names for some of them and could recognize them by the way they walked, or by their favorite roosting places. Now I realized how much leaving them had cost me. Watching the pigeons on the roof of the barn, I was ecstatic.

"Dad, I'm going down there to see if there are nests!"

"Sure. Do that."

I barreled down the steps, through the vast, dirty kitchen, and out the back door. As I started down the weedy slope to the barn, I saw that it must be a pigeons' paradise for roosting. There were dozens of broken boards that would allow birds easy entrance and exit. Pigeons will nest in trees, but they don't like it. Their large, sloppy nests fall out of the branches at the first good wind. They prefer a cranny in or on a building, where the male brings his motley collection of twigs, leaf stems, and dried weeds. The female sits inside the chosen place, arranging each tidbit as the male brings it to her.

Because they are such devoted parents, pigeons care about their nesting places more than anything. And I could see that they considered the barn theirs; they simply watched my approach, craning their necks this way and that to get a better look at me.

"Hello, pigeons," I called softly.

I opened the rickety barn door and stepped inside. Light filtered in from the holes in the walls. Two or three birds flew instantly as I entered, darting out holes. As the flapping of wings subsided, I could hear the tiny *tick-tack* of the birds' talons on the metal roof. Looking up at the rafters, I saw the edges of several nests. Later I could climb up and observe the eggs, guess when they would hatch, and monitor the growth of the chicks. I felt better than I had in a long time. I was going to like this place!

BY NIGHTFALL my mother had worked us to a frazzle, and the airy old house had begun to smell of strong soap and water rather than dust and dry rot. All the floors had been scrubbed, the walls and ceilings rubbed down with cloth-wrapped brooms, and the windows washed. My father had repaired kitchen cabinet doors and the cooking stove damper. I had been sent up the road to the company store, to come back with a small bag of beans, some salt, coffee, three potatoes, and flour. The evening meal consisted of the beans, and my mother delayed that while she mixed some of the flour and water with a few potato shavings to start the sourdough for bread she would make later in the week.

We were still sitting on the front porch steps, holding our plates after the meal, when the lights of an automobile appeared at the end of the road. We watched as they grew closer and finally a Ford stopped at our gate. My father stood as two men came toward us.

"Good evening!" a familiar voice called. It was Mr. Jones, the H&O division superintendent, with a taller, beefy-faced man we had not met. "This is Mr. Slattery," he said. "We just wanted to drop by to make sure you had found the place all right."

"Yes, sir, we did," my father said. "Everything is just fine."

Jones put a cigarette in his mouth and cracked a match on the porch post. The flickering yellow light carved shadows in the hollows of his cheeks and eyes, giving him a cruel look. Then the match was out and only the glow of his cigarette remained.

"I assume, Keller, you will be in the office bright and early tomorrow?"

"Yes, sir. I'm looking forward to it."

"Good. I appreciated your quick thinking today when you recognized Mr. Harris and notified the manager. You realize, of course, that you are on probation here. But you've made a good start."

My father gave a little bow of his head. "Thank you, sir. I'm going to try my best. I appreciate the opportunity very much."

"Good man," Jones said. "As I'm sure you know, the H&O has had to let some people go lately. We have some minor labor problems as well, troublemakers trying to agitate a general strike. Every man in the company has to pull his weight."

"Yes, sir," my father said.

"You'll probably hear things," Jones went on. "The agitators like to spread vicious rumors. They would like nothing better than to cripple our nation by bringing the railroads to their knees. Our mission, Keller, is to prevent that kind of disaster. You are part of management now. It's up to you to help keep the troublemakers in line."

There was a pause. Then my father said carefully, "I owe a lot to the H&O, sir. I'll always be loyal."

"They'll try to subvert you," Jones said. "You'll hear talk about low wages, long hours, unsafe conditions, all the usual claptrap. I expect your total cooperation with company policy."

"You can count on me, sir."

"Good. You will report to me the names of everyone you hear

spreading this poison. You can be sure they won't be around long enough to continue their tactics."

"I'll . . . cooperate, sir."

"Excellent." Jones removed his foot from where it had been propped on a step. "Now, let me ask you this: Is there anything the company can do to make your new home more pleasant?"

"I can't think of a thing, sir."

"Good. I thought not. We plan to send a crew out here tomorrow to mow the weeds and repair the fence and barn. After that, maintenance will be up to you. Keep the premises in good order, be prompt with your rent, and there will be no difficulty. Oh, and tomorrow the crew will rid the area of pests."

"Pests?" my father echoed.

"Rats," Jones said. "And I believe there are also some pigeons infesting the barn. Poisoned bait will be put out for the rats. Be sure to caution your children about the bait. We had an unfortunate incident this winter when an employee failed to watch over his children around poisoned rat bait. The pigeons are simpler. We'll kill every one we can find tomorrow."

"You can't kill them!" I blurted.

Jones turned stiffly. "Eh?"

"You can't kill them!" I told him. "We *like* the pigeons! We—"

"This is company property," Jones cut in. "Don't ever forget that. The pigeons cause wood rot with their filthy nesting habits. Where you have pigeons, you have roaches and other vermin. My policy is to exterminate them. Seven o'clock tomorrow, Keller?"

"Yes, sir," my father said.

"Good." Jones turned to his silent companion. "Come on." The two men walked back to the car.

"Dad, you *can't* let them kill all those pigeons!" I said, when they had gone. "Those pigeons have babies and everything, and he's crazy, they don't cause bugs, and—"

"Bobby," my father interrupted sharply, "there's nothing we can do about it. Be a man! Learn to take orders!"

"Is that what being a man is?" I shot back. "Laying down and letting people run over you and kill your pets?"

My father moved. His hand cracked across my face. It stung

401

more than hurt, but it shocked me because it was so unlike him.

"Oh, Ned—" my mother began.

"No," he said angrily. "I won't have trouble over a few wild birds. How many times do I have to tell you, Alma? *This is my last chance.*"

My mother hung her head. I knew argument was hopeless. This job meant everything to my father, and nothing—and no one—would be allowed to interfere. I went into the house before they could see the tears.

Later, while I was lying on my straw mattress in the small back room, my mother appeared in a nightgown and robe. She knelt beside my pallet. "Bobby?" she whispered.

I had my head partly turned and pretended to be asleep.

"Don't be scared, my little boy," she murmured softly, as if saying it for herself. "I know it's hard for you, but it will be all right. He didn't mean it, you know."

A board creaked in the hallway. "Is he asleep?" my father whispered.

"Yes." Her hands tucked the blanket around me.

"I'll . . . make it right with him."

"I know."

"I didn't mean it."

"I know."

"Come to bed now."

"Yes." She rose, moved away from me, went down the hall with him. I lay still, looking out the window at the vast night sky, knowing my pigeons were doomed.

TWO

Starting in a new school the next morning was not something I anticipated with pleasure.

"Keep hold of Mary Eleanor's hand on the road," my mother lectured me on the front porch. "And hurry on or you'll both be late. Mary Eleanor, take your brother's hand."

Mary Eleanor, in a gray dress with her hair dilly-dollied up in

402

curls, wriggled with mortification. "I'll look silly as anything!"

We waded out through the weeds to the road and turned south. I carried the lunch pail, which contained a piece of boiled potato and a small jar of cold beans for each of us. The sky was overcast, smelling of rain. As we walked, some of our pigeons swooped overhead in formation, banking sharply left, then right, gaining altitude and diving again, seeming to take pleasure in their own aerobatics. I turned, walking backward to watch them wheel over the barn and come down for landing.

"Great flying!" I said aloud.

"Will they kill all of them, Bobby?" Mary Eleanor asked.

"No, they won't get them all," I lied.

"Why do they want to kill them anyway?"

"I don't know."

She looked up at me, and there was fear in her eyes. "I don't like Preacherville. I think I'm going to hate this school."

I sighed and did not reply. It was a trick I had learned from Mom. When you don't have an answer, you heave a big sigh and pucker your mouth just so and look irritated. Mary Eleanor had always been a fool for that gambit, and it worked now.

School was a low brick building a mile or so down the road. Kids of all ages were walking toward it, and by the time we crossed the dusty playground we were surrounded. The building was old and smelled musty. There were four classrooms, each teacher handling three grades. Mary Eleanor was in the third grade. That put her in room one with a woman named Mrs. Clover.

My room, number three, was at the end of the hall. I walked in just as the bell clanged. Nearly every desk was occupied, the girls sitting still, hands folded, being nicey-nicey, the boys looking miserable and squirming in their seats. I looked toward the front of the room, and my heart sank.

The woman standing there, lightly tapping a birch rod against the palm of a bony hand, was dressed all in black. Her hair, also black, was tied behind her head in a tight bun. Gold spectacles perched on a beaklike nose. She was tall, angular, and unsmiling. A sign on her desk said MRS. MEAD.

I marched up. "Mrs. Mead?"

403

She looked down at me. "What is it, boy?"

"I'm Bobby Keller, and I'm new in the seventh grade."

"Do you have your papers?"

"What?"

"You don't say 'What?' You say 'Please, ma'am?' if you don't hear!"

"Please, ma'am?"

"Your papers."

I began to sweat. Everyone in the room was watching. Desperately I pulled my tablet out from under my arm. "This, you mean?"

The classroom erupted in laughter. Mrs. Mead looked up, spied a boy in the front row who was whooping louder than most, and reached him in two long strides. *Crash!* The rod in her hand slammed onto the desk. He stopped laughing instantly and the room went silent.

Mrs. Mead turned back to me. "I'll see about your papers later. Seventh, you say? Over there. By the window."

During the morning Mrs. Mead constantly roamed the aisles, calling on people in the upper grades to read or answer questions, and occasionally rapping one of the older boys with her rod. The biggest boy, Thurman Black, was called upon and whacked three times before recess. Each time Mrs. Mead called on him, she used his full name. "Thurman Black, please tell us the name of a key battle in the Revolutionary War."

Thurman Black looked up from the tangled shelf of dark hair in his eyes, grinned, and said, "Gettysburg?"

"Thurman Black!" Mrs. Mead cried, advancing on him from behind while he shrank down in his seat. *Wham!* "You don't even know what war we're talking about!" *Crack!*

And a little later: "Thurman Black, what answer did you get for number seven?"

"Uh . . . I didn't get that one, Mrs. Mead—"

"Thurman Black!" *Slam! Whip, whip, whip!*

What impressed me was Thurman Black's bravado. Every time he got whipped, the moment Mrs. Mead turned her back he popped up, made a face at her, and winked at someone. And during recess he walked right over and talked to the oldest boys in the yard—the

404

handful of eleventh and twelfth graders, who stood off by themselves and sneered at everyone else. He was obviously very tough—which began to impress me all the more when he left that group and headed toward me.

"What's your name, kid?" he asked. His shirt tail was out and his knickers drooped to his shoes, and I smelled tobacco on him.

"Bobby Keller," I said.

"Whose side are you on? Strikers or hoboes?"

"I don't know," I said, adding, "sir." He was a full head taller.

He grabbed the front of my shirt and pulled me toward him. "Listen," he said. "Everybody is on a side. Which side are *you* on?"

"I don't know what the sides are!" I squeaked.

"Your old man is with the H&O, ain't he? Yards? Brakeman? What?"

"Office! He's in the office."

Thurman Black released me. "Office!" He spat.

"He's got a—one of his hands got cut off," I explained, hating myself for the fear. "It's the only thing he can do. . . ."

"Okay. You'll have to start off being a hobo, then." He jabbed an index finger into my chest. "And you better watch out."

I stood petrified as he turned and strode back to the older boys.

Two boys my own size and age sidled up to me. "What did he tell you you are?" asked a plump boy with yellow hair.

"A hobo," I told him.

"Hobart-Grimes. Oh boy," he groaned.

The other boy stuck out his hand. "I'm Chuck, and this is Donald. And boy, are you in trouble."

"*I* don't want to be a Hobart-Grimes!" I said.

"You are one," Chuck said. "Thurman Black said só, didn't he?"

"What do I have to do?"

"We play it most days after lunch. The teachers say we can't, so we make it look like capture the flag. What you do is, if you're a hobo and you find a striker that's smaller than you, you punch him."

"What if he's bigger than me?"

"Then he beats you up."

I was beginning to get the picture. "What's Thurman Black?"

"Oh, he's a striker. All the bigger kids are strikers"

I looked at my two new companions. "What are you guys?"

"I'm a hobo," Donald said, pointing to his faintly discolored left eye, a shiner almost healed. "See?"

The bell clanged. I turned to Chuck. "What are you?"

"A striker," he said, and punched me in the stomach.

AFTER RECESS it was my grade's turn to perform. I cringed, waiting to be called on and certain I would get switched. However, Mrs. Mead did not call on me. The day began to warm, low clouds bringing in unseasonable humidity, and the classroom windows were opened. Shortly afterward, I became aware of a hollow cracking sound in the distance. At first I did not make anything of it. Then it dawned on me that the sounds were shots. They were shooting my pigeons. Sitting there, my mind filled with visions of the horrors taking place at home, I had no idea what was going on around me. All at once I was brought back by the sound of tittering and the rustle of dress material.

Mrs. Mead was standing beside me. "Well?" she said. "Did you hear what I asked you?"

I saw the switch trembling in her hand. "No, ma'am. I was—you see, with the window open I could hear shots, and there are these pigeons out at our new house, and the shots mean the crew is killing them, and—"

She shocked me by uttering a sharp, barking laugh. "I've heard every excuse in the world, but I've never heard someone blame pigeons for inattentiveness!" She waved the switch at me. "Don't let it happen again. There are no second chances!"

"Yes, ma'am."

At lunchtime, after giving Mary Eleanor her share, I looked for a table in the lunchroom where I could sit alone. I was mortified about the incident with Mrs. Mead and scared of what was going to happen in the strikers-hoboes game. Keeping my face down as I ate, I pretended not to see the older boys saunter by, Thurman Black among them.

"Hey, there's the pigeon boy," one of them said.

"Here Pidgey, here Pidgey," Thurman Black called. They all guffawed. Then, as they reached the door, he turned back and said

406

in a tone meant for me alone, "We'll see you outside, hobo."

The food turned to stone in my belly, and as hungry as I was, the last of the beans and potato would not go down. Putting the remainder in my lunch pail, I returned to our classroom. Outside I saw the older boys, and some of the younger ones, downslope from the building, chasing one another in what looked like a spirited game of capture the flag. Watching, I noticed what a teacher might not: it was always smaller boys who attacked, and they always got run down and pummeled.

I decided to stay inside, miserable in my cowardice. But just then Mrs. Mead walked in. She glared. "What are you doing in here?"

"I—I thought I'd stay in. I feel sort of sick."

She felt my forehead. "You're not sick. Get out and play with the others. It's good for you!"

I obeyed, with forebodings of doom. As I stepped into the yard, a pair of strong hands clasped my arms on each side.

"Hello, Pidgey-widgey," a familiar voice said. My right-hand captor was Thurman Black. The other one was bigger.

"Lemme go!"

"We're going to play," Thurman Black leered. "We're going to have fun."

They propelled me across the playground, past the swings and a group of girls. I managed to cast a despairing look toward the school building, and there in the window was Mrs. Mead, arms folded. She obviously had no idea I was being escorted to my death.

Down the slope we went, and into the creek bottom that was hidden from view of the building. To my horror I saw three more boys standing under the trees, smoking cigarettes. My captors brought me before them, pushing me forward so that I sprawled at their feet.

"What have we got here?" the biggest boy asked.

"A new hobo," Thurman Black replied.

"What's his name?"

"Pidgey," Thurman Black said.

"Get up, Pidgey," the biggest boy ordered.

Shaking, I obeyed. They formed a rough circle around me. I could not escape.

"Just remember, hobo," the biggest boy said, "the strikers always win." He spat in my face. "You understand?"

I scoured his spit away with my shirt sleeve. "Don't do that!"

"What?" He looked amazed.

"You got no right to do that!"

He grinned at his pals and made a hawking sound in his throat.

Where I got the nerve I will never know. But I went after him. It was so unexpected that for a second I had an advantage, driving him backward as I hit him with my shoulder in the midsection, pounding at his lean, hard body with my fists. But then a paralyzing blow erupted in my stomach and the breath was driven out of my lungs. I found myself on my rump, sparks yellow in my vision. Now the biggest boy had hold of my hair.

I scarcely felt the blow that knocked me backward. My whole being was intent on the fact that I was unable to breathe. Paralyzed, I fought to expand my lungs, but no wind came. I climbed to my feet, tasting blood. Bent almost double, I tried to signal frantically that someone should pound me on the back. The world was starting to go gray. I fell to my knees.

Suddenly the legs around me began to scatter. I managed to look up. Mrs. Mead was coming down the slope, dress flying, switch waving. Boys ran in all directions. She swung mightily and cracked someone over the head, bringing the whip back the other way to slash someone else in the chest. Then she was beside me, on her knees. She understood immediately. The heel of her right hand crashed into the middle of my back. "Those big bullies!" *Thump!* "I'll make them pay for this!" *Thump!*

The pounding jarred me loose inside. I managed to gasp in the smallest fraction of a breath. She kept pounding. My lungs creaked open a bit more, and suddenly I gasped a full, blessed breath. I sat there in the dirt, tears coursing down my cheeks.

Mrs. Mead had had a bad fright. She used her own white linen handkerchief to wipe my face. "What were they doing?"

"Strikers and hoboes," I gasped.

"Oh, how they'll pay for this!" she hissed.

"No," I pleaded. "I'm all right!"

It was the beginning of an afternoon I would have done much to prevent. Strikers and hoboes, it seemed, was a game forbidden by every authority. Mirroring tensions between real strikers and company detectives, it was not only dangerous to the students but likely to raise passions in the adult population.

Mrs. Mead did not punish the boys she had recognized around me in the ravine. That chore was handled by the principal, a tall, muscular man with arms bigger than my thighs. The boys were called out one by one, and each was gone for a very long time. When Thurman Black returned, his swagger was missing and he was the color of old stove ashes.

"The principal uses a strap," a girl sitting near me whispered, "and he *likes* it!"

I knew then that my troubles were only beginning. For I had caused the whippings.

I FOUND Mary Eleanor as quickly as possible after school and set out for home. I was sure retribution would be hot after me.

Amazingly, no one challenged us as we hiked up the road, nor did I see any of the bigger boys. As we reached our own road, thunder sounded, and a few raindrops pelted down, making little dirt balls in the dust.

"I don't like it," Mary Eleanor said, making a face at the clouds.

"It's spring. You've got to expect rain in the spring."

"I don't mean the rain, ninny. I mean *everything!*"

"We got to like it, Mary Eleanor. This is important for Dad."

"The school is ugly and Mrs. Clover likes the boys best and they shot our pigeons and our stuff from Henryetta will probably *never* come."

"It'll come, it'll come."

"And did you know about all the trouble?" she asked. "There's going to be a strike."

"Naw! Who said that bunk?"

"Ellen and Sue Ann did. They said why did we move here when there's going to be a strike any minute. They told me all about it. A lot of the railroad companies have made new deals with their workers for more money and not so much work, and the H&O hasn't, and it's getting worse every day, and more workers are

409

getting mad, and everybody just *knows* there's going to be bad trouble!"

"That's gossip," I said, not very convincingly. "You shouldn't listen to gossip. Besides, Dad wouldn't come here if there was going to be trouble, would he?"

"You mark my words," she insisted, aping my mother to such an extent it was eerie. "There's going to be trouble and *everybody* is going to have to pick a side, even Daddy. And we will, too."

"Will you *stop*, Mary Eleanor?"

It was raining harder as we hurried up the road, past the small, vacant house about fifty yards from ours, then through our own gate. The fence had been mended and the weeds cut, and I looked out toward the barn and saw no sign of life. I went into the house, a lump in my throat.

Inside, we had company. My mother and four other ladies were sitting on boxes in the living room, having tea. I knew the ladies must have brought the boxes, the tea, and the cups, because our own things had not had time to arrive.

"Children," Mother said, smiling broadly, "these are some of our neighbors. My goodness, you're both soaked! Say hello and then run and change before you catch your death. Mary Eleanor, Bobby, this is Mrs. Smith, and Mrs. Murphy, and Mrs. Conrad, and Mrs. Crowder."

Mary Eleanor curtsied just like she had good sense, and I shook hands with the ladies. Mrs. Murphy rolled her eyes at me. "Aren't you a handsome little man! You must be in about the fourth grade."

"Seventh," I said, angry with her.

"Seventh!" she repeated. "I swan! You're a little fellow."

"Yes, ma'am." I cringed.

As we were leaving the room I heard one of the ladies sigh. "As I was saying, Mrs. Keller, we face serious times. We're not only neighbors, but the wives of workers. We must be close to one another."

I went upstairs to change. As I was about to unbutton my shirt, however, I looked out my window at the barn, again struck by how lifeless it looked. Hadn't they missed a single one? I had to know.

My mother would forbid me to go outside in the rain if I went

410

back through the house, so I raised the window, slid through, and worked my way to the edge of the porch roof. Then I jumped to the ground, thumping hard in the muddy soil and really making a mess of myself. Half expecting to hear my mother yell at me, I ran down the slippery slope to the barn.

Near the door I saw feathers scattered in the mud and a puddle of blood. I darted inside. The rain was loud and steady on the metal roof. The interior smelled of rot and moisture and pigeon droppings, but I saw no sign of life. I glanced up to where I had seen the shaggy edges of nests on a beam. The beams were bare now Advancing deeper into the gloom, I saw what had happened. The crew had known a little about pigeons. The female bird guards the eggs, and later the young, from late afternoon to midmorning. The male works a shorter shift, from about ten in the morning to about five in the afternoon. The crew had known this—had recognized that many of the males would have stayed with the nests even as the females were being shot outside. So they had come in and scattered and killed the males. Then they had destroyed the nests, leaving a wreckage of straw, twigs, and broken eggs on the floor. What had Mr. Jones said? Pigeons were filthy and a nuisance. There would be no more filth or nuisance here.

The rain had eased off. I was shivering. I looked around, wishing I might find an old ladder that would allow me to climb back to my room undetected. I saw nothing that would help. With the rain slackening, the silence in the barn was deep. That was when I heard a sound that electrified my senses. Sharp, insistent, it came from high up in the barn, in a corner where two timbers joined. *Peep, peep, peep*—unmistakable! Babies complaining for supper!

Hauling a broken nail keg to the wall, I climbed onto its unsteady edge and got my hands onto a horizontal beam halfway up the lower wall. I heaved myself up. A hole in the outer wall gave me a new foothold, letting me swing onto one of the lower roof beams. I shinnied along it toward the corner.

Looking around the supporting post, I stared into a small nest containing two pigeon chicks. They had stopped making a sound the moment I appeared, and huddled together now, their heads erect with fear. They were about a week old, each the size of my

fist, with their pink flesh shining through the beginings of their feathers. The feathers of one were dark blue, but the other was going to be all white.

Crouching there in my uncomfortable, precarious position, I scanned the remainder of the barn. I saw no other nests, heard no other sounds. Only these two babies had been missed.

I reached for the blue, and both pigeons reared up on their little legs, holding out stubby wings and puffing their throats, making themselves look twice as big and formidable. The natural defense did no more good against me than it would have against most real predators. I felt the blue's throat crop. It was collapsed in on itself; the baby was hungry.

There were two pockets in my wet shirt. I put one of the birds in each. As I scrambled down and ran back to the house, I could feel their intense body heat and their trembling.

The back door into the kitchen was unlocked, and I tried to creep from kitchen to stairs without being detected. Just as I reached the steps, my mother called from the living room.

"Bobby? What are you doing in the kitchen? I told you to change those wet things!"

"I'll do it right now, Mom!"

I climbed the stairs and closed the door of my room. Then I carefully set the two baby pigeons on the bed. One of them promptly voided on the cover.

My mother was going to kill me. I took off my wet shirt, balled it up into a loose nest shape, and put the chicks on it. They cuddled down, shivering, close together.

"You're going to be all right now," I told my babies softly. "I'm going to be the best dadgummed momma you ever saw."

The problem was, how? I knew chicks were fed several times a day by their parents, who regurgitated moisture and partially digested grain into the babies' gaping throats. What was I going to feed them, and how? And what was my mother going to say?

WHILE I CHANGED into dry clothing, I heard my mother bidding the ladies good-by at the front door. This meant I would not have them to keep her occupied while I pondered my problem.

As I was buttoning my pants, the door swung back and Mary Eleanor poked her head in. When she spied the chicks, her eyes got round and huge. "What's *that?*"

"Baby pigeons, dummy," I said coolly.

"They're ugly! They're filthy! Ugh!"

"I'll clean them up," I said. "Be quiet."

"Bobby," Mary Eleanor said, "Momma is going to *kill* you!"

"I said be *quiet!*"

Mother's voice came from the hallway. "What's going on in there?"

"Stay out!" I called.

Too late. She swung the door back, pushing Mary Eleanor ahead of her into the room. "What in the world?" she said softly.

"They're babies," I told her. "Those guys killed all the pigeons, they thought. But they missed these two babies, Mom, and I know you're going to say 'Get them out of here!' But these are the only ones left and I've got to keep them alive, do you see? They won't eat much and I won't let them make a mess and I'll take real good care of them." I gasped for a breath. "Please, Mom?"

She knelt beside the makeshift nest. "My, they're ugly."

"They'll get prettier, Mom. I promise!"

She looked at me quietly and raised a hand to brush my hair out of my eyes. "What would they eat?"

"I'll squish up some bread and water and kind of shoot it in their mouths with our big medicine dropper. And then I'll teach 'em to eat grain, or whatever we've got. And if we don't have anything, I'll get seeds off of weeds and feed that to 'em!"

She reached toward the chicks. They did their frightened rearing-up act. "Why, you nasty little things," she said, smiling.

"Can I, Mom?" I asked. "*Please?*"

413

"We'll have to ask your father."

"Can I feed 'em in the meantime? They're hungry."

"I suppose that wouldn't do any harm," she said resignedly.

I was delirious. We went downstairs and she found the medicine dropper. I took a piece of bread, powdered it with my fingers, then added a few drops of water. The dropper would suck up almost a teaspoon of the gruel at a time.

Back upstairs, holding the wriggling white chick in my lap, I held the tip of the dropper to its beak, confident the odor of food would trigger the opening mechanism. The chick turned its head and tried to writhe out of my lap. With Mary Eleanor and Rachel both watching breathlessly, I held the chick's head and managed to get the tip of the dropper in its beak. I squeezed the bulb. White goo frothed out onto the chick's chest, and it pulled its head loose and got the remainder in its eye.

"You're killing it!" Rachel cried in alarm.

"Be quiet, you dummy! I'm having enough trouble!"

Eventually I got the hang of it. Hooking my fingers over the chick's head, I could control most of its wriggling. By pinching with the tips of my fingers I could force the beak open. Then I shoved the dropper down the throat, discharging the food deep inside as the parent did. The chick gasped and shuddered but seemed to like it. I had plenty of food but didn't know how much to pump in. As I shot in more dropperfuls, however, I noticed the chick's little crop in front beginning to swell.

"You're gonna blow him up!" Rachel said.

"I know what I'm doing," I growled, but I quit and started feeding the blue bird. This one was smaller than the white and did not struggle as much. I pumped the food in and placed the bird back in the nest. It opened its mouth hugely a few times, as if belching, and then half-rolled onto its side, stretched its neck, and slept.

"It's *dead!*" Rachel gasped.

"It's asleep, Rachel. Will you stop yelling like that?"

"You think you're so smart!" Rachel shot back, and flounced out.

I turned to meet Mary Eleanor's steady gaze. "Well? What are you looking at?" I demanded.

414

"Daddy," she pronounced solemnly, "will never hear of it."

I knew what she was thinking. My father wanted to get along here. The H & O wanted no pigeons. My father was an H & O man.

BY SIX O'CLOCK the rain had ended. Much to my mother's irritation, I made another trip to the barn and gathered twigs to form a more natural nest in my room. Dark came. We lighted a candle in the kitchen and waited for my father.

It must have been past eight o'clock when we heard voices on the road. Leaving the candlelit supper table ready for the meal, we went through the house and saw four or five workers walking past our gate. One of them spied us on the porch and held up his hand. "Evening!"

"Good evening," my mother called back.

They walked on. The road was empty again. I began to worry. It was crazy, I told myself—you didn't get hurt in an office.

Another figure became faintly visible on the dark road. It moved closer, loping along, clearly not my father, because this shadow was lankier. A deep-pitched voice sang out, "Bob-by!"

Recognizing the voice, I wished I were somewhere else.

"Why," Mother said, "you have a friend visiting! Isn't that nice!"

"I don't know him," I said.

"You haven't gone yet to see who it is."

"I know who it is, and I don't know him."

The voice from the gloom sounded again. "Bob-by!"

I was standing on the porch steps. "I gotta go check my babies."

"You're going to see your friend! March!"

Telling myself that he couldn't kill me in front of my family, I walked slowly down the steps and set out across the yard. As I neared the gate, I was able to see him more clearly—stoop-shouldered, hands jammed in his pants pockets, a dark cap pulled down onto his ears. In the dark, Thurman Black looked even bigger and more formidable.

"There you are," he growled as I reached the gate.

"Hello, Thurman," I said.

"Don't think you got out of it," he said.

"Don't think I got out of what?" I asked, knowing.

"You got a bunch of us whipped. You're going to pay. That's what I come to tell you. One of these days, when you least expect it, we're going to get you."

"I ain't scared of you, Thurman Black."

He moved swiftly, his fist catching the front of my shirt, yanking me painfully up against the gate, which clattered loudly. "You'll see what we can do, you little—"

My mother's voice interrupted. "What's going on out there?"

Thurman Black released me. I staggered backward. He turned and broke into a run.

"Wait!" my mother cried. She hurried up beside me. "Who was that? What were you two doing out here?"

"Nothing, Mom."

"You're shaking! Did that big boy hurt you?"

"I'm fine! He's a friend of mine, just stopped to say hello."

Frowning, she put her arm over my shoulder and led me back toward the porch. I was very, very frightened.

WE WERE still on the dark front porch when we heard yet another sound on the road, a faint tinkling that gradually grew louder. "What on earth?" my mother said, standing.

"It's a fire!" Mary Eleanor said. "That's the fire wagon!"

"A little tinkly bell like that ain't no fire wagon," I said.

"Isn't," my mother corrected automatically.

"Well, what *is* it, then?"

Another dim figure could now be made out on the road.

"It's Daddy!" Rachel yelped, leaping up.

And so it was. He moved bent, as if very tired. But as we hurried out to meet him, his grin was tremendous. He was leading what I took first to be a dog, but it had a small bell tied around its neck, its legs were too long, its body all wrong, and there was something— a pair of something—on top of its head. It struggled against the rope as we moved nearer, and I figured it out. "It's a goat!"

My father, still grinning, handed me the rope. "Hang on tight, son. He's a real fire-eater!"

"A *goat?*" my mother said.

"He'll keep the grass mowed down for us," Dad said. He chuckled and shook his head. "At first I also thought we might get some milk. But then I found out why Slattery was giving him away; he's a billy goat, and he's ornery as the dickens. Tell you what, Bobby—tie him to that post there in the middle of the yard. Tie him good. I'll have to find some chain, or some stout wire—"

"What's that?" Rachel squealed, grabbing at a bundle my father had under his other arm.

"Be careful," he warned, unwrapping the object in his coat to reveal a lanky gray cat.

"It's a kitty! Oh, he's beautiful!"

"It's a she, baby, and she's already a good mouser."

Rachel jumped up and down, clapping her hands. Mary Eleanor petted the scrawny beast, her eyes shining.

"A goat," my mother said dazedly. "And a cat."

"Children need pets, Alma."

"You need pets," she corrected him sternly.

"Well . . ."

"They'll eat us out of house and home!"

"The billy goat will eat weeds, and the cat will eat mice. And the kids will enjoy them, Alma."

I tied the goat, which promptly began gnawing the rope. My father scouted up a length of fence wire and tied him with that. The goat began gnawing on the wire. We went on into the house. My father put the cat down. "We'll let her get acquainted awhile."

The cat looked around, got her bearings, and tore off upstairs.

"*No!*" I screeched, and went after her. I got to the top of the stairs just in time to see her tail vanish around my open door. I threw myself into the room and just managed to get in front of her as she was crouching before the nest. "No!" I gasped again.

There was noise on the stairs, and then everyone came in at once. My father looked at the cat and at me, and then at the chicks.

"Well, I'll be . . ." he said softly.

"If I don't take care of them, Dad, they'll die! The guys that came killed their mom and dad and all the others."

He looked down at me. Mary Eleanor watched from behind his legs, with a look that said, Now you're going to get it! Rachel

417

sucked her thumb and seemed to be thinking about crying. My mother watched Dad, a slight line across her eyes. I expected the worst.

"You heard Mr. Jones, son. The company doesn't like pigeons around, soiling their buildings, eating grain—"

"I'll build a house for them, Dad! I'll train them to always go back in their house and they won't be any trouble at all. I promise!"

My father took a deep, slow breath. "You'll have to be careful to keep your door closed. I don't ever want you blaming Napoleon if she gets in here and kills them. That's just a cat's nature."

So now I knew: it was going to be all right about my pigeons, and we owned a female cat named Napoleon.

Three

With the first light of dawn the next day, I rolled over on my bed to see how the chicks had endured the night. The white baby was sitting up in the nest, blinking at me. The blue chick lay on its side, cold and stiff.

My father was shaving in the kitchen, his suspenders hanging down his pant legs, when I went downstairs with the dead baby in my cupped hands. He turned and his face drooped.

"What happened, son?"

"I don't know, Dad. It just died."

He took a deep breath. "What are you going to do?"

"Bury it." I saw his eyes move, and turned to spy Napoleon slinking in from the front room. "Deep," I added.

He reached out and pulled me close with his left hand curled around the nape of my neck. "I know you're disappointed, son. But maybe the white bird will live, and you know pigeons. Golly, you can't keep them away once they've decided they like a place. I'll bet others will be back, and even the H&O won't be able to stop them."

In the days that followed, my white pigeon chick grew at an astounding rate. Although he quickly learned to recognize me as his source of food, and began wiggling his wings and peeping the moment I knelt beside his nest, he never seemed to get the hang of the medicine dropper. I always had to hold him in place, wedge his head between my fingers, and pry his mouth open before shoving in the dropper to discharge the soupy gruel. But once the ordeal was over, he perched contentedly in the nest.

Napoleon *knew* the chick was in my room. The cat had never been allowed so much as a peek in the doorway since her first look at the nest, but every afternoon that first week, when I came back from school, I found her sitting vigilantly in front of my door.

"Napoleon, get away from there!" I would scold, and she would swish her tail and slink off, to return the moment I turned my back.

Billy the goat was a worse problem. He gnawed through the fence wire the first day of his residence, and was brought back late in the day by neighbors from a mile away. After this, my father found some heavy chain. Billy worried at it for a day or two and then seemed to become more placid. The front yard soon resembled a carpet.

At school, the retribution by Thurman Black did not materialize quickly. By the end of the week the lack of any overt action against me had become more frightening than attack. Obviously something truly terrible was being planned. Miserably I stayed in the younger children's part of the playground while the daily game of capture the flag raged on. On several occasions I happened to meet the eyes of Thurman Black in the classroom or a hall, and the brooding hate there unnerved me.

The Black family was well known in Preacherville. Justin Black, Thurman's father, was the engineer on the *Blue Ridge Express*, the crack passenger train that came through town every morning at nine o'clock. The *Blue Ridge* formed up each morning at Pittsburgh and rifled southward through our area to terminate at Richmond. It was said that the citizens of three states set their clocks by Justin Black's liner, and that any man—from the lowliest loader to Nathaniel Harris himself—would feel the force of Black's knuckles if he did *anything* to impede the train's run. Clearly, Justin Black was one of the great railroaders. I envied him his lofty and glamorous job every evening, when my own father trudged home, gray-faced with fatigue and tension, always with his quiet smile put on for the benefit of his family. My father could have been a Justin Black, I thought, if his luck had been different.

It was about ten days after we arrived that I met Justin Black. Sunday church services had been at ten o'clock and we had stayed awhile afterward, standing on the lawn to visit with some of our new friends. The morning was warm under a hazy sky, and a light breeze was blowing. As my mother and father finally turned to walk with us toward the road, a tall, barrel-chested man with a dense black beard intercepted us. He looked uncomfortable in his white shirt with a dark bow tie and navy trousers and suspenders, but he bowed slightly to my mother and extended a big hand to my father.

"Mr. and Mrs. Keller? I wanted to speak with you. I'm Justin Black."

My father stopped, smiling, and extended his left hand for an awkward shake. "I know of you, Mr. Black, and it's a pleasure. May I present my wife, Alma."

"A pleasure, madam," Black said, taking my mother's hand. His eyes took her in from head to toe in a split second, and his pleasure in the glance was evident. There was nothing ungentlemanly in it, but I saw how he very briefly turned every molecule of his being upon her, intent on pleasing her. If this pleased her, it did not me. I knew I was not going to like him any better than I did his son.

My mother's cheeks colored ever so lightly. "How do you do."

"Very glad to see warmer weather," he told her. "The *Blue Ridge* had problems several times this past winter with the heavy snow. I like my train to be on time."

"That's the kind of talk the H&O likes to hear," my father said.

"Damn the H&O!" Black retorted. "Pardon me, madam." He returned his gaze to my father. "I run the *Blue Ridge* on time because it's *my* train. I don't operate—or run my life—for the likes of Nathaniel Harris."

"It all works out," my father said pleasantly, a slight frown on his forehead. "Our interests and those of the H&O are the same."

"That's dangerous talk right now."

My father's face hardened. "I don't know what you're talking about."

Black hiked one foot to the edge of the low stone fence surround-

420

ing the church grounds. "That's why I wanted to meet you, Keller. You're new. It's important you know what's going on."

"Are you referring to the strike rumors?"

"They're not just rumors, man! It's *coming!*"

"I'm being paid a fair wage. I have no grievance against the H&O."

"You're a workingman, the same as the rest of us. Being in the office doesn't change that. *You're* not getting rich while crews work a seventy-two-hour week. *You're* not riding in a palace car while men get laid off for no reason. Look! You've already given this company a *hand!* How much more will the H&O take from you if you're not willing to stand up and be counted?"

"I've heard tales about long hours and all the rest of it," my father said. "Frankly, I don't put a lot of faith in such talk. *I* haven't seen any of that."

Black's face had grown steadily redder as he labored to control his anger. Now he made a slashing gesture with his hand. "Listen, Keller! There will be no neutrals when this thing breaks open. *You* live among the workers. You walk these roads with the workers. Do you think the hoboes will be able to save you if you turn Judas on your own kind?"

My father turned glacial eyes to my mother and us, standing silent. "I think we can go home now." He took my mother's arm.

"Remember, Keller!" Black said. "Think about it!" But he made no attempt to detain us.

"I'm sorry," my father said softly, after we had walked away.

"I don't like the children to hear talk like that," Mother said. "And at church on Sunday! He should be ashamed!"

"They told me some of the men had had their minds poisoned by that radical talk," Dad said grimly. "Well, they won't get *me.*"

"Why," I asked, "would somebody lie to start trouble?"

"Son, I didn't call the man a liar."

"Well, you said *you* hadn't heard about the troubles he was talking about. That was when he got the maddest, when you acted like there wasn't any reason for a strike."

"There isn't any reason for a strike," my father said. "The point is that I agreed to work for the H&O for a certain wage. I do what

421

I'm told; they pay me what they promised. I have no right to start causing trouble because suddenly I hear that someone in Erie or Freeport is making a little more or working a few hours less."

"Dad, either the H & O is being fair or it isn't. *Somebody* has to be lying, don't they?"

"No," my father said. "I don't agree with Mr. Black, but disagreement doesn't make a person a liar. Besides, Bobby, I gave my word to work for the H&O. What does it make me if I go back on my word?"

I did not reply. We walked on.

THE NEXT DAYS and weeks were not happy ones for me in terms of my relationship with my father. The day our household goods arrived there was a flurry of excitement as we rediscovered items we had momentarily forgotten. A chair, however, was so badly broken that it could not be repaired, and two boxes of my mother's things had been crushed. She was a strong woman, and the last thing she would ever have done was let any of us children know that she was upset. But when my father came home late that night and she started to show him the crushed boxes, her voice faltered and she wept.

"It will be all right, Alma," he said huskily, taking her into his arms. "I know the company is fair. They'll pay for shipping damage."

She got herself quickly under control and turned, dabbing at her eyes, to the three of us standing in mute shock across the room. "You children scat now! I'll be all right. I'm just a little tired today."

We obeyed, but Mother, we knew, was *not* all right.

Late that night something awoke me. I opened my door gently, vigilant, but Napoleon was not in view. I listened and heard nothing. Then I saw the faintest illumination filtering up the staircase from below. Curious, I padded silently on bare feet to the stairs. The yellow light issued from the living room. I slipped down the stairs and peered around the doorframe. A small candle stub on a saucer flickered from a table by the window. In the center of the floor, beside the crushed boxes, my mother knelt, clad in her long nightgown.

422

She had opened both boxes earlier, but now she had removed many of the contents, and they were spread around her on the bare wood floor: shattered plates and cups, the wreckage of a lamp, an old doll that had been so battered in transit that its stuffing had spilled around it on the boards, a crushed music box. My mother was, however, looking at none of these. In her hands was a framed picture, the glass broken, the picture itself wrinkled. It was a picture of her parents, and the candlelight made the rivulets of tears on her cheeks golden. Near her, sitting quietly, was Napoleon.

I must have made a sound. My mother turned and saw me. She put down the picture and held out her arms. I went to her and she held me close.

"My poor little boy," she whispered. "Everything is all right, Bobby. It's just fine. Don't cry."

"I'll get you more stuff," I promised. "I don't have to go to school much longer and then I'll get a job and I'll get rich. I'll get you everything, Mom. And I'll find out who on the H&O broke this stuff and I'll go and kill him."

"Hush now," she said. "Hush now. . . . Everything is fine."

A few of my mother's things were salvaged from the boxes, and the rest taken to the attic. A few days later I heard my father explaining to her that the H&O could not be blamed for rejecting the claim for damages, because perhaps the boxes had been insufficiently strong, as the company said, and the shipment had, after all, been free—a company benefit. It was with this development that I began to see that my father might have an infinite capacity to forgive and rationalize the railroad's actions.

Every night now he brought work home, bulky ledger books into which he endlessly entered the tiny figures that were the results of his calculations from invoices, bills of lading, and other ledgers. He became quieter, with a gaunt look around his eyes. On the occasional nights when he was not working on his calculations and digits, he was at the same small table in the living room, shoulders hunched as he pored over pamphlets, letters, sheaves of company regulations.

"Momma," Rachel said one evening, "why does Daddy work *all* the time now?"

424

"He has a very hard job, dear. There's a lot to do and learn."

"But why doesn't he ever play with us anymore?"

"He has to get his work done first, dear. You know men are being laid off. Do you want that to happen to us? Now scoot."

THE HILL COUNTRY was treating us to a glorious spring. Forsythia and azaleas and a profusion of fruit trees and dogwoods covered the slopes and yards with color. Horse-drawn plows opened the earth for seed and the gentle rain.

Through this time my white pigeon grew at an almost alarming rate. His size and weight doubled, then doubled again. The prickly, spotted feathers grew, too, his wings taking full form. He had changed from an ugly, ungainly chick to a handsome, slender bird.

From the start, remembering the men with guns, I was intent on training the pigeon to answer my call. I found in my small parcel of belongings a little brass whistle that emitted a single high-pitched note. I experimented with the pigeon, and his head turned sharply whenever I sounded it. After that, I made it a point to blow the whistle every time I was about to feed him and whenever I wanted him to come to me across the floor or bed.

"It won't work," Mary Eleanor said. "Pigeons are too dumb to learn stuff like that!"

For a while I tended to agree with her. One day I conducted another experiment. I skipped his morning food altogether and made him wait until the afternoon for his meal. When I got home from school, I prepared his food—small grain now, mixed with water and squished into him by fingertip—and put a bowl of it on the bed and opened his box. He hopped up onto the edge at once, turning his head ninety degrees to the left, then to the right, the better to fix me in the focus of either eye. I stroked his head with a finger, then walked away.

He immediately hopped to the floor with an inordinate amount of wing flapping and walked after me, head bobbing in an eager strut. I sat on the edge of the bed and picked up his food bowl.

"Here you go, chick," I said. "You want to eat?" He ignored me and began pecking around on the floor.

I picked up the whistle and blew a single hard note. The pigeon was transformed. He turned and, half spreading his wings, *ran* across the floor to my feet. Then he burst upward, actually flying for the first time, lighting excitedly on my lap and right in the bowl.

Mary Eleanor heard me laughing and came to the door. I explained to her what I had just proved. She did not quite believe me, but no matter. This pigeon was well on the way to the kind of obedience I knew he must have. I could not keep him inside much longer. He would fly free soon during the hours when I was home, while I watched for the men with guns, my whistle ready to summon him to hiding.

THE THIRD WEEK in May saw the tensions in Preacherville sharply escalate. It also saw us get a new neighbor.

Although there was still no formal strike against the H&O in our area, we knew that isolated crews had walked off the job in Erie, Pittsburgh, and Wheeling. The men who walked out were immediately fired. The local newspaper said nothing of this, however, and except for the wildfire spread of rumors, we might have been unaware of what took place even in our own town that Tuesday afternoon when, it was said, as many as fifty men gathered on the main street downtown. Until then the usual number of pickets had been a dozen or less.

The pickets had formed a ragged line around the depot. About an hour later eight policemen—virtually the entire Preacherville force—arrived on the scene. Assistant Police Chief Kerby told the pickets to disperse; he said they were blocking a public street and creating a nuisance. Some of the pickets argued. Kerby grabbed a man by the arm and told him he was under arrest, and several other pickets swarmed over Kerby and started beating him with their signs. Police fired a shot; a volley followed. The pickets scattered, leaving Kerby and two pickets sprawled on the sidewalk. The two pickets were dead on the spot, and Kerby died three hours later, a bullet in his spine.

Witnesses reported that Kerby had been felled in the fusillade from his own men. H&O division superintendent William Jones issued a statement that some of the pickets were armed and had killed Kerby in cold blood. Rumor had it that a trainload of Hobart-

426

Grimes detectives would arrive soon to supplement the H&O's regular security men.

It was the next night that we saw lantern light in the little house down the road, and the next day on the way to school I had my first look at the man who turned out to be the lone occupant. He was standing on his porch repairing the front door. The sharp pinging of his hammer as he drove nails into the wood frame caught my attention, and I slowed my pace to study our new neighbor.

He was a tall man with a massive chest and a head of gray hair flowing down into a full beard. He wore bib overalls and a long-sleeved underwear shirt despite the warmth of the morning, and he gave the appearance of great strength. But he was no longer young, and when he moved across the porch to get more nails from a brown paper bag, it was with a severe limp. He had to work for the railroad to be in this house, and I wondered what he could do with such an infirmity.

That afternoon I had planned to take my pigeon out for his first free flight. I would have delayed the ultimate test, but my mother would have no more of the bird in the house at all times. When released from his carton, Chick—as I now called him—flew back and forth in my room constantly, his droppings everywhere. Once when I left my room, he even got downstairs, where he sent Napoleon into fits and did something unfortunate on the dining table. So I gave little thought to our new neighbor when I got home from school. I was preoccupied with Chick's trip out-of-doors.

"Well," I said nervously, walking downstairs with Chick perched atop my head, "we're going outside now."

"Aren't you going to tie him?" my mother asked.

"Mom, you can't tie a bird! He might fly out to the end of the string and break his foot or something."

Rachel ran into the room. "What're you going to do, Bobby?"

"Fly my bird."

Rachel called up the stairs, "Mary Eleanor! Come quick! Bobby is going to take his pigeon outside and let it loose and it's going to fly away and never come back! Hurry!"

I went out the back door into the yard, aware of the three faces at the kitchen window. A light, warm breeze blew out of the south.

427

Chick walked around nervously on my head, tickling my scalp. Napoleon, her belly hanging low with her load of kittens soon to be born, slunk out from under the porch and started stalking us. I reached up and took Chick off my head. He cocked his head to study me with his left eye. I could feel his heart thumping rapidly with excitement.

"Now listen," I told him. "I'm going to toss you up and make you fly. But when I blow this whistle, you've got to come back to me. Understand? You fly around and have all the fun you want. But when I blow this whistle, you come back!" My heart in my mouth, I lowered my hands and then tossed him upward.

He exploded into erratic movement, darting first toward the house, then around in a sharp circle toward the barn. Bobbing this way and that, he soared higher, turning a lovely dome-shaped figure against the sky. Then he banked sharply, swooped, and glided rapidly toward the barn roof. His wings flared at the last instant, and I heard the sharp little report as he hit somewhat heavily, regained his equilibrium, and turned to stare my way.

Mother, Mary Eleanor, and Rachel had come out onto the back porch to keep him in view when he soared above the roof. Mary Eleanor was clapping her hands. "He's beautiful, Bobby!"

Rachel shrilled, "He'll never come back!"

The pigeon strutted up and down the sharply sloping roof. Napoleon, meanwhile, had continued to slink, and now bounded heavily across the little creek to steal closer to the barn. Without warning, the pigeon attacked.

He hopped off the roof and came down on Napoleon like a hawk. The cat took one look and went to her belly in the grass. The pigeon dived swiftly and so low that I thought he was going to crash into the cat's back. At the last instant he banked, flapping wings loudly as he gained altitude. Then he did a half-roll and started down again. His wing tip swiped across the cat's fat back, and Napoleon went straight up in the air and took off for the porch. The pigeon did a roll across the sky and dive-bombed her again near the middle of the yard, then did a one-hundred-and-eighty-degree turn and attacked Napoleon head-on.

The poor cat veered sharply and vanished under the porch. The pigeon swooped high and lit on the porch roof, panting with excitement.

"Why," my mother said in amazement, "that pigeon is vicious!"

"Vicious!" Mary Eleanor laughed. "That's his name!"

"Vicious?" I said, looking up at him, and he at me. I reached for the whistle in my pocket and blew. "Here, Vicious!"

Vicious hopped off the roof and lit on my head. He was enormously wrought up. I held him to my chest and stroked him.

"He wasn't raised with other pigeons," I explained to my mother. "He doesn't know he's supposed to be scared of cats!"

My mother was smiling broadly. "Come on, girls. We'll watch from the window. We don't want that poor bird to have any more excitement. Look at him! He's gasping as if he just flew all the way from Henryetta."

"He'll get in shape," I said. "Hey, Vicious, you want to fly again?" I held him out at arm's length. He needed no urging. With a downthrust of his legs, he careened through the air to the roof of the barn.

My mother took Mary Eleanor and Rachel inside, and I walked down the slope toward the creek. Vicious stood on the roof, watching me. As I hopped across the creek, I heard something surprising: male laughter. Off past the barn, leaning on the fence that separated the properties, was our new neighbor. An old pipe stuck out of his bearded mouth. He was laughing and wiping his eyes with a blue bandanna.

Feeling an instant's resentment, I walked to the side of the barn and blew my whistle. Vicious flew down to me. I held him to my chest and walked partway across the garden plot toward the old man. His voice was still weak with laughter when he spoke.

"Hello there, youngster. I'll tell you, I've never seen anything like that in my life!"

His voice was kind, so I walked nearer, beginning to grin myself. "Old Napoleon didn't either, I'll bet you."

"Napoleon? Is that the name of that kitty?"

"Yes, sir."

"I guess you know she's full of kittens."

"Yes, but we call her Napoleon anyway."

He began chuckling again, his massive chest and belly jiggling. "A pigeon that attacks cats and comes to the tune of a whistle!"

"I'm Bobby Keller," I told him. "I live here."

He stowed his bandanna in his hip pocket, allowing himself one more snorting chuckle. "How do you do, Bobby?" He stuck his hand out over the top of the wire fence. "My name is Flanagan."

I shook his hand, which was huge and work-gnarled. "Glad to meet you, Mr. Flanagan."

"It's a pleasure to meet *you*, Bobby," he said. "How in the world did you ever train that King to act that way?"

"King?" I echoed.

"Isn't that what he is? Why, sure. He looks like a purebred white King."

"I don't know anything about kinds of pigeons," I told him. "He was a baby in the barn and most of the other pigeons were blue, but there were a few other white ones, too."

Flanagan looked toward the barn. "Other pigeons?"

"Well, it's a company house, and Mr. Jones said he didn't want pigeons there, so they shot 'em all."

Flanagan's eyes narrowed. "All but this bird. And you raised him?"

"Yes, sir, I did."

Flanagan nodded with appreciation. "Well, it won't be long now until you have more pigeons to keep him company, if you intend to let him fly around much out here."

"You think others will come?" I asked.

"I guarantee it, lad. You let Vicious here fly around and sit on that barn a few days, and other pigeons will find him! You're going to have a flock here soon, and then we'll have some real fun."

"You like pigeons, then?"

"Like them! Bobby, I've had pigeons all my life! When I didn't have any of my own, I would go find a park in whatever city I was in between runs, and take a bag of peanuts and sit on a bench and put a little food on the pavement to visit with them. Did you ever think of what some of these big cities would be like without the pigeons, Bobby?"

"I've never been in a place bigger'n Preacherville," I admitted.

"Well, I've been in many big cities. The only thing you'll likely see as a sign of natural life, amongst all the wagons and automobiles and streetcars, are the pigeons. Instead of those big, empty squares, you can look out and see a flock spring up off the pavement and turn everything into life and movement, and there's nothing more beautiful in my mind than that."

"You said Vicious is what kind of pigeon?" I asked.

"A white King. Yes, sir! He'll grow to be a fine big bird, heavy in the chest and handsome." Flanagan moved, standing straighter. A ghost of pain moved across his face. "A little stiff today."

"That's a bad injury you've got," I told him, nodding toward his crippled left leg.

"I've had it a long time now. But there are days when it bothers me worse than others."

I stared at him, wanting to ask how it had happened. For all I could tell, there was an artificial leg. I glanced down at his sturdy work shoe but could get no clue.

"And does your daddy work for the H &O?" he asked.

"Yes, sir. He works in the office."

"The office. Well, he must be a very important man. My own duties here commence tomorrow. I'll be working nights, mostly, so might be a chance we'll be seeing more of each other. I ought to be getting up about the time you're getting home from school."

"What do you do for the railroad?"

"I'm a telegrapher."

"You send the messages with a key? Gosh, I'd like to learn how to do that! You sit there and talk to people way down the line, in other states, even! That must really be exciting."

"Well, it is, sorta. I was a conductor in my younger days. *That* was exciting. I had my own caboose switched from train to train. Number 304. Ah, she was a beauty. Now that's a real job. You can see the country and get good pay, and it's like you never leave home."

"Is that how you got hurt?" I asked. "Being a conductor?"

"Being a telegrapher isn't bad," he said, as if I had not spoken. "Tell you what, lad. If your parents were to say it was all right, what if I took you into town one day soon and showed you where

431

I work? We could hike on down to the roundhouse if you wanted, and all around. Have you seen the roundhouse and yards?"

"Just from the train when we came in."

"You haven't seen a hundredth of it, then! Tell you what: ask your momma and daddy, and if they say yes, we'll set a day."

"Great!" I said. Vicious, still clutched against me, seemed to be stirred up by my excitement. He squirmed to be free. I let him go and he flew back to the barn and started walking up and down.

"He sure is beautiful," I said. "You really think he'll bring other pigeons?"

"I guarantee it. And I'll tell you what we might do, just to make sure the company crew doesn't come along and start shooting again." Flanagan pointed toward the back of the property, behind the barn, where the land sloped to the creek. "We could put up a pigeon house·down there, say six apartments. Then when the other birds did come and the mating started, they would spend their time down there out of sight from the road."

"How do you know they'd use the pigeon house?"

"They're smart. They seek out the best nesting place available, and the house would be it. We would sit it up on a pole, see, with each apartment about a foot square, with a smaller door. I've got some boards left over from fixing up the house, and plenty of nails."

"It sounds good," I said.

"Now, if we could come up with a post of some kind, to nail the roost on so it would be eight or ten feet off the ground . . ." He scratched his beard thoughtfully.

"What," I asked, "if I go down into that draw and pick out one of those little trees? I could climb up and saw off the top. Then we could nail the house on top of the stump, and we wouldn't have to set a post."

"That's a fine idea! Shall we be planning to do it, then?"

"Yes!"

He chuckled. "Good lad. Well, I've got some more mending to do now, so I'll get back to my house. Mind you ask your momma and daddy about our making a trip to the roundhouse."

"I sure will, Mr. Flanagan, you can depend on that!"

"Good day to you, then," and he turned and hobbled away.

432

When my father came home that night, my excitement led me to deviate from the usual supper-table procedure. We children ordinarily were quiet, and spoke only when spoken to. My father spent much of the meal telling my mother of the day's events. She would listen and nod occasionally as he spoke of weight estimates, bills of lading, and the shortage of boxcars, which were always off on a siding somewhere like Omaha or Chicago. I understood little of it, and doubt that my mother understood much more. But we listened, and it sometimes crossed my mind that my father told us these things because he somehow needed to reassure himself that the job was vital and interesting.

Tonight, however, before he could launch into his recitation, I started telling him about meeting our new neighbor. I told him Flanagan was a telegrapher and knew all about pigeons. "And he said he would take me to the roundhouse if you would let me go."

My father looked up from his plate. "I don't know, son. We don't know this Mr. Flanagan. And I've been thinking *I* would take you to the roundhouse one day."

"Yes, sir, but Mr. Flanagan said he would take me soon, and you're always too busy."

My father's chest heaved silently. "We would have to know Mr. Flanagan before we said you could go into town with him."

"He works nights, but he hasn't started yet," I said. "I can bring him over tonight."

My father looked at my mother. She smiled faintly.

"All right," Dad said. "But I can't visit long. I have all these reports to get done tonight."

It was full night when we finished eating, and Dad said I could go over to see if Mr. Flanagan would like to join us for a cup of coffee. Excited, I ducked out the front door and sprinted through the moonlight to the house down the way. There was lantern light in Mr. Flanagan's front window. I went through the gate and onto the small porch. As I raised my hand to knock, I heard a strange series of sounds coming from inside. I paused. It was clicking— a short, sharp click of some kind broken up into an irregular, nervous-sounding pattern. Dots and dashes. Mr. Flanagan was sending messages in Morse code!

433

I moved across the porch to the window and peered inside. My view was partly obscured by a thin curtain; but I could make out Mr. Flanagan, his back to the window, hunched over a table on which the lantern rested. Beside him were a battery, some loops of wire, and a small black box, and in front of his right hand was a telegraph key. As Mr. Flanagan's thumb and index finger waggled side to side, the key vibrated, making dots and dashes. The sound was only of his code. I saw no headphones or speaker to indicate he was receiving from anywhere. There were papers strewn on the table, a glass, an open bottle of whiskey.

I went to the door and rapped. Inside, the code abruptly stopped. There was the sound of a chair scraping on the floor. "Who is it?" Flanagan's voice called, sharp and tense.

"It's me, sir. Bobby. From next door."

The door swung open. Mr. Flanagan, swaying slightly, looked down at me. His face was red, and sweat dripped off his chin and nose. His eyes were funny. "What do you want?" he asked.

"I was telling my mom and dad about you—how you said I could go to the roundhouse with you—and they said would you like to come over to say how do you do and have some coffee."

"Uuunh," Flanagan grunted, rubbing a big hand over his face. "Now, you say?" He took a deep breath. "Tell your parents I accept with pleasure. I will need . . . ah . . . they can expect me within thirty minutes."

"I heard you sending code," I told him. "Can you talk to other people from your house? Could I see your key? I—"

"Boy," he said sharply, "run give my message to your parents. I'll talk to you about this later." His appearance was so threatening that I turned and beat a retreat.

The waiting was agony. Was Mr. Flanagan drunk? I didn't know, but evidently he did drink. The bottle and glass proved that. So did his demeanor. What if he came over here and acted terrible? Both of us would be in disgrace.

Twenty minutes passed. Then thirty. My father looked up in irritation from his books to scrutinize his watch. Possibly Mr. Flanagan would not show up, and what would they make of that?

Just then boards creaked on the front porch. Someone tapped.

"I'll go," I said, and rushed to the door.

Mr. Flanagan smiled down at me, a brown paper bag under his arm. "Good evening, lad. Here I be."

It was too dark to be sure, but he sounded all right. "Come in," I said, and led him in to where my father stood waiting beside the table with his work. I made stammering introductions. Mr. Flanagan, wearing a black suit and shiny black shoes, limped forward on a cane and shook hands with my father. Flanagan's face was pink in the lantern light, and sweat beaded his forehead. But it was *my* Flanagan, the one of the afternoon.

"This is a pleasure, sir," he told my father. "You have a very bright boy here." My mother came in from the kitchen. Flanagan bowed, a gentle giant before her, and repeated his praise of me. Mary Eleanor and Rachel appeared, and he bent to hug Rachel and to chuck Mary Eleanor under the chin. "Three fine children!" he exclaimed. "You're mighty rich people, Mr. and Mrs. Keller!"

My mother was all smiles, obviously won over. "Will you have coffee and a cookie, Mr. Flanagan?"

Flanagan turned to my father. "If we will not be too much interrupting your work, sir?"

"Plenty of time," my father said, pushing the work to one side. "Sit here, Mr. Flanagan. Bobby tells me you're a telegrapher."

Flanagan sat down at the table, extending his bad leg straight and leaning his cane against it. "Indeed I am, sir. I've just reported here for duty. I have been out of telegraphy for a number of months now, and the hand and ear get rusty. When your son came over a while ago, he found me practicing my sending to be ready."

"So that's what you were doing," I said.

Flanagan opened his brown bag. "I won't be having time for practice after tonight; I'll be doing the real thing. So I brought this over, Bobby. Thought you might like to try it out." He reached into the bag and took out the battery, its wires, and the sounding box. Finally, out came the key. It was perhaps six inches long, a paddle and vibrating rod mounted on a heavy metal base. As I watched, he deftly hooked the battery wires to two terminals on the side of the base, set the key in front of himself, and gave the paddle a few finger flicks. A swift Morse code shot from the sounder.

435

"Hardly a real clicker," he said. "But when you're after hearing your character spacing, this sounder does fine. Like to try it, lad?"

"Can I?"

"Lord love you, that's why I lugged it over here!"

Standing beside him, I gingerly touched the paddle. The sounder clicked and went dead. I pressed the paddle in the opposite direction, to my right with my thumb. The steel rod at the far end of the key flipped away from its contacts, then vibrated back and forth rapidly, sending a long series of dots. "So *that's* how it works!" I exclaimed.

"The lad expressed an interest," Flanagan told my father. "I hope you don't take offense if I encourage him."

"I think it's fine," my father said.

I sent some random dots and dashes, discovering that it was harder than it looked to control how many automatic dots the key sent before you released pressure. "How do you spell words with it?" I asked.

Flanagan grinned and took a small card from his inside coat pocket. "Here. This card shows the Morse. You see? The letter *A* is *di-dah.*"

"*Di-dah?*" I repeated. "It shows dot-dash."

"The worst mistake a man can make, trying to learn the Morse," Flanagan said, "is to think about the way dots and dashes *look*. You've got to learn to *hear* them, not see them. So right from the start you should think of a dash as dah and a dot as dit. But the dits are sent so fast you don't even have time when you're saying them to put in the *t*'s. So the letter *A* is *di-dah.* And *B* is *dah-dididit.*" He reached over to the key and casually touched it. The sounder squawked a perfect *dah-dididit.* "You see? Learn to think of the sound, and you're after taking the first step to being a telegrapher!"

"I'll go copy this list," I told him, "and start memorizing it right away."

Flanagan chuckled. "You won't be needing to copy the card. I brought it for you, same as I brought the key."

I stared at him, scarcely able to comprehend. "You mean I can . . . you mean you . . . My gosh!" I touched the key and sent some dits.

436

My mother came into the room again with cups and a platter of cookies. "What *is* that racket, Bobby?"

"Ah, madam," Flanagan said, "it might be the sound of a young man starting on a career!"

THEY LIKED HIM; I could tell that by my mother's smiles and my father's respectful questions about telegraphy.

"It's a good time to have jobs like ours, Mr. Keller," Flanagan said, after the cookies had been eaten and the coffee drunk. "The railroads will come out of the present turmoil ready for a new period of growth."

"As long as this strike business doesn't get out of hand," my father said.

"Yes, sir, that is a worry. But we can hope and pray that common sense prevails."

"I don't understand why the trouble seems to be worse here than at most other terminals," my father said, scowling.

"Of course you understand the way the H&O works," Flanagan said. "As division chief, Mr. Jones has a free hand in Preacherville. Mr. Harris and the others at the top don't take part in day-to-day decisions down here. It's up to Mr. Jones. So maybe he needs to be looking at some of the other terminals to see how *they* keep calm."

"I would never say anything against Mr. Jones," my father said.

"Nor would Mr. Harris," Flanagan replied. "That's my point. Mr. Jones *is* the H&O around here. As long as these ledger books show a profit, no one is going to come down from Pittsburgh or New York and interfere. So we'd all better be hoping Mr. Jones is a good man, sir. Preacherville's fate is resting on his shoulders."

The two men exchanged looks. I saw that they shared some view I could not penetrate. It was a somber moment.

Four

My father said it would be all right for me to go to the yards with Flanagan, but in the next few days I did not see our neighbor much. His night job evidently required more daylight sleep than he

437

had anticipated. We did have one brief session on his porch when he showed me how to hold my hand farther from the telegraph paddle to avoid splattering extra dits. When he sent me a few characters slowly, and I managed to copy most of them, he was amazed. "You've memorized the whole Morse this fast?"

"Yes, but I've still got to think before I can figure out what each letter is," I told him.

"Lad, you've already learned more than many men ever do. The only way to pick up speed now is to practice sending and copying. We'll have to start having regular sessions. I can see that."

The idea excited me, but I was disappointed that he did not again mention our going to the yards. Between the practice of the code and the arrival of four new pigeons, however, I had enough to occupy me.

The pigeons, three pale blue ones and a young brown-and-white one, came home with Vicious one day after he had been out beyond my sight for about thirty minutes. This had worried me, but when he flew back and alighted on the barn roof, I noticed how excited he seemed. Thoroughly out of breath, he walked up and down, bobbing his head and turning this way and that. Then the other four birds clattered onto the tin roof and began moving around at random. The brown bird scampered as the largest blue strutted up toward him, puffing out his chest feathers and showing off like a boxer on his toes. Vicious walked toward the dominant blue. The blue fanned out his tail feathers so that they dragged the roof, then made a little charging run at Vicious. Vicious turned and walked a few steps away. The blue pursued, making a deep warbling sound of combat, and struck at Vicious with his beak. Which was a mistake. Vicious pounced on him. Wings clattered on the roof. Feathers flew. Vicious got a grip on the blue's neck and clung even as the blue tried to run away across the roof. When they separated, it was the blue who took off, landing at the far end of the barn.

"Mom!" I yelled. "Vicious went off and brought back some friends."

My mother came to the back door and smiled. "He won't be lonesome anymore."

"I'm still going to bring him in at night," I said.

"I hope you still can."

The thought alarmed me. I walked out near the barn, moving slowly to avoid frightening the visitors. Vicious cocked his head to look down at me. I got the whistle out and tooted it.

Vicious ignored it. Instead, he went over to the small brown-and-white bird and did what the blue had done earlier. His throat swelled to twice its normal size. He pranced in little circles. His tail fanned out, dragging on the roof. For the first time I heard from him the warbling fight sound. The brown bird moved nervously away. I blew the whistle again. Vicious kept on ignoring me. I blew a third time.

This time he hopped into the air and came to light on my head. I reached up and caught him and held him against my chest. It was not his heart beating wildly now but mine. If his new friends stayed, and made him wild, I did not know what would happen to my careful plans to make sure he remained alive.

"WELL, SIR," Flanagan said when I told him about the incident, "It's high time we got that roosting house built."

"But what if that crew from the H&O comes back, and Vicious won't come to me? I thought maybe I could train the rest of them to be like Vicious, but it looks like they're training him to be like them."

Flanagan's eyes showed the smile hidden by his beard. "It's nature's way, lad. Sounds to me like Vicious has gone off and brought back a bride and her whole family. We'll get the roosting house up right away and everything will be fine."

"But the crew—"

Flanagan put a hand on my shoulder. "Son, I think the H&O crews have better things to be doing right now than to shoot pigeons off a barn."

I looked up at him. "What's happened?"

439

He sighed heavily. "A little accident. Some track was damaged west of here. A switcher went off with four cars. That's the second incident in two days, and the story is that someone sabotaged the track in both cases."

"Strikers?"

"Mr. Jones says they can't be strikers, because there's no strike. Look, let's start on that pigeon house. Is Vicious out there with the others?"

"Yes, sir. He's strutting all around that brown one and spreading his tail out and making a fool of himself. The brown one acts like he doesn't like it, either."

Flanagan chuckled. "We better hurry, then. And I think you'd better stop calling the brown one him. Sounds to me like the brown one is a she, and Vicious figured it out before you did."

RAIN CAME only hours after we had taken the first steps on building the pigeon house, and in the morning my mother said Mary Eleanor, who had the croup, should not go to school. I went alone, slopping along in the mud. It was a dreary day. By the time school was over, however, the rain was down to a fine drizzle and the clouds looked higher. Thinking there might be a chance to work more on the pigeon house with Flanagan, I hurried along the road, walking with my head down, avoiding the worst puddles.

It was not until I was almost upon them that I realized they were there. "Hey, kid," a voice said. I looked up sharply. Thurman Black and three of the bigger boys stood blocking my way. Thurman stood slightly ahead of the others, his fists on his hips, a crooked grin twisting his features.

I made a desperate attempt to pretend I did not know why they were there. "Hello, Thurman! You guys sure ran fast from school!"

Thurman Black advanced on me, big hands swinging loosely at his sides. The grin was gone and he seemed to be working on getting himself angry. "You got me beat. You told Mrs. Mead about strikers and hoboes."

I turned in hope of seeing someone else on the road behind me. It was empty, gleaming brown and puddled under the light rain.

"You're not getting away," Thurman Black told me.

It was closer to my house than to any other source of help. I thought surprise might get me by them—or perhaps sheer panic took over and I did no thinking at all. My explosion into action took me past Thurman Black, but my feet slipped in the mud. I went sprawling, and they were all over me, shoving my face into the cold slime. Then they dragged me to my feet, coughing and panicked for breath.

"Off the road!" Thurman Black ordered. "Over there!"

They dragged me into the brush, perhaps twenty yards off the road, before throwing me down on sodden earth covered with last winter's decaying leaves.

"You're going to learn, once and for all," Thurman Black told me. "Get up and fight."

"Against *all* of you?"

"We're going to be fair. We'll fight you one at a time."

If I hadn't been terrified, I could have laughed. The smallest of their group was more than a head taller and twenty pounds heavier than I. There was no one here I had a chance against.

"I won't fight," I said.

"Then we'll just take turns beating you up anyway. Get up!"

Shaking, I climbed to my feet. "I didn't do anything to you guys—"

"Herman," Thurman Black said. A thickset boy with almost white hair stepped forward. His close-set eyes showed a hot excitement. As his fists balled, I tried to hunker down the way I had seen boxers do in pictures. He stepped in close, and his fist exploded in my midsection. My air gushed out and I staggered. His other hand slammed into my face. I found myself on hands and knees with blood in my mouth.

Other hands hauled me to my feet. I saw the face of an Italian boy with protruding teeth. I swung wildly, missing. His hand chopped down beside my ear and I hit the wet earth again. He pulled me up to a kneeling position and punched me in the chest, knocking me over backward.

They waited. I rolled over and knelt. The third boy moved in, and I tried to tackle him. He jumped on top of me, pummeling. As I tried to roll over, one of his blows smashed into my left eye,

441

another into my nose. They were going to kill me. I was sure of that.

I managed to scramble up, leaning against a tree for support. I was choking on blood and could not see out of my left eye. The sounds of hammers on anvils rang in my ears. And now Thurman Black, the source of all my troubles, was facing me. Something primitive within me was unleashed. I screamed as I charged him.

I hit him hard enough to take him down, and for a heady instant I was astride him, pummeling his face with ineffective fists. Then he threw me off and swung a roundhouse right that crashed into my ear. I scrambled up again and tried to charge a second time. He was ready with a blow to my midsection that felled me.

Kneeling, with the hot, acid remnants of my lunch spilling up onto the wet leaves, I wanted only to have this over with. But the animal anger I had never suspected in me was still there, suicidal in its intensity. Thurman Black moved close, leaning over to look at me. There was an expression almost like concern in his dark eyes. I swung at him, connecting feebly on his shoulder. He danced back. I sprang to my feet and moved at him.

"That's it, kid," he said, panting a little. "You've learned—"

"No!" I charged him again.

With a look of grim determination, he dodged my rush and brought a cocked elbow around in a neat, tight arc. I ran right into it. Everything went out. A moment later I found myself sitting on the vomit-fouled earth. Thurman Black and his friends were walking away.

THE RAIN had stopped by the time I walked unsteadily up my own road. Flanagan was out on his front porch at work. He had part of the pigeon house put together, rounded-top doorways in the sides of the pentagonal structure. He waved cheerily at me, then stood aghast as I limped up his walk. His strong hands grasped my shoulders. "Who did this to you, lad?"

"I had a—fight," I said.

He hugged me against his body, enveloping me in the strong smells of sweat and laundry bleach and tobacco. "Don't cry, boy, don't cry! Lord bless you! We can't be letting your mother see you like this! Come inside and let's clean you up a mite."

While he bathed my face and arms in water warmed on his stove, I told him the whole story. Telling my disgrace calmed me, and by the time he was trying to rake some of the mud off my clothing, I was only hiccuping now and then in the aftermath of the tears.

"Will you be telling your momma and daddy what happened?"

"No," I said. "I'll just say it was a fight. I can't get Mom all upset. And Dad has too much on his mind already. This job is his very last chance."

Flanagan sighed. "Life is filled with last chances. There's seldom one that's really the end of the road. Are you sure you're not taking too much on yourself, hiding the truth from them?"

"They've got enough to worry about."

He gently tousled my hair. "You'd better scat on home, now. If your mother lets you, after seeing you, why, then come on back over. With the rain eased off, we might go down the creek and see how this apartment house will sit on one of them tree stubs."

Mother was upset, but in no way as shocked as she might have been had Flanagan not gotten me cleaned up. "A fight!" she said, kneeling to examine me. "Oh, Bobby! How could you?"

"I had to," I said, trying to squirm away.

"What was the fight about?"

"It just started, Mom. I'm okay. Lemme go, please."

She gave up struggling with me. "Your father will hear of this when he comes home, mark my words!"

I muttered something grumpy and hurried upstairs. In my room, Vicious perched on my head while I looked at myself in the mirror. My left eye was swollen half shut. My lips were puffy, the lower one split and purple. One of my front teeth moved when I touched it. My side hurt, too, but I decided I was going to live.

I took Vicious outside, as I did after school each day now. The moment I was clear of the porch roof he exploded into eager flight, soaring against the sky and gliding toward the barn roof, where his pigeon friends sat waiting for him. I left him with his kind and went back to Flanagan's, skinnying through the fence.

Flanagan was sitting on his porch steps looking at the finished roosting house. He did wonderful carpentry work. Every corner was perfect, each doorway symmetrical behind its little porch.

443

"Well?" he asked. "What did your mother say?"

"She said Dad would have to hear about it."

"And you plan to deceive him?"

"It's for his own good," I said uncomfortably.

Flanagan scratched around in his chin whiskers. "Well," he said finally, "shall we go look for a good tree for this house?"

We made slow, awkward progress carrying the heavy house downslope to the small grove of trees beyond the barn.

"You think Vicious is really a male bird and the brown-and-white one is a female?" I asked.

"I think so. I think that's what Vicious thinks, too."

"He isn't very big."

"No, he has a lot of filling out to do. But I'd say he's mature enough to nest. If that little brown-and-white lady is ready, too, we'll see a nest in one of these apartments real soon."

"Since the male guards the eggs during daylight, I guess I'll have to let Vicious out in the morning and not call him until she takes over again late in the afternoon."

"I hope it works out, son," Flanagan said, sweating with his half of our burden. "Vicious will have responsibilities to his family, once he starts it. Day might come when he decides he just can't come back to you anymore."

"I've trained him too good," I said, with more certainty than I felt.

"A male likes to roost near his nesting mate," Flanagan told me. "He won't often sleep right at the door, because instinct tells him not to draw attention to the female and the eggs inside. But he'll sleep close by, where he can watch."

"Vicious won't be watching," I insisted. "He'll be inside. With me."

"If you hold a bird too tightly, lad, he may die."

"But if I hold him too loose, he may fly away and never come back!"

"If you find just the right hold, maybe you'll be all right."

"I will."

Despite his exertion, Flanagan smiled sadly. "A lot of parents have tried and failed at that trick, lad."

444

Down the creek slope we located a small wild cherry, and I ran back to the house and got Flanagan's saw. He bent over and let me stand on his back while I sawed off the top. Then we hefted the house up onto the tall stump. I stood on a packing box and balanced it while Flanagan nailed it to the tree.

"I've seen pigeons nesting," I said when we had finished, "but I never watched right from the start. How will they pick it out?"

"Well, it's the male who picks. He'll select a hole and get inside and start making the most golly-awful moaning sounds. Sort of his love song. If a female is ready, she'll go in and join him. Once they've cuddled down for a while, it's a pretty sure thing."

I took out the whistle. "Let's see how old Vicious likes it!" I blew once, then again. There was no response from the barn. "Maybe we're too far away," I said, knowing better.

We hiked up through the field nearer the barn. As we rounded it, we saw the pigeons on the sunny side of the roof. Vicious and the brown-and-white female were off to themselves a bit. She was resting on her belly, and Vicious was at her side, reaching back to preen his back and tail feathers. It was a nervous, jerky movement. As we watched, the female reached out and pecked at the side of his head. He pecked back, but gently.

"Vicious!" I sounded the whistle again. He did not react.

"I think you might wait awhile, until he's not so preoccupied," said Flanagan, grinning. "Right now his mind is full of true love. Looks like we got the house up just in time!"

WHEN MY FATHER came home that night, he was later than usual. There had been trouble at the offices. A crowd had thrown rocks through windows, and the company guards had rushed in. My father said it was an isolated incident, and as long as Mr. Jones continued being tough, there would be no worse developments.

My mother told him how I had come home from a fight. He examined my face and asked me if I hurt anywhere else. I said I was fine.

"What was the fight about?" he asked soberly, walking with me into the room where his work was already spread out on the table.

"It was just a fight," I told him. Now he would press me and I

445

would finally have to tell him about Thurman Black and he would be alarmed and take some action to protect me. I wanted that, even as I knew it was incumbent upon me to force him to squeeze the information out of me.

"Just a fight?" he echoed, sitting down and frowning at his ledger pages..

"Yes, sir." Now he would press me.

"But you're all right?"

"Yes, sir." *Now* he would.

He looked up at me. "We don't like you to fight, Bobby. Never fight if there's any other way. Do you understand me?" He bent his eyes back to his ledgers. I waited for what seemed a long time, but he did not look up again. I quietly left the room.

THE NEXT MORNING two of the new pigeons had located the roosting house and were sitting on top of it. That afternoon Vicious and the brown-and-white female began making inspection trips back and forth from the barn. And with each day of the next week Vicious showed less eagerness to return to me when I sounded my whistle before dark.

That Saturday my attentions were drawn from the pigeons by a trip to the Preacherville yards with Flanagan. I think he waited a few days for my facial wounds to heal.

"Preacherville is a vital link for the H&O because of its central location," Flanagan explained as we neared the yards on the electric streetcar. "The valley makes a natural channel for tracks both north and south and east and west. Today we'll see cars for ten or fifteen railroad companies all here in our yards."

We left the streetcar near the depot and walked toward a gate in the high metal fencing of the yards. A sullen group of six or seven workers, caps pulled down over their eyes, watched us from across the street as we approached the gate. The guard appeared nervous as he examined the card Flanagan handed him. "Who's he?" he asked, nodding at me.

"A lad who wants to see the trains," Flanagan said.

The guard hesitated. "Rules say—"

"He's just a boy, Starbuck!"

446

"Well, being it's you . . ." The guard slid the bars back and moved the gate enough for us to slip through. Our feet crunched on a gravel walk blackened by coal dust. Behind the gatehouse, hidden from view of the street, was a flatbed cart. A dozen or more men, wearing lumpy business suits, lounged on the cart. Rifles and shotguns leaned against the back of the building. The men looked uniformly heavy and tough and serious.

"Who're they?" I whispered as we passed. "They act like guards, but they're not wearing uniforms. Are those guys hoboes?"

"Don't concern yourself," Flanagan said, limping on.

So it was true. Detectives from the infamous Hobart-Grimes Company had been called in. I was astounded. My father had not mentioned this. Why had he kept such an ominous development from his family? Did he want to pretend that things were not as bad as the presence of these notorious strikebreakers indicated? Or was he trying to protect us? I did not know, but I felt betrayed. He should have told us. If labor violence threatened the company, it threatened all of us.

Flanagan's every step, meanwhile, took us deeper into the yards. We passed a huge steel building filled with the clamor of machinery. Inside, men stood beside gigantic engines, using their welding torches on wheels taller than anyone among them. A crane held aloft the front of a great black Harriman Standard Atlantic locomotive. The plates of its huge boiler had been peeled back on one side, and men worked inside the cavern with torches and hammers. Piled everywhere, like bones of prehistoric giants, were wheels and pistons, tubing, bolts as big around as my wrist, sheet steel, bearing assemblies the size of a bathtub. We were past the doors, then, and heading out across a clutter of tracks toward an area of billowing steam and smoke.

There was a brief, ear-shattering whistle. A huge black switching engine chuffed by, pulling half a dozen cars and a caboose. It moved so slowly that I could make out every articulated gear and spinning mechanism in the wheel housings; catch a scent of the blinding steam that hissed onto the scarred track from an overflow hose under the cab; look up, startled, and have time to wave to the engineer, a man of middle age, who gazed down at us from under

447

the bill of his gray cap and raised a heavily gloved hand in salute. In the caboose another man bent over a table, working with a pencil. Two workers strode along behind on either side of the track, swinging lanterns.

The way clear, we proceeded again. The roar and turmoil of the roundhouse enveloped us as we climbed onto a railing to watch.

The platform, a circular, rotating platter, was immense. Tracks fanned out from it like spokes of a wheel. Eight engines were nosed in on the gigantic revolving disk. Steam issued sullenly from vents. I had a glimpse of a fireman stoking coal into the brilliant red of a furnace. Sound and smell and vibration surrounded me.

As I watched, the turntable lurched to a stop. Two men moved out in front of one of the locomotives and did something to a switch. Then another man waved his hand slowly left and right to the engineer, who was leaning from his window. The great engine snorted and chuffed, and a puff of dark smoke gushed from the stack. Groaning, the engine began to inch backward off the platter onto its designated track.

We watched a while longer. Then Flanagan led me farther out into the yards, down endless lines of silent cars, and into that part of the operation where the trains had been assembled and now awaited their orders to travel. One such train—a long freight headed east—was now in motion, and we stood on the graveled siding, almost close enough to touch the massive wheels as they ground by us. I watched the heavy steel rails bend downward slightly as each pair of tandem wheels rolled over a spiked joint just in front of us, and registered the identifiers on the cars: H &O, Wheeling, Pennsylvania, Santa Fe, B&O, Lackawanna, Erie, Gulf. The train was gathering momentum now, and far to our east I heard the hoot of the whistle as the head neared the crossings on the far side of Preacherville. Still the cars rumbled by, more than a mile of them, shaking the ground, deafening me with their thunder.

I turned to Flanagan. He was watching the cars, too, a slight smile on his lips like one I had seen on my father's face. I could understand it in this moment. There was something vital and elemental and exciting and right in this; it was the way things were supposed to be. Number 482, for New York; out on time.

We visited the section where passenger trains were made up, and climbed up into one of the extra Pullman cars. A thin layer of dust covered the leather seats, and I could smell soot and old cigars. We walked through to a dining car, and I gawked at the tables and cabinets and rows of gleaming flower containers. A stray menu, beautifully printed, was on one of the tables. I looked at the list of exotic dishes and marveled. Passengers here could even order French champagne for two dollars a bottle. I was amazed that anyone could be so rich.

"My dad was going to be a conductor before he got his hand cut off," I told Flanagan as we walked slowly along other lines of passenger cars. "If I work for the railroad, I'm going to be an engineer. I'll be up there in the cab with the big headlight shooting out ahead, and I'll hang my head out and feel the wind pushing against me, and we'll go through little towns and I'll blow my whistle and people will wake up and hear me and think, There's old Number 14, the candy run to Philadelphia, right on time!"

"If that's what you really want, lad, then I hope you get it one day."

"If you really try, you can get anything. Right?"

The question seemed to bother Flanagan. His forehead wrinkled. "We can always hope so." He pointed. "Look. This is a special one."

The train we were approaching from the rear was very short, only five Pullman cars, each unit in perfect condition. Out in the narrow canyon between the spotless Pullman cars and another passenger train parked on the next track stood a small group of men in dark business suits.

"Must be somebody important!"

"I wouldn't be surprised."

We walked nearer. There was something familiar about the largest man, bulky in his dark suit, with diamonds glittering on his fingers as he gestured. Then I recognized him. Leaving Flanagan a few strides behind, I hurried closer. "Hello, Mr. Harris!"

Nathaniel Harris and his companions turned, surprised. I saw that he didn't recognize me. "I'm Bobby Keller. We met one day when you came here and my father was just starting to work here and—"

"The young man who does his arithmetic in his head!" Harris smiled. "Hello! What are you doing in the yards, Bobby? You said you would only own a railroad, not work for one."

"Mr. Flanagan is showing me around. Have you met Mr. Flanagan?"

Flanagan's face was the color of dough. He limped forward. "How do you do, sir."

"I seem to remember you," Harris said, frowning. "Aren't you—"

"A telegrapher, sir," Flanagan said quickly. "Telegrapher on the night shift here now."

"Yes," Harris said, and in some way I did not understand, his expression closed. "Of course."

"Are you here because of the trouble?" I asked.

"Lad," Flanagan whispered warningly.

"Just a brief visit," Harris told me, ignoring Flanagan. "I don't think there's anything too serious going on in Preacherville, do you?"

"It's serious enough!" I told him. "More men out of work, extra guards. I heard—"

Nathaniel Harris silenced me with a hand on my shoulder. "Bobby, when you own your own railroad, you'll understand that no single hub makes a rail line. The first principle of management: let the local man handle the situation. Right, boys?"

The other businessmen chuckled and nodded.

"Come on, son," Flanagan said, pulling at my arm.

"I think you ought to keep in touch with stuff going on here now, though," I told Harris.

"Oh, you do, do you!" Harris's laugh came from deep in his body. "I'll tell you what, Bobby. I'll do my best to stay on top of the situation. But if you ever have anything extra special to tell me, you just feel free to contact me."

"I'll sure tell you if I think I know something you ought to know," I promised.

Nathaniel Harris guffawed. "Splendid lad!"

Flanagan finally succeeded in dragging me on down the tracks. I saw to my surprise that he was sweat-soaked with nervousness. "Come on, lad. Let's be getting over to the telegraph shack."

451

"Why were you nervous about me talking to Mr. Harris?" I asked. "He didn't mind."

"Nathaniel Harris," Flanagan muttered, "is a very rich man, son. And very powerful, to boot."

"I don't understand why, just because somebody is rich, people like us should be scared of them."

"I hope you never do understand that, Bobby."

It was obviously one of those adult perceptions that was beyond me. I lapsed into silence and followed my friend across a clutter of trackage to a small brick building next to the depot. Flanagan opened the door and gestured me in. I already heard the clatter of the telegraph.

Inside, desks were banked along one wall and wire loops criss-crossed the ceiling. Two of the desks, equipped with copy hooks, ledgers, telegraph keys, and amplifying horns, were vacant. At the closest desk a bald man in a green eyeshade was running his key, looking down at a sheet of paper in front of him. Despite the enormous speed of the Morse, I picked up some letters.

"Hello, Henry!" Flanagan said, closing the door.

"Greetings," the bald man said, never breaking his sending pattern. "Hello, young feller. Be with you in a minute."

We stood waiting. The room was the most complicated and hectic place I had ever been in. The box over Henry's operating position had a series of lights, and the words WESTWARD and EAST-WARD stenciled on the front. I wondered where the operator was sending his code.

At that moment, the man sent a quicker burst of Morse and moved his hand to close a relay at the base of the key, which closed a circuit and allowed the operator at the other end to return a message. He swiveled his chair and held out his hand. "Howdy do, young feller. I'm Henry Ball."

"Bobby Keller," I mumbled.

Behind Ball the sounding apparatus began to clatter as a return message came in. Ball seemed to pay no attention. "You're the young man who's taken to the code, aren't you?"

"I'm trying," I admitted.

"You copy any of that message I just sent?"

452

"Well, it was awful fast. I think you sent the numbers four two eight, and you sent the word 'siding' a couple of times."

Ball's mouth fell open. "Flanagan, this youngster is copying over thirty words a minute! And copying in his head! That's plumb amazing! Young feller, copying the code is a talent, and—oops! Wait a minute." He swung back to his key, flicked the blade switch, and sent off a quick burst, then turned the switch once more. A few dits came back, and then the sounder fell silent. Henry Ball had been copying the code from the other station while talking to me. I was awestruck.

Ball, however, was much more interested in me. "Flanagan," he said, "this youngster is a born telegrapher!" He got up from his chair and pushed me into it. From a niche in the rear of the desk he pulled out a second key and quickly hooked some wires to it. "All right, this won't go out now, but we'll hear it. Send us something. Say 'Hello, how do you do, my name is Bobby and I live in Preacherville.'"

I hesitated, worried I would make a fool of myself. Then I took a deep breath and struck a few dits to get the feel of the key. It seemed stiffer than Flanagan's, but that might make it easier to control. Resting my forearm on the desk top, I sent the words, trying my best not to splatter extra dits.

"That's fourteen words, and letter-perfect," Ball said as Flanagan grinned proudly. "Youngster, you've got a God-given talent for this! You're going to be a telegraph man!"

"I like it a lot," I admitted. "But I don't know what I want to be."

"You will," Ball said. "You're going to be a telegraph man!"

"Why," Flanagan asked, "is 428 on the siding over at Waterloo?"

Ball sighed. "Track damage."

"Somebody do it?"

"Looks like. There will be Hobart-Grimes people on the repair car with the crew. I tell you, it's not helping, sending the Hobart-Grimes out on every incident. Did you ever know a group of men so completely hated by everyone else? Even our own regular guards fear them."

"It's a powder keg," Flanagan said grimly. "If there are more layoffs, I worry what might happen next."

453

"The Hobart-Grimes will provoke an incident one of these days if all the other things don't do it for them."

"What other things?" I asked. "Has there been more trouble?"

Both men seemed to remember me with a start. Flanagan gave me his slow grin. "Nothing to worry about, lad. We're just two old men who worry too much because we don't have anything better to do." Nevertheless, the news of trouble up the line seemed to have taken the fun out of the day for him.

Five

The next day was Sunday, ordinarily the only day of the week when my father was not poring over his paperwork. We had not been home from church long, however, when Superintendent Jones paid us the visit that changed everything.

I was downslope of the barn, watching life progress for the pigeons. The largest blue male had moved into an apartment in the roosting house and had enticed one of the blue females to join him. Now he was making endless trips to and from the nesting site, bringing tiny twigs and leaf stems.

Vicious was in a hole on the far side of the house, making pitiable sounds. The object of his love song, the brown-and-white female, walked around on the ground below. After a while he flew down beside her and began strutting around. She walked away. He pursued, fanning his tail feathers and puffing out his breast. She pranced in a circle with him. Then simultaneously both birds broke into flight. Shading my eyes with my hands, I watched them climb joyously and turn in diving loops, soar upward again, and head for the roosting house. Vicious landed on the ledge of the apartment he had selected, and the female landed on the roof. Vicious peered up at her and she flew into the hole. A moment later his cooing started. Then her voice joined his, softer, gentler.

So there was going to be a second nest started, I thought, wondering what this new development would do to my training of Vicious to come in each night.

"You're just going to have to work it out," I told them. "I'm not

454

going to let you go wild, Vicious, and you might just as well get used to that."

It was at this point I heard the unaccustomed sound of a car out on our road. I left the pigeons and walked uphill. A black roadster with three men inside was coming up the road at moderate speed, leaving behind a faint trail of yellow dust. As it neared our gate, it slowed and then halted. The passenger door popped open and Mr. Jones stepped out. The other two men remained in the car as he walked through the gate and approached our house.

Curiosity impelled me to go around to the front porch, where I found Jones standing at the foot of the steps, looking up at my father. Jones appeared grim, angry. My father's expression was one of guarded surprise. "Would you like to come inside?" he asked.

"No, Keller," Jones said, "I have other stops to make. It's better to talk out here anyway." He removed his hat, mopped his forehead with a handkerchief, and sat on the step.

My father, not seeing me, joined him. "Has something happened?"

"I need you in the office. I assume you can leave right away?"

"Well," my father said slowly, "my wife is fixing dinner, but . . ."

"You know we almost had a derailment yesterday," Jones snapped.

"Yes, sir, of course. Terrible thing. I—"

"Our Hobart-Grimes operatives captured three suspects in the area. They've been questioning them right through the night. We have confessions, Keller, and a list of the ringleaders."

"The men who were captured gave the names of others?"

A little smile quirked Jones's mouth. "There are ways to make people give information, and Hobart-Grimes invented most of them. So now we'll move immediately, to cut the head from this monster once and for all."

My father watched his employer with narrowed eyes. "How many names do you have?"

"Seventy-nine." Jones balled a fist. "Every troublemaker. Every malcontent. Every cancerous growth that will be cut from the company and never given a chance to work for any railroad in this nation again."

"Seventy-nine! I can't believe there were that many planning the track damage up there!"

Jones made a gesture of dismissal. "Oh, few of them were in that. But they were all in *something*. We have the names of radicals who spoke out against the company at a meeting two weeks ago. And we got the names of their friends."

"What do you intend to do?" my father asked softly.

"First, termination papers. That's part of your job. Then a public notice tomorrow noon, and a promise of similar treatment for anyone we may have missed. But that isn't all you have to help with, Keller. These dismissals mean wholesale reshuffling of job assignments all the way through the division. You'd better bring some food with you. We may be working right through the night."

My father said huskily, "What a blow for all those families."

"We're going to be humane," Jones replied. "We're giving those of them who live in our houses a week to vacate company property."

"Are you going to have hearings?"

"Hearings? What do we need hearings for? We have confessions."

"But what if one of the men who confessed made a mistake? Or he could have had some enemy, and put him on the list just for some old grudge. Without due process—"

"Don't lecture me about due process!" Jones's face had gone white with rage. "This division has lost thousands of dollars, not to mention two lives, because of this. Only yesterday Nathaniel Harris was through here and gave me a direct order to get this straightened out! I mean to rid us of the rabble here and now."

My father also had gone pale, and the sunlight gleamed sickly on the sweat now visible on his forehead. "Mr. Jones, I feel compelled to tell you my feelings on this. Terrible injustices could be done. Many loyal workers—men who have never said an unkind word about the H&O—could be angered. The situation is already incendiary—"

"That's enough, Keller!" Jones said, tight-lipped. "You've been given an order. Report to the office at once. Any questions?"

I watched my father almost speak again; then a terrible control turned his face to a pale mask. "No questions, sir."

Jones stood, replacing his hat on his head. "Good. Just remember,

Keller, this is a time that will test the loyalty of every man in this division. I am determined to weed out every undesirable."

"Yes, sir," my father said almost inaudibly. "My only point—"

"Do you know what happens to people in management who can't get the job done?" Jones said in a soft, hissing voice. "They don't last long."

My father watched him, saying nothing. I could see his strain, the intense pressure. Come on! I thought. Say something—don't be like Conductor Stein. Don't just take it. If you take it now, you'll always take it. And you'll be a cripple in that way, too. But he said nothing.

"I fought to get the position I hold," Jones told him. "There are men all up and down the tracks who would slash me down in a second if they thought they could replace me. It's my job on the line here, Keller. And it's your job, too. You fight me now and I'll sacrifice you in an instant, if I have to. Understood?"

"I'm sorry if I said anything out of line, sir."

Jones seemed to relax slightly, now that my father was not only beaten down but beginning to grovel. "We'll say no more about it. I'll expect you at the office within the hour. Good day."

My father stood as if rooted, watching Jones stride angrily back to the car. The door slammed. The other men moved to make more room for him as the engine started. For an instant I saw something thin and cylindrical against the sky behind them. They had rifles with them, I thought. The car jerked away and headed up the road, gathering speed. My father stood with one hand against the porch post. He did not move.

"Are you going to do it?" I asked.

He started violently and turned to me. "You heard all that, son?"

"Yes. Are you going to do it, Dad? You told him it was wrong to just fire those men."

"I work for the H&O, son. Mr. Jones is my boss."

"I *know* that! But you said yourself some of those guys might not have done anything! Mr. Jones is the nastiest, hatefulest man I ever saw! He's crazy. You aren't going to help him, are you, Dad?"

He walked closer to me. I had never seen him so grim. "We'll

457

say nothing about this to your mother or sisters. As far as they're concerned, I've just been called in to do some extra work."

"If you take up for Mr. Jones's side, won't people hate you, too?" I demanded. "If it's wrong, won't you be doing wrong when you help him?"

"Bobby, I work for the H&O. I love the H&O. When you're a man, you do what you're told on your job. Maybe everything I said to Mr. Jones was wrong. Maybe he knows best. It isn't for me to decide. I take my orders. Someday you'll understand that."

"I hope I *never* understand that!" I cried, and burst into tears.

He stared at me, and I thought he might strike me. Instead, he turned and went without another word into the house.

MONDAY, the opening of the last week of school for the year, was marked with the traditional school picnic at the small city park in Preacherville. Everyone was excited when they arrived in class. Even Mrs. Mead had forsaken her usual browns and blacks for a summery-looking dress in pale lavender. She joked with the girls and only whipped one boy as we assembled our picnic baskets and lined up to walk into town.

If anyone else was aware of the sword about to fall on so many H&O workers, they did not show any sign of it. The mood was exuberant as we set out. Mr Jones had said the news would be made public at noon. We would be back in school by then, and safe.

Safe, of course, like all words, is relative. As we trooped toward the park, the head of our line, four abreast, turned a corner past a business building. The teachers at the head were screened from view temporarily, and I suppose the teacher at the back of the line was looking the other way. Whatever the explanation, a smaller boy named Tommy Mitchel, walking just in front of our class, was tripping along joyfully when one of the bigger boys, the white-haired Herman Towers, stepped forward and stuck his foot out. The smaller boy went sprawling. His picnic basket sprang open and a jar of milk shattered on the pavement. His sandwiches, too, spilled out, along with a banana. Before he could react, Herman Towers kicked the banana into the street, and Thurman Black stepped on the sandwich. All the bigger boys broke up. As Tommy

Mitchel got up, Thurman Black kicked him in the backside, making him sprawl again.

The line had been moving steadily forward while this took place, with the result that I was beside Tommy Mitchel when he scrambled up the second time. I bent to help him. "Hey, are you all right?"

Mitchel was crying. "They ruint my whole lunch!"

"I've got plenty, Tommy. I'll share. Just get your basket and—"

A paralyzing blow descended on my shoulders. "I told you to keep up with the line!" Mrs. Mead hissed. "What are you doing here?" The switch raised to hit me again.

"He didn't do anything!" Tommy Mitchel cried.

"You keep quiet!" Mrs. Mead ordered. She swung back toward me. "You should be ashamed of yourself!"

I knew I should keep quiet, but my sense of outraged justice was too strong. "*I* didn't shove him down!"

"Who did, then?" she demanded.

I looked up the line. Thurman Black and his cronies were walking backward, giggling and shoving one another. I pointed at them. "They did! Herman Towers tripped him and Thurman Black kicked him!"

Mrs. Mead looked, saw the hilarity suddenly stilled, and charged ahead, reaching the group just as that part of the line turned the building corner. Back came the sharp reports of the switch and someone's pained yelping.

"You shouldn't have told!" Tommy Mitchel said. "They'll kill you!"

"What do you want to do?" I shot back. "Let 'em push you down the rest of your life?"

"You can't fight 'em, Bobby," Tommy Mitchel said, with the resignation of an eighty-year-old man. "You made a terrible mistake, and now I can't eat part of your lunch. They'd kill me, too, if I did that."

"You've got to do what you think is right. How are you ever going to be a man if you always let other people run your life?"

"I'll be a man, don't you worry about that! And then I'll be big enough and they won't push me down anymore."

"That's where you're wrong, Tommy. By the time you're big

459

enough to fight back, you'll have been taking their guff so long that it's a habit, and they'll walk over you all your life."

"And what are you going to do when we get to the park and they beat you up?"

"I'm going to fight 'em," I said, thinking suddenly of my father. "I'm never going to let people boss me around when they're wrong."

We rounded the building. Mrs. Mead was waving her switch and berating the bigger boys up ahead. Thurman Black's eyes were bright, almost as if she had managed to beat tears out of him. Herman Towers *was* crying. Thurman Black managed a quick look back at me. His eyes were murderous. My new-found resolve vanished in a gust of fear. What had I gotten myself into?

IT DID NOT take long to find out. The line reached the park, a pleasant, slightly hilly bit of terrain with a creek running through it. For a town the size of Preacherville, it was quite large. We assembled at the shelter house, and our principal told us we would eat promptly at eleven o'clock, and that we could play anywhere in the park for the next hour. Kids broke, running in all directions. I decided the safest place was the shelter house, with the teachers. I walked in.

Mrs. Mead spied me at once and marched over. "And what do you think you're doing in here? Get out and play!"

"If I go out there, Thurman Black and those other guys are going to take me off and punch me for telling on them!"

Mrs. Mead smiled. "Don't be a coward, boy. Face the medicine."

"Mrs. Mead, they're a lot bigger than me. I'm scared."

"You should have thought of that before you were a tattletale."

I was thunderstruck. She *wanted* me punished for telling. She admired Thurman Black and his ilk. *I* was the one for whom she felt contempt, because of my size or weakness or some streak of difference within me that I had not yet identified by name.

I turned and walked out of the shelter house. The game of capture the flag seemed to be ranging along the street side of the park, so I turned in the opposite direction, toward the creek. I felt ill. I had helped Tommy Mitchel, so he had rejected me. I had told

460

Mrs. Mead who had done wrong, so she despised me. You get along by being weak and not standing out in the crowd. Did this explain my father? I was filled with bitterness.

I had progressed only a few yards past the playground equipment when motion to one side caught my eye. I turned, nerves tingling, and saw Thurman Black and four of his friends walking briskly toward me.

"Hey, Keller!" Thurman Black's voice sang out. I walked faster. They broke into a jog.

"Keller!" Black called more sharply. Fear took over. I started running. It was downhill, and I thought that I might somehow escape if I could make the nearby trees. Dodging some shrubs, I raced around the water fountain and skirted some benches. I knew the others were gaining on me fast. Oh, to be like some of the boys in books I read, able to run faster than any Indian in the forest!

I reached the first trees and ran between them, cutting to my left nearer the creek. But someone had trimmed out some of the smaller trees, leaving scattered bits of logs and limbs. I tripped and plunged headlong, and they were upon me. Two of them grabbed me and pulled me up. Thurman Black started walking toward me, fists balled. "Let him go. I can handle it from here."

His aides released me. I turned to see if I could try to run again and instead saw on the ground beside me, in easy reach, a piece of tree limb about three inches in diameter and over two feet long. I snatched it up and turned back to Thurman Black, swinging blindly. My makeshift club crashed into his forehead. He went over like a sack. My God, I've killed him! I thought.

Thurman Black, however, was not seriously injured. The blow evidently had caught him off-balance and he had fallen more from surprise than force. He scrambled to his feet, blinking in confusion.

"Kill him, Thurman!" someone urged.

Thurman Black stood his ground. He pointed at my club. "You *hit* me with that," he said in quiet wonderment.

"And I'll hit you again, you bully!" I was crying now, heaven help me.

"You're all right, kid. You're about half my size, but you hit me. That took courage!"

461

I stared at him, hefting my club, completely confused.

"When you get some size on you, you'll be a real jim-dandy fighter. You know that?" He turned to his pals. "Guys, this little mutt is tough." He turned back to me, grinning. "From now on you can be a striker, kid. What do you say?"

I was too surprised to respond. The reversal was too dramatic. Was it a trick? No, the other boys were grinning, too. They admired spunk above all else, and in my desperation I had shown some.

"What do you say, kid?" Thurman Black repeated. "How about being one of us, huh? Come on. We'll go up by the shelter house and scare some of those kids in your class."

"No," I said.

Black's eyes bulged. His mouth actually fell open. "Huh?"

"I'm not going to beat up other kids," I told him.

"You just *proved* yourself. Now you're on our side."

"No," I repeated, wondering if I were insane. "I'm not on your side."

"Then we've got to beat you up again!"

"I'm not on anybody's side, Thurman! If you think that means you've got to beat me up, well . . . come on." I readied the club, sure I would never get a chance to use it now that they were forewarned.

"Kid—"

He got no farther. Across the park at that instant came the sounds of shouting, followed by a series of booming reports.

Gunfire.

WE RAN, all of us, to see what was happening. Thurman was in the lead, with the other boys just behind. I stayed close as we encountered other children and a few adults rushing east through the park toward the train yards, the direction of the shots.

In the street near the depot and the yard gates, wispy smoke drifted into the hazy, sunny sky. Everyone was milling around, some bystanders not wanting to get any closer, while others pushed past them. I skirted the end of the line and got a clear view of the street. To my right was the corner of the yard fences, with the depot farther away. The nearest gate stood ajar, and in front of it were ranged half a dozen regular company guards and about fifteen business-suited Hobart-Grimes operatives. The hoboes had rifles and shotguns.

Ranged against them, to my left, was a ragged band of fifty or so railroaders. A few signs lay on the street, but I also saw lunch buckets, indicating active workers were part of the melee. One man was down on his knees, clutching a shoulder dark with blood. Another was being dragged to the rear, where more workers were running to join, or to observe. I saw several workers pick up rocks from the curb area and hurl them toward the guards.

The hoboes did not even dodge. A tall man in a derby hat, evidently their leader, said something sharply. The hoboes raised their guns and fired deafeningly into the air, discharging another cloud of gun smoke.

Our teachers were running around frantically. "Back to the shelter house, children! Back to the shelter house!" Some of the younger children began reluctantly to obey. Others held their ground, eyes wide at the spectacle. More and more adults were coming to witness the confrontation now. The sidewalk on the far side was jammed. Carriages and a few motorcars were parked in every direction at the far corner in a traffic jam like none Preacherville had ever seen.

Off in the distance came the clattering of a police bell. Responding to the sound, the workers began retreating up the street from the gate. The hoboes held their ground, watching the attack dissipate. I thought it was over as quickly as it had begun. Then, however, a police wagon careered around the far corner and plowed to a halt behind the workers, the four-horse team rearing and tearing at the harness. A dozen or more uniformed officers piled off the wagon and made for the workers, wading in with their clubs. The workers milled in confusion, retreating again—being driven back *toward* the waiting Hobart-Grimes men.

A second police wagon rounded the corner and was reined to a halt. More policemen piled off and joined the savage attack. I saw a worker clubbed and go down as if dead. Another was knocked sideways, where he lay sobbing on the pavement, his face a mass of blood. The workers were trying to fight, but they had nothing to

463

withstand the clubs. The police drove them back into the middle of the street, nearer and nearer the Hobart-Grimes position. I saw some of the hoboes stacking their rifles inside the fence. For a moment I thought they were going to let the police handle it. But then they came back out, each of them holding a length of two-by-four lumber with one end rounded to the shape of a handle. They moved up in front of their fellows with the remaining guns and waited, patting their clubs into their palms.

The workers were within ten yards of the gate now, in steady retreat. With each step another of their number was felled, and the remainder put in worse peril from attack both front and back. The path of their retreat up the street was littered with bodies.

One of the remaining workers had time to see the plight. Looking around desperately, he bellowed over the din, "*The park, boys! Run for it!*" Bowling over a lanky policeman, he broke through the line and ran raggedly toward where I stood. All of us scrambled out of his way. Three of his fellows also broke free, following him.

Several policemen saw the escape try. Yelling, they left the central fight and also ran my way, waving their clubs. They intercepted the workers right at the curb, not a dozen paces from where I stood. The first officer caught the lead worker with a shoulder tackle, driving both men to the ground. The next two workers tripped over them and also sprawled. Then the other police were on hand. The first worker tried to get up. His face was contorted with fear and desperation. "All right, boys!" he yelled. "I give up! I—" He got no farther. The nearest policeman stepped past his out-stretched hands and swung his club, the hard wood striking the man's skull with a sound like a hammer hitting a thick steak. The worker keeled over. The other workers were also knocked down, then clubbed a second and sometimes a third time.

"Stop it!" screamed a woman. "My God! *Stop it!*"

In the street beyond, a whoop announced that the hoboes had moved into the remaining few workers from the rear. Clubs swung. Red splattered. It was over in a few seconds, the last of the trapped workers going down. Suddenly it was silent around the square. A few wisps of smoke drifted through the trees. People lined the sidewalks, their faces white, their eyes fastened on the scene. Here and there a worker groaned, or moved slightly in his prone position on the cobblestones. The police and Hobart-Grimes operatives conferred. The clubs were at their sides now and they looked calm and businesslike.

Near me a woman was sobbing hysterically. I turned to look at her, and as I did so I came face to face with the nearest policeman. He looked quickly away, but the instant of full frontal view had been enough to send a shock through me. I knew him. He had a peculiar darkened area on his left cheek. I had noticed it on Saturday when Flanagan led me through the gate and past the group of waiting Hobart-Grimes men. He was dressed as a policeman, had come on a police wagon. He was not a policeman. He was Hobart-Grimes. And there, standing in the street, were all those other city officers—far more policemen than Preacherville had ever had on its force before this day.

Something hammered onto my back. I ducked frantically in terror. Mrs. Mead was beside me, her switch raised for another blow. Behind her, all the children were scurrying back toward the other area of the park. "I said move!" Mrs. Mead screamed at me.

As I hurried to join the safety of the throng, I tried to cope with the realization that had been forced upon me. The police and Hobart-Grimes had become one and the same. The H &O now was the law in Preacherville. I still had no clear idea how the confrontation had started, but I now knew it had been a carefully orchestrated slaughter.

THE EXCITEMENT ABOUT the fight at the gates was so intense that the picnic was canceled, and all of us marched back to school for regular classes. Any academic undertaking was virtually impossible, and the classroom all day was chaos that not even Mrs. Mead could control. I expected some aftermath to my scene with Thurman Black and the older boys just prior to the street attack, but even that event had been obliterated by talk about what some were already calling "the riot."

"I guess those strikers got what they had coming to them!" Mary Eleanor said as we walked home that afternoon.

"You'd better not say that too loud," I told her.

"I know," she said breezily. "But Daddy knows what's right, and we've both heard him say those men are just troublemakers!"

I didn't argue. Watching Mary Eleanor trip along the dusty road, swinging her picnic basket, I felt a million years older than she. Perhaps my knowledge had moved me nearer to being an adult. If so, being an adult was not a comfortable station.

Mother met us at the front gate, bending to hug Mary Eleanor and then scan my face with anxious eyes. I realized that she had heard about the trouble in town.

"Are you both all right?" she asked. "The school sent people around to tell all of us you had been taken back to the building. They asked us not to interfere with the normal day." She shuddered. "They think it can be a normal day, after children have witnessed a bloody riot?" She took a turn at hugging me; she smelled of apples and cloves.

"It was *awful*, Momma!" Mary Eleanor cried, deciding to shed a few tears. "There were men with guns and clubs, and those bad strikers fought with them, and I saw blood and everything!"

"Come in the house, both of you, and I'll give you some pie!"

As much as I would have liked a second slab of pie, I could not bring myself to join Mary Eleanor's grotesque exaggerations of what had taken place. At first it was a big fight with a few signs of blood; Mother gave her more pie; Mary Eleanor rewarded her by specifying just how much blood she had seen, going on to draw a battle scene worthy of Gettysburg. At this point I could take no more, and went to my room.

Vicious flew out of his carton the instant I lifted the lid that had been weighted with a rock on top. He hopped onto my shoulder, panting, and then flew to the windowsill with a great wing flapping. From outside came a replying clap of wings. The brown-and-white female had somehow located his prison and was waiting just beyond the glass.

"All right," I sighed, opening the window. "Just remember who your momma is when I blow the whistle." The brown-and-white female flew off. Vicious leaped into the air after her. They arced high, joyfully, and made a beeline for the roosting house.

Unwilling to face more of my mother's probing looks, I changed clothes quickly and exited via the window and the back porch. Climbing down the ladder I had made, I went over to Flanagan's. I pounded on the door, but there was no response. He must have gone to work early. Still pondering what I must do with my secret knowledge, I hiked down the slope to the pigeon house.

The female blue sat on a tree limb not far from the house. I could see into the apartment she and her mate had been frantically furnishing in recent days. The male was inside, sitting very still in the nest. I saw his eye roll to watch me, but he did not move. Earlier, either bird would have flown off as I approached.

My curiosity stirred by the male's new boldness, I hurried back to the house, got my ladder, and set it up against the tree that was the base for the pigeon house. I climbed carefully. As I poked my head over the level of the floor of the house, the male was finally startled enough to break into escape flight. Feeling a bit guilty, I peered into the apartment. In the bottom of the nest was a single pale egg, about the size of a mature radish. I reached inside and touched it. Its smooth surface was hot.

Climbing down, I took the ladder away. A second egg, I knew, would be laid by the blue female, probably early in the morning. And in less than three weeks there would be chicks. I was conscious both of my pleasure and excitement on the one hand, and of how part of this experience had been spoiled for me by the day's earlier events. The fight in the street signaled worse trouble ahead. When my father came home, I had to tell him about the Hobart-Grimes men mingling with the police. When he heard what I had seen, I thought, he would have no choice but to join whatever action dissident workers might plan.

AT THE SUPPER TABLE my father was greatly agitated. "No one knows how the list of dismissals got out early," he told my mother. "The notices were supposed to be posted at noon, but a hand-written copy was on the street more than two hours early."

"How could that happen?" my mother asked.

"It means a traitor in the office somewhere. Mr. Jones brought four Hobart-Grimes detectives in this afternoon, and I can tell you they asked hard questions!"

"You mean they questioned *you?* You've always been loyal!"

"Alma," my father said patiently, "in times of crisis you can't trust anyone."

"Are you still under suspicion?" My mother was pale.

"I've been cleared," my father said. "I was busy on records of the earlier strikers. Besides, I had someone with me at all times."

"And if you hadn't," Mother said indignantly, "what would they have done? Broken your thumbs?"

"Alma."

"I don't care! I think it's terrible when a man of your character has to be questioned! What is the H&O coming to?"

"What it's coming to," my father said, "is the settlement of who owns the railroad: the management or the workers. Those workers today were troublemakers. According to the evening paper, most of them had hidden weapons. If our guards and the police hadn't been heroic, we might have had far worse bloodshed."

"None of that is so," I blurted.

My father turned amazed eyes toward me. "Are you saying your father is a liar?"

"We saw it. Mary Eleanor and me. We were at the park and saw it, and it ain't the way you said at all."

"Isn't," my mother murmured.

"What part do you think you know more about than Mr. Jones or the newspaper?" my father shot back.

"All of it, if what you just said is any sample."

My father started to rise from his chair to whip me. My mother's hand stayed him. "Ned. They were there. Hear him out."

Dad sank back, still glaring. "The troublemakers stormed the gates. Our Hobart-Grimes held them off until the police could come," he said.

"No, sir," I said. "The hoboes shot over their heads, and maybe shot *at* and hit a couple of them. Then the workers started backing up. The police came up behind, and that way they had the workers stuck in between them, and the hoboes—"

"Hobart-Grimes," my father said curtly. "Don't call them—"

"Hobart-Grimes. Then the police started beating on them and driving them back to the Hobart-Grimes, and then the Hobart-

468

Grimes joined in, and it was a slaughter, Dad! And none of the workers had a gun or a knife or *anything*."

"Why did the paper say they did, then?"

"Maybe because the paper is on the H&O side. I don't know. And I'll tell you something else, Dad. Some of the police weren't police. They were hoboes wearing police uniforms. I recognized one of 'em!"

"Oh, my word," Mom whispered.

"I can't believe that," my father said. "You were mistaken."

"No! I wasn't!"

My father rubbed his palm over his eyes. "Well," he said.

Silence hissed in the room.

"Well," he repeated, "even if what you say is true, it doesn't change the basic facts."

"But hoboes dressed like cops?"

"What difference would it make? Both groups are on the side of law and order."

"Dad! Mr. Jones fired guys when he had no evidence, no—no *due process*. Then he sends the hoboes out there to beat guys to a pulp, dressed like police, and if that isn't a cheat, I don't know what is! And you say it's all right! Dad, I—"

"We'll hear no more of it," my father snapped.

"Ned—" Mother said tentatively.

"No! I've heard enough, Alma! This boy is getting too big for his britches." He swung back toward me, pointing a finger. "There will be no more disloyal talk under this roof, do you understand?"

I was stunned. "Yes, sir."

"*I* earn the food and shelter for this household. *I* have to hold on to the job. You may be growing up, Bobby, but you're still a child. Until you earn your own keep, you'll keep ideas like those to yourself."

I stared at him, near tears. His outburst was totally unexpected, more savage than anything my upbringing had prepared me to cope with. For the first time, perhaps, he was treating me as an equal, a man. But in the equality was rejection.

"Now go to your room," he added, softening his tone.

I fled. That night when I sounded the whistle, Vicious did not

469

come. I crept down the ladder and went out near the roosting house and located him in a tree nearby, a white blur in the starlight. I sounded the whistle and spoke to him. He did not move. I went back to my room alone.

Six

In the following days of grief and shock a deceptive calm fell over Preacherville. One of the men caught in the street fight died of his injuries, and it was said that the crowd attending his burial service was one of the largest ever assembled in the area.

According to the newspaper—which I thought might be accurate on this item—the H&O had finally dismissed fifty-three men. Criminal charges had been filed against seventeen. Only two of them had been able to post bond; the other fifteen were being held in the county jail. Rumor said there had been minor violence up the line, near Wayne. But it appeared that serious problems existed only in Preacherville.

"If the trouble is only here," I heard my mother ask my father one night, "doesn't that mean something is wrong with the management here?"

"No," my father replied quickly. "It's a matter of sheer bad luck. Obviously management trusts Mr. Jones to handle it."

"The Buswells and Abernathys have to move out, Ned. It's terrible."

"If they're innocent, they'll be cleared."

"In the meantime, what do they eat?"

"We'll not discuss it, Alma."

At school, my relationship with the older boys had changed. They seemed puzzled, and ignored me. "Look, kid," Thurman Black told me one day during noon recess, "the guys want to be friends with you. Why don't you join us after school? Towers hooked some cigarettes. We'll all go down in the river bottom and smoke."

"I can't," I told him. "I've got a lot of work to do at home."

Thurman looked baffled. "You're either with us or you're against us. Do you *want* to be enemies?"

"No! Just lemme alone, Thurman. Just let me be my own self without being on anybody's side. Please!"

"I don't understand you, kid," Black sighed, and walked away.

"DO YOU UNDERSTAND what I meant?" I asked Flanagan that afternoon. We were sitting on his front porch and he was whittling on a stick, the yellow shavings falling around his feet.

"Sure," he said. "You want to be your own man. It's not so hard to understand, lad. It's that it's so hard to live that kind of life."

"You live your own life, don't you?"

Flanagan stopped whittling for a minute and looked at me with an expression of regret that I could not understand. "Well, lad," he said finally, "some would say yes and some would say no."

"You've got a good job, on your own terms. You don't have to live your life the way other people tell you to. That's all I want, to be like you."

He glanced sharply at me, and for an instant there was a wetness in his eyes. "Ah, Lord love you," he said quietly. "You're still mighty young."

"Maybe I am," I retorted. "But I know what I believe."

"Do you, now?"

"Yes! I believe in telling the truth, and doing what's right, and being your own man."

"Just about everybody believes that, sonny."

"You think Mr. Jones does? I *know* Mr. Jones is a liar."

"Maybe he's afraid, lad. Did you ever think of that?"

"With all his hoboes and guards and police?"

"A man can have all the force in the world on his side, and still be afraid. Fear doesn't come from outside. It comes from in. Everybody is afraid."

"What have you ever been afraid of?"

"Afraid of dying. Afraid of being gone and dead, and nobody caring or even knowing I was ever here."

"*I'll* remember."

His smile was thin, sad. "One day you'll be gone, too."

I paused. "Sure, but it won't happen for years and years. So I just don't think about it."

471

"You can talk like that when you're young. When you get older it's different. People you knew are already gone, and you know it's going to come your turn. Moving around, changing jobs, losing friends—they're all little parts of dying, Bobby. Most folks don't die all at once. They die a little bit at a time—first the dreams and hopes, and then most of what they used to believe in."

I had never heard him talk like this before, or seen him so somber. I felt a little shiver of dread, and changed the subject.

WHEN I GOT back home, I found three of the neighbor women in the parlor with my mother. Two of them were crying. My mother shooed me off to my room. I obeyed, leaving the door open a crack to try to hear the conversation below. I could make out only brief bits and pieces.

"Have to go somewhere . . ." Mrs. Corbett said.

"Could possibly," my mother said, and then I lost some words and caught, "into temporary storage."

"Someone in the area . . ." That was Mrs. Buswell.

"I don't know who. . . . Such a risk . . ."

It went on and on. Unable to make out enough to understand, I gave up and practiced with my telegraph key. I was getting better all the time, working diligently to imitate Flanagan's swift, lilting rhythm. After about an hour of it, I went outside, via the roof and ladder, to visit the pigeons.

Vicious was walking around on the ground, but not gathering twigs today. His female was inside the nest, motionless. I strewed some feed on the ground, and Vicious walked up to me and began pecking. I knelt in the grass and reached out to him. He backed away nervously. "Dummy," I said softly, holding my hand still.

He walked back to peck at the grain, allowing me to steal my fingertips along his sleek, plump feathers. He had grown. Each day he seemed to fill out and become more handsome—white without blemish, the curve of his head and neck a regal line. I stroked him.

"I ought to grab you and take you in the house and keep you there," I told him. "That way you'd know who's boss. I raise you from a chick, then you stop coming when I whistle. What's the matter with you? Don't you know it's for your own good?"

472

Vicious tilted his head to look up at me. He understood me. Not the words, maybe, but the message. He would always trust me, I thought. But he had had to break away from me to live his own life. Possibly I was doing with my father what Vicious was doing with me. We both had to establish our independence, even if sometimes it hurt. Perhaps, in Vicious as in me, there would always be a child who wanted only to nestle close and feel the perfect security of having no doubts, no worry I wondered if Vicious ever wished it didn't have to happen, this growing up.

THAT EVENING, after we children had been sent off to bed, we had late visitors. Awake in my room over the kitchen, I heard the hushed voices. There were several people downstairs with my parents. They were all trying to keep us from hearing them, but the sounds carried well because there was a register in the floor, a hole with a grating over it to allow heat from the stove to circulate upstairs. Since it was summer, I had placed a piece of rug over the register to cut down light coming up at night.

Now, however, getting out of bed, I crept to the corner register and silently pulled the rug off. The register was too far off to one side to provide a full view, but I could see most of the table and the people around it. A lantern rested in the center of the table, bathing the room in yellow light. My father stood behind his chair at one end, my mother sat close by, along with Mrs. Buswell and Mrs. Abernathy, a thin, somewhat older woman. Their husbands, both railroaders who had just been laid off, stood near them. The atmosphere was tense as my father spoke. "I don't see how anything can be done." His face was grim.

"All we want is some kind of hope," Mrs. Buswell said. "We can find a room in town, or even go somewhere else. But we can't take our furniture and things with us. We have no money. What are we to do? Just leave everything out in a field to rot or be stolen?"

"We have to be out tomorrow," Abernathy said. "If we haven't vacated the company houses, the hoboes will throw everything into the road, and probably burn it."

"If we could just store everything somewhere," added Buswell, a dark, bearded man.

"If there was anything I could do . . ." my father said. "But I'm just a clerk down there. Even if I asked for leniency or some kind of extension, no one would listen."

"We understand that," Mrs. Buswell said. "But talking with Alma today, we thought of another way you could help us. You have a barn—"

"Oh, no," my father said quickly. "No. That couldn't be done."

"We have to be out tomorrow," Abernathy repeated intensely. "We could bring everything over yet tonight. It's dark. No one would see. We could hide it all inside your barn."

"Alma," my father said, "did you suggest this?"

"We . . . discussed it," my mother said, her hand at her throat.

"You know Mr. Jones would fire me on the spot if he found us doing it. The orders are explicit: no assistance to families that have been laid off."

"But these are our neighbors," my mother said, color appearing in her cheeks. "These are our friends."

My father stared at her, then slowly around at the others.

"No one would know," Buswell told him softly. "It could make all the difference for us. We wouldn't lose *everything*."

"We know it's some risk," Abernathy added, "but—"

"*Some* risk?" my father repeated. "Just my home, my family— my job!"

"We can't force you," Abernathy said. "We haven't asked you to join our cause. That has to be every man's own decision. All we ask is a chance—a place to store our things until we can get our jobs back or win a decision in the courts."

My father's agony was clear on his face. "I wish I could help you. . . ."

Buswell looked at his wife. "I told you it would never work."

Mrs. Buswell smiled, her eyes bright and wet. "Mrs. Keller, we'll never forget that you wanted to help." She stood, her chair scraping, and held out her hand to my father. "Don't think we blame you. Perhaps if the positions were reversed, we would have to make the same decision."

Abernathy faced my father. "I can't quite shake your hand yet. But I know you would help if you could."

474

My father turned to my mother, who had remained seated. "You're willing to risk everything we have here this way?"

She looked up at him with pale calm. "It was my idea, Ned."

My father rubbed his hand over his eyes; his shoulders slumped. "No one else must know," he told Abernathy. "No one."

Abernathy's face began to light up. "You'll—do it?"

"We'll have to move everything tonight. And I can't help anyone else. If word starts spreading—if *anyone* knows—I'm finished."

Everyone but my father was smiling broadly. My mother hugged him. Abernathy and Buswell took turns fervently shaking his hand. Lying there on the floor, my face welted from being pressed against the rough metal grating, I could scarcely believe it. He had done something against the company. He had done something on his own. He had confounded all my new, fragile conceptions about him. He was a hero again.

THE TWO COUPLES departed almost at once. Then I heard the back door slam. Going to my window, I was barely able to make out my father's dim figure as he went away from the house into the shadows and vanished with the faint squeaking of the barn door hinges. I watched and waited, but saw no light and heard nothing. He must have been in total darkness, moving things around to provide maximum room for the items that soon would be brought for secret storage. The walls leaked too badly to allow him a lantern as he worked.

In a little while—perhaps an hour—the night silence was broken by a slight creaking and jangling on the road out front. In the faint starlight I saw two small wagons, each drawn by a single mule, pulled through the yard and near the barn. I guessed it was Mr. Abernathy in one cart and Mr. Buswell in the other. Each wagon was piled with boxes, barrels, and items of furniture. The shadowy figure of my father appeared, and the three men quietly unloaded first one cart, then the other.

I grew sleepy watching them, but at the same time was filled with nervous apprehension. If rumor was true, motorcars filled with Hobart-Grimes operatives were touring county roads at all hours, gliding along in the night without lights, on the lookout for

475

supposed meetings of agitators. And if my father was correct, we could not be sure who among the workers were friends, and who enemies.

THE FOLLOWING MORNING my father headed for town early, as usual. When Mary Eleanor and I left for school, I cast a long and searching look at the barn. I could see faint wagon tracks in the yard, but I did not think anyone else would see them unless he looked closely. The barn itself appeared as always; its door was closed. I told myself everything would be all right.

After school, Flanagan was nowhere to be seen around his house. There was still no sign of trouble at our place. If anyone had seen the transfer of the household goods to the barn, I did not doubt that the H&O would already have taken some action.

Late in the afternoon I went down to the pigeon roost. I found the blue male on his nest, and Vicious's brown-and-white female on hers. Vicious, the blue female, and the other two pigeons sat in a nearby tree. For them, life was better than it had ever been before. They were lucky.

Turning my head, I caught sight of Flanagan coming slowly through the brush. I waited, glad to see him.

"Well, well," he panted, reaching my position. He leaned on his cane as he mopped sweat from his face. His big chest was heaving from the exertion of the walk. "Those birds are really doing their housekeeping now, aren't they, lad?"

"They sure are," I agreed. "I think Mrs. Vicious is fixing to lay her eggs anytime now. How come you're not at work, Flanagan?"

"Day off."

"Is there more trouble?"

He studied my face, as if deciding how to reply. "There's talk about a general meeting—all the workers—I suppose to decide on a strike."

"If they try that, the hoboes will kill them!"

"Oh, the Hobart-Grimes can't kill everyone, sonny."

"But all the workers won't attend, right? I mean, some will be afraid. If *everyone* was together, it might be all right. But some workers won't meet or even talk about it. And that gives Mr. Jones and his guys enough help to keep things running. So those who do meet will just get beat up or fired. Right?"

Flanagan sighed. "You might be right."

"The H&O," I told him bitterly, "doesn't care a hoot about people. Did you know the Abernathys and the Buswells moved today?"

He nodded solemnly. "It's a sad thing."

"Nobody should have a right to throw people out like that."

"It's business, Bobby. You don't understand all of it."

"Now you sound like my dad!"

"Don't be too hard on your father, boy."

"I'm not hard on him anymore." I hesitated, then knew it was all right to tell this good friend. "My dad is loyal. But he cares about people, too. Our barn up there is full of stuff right now!"

Flanagan slowly turned to stare up at the barn. "Stuff?"

"The Abernathys' and the Buswells' stuff. They didn't have any place to put it, so they asked, and Dad said it was all right."

Flanagan's eyes widened as he felt the impact of my words. He became grave. "It's in there now?"

"Sure! See? My dad isn't like Mr. Jones!"

"Lad," he said, grasping my shoulder, "you must tell no one about this. If your father was found out, it would be his job."

His grip hurt. I tried to pull away but was powerless. "Sure! Sure! I'm not telling a soul!"

Flanagan seemed to relax. "All right, then."

THAT NIGHT WE again had callers. The sound of their voices awakened me even though they were out in front. I hung out my window but could not make out all the words. There were at least four men out there in the dark with my father; they were trying to persuade him to come to a secret meeting the next night.

"We band together or we have no chance!" one man said.

My father's response was lengthy, hushed. The replies were angry. "Just remember, Keller! If you don't support us, you're one of the enemy!"

Then my father's steely retort was, "Don't threaten me, Black."

So Justin Black was in the group. I heard his reply. "There can't

477

be any neutrals! Join your own kind, or pay the consequences!"

One of the other men remonstrated then, lower, more calmly. The conversation became muted. It went on for a long time.

Finally they left. I opened my door and heard my father coming wearily up the stairs. At the top he paused. "Son? Is that you?"

"Yes, sir," I whispered. "Are you going to the meeting tomorrow night?"

"No. Now go to bed."

Disappointed, I obeyed. I could not understand this man! He had already risked everything to help his friends, so his refusal to attend a strike meeting could not be traced to cowardice. It seemed that in trying to walk a line between the factions, and maintain his private concept of loyalty to the company, he was in danger of becoming the target of hate for both sides. No one understood a neutral—not in adult life, not even at my school. My father was being pressed harder and harder against the wall. I did not think he could refrain from taking a position much longer.

THE CLOSING of school left me with time on my hands. The trouble in our area had eliminated any chance for a part-time summer job. Shopkeepers, their business down due to unemployment, were cutting back everywhere they could, and had no margin that might have allowed hiring a boy to carry sacks or sweep floors. There were grown men on every street corner looking for these jobs, if any had been available. I practiced daily on my telegraph key, did my chores, and watched my small flock of pigeons; Vicious and his mate, like the blue pair, were now taking turns sitting on a pair of small ivory eggs.

We might have been moving into a routine for the summer during that first week away from school, but on Thursday—a week and a half after we had hidden the belongings of the Abernathys and the Buswells in our barn—the worst happened.

It was a warm, hazy morning, about ten o'clock. Mother was washing dishes and I was scrubbing the floor. Mary Eleanor and Rachel were out in the back, playing in a sandbox Flanagan had built for them. We all heard the sound of automobiles coming along the road, and then brakes squealing.

"Momma, some people are here!" Mary Eleanor called.

My mother was already drying her hands and on the way to the front of the house. "You and Rachel stay there, Mary Eleanor."

No one had said anything to me, so I got up and went to the parlor. From there I had a good view out to the porch and yard, and I could also see my mother inside the door.

There were four automobiles parked on the road. More than a dozen men, most of them in suits despite the heat, had come into the yard. Two of them, a tall thin man and a tall, bulky companion, walked up onto the porch.

"Yes?" my mother said, looking out at them through the screen.

The bulky man removed his straw hat. "Mrs. Keller? My name is Beggs. We'll be having a look into your barn over there."

"You will not!" my mother flashed. "That's private property!"

Beggs's face furrowed. "This is H&O land and H&O buildings."

"Now you see here. My husband works directly for Mr. Jones, and when he hears of this, you'll probably all lose your jobs!"

It was a fine act and I was proud of her. Beggs, however, showed no effect. "Yes, ma'am. Now, I advise you and the children to remain indoors, out of harm's way." He turned and waved his arm. The men in the yard started toward the barn.

"You're going to regret it!" my mother said shrilly.

Beggs took a cheroot from his coat pocket, struck a match on the doorframe, and puffed smoke. "Just stay inside, Mrs. Keller."

My mother was worked up. She shoved the screen door outward to go onto the porch. "Now you see here!"

Beggs moved a few inches, his big hand catching the door and slamming it back into my mother's face. "*Inside,*" he repeated, his voice sharper. Then he turned and walked off the porch, puffing smoke.

"Oh, my God," my mother murmured, walking back and forth in the hall. "Oh, what are we going to do?"

There was nothing to do. She went to the far windows to look out toward the barn. I joined her, and then Mary Eleanor and Rachel came in looking scared and stood with her, too. We watched two of the men open the barn doors and step inside. One of them peered out, nodding, and called to Beggs, who went in to join them.

When he came out, it was to motion toward the other clustered men. Some of them, doffing their coats, went into the barn. When the first one came back out, he was carrying a small table and lamp. Beggs pointed. The man carried the table and lamp into our side yard and tossed them onto the ground. His fellows began making trips into and out of the barn, carrying out the possessions of the Abernathys and Buswells: beds, boxes, chairs, everything. The men tossed it all together carelessly into a small mound in the side yard. Even Mary Eleanor and Rachel did not speak. Even they knew, I think, what was coming.

Finally the last box was carried out and dumped on the pile. Beggs went to one of the cars and came back with two fat red cans. Handing one to a helper, he began splashing the clear liquid onto the mound. His helper went around on the other side and started doing the same.

"No," my mother pleaded hoarsely. "Not that." She ran to the front door. Trying to swing it open, she was blocked by a beefy detective standing on the other side.

"Let me out! You can't just destroy those things!"

"Stay inside, ma'am."

Somehow she managed to get the screen partly opened and almost slipped through. The man grabbed her arm and shoved her back. She sprawled on the floor, sobbing. I think I went a little berserk. I seized the umbrella and ran at the big man. Laughing, he pushed me back inside the house. "You big bully!" I screamed.

A huffing roar from the side yard drew the attention of all of us. Beggs had tossed a match onto the gasoline-soaked pile of household goods, and a sheet of flame gushed up thirty feet high, making a dense black plume across the sky. I knelt beside my mother on the floor and clung to her shoulders as she wailed.

IT DID NOT TAKE long for the flames to change the pile of household possessions into an ugly smoking pile of black rubbish. The men stood around the blaze with burlap bags they had wet at our well. Whenever a tendril of flame tried to creep across the grass, they quickly beat it out. Finally the flames vanished, and only white smoke and a few glowing mounds of ashes remained. The men

480

carried buckets from the well in relays and soaked everything down—I suppose to make sure no H&O property could possibly be damaged by stray sparks. Then they went back to their cars and drove away. My mother, her face tear-streaked, walked outside to stare at the wreckage. We followed, knowing enough to stay on the porch and let her near the charred black heap alone. Rachel and Mary Eleanor stared with big round eyes.

Standing there, I looked over at Flanagan's house. It was too early for him to be at work; indeed, this was the time he ordinarily limped over across his property and down to the pigeon house. Today, however, his small house appeared deserted. Where was he? Had something happened to him? I wondered. I ran down to the rear of his house. "Flanagan!" I called.

There was no answer. But the back door stood open, and I caught the aroma of the rich coffee he always boiled in the morning. I walked onto the porch and peered into the dim kitchen. "Flanagan?"

Coming from the bright sunshine and trying to see into the shaded interior, I would never have spotted him if he had not given himself away with a slight movement. He was sitting at his small table, an empty cup clutched between his hands. I could not make out his features. "Flanagan?"

He turned toward me. "Go away." His voice was blurred, as it had been that other time when he had been drinking.

Something—concern for him—compelled me to step inside. "Flanagan, it wasn't your fault. Nobody expected *you* to stop 'em."

"Get out, boy," he ordered. "Don't you understand yet?"

I could see his face now. The mouth was drawn downward by bitterness. His eyes were liquid darkness, expressing a sickness like none I had ever seen. I could smell the liquor.

"Understand?" I echoed. "Understand what?" Our eyes met.

Then I knew—I did understand, the import of my sudden knowledge racing like sludge ice through my system. "Oh, you—oh, no!" I groaned.

He reached down beside his chair, brought up a half-empty bottle, and poured the fluid into his cup.

I might have cried out. I know that I struck my face against the screen in my rush to escape. I know that my mother was back inside our house when I ran through the kitchen on the way to my room. She rushed upstairs after me. By the time she was at my door, however, I was on the way back out, bumping into her as I went past. "Bobby!" she called as I plunged down the steps again. "Where are you going with that? Bobby!"

I ran back through the kitchen and into the yard. I threw the gleaming telegraph key into the dirt, wires flying. I picked up a rock. Kneeling, crying, I began smashing at the key with it. Parts flew off. The bright nickel plate shattered. The vibrating rod was crushed, springs flew, parts disintegrated. Hysterically I pounded.

"Bobby!" my mother cried, throwing herself down beside me. "Stop it! What are you doing? What's happened to you?"

"*He* did it!" I sobbed, hammering again at the key. "Flanagan did it! I thought he was our friend and I told him, and he told them about the stuff in the barn. He's one of them, Mom! He's a hobo!"

AFTER A WHILE she was able to calm me. I was taken to my bed and told to lie still. I closed my eyes. I felt feverish. My grief and sense of betrayal were overwhelming. The one person I had trusted was a traitor. And my stupidity had cost us everything.

My mother cautiously opened my door and peeked in. "Awake?" I opened my eyes. "Yessum."

She came in with a plate of sugar cookies and a glass of milk. "Mary Eleanor and Rachel are having lunch. I thought you might like something." She sat on the edge of the bed and put down the plate. "I'm so sorry, Bobby. I wish it hadn't happened to you."

"The Buswells' stuff is gone, burned up. The Abernathys', too. And now Dad is probably getting fired. And it's all my fault!"

"You think Mr. Flanagan is a Hobart-Grimes?"

"I know it. I went over there and he was drinking and I told him it was all right he didn't try to help us and he said, 'Don't you understand yet, boy?' and the way he looked. He *is* one, Mom! Has been all this time!"

She touched her fingertips to my hair. "It will be all right, Bobby."

"No. It ain't ever going to be all right."

"Isn't. But it will be. You'll see."

AN HOUR LATER my father came home. That he appeared so early in the day was evidence enough. And one look at his face confirmed it.

He walked through the gate, up to the front porch, and through the door into the front hallway. There my mother met him, with me standing back in the door to the kitchen, watching. His lunch pail was in his hand. He was very pale. His eyes had a dazed, puzzled look, as if he were not quite focusing on her. "I see they came," he said.

"They . . . burned everything."

"But you're all right? And the children?"

"We're fine."

His chest heaved. "I've been . . . discharged."

My mother's hand went to her throat. She did not speak, did not move.

He looked up from the floor into her eyes and I saw his havoc. "I'll get no pay that's due me. We'll have until the weekend to pay the store . . . be out of the house." His bitterness surfaced in a terrible smile. "Mr. Jones said he was taking my past loyalty into consideration, giving me so much time to settle our accounts."

"What did you do?" my mother asked.

"What could I do?" he shot back. "Beg? Try to convince him I wasn't betraying the company by helping our friends?" He raised his stump and shook it under her nose. "Hit him? With this?"

"Ned!" She seized the arm in both her hands and held it against her breast. "Ned! Don't take it that way! We'll manage!"

He looked past her suddenly and his wildly angry eyes found me. "I guess you were right, son. You *said* he was a bad man."

"Oh, Ned," my mother whispered. "Spare the children—"

"How can we spare them? Didn't they see the Hobart-Grimes people come and burn those things from the barn? How do we hide any of it from them: the fact that I've lost my job, that we're in debt, that we have to move again, like paupers?"

"We can . . . have our dignity."

"Dignity?" His voice dripped sarcasm. "When we don't have a dime, and owe the company for our food? When we might not even be able to move these few things we have left out of this damned H&O house?"

483

I said desperately, "We'll figure something out, Dad! We can find us a cart and haul our stuff, and I can get a job—"

"It's not the H&O," he cut in.

"What?" I said, confused by his change of pace.

"It's Jones. It's the way he's running the division here. Remember that, Bobby. If Mr. Harris—if some of the men at the top knew what was going on, things would be different. It isn't the H&O."

"Somebody ought to tell Mr. Harris, then!" I said.

"Of course. I'll hitchhike right to New York and walk into the boardroom. I'll show them this"—he held up his stump—"and I'll say, 'Gentlemen, this is the hand I gave for the H&O. Being a cripple makes me an authority on how to run your railroad!'"

"Ned!" my mother cried. "Stop it!"

He stared at her for an instant and then tears sprang to his eyes. "I tried, Alma. I tried."

My mother took him into her arms. They clung together and his shoulders quaked. I had never heard a sound like the broken sobs that seemed to be wrenched out of his depths.

It was more than I could endure. I turned and fled upstairs to my room. I would have moved the world for them. But there was nothing within my power . . . *nothing*. I knelt by my bed and pounded it with my fists.

Seven

Our neighbors seemed to know about my father's dismissal almost as soon as we did. He had not been home an hour when other workers came to the house to talk with him. Then some of the area women appeared, in twos or threes. Some brought covered dishes, as if for a wake. I was amazed to see my father sitting on the steps of the back porch with the men, talking quietly, almost as if nothing had happened. The initial emotional outburst was already a thing of the past. In some way I could not understand, adults got themselves back under control very quickly. I was too young to understand that the calm exterior was the thinnest façade over emotions rubbed raw by anguish and uncertainty.

I worried about Hobart-Grimes operatives touring the road and seeing my father with the other men. Perhaps that was why our visitors stayed at the back of the house. Or perhaps there was no real problem, since everyone had already felt the weight of H&O wrath. At least there was no worry about Flanagan. I had seen him limp away toward town shortly after my father's arrival. I would get Flanagan, I thought. Crazy schemes ran through my brain.

"What will we do?" Mary Eleanor asked, sitting cross-legged with Rachel on my bed.

"Go someplace else, I guess," I told her, determined to put the best face possible on things.

Mary Eleanor bounced up and down nervously, bouncing Rachel with her. "But what about school?"

"We'll go to a different school, Mary Eleanor, wherever we are."

Rachel piped up, "Can I take my doll?"

"Sure," I told her.

"And Napoleon and her babies?"

"Sure," I lied.

"And Billy?"

"Heck, yes, we'll even take ole Billy."

"How about the pigeons?" Mary Eleanor added.

I could have slapped her. "I'll figure out something."

"You can't take the pigeons! They're going to have babies and they'll want to stay here!"

"I'll fix up a net and catch them and put them in a box with wire on it, and when we get to our new place I'll keep them locked up for a long time and then I'll let them out and they'll be homed."

"And then we'll move again. We're always going to move again."

"No, we're not, Mary Eleanor, and you stop talking that way! Mom and Dad will take care of everything."

"Not the pigeons," Mary Eleanor put in.

"Will you be quiet about my pigeons?" I snapped.

She leaped off the bed. "I can tell where *I'm* not wanted!"

I let her flounce out, dragging a bewildered Rachel with her. Alone in the room, I worried about what she had said. Mary Eleanor might be right. This impending move might mean losing Vicious and his friends.

486

As darkness settled in, our visitors left and the house fell quiet. I went downstairs and found my mother in the kitchen preparing mush. My father was at the table, going over some sort of printed handbill. I could only make out the larger heading: BAND TOGETHER, it read. Both of them were very calm and controlled.

When we had almost finished eating supper, my father squared his shoulders, a sign he was about to deliver himself of something important.

"We all know," he said slowly, "that we face some problems right now. I'm going to be changing jobs. We'll be moving again. Now I don't want you worrying about this because everything is going to work out. I'm going to be checking into some things the next day or two and as soon as I have some information I'll share it with you kids. In the meantime just be good. Don't create any extra problems for your mother. We're going to be fine. Your mother and I are going to take good care of you. That's what moms and dads are for, right?" He winked at Rachel, and she giggled.

Late that same night I thought about Rachel and realized how lucky she was. She was not old enough to understand that this was a time to be really scared.

THE MORNING was almost like a normal day. My father had gone to town early. Billy got away, and I had to track him half a mile up the road, where some neighbors named Armbruster had caught him. My mother made a batch of cookies.

A little before noon I went down to the pigeon house. I found Vicious ensconced in his apartment and his brown-and-white female walking around on the ground. My pigeon-food can was nearly empty. I put a handful of the grain on the ground, and the female pecked at it. Vicious did not stir. The evidence was clear enough. Vicious and his mate now had eggs to attend to. Guided by a wisdom I could not fathom, they had fallen into the universal pattern that put the male on the eggs from midmorning to late afternoon. It would make it harder to trap them together if I were to take them with me when we moved.

A sound nearby caught my attention. Turning, I saw Flanagan hobbling down through his lot, evidently heading in my general

487

direction. He saw me glance his way, and waved as he hurried faster. It infuriated me. After betraying us, he wanted to make up? I started for the house.

"Lad!" he called.

I ignored him, ran to the house, went up to my room. Something compelled me to do something normal, to ignore his unbelievable attempt to act as if yesterday had never occurred. I picked up a book and tried to read it. My heart was pounding fast.

Moments later he rapped on our back door. I heard my mother's voice, then Flanagan's. I strained to hear.

They conversed for a moment. Then there was silence. Then my mother called up the stairs, "Bobby?"

I stayed where I was, hoping she would give up.

"Bobby?"

No use. I went to the door and opened it. "Yes, Mom?"

"Mr. Flanagan is here to see you."

"No."

"Bobby." There was no arguing with that quiet tone of voice.

In the kitchen, Flanagan stood near the back door, leaning on his cane, clutching his cap. Sweat beaded his forehead. He did not look well. My mother sat at the kitchen table and motioned toward another chair. He shook his head. I held my ground near the hall entry, trying to decide where to look.

"Hello, lad," he said softly.

"Hello."

"I was coming to talk to you at the pigeon place. You run off."

I looked directly at him. The conflict between anger and thwarted love made me incapable of anything but sullen silence. I hated the man. I wanted him dead. But I did not want to see him hurting this way. What *did* I want?

Looking from me to my mother, Flanagan tried solemnly again. "I can't be blaming the boy, Mrs. Keller. I'm sure he has told you."

"You're Hobart-Grimes," my mother said tonelessly.

"It was why I couldn't aid you when they came here yesterday. But I had nothing to do with what happened. My assignment has been to work in the telegraph office and watch out for attempts to hurt communications. Nothing more."

"If that's true," my mother said, "why did you have to keep it such a secret that you're Hobart-Grimes?"

"Would any of us have been friends if I had told you? Do you imagine I would even have been *safe* if the word was out?"

"Then why tell us now?" I shot at him.

"Because you think I told about that stuff in the barn."

"*Didn't* you?"

"No! I swear it, lad!"

"I told you about it," I said, "and then your pals came. You're a hobo and they're hoboes and you're all alike!"

"When I saw them coming," he said hoarsely, "I knew what they were coming for. There was nothing I could do. That's why when you came over you found me drinking."

"Yeah," I said. "That helps a lot, getting drunk!"

His chest heaved. "Were you thinking I—or any man—was perfect?"

"I thought you were my friend!"

"It was not me that told the company!"

"Mom, can I please go back to my room? Please?"

"Mrs. Keller," Flanagan put in quickly, "do *you* believe I betrayed you?"

"Mr. Flanagan, I don't know what I believe. I don't know that it makes a whit of difference. The result is the same . . . for us."

"You'll be leaving?"

"I expect so."

Flanagan reached into his pocket and removed a well-worn brown leather purse. "It would be a kindness if you would allow me to help—"

"No. No, that's quite out of the question!"

He stared imploringly at her. "I have no family, Mrs. Keller. Your son has been a source of great joy to me. If we could consider it a loan . . ."

"You would have to discuss that with my husband, Mr. Flanagan, but I feel sure he will decline. He's a very proud man."

"Yes," Flanagan sighed. "You are that, all of you."

"Ain't you afraid your hoboes would find out and fire *you*?" I asked.

His lips curved in a bitter smile. "My risk, Bobby."

"I broke your key," I told him. "I took it out and smashed it to smithereens with a rock. So what do you think of that?"

He studied me with those tormented eyes. "Lord bless you, it was yours. I gave it to you for keeps. If you wanted to break it, that was your right."

I stared straight back at him, but my insides were quaking. If I cried now, I would kill myself. I gnawed my lip.

Flanagan looked back to my mother. "I would be obliged if you would tell the mister about our conversation. I must go over to the yards, but he and I could talk about it in the morning."

"Thank you, Mr. Flanagan," my mother said.

He stood another few seconds, shifting his weight from one side to the other. My mother said nothing. I stood frozen. There was an insane impulse in me to run to him, hug him, tell him *he* didn't have to be hurting inside, too. But I did not move, and in another moment he was gone.

BY MID-AFTERNOON I had begun to worry about where my father was. I saw my mother look repeatedly from the kitchen window, scanning the road, and knew he was in her mind as well.

It was past four o'clock when I saw the bicyclist coming up our road. A few bikes went by from time to time, but this rider was not very good at what he was doing, veering from side to side in frantic attempts to maintain his balance, and pumping dangerously fast, considering his skill. As he drew nearer, I watched him with interest, and was surprised to recognize Thurman Black.

He drove crazily along the rutted dirt road, almost falling as he cut across depressions heading toward our gate. By the time I ran from the back of the house to the front porch, he had dismounted, letting the bike crash against the fence as he vaulted the gate and ran toward me. The sound of his breathing was like air escaping a tire. His shirt was soaked with sweat, and his face was bright red.

"Where's your mom?" he gasped, grabbing me by the arms.

"Inside," I told him. "What—"

"Mrs. Keller!" he yelled. "*Mrs. Keller!*"

My mother appeared in the doorway. "What—" She saw

490

Thurman's face and staggered as if she might fall. "Oh, God . . ."

"There was a meeting," Thurman panted. "My dad was there. Mr. Keller, a lot of guys. The hoboes came, and the police, and arrested them."

"*Ned?*" my mother cried unbelievingly. "*Arrested?*"

"They're in jail right now and they're going to be taken into court and my old lady sent me to tell you. I don't know what's going to happen. You better come quick!"

AFTER A MOMENT'S dazed silence, my mother turned from Thurman Black to me. "Bobby, I'll go to town. You stay here with the girls."

"I want to go!" I protested.

"Bobby, your father is in trouble. My responsibility is to find out what the situation is. Yours is to stay here and care for your sisters." Her calm was preternatural. I sensed what a burden she was under. Swallowing my disappointment, I nodded. "They're upstairs. I'll go tell 'em—"

"I'll tell them," she said quietly. "Wait here." She turned to Thurman Black. "Can you go with me back to town? Show me where . . . ."

"Yes, ma'am," Thurman said.

"Good," she said, and headed for the stairs.

"I got to hand it to your old man, kid," Thurman said softly. "I was outside. The hoboes busted in from the back before anybody could do anything and then the police rushed up in front. When they brought the guys out, some of them was crying, some was screaming and yelling bloody murder. But your old man and my old man was side by side, walking with their heads up, looking looks that would kill a man."

"Your dad thought mine was a coward," I said bitterly.

Thurman nodded. "Maybe before. But everybody knows how your old man tried to hide that stuff for them families. He got fired for it, and now he's in jail. So we're on the same side now."

"He's the same man he was, Thurman. Only before, some guys was acting like he had leprosy or something."

Thurman Black frowned. It was clear he had no idea what point

491

I was trying to make. I gave it up. "What was their meeting about?"

"I dunno exactly. I heard my old man talking before about calling for a general layoff day, and sending men to Philadelphia or New York, wherever the big shot, Harris, is, to talk to him."

"How could they be arrested for that?" I asked.

"Don't ask me, bud. I guess what Mr. Jones wants, he gets. All I know is, when my old man walked by he said, 'Go tell your momma.' And your old man said, 'Will you tell my wife, too?' So I did."

I turned as my mother came back downstairs, a shawl over her arm. Pink splotches on her cheeks emphasized her pallor. "Now, Bobby," she said, "I've told the girls I have to go to town to meet your father to make some arrangements. That's all I told them. Do you understand?"

"Yessum," I said.

"I'll be back as soon as I find out what we have to do. You keep the girls calm and give them their supper. There's some bread and milk, and you can reheat the beans. And don't eat all the cookies. I don't want anyone making himself sick."

It struck me as odd that she could concentrate on things like the cookie ration at such a time, but mothers were like that. I nodded, understanding.

"Yessum."

She turned to Thurman Black. "I'm ready."

Mary Eleanor and Rachel had stolen downstairs, so there was nothing more I could say. Mother and Thurman went up the road together. He left his bike by our porch. I watched them go, then turned to my sisters with a big, phony smile. "Want to play something?"

"Daddy is in trouble, isn't he?" Rachel said.

"Naw! That's silly!"

Mary Eleanor added, "Now we don't have a job and no house and no daddy, and we'll all *die*."

"Go play dolls or something," I sneered. "You're talking like babies."

It was just the thing to say. Perhaps they figured I couldn't be

492

my usual nasty self if there was trouble. Brightening, they skipped back upstairs. In a few minutes I heard them playing house; Mary Eleanor was Mother, Rachel was Dad, and the doll was me. I was being punished.

As darkness came on, I got a small fire going in the cookstove. The lantern on the table helped dispel the gloom. Mary Eleanor and Rachel came down and played quietly on the kitchen floor. I made it a point to whistle like nothing was wrong, but the world was vast beyond the kitchen windows, and it was as if we were the only inhabitants of the planet.

I fed my sisters and ate some myself, allowing myself four extra cookies. Full night came on. I made Mary Eleanor help with the dishes, and we got the kitchen all clean again. Mentally I had reviewed Mother's supposed progress a number of times. By now she's in town, I told myself while we ate. She's at the courthouse right now. While we did the dishes I told myself, They've had the court by now, surely, and it's all right, and she's walking out of the courthouse with Dad.

Much later I read to Mary Eleanor and Rachel in their bedroom. When they finally fell asleep, I crept out, taking the candle with me, and went back downstairs alone. The house creaked spookily, and I avoided looking at the windows for fear I would see someone looking back at me.

Time passed. I went to the front door and peered through the screen. A warm wind stirred the trees and bushes, and a crescent moon looked down through ghostly-looking clouds. The road was empty.

I mentally retraced the entire trip with my mother, allowing for delays in court, conversations after the hearing, stopping somewhere to have a meal at someone's house. It had to be near midnight. My eyes felt sticky, and once as the wind made a sound in the attic I jumped in the chair and I realized I had almost fallen asleep. I roused myself and slunk through the creepy house and had six more cookies. Somehow I felt I could not be killed if I was awake.

What seemed a long time later, I heard faint voices outside. I ran to the door. Two figures—no, three!—were coming up the

493

road. Heart pounding, I got the lantern from the kitchen and carried it to the door. The figures came up onto the porch: my mother, her expression one of crushing fatigue; Thurman Black, also pale and tired; and a woman I had never seen before.

"Where's Dad?" I asked as they came in.

My mother led the way to the kitchen, put a bit of wood into the stove, and poured water from the bucket for coffee. She walked over and joined Thurman and the woman at the table. I waited.

"Your father," she said grimly, "is still in jail. They had a court hearing. Each man was placed on bail of two hundred dollars pending a preliminary hearing tomorrow afternoon."

"Two hundred dollars!" It might as well have been a billion.

My mother seemed to remember her companions at the table. "Mrs. Black, this is my son, Bobby." Mrs. Black gave me a wan smile. "Mrs. Black is staying here with us tonight," my mother said. "You can sleep on the couch, Bobby."

"Thurman," Mrs. Black added, "is going to my sister's house to make sure they know what's happened. You can sleep there, Thurman." Thurman nodded, chewing on a cookie.

"What happened in court?" I demanded.

"They were charged with loitering, disturbing the peace, and conspiring to riot."

"Are they crazy? Would Dad plan a riot?"

"If Jones has his way," Mrs. Black added, "every man who was at that meeting will serve jail time, as an example."

"As a warning," my mother corrected, getting up to put coffee into the pot. There was little left in the can, and she emptied it.

"Have they hurt him?" I asked. "If they're treating him bad, I'll—"

"He's fine. They allowed us to talk for a few minutes. He said something will be worked out. He said when Mr. Harris learns what's happened, the decision by Mr. Jones to prosecute will be reversed."

"Your husband is a fine and gentle man," Mrs. Black said. "I think he really believes that, bless him. But even if Mr. Harris *is* a decent man, how will he ever hear what's really been happening around here?"

494

My mother's eyes widened. "Why, he'll just . . . *hear*."

"How?" Mrs. Black asked with a sad smile. "When he comes to Preacherville, it's on that fancy car. He gets off the train and hobnobs with . . . who? With Jones. Things like the so-called street riot—and this arrest today—don't go in formal reports. Jones certainly will never tell anyone higher up. The newspaper prints what Jones says is proper. Mr. Harris and all the other higher-ups never talk to anyone like us."

"But this is so unjust!" my mother cried.

"Of course it is," Mrs. Black said.

"What are we going to do?" I asked.

"We stopped and found a lawyer. He'll meet us at the court tomorrow and represent the men who were arrested."

"And then what?" I asked angrily. "The judge will believe what the railroad tells him. Then he'll send Dad and everybody else to jail."

"I have more faith in the justice system than that," my mother said. But I caught the haunted look in her eyes and knew she was as frightened as I was. She poured coffee, and we sat around the table, talking about what had been said in court . . . what would happen tomorrow.

While part of me listened to the conversation, another part was thinking of what had been said about Mr. Nathaniel Harris and the higher-ups. I thought back to the two brief times I had met Harris. What was it he had said to me the second time? "You just contact me!" Of course it had been a joke, to make his friends chuckle.

But what had Mrs. Black just said about Mr. Harris never really being given the straight story? It was then that I had the first glimpse of my incredible idea.

I examined it. My pulse began to race. The idea was insane. But as I thought about it, my imagination began painting in details.

Thurman Black brought me back to reality by shoving his chair away from the table. I noticed the cookie plate had been emptied. "Well," he said with a soft belch, "I better get to Aunt Tella's." He nodded to me. "See ya in the morning, kid."

"Listen," I heard myself say, calm as anything. "Since I have to sleep on the couch anyway, why don't I just go with you?"

495

Thurman looked blank.

"Tella has lots of room," Mrs. Black said.

"I really would like it better if you stayed here," my mother said.

"Let me go, Mom. I'll be back bright and early. Right, Thurman?"

"Sure!" He grinned. The idea of company seemed to cheer him up.

"Well," my mother sighed. "If you really want to. But be careful, and get back early. If anything were to happen to you . . ." She frowned and left the rest unsaid.

"Come on, Thurman," I said.

Out on the dewy lawn, Thurman reached for a cigarette. "Might as well walk. Kill ourselves trying to ride that bike double in the dark."

"No," I said. "We'd better take it. It's a long ways to town."

"Town?" He stopped to stare at me.

"Listen," I said, and told him in a rush of words what I had in mind.

"You're nutty," he said when I finished.

"It's our only chance, Thurman."

Thurman Black thought about it, his face somehow more mature under the moonlight. "Wow. Could you *do* that?"

"Sure," I told him. "You do your part, I'll sure do mine."

"You're nutty!" he repeated.

"You rather go to court tomorrow and watch that judge send our dads to jail?"

Thurman struck a match and lit his cigarette, the light flaring into narrowed eyes. I waited. It was up to him now.

He dropped the cigarette to his side, turned, and pulled up the bicycle. "You think you can ride the handlebars?"

"I can if you can pump me," I said.

"Let's get started and find out."

THE USUAL SMOKE and haze hung over downtown Preacherville, blanking out the moon and stars and making a halo effect around every streetlight. We left the bicycle near the edge of the park and crept behind low bushes to survey the side of the yards now facing us. To our right was the gate area with its guard shack. Ahead was the brick wall of the depot. Beyond its roof, spotlights inside the yards shone with an eerie yellowish effect on clouds of steam and smoke billowing up from the roundhouse and tracks. The street was empty. We could make out the figures of two or three guards inside the shack.

"Are you sure you can do it?" Thurman asked, his eyes on the high wire fence with its topping of tangled barbed wire.

"I can do that part," I said. My heart was hammering.

"Do you want to think about it some more?"

"No." I took a shallow, ragged breath. "Let's get it over with."

Thurman Black stood and hitched up his trousers. He turned to me and grinned, the old reckless look lighting his expression. "I'm ready, buddy."

I also stood, on legs that felt weak. Leaving him there, I strode out into the street, in full view, and started toward the guard shack. I tried to whistle, but my mouth was too dry. I walked boldly, swinging my arms. As I neared the shack, a figure inside moved in the lantern light. I heard a wood-framed window slide. Ignoring this, I walked on up to the gate. "Hey, inside!" I called cheerfully.

"What do you want, kid?" a voice came from the shack.

"I need to see old Mr. Flanagan. In the telegraph shack."

"What for?"

I held up the wadded rag in my hand. "He forgot his lunch!"

"Leave it. Bring it over here."

"No! I want to see him a minute!"

"Leave it or take it, but get going, kid. That's an order."

"Aw," I growled, "Flanagan is going to be really mad!"

"Git!"

I turned as if disgusted and started walking away from the shack, down the line of the eight-foot fence. My pulse was racing. My legs were water. The two-inch diagonals of fence wire beside me seemed blurry. What if I wasn't strong enough?

Behind me, there was a sharp cry in the street. Thurman ran out of hiding and stood in the middle of the cobblestones. He had several rocks cradled in his arms. He reared back and hurled one toward the guard shack. "Scabs!" he screamed. "We'll get you!"

To my amazement, glass tinkled loudly and I heard the guards cursing as they rushed from the shack. His first rock had hit a window.

"Get him!" one of the guards called, running toward the street.

"Kill!" Thurman yelled, chucking another rock. "Murder! Riot! Come on, men! Now we've got 'em!"

One of the guards near the shack yelped as a rock hit home. With a shout, he, too, started after Thurman Black. Thurman threw another rock, then turned and raced for the park. Another guard shouted and tried to cut across the pavement to head him off. Two more guards appeared at the gate and joined the pursuit.

There was no more time to watch Thurman's diversionary tactics. It was now or not at all. Turning to the fence in the half-light, I linked my fingers in the wire strands and jumped as high as I could. My shoe tips hitting the wire made a fearful clatter, but I grabbed another handhold and scrambled upward. I went at a frantic pace, certain that a guard's shout—or a bullet—would find me at any instant.

I got one arm over the top rail and snagged my shoulder on the barbed wire at the top. At the same instant, two echoing booms racketed in the park. They must be shooting at Thurman! I skinnied under the wire and threw myself sideways over the top rail, feeling hot pain where the wire had torn my shoulder. Losing my grip, I plunged downward. I hit on my feet with stunning impact and rolled over backward.

Sitting up, I thought I had been blinded. I had plunged into the darkness between the fence and a wood storage building, in a very narrow area. Getting to my feet, I felt sharp pain in both knees, but my fear drove me into movement along the side of the building. At its corner, I paused and peered out. A security light cast a puddle of illumination onto a brick sidewalk. At the far end of the walk I saw the smoke of the roundhouse area, and knew where I was. There was no one in sight. Moving from behind the building, I broke into a run, sure that someone would reach out and grab me at any moment. I was just short of panic. What had happened to Thurman?

I reached the far end of the walk and crouched behind a pair of

498

trash barrels. Two workmen strolled into view, their tools in hand. I waited, sobbing for breath, until they were out of sight. Then I darted to the corner of the next building. There, across a small paved yard, was the telegraph shack. The windows were open and I could hear the faint clatter of the key. By moving carefully in the shadow of the wall, I was able to get a good view into the shack.

My hopes were realized. Only one person was inside the office at this hour: Flanagan. He sat at the middle desk in his swivel chair, copying with a pencil as some message clattered in over the wire. He sent a brief reply, then leaned back, his hands behind his head, and stared into space.

Hunkered in the dark, I knew Flanagan must have to leave the office two or three times during his long shift. He was probably on duty alone until dawn. There was nothing for me to do but wait.

WAITING, I worried about Thurman and about what might happen to me after I did what I had to do. Mentally I rehearsed my message, honing out words, making it simpler. I would not have much time. It had to be clear. It had to be right.

After about an hour Flanagan stood up and stretched. The telegraph key had been quiet for some time now. Reaching for his cane, he limped to the door, looking out into the night.

Come on, Flanagan. Stretch your legs!

He yawned and opened the screen. He stepped outside, looked left and right, then turned left and limped down the walk, going out of sight around the depot.

My legs, cramped from my long wait, almost collapsed as I jumped up and ran for the door. I dashed inside and threw myself into the chair in front of the center key. I opened the switch and started hammering out the Morse.

NATHANIEL HARRIS, I sent, PRESIDENT H&O PHILADELPHIA . . . URGENT . . .

My desperation drove me to send faster than I ever had before. Sweat dripped off my nose, splashing on the wood surface of the desk. The key flashed in the light. My arm began to cramp. I did not dare ease my position for fear of error. Flanagan would be back

499

soon, and then I would be in terrible trouble. I made a mistake, corrected it, plunged on. I tasted salt and copper in my mouth, and realized I had bitten my tongue. Had I done it falling over the fence, or now, in my anxiety?

I was nearing the end of the message. Would Nathaniel Harris believe any of it? Would he take it as a prank? Was the Philadelphia operator even at his desk to copy? If he did copy, would he pass the message on, or throw it away?

I flicked out the last words: EVERY BIT IS THE TRUTH . . . YOU ARE ONLY HOPE . . . ROBERT KELLER . . . PREACHERVILLE. Pushing the key closed again, I leaned back in a virtual collapse. For an instant I simply stared. Then I remembered Flanagan. I had to run again. Swinging the chair around, I jumped to my feet and started for the door. Then I skidded to a halt. Flanagan stood in the doorway, looking down at me with a combination of anger and astonishment.

Escape was the only thought in my mind. I darted for the door, trying to get past him. He moved easily, catching me with one big hand.

I struggled. "Lemme go, you—"

"Wait, lad," he said. He held me at arm's length, looking down at me. "Do you think that message will do you any good now?"

I glared at him.

"It was good code," he told me. "I suppose if anything makes the man come, it will be your message."

"What are you going to do to me?"

Flanagan, to my amazement, released me. "Well, sir, you'll just have to stay here with me until my relief comes. Then we'll have to be seeing if we can get you out of the yards." His smile came then, gentle and filled with pride. "You're an amazing lad. I think I told you that once before. I suppose if you got yourself in without being caught, the two of us can get you back out the same way."

I could hardly believe it. I saw that I had misjudged him—that his protestations of friendship had been truthful all along. Whether in relief that I would not be immediately thrown into jail, or gladness that Flanagan was again my friend, I went to pieces. I clung to him, and his arm went around me.

Eight

Flanagan walked me out of the yards in the morning, unnoticed amid the confusion of departing and entering crews.

"Do you think Mr. Harris will answer me?" I asked as we walked slowly past the park.

He smiled faintly. "Well, he didn't during my shift, did he?" He paused, then added, "You sent a good message and your Morse was solid. Now all we can do is wait."

As we neared the streetcar station, a familiar figure walked out of the park toward us. The sight of him made my heart bound. "Thurman!"

He approached cockily, hands jammed in his pockets. "I see you made it, kid."

"*You* made it!" I said, grasping his arms.

"Sure! Oh, you probably heard them dummies shooting. They never even seen me. I dunno what they was shooting at."

I introduced Flanagan, who had already been told about Thurman's diversionary tactics, and explained how he had gotten me back out of the yards just now.

"Boy," Thurman murmured, "if there's no answer, you're in trouble, too, Mr. Flanagan."

"Well, sir," Flanagan said, "if there is no answer, and they come for me, why, I was on my relief and knew nothing."

On the streetcar ride home, Thurman explained how he had eluded the guards in the park, then had watched for signs of my discovery inside the fence. Assuring himself that I had either been captured or was in free, he had biked cross-country to his aunt's house, where he had caught two hours' sleep. He had been back at the park, waiting to learn my fate, since five o'clock that morning.

We walked to our road from the edge of town in the slanting rays of the morning sun. It was going to be hot. My stomach felt like a quart of battery acid had been poured into it. Flanagan, still in good spirits, waved us farewell in front of his place. Thurman and I walked on to my house. We found my mother and Mrs. Black in the kitchen, preparing a breakfast of mush. Both were in their

Sunday best, but their faces betrayed how little sleep they had had.

"Did you boys sleep well?" Mrs. Black asked.

"We sure did," Thurman lied glibly.

My mother told me, "Mrs. Black and I are going into town to see the lawyer. You stay here with your sisters, son."

"Mom, I want to be in town to see what happens!"

"You'll do as you're told."

I was downcast, but by the time I had some mush, the need for sleep was overwhelming. Thurman left with our mothers, looking amazingly chipper. Mary Eleanor and Rachel played quietly; their voices began to lull me, and after admonishing them to stay in the house, I climbed the stairs and fell across my bed, instantly asleep.

I AWOKE with a guilty start, sticky with sweat. The room was stuffy. I went to open the window and peered outside. The sun was past its zenith. Some dust was settling on our road. Had I been awakened by the sound of some passing vehicle? Downstairs the front screen door slammed. I heard voices and Mary Eleanor's cry. *"Daddy! Momma!"*

I went down the stairs three at a time and ran onto the porch. A black roadster was pulled up at our gate. A man in a dark suit— a Hobart-Grimes?—sat behind the wheel. My father and mother were coming through the gate as Mary Eleanor and Rachel ran to meet them. My father was disheveled, dirty, and had beard stubble darkening his face. He gave me a lopsided grin. "Hello, son!"

"What happened?" I asked.

"Everything," he said, dropping wearily to the porch steps. "We've all been released. Preacherville looks like the Fourth of July, everybody's out on the streets."

"Are you all right? You don't have to go to jail?"

"All the charges have been dropped. There are all kinds of rumors. People are saying Nathaniel Harris's special car came in an hour or two ago. There's supposed to be a big meeting going on at the office. A man from the Philadelphia office was outside the courthouse. He said Mr. Harris is personally investigating the situation in Preacherville."

I whooped. I stood on my head. I think they thought I was crazy.

"Are you all right, Bobby?" my mother asked.

"I'm fine, Mom! I'm just great!"

My father was laughing. "Is there any coffee?"

"There's a little left from yesterday," my mother said. "We ran out—"

"Your coffee a year old will be better than anything I've had lately." We trooped into the kitchen. Mary Eleanor and Rachel sat with eyes shining as our parents babbled like children. I could hardly believe it. I had had, if the truth were known, only a faint hope in my telegraph message. It had worked beyond my dreams.

"Will you get your job back?" I asked.

"That might be a little too much to ask for. We'll wait and see."

There was a rap on our back door. My mother opened it and her smile died. "Hello, Mr. Flanagan," she said coolly.

"Mom!" I said. "*He* didn't tell about the stuff in the barn!"

Flanagan stood uncomfortably, leaning on his cane.

"There was talk in jail," my father said. "Our barn was not the only secret someone gave away. Someone—some two or three people, maybe—gave secrets to the company."

"It wasn't Flanagan," I repeated.

My father rose and walked to the door, opening the screen. He extended his hand. "Come in, sir. We can offer you coffee."

Flanagan entered, sat heavily at the table. His smile was there, but faintly. I detected a tension in him that I could not understand.

"I saw your return," he said. "I came to congratulate you."

"The judge dismissed all of us," my father told him. "Nathaniel Harris is in town. There's a big meeting at the office."

Flanagan's heavy eyes rolled toward me. "Is there, now."

"How it happened, we don't know," my father said. "But somehow or other, he decided to take a hand directly. I wouldn't like to be in Jones's shoes right now!"

Flanagan was watching me as this was said. "Have you given your momma and daddy your ideas of why Mr. Harris might have taken a hand, lad?"

"No," I said quickly.

"Why should Bobby have ideas?" my mother asked. "He's just a boy!"

"Ah, yes," Flanagan sighed.

Perhaps I should have spoken then. But I did not know how things would turn out. And Flanagan might still be in trouble. I kept my silence.

THE NEXT TWO or three hours were a blur. Neighbors started coming by. I heard all the speculations repeated. Justin Black and his family appeared, and he and my father clasped hands like long-lost brothers. Thurman got me aside and asked if anyone knew what we had done.

"I haven't told anyone," I whispered.

"Why not?"

"For one thing, what we did was breaking and entering."

Thurman's face went blank. "Oh," he said.

A little later, when Flanagan had gone home and the Blacks were preparing to leave, we heard the sound of another motorcar on the road, then the slight squeak of its brakes. My father went to the front door and looked out. I saw his back stiffen. "Alma!" he said sharply.

My mother left Mrs. Black's side and joined him. She stared through the screen. "Oh, my word," she said softly.

"It *is* him," my father said. "Isn't it?"

My mother turned from the door, primping at her hair with one hand. "Oh, my! Everything is a mess." She rushed to the end table and frantically rearranged things on it.

I went to the door and looked out. My stomach dropped. It was the biggest motorcar I had ever seen, black leather and nickel plating gleaming in the afternoon sun. Four or five men were getting out, but I saw only one with any clarity. He was massive, handsomely dressed in a dark suit, with a diamond pin in his vest.

"What does he want with us?" my father asked, aghast.

"Who is it?" Mr. Black asked sharply.

"Nathaniel Harris!"

The front porch groaned as Nathaniel Harris and two of his aides came up the steps. My father went outside to greet them.

"It's a pleasure to see you again, Mr. Keller," Harris said. Then he spied me in the door. "Ah! Good. Our hero."

My father escorted Harris inside. After a confusion of introductions, Harris turned his attention back to me. "Thank you for
your message."

My father and everyone else stared blankly. "Message?"

Harris grinned at me. "You didn't tell them?"

"I didn't tell anyone," I said.

"I came to Preacherville," Harris told the others, "because of a
remarkable message." He reached into his coat pocket and with-
drew a crumpled sheet of paper. "I have the copy here, as received
at the main office last night. We have all been concerned about the
situation here, but until I saw this, I was determined to allow local
management to work things out."

"I don't understand," my father said. "Who sent the message?"

Nathaniel Harris looked back at me.

"*What?*" my mother and father said at the same time.

"Somehow," Harris told them, "this astonishing son of yours
got to the telegraph office. I believe he sent me this message
himself. Right, Bobby?"

"That's right," I said, swallowing hard.

"A remarkable message," Harris said. He extended the sheet to
my father. "Your boy is a crack telegrapher, according to the man
who copied it. He is also a master at succinct, persuasive language."

While my father and Mr. Black frowned over the message, my
mother grasped my arms with both hands. "*Son?* Did you really *do*
this?"

"Yessum," I admitted.

"How? When?"

"When Thurman and me left last night, we went to town.
Thurman chucked rocks at the guards, and I climbed the fence."

"You climbed the fence at the yards?"

"You helped him?" Mrs. Black said to Thurman. "I can't believe
it!"

Mr. Harris asked me, "Did you have an accomplice in the
telegraph office?"

I wanted Flanagan to have credit, but not trouble. "Well—"

"If some operator allowed you to send this, it took courage. I'd
like to reward him."

506

"It was Flanagan," I said. "He lives next door. He's the one you met with me in the yards, the one that taught me how to use the key."

"Flanagan," Harris said. "Oh, yes. But he's—"

"He's Hobart-Grimes," I supplied. "But he helped me. I got in by myself, but he found me. He could have stopped me, only he didn't."

"I would like very much to speak to Mr. Flanagan. I'll stroll over there in a moment." Mr. Harris turned to my father, who stood staring, the message in his hand. "Mr. Keller, your son's message decided me to take personal control here. I should have done so long ago, but Jones had a good record and I believed his reports. I hope that you—and you, sir," he added, flashing a look at Mr. Black, "will be willing to return to your jobs. We are going to need good men to get the division rolling again."

"I'll do everything I can, sir," my father said, his face radiant.

"And me," Black said. "If these two little squirts can do what they did, we can all work together and get everything back on an even keel in no time!"

Nathaniel Harris smiled but shook his head. "Jones has been sent packing, along with his stooges. But make no mistake: we have a heavy backlog of misunderstanding to work out." He squared his shoulders and brightened again. "But with goodwill . . . we can have a start at it."

"I'll help all I can," my father said.

"Good. I'll have a new assignment for you in the office here. We can discuss that in the morning. Meanwhile, I have much to do." He turned toward the door, then looked back at me. "As for you, young man, you did a man's work last night. You'll receive a man's cash bonus for it."

"I don't want anything!" I protested.

"Take it," Harris said sternly. "You want to own a railroad someday? Take it!"

"Yessir."

"I will consider it an investment. One day I may want a new crack telegrapher, and I want you on my side. Now. Shall we walk next door to see our friend Flanagan?"

We trooped down the road to Flanagan's place, all of us, while Nathaniel Harris lectured us about the complexity of railroading, and how subordinates had to be trusted. I think we were all too dazed to pay close attention.

As we walked up to Flanagan's house, I expected him to appear in the doorway. There was no movement. "Flanagan!" I called. We went up onto the porch. I rapped loudly. "Flanagan?"

"Maybe he went to work," my father said, frowning.

"Not this early!"

"Try the door," Nathaniel Harris suggested.

I opened the screen. The inside door was halfway open. I poked it with my finger and it swung wide. I looked in. The table and chair stood neatly together in the center of the room. The little brass lamp that had rested there was not in sight. Flanagan often left dirty dishes on the table, but there were none. Something about the look of the place sent panic gusting through my belly. I stepped inside.

It took only a moment to verify the growing suspicion. The house was vacant, stripped and cleaned. Flanagan was gone.

"Why?" I asked, facing the adults in the empty front room. "He was just over at our house! He must have been ready to go when he was over there, but he didn't say a word!"

"I think I understand," Nathaniel Harris said heavily. "Flanagan was a chief inspector for Hobart-Grimes. I recognized him in the yards that day, lad. He allowed you to send the message last night. He could hardly afford to stay around after his role became known. Some of his own agents might want to take revenge on him."

"It doesn't make sense," I protested. "He helped solve things!"

"Ah," Harris said. "But Hobart-Grimes was brought in by Jones, correct? In terms of the job the agency was paid to do, what Flanagan did was betrayal. Your friend feared for his life, lad. That was why he left the way he did."

"And didn't even leave me a note? That's not like him!" I stared at them, my disappointment welling up inside me. I thought of the good times Flanagan and I had had. Could he leave me like this? Then I got an idea.

Without a word, I turned and hurried out in back of the little

508

house. Flanagan's many trips down to the roosting house had beaten a narrow path through the weeds, now lush and high in the summer heat. I ran, tearing my shirt as I went through the fence. The blue female and one of the other blues fluttered to the sky in alarm as I approached the pigeon house. Sure enough, a small sheet of paper was pinned to the tree. I pulled it loose and read it.

Lad,
    Safer for me to move on. I will see you again someday. Be good. Love your pigeons. Work on your Morse. You are a one in a million.

Flanagan

I read the note several times. It became blurry. I sat down on the grass and stared at it, and to my surprise Vicious flew down from his apartment and walked up to me, cocking his head to the side and viewing me with intense concern. He had no experience with someone crying.

THAT DAY marked a major turning point for all of us. My father eventually became first assistant to the new division manager. Mr. Black went back to running his crack train, and Thurman joined the company as a fireman a year later.

Nathaniel Harris's direct intervention did not spell an immediate end to labor problems, but Preacherville became a model division and was spared much of the violence that came to many railroad areas in the years that followed.

We moved to a larger house nearer town. I trapped my growing flock of pigeons and homed them to the new location. Vicious lived to the ripe old age of ten, and left countless children and grandchildren, whose murmuring wings and joyful flight gladdened our days.

Later I became a telegrapher for the railroad. It was always my dream that one day Flanagan would come limping into my shack, or I would recognize, coming down the wire from some distant station, that immaculate, lilting code that was so indelibly his. And it happened late one night when I was alone, tending a quiet circuit. As the code began coming in, I sat up straight, chilling from head to foot. The message was routine, but there could be no doubt.

The exchange had been made between Flanagan's station, in Altoona, and Pittsburgh. Shaking with excitement, I sent a burst: ALTOONA . . . FLANAGAN . . . THIS IS PREACHERVILLE . . . BOBBY.

Without a pause his reply came back: PREACHERVILLE . . . ALTOONA . . . YES LAD . . . GOD BLESS . . . NOW MIND YOUR DISCIPLINE . . . END.

The old pro was reminding the relative novice that personal messages were not sent on the company wire. I sent the letter *R* to show I copied, and sat back, suddenly wet with perspiration.

I went to Altoona on my next holiday. I found Flanagan in a little house not far from the yards. He was very old now, and as we embraced, both of us were weeping. We had that afternoon together, and he told me how he had quit Hobart-Grimes and gone west for a long time to allow tempers to cool, and how he was back only as a relief operator until he retired in another few months.

"Where will you go when you retire?" I asked.

"West again," he said. "Omaha."

We looked at one another. "Will you write?" I asked.

"Of course," he said, in a tone that told us both that he was lying.

I never saw or heard from him again after that day. But I shall never forget the summer he was so central in our lives. And to this day, when I am around a telegraph shack I catch myself listening for the sound of his key. Somehow I think I'll hear it again, and answer.

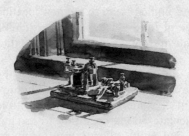

Jack Bickham

Dinah, Blow Your Horn is fiction. However, the book's setting and its main characters are drawn from Jack Bickham's own life. Having grown up in eastern Ohio in the 1930s, Bickham knows firsthand the nearby Appalachian hill country of Pennsylvania and West Virginia, which provides the setting for the fictional town of Preacherville. And it was Bickham's grandfather Arthur Miles, an old railroad man, who inspired the character of Flanagan. "He's also a little like Bobby Keller's father in the book," says Bickham. "He lost a hand in a coupling accident, but, like Ned Keller, my grandfather still loved the railroad. A lot of the railroading incidents in the book are based on stories he told me when I was a kid—the railroad detectives beating up the strikers, for instance." Bickham has repaid the debt for all those stories by dedicating *Dinah* to his grandfather.

For the novel's fund of pigeon lore Bickham needed to look no farther than his own backyard in Norman, Oklahoma, where he's been "homing" a small flock of pigeons for nearly five years. "I've been keeping records on their mating and nesting habits all along, just for my own amusement," Bickham says. "So when I started writing about pigeons in *Dinah* I didn't need to do any research." Vicious, the novel's strutting cock of the flock, is based partly on a friend's pigeon that loves to terrorize cats, and partly on a foundling that Bickham himself raised to adulthood. "He used to fly upstairs to the room where I work, and sit on my typewriter while I wrote. But he got too big for that and I had to let him out to join the flock. He's raising a family now."

Jack Bickham's own family includes his wife, three sons and a daughter, as well as an assortment of dogs, cats and tropical fish. A onetime newspaperman, Bickham now teaches writing at the University of Oklahoma's school of journalism and maintains a writing schedule of ten thousand to fifteen thousand words a week. His more than fifty published novels include *Baker's Hawk*, a Condensed Books selection in 1976.

DD111